Also by Edgardo Vega Yunqué

The Comeback

Mendoza's Dreams

Casualty Report

The Lamentable Journey of Omaha Bigelow into the

Impenetrable Loisaida Jungle

"In prose that flows like itself and makes reading an act as natural as singing or crying, Yunqué amalgamates all. . . . Let the book read you. With this magnificent novel, that's all you have to do."

—Laura Restrepo, author of *The Dark Bride*

"Masterfully crafted and complex . . . I couldn't put it down, and was saddened to leave the plethora of vital, cruel, loving, and questioning characters who I now feel are part of me. Absolutely amazing."

—Ntozake Shange, author of *For Colored Girls Who Have Considered Suicide When the Rainbow Is Enuf*

No Matter How Much You Promise to Cook or Pay the Rent You Blew It Cauze Bill Bailey Ain't Never Coming Home Again

Edgardo Vega Yunqué

Picador

Farrar, Straus and Giroux / New York

www.picadorusa.com

Picador® is a U.S. registered trademark and is used by Farrar, Straus and Giroux under license from Pan Books Limited.

For information on Picador Reading Group Guides, as well as ordering, please contact the Trade Marketing department at St. Martin's Press.
Phone: 1-800-221-7945 extension 763
Fax: 212-677-7456
E-mail: trademarketing@stmartins.com

Grateful acknowledgment is made to the following publishers and holders of copyright for permission to quote from and/or reprint copyrighted material: "Just One of Those Things" by Cole Porter, "She's a Latin from Manhattan" by Al Dubin and Harry Warren, and "Zing Went the Strings of My Heart" by James F. Hanley, copyright 1935 (renewed) by Warner Bros. Inc., used by permission of Warner Bros. Publication U.S. Inc.; diagnostic criteria for post-traumatic stress disorder from the *Diagnostic and Statistical Manual of Mental Disorders, Third Edition*, © 1987 by American Psychiatric Association; *Atlas of the North American Indian*, revised edition, by Carl Waldman, © 1985, 2000 by Carl Waldman. Reprinted by permission of Facts on File, Inc.; "If the Drum Is a Woman" by Jayne Cortez; "Loveliest of the trees, the cherry now" from "A Shropshire Lad," from *The Collected Poems of A. E. Housman*, authorized edition, copyright © 1939, 1940, 1965 by Henry Holt and Co., © 1967, 1968 by Robert E. Symons.

Designed by Jonathan D. Lippincott

Library of Congress Cataloging-in-Publication Data

Vega Yunqué, Edgardo, 1936–
No matter how much you promise to cook or pay the rent you blew it cauze Bill Bailey ain't never coming home again / Edgardo Vega Yunqué.
    p. cm.
    ISBN 0-312-42402-7
    EAN 978-0312-42402-2
    1. Lower East Side (New York, N.Y.)—Fiction.   2. Vietnamese Conflict, 1961–1975—Veterans—Fiction.   3. Irish Americans—Fiction.   4. Jazz musicians—Fiction.   5. Race relations—Fiction.   6. Puerto Ricans—Fiction.   7. Birthfathers—Fiction.   8. Stepfamilies —Fiction.   9. Young women—Fiction.   I. Title.

PS3572.E34N6 2003
813'.54—dc21

2003044064

First published in the United States by Farrar, Straus and Giroux

First Picador Edition: September 2004

10   9   8   7   6   5   4   3   2   1

This book is dedicated to

Alyson

The book also honors all the women ancestors of our family, but particularly our most recent:

Patricia Schumacher Vega (b. 1940)

Abigail Yunqué de Vega (b. 1916)

Harriet Turner Schumacher (b. 1920)

Laura Vega Lebrón (1890–1909)

Asunción Martínez de Yunqué (1886–1990)

Hattie Tuchtenhagen Schumacher (1892–1982)

Mary Magnussen Borg (1888–1978)

And the others before them and the ones to come, each one teacher, nurturer, and defender of our bloodline, extending to the East and West, to the North and South, across oceans and deserts, mountains and forests, jungles and savannahs, across ice floes and tundra, into all parts of the world and into time past, present, and future.

But men have no secrets, except from women, and never grow up in the way that women do. It is very much harder, and it takes much longer, for a man to grow up, and he could never do it at all without women.

—James Baldwin, *If Beale Street Could Talk*

There is no rule for painting al fresco. Every artist may do as he pleases provided he paints as thinly as possible and only while the plaster is wet, six to eight hours from the moment it is applied. No retouching of any kind afterward. Every artist develops his own way of planning his conception and transferring it onto the wet plaster. Every method is as good as the other. Or the artist may improvise without any previous sketches.

—José Clemente Orozco, Mexican muralist

Music, though it does not employ human beings, although it is governed by intricate laws, nevertheless does offer in its final expression a type of beauty which fiction might achieve in its own way. Expansion. That is the idea the novelist must cling to. Not completion. Not rounding off but opening out. When the symphony is over we feel that the notes and tunes composing it have been liberated, they have found in the rhythm of the whole their individual freedom. Cannot the novel be like that?

—E. M. Forster, *Aspects of the Novel*

Contents

Second Movement The Horizon

Third Movement The Journey

Fourth Movement The Drum

First Movement

The Quest

1 Here and There

In the not so merry month of May 1988, when her studies had evolved into a drag, Vidamía Farrell, finishing her sophomore year of high school, again became as restless as she had the previous four years. In spite of ample evidence of her eventual metamorphosis into a scholar of consequence, the upcoming end of the school year had become an extra-special time ever since her parents, but mostly her mother, and perhaps for the wrong reasons, had come to the understanding that it would be ethnically beneficial for Vidamía to spend part of the summer with her father.

As she stood rigidly inside a quadratic equation and stared at a sky full of nimbusian elephants, Vidamía thought again of her father, Billy Farrell, in her mind a figure of considerable mythic qualities, whom she both admired and pitied once she got to know him, and decided that it was in everyone's best interest to help him make a reentry into more acceptable human society. She didn't meet her father until the age of twelve, when she learned that once upon a time her father had sat in the middle of a Vietnamese rice paddy, under a shower of steel, cradling the broken and forever useless body of her uncle, Joey Santiago of Rivington Street on the Lower East Side of New York City, whom she would never meet since time and space didn't allow for such stratagems.

Billy Farrell had cried while he held the eviscerated corpse of his ace, his homeboy, his reefer-smoking main man. Such was the shock, that Billy didn't notice that the drizzle of steel, while it had barely touched his own head, had meticulously erased his catalogue of the musical techniques of Thelonious Monk, Bud Powell, Dave Brubeck, Oscar Peterson, and other jazz pianists. However, even if that aspersion of steel had not removed from consciousness the complex knowledge of flatted sevenths, augmented ninths, intricate harmonic patterns, and improvisational virtuosity that Billy had at one time displayed, he would have been unable to perform adequately, he believed, his own renditions of such standards as "Moonlight in Vermont," "April in Paris," "Back Home Again in Indiana," or "Autumn in New York" not because he lacked a geographical metronome, but because that baptismal of steel had neatly severed, at the root, the middle and pinkie fingers of his right hand, rendering him an eight-fingered jazz pianist, a phenomenon more rare than an arctic orchid.

As Billy recalled, the medics finally appeared. Making their way through the sticky heat and the soupy stirfry of growing rice, detached limbs, and involuntary bowel movements, and the monotonic keening of thousands of flies, the medics removed the lifeless body of Joey Santiago from Billy's semi-catatonic, eight-fingered, shock-induced clutches and placed it in a body bag. They then saw Billy's lacerated scalp and the empty places in his hand, shot morphine into him, and whisked him off in a medevac helicopter.

At the hospital in Da Nang, while they shaved his skull as preparation for neurosurgical engineering, the doctors, after cleansing and disinfecting the wounds, sent Billy, by way of various anesthetics, into a never-never land of painless musings. They then stretched the torn and jagged epidermis of his right hand over the first knuckles of his middle and pinkie fingers and stitched them up. Not a minute elapsed before the surgeons addressed Billy's cranium. The shrapnel had removed one and a half centimeters of bone from the upper-left side of his head above the ear. After inserting a minute metal plate where the hole had been, the surgeons sewed up his scalp. Ironically, given Billy's preference in music, on certain ionospherically hospitable nights, the metal insertion picked up a country-music station in Wheeling, West Virginia, so that his battlefield nightmares were now accompanied by music more suitable to the soundtrack for a moonshiner and revenuer film starring Robert Mitchum and his sons.

The doctors, having failed, in his view, to scoop up from that rice paddy the spilled Thelonious Monk, Gil Evans, McCoy Tyner, Horace Silver, Red Garland, *et al.*, plus his personal repository of blues, ragtime, Dixieland, swing, bop, West Coast, and progressive solos of hundreds of musicians ranging from Blind Lemon Jefferson to Ornette Coleman, were left wondering why Billy said nothing but simply stared at the ceiling. He often held up his right hand, now bandaged against infection, and, within that mitt of gauze, attempted to wiggle his absent digits, which at one time, together with the perfectly matched fingers of his gifted left hand, had surrounded intricate melodies as would the hands of a child a delicate spring butterfly, admiring it briefly and then letting it go to watch it dance lepidopterally away.

For eight months, first at the hospital in Vietnam, then one in Japan, and subsequently in the States, Billy Farrell sat and stared bleakly at his crab hand, not recognizing it as his. Doctors and counselors and chaplains came and went, but none of them apologized for their failure to retrieve the music from the rice paddy. Having lost, along with the spilled music, his temperament, inventiveness, and musical technique, Billy Farrell had only love left. Eventually he told everyone he was fine, thank you very much and God bless you. When they asked him where they should send his disability check he said please send it care of my grandpa, Buck Sanderson, in Yonkers, New York, the chaplain has the address.

As Vidamía grew up and learned that other girls were called Jane, Joan, Jean, Jeannette, Ginny, Ginger, and even Gloria, Carmen, María, Teresa, but not Vidamía, and if they had mothers who looked like her mother they had last names like Rivera, Rodríguez, Vásquez, López, but not Farrell, she demanded to know everything about her father. When her mother, Elsa, ignored her, brushing off her concerns as unimportant, she went to her grandmother, Ursula Santiago. All Grandma Ursula would say was that her father had been in the war with her uncle Joey. Her uncle had been killed and her father had been hurt. His name was Billy Farrell and he had blond hair and blue eyes and used to live in Yonkers.

"How did they meet?" Vidamía had asked on one of those rare occasions when her mother brought her into the city and left her with her grandmother. "How? He and my mother, huh, *güelita?*" Vidamía inquired, practically pinning her grandmother against the stove where she had been stirring a pot of red beans in sauce for the better part of an eternity.

"You have to ask your mother that," Ursula said, in the accented English of the Island of Enchantment, *Puerto Rico, tierra de mis amores, jardín de flores donde yo nací,* linguistic cha-cha. "I'm sure she knows, *mijita.*"

"She won't tell me."

"She must have her reasons."

So in the summer that she turned twelve, aware that in riding the train back and forth between Tarrytown and New York one of the stops was Yonkers, she created a plan. Having saved six months' of allowance, Vidamía set out to find Billy Farrell, going off one Saturday, ostensibly to visit the Guggenheim Museum with her friend from summer camp, thirteen-year-old Janet Shapiro, who lived on Sutton Place. Artfully coordinating her cover and promulgating the lie with the skill of a graduate of one of your best disinformation finishing schools, rather than making the complete journey to Grand Central Station she got off the train in Yonkers. Filled with trepidation but determined in her resolve, she went forward. Like some fear-maddened mammal, she burrowed into the telephone directory, digging down through the alphabet until she reached the required depth. Methodically, she copied the name, address, and telephone number of every Farrell in town. After an hour or so of changing dollar bills into dimes and making useless Saturday-afternoon telephone calls to unsuspecting Farrells, in which, by deepening her voice or holding a handkerchief over the instrument, she masqueraded immaturely as officials of governmental bureaus, banks, or insurance companies, Vidamía began to feel the frustration of the amateur sleuth and, overcome by her despondency, sat on the curb to ponder what she must next do.

So overwhelmed by the desolation of defeat did she appear, that a policeman by the name of Arnold Tyson decided she must be a runaway and inquired as to her predicament. When she explained her quest, Officer Tyson, who had gone to high school with Billy, dutifully drove Vidamía in his patrol car across the bridge to see Maud Farrell, Billy's mother, who was also known as the big, good-looking blonde who tends bar at O'Hanlon's in Mount Vernon.

"Mrs. Farrell, this little girl's looking for Billy," Officer Tyson said, urging Vidamía up on a barstool. "Says Billy's her father."

"You want a ginger ale?" asked Maud Farrell.

"No, thank you," Vidamía replied.

"What's your name, darling?" Maud Farrell then said, scooping up ice cubes with a glass from the bin behind the bar.

"Vidamía. Vidamía Farrell," said the little Spanish wisp with freckles on her nose as Maud later described Vidamía to her friend, Ruby Broadway, also known as the good-looking Negro woman who ran the house where firemen, policemen, and railroad men went when they grew tired of listening to their wives talking about coupons, color TVs, and new skin-care products.

"And you know my son?" Maud said as she set a glass on the gleaming surface of the bar.

"No, but I know he's my father. He and my uncle were in the war. My uncle died. Here's a picture."

And from the large leather bag she carried slung over her shoulder as if she were a bona fide teenager, Vidamía produced the worn picture of Billy Farrell and Joey Santiago in Vietnam that she had discovered in one of her mother's trunks while Elsa was in the Bahamas with her stepfather two weeks prior.

"Could be," Maud said, looking at the picture and then at Officer Tyson before pouring ginger ale into the glass. "As Irish a face as you'd want," she added as she scrutinized Vidamía's physiognomy. "Same shape mouth as Billy. Drink up, honey."

"No, thank you," Vidamía said.

"Look, if I'm gonna be your grandmother, you better do as you're told," Maud said, depositing her formidable bosom on the bar and squinting her eyes like *I Love Lucy* on TV so that Vidamía was charmed into smiling. "It's free and it'll make your nose tickle."

"Okay," Vidamía said, taking little sips and letting the bubbles strike her face.

And so Maud Farrell became a grandmother to Vidamía and on Saturday afternoons when she was off from O'Hanlon's she fed Vidamía bologna sandwiches and ice-cold root beer and brought her carefully in touch with her lineage, explaining, through family anecdote, fable, and myth, that Billy had indeed been in the war and had suffered a life-threatening injury that had left him in many respects incapacitated, but not in *that* way, she said, meaning his capacity to reproduce, saying it not luridly but thankfully, so that huge maternal tears emerged from her big blue eyes and she hugged Vidamía to her, making the girl cry and laugh at the same time and say, "Grandma, you got mayonnaise on your cheek."

"The Kid," Maud Farrell called him, telling Vidamía he had been so christened in his Yonkers–Mount Vernon boyhood for no apparent reason by his maternal grandfather, Buck Sanderson, of banjo-playing fame, of whom it was told—mostly by him—that he had played on Mississippi riverboats and knew a thousand-and-one tunes which he taught the boy from the time he was one and a half years and was labeled a musical genius, by the same Buck Sanderson, grandfather, who, after playing "Mary Had a Little Lamb" on a Christmas xylophone had handed the infant Billy the mallet and the boy, not yet able to form coherent vocal sounds, had, without any hesitation, reproduced every note of the song flawlessly from "Mary had" to "sure to go." When everyone had applauded, Baby Billy looked at them totally surprised at their glee, and they swear to this day that he had a look that chided their naïveté, as if he knew there was little complexity to the tune.

It turned out, Vidamía learned, that when Billy was released from the hospital, he'd flown from California to New York, staying with his mama's parents, listening to the two of them bickering about everything as he always had in his childhood.

Between unbidden flashbacks of the war, Billy permitted his grandfather to teach him the guitar, letting the big old man hold him while he cried when he couldn't form a B7 even with his good hand. Somewhere in the distance of his personal history, in some placid place of guarded memory, he knew that at one time the chords poured into his mind fluidly, the music going directly to his left hand, that wonderful, rambling-and-walking left hand, chording, laying down the music as if it were a road filled with beautiful landscapes. Patiently urged by his Grandpa Buck, Billy persisted and after a while, when he knew twelve or so chords and could play and sing folk songs such as "The Fox" and "Go Tell Aunt Rhodie" together with some Leadbelly like "Easy Rider," or "John Henry," he called his mother and said he was going into the city, meaning Manhattan.

Maud, with the concern only a mother could have, said that he should be careful and that if he was starting to get restless and in need of companionship, there were plenty of girls right in the neighborhood willing to douse his ardor, especially Margie Biancalana, the little Italian girl whose father owned the barbershop and who just last Saturday had said, "Hi, Mrs. Farrell, how's Billy?" Or maybe Adele Botnick, who was studying to be a doctor but always liked jazz and had been asking for him.

So Maud, feeling foolish for bringing up the subject, went on to say that he was welcome to use her apartment while she was at O'Hanlon's during the day, as long as he changed the sheets and straightened up after he was finished, because she sometimes got the same way and had men friends because she was still a relatively young woman, and that she hoped that he didn't think it was because she hadn't loved his father—may he rest in peace—because she had and still did, or that he wasn't angry now because she was discussing adult matters.

"Naw, Ma," he said. "It's nothing like that. Thanks, anyway. Don't worry."

"That's what you told me last time, you big jerk," big, good-looking Maud said, acting like a mother. " 'I'll be all right,' you said, and they shot you full of holes, like they did your father in Harlem, the spic bastards."

In retelling the story the phrase "spic bastards" had been censored and no mention made of Puerto Ricans or the more sanitized "Spanish" as the perpetrators of her life's tragedy, now that Vidamía had deposited herself with absolute charm in a very special place in Maud's heart, causing Maud to feel immense pride in her grandmothership.

"I'll be fine, Mom," Billy Farrell had said. "Really. Don't worry, okay?"

"Billy?" Maud said, her voice starting to break on the phone.

"Don't, Ma."

"You got enough money?"

"Yeah, the check came yesterday. I'll be back tonight. I just need to get out. I'll call you."

"I love you, you big son of a bitch."

And, like he always did, he reminded her of what that made her. She laughed and said, "That's right and don't forget it" and they said goodbye; and he said goodbye to Grandpa Buck and Grandma Brigid. Dressed in jeans and a green fatigue jacket, unaware that he was making a social statement, one which forever set in motion the consciousness of war in America not as a romantic John-Wayne-from-the-Halls-of-Montezuma-to-the-Shores-of-Tripoli-come-back-and-kiss-ecstatic-girls-on-the-front-page-of-*Life*-magazine experience but a real spilling of blood, tearing of limbs, shredding of flesh, concussive, loud, horrific encounter with fear and death, he walked down from his grandpa's house until he reached Broadway and then, leisurely, walked the forty or so blocks to the hit-the-elevated-train road, jack.

Forty blocks was nothing. A stroll. He was used to humping uniformed and booted, loaded down with ruck, canteen, bolo, .45 in its holster, C-rations, his big .60-caliber machine gun and enough ammo to stop a regiment, should they come across one; sneaking through elephant grass and woods, across rice paddies, up into hills; fighting the heat and the bugs and the leeches and constant wetness of the rainy season; looking out for booby traps; humping at night, looking to set up an ambush for the North Vietnamese regulars, or the fucking Cong gooks, to use the correct parlance, who never once gave up trying to infiltrate their perimeter, even after they'd surrounded it with concertina wire, a minefield, and more concertina.

"Man, they don't give a fuck," the sarge had said. They would simply lay down a homemade Bangalore torpedo, which was a long bamboo filled with explosives, and blow up all the claymores and antipersonnel mines and in they'd come, raising hell at all hours of the night. So they'd just go out and mess them up before they had a chance to strike. Six or seven gyrenes sneaking around at night, walking in line by holding on to a wire that the point man held so they wouldn't get lost or separated or step on their own mines. Every once in a while they established contact and all hell broke loose and then he'd set up and let the gun do its thing, the fear tearing at him and his mouth getting dry. And then inside of him everything happening very slowly as he observed the red tracers cutting up the night and at the same time watching the enemy tracers like rapidly traveling lightning bugs whose slow delicate paths he'd followed in early summer evenings when he was a boy. Ours were red and theirs green, the bullets crossing each other in the night, each one carrying instant death. "Fucking spectacular!" Pete Farrentino had said when he first saw them. "Like fucking Christmas," he'd said. "Yeah, peace on Earth and good will to men, mothafucka," Bobby Carson had said. Bobby Carson was from Wichita, Kansas, and Pete was from someplace outside Detroit. Pete, the son of an Italian shoemaker, had been the quarterback on his high school team, but was too small to get a college scholarship so he joined the Corps.

The two of them got it one day after they went and swept the road outside the gate, going almost a klic in either direction with the mine detectors and the dogs from the K-9 detail. When they were done and were walking back, a truck came by and hit a mine they'd missed. Afterward, they didn't find diddly-squat, except maybe some dog nuts, teeth, and a collar and a combat boot with stockinged toes in it and dog tags with neck sinew and skull fragments where their chained metal tags with name, rank, serial number, blood type, and religion had shot up through the head. The truck had been carrying ammo so that for about twenty minutes the air was filled with round after round of all kinds of ordnance: .45s, .60s, frags, mines, our own Bangalore units, all of it going off like one big Fourth of July party forcing everybody to stay in the bunkers, some of the newer men chattering and asking if they were under attack.

Death was a constant. One day somebody was there and the next day he was gone; sometimes it happened right next to you and other times you'd hear the stories, each one worse than the last, not exaggerated but amplified by the fear that eventually death, dressed in black pajamas, a straw hat, and rubber-tire sandals, would come calling. Once in a while you'd hear of lucky hits like getting a round that slid through your arm or shattered your shin and you'd be awarded a Purple Heart and be gone a while. If you were lucky you went back home a hero.

At times, they'd stay inside the compound, waiting. Word had come that the North Vietnamese Army was spotted heading their way, and Billy'd set up above the sandbags, looking out over the wire and the minefields, the sea to the east shimmering in the sunlight, reminding him of the times he and his father went fishing on Long Island Sound in his friend's boat. To the west was Laos, another country, and the Viet Cong could as easily come that way; always looking north for the enemy, with daylight fading and communications calling for artillery, measuring the distances, until the shells, deafening and deadly in their insistence, came within a hundred feet of their bunkers; setting up the defenses in case the NVA decided to attack at night.

If the enemy attacked, they'd just call Camp Caroll or the other artillery encampments and they'd set up a ring of fire around their outpost. It didn't matter, the Cong still came. With howitzer shells raining all around their perimeter they came. Sometimes you could just tell they were out there, you could feel their presence. He'd then fire a couple of flares to see if he could spot them. It never ended, day after day, looking for them and waiting, wanting them to come and then when they came, wanting it to be over; day after bloody, noisy, wet, hot day; choppers overhead, mortars and sporadic machine-gun fire, jet planes dropping napalm, and beyond it all, high above, the droning of the bombers as they headed north.

There were times when nothing happened—quiet, hot days, with just a slight breeze blowing from the sea, bringing memories of peaceful summers at Jones Beach or on the Sound. They patrolled the road and watched the people: small, their brown-yellow skin tight and their hair black under straw hats; sometimes a farmer herding a hundred or so ducks, all of them walking in a row; boys five and six years old controlling a huge water buffalo by grabbing the animal's nose. Sometimes a squad went up into the wooded areas and encountered wild dogs. Marines walking, not knowing what would happen next, wondering if the enemy felt fear in the same way they did. None of them wanted to believe that some GI had been glommed by a tiger, in-country—just grabbed him and carried him off. All they found were shreds of his fatigues and torn-up combat boots, the head chewed to the bone, everything sucked out. He was fascinated by the old women with their teeth blackened or dull red from chewing betel nuts, the areas around their lips wearing the same colors in darker shades.

So he went through the streets of Yonkers with old men who had seen combat and the women who had lost men in the war staring at his desolation, knowing from his attire and his demeanor, his detachment from the pain, that he'd been in Vietnam. He crossed into the Bronx, past Van Cortlandt Park, where he'd spent long summer afternoons mowing them down with his fastball until that, too, had passed and he began drifting, more and more to the music, deciding that his life was about jazz and he had no choice but to go with it. But something had happened and he couldn't recall much except Joey Santiago dying in his arms.

He brushed back his long blond hair with his left hand, keeping his right one in the pocket of his fatigue jacket and then combed his beard with his fingers and climbed the stairs to the 242nd Street elevated station and took the train to Manhattan driven by a need to apologize to Joey's mother for letting her boy die.

2 Name That Girl

That first instance of Billy's return from the jungles of forgetfulness and into the lunacy that was American society and life in New York City was in 1971, when he was sitting by the radio and word came on July 6 that Louie Armstrong had died. As if a jolt of electricity had shot through him, he sat upright and was surprised to find himself in the present, so that his distant past, dormant except for his fixation on Joey's death, began streaming to him clearly. He recalled Pop Butterworth taking him along to Mr. Armstrong's house to bring him an arrangement. Billy was thirteen years old but knew about the great jazz showman from listening to his grandfather talk about "Satch" and seeing him singing "Bill Bailey, Won't You Please Come Home?" in a film with Danny Kaye about another jazz musician that his grandfather knew. Something about pennies, but he couldn't recall the name of the film.

That day Pop Butterworth had said, "Louis, you remember Buck Sanderson? Played banjo down in Memphis. We came up to New York in the thirties. Used to play Dixieland with Pee Wee and those fellas. This is his grandson, Billy Farrell. He plays a very fine piano."

Mr. Armstrong laughed, his eyes all crinkled, and touched Billy's blond head, looked into his eyes and said, "Well, Pops is gonna have to sit down and play with the young man one of these days. Is that okay?" Billy looked confused and, pointing at Pop Butterworth, said, "We've played together a few times." Mr. Armstrong laughed and made a raspy noise of delight in his throat. Mr. Butterworth later explained that Louis Armstrong called himself Pops.

Now, as if he had awakened from a long sleep and was walking through a thick haze, Billy began to take notice of the world around him. It should also be noted that during 1971, the last year on planet Earth of Louis Daniel "Satchmo" Armstrong, he of the voice, the trumpet, and the handkerchief, an additional number of noteworthy events took place. Richard Nixon, then president of the United States, announced a trip to the People's Republic of China, for "Ping-Pong diplomacy," as the press labeled his efforts. To prepare for this momentous event Nixon said that there was no reason why that vast country shouldn't be admitted into the United Nations. Also during this year the Reverend Philip Berrigan was indicted, along with five others, for conspiring to kidnap U.S. Secretary of State Henry Kissinger. Everybody was reading Jerzy Kosinski's novel *Being There*, about the effects of TV on American society. Wishing to capitalize on this massive interest in television, the government, with cameras recording everything, killed twenty-eight prisoners at the Attica State Correctional Facility in upstate New York in a concerted air and ground attack of unprecedented brutality in which 1,500 law enforcement officers participated.

In Super Bowl V, the Baltimore Colts beat the Dallas Cowboys 16–13. The Pittsburgh Pirates won the World Series and Roberto Clemente from Puerto Rico won the Most Valuable Player Award. In other sports, meanwhile, 1971 was the year William Calley was convicted of massacring more than a hundred women and children in Vietnam, in the village of My Lai. During this same year, the *New York Times*, convinced that their mission truly is to bring us all the news that's fit to print, published *The Pentagon Papers* on the official role of the United

States in Vietnam. Daniel Ellsberg, who leaked the information, was indicted for being an ethical fink. On the other side of the planet, the United States continued its massive air bombardment of North Vietnam, while in Washington, D.C., where the orders originated to pound the little slant-eyed, black-pajama-wearing, rubber-tire-sandaled, rice-eating, conical-hat-wearing, tunneling little bastards, the Weather Underground caused $300,000 worth of damage when they placed an explosive device in a Senate bathroom. The significance of the target has been lost on many but perhaps these self-proclaimed patriots, in spite of the seriousness of their mission, had a sense of humor and were forecasting the phrase "shit happens."

Drifting in and out of his walking delirium, oscillating between reading subway signs for SALEM cigarettes (get some they're cool; no, not Kool, cool, minty) and seeing red and green tracer bullets in the night and hearing the rumbling of bombers as they headed north, everything about him *boku dinky dao*, Billy Farrell thought about God and wondered how He chose this one and not that one for extended duty on the planet and in the case of that one why He had visited so much misery on him, meaning Joey Santiago, who got hit but remained alive more than an hour moaning and crying, one hand gone and a leg shattered; PREPARATION H: for your hole, that's what the H stands for ("Yeah, up yours, too, Flanagan"), and afraid and shocked that his young life, which had only a few memories in it, would suddenly cease to exist, Billy's own brain like a camera fixed on the scene but unable to push down on the shutter button to complete the picture, instead taking in each and every detail, such as the way the rice grass in the paddy was bent and how the water drifted in little circles, everything together, like a multiple-exposure photograph.

As the wound in the middle of Joey's chest began to dry in the sun—TRAIN FOR COMPUTERS ("What about a train for people?" "Yuck, yuck, Flanagan, you're a sick fuck")—Billy watched as the flies came to feed and lay their eggs, from which maggots would grow and produce more flies, which would find other dead and dying soldiers or dogs or water buffaloes where they could rest their weary bodies and deposit life because they didn't know any better; his own body, as if joined to Joey's, becoming more and more rigid. Numbed by the desire to join his friend and buddy and also be dead, Billy eventually decided to forgive the flies for swarming around Joey and entering the punctured helmet to sit on his own head. In the middle of that rice paddy and the horror of that experience, Billy prayed with the fervor and trust of his childhood and vowed then to never allow anger to be part of his life.

The Lower East Side reminded Billy not of his high school days, when he'd come down with his friends to cop grass, but of Da Nang—people talking and him not understanding and the smells so foreign that he had numerous flashbacks of explosions, rapid-fire shooting, whining mortars, and whirring helicopters. He controlled himself and didn't run for cover but nervously kept telling people he was looking for Joey Santiago's family, going up and down from Fourteenth Street to Houston and from Houston to Canal Street, from Third Avenue to Alphabet City and the FDR Drive and then cutting back over Houston and crisscrossing the streets down to the Henry Street Settlement, talking to junkies and housewives alike, to little kids and Jewish peddlers—pleading with them and showing them the picture of Joey in a green undershirt with his dog tags around his neck, until he found Elsa Santiago, who would become Vidamía's mother, on Orchard Street, walking home from Seward Park High School.

What Ursula Santiago didn't want to tell her granddaughter, Vidamía, was that her father had somehow managed to get himself down to the Lower East Side and over a period of a week had located Joey's family. Utilizing every spare moment, he asked one person after the other until he found Elsa and came up to their apartment, looking like some lost soul, pale and thin and like the life had been drawn out of his eyes, and said he'd been with Joey when he died. "Viet Cong grenade, mortar maybe," he'd said. "I'm not sure." He told them that he and Joey were best friends. Elsa Santiago, just fifteen years of age, who had brought Billy into the house, watched him worshipfully, so that Ursula knew that her daughter was smitten and the first time she got a chance she'd go off with him like a bitch in heat. And that's exactly what had happened.

Elsa remembered a letter she had received from Joey with a picture of him and Billy, their hair in crewcuts, smiling and without a care because they were Marines. Semper Fi, you hump. It was like a dream come true, because reading the letter she had fallen in love with the handsome blond boy and recognized him now even through the beard and the sadness, which he wore permanently. Smiling boldly, she said, "You're Billy Farrell, ain't ya?" and knew that someday she would marry him (so went her fantasy), so that before they had spoken ten words or taken ten steps there had been an enormous outpouring from Elsa's primed Bartholin's glands, which caused the nylon and cotton fabric covering her virgin loins to become soaked and fragrant with love. Her eyes became blind to Billy's manual disability so evident to everyone who saw him when he had to display both hands—such as the times he had to cut steak or read a newspaper or a book in public or help someone lift something.

Vidamía sat staring out of the window of her Tarrytown prison, confined there by her mother, the former Elsa Santiago of Rivington Street in the Spanglish-speaking Warsaw Ghetto of Latin America, from which Elsa had eventually escaped through effort and travail to obtain a Ph.D. in psychology. Thus armed, Elsa had established a private practice of psychotherapy-cum-counseling-of-marital-irregularities-and-discords. And when Vidamía was six years of age, Elsa, having just finished her undergraduate work at Hunter College, wed a certain Mr. Barry López-Ferrer, a C.P.A. of considerable art, who, it was rumored in business circles, could balance and make dance any number of accounts on the head of a financial pin, provided you gave him enough *música* for tax write-offs. Together the two made money faster than it could be printed. They took this inky currency and invested it every which way, in mutual funds, real estate, stocks, and municipal bonds, so that in eleven years this hyphenated conglomerate of Puerto Rican ingenuity, without much beating around the pubic area—and in spite of anything one might hear about this other chosen people's lack of git-up-and-go—was worth two cool million dollars, give or take a couple hundred thou. They now affected the lifestyle of the rich and famous, complete with *muchos* Mercedes (and not Santiago or López, but of the Benz variety), together with cabin cruisers, multiple homes (*and* orgasms), trips to Europe, memberships in private clubs, and enough plastic pecuniarities and credit ratings to re-build a small underdeveloped country or even the South Bronx if they so wished—which they did not—opting instead to do good deeds in their own community of Westchester County through the United Way and recognized hospital and church charities, taking care of the homefront, so to speak, where it could be more appreciated since it is a well-known fact that truly poor ghetto denizens have, among their many flaws, a horrid sense of gratitude. And in any case if the Puerto Ricans who were left behind were going to make anything of themselves they had better do it as Elsa and Barry had, by pulling them-selves up by their own bootstraps, referring to Operation Boot-strap, a U.S. program to further justify colonial rule on the island.

Mrs. Barry López-Ferrer, née Elsa Santiago, had forgotten, as if her graduate studies had culturally lobotomized her, that at one time she was a Latin from Manhattan who with her mother,

Ursula Santiago, shopped on Orchard Street for bargains and on Saturdays accompanied her to the Essex Street Market to buy chicken and chops, listening to her mother say *shiken* and *shops* and not being ashamed of her like some people, because back then she was proud to be a Puerto Rican, ready to throw down and deal if anyone black, white, or Oriental got it into their heads to be fucking with you. "Girl, what's wrong with you that you be coming around with your bad self selling tickets? You better dig yourself, homegirl, and don't be sniffing around my man like some stray *perra puta*. You know what I mean? Cause if you don't I'ma teach you something you ain't never gonna learn in school, chile." All the while talking her modified black English as if the down-home accenting of her Puerto Rican phrases carried with them the malevolent authority of the *morenos*, whom she, as a Rican, feared and secretly admired for their style in dealing with white people.

In high school, homegirl par excellence Elsa Santiago of Rivington Street had her crew at Seward Park that went back to grammar school. She was down with Sonia Escobar, Mandy Lugo, Denise Aguayo, Baby Contreras, Daisy Marrero, Carmen Texidor, Hilda Pantoja, and Josie Villegas, who became a cop— and who would've thought it since she was the baddest of all her homegirls and the one who, when they were eleven or twelve, introduced them all to pot, all of them playing hooky one afternoon and lighting up the joint in Carmen Texidor's basement apartment while Carmen's mother, who was the super, was in the hospital having the twins, and all of them getting high and giggling at the slightest little thing, talking about boys, getting hungry, and cleaning out the entire kitchen of all food.

And now this little spic-mick, this Hibernian *boricua*, this idiotic blend of blarney and *pimienta*, of bagpipes and *salsa*, this San Juan Dubliner was making her recall how painful that existence had been and how far she had come from that wretched childhood and how stupid she had been, how utterly romantic she had been about Billy Farrell and his frayed psyche, how desolate everything had been, knowing she would never see her brother Joey again. In later years, when she had the opportunity to be psychoanalyzed, she learned how bad she felt that she didn't miss Joey or care what had happened to him in Vietnam, not because she was trying to block out the pain that should've been there, but because there was no pain at all. Her only concern had been this animal hunger which she felt deep inside her tiny womb, that void crying out to be filled with this Billy Farrell, who permitted himself to be led by her into a love which she herself eventually learned was mostly her own youthful fantasy.

But back then, at fifteen, latching on to that fatigued arm as if it were the most natural thing for a girl to do in the middle of Attorney Street, and, crossing Houston Street, unconcerned by time until they hit the number streets and the alphabet avenues and found themselves down by the river, watching the cars going over the Williamsburg Bridge into Brooklyn and her life crying out for him to possess her, to be inside of her, and not knowing what the hell that was about since all her homegirls did was talk and none of them had done it yet, not even Mandy Lugo, who was a year older than all of them—talking bad but being the good girls their *mamis* and sometimes *papis* had brought them up to be. But feeling all the knowledge inside of her and knowing that she was going to have a child by him and therefore instinctively setting up a nest at Sonia Escobar's apartment in the projects on Avenue D while Sonia's mother was in P.R.

Elsa, Vidamía's mother-to-be, came to her homegirl, Sonia, with a story about a friend of Joey's from Vietnam. He'd been messed up by the war, and not being from New York had no place to stay and he couldn't stay at her house. "Because you know how mothers are about boys. Yeah, a *gringo* white boy, who was all lost and whatnot, *un americano, panita de* Joey"—not wanting to admit to Sonia how much she had been affected by

Billy. Sonia gave Elsa the keys and instructed her that if anyone asked what she was doing to say she was a cousin of Sonia's, watering the plants while her aunt was in P.R., okay?

And then going to the apartment and setting up house early in the morning when she was supposed to be going to school and one thing led to another and she couldn't believe what was happening. Just kissing at first and then his hands were all over her and he was removing her blouse and her bra, then her pants and underwear and she was naked on the couch and his finger and tongue going into her at the same time and far away she could hear herself moaning and the pleasure coming from deep inside of her so that it hurt but not really. And then they were on that big huge bed and she feeling the way she did, so open that she couldn't tell when his *coso* actually went in and didn't even hurt that much like it was supposed to and after the third day liking the full feeling inside of her and it all came out, the feeling and the words that went with it, crazy stuff, but saying those words of love with all her heart in English and Spanish and punctuating it all with *Sí, sí, vida mía, sí.*

After a while, when it was over, he asked her what she was saying and she said, "Nothing." But he insisted and said, "I'm sorry I don't understand Spanish, but it sounded like a sweet rose or something like that." She couldn't recall her exact words but she relented and said, "What?" " 'Vidamía,' what does it mean?" he said. And she said, "It means 'my life.' " "Like I'm your life, or my life belongs to you, or something like that?" he asked, and she said, the words insignificant, but listening to the life growing inside of her, "Yes, something like that." And she held him while he cried and said, "Thank you and God bless you, that's the most beautiful thing I ever heard."

By Friday, her mother, Ursula Santiago, knew what was going on because all the baby fat and innocence had vanished from Elsa's body and her hips were wider and her breasts fuller and she talked with the confidence of *una mujer encinta*, which she

23

was—pregnant—categorically and unarguably from the first emission of love which Billy Farrell shot into her virgin Puerto Rican womb. So her mother asked what was she going to do with a child to raise at such an early age and of course Elsa denied everything and cried, but her mother knew there was another life coming so she added one hundred more grains of rice to one pot and fifty extra beans to another and continued stirring the food at her stove of Caribbean desolation.

They made the best of it, and even tried having Billy live with them, and that was okay because he contributed mightily to the household income from his disability check and even got a job handing out flyers for an exercise studio down on Wall Street to bring in extra money. But the arrangement didn't work and the more pregnant Elsa became, the sorrier she was she had allowed an intruder into her body, meaning Billy, the stranger who would forever complicate her life. She cried and carried on and was forced to drop out of Seward Park High School and was used as an example by wary mothers and overzealous guidance counselors. She eventually considered an abortion, but by the time she had that thought it was too late.

Nevertheless . . . once she found out exactly what happens during birth and how she would be ripped apart by this thing growing inside of her—she drove Billy away with her prepartum dementia, unconcerned with how much she and the baby meant to him after going through the shock of Joey dying in his arms, which (as a foretelling of her eventual psychoanalytic leanings) she encouraged him to talk about and get out of his system.

Trusting her with his life, since she indeed was carrying part of him within her, Billy attempted to reveal every gruesome detail, down to the fact that he could actually see Joey's mangled heart lying inside his open body and his face frozen into, not a pained look, but one of annoyance, so that all Billy could think about was of someone who has just stubbed his toe out of carelessness, making him feel so bad that a few days later, in front of her mother, Ursula Santiago, who knew genuine pain when she encountered it, he again apologized for letting Joey die and said, whatever they did, if it was a boy please name him Joey.

"And if it's a girl?" Ursula said.

"Vidamía," Billy Farrell said, looking longingly at Elsa.

"Yeah?" Ursula asked, looking at Elsa.

"Yeah, sure," Elsa said, looking at the linoleum in the kitchen.

"Here's my number," Billy said, handing Elsa a piece of paper. "And I'm sorry. If you and the baby need anything, let me know."

And that was that.

In the fall Billy Farrell returned to the park in the Lower East Side many times until one day he saw Elsa, her stomach flat once again, pushing a baby carriage. He didn't dare approach her, fearful that upon seeing the child he'd want to hold it and keep it and the pain of not being able to do so would be too great, convinced, perhaps as a wish, that it was a boy and his name was Joey, so that at least he could believe that he had brought his poor friend back to life, though he learned subsequently that the baby was a girl, from the pink baby clothing she was wearing.

When Elsa was brought the cleft product of her despair, she told her mother that she wanted to name her Katherine Ann, or maybe Stacey, and her mother asked her what kind of people did she think they were, promising the father what the child would be called and then going back on their word like some backstabbing, conniving sneak, stressing that being poor wasn't a good enough excuse for lying or cheating. So no matter what she may put forth as an argument, it was useless because she had given the child's father her word.

"Vidamía, just like the father asked, and make sure you spell his last name right to the nurse for the birth certificate because he's a veteran and the government checks on things like that for benefits," adding that if Elsa was too young to have sense enough to care for her daughter, she, as the child's grandmother, wasn't.

"He ain't gonna find out, *mami*," Elsa said.

"No, Elsa, you gonna name her the way he wanted."

"Vidamía?"

"That's right."

"Vidamía? Vidamía Farrell?"

"Yeah, Vidamía Farrell, just like the father said."

"That's it? No middle name, no nothing?"

"Yeah, that's it. No middle name and no nothing."

"That ain't no name, *mami*."

"It is now," Ursula said.

3 Creature Discomforts

And so Ursula Santiago prevailed, and Elsa, thwarted in her efforts to rid herself of the shame that she felt in giving her daughter such an unusual name, celebrated her sweet-sixteen birthday not only having been kissed but deflorated in a love-crazed episode of confusing sensations of pleasure and guilt. Inducted into motherhood, she found, as the years passed and she peeled away layers of her mind, that she not only hated her own motherhood, but was incited to that emotion by her own feelings toward her mother, whom she saw as weak and sacrificing. In Elsa's opinion her mother was a fool, for Ursula Santiago sacrificed herself first to an ungrateful husband and then to her children, rising early in the morning and standing by the stove, year round, to prepare their breakfast; slaving the rest of the day at making beds, cleaning the house, and doing laundry, often by hand. When not attending to these tasks, Ursula stood sentinel-like by the mailbox to make sure her Aid to Dependent Children checks were not stolen. Additionally, she waited defiantly in line to receive welfare food and then devised ways of making the food palatable.

Whenever there were family gatherings now, Elsa still recalled fondly the large, ripe plantains carefully hollowed out and filled with a core of welfare cheese from the big five-pound bricks which, as if by some magical family tradition, sat like a beneficent icon in their refrigerator, seemingly never diminishing in size, like some sort of self-generating entity. Like all children of the state, she remembered the thick peanut-butter-and-jelly sandwiches, and the rich butter which they spread liberally on bread and ate whenever hunger attacked them, conflicted as she grew up because the food quelled her hunger but, as she matured, made her curse her fate as a Puerto Rican for suffering the indignity of having the government take care of her.

Her mother even found use for the white flour, which everyone in the neighborhood threw away and which she bought for pennies a pound from them, storing it in large metal Sultana cracker containers which she obtained from *bodegas* in the neighborhood. She'd buy dried codfish, soak it in water to desalt it, cook it, remove the bones, and tear it into small shreds. She then made a big flour batter which she seasoned with spices. Pushing a supermarket cart that held a can of lard, a large cooking pot, a folding table, frying utensils, paper napkins, her apron, and a money changer she'd bought in a thrift shop, she'd leave early on weekend mornings during warm weather with Joey and Elsa, who were the youngest, while their sisters and Bobby worked at stacking grocery stores or clerking. Trailing their mother and picking up pieces of wood, which they put in a beat-up red wagon, they would make their way east on Houston and across the footbridge to the baseball diamonds.

There in the park, upon a structure of gathered bricks and a shelf from a discarded refrigerator, she lit a fire and placed the large pot on it. In the pot, three-quarters filled with boiling lard, she cooked crispy *bacalaitos*, which when done, she placed on a large dish and sold for fifty cents each. Hundreds of them in a day, her white fingers and hands shiny with the grease, dropping large spoonfuls of the codfish-laden batter into the boiling shortening, the batter coalescing into big cracker-like golden fritters which people loved, buying them up so fast that she took to preparing three large plastic containers of the batter which Elsa and Joey had to return to the apartment a couple of times during the day to get from the refrigerator and bring back to their mother in the shopping cart. Ursula Santiago always picked the fritters up with a napkin in her left hand, took the money with her right, and quickly maneuvered her coin changer when it was necessary. When she had to deal with large bills she went into her apron and deftly counted out the change, always smiling and thanking everyone. She never had to hawk her wares like other people, possessing a natural magnetism which Elsa, in spite of her feelings, found remarkable and secretly admired.

On days when it rained, her mother sat by the window, bereft of any joy, and lectured them on how important it was to learn and to work hard. But there were more sunny days than rainy ones and on Mondays she would go to the Banco Popular on Delancey Street with a paper bag filled with greasy bills and the pennies, nickels, dimes, and quarters which had been divided into their proper plastic containers—and washed with detergent and dried—before being placed in paper rolls so that the grease didn't soak through the paper, thus giving the term "money laundering" a whole new meaning. With the money her mother earned she was able to buy everyone extra shoes and winter coats and for their birthdays and Christmas always some special gift or treat. Elsa loved and admired her mother in those days, but somehow something had gone wrong, and she hadn't figured out yet what that was.

Ursula Santiago, once a shy, plain-looking peasant girl who

had come from the town of Cacimar in the mountains of Puerto Rico in 1946, was so strict as to be tyrannical when it came to school, manners, respect for elders, and being truthful. Always encouraging her children with her simple philosophy that if you did good, good things would happen to you, intolerant of sloth and mendacity. Hilda, Bobby, Milagros, Nancy, Joey, and Elsa, all of them stuffed into that two-bedroom apartment, the girls, all three of them, sleeping in the big double bed, Bobby and Joey in the bunk beds in the other room and Elsa, being the baby, with her mother on the sofa bed in the living room. Every couple of weeks their father showed up and she yielded her place and slept with her sisters and listened to them talk about boys.

As Elsa grew up, something that she had never been willing to label hatred crept into her view of Ursula Santiago. So pervasive was this loathing of her mother's values that it provided the impetus for her master's thesis. Her study was titled, with a certain measure of self-reflective irony, *The Martyr Complex in the Puerto Rican Immigrant Woman and Its Deleterious Effects on Her Children*. Elsa refused to acknowledge that her own drive to excel had been nurtured by her mother, nor was she able to justify, under her theory, how her brother Bobby had supported his family by managing a supermarket and, over the years, had acquired a business degree; nor how Hilda, Milagros, and Nancy had attended college and worked as teachers, Hilda rising to the position of principal at a grammar school in the Bronx.

According to her thesis, the Puerto Rican woman sacrificed herself to such an extent that it made her offspring socially docile and extremely pliable. This docility eventually placed the offspring in various high-risk groups for people suffering sundry mental disorders with their attendant physical problems. As an antidote to this social propensity, and perhaps to justify her distant attitude toward her own daughter, Elsa Santiago considered herself a paragon of scientific objectivity. In every respect she distanced herself from the commonality of simple human emotion, viewing everything in behavioral terms and attributing all expressions of feeling, whether of a negative or positive nature, to aberrational conduct.

Back then, she hated, with even greater passion, her father and everything he represented, for his sins were unforgivable: the carelessness in living, going from one Latin band to another as if he were a hired gun; instead of *pistolas*, toting his congas from one club to another in the *cuchifrito* circuit; drinking and womanizing; the future and its dangers of no concern to him. She despised him—and, above all, his Latino pride, his Puerto Rican insistence on personal independence, even though he was enslaved in the most basic of ways.

On the issue of personal freedom she was most critical, since she was a staunch believer in the independence of Puerto Rico and aligned herself with the intellectuals who espoused the belief that a great injustice had been done to the island by the United States. At parties and dinners she still regaled guests and friends with her stories of having met William Morales, allegedly of the FALN, when she was a student at Hunter and he at City College, condemning anyone who called him a terrorist and defending his actions against the U.S. as those of a Puerto Rican patriot, someone who was fighting for the independence of his homeland, or at least his parents' homeland, pausing to make reference to her father's life, without mentioning him, as an example of certain Puerto Ricans who had no political pride. Even today she could only recall with repugnance his awful accent and his dark skin, oblivious to anything around him except his music, promising to bring her weird stuff like the time he said he was going to bring her a crab.

"Where you going, *papi?*" she'd once asked.

"I gonna play with *Machito en Puerto Rico, mijita.* Ju be googel, helpy ju motha and I bringy ju a *cangrejo*," he'd say, playing with her.

"What's a cangreho, *papi?*"

"Ha, ha. Ju no, a *juey*."

"A whohey, *papi*?"

"Jezz, a *juey*," he'd say, laughing, picking up his congas in their bags and waving at her as he went out the door, never kissing her or hugging her, and Hilda and Milagros laughing and explaining that a *cangrejo* and a *juey* were the same thing.

"A crab, dopey," Hilda said. "He's gonna bring you a crab."

"Really?" she'd said, truly excited by the prospect.

"Yeah, really," Milagros said and she and Hilda pushed each other and laughed.

Years later, at a friend's house, where they had prepared one of the most delicious dishes of Puerto Rican cuisine, *salmorejo de jueyes*, she recalled her father and refused to give herself the pleasure of enjoying the crab dish. She still recalled times when she wanted to sit on his lap and he got up at the last minute. She hardly ever saw him while she was a little girl. He never played with her or took her anywhere, dropping by so seldom that the first few years she hid whenever he came in. After her seventh birthday, he stopped coming around.

Later on, after she had studied and observed people she realized that her father wasn't unique. There were men who couldn't face up to the responsibility of marriage and children. Milagros, her oldest sister, who had gotten married and moved to the Bronx, came back one Christmas when Elsa was twelve and said she'd seen their father.

"Did you talk to him?" Elsa had said.

"Are you kidding?" Milagros said. "No way. Anyhow, he was with a woman. *Una mujer trigueña*. Darker than him."

"Was she pretty?"

"Yeah, she was sort of cute. Young. Maybe a couple of years older than me. Looked a little like your friend. What's her name?"

"Baby Contreras?"

"Yeah, Baby. *Trigueñita así*. Like that. Her color."

She had gone into the bedroom and cried, unable to stop her tears for nearly an hour. When she was finished she washed her face and swore that she'd never see him, talk to him, or think of him again. But he was always there, grinning at her, his gold tooth glimmering below his mustache and his hair slicked back, *pelo estirao*, his hair straightened because otherwise it'd be all kinky. But she had good hair, and her skin, although not totally white because who needed that, was a nice creamy color and golden when she was out in the sun.

The day word came about Joey, she had called out to her mother and, receiving no answer, found her lying on the bed with Joey's picture in his Marine uniform clutched to her breast, crying quietly in the darkened room so that Elsa immediately knew her brother was dead— recognizing the presence of death to which she had grown accustomed, having seen death consistently since she was a child, beginning in the second grade when her friend Gigi Flores was shot walking to school on Stanton Street when a couple of drug dealers decided to settle things near the Pitt Street Pool and one of the bullets ricocheted off a building and a fragment traveled uncannily at the precise angle to strike Gigi below her right jaw, penetrating the neck just deeply enough to sever the carotid artery so that she was dead within minutes. Or the friends who died of overdoses or were murdered by phantoms, no one ever knowing why or what had happened. Late at night she tried counting all the people she had known who had died before they were thirty years old. She would lose count up around seventy, all of them lying in their caskets quietly, no longer talking back or protecting their dignity, but silenced forever.

That her brother Joey, whom she loved and felt closer to than any of her other siblings because he was always her supporter and had fought countless battles on her behalf, was dead, left her numb for months. Eventually the numbness turned into glacial indifference, and, like the other deaths, she accepted it with the same resignation that life in the neighborhood imposed on everyone. It was as if the area were the center of a thought system that without saying so imposed every tenet of a determinist philosophy, a mutually agreed-on predestination which left human beings spiritually limp and without true will.

Her pregnancy had simply happened to her, and once that recklessness, that abnegation of responsibility in becoming pregnant became apparent to her, she began having second thoughts. She recalled those first weeks after she'd told her mother that she was going to have a baby and could Billy move in with them since he was the father and anyway she was the only one left in the house and it would be good to have a man around. Her mother had nodded bravely and said she'd start cleaning out the room, explaining that the only condition was that he help with the household. Elsa reassured her mother that Billy would help out and she set about making their room a love nest, using the money from her weekend baby-sitting jobs to buy curtains and new sheets and a flowered bedspread. She loved walking down the street with Billy, his big strong arm around her waist and her own around his, usually hooking her thumb in the pocket of his jeans and feeling his buttocks with the rest of her hand.

He was taller than most people she knew, but the way he talked made him seem shorter and like he was one of them. He talked like he was black, not exactly like the *morenos*, but not unlike them. "I can dig it," he'd say. Or in greeting someone he'd say things like, "What's happenin', brother?" And when the person answered, his head'd be nodding patiently, his eyes half-closed like he was high, which sometimes he was when they smoked and listened to records up in the room, and he'd say, "I hear you, man. Most definitely." And he'd always refer to guys as "cats." But most of the time he was quiet, like his mind was far away.

They'd walk around the neighborhood and go shopping for her mother and once in a while they'd go over to Greenwich Village and walk around late at night and then he'd grow very quiet and a couple of times they'd stopped by a club on Seventh Avenue, the Village Vanguard, or Boomer's, or the Village Gate on Bleecker Street, and he'd stand listening to the music, his head keeping time. She'd ask him if he wanted to go in, but he'd shake his head and walk down the street, his step hurried. She'd chase after him, asking him what was the matter, but he'd never answer and then they'd go over and sit in Tompkins Square Park until whatever was going on with him passed. Eventually, he told her he used to be a musician and played jazz, but she didn't know what jazz was and hadn't pursued the discussion, not finding out that he was a pianist until Vidamía got it into her head that she wanted to help him.

The first few months of the pregnancy were both heaven and hell. She'd heard about morning sickness before but never imagined it would be as devastating as it was. At first the notion that she was pregnant gave her a feeling of absolute power. When her girlfriends found out that she was expecting, she became a celebrity and overnight she was an authority on lovemaking and pregnancy, subjects of almost obsessive proportions with the other girls.

"What's it feel like in there?"

"The baby?"

"No, the thing."

"Does it hurt?"

"Is it really hard?"

"What if you have to pee while it's happening?"

"Suppose *he* has to pee?"

"My sister, Vilma, says the stuff is all sticky and smelly, but she likes it and she says it turns her on. She said she even tasted it."

"Yecht!"

"Yeah, I betcha it feels good."

"No way."

"Yeah, way. My cousin Maritza took a hot dog and put it in her *tontón*."

"With or without sauerkraut?"

"Gaw, Yolanda, you're such a stupid."

All of them talking at once and she feeling like she was in total control, explaining that you get sick and throw up the first couple of months, but it wasn't too bad, minimizing the experience but dreading waking up the next day. And the next morning she would be sick and vomiting and one day she'd even gone with Awilda and talked to a *comadre* of Awilda's aunt who knew a doctor who did abortions but he wanted five hundred dollars, and where the hell was she going to get that kind of money. She thought of asking Billy, but that would have been too cruel.

The feeling of wonder at being pregnant and living with a boy lasted into her fifth month of pregnancy. He seemed insatiable in his desire for her—the big blond boy who held her and kissed her passionately and went into her with a hunger that left her drained until she finally could no longer take the burden of absorbing the pain that poured out of him along with his orgasms and told him he had to leave, her ambivalence about him even puzzling to her.

"Please, Elsa," he'd said. "I love you. I want to marry you. I'll go to school. I'll learn to do something. Please, don't do this. Please."

"Oh, God, Billy," she'd replied, sitting on the bed, her belly beginning to show a little, making her skirt tight and uncomfortable. "I can't, I can't."

"Is it my hand?"

"No, no, it's not your hand," she'd screamed. "I don't even want to have the baby."

"Please don't say that. Please don't. It's going to be all right. It's just a helpless little baby, Elsa. It's never done anything to anybody. It's our baby."

"I don't care."

"Don't you love the baby?" he'd asked.

"I don't know," she'd answered honestly. "I'm supposed to, but I just feel so sick all the time. I'm sorry."

And he'd hold her and she'd cry and then they'd go to bed and he'd make love to her, calling her name and saying "I love you" and always he'd cry, quietly most times, but once in a while a great racking sob would escape his chest, and then she'd hold him and her own tears would come and after a while she'd fall asleep. Getting rid of Billy didn't improve the situation. She cried constantly, feeling abandoned and confused, needing to have him touch her and yearning to feel wanted again. And each day the creature inside her grew larger. "Creature" because that is what her mother and the people who spoke in Spanish called it. *La criatura.* She knew that in Spanish the word carried tenderness and fragility, while in English the word was close to "monster," something from another planet, or else like that movie they showed from time to time on TV, *The Creature from the Black Lagoon,* so that she imagined giving birth to an ugly, web-footed monster she would eventually have to kill.

◢ Zing! Went the Strings

Maud Farrell watched Vidamía fold the piece of paper with her address and telephone number on it, remove her wallet from her bag, slide the paper into a plastic slot, and drop the wallet back into the large bag. She liked the girl's spunkiness immediately. And then in a gesture that left Maud Farrell shaking her head, wondering how the girl could be so mature and so poised, Vidamía extended her hand across the bar and thanked her. Maud Farrell took the hand, feeling foolish, and shook it, thinking,

"This is crazy." This was her granddaughter, and she ought to put her arms around her and kiss her. She remained behind the bar, her heart swelling with pride, and decided there would be plenty of time for that. The girl left with Arnold Tyson and got into the patrol car to be driven to the train station so she could return home. Through the bar's window Maud watched the girl wave to her, those eyes pleading for her to keep her promise to let her meet her father soon.

When the patrol car was gone, Maud Farrell sat pensively, attempting to fashion the best way to let her son know that his daughter had come looking for him. At first she was angry that the entire matter had resurfaced. Back then, after he returned from Vietnam, she had been bothered that Billy was living down on the Lower East Side—with Puerto Ricans, at that. When he got involved with his friend's sister, she had kept her counsel because the war had damaged him too much for any emotion on her part to be of any help. But she'd hated Puerto Ricans because they'd shot Kevin, and she could never forgive them. She knew the hatred was irrational, against God's teaching, but she couldn't help feeling as she did.

As she finished setting up the bar and turned on the air-conditioning, she experienced the pleasure of recalling Vidamía: her green eyes large and bright, the lashes long, shading the eyes so that the golden specks in the green appeared to shimmer. The bridge of her nose was thin and perhaps too bony, its tip slightly turned up, the slight upward tilt reminiscent of her own mother, Brigid. She wasn't perfect but she was her granddaughter, and perhaps she saw greater beauty in her than was there.

That evening when Maud Farrell got off work, she met Ruby Broadway and they sat in the coffee shop up the street from Ruby's house and she told her about her granddaughter.

"Is she dark?" Ruby inquired.

"Is she what? Dark?"

"Yeah! Dark!" Ruby said.

"No, I told you," Maud answered. "She's sort of a golden color. Tawny. Like a lion."

"Yeah, what we call high yella," Ruby said. "What kinda hair she got?"

"Brown and wavy."

"Yep, sounds like a high yella gal to me," Ruby said. "You say her mama's Porto Rican?"

"Yeah, Billy met her down on the Lower East Side."

"Makes sense. Porto Ricans got plenty of black in them. Is she small or big?" Ruby said.

"I don't know. Tall. Maybe five seven. Gangly now, but a looker," she said and described the prominent cheekbones and full lips that gave Vidamía an exotic beauty which she couldn't quite place as belonging to any group or race so that Maud felt as if she had met someone so different from anyone she'd ever encountered. She'd have to ask the girl to bring her a picture.

"Oh, she is a lovely girl, this Vidamía. Just lovely," she told Ruby.

From Ruby's smile anyone could tell their friendship was a true one.

"You're sure one proud grandma, ain't you?" Ruby said.

"Yes, I am," Maud said.

They both laughed and ordered more rice pudding and coffee.

That night, before she fell asleep, she suddenly realized that the feeling of satisfaction which she had been experiencing since Vidamía left the bar was the same fierce, possessive, all-consuming maternal love that she felt for Billy. And then as if she were standing outdoors and the skies suddenly loosed a heavy downpour, the realization hit her. Billy's child was the girl she'd wanted to have with Kevin and never could; time after time carrying the child and in the second or third month losing it, until she dreaded becoming pregnant. And then Kevin was shot and gone forever. That ended any hope of ever again having a child because one thing she could never bring herself to do was open up her heart to another man. God help her, but it was one thing to need the company of a man, to need to have them touch you and feel their roughness and hardness, and another to love someone enough to want to have a child by him, and that time was gone now, receding like the delicate colors of a sunset.

She recalled being not yet seventeen years old and standing in the bleachers at Gaelic Park on Corlear Avenue in the Bronx with her girlfriends Rita Lyons and Trish Cunningham, who were older and worked as stenographers in Manhattan, watching the hurling game, the sticks flying and the young men in their short pants bouncing off each other, having gone there because Trish was dating Tommy Corcoran, who was a fireman. It was 1949 and all the boys had returned from the big war but everyone was already talking about another war, in Korea. All the girls had fellas and she was still in high school. Rita's fella was a sailor she'd met at a dance the previous year. He'd gone back home to West Virginia and wrote her long, tender letters. They were planning a June wedding and Rita had a beautiful diamond ring. After the wedding they would move down south where the family had a dairy farm. It was all so exciting that Rita looked dreamy-eyed most of the time.

When the game was finished, Tommy came over with a great big brawny boy with sandy brown hair and the bluest eyes and loveliest smile she'd ever seen. Her heart immediately began beating uncontrollably and all she could think of was the lyrics to the song "Zing! Went the Strings of My Heart," which she used to sing standing by the piano on Saturday afternoons when her father's friends came over to the house in Yonkers and played music. Candy Donovan, who used to sing down in the clubs and who was sweet on Charlie Parker, or so the rumors went, taught her how to sing the song.

"Hi, girls, this is my pal, Kevin Farrell," Tommy said, and

her knees were shaking. "Turns out we were with the same Marine outfit over in Europe. We didn't know it until we met at Charlie Dolan's in the Bronx. Kevin, this is my girl, Trish Cunningham. Ain't she a beauty? And this is Rita Lyons and the cute blonde is Maud Sanderson. Don't get any ideas, buddy. The redhead's engaged and the blonde is underage."

"Pleased to meet you," she'd said, cordially, avoiding looking at his eyes because the words of the song nearly burst out of her:

> *Your eyes made skies seem blue again,*
> *What else could I do again*
> *But keep repeating through again,*
> *"I love you, love you."*

When she next looked up, Kevin Farrell was looking at her and he said the strangest thing. Trish and Tommy had gone off, and Rita had followed, leaving her standing there, feeling like a fool. And then he said:

> *O blessed, blessed night! I am afeard,*
> *Being in night, all this is but a dream,*
> *Too flattering-sweet to be substantial.*

The words sounded so familiar. She went crazy for the next two weeks trying to remember, and then being positive it had to be Shakespeare, but what? She had no choice but to ask, so she went to Sister Agnes, the English teacher, and repeated what she could recall: ". . . all this is but a dream, too flattering-sweet to be substantial."

"*Romeo and Juliet*," Sister Agnes had said, a bit of a twinkle in her eye. "Is it some young cad said this to you, Maud Sanderson?"

"Oh no, Sister. It was my cousin, Margaret, that called me. She goes to Cathedral in Manhattan and she had a quiz. *Romeo and Juliet*. Thank you, Sister. I'll be sure to tell her. Thank you," she said curtseying twice and blushing as she backed out of the classroom, her heart beating wildly.

"What?" she'd said, standing in front of Kevin that first time in the cold afternoon wind, the autumn leaves turning in whirlpools on the ground and the ends of her kerchief flying at her face, her eyes riveted to her black-and-white laced shoes. "Was that a poem?" she said.

Kevin laughed, his voice like tinkling glass, strong and gentle at the same time.

"Yeah, a poem."

"From what?" she asked.

"The Bard," he said.

"The what?" she said, stupidly.

"Never mind," he said, pawing at the dirt with his cleats. And then looking up, smiling. "Will you come to the movies with me next Friday? There's a pretty good musical playing. You like music, don't you? Tommy says you like to sing."

"Oh, yes. Very much," she answered.

"Well, I'm a lonely guy and you're the most beautiful girl I've ever seen, and if you're underage, then let them take me to jail."

How could this be happening to her, she thought.

> *Dear, with your lips to mine,*
> *a rhapsody divine,*
> *Zing! went the strings of my heart.*

"So you'll go with me?" he said.

"Oh, I can't."

"Why? Do you have a fella?" Kevin asked.

"No, but I can't. I'm still in school," she said.

"It's a weekend. Friday."

"I'm not very smart, so I have to study hard to graduate," she said.

And then she opened up and didn't know why but explained that she had trouble reading and got things backward and everyone had always thought she was stupid, but she could do mathematics real well so she might go in for working as a clerk in a store and study bookkeeping at night. And then he said he was sorry and she asked why, and he shook his head and said he wasn't too smart either and hoped she'd change her mind and let him take her to the movies sometime.

"And then as openly as a little boy, Kevin asked her if she liked him at least a little bit, holding index and thumb but an inch apart, the hand up in front of his face so that his blue eyes were peering over the fingers. She smiled and felt herself blush, but she said, too boldly for her to believe, "Oh, a lot more than a little bit," and then ran off, calling to Rita to wait for her, but not before hearing Kevin let out a whoop of delight.

What a lovely man he was, always so honest and gentle. And they'd shot him, and she had been numb for more than three years so that not even Billy could penetrate her despair, the desolation in her heart so profound that more than once she had stood watching the railroad tracks below the bridge crossing into Yonkers and considered climbing down and lying in the path of a train. But it would be a terrible sin and she would burn in Hell forever.

She was glad now that she hadn't killed herself, but back then her loss had been unbearable. The understanding that she would now have partial responsibility for the well-being of a young woman produced both joy and sorrow in her. She cried quietly into her pillow, thinking, of all people, about Candy Donovan, pining away for Charlie Parker, following him from club to club and waiting until the club closed and other musicians came in for the early-morning sessions, listening to them jamming. Every once in a while they'd let her sing and she always sang things like "Lover, Come Back to Me!" or "Love for Sale," or "Just One of Those Things," with everyone playing up-tempo, and Candy breathless, wanting to scat but the nonsense words not coming out of her. At some point the musicians took a break and they'd light up some reefer and Candy Donovan smoked with them, just looking at Bird, her eyes brilliant with the love she felt for him, until one day he finally noticed her and they went off, Maud's father, Buck Sanderson, told her later, and stayed locked up in some Midtown hotel for about a week. After that, Candy, who could've never been a true jazz singer but definitely had some promise as a popular singer, certainly as good as, say, Teresa Brewer or Jo Stafford and girls like that who came later in the fifties, went a little crazy and started following Bird around. When he married his fourth wife, Chan, in 1950, and moved with her into an apartment across from Tompkins Square Park, Candy stood out there in the park for hours watching the windows, sometimes in the rain or snow, shivering and totally without hope, and when Bird came out she'd run away crying. Candy's girlfriend, Dotty Gagliano, told her about it when she came to Billy's christening. She said she went on like this for another six months until she finally dropped out of sight, and someone said her family kicked Candy out for hanging around with niggers.

Human beings were a silly lot, Maud thought. How they let their hearts rule their lives. And yet how could a person help herself? How sweet love had been with Kevin Farrell, and how sadly everything had turned out. They made love one summer evening after they were married a year and were living in the small apartment in Mount Vernon. In those days she was shy and unsure of herself, but he would spend time holding her and touching her in a very special way so that after a while she was lost and wanted him inside of her, and then he'd be inside, just resting there full and still and she couldn't help moving and then she could feel him surging up into her and the feeling was indescribable because he loved her so much. When it was over they lay very still, holding each other. The window was open and through it they could see the moon nearly full so that she saw their bodies clearly as she rested on his arm, his long fingers creating what looked to her like a shadow netting around her breast closest to him. She had always thought the size of her breasts excessive until he undressed her when they made love for the first time at his mother's apartment, in Hell's Kitchen in Manhattan, while she was working. He went crazy and praised their ampleness and beauty, kissing the nipples and caressing her so that his enthusiasm for her made her feel more sensual than she had a right to; afterward she felt sinful and confused, but at the same time happy.

"I'm sorry," he'd said that night with the window of their bedroom open and the moonlight streaming in to bless their marriage.

"What about?" she said, turning her face to look at him, her eyes hungering to see herself in his.

"About what I said to you when we first met. I didn't know you had trouble reading."

At first she couldn't recall what he'd said but then when it came back to her she told him she hadn't been hurt but just couldn't remember what he was quoting from and had to ask her English teacher.

"It was very embarrassing, I'll have you know," she said. "The sister could tell how smitten I was by your blarney."

He laughed and kissed her lips and said, "I love you, Maud Farrell. You're my girl." And she said, "Do you really?"

And he said, "Lady, by yonder moon I swear . . ." The lace curtains billowed out and on the gust of wind a dark shadow entered and a bat, sick or lost, had flown in and entangled itself in the cloth, shrieking its despair. The shadow, like an omen, invaded her heart. All night, even after Kevin swatted the animal with a broom and drove it out, she lay awake wondering what she'd done for this evil to enter her life. Her mother had shaken her head and said, "*Sciathan leathair*," when she told her about it. When Maud asked what that meant, her mother said it was Irish for bat, never calling the language Gaelic but insisting that it was Irish. "Leather wing," she'd said. "Ugly little beasts that suck your blood while you sleep."

The image of the desperate, keening animal fighting to free itself again rose up like a specter to cast a shadow against her future so that she felt unprotected, as if God and the Holy Mother and all the saints had deserted her. Whenever Kevin left her to go to work, the time he was away was beyond torture, long hours of profound desolation in which she imagined the worst and knew that someday word would come that her blue-eyed, lovely man was gone forever, taken away on the wings of angels because he was so good and was needed in Heaven. And she would grieve an eternity and never marry again.

How long had she gone on grieving? Six years. And then at Christmas of the sixth year she'd gone to her brother Michael's in Queens to celebrate the holidays. God forgive her, Nick, the second man she would make love to in her life, was there, his heart broken by the deaths of his wife and daughter in an auto accident while visiting relatives in Schenectady for Easter the previous spring. Nick Andreadakis worked with her brother at the firehouse, the two of them buddies, so she had felt at ease. He was a short, stocky man with black, sorrowful eyes and a thick mustache, about Michael's age, thirty-one or -two at the time. When it was time to leave, Nick said Michael didn't have to bother and he'd drive her back to the city. She said, unsure of herself, that it would certainly save Michael a trip, but she lived in Mount Vernon. He said that was no problem at all.

When they arrived at her apartment she thanked him and began getting out of the car. But he said, "Wait a minute," with the fierce urgency of someone whose life depended on what he was going to say next. He berated himself for not honoring his wife's death, but asked her if he could see her again. He seemed so vulnerable that she had no choice and said, "Sure, write down my number."

The following week he came and picked her up and they drove over to White Plains listening to the radio. Every other song was from the Beatles' *Sergeant Pepper's Lonely Hearts Club Band*, which had come out that year. They had dinner and then saw a movie. Halfway through the film, which she couldn't recall, she could feel Nick squirming around, trying to decide if he should take her hand. She was reminded of Kevin the first time they'd gone out, and all at once she felt a great feeling of joy lift up in her heart and she was there again, feeling the excitement of those first moments alone in the dark with him after the show was over and as the applause died down the place went dark and the newsreels came on. For the first time in six years she again felt the hot feeling in the middle of her body. She shifted in her seat so that she was closer to Nick and he put his arm, which was resting on the seat, around her shoulder and she snuggled against him and could feel him release a sigh of relief.

They went out a few more times and then one Saturday afternoon he picked her up at work. She asked him if he'd like to come to her apartment, she'd cook supper for him. He nodded and they drove off in silence, both certain of what would happen. Once they were inside her apartment and she removed her coat and he removed his, he was immediately on her, kissing her with an animal passion she had never experienced in a man, God forgive her. His swarthy face and mustache aroused her so much that she was clutching desperately at him, her tongue searching for his, her sex thrusting against him. She led him to the bedroom and when they were undressed rather than going up into her he knelt and lowered his head between her legs, which she had heard about men doing to women and women doing to men but which she and Kevin had never done. A moment later his

46

face was on her and his tongue was lapping at her little button and she was calling out to God, over and over, holding his face down, imagining the mustache knitting itself with her own hair, creating a wide, woven ribbon of black and blond that went on and on as the pain of the release left her in wave after wave of sobs and tears. When she thought there could be no sweeter pleasure, he was in her, immense and rigid, pounding her so that she was feeling release again and then felt his own orgasm in violent thrusts that later made her ache.

They were together three months, always making love with the same intensity and then one day he announced that he couldn't see her again because he'd met a young girl, recently arrived from Greece, and he was planning to marry her and that he hoped she understood. She was slightly hurt, but not as much as she had thought she would be. She wished him luck.

She missed Nick for a month or so and then she went to Atlantic City with Dotty Gagliano and her husband and they introduced her to Dotty's cousin Louis from Philadelphia, who was in construction and drove a convertible and the first night they were together they made love and that was fine because they laughed a lot and he said he'd come to New York and see her, if his wife let him. And they laughed some more and that was it. She understood then that she needed a man from time to time, and she began cultivating friendships with three or four men, married and needing her companionship; she had dinner with them and then they made love and they usually talked about their children and she listened and then they said goodbye and that was that—everything neat and orderly with no regrets and no attachments. She often thought of Kevin, but never while she was with someone else, feeling sinful then and not liking the feeling, yet able to separate the experiences, one a memory and the other a need.

She again thought of Vidamía and recognized that there was

something of Kevin in the girl, a deep, passionate love of life and a poetry which always remained a mystery to her, being as he was so gentle and such a big, rough man. There had always been something at the forefront of his existence, accessible and at the same time elusive. It was like his voice, which even in a whisper commanded attention. It was like what Candy Donovan had once said about singing: "Let the song sing you, honey." That was how she perceived this little Spanish wisp, like a powerful force over which she'd have no control. Maud could only bask in her radiance and be thankful to God that Vidamía had come into her life. Kevin had been like that, fragile and yet solid as granite, a paradox. She prayed fervently and sincerely that God keep her new child safe. When she was finished she crossed herself and felt better, seeing her granddaughter's face again until she drifted off to sleep.

5 A Latin from Manhattan

The torture of the pregnancy was unceasing and Elsa's visits to the maternity clinic interminably long. On the days that Elsa didn't skip school she acted unconcerned. If teachers asked her what was the matter, she said, "Nothing." When she began showing, in her sixth month, word finally got to the principal. The guidance counselor set up a time when she had to bring in her mother. Carefully, in very bad Spanish, they explained that her daughter couldn't stay in school if she was pregnant. They recommended a GED certificate or night school after the baby was born. Her mother nodded politely, never letting on that she read, wrote, and spoke English quite adequately. When she got outside she spit on the ground and cursed mightily. "They don't have mothers!" she said in Spanish, dismissing them all as sons of bitches. It was March. New clothes. Easter. Bonnets. Her mother bought her a beautiful maternity dress and a hat and they went to church, and in the afternoon Milagros's husband came to pick them up to go to their apartment in the Bronx to eat dinner.

In time Elsa got used to being alone, and the weeks began to pass more quickly. Then she was finally in the maternity ward of Bellevue Hospital, rushed there by her mother when her contractions began coming twenty minutes apart. When her water broke it was nearly two o'clock in the morning. She was lying in bed dreaming of being at Orchard Beach, where she often had gone with her homegirls. To get to the beach in those days, they would all walk over to Spring Street on summer mornings and take the Lexington Avenue Local, christened the Number 6 line by the Transit Authority in the winter of 1947, though always known as the Pelham Bay Local until 1967, when everything was spiffed up and made modern and the lines were color-coded on the maps so that everybody began calling it the Number 6— "El Número Seis"—Bobby Rodríguez y La Compañía's *salsa* number about the train that was their link to the sea, running from the Lower East Side up to East Harlem and into the South Bronx.

The neighborhoods were like towns in Puerto Rico. *El Barrio*, *Loisaida*, *Los Sures*, *Bushwee*, and, of course, *El Bron* which was their very own even though they had not yet colonized it, or brought it into the hegemony of *salsa*, Spanglish, the insouciance of being Rican and of *mañana* being synonymous with the next party. Hers was the Lower East Side which extended, in her childhood, from Fourteenth Street to Canal Street, at one point bisected so that north of Houston Street became the East Village, part of which would be christened *Loisaida* by the Celestial Warrior, Bimbo Rivas, converted into the Loisaida of poetry and dreams, with its bohemian ambiance and garishly painted *bode-gas* and restaurants and signs in Spanish.

Among his other tunes Bobby Rodríguez had one which they liked even more. It was kind of a Charleston with a Latin tempo. "She's a Latin from Manhattan" was like nothing they'd ever heard. They sang it in a chorus, all of them going crazy as they danced to it and sang to each other like it was a dialogue between several people:

> *Fate*
> *Sent her to me*
> *Over the sea from Spain.*
> *Ah! She's the one in a million*
> *For me.*
> *I found my romance*
> *When she went dancing by;*
> *Ah! She must be a Castilian,*
> *Sí, sí.*
> *Is she from Havana or Madrid?*
> *But something about her is making me doubt her,*
> *I think I remember the kid.*
>
> *She's a Latin from Manhattan,*
> *You can tell by her "Manyana."*
> *She's a Latin from Manhattan*
> *And not Havana.*
> *Though she does the rhumba for us*
> *And she calls herself Dolores,*
> *She was in a Broadway chorus,*
> *Known as Susie Donahue.*
> *She can take a tambourine and whack it,*
> *But with her it's just a racket,*
> *She's a hoofer from Tenth Avenue.*
> *She's a Latin from Manhattan,*

She's a Forty-second Streeter,
She's a Latin from Manhattan,
Señorita Donahue.

One time when she was thirteen, her sisters Hilda and Nancy dressed Elsa up. They put lipstick and eye shadow on her and did her hair so that when she looked in the mirror she didn't recognize herself. Her sister Milagros, who was married and pregnant with her first child, said she looked like Ava Gardner. Elsa felt her face get red and flushed, because Ava Gardner looked so beautiful in her films. The three of them had gone up to Hunter College for a Bobby Rodríguez concert—Hilda already engaged to be married and Nancy about to graduate from Seward Park. It was the first concert of any kind she'd gone to and she couldn't believe how excited she felt, sitting in the dark, wanting to get up and dance, wishing Joey was there to dance with her.

After Bobby Rodríguez y La Compañía played "She's a Latin from Manhattan," some homegirl interrupted Bobby Rodríguez while he was introducing the next number and said, "Why you gotta call the girl a hookah, huh? Why? Cause she's Rican, huh?" Bobby had pointed his clarinet at the girl and said, "Not hooker, darling. Hoofer. A dancer." And he made a little step and the audience applauded and then the orchestra played "El Número Seis" and Elsa couldn't stop smiling she was so happy. She thought about what she'd say when answering Joey's letter. He was in a place called Camp Lejeune.

For a time she thought she'd like to become a dancer. She recalled Joey and herself, the two of them dancing the fast *salsa* numbers, spinning and twirling, her feet so quick and light and her entire body feeling smooth and easy as they went through the complicated steps, the two of them like they were electronically synchronized, so well did they anticipate each other. Whenever they went dancing, people moved into a circle to watch them do their routine. Joey even talked about starting an act or maybe competing in ballroom-dancing contests. Joey knew every dance there was, but *salsa* was his thing.

Elsa loved those times with her homegirls, learning new steps and listening to records and laughing and carrying on. Her sisters all agreed that the girl in "Latin from Manhattan" had to be Rican.

"She's not from Havana or Madrid, right?" Hilda had said.

"Yeah, right," said Nancy.

"And she's a Latin from Manhattan."

"Yeah, so?" Milagros said, looking up from a book. "What's that gotta do with it?"

"What Latins we got the most of in Manhattan?" Hilda challenged, getting up from the couch. "Ricans, right?"

"Yeah, right, but what's this booshit about Señorita Donna Who?" Milagros said. "She lives on Fifth Avenue. That sounds like some rich girl to me."

"Oh, that just means they're making fun of Americans, girl," Nancy said.

"Yeah, cause they can't pronounce *Doña* and they're trying to figure out who this girl that can dance up a storm is," said Hilda, sitting back down.

"She's a Latin from Manhattan." Nancy took up the argument once more. "She's from *El Barrio*, from up there on Fifth Avenue, maybe around 110th Street. I can tell from her *mañana*, cause they probably picked up on our accent. They probably asked her when she could start and she probably said, 'Yo, *mañana*,' and whatnot. I'm sure when Bobby Rodríguez wrote the song he was talking about a homegirl called Suzy Dolores Rivera and they probably asked her mother's name and she said Doña Moncha or Doña Suncha. And when the American didn't understand, he said: Dona Who? So they call her Señorita Dona Who? Like, what do Americans know about our shit and what-not?"

That was as good an explanation as any, until last year, when Elsa was at a party out on Long Island at one of Barry's friends', and they were talking about old times, and Barry's friend, Tony, brought out some old records and they played "She's a Latin from Manhattan," this more than twenty years after the concert. Everybody agreed that the girl had to be Puerto Rican except Nando Alvericci from WBAI, who had a Latin music show on Sundays. He was an authority on the history of Latin music. He said that the song was really about an Irish girl, Suzy Donahue, who's trying to pass herself off as a Latin dancer called Dolores.

"The song is from the thirties," Nando said. "A show tune. I think it's in a movie, but I can't remember the name of it or who was in it. Bobby Rodríguez and La Compañía made it Latin. The girl's Irish. Suzy Donahue."

Everyone questioned his opinion, but he asked everyone to listen to the lyrics more closely and each person at the party began to nod their agreement.

"What's this stuff about Fifth Avenue? That's gotta be in *El Barrio*."

"The Irish lived on Fifth Avenue, up in Harlem," Nando said. "In those days Fifth Avenue was Irish. Maybe being a Forty-second Streeter just meant that she was a Broadway dancer. Bobby didn't write the song. I think the composer was Harry Warren."

They played the song three or four times in a row and she listened, feeling like somebody was forcing her to drink poison. But Nando was right. It was so clear. That the girl in the song was Irish made her blood boil.

She went out on the back porch of the house and stared out at the sea, digging her fingernails into her palms in rage. Barry came out and asked her if she was all right, knowing she wasn't and, beyond that, knowing it was best to leave her alone. He asked if she wanted a drink. She said scotch would be fine. A bottle if there's one handy, she said. After Barry returned with a half-bottle of Johnny Walker Red and handed it to her, and then a glass, which she refused, she took off her sandals and went down the stairs to the beach.

Dolores, she thought as she walked, tilting the bottle back and letting the liquor burn her throat, the alcohol making her woozy. She walked on and on, her feet digging into the now cool sand, the beach desolate as the sun began setting; walking and her heart raging at everything that was wrong with her life until the sun went down and she sat on the sand, drunk by then, and listened to the sea and cried. Billy Farrell, Irish. Suzy Donahue, Irish. Vidamía Farrell, her daughter, Irish. She was never prejudiced and now all this hatred was surfacing in her life, threatening to choke her, maybe turn her into a drunk. Wouldn't that be lovely. The Irish were supposed to be the drunks, but P.R.s could outdrink the bastards any day. She lay down and heard the sea far away as she drifted off. When Barry and Tony found her, the incoming tide was lapping at her feet. A few more minutes and she would've been carried off, Barry later told her. He wanted to know what had happened, but she couldn't discuss it with him. It had to do with Billy Farrell, and she didn't want to talk about him.

When Monday came she still couldn't believe the entire matter of the song and canceled all her appointments for the next two days as she made call after call to music stores, trying to get the sheet music to the song. She finally was able to get it at the Colony Record Shop, on Broadway at Forty-ninth. She looked at the lyrics and there she was, Suzy Donahue, except that the name on the music was spelled Susie, not Suzy. The more she read, the angrier she grew. She asked the man who'd brought her the sheet music about the song back in the thirties, expecting that somebody like Xavier Cugat had performed it. The man was in his seventies, gray hair and skin, his eyeglasses thick.

"Jolson," he said, matter-of-factly.

"Al Jolson?" she said, unbelieving. " 'Old Man River'? . . . 'Mammy'? . . . 'Swanee'?" Her display of the knowledge of America made her feel as if she were superior.

"That's him. Nice Jewish boy from New York whose papa wanted him to be a cantor."

"Do you have the recording?"

"I got a tape. You want it?"

She nodded, and when the old man came back with the tape she took it and began to go into her wallet for her credit card, when she saw him reach up to adjust his glasses. As his sleeve crept up she noticed the faded blue numbers on his arm. Tears filled her eyes, the numbers reminding her of the fate of the parents of her old therapist, Barbara Gelfand.

"He sang it in a movie," the old man said.

"Really?" she replied, feigning brightness. "The song? What was the movie?"

He smiled, his dentures too large and yellow—she guessed the Nazis had probably pulled out all his teeth—and told her that the film was called *Go Into Your Dance* and featured Al Jolson, Ruby Keeler, Helen Morgan, Phil Regan, Barton McLaine, Patsy Kelly, Betty Rubin, and Glenda Farrell.

"It was the only film Jolson and Keeler did together," the old man said. "They were husband and wife."

"Really?" she said, once again annoyed, but not sure why.

The coincidence of the name didn't hit her immediately. She paid for her purchases, hailed a cab, and headed for Grand Central for her trip back up to Tarrytown. Once again she heard the lyrics in her mind, and the words cut through her. And then she heard the old man again reciting the names of the actors. Glenda Farrell. She couldn't believe it. Farrell, like the William Farrell of her impulsiveness, of her *bollo loco* days. Irish. She read the lyrics on the sheet music and there it was. Of course. *"Tenth Avenue . . ."* Hell's Kitchen! That's where the little bitch lived. Passing herself off for a Latin, the cunt.

As the train moved, she heard the lyrics again and felt her fingernails digging into the palms of her hands. *"She can take a tambourine and whack it, but with her it's just a racket . . . She's a Latin from Manhattan, Señorita Donahue."* Who was Harry Warren? She was positive that, like Al Jolson, he must be Jewish and had simply changed his name.

When she got home she made Barry sit with her and listen to the Al Jolson rendition of the tune. It sounded dopey, outdated, the Latin music like something out of a Carmen Miranda movie. The year was 1935 and they were making a movie with a song about a Latin in Manhattan. Some of the lyrics made her laugh, but the laughter hurt. Bobby Rodríguez's version excluded certain lines but she couldn't imagine why. Barry, who knew a little about music said maybe they didn't fit with a *salsa* beat. He was right. *I found my romance when she went dancing by. Ah! she must be a Castilian. Sí, sí.*

The next day, having induced sleep through a combination of pills, she went back into the city and went to the library and learned that Harry Warren had been born in Brooklyn. His parents were from Calabria, Italy. His name was Salvatore Antonio Guaragna. He was Italian.

Harry Warren, who was Italian, wanted to be American. What did Señorita Donahue want? What did anybody want? Maybe Susie Donahue just wanted to eat good food and wear nice clothes and be around classy people, like she did. The recognition that her desires were so petty made her hate herself even more. She knew she had no burning desire, as a psychologist, to heal people. It was a means to an end. She wanted to be wealthy and forget where she'd come from. She heard the lyrics once more and then began drifting off.

Though she does the rhumba for us
And she calls herself Dolores,
She was in a Broadway chorus,
Known as Susie Donahue.

Back then, Elsa and her homegirls left early in the morning, hauling big bags full of sandwiches, beach towels, and suntan lotion and combs and brushes and makeup, "darling, because you never know when some fine *papi*'s gonna come along and you looking like the Wicked Witch from the West Village, honey"; and giggling and talking loud about boys as they rode the Number 6 all the way up to Pelham Bay Park, thirty-five stops; refusing to take the express train, "because how you gonna go all the way up there to Orchard Beach standing up? Like, what am I, some sort of *pendeja*, I gotta stand up while all these *blanquitas* are sitting down warming their white *culos*? Fuck that booshit, girl." Twelve or fifteen overactive Puerto Rican girls on the loose, talking all at once in English and Spanish, going back and forth from one language to the other with the ease with which they and their relatives went back and forth from the States to the island so that later on, when she was in college, she heard someone say at a party that with the money Puerto Ricans had spent on airfare coming and going between Puerto Rico and the States, they could have built themselves a bridge and simply driven to the island. But back then giggling and singing and playing hand-clapping games like they were still in grammar school. Lining up and down the middle of the subway car like a chorus line, while their big bags held their seats, they sang and danced to the Wallaby song.

This is the way we wallaby, wallaby, wallaby.
This is the way we wallaby all night long.

Step back, Sally, Sally, Sally.
Step back, Sally, all night long.
I called the doctor and the doctor said,
I got a pain in my stomach cause my baby's dead.
I got a pain in my side cause I went for a ride.
I got a pain in my back cause I sat on a tack.
Roll 'em, roll 'em, cigarette man.

Or else they'd do a cheer they had learned in summer camp from a little *blanquita*-looking girl with blue eyes from Uptown that had a Rican father who'd married some white woman. The *blanquita* girl's name was Ali Sue, some name like that, she thought. "And she was Rican?" somebody said. "Yeah, she speaks Spanish better than dopey Mandy Betancourt and her sister Connie who think they're guineas and whatnot."

Eenie meenie pepsodeenie
Ah bah boobaleenie
Achy, pachy Liberace,
Ann's brother George got a peach, got a plum,
Got a stick of cherry gum.
And if you want one,
This is what you say:
Amen, Amen, A-mendiego, San Diego
Hocus Pocus Dominocus
Brave Eagles
Sitting on a bandstand, beating on a tin can.
Gees, gees, gees boom bah.
Horses, horses, yah, yah, yah.

Crazy-ass shit but she still remembered it all. Everything happened so quickly. One minute they were all girls wondering what boys were all about and the next they were women, all of them having done it, with differing degrees of success, some claiming that they couldn't believe what the big deal was about and only a few, like Carmen Texidor, who was always the hippest of them and always reading weird shit, saying dopey things like, "Man, it's better than ice cream, girl. You just gotta relax and tighten up your butt and move your thing."

And they all went, "What?"

"Girl, wherechuget that?"

And she said, "*Cosmo*."

And everyone looked at her like she was crazy.

"*Cosmo*?"

"Yeah. It says you tighten your butt like when you have to go *caca* and you don't wanna let it go cause you in the elevator going to your house and whatnot."

They all giggled and looked at each other but they all started doing it in the park and Lily Betancourt said, "Oh my God. Girl, that is too much. How much it costes, that magazine?"

"What are you ohmygodding about, girl?" said Baby Contreras.

And Carmen Texidor stepped in and said that maybe Lily was having a thing.

"What thing?" they all said.

"A orgasm," Carmen said and they all went: "A what?"

And now they really giggled and gave each other fives and pushed each other and Beatrice Cordero called it an *oregano* and that's what they all began calling it and eventually read in *Cosmo* about multiple *oreganos*, which she herself now reported had happened with Billy Farrell when she had been on top of him and moving and all at once her *tontón* had started moving on its own and she could hardly breathe and all she could do was throw herself on him and hold on and her body felt like it was flying away from her and her head like it had gone totally blank so that when she told it all her homegirls looked at her with their mouths open and said things like, "For real?" But it stopped happening soon after for Elsa and hardly ever happened with

Barry, except the first year or so. It didn't matter. Her homegirls had all gone and gotten pregnant over and over; some of them had kids by three different guys and some didn't even know who their kids' fathers were. It was like she had started the whole thing with her stupid infatuation with Billy Farrell, damn him and his destroyed life.

Twenty-two hours she had to wait for her to be born.

6 Identity

Finding her father and having another family gave Vidamía's life a different purpose. It confirmed what she had always thought about her existence. It was like the proud feeling she experienced when she placed her hand over her heart each morning and pledged allegiance to the flag, or whenever they played the national anthem, believing in her fantasies that she was one of the drummer boys of the American Revolution, or a soldier in the Civil War, fighting on the side of the North because she felt so bad for the slaves, whose families were sometimes broken up—the mother going one way and the children the other and the father still another, all of them sold as property.

She recalled two years prior being in a restaurant in New York City with her mother and overhearing a black couple talking about a book called *Roots* in which a black family was separated. Coming home on the train, she asked her mother if she had the book. Elsa said the book was probably in their library. As soon as she entered the house she went to the library of the very well-kept Santiago López-Ferrer home, fifteen spacious rooms spread over three floors, and searched until she found the book. She kicked off her white Reeboks and curled up in Barry's big leather chair and read until Mrs. Alvarez came for her to eat supper. She couldn't stop reading the book, so she brought it with her and read while she ate at the kitchen table. When she was finished she took the book up to her room and continued reading until she fell asleep in her clothes. Around eleven p.m. she woke up, got into her pajamas, and went to sleep.

That night she dreamed that she was traveling in a canoe down a wide river. On its banks African people were waving at her to come ashore, but no matter how much she paddled she couldn't make it and soon the current of the river became swifter and she was going faster and faster until the canoe turned over and she was being submerged and tumbling, over and over, in the rapids. When she finally came to a stop in a calm pool, her skin was a shiny, ebony color. In the morning she felt ill and got up to look at herself in the mirror, expecting to find herself transformed. She didn't go to school that day but instead remained in bed, reading what she now called "the African book." When she was finished reading *Roots*, she was outraged and couldn't understand how so many injustices could be perpetrated on the characters in the book. When she told her mother about it, her mother laughed.

"Mom, Kunta Kinte was in his home in Africa. He went out to get a log to make himself a drum and they captured him, brought him to the United States, and made him a slave."

"The book is fiction, baby," her mother said.

"No, it isn't, Mom," she replied, indignant, her hands on her hips. "It's real. It really happened to Mr. Haley's family."

"He made it up," her mother said. "That's what most writers do."

"No, he didn't. I bet you haven't even read it," she shouted.

"No, I haven't," Elsa said.

Vidamía ran out of the kitchen and into the woods behind the house, where she sat in her special place under the pines and cried and everything in her was mixed up. She had never given much thought to Marjorie Green or Juanita Dell in her class.

They were black girls who smiled shyly at her and always said hello, but hurried off as soon as school was over and even at lunch stayed by themselves with other black girls. She wondered now if Marjorie or Juanita felt like the characters in the book. Were Marjorie and Juanita descended from slaves? Perhaps they weren't at all shy, because at times she saw them laughing brightly and talking animatedly with each other, their speech filled with a language all their own, like she and Elizabeth Wright had, with their words for the seasons and directions and times.

"It's not fair," she argued after class, when she stayed to speak to her teacher about the book. Elizabeth had stayed with her since Mrs. Wright was picking them up. Ms. Robertson listened attentively, nodding politely. It appeared, however, that she hadn't read the book. She kept looking at her watch. She said Vidamía was absolutely right and perhaps she ought to read more about slavery and the subject of African-American contributions to society, and that, by the way, there had been a television miniseries based on the book. This idea spun around in Vidamía's head, and when Mrs. Wright came to pick them up—it was the day of the week when both her mother and stepfather stayed in New York late and Vidamía slept over at the Wrights'—Vidamía couldn't stop talking about the book and the characters in it.

Mrs. Wright had read the book and seen the television series, and said they were both wonderful, beautifully dramatic examples of Americana. Mrs. Wright spoke like that. She used phrases like "dynamic in scope," "vast in its humanity," and "metaphorically tragic." It annoyed Elizabeth, but Vidamía loved listening to her—even though sometimes she didn't understand what Margaret Wright was talking about. Mrs. Wright drew delicate, pastel landscapes for a greeting-card company, and everything about her was like thin crystal, delicate and fragile.

"Do you think they'll show it again, Mrs. Wright?" Vidamía had asked.

"Well, if they don't it would be regrettable, because it is simply breathtaking in illustrating the plight of the Negro in America."

"Black, Mom," Elizabeth corrected.

"Yes, of course," Mrs. Wright had said. "Thank you, dear." They had stopped at a light, but when they were moving again she made a suggestion. "Perhaps you ought to write to the network and ask them to retelevise the series. I believe it was the American Broadcasting Company. My friend Helen from college works there and perhaps I can get the name of the person to whom you should write. I think it would be a wonderful project for the two of you to work on."

"ABC, Mom?" Elizabeth said, hooking a question mark on the end of her reminder to her mother that she need not go into such painful detail about everything. "And it's Vidamía's project?"

"Very well, then I will make sure that Vidamía has all the necessary information so that she can write to the powers that be."

The girls looked at each other and shrugged. When they got upstairs they rolled around on the floor of Elizabeth's room, laughing and saying the phrase over and over, until, exhausted, they came downstairs, and Elizabeth asked her mother who "the powers that be" were.

"Oh, my," Mrs. Wright said as she patted the lettuce dry. "The powers that be are the people who make the decisions."

"Shouldn't it be the powers that are?" Elizabeth said. "It makes it sound like Mrs. Washington. She says things like that. 'Who it be gonna pick up you room when you be married, Lizabef? Who it gonna be?'" Elizabeth said, imitating their cleaning woman.

"Elizabeth!" Mrs. Wright said, turning to face them. "I will not have you making light of other people's ways of expressing themselves." And then she apologized to Vidamía: "I'm very sorry, dear." And then back to her daughter: "Mrs. Washington is a kind woman who loves you very much. I will not have you ridiculing her or demeaning her person."

"I'm sorry, Mom," Elizabeth said.

"That's quite all right," Mrs. Wright said, back to her cheery self. "Now, go and wash up. Your father went to pick up your brother from basketball practice. They should be here any minute and then we'll have supper."

Vidamía wrote the letter to the American Broadcasting Company and they wrote back, addressing her as "Ms. Farrell," thanking her for her wonderful suggestion and informing her that in the very near future they would consider rebroadcasting the series. She was ecstatic and brought the letter to show Ms. Robertson. The entire matter had been perfect and reassured her that being American was a most wondrous thing. She wrote back and thanked the network and asked if it was possible to obtain copies of the tapes. They replied that it was not. She was despondent, and then Barry said he'd see what he could do. Three weeks later he walked in with a box full of videotapes. When her mother asked Barry how he'd managed to get the tapes, he replied that at ABC there were all manner of Riveras, Pabóns, Colóns, Rodríguezes, Lópezes, and even Santiagos running around doing one thing or another.

Vidamía didn't understand much of the interchange, but she was grateful for the opportunity to see the series. She and Elizabeth watched nearly twenty-five hours of the epic. As she saw each segment, she again cried, as she had when reading the book, everything so realistic that she was irate at the injustice, angered over the treatment of black people, shaken with rage.

They were Americans and they were treated so awfully. How could it be? Maybe they would've treated her the same way because she was Puerto Rican.

But she was American—just like anybody else, even though she spoke Spanish and was Puerto Rican in a way, although that part was a little vague. From observing her mother and stepfather she absorbed that being Puerto Rican was something special. Even though her mother and Barry were born in the United States they spoke proudly about the island and their identity. As she grew up, she understood that their pride was a mixture of knowledge acquired through education combined with a need to be distinct from other Latinos and perhaps even from blacks, embracing their culture as both a social and a political statement. Barry often spoke about his firm being the largest Puerto Rican–owned accounting firm in the United States, employing more than six hundred people, and having an impressive list of clients.

She went to Puerto Rico with her mother and Barry when she was ten, just after her *Roots* experience, and loved the beaches with their turquoise waters. She marveled at the distant mountains—then you were on them, the car climbing higher and higher and the perfumed wind hitting you in the face and making your hair dance away from your ears. She stared in amazement at the small houses perched on the sides of the hills, sometimes supported precariously by long stilts; the people, rendered doll-like by distance, climbing the hills on ribbon-like paths of red clay; the car traveling on the narrow roads so that there were times when she looked out the window on her side and all that she could see was a precipice and below it a valley with a river snaking in and out of the land, appearing and disappearing, the mountains in the distance dark green and the air smelling of flowers and fruit.

They had gone up into the mountains to her mother's uncle's house, so far up that sitting on the porch of the big house—there was an Indian cave on the cliff on the other side of the narrow, two-lane road—she had begun yelling that the fog was coming. Her uncle said that it wasn't fog but a cloud, and that if she remained sitting as the cloud passed the house she would feel the rain within. She sat there unbelieving as the cloud approached and enveloped everything in gauzy moisture so that even the inside of her nostrils and ears became moist and the dormant rain made her skin tingle. Her mother's uncle, Bernardo, said the Indian spirit of Yukiyú traveled in the cloud and now that it had touched her, she was a real Puerto Rican. He also told her that if she saw the elusive *coquí*, the diminutive tree frog that filled the evenings and nights with its chirping cry, it meant that she would return to the island again and again.

During the week that she was there, she searched day and night with her cousin Ileana, crawling through the undergrowth and lifting leaves, at night the *coquí*'s cry so close she was certain she would find it but always coming away disappointed, not believing it was possible to see one. The evening before they left she came outside after supper and sat on the porch swing, moving the seat ever so slowly, the night air carrying a slight chill and the sky above brilliant with stars. Out of the corner of her eye she saw it. The tiny tree frog had jumped and attached itself to the louvers of a closed window, the porch lights making the yellow skin translucent. She moved her head ever so slightly and saw how truly small the animal was, perhaps no bigger than half of her thumb. And then the *coquí* emitted its two-tone cry once, and then again and in a prodigious leap gained access to a hibiscus bush more than a dozen feet away. Dazzled by the sight, she went immediately to where the tiny tree frog had jumped but saw nothing. She then ran inside, ecstatic, yelling, "*Lo vi, lo vi. Vi el coquí.* I saw it. I saw the *coquí*." After her return to their home in Tarrytown, for weeks she woke up hearing the island birds and in the evening the tree frogs and at times she heard the surf as it struck the shore.

She was aware that she was Puerto Rican, but she was Irish as well. Above all she was American. Not Italian or Irish or Spanish or black but American. This meant a great deal to her growing up, because she didn't have to explain much about herself. In spite of the fact that Farrell was an Irish name, it was also from across the ocean, from the British Isles, and as she had read, linguistically the name was Gaelic, Celtic, and therefore more connected to English than, let's say, her mother's name, which was Santiago, which she was equally proud of. Sometimes she wished people in the United States carried both parents' names like they did in Spanish-speaking countries. In Puerto Rico she had seen houses that had signs on them stating the names of the family: Pantoja-Ramos or Díaz-Linares. One house had Vizcarrondo-Vizcarrondo and her cousin Ileana, who was eight years old, had asked if a brother and sister had gotten married, and her mother had called her a *boba*, which meant dopey, and explained that the husband and wife's families both had the same last name. If she were living in Puerto Rico or Spain or anyplace where they spoke Spanish she would be Vidamía Farrell Santiago, carrying both the father and the mother's name, which was sort of cool. But in the United States people didn't understand. She liked Farrell, though. It sounded American, and that's what she was. And yet there had always been something missing, like when someone is speaking and you missed it and ask the person to repeat what they've said and the person's forgotten and you're left wondering what it could've been. Like that. Something not quite stated about her life. She thought it could be the fact that she'd never known her father.

The day that Officer Arnold Tyson brought her to O'Hanlon's, when she was twelve and she met Maud Farrell, would sustain her forever as a moment that gave meaning to her life. No matter what happened afterward something wonderful had taken place then, so that when she returned to Tarrytown and her mother asked her, "How was the museum?" she said confidently that the museum was fine, feeling entirely justified in her deception because under what category other than museum could she file going back and discovering her past? But at dinner that night, while they were having dessert, not tormented by guilt but, buoyed by the pride of her accomplishment and her wish to have it noted, she told Elsa and her stepfather that instead of the museum she had stopped off in Yonkers and found her grandmother.

"Grandmother? What grandmother?" Elsa said.

"Grandma Farrell," Vidamía said. "My father's mother."

Elsa got a very odd look on her face, much as if someone had insulted her and she didn't quite know how to respond. Without the least preamble, she informed Vidamía that as far she was concerned her father didn't exist and that she ought to be grateful that Barry was willing to serve in a surrogate function as her father, which she should realize, even though she was only twelve and didn't understand about such things, was quite important in the social development of children. Vidamía responded that she was grateful, but that she still wanted to meet her father, and there was nothing wrong with wanting to do so. She said that even though she was only twelve and had no right to understand such things, hadn't Elsa said how important it was to a healthy ego to be able to make decisions that were beneficial to one's life?

Elsa Santiago López-Ferrer sat stunned, not wanting to admit to herself that Billy Farrell would have proved a burden to her and that she could never have achieved all she had if she had taken care of him. There was no way she'd sacrifice herself like her mother. She knew she had made the right decision back then. She looked to Barry for help, but all he did was shrug his shoulders and say, more out of a wish to help a child for whom he'd always felt affection, that he thought Vidamía was right and she ought to meet her father, and she could decide where to go from there.

"I can't believe you'd say something like that, Barry," Elsa said.

"What?"

"That she can just go off on her own like she did and you condone it. How do you know where she's been?"

"If you didn't make such an effort to keep her father out of her life maybe she wouldn't have had to do what she did," Barry said, rising from the table.

"Thank you very much."

"You're welcome," Barry said, and left the dining room. Elsa sat, her face turned to the windows as if she were searching for something in the night outside.

"I'm sorry," Vidamía told her mother. "I had to find out."

"Well, you could've asked me," Elsa said, turning back to her.

"I did, and you said it was none of my business, Mom," she replied.

"I most certainly did not," Elsa countered, then thought a moment and reconsidered. "I was upset. I'm sorry." She paused again and finally asked if she'd met her father.

"No, Grandma Farrell . . . I mean, she's going to let me know when I can," Vidamía replied, and then hesitantly asked what had happened. "With him, Mom? How did you meet him?"

"I really don't want to discuss that right now," Elsa said. She removed the napkin from her lap, dabbed her lips, got up from the table, and went upstairs. Vidamía finished her dessert alone and then sat in the kitchen while Mrs. Alvarez cleaned up. She told the housekeeper about her other grandmother, smiling as she spoke in Spanish as well as she could, describing Maud Farrell as an *abuelita rubia*, a blond grandmother, telling her how she was going to meet her father and how upset her mother had been. Mrs. Alvarez listened carefully and then asked her if she wanted another slice of cherry pie with ice cream. Vidamía looked around to check that no one was coming, because she wasn't permitted seconds on desserts, and nodded happily. *Una celebración*, Mrs. Alvarez called the treat.

Mrs. Alvarez said it was wonderful that she had found her father. She then sat down and told her that once there had been a beautiful young woman by the name of Pilar Fernández in the town of Buenaventura on the Pacific coast of Colombia, where she was from. This girl had fallen in love with a young man by the name of Alonso, a sailor from a Chilean ship, who promised that someday he would return and marry her. One year went by and then another and then a third one and Alonso still hadn't returned. Every ship flying the Chilean flag brought new hope, but as she stood waiting for the sailors to come ashore, Alonso was never with them. When she showed the other sailors Alonso's picture and asked if they knew him, no one knew who he was.

One day when Pilar had almost given up all hope she asked an old sailor if he knew Alonso, and showed him the nearly faded photograph. The old man squinted at the photograph and then shook his head sadly, explaining that although he had only seen him a few times he was sure he was the young man who'd had the accident. The pain in Pilar's heart was as intense as if someone had plunged a knife into her chest.

"Is he dead?" she said, nearly on the point of fainting.

"No, but he lost his right leg," the old sailor said. "It was amputated above the knee."

"Does he still live in Valparaíso?" Pilar asked.

"Yes, I believe he still lives there with his family."

"Do you know if he's married, sir?" she asked, timorously.

"That I do not know, *señorita*," he said.

"Thank you," Pilar said, and walked away clutching the photograph to her heart.

With tears in her eyes she walked home in the rain, unable to know what she would do next. That evening she couldn't eat and remained awake the entire night. The following week, desperate, and her heart aching to be with Alonso no matter what his condition, she packed a few belongings and with the small amount of money she had saved began a journey that took her along the coast of South America through Ecuador, where she worked as a maid for a wealthy family for six months in Guayaquil, before going on to Lima, Peru, and doing the same for a year. Her suffering and love for Alonso made her even more beautiful and in each place where she worked, suitors came and sought her hand in marriage. Pilar thanked them but explained that she was already engaged.

Eventually, working and traveling, Pilar was able to reach the city of Valparaíso, Chile. She again found work, this time as a seamstress, a trade she had learned while in Peru, and spent her days working in a dress shop and her evenings searching for Alonso. One evening, after she had put the finishing touches on a wedding gown for one of the young women of the city, she left her place of employment and, crossing a small square, saw a young man ahead of her. He was walking with crutches, his right pants leg folded and pinned halfway up. Without the least hesitation, knowing she had found her love, she called Alonso's name. The young man stopped, turned, and, puzzled, peered into the failing light of day. She moved forward and it was indeed Alonso. The young man was struck dumb by what he saw before him.

"Pilar?"

She nodded and threw her arms around him with so much emotion that she nearly knocked him off balance. The young man laughed and sat on a bench in the square. He explained that he had lost his leg in an accident at sea and was ashamed of his appearance. He thought she wouldn't want to marry him. Pilar shook her head, put a finger to Alonso's lips and said she loved him and even if he had lost both legs she would want to be with him.

"Those were my parents," Mrs. Alvarez said. *"Mi madre y mi padre, que en paz descansen,"* she said, may they rest in peace.

Vidamía, her eyes moist and her mouth red with cherry pie, said it was a beautiful story and then asked Mrs. Alvarez if she thought she'd done the right thing in looking for her father.

"Yes, I think so," Mrs. Alvarez said. "Always do what your heart tells you. You're a good person and your heart will not lie to you. There, wipe your mouth and get upstairs before your mother comes down," she added handing her a paper towel.

Vidamía stood up and hugged Mrs. Alvarez and said I love you and then ran upstairs feeling light and wondering if someday she would fall in love like Pilar. But that would be much later, she thought. Now she was going to meet her father. She couldn't wait to tell Martha Coburn, who was her very best friend now that Elizabeth Wright had moved away.

7 From A to Z

Nearly three weeks passed before Maud Farrell, familiar with the complexities of Billy's fragile mind, phoned her son to tell him that his daughter, Vidamía, had come looking for him. For the past eleven years Billy Farrell had settled into a new life fashioned out of his confusion, and the concern of his grandfather, Buck Sanderson, who had brought him down south, to his part of the country, to help him find a wife. Of greater importance to this relatively calm life was the inventiveness of said wife, one Lurleen Pierce Meekins from Wilkins, in central Tennessee, population 328, who managed to steer him carefully away from his memories of Vietnam and into a structured present and a safe, albeit indefinite future.

Billy Farrell listened carefully as if his mother's words were drinking glasses that were being stacked atop each other, each new level of understanding threatening to topple the entire structure. Hearing his mother request that he come up and discuss the matter coupled with the realization that he would have to meet this child, to whom he was a stranger, and inflict upon her the sight of his ugly hand rattled uncomfortably inside of him.

"Let me think about it," he'd said.

Recalling his time with Elsa Santiago produced memories of Joey and Vietnam, and for nearly four days he sat in his rocker, staring out at the city, not saying anything. The children played around him but he was oblivious to them. Lurleen brought him food and drink. He ate without tasting anything. At night she guided him to bed so he could at least rest if he couldn't sleep. He remained awake, seeing vividly himself and Joey running across the rice field; and then not hearing the explosion but feeling the force of the blast and then the blackness.

His mother's phone call came one evening, after he had spent the day emptying out an apartment on Orchard Street. An old, presumably Jewish, man had died. They always came over and got him when the person was Jewish.

"Farrell's a Jewish name, right?" Raymond Marcano had asked him some years before. He'd shaken his head and shrugged his shoulders, not considering the question important.

"Irish," he'd said, but Marcano either hadn't heard him or didn't believe him.

In the eyes of the neighborhood he was white, with a beard that was beginning to gray, and that must have reminded them of the Hassidim who trekked from Brooklyn across the Williamsburg Bridge every Saturday to the many synagogues of the Lower East Side. It didn't matter what he was. Everyone was heading down the same road to death. This time the man hadn't been Jewish. "The man's family came and took a watch and some silver candlesticks and frames," Marcano had said. But most of the belongings remained, including a wooden crucifix and a Bible and the man's clothes: big, cracked shoes; and, in the drawers, frayed underwear and old dark socks, everything smelling of the old man, musty and forgotten. Sánchez and Marcano had a superstition concerning the Jews. Sánchez explained that it was a sin for Christians to touch a dead Jew's belongings, especially his clothing, but Billy'd heard that when the Jewish lady on Rivington Street died, Sánchez found a gold watch in her apartment and kept it.

Billy got the key from Marcano. Once inside the apartment he opened the windows to get rid of the smell of death. He went through the closet, tossing everything into one of those tough, large plastic bags they used in the projects for trash. He kept the socks that were still usable and a maroon sweater with two buttons missing. He found mail addressed to a Mr. Albert T. Zorich—a Con Edison bill and bills from magazines, some mystery novels and a few Christmas cards with postmarks from different places but no return addresses. Lincoln, Nebraska. Ames, Iowa. Lawrence, Kansas. His children? Friends? Relatives? When he was finished he looked under the bed to make sure there were no other shoes there.

Beneath the rusting metal bed there was an old suitcase. It was an odd make, unlike anything he'd seen in the United States, combining cloth and woven cane, and on the corners triangular metal reinforcements. He pulled out the valise and inside he found hundreds of photographs of what he assumed was the old man. Albert T. Zorich. He was a tall, angular man, sharp-featured and reserved. There were members of his family with him, which he deduced from their resemblance. A wife and children. Parents and grandparents, aunts and uncles. Family picnics. Beach scenes with the people dressed in old-time bathing suits, the women's lips painted in cupid bows; self-conscious, smiling people standing on the edge of the woods, near automo-

74

biles, waving from trains and buses, shopping in fruit and meat markets; children playing in the snow, their faces ruddy as they held their sled ropes. And there he was, Mr. Albert T. Zorich, smiling with his mouth, but his eyes wearing an overwhelming sadness as if something tragic had happened. Billy dug further down and found pictures of Zorich as a younger man. In those photos his eyes were bright and smiling. Then he saw still others. They were pictures of Mr. Zorich as a soldier in spats and a World War I helmet, the date and place in beautiful script on the back of the picture: Albert, France, 1916.

Billy closed the suitcase and began to look through the apartment, trying anxiously to find an address or telephone number that would tie Zorich and his history together so he could return the photos to the family. Quite unexpectedly, in his mind he heard Miles Davis's muted horn in an improvisation on "Autumn Leaves," the phrasing clear and melancholy. He felt a panic, as if hearing the music again meant something sinister, something which he would be unable to decipher. He sat on the old bed for nearly an hour, too numbed to move and unable to turn off his mind from recalling passages of music with their chord structures and the difficult runs that made tunes dazzling in their beauty. What was the connection between the photographs and the music? He didn't want to remember playing jazz, didn't want to recall sitting at the piano, his hands moving almost independent of his volition, the figures of music instinctive as he bent over the keyboard and his life hummed the improvisations before they got to his fingers, or simultaneously. He never could figure out the process nor had it mattered since the music flowed endlessly, effortlessly from him. He didn't want to think about Miles and those days. He'd made the right decision when he went into the Marines. It was what his father would've done. It was his duty.

In the end he gave up trying to figure it out. He lugged the large bag and suitcase over to Ludlow Street and sold the clothing for ten dollars to a thrift shop. He took the suitcase home and after supper told Lurleen of his find. He didn't tell her about the music, hoping it would go away. The music remained. He could now hear clearly Dave Brubeck's *Jazz Goes to College*—the entire chorded piano solo of "Le Souk" and a few other tunes. Photos of Mr. Zorich reminded him of Dave Brubeck, as if the sensitivity of the music and what Brubeck saw of humanity made him sad.

When the children were in bed asleep he opened the suitcase and showed Lurleen the photos. Together they laid them out on the long dining table, trying to place them in rough chronological order, aided at times by the date and place written on the backs of the photos, other times by their recollections of fashions and the condition of the photos. After more than three hours they were able to establish that the man had lived on the Lower East Side all his life; that his father had owned a hardware store around the turn of the century; that Albert T. Zorich had been born around 1896, had gone to grammar school at P.S. 160 on Suffolk Street, had been trained as a lathe operator, joined the army and had seen service in Europe in WWI; that he had returned home, married his high school sweetheart, Greta Wyche, had raised five children, two boys and three girls, and that all of them had graduated from City College. They further established that Albert T. Zorich had retired from work and his wife had died around 1964, when she was sixty-six years old and he was sixty-eight; that he had gone on living, probably alone, another twenty years until his death.

Exhausted by the effort, his mind taxed by the attempts to decipher Zorich's life, Billy sat down and separated the pre-WWI pictures from the ones after the war. It was obvious that something had happened to the dead man in the war. Whatever horrors he had seen had shocked him permanently and caused his face to be contorted by profound sorrow. Billy thought that perhaps God was sending him a reminder of what he had done; perhaps Albert T. Zorich had allowed his friend to die, as had happened to him with Joey.

He couldn't handle the speculation, returned the photos hurriedly to the suitcase, closed it, shook off Lurleen's arm as she tried to stop him, and took the large loft elevator down to the basement. Racing, such that he scratched his arm on a nail as he let himself into the boiler room, he headed for the furnace. He burnt his fingers as he threw the door of the coal burner open, its low summer fire illuminating the room in a shadowy, red glow. Without opening the suitcase he attempted to shove it into the fire, but it wouldn't fit. He then opened the suitcase, grabbed at the pictures in handfuls, and threw them into the furnace. When he was done and the only trace of the pictures was the odd smell of photographic chemicals, he began, with his bare hands, to tear up the suitcase. His anger mounting with each effort, he used his foot to hold the suitcase down as he tore at the hinges and threw the pieces into the fire.

What the hell difference did it make what you were? Maybe Albert T. Zorich was a Jew living as a Christian. It meant nothing. He was Irish living like a shadow, Billy Farrell, a dumb mick, a harp, a stupid son of a bitch paddy who had let a buddy die. Dumb friggin' Irishman. Whether in Dublin or Belfast, New York or Chicago, Toronto or Durban, he was Billy Farrell. There were likely a thousand Billy Farrells in the world. At least five hundred in the U.S. Three or four hundred in Ireland. Some in Canada, others in Australia, New Zealand, and even South Africa. Wherever the Irish had gone they'd sprouted Billy Farrells. Just like they sprouted Kevin Donovans, Johnny O'Connors, Tommy Loughlins, Jimmy Quinns. What difference did it make? Italian, Jewish, Polish, Puerto Rican, black, white. Nothing made sense anymore. So what if he was Irish. He returned upstairs and sat in his rocker, feeling a headache coming on and the music attacking him. Bird, Diz, Monk, Miles, all calling to him.

He wished he was a little boy again and could start over. He remembered everybody at St. Luke's School making a big deal of St. Patrick's Day—everybody, lay teachers and nuns, involved in preparations for going to the parade, everybody wearing green. That had been 1961. Later in the year, Maris and not Mantle was threatening to break Babe Ruth's homerun record. He was angry because Maris wasn't a real Yankee. He had been traded from the St. Louis Cardinals. It wasn't fair that a non-Yankee might break Ruth's record. But his father said that Babe Ruth had been traded from the Red Sox to the Yankees. He was surprised to hear this. Ruth had been a pitcher. And then it was okay, because *he* was going to be a pitcher and pitch for the Yankees and, like Whitey Ford, they'd call him Whitey Farrell. He didn't want Maris to feel bad, so he rooted for him, and Maris broke the record.

The only thing he'd enjoyed about the parade had been the bagpipes since it was the first time they were marching in front of the Emerald Society and his father's friend Danny Condon, who'd taught him how to throw a curve ball, was playing the big bass drum for the pipers. He wanted to see his father marching with the other policemen. He recalled standing with his mother, holding her hand tight, and hearing the bagpipes way off at the other end of Fifth Avenue—their eerie sound penetrating the music of some brass band from a high school on Long Island passing in front of them—and he looked down the street, his heart beating wildly with eagerness, imagining how his green tie would be flapping if he didn't have a chest. But he mustn't think about that because then he'd think about Joey in Nam, his chest burst open. The sound grew louder and more insistent and he had an urge to go out and march with his father when the Emerald Society contingent reached them.

"Listen, Mom," he'd said. "I think it's the pipes. Listen." And then he'd tried imitating the sound. "BNEEEE, BNEEEE, BNEEEE. I can hear them, Mom. They're coming."

The pipes got louder and now there were drums. He broke away from his mother and got down on his hands and knees. Through the legs of the people, he saw them marching up Fifth Avenue in their big brogans and knee socks, large bright kilts and bonnets. The sound was now deafening, the skirling going through him so that he wanted to run out into the street to join them. And then they passed by him, the piping in the marrow of his bones making his body vibrate with something he'd never felt. He looked for his father. Row after row they came, all of them neat in their blue uniforms with their badges and ribbons and caps. And then he saw him and yelled, "Daddy, Daddy, Daddy," and his father had smiled and winked, waved his hand and pointed Billy out to his friend Jimmy Dougherty marching next to him.

That year when the pipers played for the first time, the parade was great. All he could think about was the pipes. He'd asked what the pipes were for and people said they were for dancing and parades. The answer didn't satisfy him. He went to his father, who said he didn't know but he'd find out from Sergeant McDonough at the 2-3, who was one of the pipers. As with all the promises that his father made, he kept it, and after supper while Billy was doing his homework he could hear his father talking to Sergeant McDonough. "Sure, he might want to learn," his father had said on the phone. "He's a damn good musician. Gets it from his mother's side, because I can't carry a tune," he'd said self-deprecatingly. "Sure. I'll drive over Saturday and bring him."

The following Saturday they drove out to Dan McDonough's house in Brooklyn, and there, in the basement, were the pipes.

His heart immediately began beating rapidly. He watched Dan McDonough pick up the pipes, bring the mouthpiece to his mouth, move his arm ever so slightly, and there issued from the pipes the same eerie sound as at the parade. Dan McDonough played "The Wearing of the Green," and afterward talked about pipes. He said ones not quite like these had been at the Battle of Clontarf in the year 1040, when Brian Boru drove the Vikings from Ireland. Billy listened, wishing to hear the sound of the pipes again. "Would you like to try, Billy?" Dan McDonough said. Billy shrugged his shoulders. Dan McDonough wiped the mouthpiece, brought the pipes over and showed him how to hold them and where to place his fingers and arms so that he could manipulate the bag.

For a while he'd gone each Saturday to Dan McDonough's to take lessons, weaving a fantasy of being on the job, as they referred to being a member of the police force, like his father, and dressing in kilts and playing the pipes. After his father died, all of that disappeared, packed away in the lonely storage of his mind's sorrows. He realized years later that he had been drawn to the sound of the pipes by the visceral reaction of wishing to go forward at no cost to himself, understanding clearly that even though the pipes were used for dancing and merriment, at the tribal level they were first and foremost a call to battle, and often an homage to the dead, and that he had also seen. That fall, a week after the Yankees beat Cincinnati in the World Series, his father had been shot, and at the cemetery the pipers played at his father's grave, and he hadn't wanted to go to the parade the following spring.

In subsequent years, when he was in high school at Cardinal Hayes, because his father and his uncles had gone to the school, his friends persuaded him to go to the St. Patrick's Day Parade. But there was no joy in it, and hearing the pipes only made him ache to see his father. Like the rest of the other boys, he drank too much and puked and rode the train back up to Yonkers that evening. He, Kevin Higgins, and Matty Dolan crawled around the Sanderson lawn, screaming like banshees, as his grandmother, the former Brigid Flynn of Donegal, said, crossing herself, and adding, the words thick in her mouth, that banshees foretold the death of a relative, alluding obliquely to his father, may the saints keep him. Everything was drinking, cursing, and loudness. When he recuperated he swore that he would never go back, and he never again returned to the parade.

Back upstairs after disposing of the photos, Billy sat for nearly an hour and then Lurleen came over and made him get up and sit on the couch. She fixed him a toddy with rum and lemon, and, as if reading his mind, she said he ought to go and meet his daughter.

"It won't do any good to postpone it, Bill," Lurleen said. "Go up there and find out."

"What am I going to tell her, baby?" he said helplessly. "I don't know if that's the right thing to do. She's probably poor and needs help. I can't offer her anything."

"She just wants to see you, Bill. She just wants to see her daddy. That's all."

"And you don't mind?"

"No, I don't mind, you big silly man. She's your first child. Why should I mind? Go and see your mama and take it one step at a time. Go on up there."

The next day he walked to Bleecker Street, took the Number 6 train, changed at Fourteenth Street to the Number 5, which had been called the White Plains Road train back when he was fourteen and had just started high school. Forty minutes later he got off the train at the last stop and walked slowly to O'Hanlon's, dreading what was to come, knowing he'd have to hide the hand from the girl and unsure of what he should say.

When he finally got to O'Hanlon's he said hello to Michael

O'Hanlon, who had been a Marine in the Korean War and now ran the bar for his father, Patrick, who had developed diabetes and had had his right foot amputated. Every once in a while he came to the bar, his wheelchair pushed by Michael's slow boy, Sean, the three blocks from the house to the bar. Patrick O'Hanlon then sat around, drinking ale and talking about the IRA and Dublin and the injustices of the British, saying that all that hunger-strike business and the women peace activists were just shameful and had done no good at all and what every good Irishman ought to do was pick up a gun and drive the British out of Ireland. "Just like St. Patrick drove out the snakes, which is what they are, the damn Brit bastards. Drive them all out," he said, gripping the arms of the wheelchair until his face was white with the rage.

"How you doing, Ma?" Billy asked, sitting at the bar.

"I'm okay. How are you doing?"

"I'm all right. I had some things to do. That's why I couldn't get up here right away."

"How's Lurleen and the kids?"

"They're okay, Ma," he said. "Horty's still having problems writing, but everybody else is doing good. I can't understand it with her. She reads all the time. Everything. But ask her to write something and she can't do it."

"She's like me, honey," Maud had said. "Don't worry about her. She's a good girl. You want a beer?"

"Sure. It's pretty hot out there."

"It wouldn't be if you didn't wear that fatigue jacket all the time. Why don't you take it off? You want a sandwich?"

"I'm okay."

"With the jacket on, or you don't want a sandwich?"

He laughed and said he was fine with the air-conditioning on, but if it wasn't too much trouble, sure, he'd have a sandwich. When Maud returned from the kitchen with a big corned beef sandwich and placed a second mug of beer on the bar for him, he asked where the girl was.

"Isn't she coming?" he asked.

"Not today," Maud said. "I just wanted to talk to you about it. I didn't want to rush things. You know, I wanted to go slow."

"I understand, Ma," he said, somewhat relieved. "That's cool. No sweat."

"Do you remember her?"

"I've never seen her, Ma," he said, taking a big bite from the sandwich. Then he lifted up the rye bread and spread more mustard on the meat. "I told you that."

"I forgot," Maud said. She was wiping the bar mechanically, gauging his mood, not sure how this would go down. "Do you want to see a picture of her?" she asked, smiling at him.

"Sure," he said, shrugging his shoulders. "Did she give you one or did you ask?"

"I asked," Maud said, then turned and went into her handbag, resting on a box near the cash register. "She called me up to see how things were going and I asked her for one. She wrote me a very fine letter, very nice handwriting."

She pulled out a square, butterfly-yellow envelope with her name and the address on it and held it under his nose for him to smell.

"It's perfumed," she said.

"Where does she live?"

"Look at the return address. Tarrytown."

"Oh, yeah? She's doing okay?"

"Looks like it," Maud said, opening her wallet and sliding it gently across the bar for him to see the picture. He picked up the wallet with the three fingers of his right hand and looked at the picture, admiring the smiling girl in the photograph for a long time and nodding his head. The picture had been taken in a studio the previous winter, right before Christmas, and Vidamía's hair had been done specially for the sitting. It was cut short and combed in a boyish way, highlighting her already prominent cheekbones and large eyes, the mouth smiling openly with profound innocence and trust. Just looking at the photograph made him anxious.

"She's a beauty, ain't she?" Maud said.

"Yeah, she sure is. She has your nose. A little bony—not perfect but cute. And your eyes."

"Does she look like her mother?"

"A little, but she reminds me of the pictures of Grandma's sister when she was a girl. The one who went into the convent."

Maud laughed and said that he was absolutely right, that she had thought long and hard about who it was that the girl reminded her of but couldn't recall, and that indeed it was Kitty Flynn, the one who had returned to Ireland and become a nun, and how she'd driven many an Irishman to drink from just looking at her she was so beautiful.

"You son of a gun," Maud said. "Your daughter looks just like Kitty Flynn. You've always had a good eye for feminine beauty."

"Just like my old man," he said, pointing at her, his eyes mischievous for a moment before they went dead again.

"Go on with you, you scoundrel," Maud said, taking the wallet back and admiring the photo before returning it to her bag.

"Are they blue?" he said. "Her eyes?"

"Green. Like huge emeralds. Bright, and just like the song."

"What song?" he said, and he almost told his mother that he'd begun recalling jazz tunes.

"What do you mean, what song?" Maud laughed. "If ever a pair of eyes were meant to describe the smiling of Irish eyes, it would have to be your daughter's. Oirish through and through," she added, affecting an accent.

"Okay," he nodded. "That song."

"Yeah, that song, you dumb mick," she said. "You think you're up to meeting her? She's real anxious to see you, Billy."

"I guess I better," he said, finishing the sandwich and taking a long draught of beer. "I'm just worried about the hand."

"Forget about that, Billy," Maud said, slapping his arm and in one motion removing the mug and refilling it before placing it back on the bar. "Just forget that stuff. You should see this kid. Remember that picture I told you about? The one of you and the girl's uncle in Vietnam? That's all she had to give her a clue about you. But when she talks about you, the love just pours out of her eyes. She needs you to be part of her life. It's so obvious it makes me cry to watch her. She's a perfect little lady. You're going to fall in love with her just like I did."

"And she's all right? I mean, in terms of money, because I couldn't give her anything."

"She doesn't want anything. From the looks of it, I think she's well off."

"That's good."

"So, I can go ahead and set something up?"

"Yeah, sure. I don't have to dress up or nothing, right?"

"I don't think so," Maud said as three men walked in and sat at the bar. "I'll call you and you can come over to the apartment, okay?" she added, and reached over and patted his arm. "It'll be all right. Don't worry."

"Yeah, sure, Ma," he said and finished his beer as he stood up to leave. He felt a slight buzz from the three beers as he headed out the door to catch the elevated train back to Manhattan.

8 Catharsis

Maud Farrell, dread and high expectations squaring off against each other in her mind, arranged for Billy and Vidamía to meet. On the agreed-upon day, a Saturday afternoon, her brother,

Michael Sanderson, now a Fire Department lieutenant living in Whitestone, Queens, but working out of a firehouse in the South Bronx, where they had grown up, drove over to Tarrytown, whistled at the opulence of the manicured grounds and the mansion-like home of Elsa Santiago and Barry López-Ferrer and banged healthily on the brass knocker with the disdain of the working class when faced with what it considers to be suburban posturing. He was asked inside, and to Barry's first questions, about his health and his relationship to Vidamía, he answered that he was feeling just fine, thank you, and that he was the young girl's grandmother's brother, her grand-uncle, he supposed. To all subsequent inquiries he replied with polite monosyllabic distance.

Eventually they were permitted to leave, and he whisked the young girl away in his car in order to discharge his responsibility and deliver her to Maud's apartment. It being a Saturday, both Elsa and Barry had been home, and after the tough-looking Michael Sanderson left with Vidamía, Elsa immediately went ballistic and said to Barry, chasing after him as he sought refuge in his den, that she had been right all along and that she had just handed her child over to barbarians. Barry turned around angrily and said she ought to stop being hysterical and overdramatizing things. And then the two of them went at it, berating each other for their lack of support, until, emotionally spent, they lapsed into silence.

Elsa went upstairs and threw herself on the bed, wanting to cry but unable to, her mind raging at Billy Farrell, who had reappeared in her life and taken her daughter away and where would it all end? Had she made it worse by denying Vidamía access when she had asked to see him? But the girl had lied when she said she was going to the museum and had gone to Yonkers looking for him. Lied. She wondered what else Vidamía was keeping from her. Hadn't she always been honest with her daughter? She thought a moment and decided that she hadn't.

For starters, she never told her how much she'd despised the name Vidamía, how she'd railed at her mother to let her change it, pleading, "It's like we're black people or something," while Ursula Santiago stood monument-like in her insistence that the child would be named Vidamía. "Like *morenos, mami.* They name their kids any old thing. They make up names. Falima. Koutrana. Latulia. Mahapi." Things like that, she'd said, making up names as she went. "That's what we're doing, *mami.*"

She had always relegated the matter of her own connection to blackness to the cultural certainty that if one had a Puerto Rican background, naturally one had to include the European, the Amerindian, *and* the African into the cultural mix. But it wasn't a question of race. They were Puerto Ricans. She thought the position of people in the United States, both black and white, was ridiculous concerning the matter of race. Even if you had one drop of African blood you were considered black. She knew Americans who were whiter than some Puerto Ricans and went around calling themselves black; while in the case of Puerto Ricans, and many other Latin Americans, the slightest shading away from black excused a person from the stigma of negritude. She knew it was a matter of culture, of people identifying themselves with Afro-American culture, but she also knew that if she capitulated to the argument, she'd have to align herself and become black, and she didn't want the burden of being one of them. In her opinion, slavery had beaten everything out of black people. The only thing that remained was the music that had developed from the experience, the destructiveness of self-loathing, and the African inflections in their speech. She hated to think that Puerto Ricans were headed in the same direction.

Her rage returned and she saw again her father's face, his dark skin and obvious African features grinning mockingly at her. *Doan gworry, negrita.* There it was, she thought. *Negrita.* My little black one. A term of endearment for Puerto Ricans. White or black, they called each other *negrito* or *negrita.* Just like black people—"nigger" this and "nigger" that. It was disgusting. She had once told her mother to stop calling her *negrita*. Although everyone used the word to convey affection, in her opinion the word was, in reality, indicative of the inbred racism of Puerto Rican society. Her mother, because she was white, undoubtedly had the same hang-ups as white people. It was inconceivable, but Elsa was certain of her mother's prejudice. In Elsa's unstable mind, it seemed obvious that her mother was trying to make herself superior, to work out her feelings of hostility toward her husband, who had deserted her and the family.

Elsa was in her second year of college at Hunter and had taken a couple of courses in the Black and Puerto Rican Studies Department when lawyers from the independence movement came and spoke at the school, and she was naturally drawn to the cause against United States colonial rule. She felt good listening to them speak in Spanish—not Puerto Rican, as most of her non-academic American friends called what Puerto Rican people in New York spoke. Though in a way they were right. The patois was a ridiculous mix of badly spoken Spanish, English, and made-up words. She hated calling a mop *el mapo,* the roof of a building or house *el rufo* instead of *techo*, and *yarda* for yard instead of *patio*. And not even *yarda* but *yalda*. Why couldn't Puerto Ricans pronounce their R's? What were they, Chinese? Why did they have to substitute L's where the R's should go? If she wasn't careful, she sometimes slipped up. She had even asked Barry not to speak in Spanish to her in public. She had gotten Vidamía away from that environment and hired Mrs. Alvarez, who was from Colombia and pronounced her R's correctly and hadn't lived in the United States long enough to be corrupted into speaking Spanglish.

But the matter of blackness bothered her. The time Elsa

made the request that she not call her *negrita* again, her mother had looked at her long and hard and told her to keep going to the psychiatrist, because she was still crazy.

"What's all this black and white crap?" she'd said. "What you got in your head? You're Puerto Rican. You're not supposed to be thinking like that. What's the matter with you? The more you go to school the stupider you get, Elsie. Just shut up with that stuff, okay? Everybody's got his little *mancha de plátano*. You understand that? Your father, you, your brothers and sisters, me. Everybody."

When Elsa opened her mouth to protest Ursula Santiago slapped her own arm.

"What's this white skin good for, anyway?" she said. "What? Answer me, *carajo*. Inside I'm Puerto Rican. You think I go around looking at people and saying he's black, she's white, she's yellow, he's red, they're brown? You think I got time for all those *boberías* when I got all kind of things to do? Wake up, Elsie. You're in a fog half the time."

"I didn't mean it like that, *mami*," Elsa said.

"Tell you what," her mother said. "I'll stop calling you *negrita*, okay? No more *negrita*. If I call you *negrita* again, don't invite me to your house again, okay?"

Elsa felt suddenly ashamed and sat at the dinette table and cried. Her mother came over and rubbed her back and smoothed her hair away from her face. Elsa stopped crying and hugged herself to her mother. She felt better and was able to say, "I love you, *mami*. I'm sorry."

"That's okay," Ursula Santiago said.

"You can call me *negrita*," Elsa told her mother. "I don't mind." She couldn't recall if her mother had ever called her *negrita* again. Whatever happened, Elsa swore not to let the matter of blackness touch her daughter. She'd made sure of that. No pictures of her own father and no mention of him. Barry was white, and as far as she was concerned, Vidamía was white, and that was that. People who saw them together didn't know Barry wasn't her father.

Elsa got up from the bed, looked at herself in the mirror, and brushed her hair. For a moment she considered her image. She was still young and attractive, her hair thick and wavy, her nose long and fine and her lips thin. No one ever questioned her own whiteness, but like a specter, her father's dark skin mocked her, constantly stalked her, making her wish there was some way of genetically erasing that part of her background. God, she sounded like a Nazi. The thought made her recall the years after she gave birth.

After the baby was born, Elsa had turned Vidamía over to her mother. Unconcerned with the consequences of her attitude, she went back to hanging out. She and her homegirls stopped singing and playing games, deciding the behavior was for little kids. But then the following summer a record came out and they developed a game around which they sang the Alegre All Stars' "Estoy Buscando a Kako," meaning "I'm looking for Kako," the band calling out each member's name. She and the other girls would go through all the names of the boys each girl liked, pointing at her and singing. Like pointing at Delia Campos, who liked Eddie Cruz, and singing. *Estoy buscando a Eddie, Eddie, Eddie, Eddie, estoy buscando a Eddie, Eddie, Eddie, dónde está?* all of them singing, and as soon as they pointed at the girl she had to get up and dance while they were singing, and then whoever was dancing got to point at somebody else and they began calling out the name of the boy she liked.

Sometimes a girl liked two or three boys and then they wouldn't repeat the boy's name, but strung one name after the other like in the case of Lizzie Delgado, who had a wild reputation and had boys after her all the time. All the homegirls knew

Lizzie was still a virgin and later realized in their last year of high school that she liked girls when she began talking about this girl named Veronica who was a dancer from Greenwich Village. Right after graduation Lizzie ran off with her dancer, which was cool because, you know, whatever turns you on and, like, she's one of our homegirls so don't be saying nothing nasty, okay? So when they pointed at Lizzie, they'd say: *Estoy buscando a Bobby, Ralphie, Louis, Carlos, estoy buscando a Jimmy, Néstor, Henry, dónde están?* and then they'd all goof and accuse each other of being a *bollo loco,* which meant literally "crazy bun" but in P.R. slang meant "crazy pussy," meaning a girl who gave it away to anybody.

After a while Elsa felt that she didn't belong because they wouldn't call out her name in the game. She felt it was her own fault, because she had given it away to Billy Farrell and none of the boys were interested in her because her reputation was that she only dug white boys. And now she had this baby who was cute and white, with curly blond hair and real bright blue eyes, which, to her distress, turned green later, perhaps signaling an upcoming dilution of her daughter's whiteness because of her own connection to Africa. Her homegirls made a big fuss about her and wanted to hold her, calling out Vidamía, Vidamía, Vidamía constantly like it was such a cool name, telling her how gorgeous her daughter was, so that she felt that they liked the baby more than they liked her; talking constantly about her so that it was like everyone on the Lower East Side knew that she had spread her legs for this *gringo* white boy and they had this kid with a weird name.

When the baby was three months old, her sister Milagros, who had also gone to Seward Park High School and now studied at Lehman College at night, went to the school and spoke with Mrs. Kantrowitz, who had taught Milagros and her other sisters. Mrs. Kantrowitz then spoke to the principal on Elsa's behalf and they let her back into the school. Although almost everyone knew what had happened, no one ever brought up the pregnancy. Nevertheless, she felt she was treated differently, even by her friends. Everything made her angry, and the only respite from the constant shame was studying. As much as she enjoyed school, she felt like she was stuck, even if her mother took care of the baby most of the time. She felt excluded, even though she and her homegirls still hung out in the summer and did crazy things and still rode the subway up to Pelham Bay, laughing at every little thing. If anyone said anything critical to them they still acted all bad like that one time when they got up to Zerega Avenue and about ten tough Italian girls with beehive hairdos and weird lipstick that glowed got on the train and Mandy Lugo had her eyes closed because they were playing the game where they had to remember what station they were at and Mandy shouted out "Buhre Avenue" and Denise Aguayo said, "Wrong, retard, it's Zerega Avenue," and this Italian girl with all kinds of eye shadow and glowing copper lipstick came over to Denise.

"Who you calling a retard, you spic bitch?" she said.

Carmen Texidor, who was the biggest of them all and already at sixteen wore dresses two sizes bigger than her mother and was named Wonder Woman by some of the boys in the playground around Rivington Street because at thirteen she'd fought a boy and broken his jaw and who wasn't only real bad but was Papucho Texidor's cousin and everybody knew Papucho dealt big time and rode around in a big car and sometimes you saw him down on Mulberry talking to the Italians, stood up in the middle of the train and challenged the Italian girl.

"Yo, who you calling a spic bitch, you guinea scumbag?" Carmen Texidor said.

"Yeah," Lily Betancourt, nicknamed Pygmy, because she was so small, said, jumping up and standing next to Carmen, shaking her shoulders and her finger pointing down at the ground and letting go like she always did with this big, loud voice, the words pouring out of her with not only astonishing regularity but unbelievable nastiness. "Don't be calling us no spics. You understand what I'm saying to you? That ain't right you talking to us like we dirt and whatnot. We Puerto Ricans, and we proud, you low-class guinea *butana*," she said, substituting a B for the P and affecting a perfect New York Italian accent from being friends with Barbara Sacco, who wrote for the paper in school.

"Big deal," another Italian girl said. "Same thing."

"Hey, fuck you, okay?" Pygmy Betancourt said.

"No, fuck you," the first Italian girl said. "And watch that 'guinea' shit. Your friend called my friend a retard. Right, Tina?" she said turning back to one of the girls.

"Right, Connie," Tina said, a little scared and not really wanting to get into it.

"Oh, you're fulla shit, girl," Pygmy said, coming back to a Puerto Rican accent. "Whyn'tcha take all that plastic hair you got on your head and trade it in for some clothes. You look like a old lady dressed like that," she threw in for good measure and turned around and stuck out her hand to get fives from the other girls, so that they were all now goofing on the Italian girls.

"Oh, yeah?" Connie Beehive said.

"Yeah," Carmen Texidor said.

And boom! This Connie Beehive does it.

"Hey, fuck you and your mother," she said.

That was all that was needed for them to go totally crazy. San Juan versus Naples for the World Cup in hair pulling. They all began screaming and scratching, hitting with their bags, which carried suntan lotion, thermos bottles, sandwiches, hair rollers and who knew what else, and talking about "Don't talk about my mother, okay, you *puta*, you bitch, you guinea cunt," slapping wildly at each other, and Denise Aguayo telling Gloria Puente, Li'l Louie Puente's sister, to "put away your nail file, okay?" cause, like her brother, she was ready to do someone, because, "Homegirl, for less than that my brother took this guy out."

Later on, talking about the encounter and Gloria Puente putting everything in perspective. "I smacked the bitch and told her never talk about my mother, mothafucka. Because, homegirl, you could almost kill a Rican, but don't talk about his mother, *no le menten la madre, coño,* because that's it."

This all happened real quick and people emptied out from the subway car except for these two Rican homeboys who looked on at the occurrence all steely-eyed, their arms crossed and their heads turned sideways, one of them with a kerchief on his head so that he looked like a pirate and the other one with his hand in his jacket, which they later found out contained a small, silver-plated, white-handled, automatic *pistola.* At Westchester Square a couple of policemen came into the train and everybody cooled out, the Italian girls sitting down on one side of the subway car, doing their nails and looking at magazines, and Elsa and Carmen and Pygmy Betancourt and the rest sitting on the other side, busying themselves with whatever until the train reached Pelham Bay and the Italian girls, glaring back, got off the train, went downstairs, and took the bus. Carmen Texidor decided it was better if they went on foot so they started walking and the two Rican boys came alongside and said they'd go with them.

"Yeah, we be along for protection," José said.

"Dig it," said his friend Victor, his hand still in his jacket. "Yeah, cause you did the righteous thing. The bitch be talking about spic this and spic that. Who she think we is, man? Is a good thing they didn't have their fellas with them or there woulda been some serious bloodshed, youunderstandwhatI'm-saying?"

"Check it out," Victor said.

So they went on talking like that, twelve girls and these two fine *papis* with their hair long, and eventually they got to the beach and had a wonderful day and the net outcome was that Pygmy Betancourt fell totally in love with Victor, while she and José started talking, and even though Elsa didn't like him that much she staked out a claim to him and said, "Oh, wow, that was my brother's name, he got killed in Vietnam." José would come down to the Lower East Side from East Harlem and they'd go to the movies and hold hands and kiss and she'd let him feel her breasts, but that was it, resisting his advances when he'd bring her home.

"Yo, baby, I understand you're a virgin and whatnot, but give a fella a break. Like I got good intentions and I'm taking the test for being a corrections officer."

"I can't, honey," she'd say and play coy, even crying one time, which made him apologize and agree that they had to wait.

But then, whenever they'd play the *Estoy Buscando* game, they'd point at her, but because "José" didn't work with the song, that made the whole thing weird. And they couldn't say "Joey," because they all knew that her brother, Joey Santiago, had died in Vietnam, so they didn't include her, but she knew it was just an excuse and had to do more with the baby than anything else. One day José stopped coming around. Baby Contreras said she thought Tita from the Baruch projects had told José that Elsa had a baby because she liked him and wanted to steal him away from her. Elsa was relieved. After a while when they played the game they'd use different guys' names and kid her because older boys who knew she'd had a baby were always rapping to her, offering her all kinds of outrageous pleasures because the myth was that once you did it and had a baby, you couldn't live without it.

She'd laugh, relishing the attention, and brush her suitors off coquettishly. Eventually, the song, like everything about their lives—the fads, the music, the clothes, the words they used—disappeared and something else took its place. Within a year after Vidamía was born it seemed like all the homegirls were pregnant. There were six weddings one summer. Then, instead of running free all over the place, having fun and listening to

95

records and dancing, they were changing diapers and pushing baby carriages and bragging about what their baby was doing and how much they ate. "Girl, this baby's going to be enormous, *mami*. Gaw, he eats everything. And he's healthy and good. Ain't you, *papito*?" cuchicooing the baby. They seemed happy, but deep inside they were dead and complained about everything and Elsa felt like she was responsible for starting a fad and every pregnancy was her fault. Although she often felt guilty, she knew she had done the right thing in breaking up with Billy and sending him away. Otherwise, she'd end up having a baby every year and she'd be stuck like her mother. She knew she had to get away from the neighborhood and the life of making babies and taking care of children.

One day as she stood watching her pregnant friends who were dropping out of school, their baby faces bloated and their eyes glazed over so that she was reminded of watching cows chewing their cuds, she flipped her lid.

9 Sanity and Insanity

A week later, at the end of the schoolday, Elsa had gone looking for Mrs. Kantrowitz and told her that she felt like she was going crazy and wanted to kill her baby. Mrs. Kantrowitz suggested she see the guidance counselor, but Elsa shook her head and began crying. Mrs. Kantrowitz arranged for her to see a therapist friend up on Park Avenue at around Seventieth Street. Every Tuesday and Thursday after school she rode the subway up to Sixty-eighth Street and sat in a red leather chair and talked to Dr. Gelfand, who was a beautiful, delicate woman about the age of fifty with very thin blond hair and skin so white and fragile that in the light from the lamps in the room it appeared almost transparent. There, in an atmosphere of clinical acceptance, Elsa began talking about herself and her fears and dreams, and, eventually, between those sessions and academic counseling at school, she decided that she would enter Hunter College under the Open Admissions Program, the trips up to Sixty-eighth Street becoming therapeutic in and of themselves, so that it was natural that she should attend college there as part of her treatment. The trips uptown seemed to her like vacations away from the oppressiveness and sameness of her life on the Lower East Side. Here, uptown in this wealthy neighborhood, she was not just another Puerto Rican girl, anonymous and without substance, a ghostly presence that blended with the others in a brown haze of insignificance. Here, in this American world, she was visible, she stood out, she was different. Years later while reading *The Invisible Man*, she laughed at the contrast between her view and that of the author, for it was in the bigger world that she found substance to her being, not invisibility. It was in that larger world that she saw her worth.

Dr. Gelfand spoke with what Elsa later learned was a German accent. She often heard her speaking what she also learned was Yiddish, recognizing words from shopping along Orchard, Essex, and Delancey streets while her mother haggled artfully with the shop owners in her Spanish-accented English. She remembered clearly her mother shaking her head and dismissing a price as too expensive, and the merchant shrugging his shoulders and saying: *Onkuken kost nit kein gelt.* While talking about living on the Lower East Side, Elsa once asked Dr. Gelfand what the phrase meant. Dr. Gelfand smiled and said it meant that it doesn't cost anything to look. But Elsa's favorite phrase, which she memorized and used liberally with her Jewish friends, was: *Kush meer in toches,* which meant "Kiss my ass," though she never used it in Dr. Gelfand's presence. She loved being able to say things like: *Bist du meshuge?* "Are you crazy?" She would have liked to follow that up with "Better that you should grow upside down in the ground like an onion," but she could never remember the Yiddish for the saying.

Eventually, when Elsa matured sufficiently and began to attend college and through study became aware of what had taken place in Europe during the thirties and forties, she discovered that her doctor had been one of the people who were persecuted by the Nazis. One afternoon while she was talking absently, watching the rain outside the window, she told Dr. Gelfand that she hated being what she was—meaning Puerto Rican—and that she often wished she were white. She began sobbing and couldn't stop crying for nearly fifteen minutes. Then she told Dr. Gelfand that she wished her parents were dead. The doctor got up and went to the window and stood there for a while. When she came back, there were tears in her eyes, but she said nothing. Years later, after Elsa had received her Ph.D. and was a practicing psychologist and therapist, but still making weekly visits for her therapy sessions, now paid for, she asked Dr. Gelfand why there had been tears in her eyes that day. The older woman, grown even more fragile and ethereal, sat behind her desk and explained.

Barbara Gelfand had lived in Nürnberg as a young girl. She explained to Elsa how at this time Nürnberg had become the center for the activities of the National Socialists and that every year in late summer Hitler held rallies there that included enormous shows of military might, and hundreds of thousands of people came to the city to celebrate their Aryan roots, since Nürnberg was supposedly the center of Aryan culture. In 1938, after the approval of the infamous "Blood Protection Laws," her father, himself a physician, grew worried because his wife was Jewish. The following year, when the laws began to take effect, fewer and fewer of her father's German patients came to be treated. It was early July, and already there were more than 20,000 soldiers in the city. One Saturday, he gathered the children—Barbara, her older sisters, Anna and Karin, her little brother, Uwe, and Gretchen, her youngest sister. Their mother packed a large wicker picnic basket, and they took the train, ostensibly to visit their grandparents in Frankfurt. In the basket's top layer were sandwiches, a large apple strudel, and some *kugel*. Beneath that layer were napkins, and beneath the napkins a family photo album. A false bottom had been constructed, and under it her father had stashed the family jewelry, their passports, birth certificates, and a few stocks. A similar false bottom had been constructed for her father's medical bag, which carried nearly ten thousand dollars in marks, and another ten thousand dollars or so in English pounds. Barbara was fourteen years old at the time, studying the piano at the conservatory and reading French literature.

Uwe, only five years old, and Gretchen, three, were restless. Eventually they ate and their father entertained them until they fell asleep. Anna, nineteen, a student of history and languages at the University of Erlangen, and Karin, sixteen, who was studying science, sat stoically, looking out of the train windows at the countryside. When the train entered the station in Frankfurt, Barbara started to rise, but her mother held her back and put a finger to her lips. And then she saw on the train platform her grandparents Joshua and Rachel, her mother's parents, carrying a smaller picnic basket. Their father helped them get on the train, and Barbara remembered they looked small and scared, but her father, who was very strong, patted their cheeks and made sure they were comfortable even though Grandma Rachel's hands were shaking.

When the train started moving again it began to rain. It rained all the way to Köln as they traveled along the Rhine, the villages of neat houses and the castles up on the hills like the miniature landscapes of the train sets displayed in store windows during holidays. Barbara knew that they would never return home to Nürnberg, and that she'd never again see Dietrich Meyer, who played the cello so beautifully and whom she loved so much even though he was nearly twenty years old. She knew also that their poor little dachshund, Fogel, who had barked and whined, running back and forth behind the fence of their garden as if he knew he'd never see them again, would eventually die of sorrow. The rain had stopped falling when they got off the train at a small town—she recalled vividly that it was Kaldenkirchen, near the Dutch border.

Uwe wanted to know where they were going as he walked, holding Anna's hand. Her father, carrying Gretchen, still asleep, said they were going to visit a friend from his days at the university who now taught at the University of Utrecht, in the Netherlands. They walked nearly a mile along a deserted road, and then in the distance there was an abandoned stone house, which she surmised decades later had been part of her father's escape plan. They went into the house, and their father announced that they would stop there for a while, until dark, then they would go on. They ate sitting on some hay bales, their mother spreading a tablecloth over one of the bales so that they were reminded of being home. Her grandparents spoke Yiddish, their faces showing worry. Her grandmother Rachel was still shaking a little bit and taking only tiny bites of food. Her mother spoke soothingly to them and her father listened attentively.

When the sun began setting her father looked out the window of the stone house. He stepped away rapidly and from his medical bag removed a small pair of binoculars and again looked out the window. He returned to the family and announced, in German, that no matter what happened, no one was to cry or be afraid, that there could be a dangerous situation coming and everyone must be very brave. And then their father asked the children to go quickly out the back door of the stone house and into the grove of birches. He handed Anna the picnic basket and gave Barbara his medical bag. And then he and their mother and their grandparents kissed everyone hastily. "Go now," he said to them. "Go. No time to waste. *Schnell, bitte*. Your mother and I will follow soon and bring your grandparents."

They went quickly out the back door, through the fence gate and across a field of tall grass and then silently into the woods. When they were in the grove, protected by the shadows of the trees and the failing light, Barbara turned and saw the car with the German officers wearing swastika armbands getting out of the black vehicle and heading for the house. They were followed by motorcycle soldiers with machine guns.

Once again Dr. Gelfand went to the window and stood there, the afternoon light making her pale skin appear paper-thin. When she turned she was smiling sadly and said that she never saw her parents or grandparents again. She and the rest of the children had spent the night in the woods. Toward early morning, led by Anna, they had crossed the border into Holland and entered a small town. Anna took them to the address that her father had given her, and they remained there for nearly a week. Then, they eventually made their way on foot, by car, and in canal boat to the house of their father's colleague, who was a professor in Utrecht. During the three months that they lived in the professor's house, they wondered what had happened to their parents. Anna, Karin, and Barbara lied to Gretchen and Uwe, telling them that their parents would be coming soon. One afternoon the professor said that things had grown worse and it was best for them to cross the channel to England. They were given warm clothing and put on a train and then a boat to England.

"I never found out what happened to my parents," Dr. Gelfand said, adding that she had tried everything possible, and that it wouldn't be quite so painful if she had at least been able to finally learn that they had been sent to Dachau or another of the death camps. Instead, they had been swallowed up by time and the brutality of war. On one of her trips to Germany she learned that her grandparents, Joshua and Rachel Altschuler, had been exterminated by the Nazis at Buchenwald along with countless others. But in more than forty years she never learned her parents' fate.

The story affected Elsa powerfully and she wondered if Puerto Ricans were being culturally annihilated as Hitler had attempted to do with the Jews. It wasn't the same as disappearing, but one could as well become a walking wraith and cease to function.

Toward the end of her junior year of college, when Vidamía was about to enter first grade, Elsa began to feel rudimentary feelings of motherhood and intimations of identification with her mother, who still lived down on the Lower East Side in the same small apartment, now made larger because she was alone. Elsa knew that those first six years had had their effect on Vidamía, and although she called Elsa "mommy" and Ursula Santiago *güela* or *güelita*, the slang term for *abuela*, grandmother in Spanish, the real mother in her life was obviously Ursula. Vidamía had quickly learned that there were certain filial responsibilities that she must respect and adhere to and she did so with remarkable aplomb.

Given Vidamía's disposition, it was fairly easy for her to overlook her mother's faults. What she suspected, but didn't want to confront, was Elsa's profound antipathy toward her. Vidamía's antidote to the pain of the rejection was to become the perfect child who lived in careful admiration of her mother, fulfilling every intellectual and social ambition her mother had for her; instinctively knowing that if she couldn't be loved by her mother she could at least gain her respect; joyfully and willingly taking test after test to determine her intelligence; serving as her mother's reassurance that she wasn't a hindrance; rising at six o'clock each weekday morning to make herself ready to go with her mother all the way down to Hunter College, Elsa having discovered in her senior year at the college that there was a Hunter College Elementary School, which she looked into and, through Mrs. Kantrowitz and Dr. Gelfand's influence, got Vidamía tested and admitted to.

This was also the year she met Barry and within six months they were married and had moved to a beautiful apartment in Riverdale. The further Elsa went with her education, however, the more time and money she spent attempting to fathom what was wrong with her life. No matter how much she tried, she remained trapped in a vague zone of her being that made her feel as if she were walking around with her eyes closed and her hands outstretched to reassure herself that there were no impediments in her way. She found herself wanting to be in command of every situation, and of everyone's life, including her daughter's. She soon realized that beneath all her emotions there was still a self-loathing that, although submerged, surfaced with disturbing regularity. The worst part was the feeling that she didn't belong to that wondrous world of intellect and exploration of the mind which so fascinated her. Upon receiving her Ph.D., she immediately sought work and was able to find employment at a hospital on Long Island.

After dropping Vidamía off at Hunter College Elementary School, she traveled each morning an hour to be at work at ten a.m. and she had to be back at five to pick Vidamía up. No matter how much psychoanalysis she endured, she couldn't get rid of the images of those summer days when she and the other girls got on the subway and felt absolutely free, and she could still hear all the songs. She kept hearing one of them over and over like a leitmotif—*Ay, camina y ven para que gozes conmigo,* translating it as "Hey, let's go so you can enjoy yourself with me." But she could never enjoy herself ever again, because she had given her freedom away. The irony of the other song, the Alegre All Stars' "Estoy Buscando a Kako," in which the singer is looking for someone, continued to haunt her and produced such anger that one day, alone in her beautiful apartment while Vidamía was at a friend's house, she began pounding her head until a torrent of tears poured out of her, the sobs in her chest so uncontrollable that she felt as if at any moment she would pass out from the emotion. She eventually fell asleep on the living-room floor and didn't wake up until Barry came in.

One afternoon during the year she was writing her dissertation, Elsa had gone into the Times Square subway station and found the record shop where there is every kind of album and tape of Latin music and purchased the Alegre All Stars' album, then returned to the Riverdale apartment and played it. A smile returned to her face as she thought of those days. And then, suddenly, in the middle of listening to the record, she realized that she would never find herself again, that her memories and who she was had been left in that lovely, quiet room, on that psychoanalytic couch on Park Avenue. But she was unable to hate Dr. Gelfand, because no one had ever shown such kindness and concern for her, which she was, of course, unworthy of, deserving nothing but hatred because no matter how many times she returned to Dr. Gelfand she could never be whole. She continued keeping her weekly appointments until one day she went to Dr. Gelfand's office and was told that the doctor had passed away. She spent the next eight months in a dangerous depression, suicidal feelings swirling around almost every subject that came into her mind. She was a horrible mother, daughter, sister, wife, scholar, therapist, lover, American, Puerto Rican—but, most of all, woman. And now her darling little mistake of a daughter, whom she had been charged with loving and who kept her constantly confused with feelings of inadequacy, had gone and unearthed the memories of Billy Farrell and his lost life.

Damn her and damn him.

10 Dear Diary

The big, red-faced man said his name was Michael Sanderson and greeted Vidamía with a nod—apprehensive and suspicious, she imagined, of the wealth that had attached itself to her person without her having any control of it. She could always tell when money made people uncomfortable. He went around to the other side of the car, and Vidamía sensed that he felt foolish opening the door for her. She was dressed in a flowered dress and was wearing stockings and cordovan loafers and suddenly she felt silly that so much money had been spent on the clothes she wore, her mother always insisting on the most expensive items. But this was a special occasion, so it was all right. She carried a small pocketbook and her hair had a small ribbon in it. There was a bit of gloss on her lips. When she was inside, seated demurely, having put her seat belt on without being asked, he got into the car, breathed a sigh, started the engine, and drove through the wealthy neighborhood—the acreages in the double figures and beautifully landscaped—computing how much each house must cost. Vidamía thanked him for coming to pick her up, calling him Mr. Sanderson.

"You're my father's uncle, aren't you?" she said.

"Yes, I am."

"Grandma Maud told me," Vidamía said. "She described you pretty accurately. I guess that makes you my granduncle. Do you have children?"

"Yes, I do. Two boys and two girls."

"What are their names?"

"Michael Jr., Peter, Maureen, and Samantha."

"And how old are they?"

"Michael's twenty-three, Peter's nineteen, Maureen's sixteen, and Sam's about your age."

"Sam? I like that. I'm twelve."

"Oh, yeah?" he said and laughed for the first time at Vidamía's seriousness.

"Sam's fourteen. I thought you were older."

"Thank you very much," she said, feeling foolish. "I guess I should wait to grow up, but being a child can be very limiting," she added, knowing she probably sounded a bit affected.

"Enjoy it, kid," Michael Sanderson said. "It doesn't last that long. After a while time just disappears on you. One day all you can do is ask yourself where your life went. Believe me."

"You're probably right. I guess we're all cousins. Your kids and me."

"Yeah, I guess you are," Michael Sanderson said. "Let's see," he mused as he turned onto the highway for the trip to Maud's. "Sure. My kids are Billy's first cousins and Billy's kids are their second cousins. You're Billy's kid, so you're my kids' second cousin. Sam's going to be very happy to hear that."

Vidamía then asked Michael Sanderson if there were any other brothers and sisters besides her grandma and him. Michael Sanderson said there had been seven of them, but Brendan had died when he was just a baby. So there was her grandmother Maud, the oldest, then Mary Katherine, Douglas, Olivia, Frazier, and himself. She asked him about the entire family, how many children each of his brothers and sisters had, so that by the time they reached Maud Farrell's apartment, Vidamía had gained nearly one hundred relatives from her connection to her father. The idea that they included people all over the United States and Canada, and even a cousin who was a sheep rancher in New Zealand, made her feel enormous pride.

When Vidamía walked into Maud's apartment she was stunned that the large blond-headed man standing there was her father. For a moment she just stared at him, looking from his face to his right hand, which was at his side, wanting to see the places where the missing fingers had been as Grandma Maud had said, wanting to see them and touch them to see if she would feel disgusted, and him just saying, barely audibly, "Hi, how are you? My name's Bill."

And then he came forward and opened his arms awkwardly so that she felt as if the two of them were magnetized figures who couldn't help but move toward each other, and she rushed, crying, into his arms and buried her face in his long hair and he kissed her face and then wiped the tears with the back of his right hand, not at all fearful that he would scare her since Maud had explained that it would be worse if he tried hiding it from her and Bill trusted his mother, who had never hurt him in any way. Maud had been equally confident with Vidamía and had told her that her father had been very brave and that the hand was like any other hand, except that it's missing those two fingers and that she ought to look into his eyes and into his heart and if she saw his love for her there, she shouldn't worry about the rest. When he began to withdraw the hand, Vidamía took it tenderly and held it in both of her hands. She then brought it to her face, kissed it, and said, "I love you, Daddy," and Billy Farrell said, "God bless you, I love you, too."

That day they sat in the living room for a good half hour, Maud the only person saying anything, telling Vidamía stories about Billy—things like the fact that when he was a boy his room had been filled with model airplanes and ships, the planes suspended from the ceiling by thread that he took from her sewing kit—fighter planes, American P-51s, German Messerschmitts, Japanese Zeros, British Spitfires, B-29 bombers—achieving this by moving his dresser, climbing on it, gluing the thread to the ceiling, and then rigging the airplanes at different heights so that at a distance they appeared to be flying. She didn't tell Vidamía how on the day Billy found out that his father had been killed his face became gray and his eyes opened wide at the shock. He'd gone to his room and locked the door and all Maud could hear was the sound of a baseball bat hitting the fragile plastic and balsa of his airplanes until, an hour later, he came out and ran to her, his face ravaged by the pain of his dual loss, a small cut on his neck where a sharp piece of plastic had pierced the skin.

Holding back her own pain in order to comfort him, Maud had held him close to her, not saying anything but absorbing his pain—so much that she feared that at any moment she would break down. She had taken him into the bathroom and washed his face, running the cold hand towel over his reddened cheeks and moistening his neck, which was burning hot. After a while she gave him a glass of orange soda and a sandwich and went into his room. Everything was smashed, shattered, destroyed. The nearly twenty-five airplanes hung in pieces from the threads, a half wing here, a tail there, a cockpit a bit above the rest. And on the bookcase and desk where he had carefully placed his ships—cruisers, battleships, even the PT-109 his father had helped him build, because it was President Kennedy's boat—everything was shattered. And then she saw the photograph of Mickey Mantle, his hero, also smashed. The Mick swinging the bat, keeping his eye on the ball and his head down, just like Billy's dad had taught him. And now he was gone. The force of the blow had driven Mantle's uniform, below the Yankee logo, into the wallpaper, the picture left hanging not by its wire and hook but by the adhesion of the cardboard and photograph to the wall.

In time she'd had someone come in to repair and repaper the walls. Billy never built airplanes again and never wanted to play the bagpipes. He withdrew into himself, spending most of his time at his grandparents' in Yonkers. Maud had to go out and support herself and Billy because Kevin's death benefits were not enough, working first as a waitress, which kept her busy and in front of people. Because when she was alone all she did was cry and imagine Kevin's last minutes, his split-second decision to go into that bar without first learning what was going on inside. Would she have done the same thing in his place? She couldn't imagine. Her only release from the torture of the tragedy was to go to confession and repeat monotonously, "Forgive me, Father, for I have sinned," and then confess to the searing hatred she felt for the men who had killed her husband, extending the hatred to their relatives, and their friends, and everyone who came from that wretched island, the spic bastards.

"They're worse than niggers," Dotty Gagliano's husband had said.

He had a beer distributorship in the Bronx and every other word with him was kike this and Polack that, sparing no one his hatred except for a small group of people who came from a particular section of Naples; everyone else was scum, even the Sicilians and the Calabrese. Dotty would just stand around and frown and shake her head. Maud supposed that Dotty's hatred was fueled by being around Lou Gagliano, but in those years all she herself could think about was that those people who had come here to collect welfare had killed Kevin.

Now here she was chatting with this lovely, innocent child, her granddaughter, for whom she felt the greatest love and a desire to protect her from a world that, in her experience, could be harsh and without conscience. After a while, Maud Farrell announced that it was time for dinner and the four of them sat down to roast beef, mashed potatoes with gravy, vegetables, salad, and a big apple pie with ice cream. At one point during the meal Maud observed Billy eating heartily, and she remembered then that Billy was always a good eater, from the time he was a little baby, always taking everything she gave him with great enthusiasm and with a gratitude that reminded her of a small puppy. He was a fierce eater, cutting his meat into large chunks and shoveling it into his mouth. She observed the contrast between his style and that of Vidamía, whose manners were very polished and her movements at table dainty. She was pleased, however, that the girl ate with an equally healthy appetite, her granddaughter looking up at one point and nodding approvingly. Maud laughed and said there was still pie and ice cream. Vidamía smiled. When Maud had served the pie and scooped ice cream on it, Vidamía finally got up enough courage to ask about her father's other children.

"Can I ask you something, Daddy?" she said, smiling at Billy across the table, not the least bit unsure even though it was only the second time she was addressing him as her father.

"Sure," he said, shyly. "What is it?"

"How many brothers and sisters do I have?"

"Oh, right," he said, relieved that it wasn't anything about how he'd lost his fingers. "Three sisters and one brother. Hortense who's ten, Cliff who's nine, Fawn who's seven, and Caitlin who's going to be a year old in September."

"Really?"

"Yeah, really," Billy said, smiling at her enthusiasm. "You want to meet them?"

"Yeah, sure."

"We'll have to see if your mother'll let you come to New York."

"Maybe next weekend," Vidamía said. "I'm sure it'll be okay."

"We'll see."

After they rose from the table Vidamía helped Maud clear the table and scrape the plates before they were put into the sink for washing. She volunteered to do the dishes but Maud tapped her lightly on the bottom and told her to scoot.

"Don't you dare," she said. "Out of the kitchen."

Maud then went into her bedroom and came out with two large albums. One contained photos of Billy Farrell as a baby, a boy, and a young man. Vidamía oohed and aahed, calling her father the cutest baby and the cutest boy and a very handsome young man, unabashedly commenting on his good looks. The display of flattery, predictably, embarrassed Billy, but, as it was coming from his daughter, he allowed himself to privately enjoy the praise. Toward the end of the album there were some pictures of Kevin, and Vidamía asked who the man was.

"That was your grandfather, Kevin Farrell," Maud said. "He was a policeman who got . . ."

"Shot?" Vidamía said, completing Maud's sentence.

"Yes."

"I'm very sorry, Grandma."

"That's all right. I'm sure he would've also been very happy to meet you."

And then she closed that album and opened the other one. This one had every conceivable picture of her siblings, taken at play, at birthday parties, in the park, at dinner, and playing musical instruments. This last detail fascinated her.

"Do they really play?" she asked.

"Oh, yes," Billy Farrell said. "Pretty well, too."

"You should hear them," Maud said. "Very talented. Just like their father."

"Do you play, Daddy?"

"A little," Billy said, suddenly uncomfortable.

"What?"

"A little guitar," he said, almost in a whisper, his mind fading rapidly, his thoughts disappearing and being displaced by memories of the battlefield.

He closed his eyes, then realized that doing that would attract her attention and excused himself to use the bathroom. When he came out a little while later, he said he felt better, but Vidamía knew something was wrong. She watched him as he sat down on the couch and smiled at her.

"Daddy, you were starting to tell me about my brother and sisters."

"Oh, yeah. You'll like them," he said. "They're good kids. Like you. I'll call your mother and see what we can do."

"Thank you, Daddy," Vidamía said, coming over and sitting next to him. He sat motionless, wanting desperately to put his arm around her shoulder to let her lean against him but unable to do so. Maud looked at her watch and said that it was getting late, and that Vidamía had promised her mother she'd be back before eight o'clock.

"Let's go, big fella," she said, mussing Billy's hair. "Mike'll drive Vidamía home and you can ride with him back to the city."

"That's okay," Billy said. "I'll walk across to the Bronx and take the subway."

"You sure?"

"Yeah, I'll be okay."

"I guess you'll have to see where I live next time," Vidamía said, not revealing her disappointment. She handed her father a piece of paper and then withdrew a small address book and a pen from her pocketbook. "Could you give me your phone number?"

"Yeah, sure," Billy said and recited the number slowly. "I'm home most of the time," he added and stood up.

And then she rushed to him and put her arms around him and reached up to kiss his face. He kissed her and patted her head, telling her to take care of herself and that he'd see her soon.

Vidamía watched as he walked out the door and into the summer evening, his thoughts weighed down by she knew not what. Worried about him, she looked out the window as his silhouette receded into the darkness, reappeared again in the light of a streetlamp, and was gone.

"Is he going to be okay?" she asked, looking from Maud Farrell to Mike Sanderson.

"Oh, yeah," Mike said. "He's a strong fella. He'll be okay. Don't you worry."

"Sure," Maud said. "He'll be fine."

And then Vidamía hugged Maud, seeking reassurance. Maud reciprocated by kissing Vidamía and pressing her to her big bosom so that Vidamía could smell the soap and powder and perfume and the special smell she associated with respect.

When Vidamía got home, her mother was waiting, her face tight and troubled the way it got when she was overwrought. Vidamía ran immediately upstairs to her room to change into more comfortable clothes. Elsa followed her, speaking rapidly and betraying her fears, demanding to know what had happened.

"Well, was he all right?" she said.

"Sure, he was fine," Vidamía replied. "Why?"

"Nothing," Elsa said. "It's that . . . sometimes he used to have these moods, and I was wondering if he was still the same."

"No, not that I could tell," she said, knowing instinctively that it was necessary to lie.

"One minute he was there—and the next minute ten thousand miles away, his eyes looking glazed."

"No, nothing like that," Vidamía replied. "I have three sisters and a brother."

"Oh, really?" Elsa said. "How old?"

She recited the names and ages of the children and watched her mother, her face a mask of forced composure.

"Well, he certainly didn't waste any time," she said.

"He wants me to meet them," Vidamía said.

"Oh, really? What did he do, invite himself here?"

"No, he wants me to come and see him in New York City. He lives in the East Village."

"I don't think that'll be possible. This was a one-time thing and that's it."

"*Mami*, stop it," Vidamía said. "How can you talk like that? He's my father."

"He abandoned us, and now he wants you to come down and see him? I don't think so."

Vidamía thought for a moment and was disturbed by the notion that it could be true that her father had abandoned them. She was silent while her mother went on talking about irresponsibility and lack of commitment, explaining that she was just a young girl full of dreams when he came along and simply manipulated her emotions with stories about his friendship with her brother, saying that Billy had used the death of a loved one in order to take advantage of her sorrow.

"I was fifteen years old, honey," she said, playing at being wounded. "Fifteen years old. Three years older than you. Going to high school. Poor as a church mouse and here comes this slick-talking young man, filling up my head about his friendship with my brother, whom I loved. About a year and a half before, we had mourned and cried over Joey when we got the news that he'd gotten killed. Now here he came, unearthing those memories in order to get at me. This is very painful for me to tell you, but I'm being absolutely honest."

"I should get his side of it," Vidamía said, suddenly dubious about her mother's version.

Elsa said that it was out of the question, adding that if Vidamía attempted to establish contact with him, or lied as she had done previously, then she would have no alternative but to place very severe restrictions on her, and she hoped it wouldn't come to that. Rarely at a loss for words, Vidamía sat stunned. A feeling of rebellion rose up in her and she vowed silently to see her father again as soon as she could.

"Do you understand that, young lady?" Elsa said.

"Yes, *mami*," Vidamía said.

"Good. Try not to abuse your privileges."

Vidamía didn't answer her mother, but as soon as she left the room and Vidamía could hear her going down the stairs, she felt a profound sadness for both her mother and her father. How unhappy they both seemed. Their sadness made her wonder what they had done to each other, or if it was all because of something they had each manufactured on their own. Whatever was the case, she had to figure it out. She'd call him tomorrow when her mother and Barry were gone. And then, once again, as she changed clothes, she thought about how her mother never called her by her name. The only time she spoke her name was when she was introducing her, although lately she had taken to asking her to introduce herself, or asking her to provide the name when it was required on documents such as school records, or when they had to get airline tickets.

When her mother was in a good mood it was honey, baby, sweetie, darling, dearie, or, in Spanish, *mijita*, little daughter, *corazoncito*, little heart, *amorcito*, little love. Never Vidamía. The thought angered her. When she was eight years old her mother had even asked her if she'd like to have her name changed. She had shaken her head. "I like my name, *mami*," she'd said. And she did, especially the way her grandmother and her aunts and everyone who spoke Spanish pronounced it. Vidamía. Vee-tha-MEE-ah, the final A lingering, then fading. Her name was made up of beautiful sounds, and there was no one she knew who had a name like it. In any case, her name meant "my life" in Spanish and that was the best part of all.

Now, as she unlocked the bottom drawer of her desk in order to write in her diary, she wondered if her father had named her. She didn't dare ask her mother, since it was obvious she didn't like the name. She brought her small trunk down from the closet and set it on her bed. She locked the door to her room, went into the bottom drawer of her desk and from beneath a stack of papers she retrieved the key to the trunk. When she had opened the trunk, she removed her diary. She opened the treasured, private book, sat at her desk, and smiled as she wrote the date on the fine blue paper.

August 1, 1984

Today, I met my father. He is approximately 6'1" tall and very strong. His eyes are very blue and his hair is blond. He has a beard with some gray hairs in it. The middle and pinkie fingers on his right hand are missing. I thought I would be disgusted by the hand, but I was not and was very proud of myself. I told him that I wanted to study medicine and he said that was a very fine thing to want to study. He plays the guitar and he is very handsome. I think I look more like him than I do my mother. Speaking about my mother, she was insupportable. I have always known this word in English because in Spanish everyone always uses it to describe the behavior of unruly children. They say: *Ese muchacho es insoportable.* I am very glad that I speak Spanish, because the more advanced the English language becomes the closer it resembles Spanish. Mr. Echebarren, who is a friend of my stepfather and teaches at a college in New Jersey, says this is because as English gets harder it becomes more Latinate (sp?). Anyway, since Spanish comes from Latin, it's understandable. *Insoportable!* That's how the mistress of the house was tonight when I got back. I'm not bragging, but the word is only used by Mother when referring to me, because, as much as possible, I try to stay away from having problems with other people unless absolutely necessary. But insupportably is the way my mother behaved today. Like a spoiled child and definitely insupportable.

I must figure out a strategy for seeing my father again. I feel like a character in *Roots*, held in slavery and separated from her relatives. I must be brave and smart and not allow anything to interfere with seeing him. Why did he leave us? Didn't he care for us? I'm not angry, but I'd like to know. I have so many questions for him.

That's all for now, my dear diary,
Vidamía Farrell

11 Jamming

Billy walked in the summer evening the fifteen or so blocks from his mother's apartment to the elevated subway station trying to figure out why in the middle of a happy occasion his mind should start acting up to trigger such awful thoughts, memories so vivid and frightening. Inside the bathroom, the door locked, they had attacked him with compassionless fury so that he was there again, lying on his stomach in the jungle, firing burst after burst from his machine gun, the steady rat-a-tat-tat lost in the din of the artillery above him ripping at trees in the distance and the exploding mortars that whined as they approached. They made you a machine gunner because your aim with a rifle was bad. But being a machine gunner made you an even more important target for the enemy.

He had grasped his head in both hands and attempted desperately to shake the thoughts out of it, as if it were a gourd and he was trying to extract the last drops of liquid from it. When his attempts met with failure, he stood looking at himself in the mirror, hating what he saw and pulling at his beard with such force that he caused tears of pain to burst from his eyes. He pounded his head with his fists until he saw stars and his skull ached. Then he poured cold water on his head, and when the water was even colder he took a big gulp and let it go into his bad tooth and the pain hurt him so badly that he nearly blacked out. He heard his mother banging on the door and calling him and he saw Albert T. Zorich's sad face after he came back from the war.

Still, the thoughts wouldn't stop coming, and with them the overwhelming feeling that he was responsible for Joey's death; whenever the subject of his hand came up he was immediately transported back to the incident that had caused the tragedy. Lately, he had become convinced that he had directly caused the fatal injury. The feeling lingered so that when he first awoke in the morning, or at different times during the day, he felt that he'd been the one who had shot Joey or tossed a grenade but was too cowardly to admit it back then and turn himself in, fabricating a lie about crossing the corner of that rice paddy and suddenly being attacked by the VC.

"No, sir, we didn't see them."

"Are you sure they were Viet Cong?"

"Yes, sir. We heard them talking."

He had said this, lying on his hospital bed nearly two months after Joey's death, trying to figure out why they were still asking him questions. He tried recalling why the captain investigating the incident had been so insistent, but couldn't remember his reasons. Everything was foggy, as if he were looking at the details of that day with Joey through mosquito netting.

On his way to the subway Billy Farrell was forced to recall the last time he walked out the door of the Santiago apartment, knowing he was leaving behind his broken heart just as Joey had left his own mangled one back in that rice paddy. Stunned by the loss of Elsa and expecting never to see the baby that would link him to Joey, he returned to his life of desolation. As if in a trance, he went back to Grandpa Buck Sanderson's place in Yonkers and stayed in his room for five months, not talking or playing the guitar, just thinking about life and trying to remember who he was and where he'd been.

At the end of his self-imposed monastic exile, Billy Farrell finally emerged, haggard and thin—his body aching from sleeping fourteen to eighteen hours a day—and moped around, relearning the guitar, reading novels about noble animals, books like the Lad and Lassie series, and some Jack London, his father's favorite author. Eventually he regained some weight and began playing the guitar more frequently, so that in time he started toying with the idea of playing publicly, in the street, to see if the pain of not being able to play the piano would leave him. It wasn't as if he hadn't tried, because Grandpa Sanderson had guided him over to the Wurlitzer upright where Billy had practiced scales as a boy over and over as if he were storing the notes within him to someday lay them down in beautiful lines of melody. But once there, with the yellowing keys in front of him, all he could feel was an unbearable pain in his head where he had been wounded and where the diminutive tin plate now resided, so that his head throbbed and he could hear, instead of triplets and chord changes, mortar fire and the pinging of bullets hitting metal.

So it was the guitar: sitting for hours in a rocker, fingering the chords with his intact left hand, hearing the harmonies, mesmerized by his three-fingered claw as it picked at the six strings. But something else was missing besides his two fingers, and he was convinced that what he had lost was gone forever and nothing could bring it back.

There were times when he sat on the porch of the big house and stared in cold or warm weather at the air and saw it change color and saw in it battles being waged in slow motion by men vastly different from one another who never bled or fell but continued crawling and running and firing; sitting there, hour after hour, feeling the cold in winter and not caring. And when the sun disappeared and night came, his grandmother Brigid came and brought a blanket and draped it over his shoulders and told him dinner would be ready in twenty or so minutes. And when she came to get him, all she needed to do was touch his arm and he came quietly, the colors of the air and the pictures in his mind remaining as he cut the meat and fed potatoes and vegetables with gravy into his mouth mechanically and buttered his bread and ate it, without tasting anything, because none of it seemed important.

At night he remained awake for hours, lying still in the hope that he could rest, but not fall asleep, so that he wouldn't have to wake up to the nightmare in which he walked in a procession dressed as an altar boy with the Sacred Heart of Jesus on a silver tray, the bloody mass crying out in Spanish, and he dutifully delivering it to the president of the United States, who was faceless, because that is what he dreamt and he couldn't switch channels.

There were also occasions when he emerged from the thick mist of misfortune that had enveloped his mind and read, played the guitar, or went walking through the neighborhood, stopping at the post office and looking at the wanted posters, wondering if any of those guys had served in Nam, as if all men were divided into two groups: those who had experienced the madness of that war and those who were too young or too old or had found some way to avoid being there. He wandered through the streets, so that everyone knew what had taken place in his life as clearly as if he were wearing not jeans and a fatigue jacket but a death shroud. He walked the streets lost in thought, sometimes crossing into Mount Vernon and stopping off to see his mother at O'Hanlon's in the afternoon, when only the old people sat there quietly with their drinks, waiting to be summoned to their death or the funeral of a friend or relative.

Wearing his sorrow without style, Billy climbed up on a stool and smiled sadly at his mother. She brought him a mug of draft beer and he remained there, sitting, sipping the cold brew in the semi-darkness and recalling places where he had played jazz. In the quiet shadows of his mind he could see everything: the musicians playing their instruments, the movement of their fingers and the expressions on their faces, the music coming in pleasant waves, but now all of it was foreign, as if jazz had never existed in his life. He enjoyed the memory of the tunes but was unable to express their complexity now, so that there might as well not have been any sound to them. This bothered him because in his memory he could even smell the cigarette smoke and hear clearly the tinkling of glasses and the buzzing of the audience as they spoke. But no matter how much he concentrated, the music wasn't there and a simple twelve-bar blues played upon a piano remained as much a mystery as the diagram of a rocket engine.

The subway train rolled on through the Bronx neighborhoods, letting passengers out and taking on more, all of them with stories to tell and memories plaguing them. He couldn't understand how suddenly he could recall tunes. He thought of the song "Summertime," and as in a dream he closed his eyes and saw himself playing again, his ten fingers still there as he bent over the piano, eyes closed, humming softly, singing the lyrics inside his head: *"Your daddy's rich, and your ma is good looking, so hush little baby, don't you cry."* The clickety-clack of the wheels on the tracks and the music in his head relaxed him. He slipped into a half-dream state and then fell asleep dreaming he was a Vietnamese boy with long blond hair leading a water buffalo, and Vidamía, as she had looked today, was riding the animal. She was holding a photo album and singing a song he didn't recognize.

"What were you singing?" he asked Vidamía.

"I wasn't singing," she said, smiling at him.

"Yes, I heard you."

"It was in your head."

"How can that be? How can you have been singing in my head?"

"I don't know. Maybe you remembered something. Maybe I was singing in your memory."

"But what was the song?"

"Oh, you know the song."

"I do?"

"Yes. It's the *Eenie meenie pepsodeenie* song."

"Well, sing it again."

"I'll whisper it to you," Vidamía had said.

She came close to him. He moved his hair away from his ear and she whispered the words—*Eenie meenie pepsodeenie, Ah Bah boobalini*—but he didn't recognize them, so he figured it was a poem. When she was finished, she asked him if he liked it. He nodded and they smiled and then went inside a marble house and had a lunch of tropical fruits with K-rations and a little dog meat. There was no one there but they were happy and he wondered why he was a boy and Vidamía such a big girl.

Billy woke up as the train pulled into Fourteenth Street, the wheels screeching as they turned into the station. He got out and walked upstairs to the street. The bright lights startled him and he walked east until he got to First Avenue. He then turned south and continued to St. Mark's Place and again walked east. He passed a photo shop and stopped to look at the albums and suddenly everything came together. There were all sorts of memories. Distant memories of happy times and sad times when he was a child. Memories of the war, and recent memories, such as being with Vidamía for the first time. The music was there, stuck between the memories of being a boy and the present memories. He narrowed his eyes and looked at the album inside the store window and sighing deeply, turned and continued walking.

He let the memories of his life flow freely now, hesitant at times but trusting himself a little more, fearful that the battlefield images might attack him, but steeling himself to them. He crossed the street at Avenue A, waved to a couple of people he knew, went into Tompkins Square Park, found a bench, and sat down.

Once, a few months after being dismissed from Elsa's life, Billy snuck back down to the Lower East Side and wandered through the streets, mingling with the ghosts of millions of immigrants who had traded in their identities, their languages, some even their souls in order to be Americans. Up and down Suffolk and Norfolk, Forsyth and Essex, Kenmare and Eldridge, Rivington and Stanton, Clinton and Pitt, the names thoroughly British, as if the area were an English decompression chamber one must enter to be cured of ethnic ills before emerging as a full-fledged citizen of the United States. He wandered through the maze of sad streets and sorrowed memories down to Grand Street, and in the park on the edge of Chinatown, by chance, he saw Elsa under the full sail of her pregnancy, big as a house, beautiful and happy, talking to some girls with baby strollers. His heart broke some more, but he knew it was no use, so he just kept walking, knowing he might as well have remained with Joey back in Nam. He didn't blame anyone but wished the hell he could turn back time.

Miles Davis brought the horn to his mouth and then back down and through the previous night's aroma of cigarettes and whiskey left in the club where they were rehearsing, said, "What you lookin' at! And don't 'I'm a pianist, Mr. Davis,' me!"—Miles cutting him off in mid-sentence when he began to explain, not needing to because Pop Butterworth must have already told Miles about him. Not even in Nam would he feel the kind of fear he felt in front of the slight, shiny black man whose eyes threatened to burn through him, the rage in them so intense that he felt literally like running from there.

"He's a pianist, Wayne," Miles said turning to the serious man holding the tenor saxophone to him like it was a child that needed comforting. The serious man, his lips pursed and his head held high, nodded. "Ain't that a bitch!" Miles said. "How old are you, eighteen?"

"Sixteen, Mr. Davis," he said. "I'll be seventeen in a few months."

"Sixteen? Oo-whee! Sit down and let's see what you can do. Herbie, get up for a minute and let this boy stretch."

" 'On Green Dolphin Street'? Yes sir, Mr. Davis, I know it."

And he sat down at the piano, saw an ebony hand pick up the mute and heard Miles count as if he were far away, and saw himself, an Irish Catholic boy still in high school, who should know nothing about the world of jazz, begin playing smooth and easy, the melodies and harmonies already part of him, as always, lost to the music as if something else were operating, something else not of his own volition, some force deep within him that had no color or form but ached to find expression in the structure of the tune. He watched out of the corner of his eye as Miles, glowering thoughtfully, put the mute to his horn and began playing just like he'd heard him on the records, the horn's voicing melancholy but not so that it made him hurt, the sound strong and defiant in its sadness. He followed Miles through the intricacies of the changes and never missed a beat when the tempo increased. He and Miles traded six or eight choruses, each time Miles daring him to come out and show him what he had learned all those afternoons at Mrs. Wilkerson's house, the only place where he could forget the horrible pictures in the newspapers of his father lying dead on the floor, his head between the legs of a barstool, the face bloody, and his eyes staring at God's face, like Grandma Brigid had said, her voice thick with sorrow though not yet crying.

Up there at Mrs. Wilkerson's house in the Bronx there had been a piano on each floor and throughout the house pictures of all the greats, all signed, and she elegant and beautiful, smiling with Duke Ellington, the Dorsey Brothers, Benny Goodman, Cab Calloway, Pearl Bailey, and Louie Bellson, even one with Charlie Parker—Bird not looking too happy about being photographed and as if he was about to turn away and reach for his ax, lying on a table by the stage. Mrs. Wilkerson saying the picture was taken down at Birdland when Parker first began playing there. Pictures everywhere so that as Billy studied and played, always hungering for more, mastering difficult techniques and always listening as Mrs. Wilkerson talked about "the music," as she called it, not ever saying jazz or black music or Afro-American, but simply "the music," being very strict about what was and what wasn't considered such.

When he played the last note of "On Green Dolphin Street," Herbie Hancock clapped and Ron Carter said, "Yeah!" Miles Davis nodded imperceptibly, deep in thought as Mr. Butterworth spoke to him.

"What did he say, Mr. Butterworth?" he'd asked when they were back outside in the wintry afternoon air, the cold burning his face and his body shivering with excitement, the midtown traffic forcing him to shout, but still hearing the muted horn and his own hands comping, weaving beneath the magnificent solo a solid, brave tapestry of chords for the great Miles Davis to ride on.

"He said you was right in the pocket and learning real good, son," Pop Butterworth had replied. "He still don't believe you're only sixteen years old."

"Seventeen soon, Mr. Butterworth," he reminded him, but back then not having any notion of time in the sense of years, everything still filled with the urgency and mystery of not knowing, and only the music having any meaning. "My mom said she was definitely going to get the piano and that you should come with us to pick it out, Mr. Butterworth. Could you?"

And Pop Butterworth said, smiling sadly, that he'd be pleased to do so.

Billy sat in the park, recalling his life, until past midnight, when he got up and headed for home. As soon as he arrived, Lurleen asked him how things had gone. He said things had gone well. Uncharacteristically, she thought later, he sat and told her all about his visit with Vidamía, but did not discuss recalling more of the music, fearful that his skill might continue to return and then he'd have to play.

12 An Ideal Scenario

Every minute she wasn't involved with one of her patients and at times even while they were unburdening themselves of their neuroses, Elsa's mind returned obsessively to her involvement with Billy Farrell more than thirteen years before. What was she afraid of? Was it that she had been too hasty in rebuking him? She didn't want Vidamía to even suspect this. Did she still yearn for his passion? There were times when she imagined what sex would be like with him now that she had matured. The thought both excited and disgusted her. In her husband's eyes there was little doubt that Elsa was succeeding in raising an independent, broad-minded, non-docile daughter. To him it was ironic because his wife's resistance to allowing Vidamía contact with her father was not for Vidamía's well-being but was meant to soothe her own fears. Beneath those fears, like a large underwater monster talked about in theory but never seen, there lurked a preponderant need in Elsa to control Vidamía's life.

Vidamía, on the other hand, continued working toward creating the right circumstances for seeing Billy Farrell again. Whenever she could, she called Maud and asked for advice on how to handle her mother, confiding in her paternal grandmother in a way she found more satisfying than she did when talking to Ursula Santiago, on whom she leaned emotionally, but who didn't understand her concerns and always encouraged her to try to see things from Elsa's point of view.

Grandma Maud talked like one of the older girls in high school, brash and knowing, except that her language reminded Vidamía of the black-and-white films of the forties, with those fast-talking, wise-cracking ladies who threw caution to the wind and barreled their way through every difficulty.

"Don't worry about it, kid," she'd say. "Just hang in there till we figure it out. And whatever you do, keep your chin up."

For Maud Farrell the matter of her granddaughter and the problems she was having with her mother created an enormous dilemma. Her own motherly instincts and feeling for Vidamía were overwhelming, and any indication that the girl was suffering because of her mother made her so angry that on more than one occasion she thought of taking the train to Tarrytown and giving Elsa a piece of her mind. Reason always prevailed and she remained neutral, sensing that to become involved would create more problems for her granddaughter. However, the picture she was getting of her granddaughter's mother convinced her that she was dealing with someone whose screws needed tightening, as she told Ruby Broadway.

"She's a bitch on wheels, Ruby," she said, as they sat drinking coffee. "It makes me wanna go up there and slap her."

"Oo-whee," Ruby had said. "You Irish people are sure one violent tribe, ain't you?"

"Well, what would you do?"

"Don't ask me. You're the mother. What would you do if somebody started messing with your child? Knowing you, they'd end up hamburger. Why she gonna be any different? Remember she's Porto Rican."

"What's that supposed to mean?"

"They're very emotional people."

"So I should just forget about it?"

"I ain't Dr. Spock, and I ain't no Einstein, but I don't think you got much choice unless you wanna make more problems for your grandchild."

For Vidamía the next few months were an emotional tug-of-war with Elsa. Halloween and Thanksgiving, usually times of great excitement and fun, turned sour with Elsa's worries and complaints. Ursula Santiago, her health beginning to fail, had come up for Thanksgiving and immediately noticed that the household was ailing. She spoke to Elsa, but Elsa denied that anything was amiss. During dinner there were long silences and looks of exasperation from Vidamía. On more than one occasion Barry looked pleadingly, for understanding, to the now frail figure of his mother-in-law. When he drove Ursula Santiago back to the new two-bedroom apartment that Elsa and Barry had bought for her in the high-rise development not far from where she had raised her children, she inquired as to the tension. Barry explained that Vidamía had found her father and Elsa was upset.

"*El rubito?*" she said, calling Billy "the little blond one."

"Yes, I think so, Ma," Barry replied. "Billy Farrell."

"I remember. He was in the war with Joey. But why is Elsa upset?" Ursula asked.

"I don't know. She's upset about what this is going to do to Vidamía," Barry said, pulling away from the tollbooth. "She's acting crazy. *Una loca*. What's the matter with her?"

"I don't know, but whatever it is, I hope she gets over it," Ursula said. "Vidamía's no dummy. Between you and me, I don't think Elsa was cut out to be a mother. That is a terrible thing to say about my own daughter. But if you ever want to have children, you better find yourself a new wife, because Elsa won't help you."

"I know that, Ma," Barry said. "Don't worry about it. Vidamía's good enough for me."

Elsa's outbursts over Vidamía's resolve to see her father were persistent and each day more strident. He was irresponsible and most likely psychotic; too damaged by the war, and who knew what his children were like, not to say anything about his wife.

"She's from the South, right?" Elsa said.

"I think so," Vidamía replied. "What difference does that make? You don't know her. Why are you judging her?"

"I'm not judging her, but she's probably uneducated and primitive."

"*Mami!*" Vidamía had shouted. "You don't even know her. As a matter of fact, she graduated from college." Grandma

Maud had said Lurleen was very kind and gentle. "A school in Tennessee. She has a degree."

"Oh, really?" Elsa said, pursing her lips and closing her eyes in what she imagined was upper-class snobbery. "What? TAC— Tennessee Agricultural College?"

"What if she did? What's wrong with that?"

"Nothing, unless you're planning to start a new kind of farming on asphalt or concrete. You did say they were living on the Lower East Side."

"Fine. Make fun of other people. Be superior. If you want, I'll find out what she studied." At that point Elsa got a strange look on her face, got up from where she was sitting, and walked over to Vidamía, curled up reading on the sofa.

"How do you plan on doing that? Are you sneaking down to see your father?"

"Mami!"

"Well, are you?"

"Of course not."

"Then how would you find out?"

"I'll call Grandma Farrell and ask her."

"You'll do no such thing," Elsa said. Whether she had reached the limits of her patience regarding the subject or the threat to her authority was too great, Elsa became even more strict. "Until further notice you are forbidden to have any contact with your father's family."

"That's not fair," Vidamía said, her eyes becoming moist, the hurt of her mother's strictness constricting her throat and chest. "You're treating me like a baby."

"Well, it's not like you're twenty years old, you know? Twelve is still pretty young for making those kinds of decisions."

"You're mean and you're just trying to control me," Vidamía said, jumping up and running out of the room, leaving Elsa calling, "Young lady, you get right back here," until she heard the door to Vidamía's room slam upstairs. The impasse lasted nearly a week, with hardly a word exchanged between mother and daughter.

On Saturday morning when Vidamía returned from one of her girlfriends', Elsa asked if they could speak. Attempting to explain herself, she pointed out why it would be detrimental for Vidamía to spend time with Billy. She tried to convince her that it would be confusing on a deep, psychological level for her to reject her paternal feelings for Barry. Vidamía listened quietly, then asked her mother if she was finished. When Elsa said she was, Vidamía turned and marched upstairs. Things became so bad that Vidamía, generally kind, well-mannered and open in expressing herself when dealing with adults, grew sullen and refused to answer the most insignificant question or carry out the simplest task for her mother. Rather than following her mother's orders not to speak with the Farrells, she enlisted the help of her friends. Within the space of two weeks following the blowup with Elsa, she managed to speak to her grandmother six times and called her father's home three times, once talking with Lurleen, who was very pleasant and expressed the hope that she would come and visit during Christmas. In the background Vidamía could hear music and laughter, and she wondered who the laughter belonged to.

Another time a young girl answered the phone. When Vidamía identified herself, the other girl simply said, "Hi, sis, how you doing? This is Cookie." The simple statement made her laugh and she said she was doing okay. "Me too," the girl said. "I just got my right ear pierced again and it hurts like hell. Above the lobe. My girlfriend Milagros Pagán's mother did it. Your ears pierced? Yeah? I'm thinking of piercing each ear six or eight times. I don't know. Maybe not. Maybe that would be too much. You wanna talk to Daddy?"

The conversation had made her feel ticklish inside and increased her determination to meet her new family. Which of the girls was Cookie? Hortense, Caitlin, or Fawn? She loved the connection to the Farrells. But now whenever Elsa spoke to her about them, she would ignore her mother or simply walk away. After a while, Elsa resorted to communicating with Vidamía through Mrs. Alvarez, or else leaving her notes. At the dinner table, instead of the chattering that usually went on, mainly between Vidamía and her mother, there was now silence.

Without much thought Vidamía knew that she could wait out her mother, believing that an injustice was being perpetrated by Elsa and that the cruelty would eventually bring about her downfall, as with the dictators they'd learned about in social studies. She imagined her mother not being allowed to practice therapy. She heard the word "impeachment" on television, looked it up in the dictionary, and wondered if a psychologist could be impeached.

One evening at the beginning of December, at supper, Barry got tired of the silences and asked how much longer the situation would continue.

"The least the two of you could do is tell me what you want," he said, removing the napkin from his lap to wipe his lips before placing it on his empty plate. "That's all. Just give me a hint of your ideal scenario and maybe we can work something out."

"I want to see my father," Vidamía said.

"I don't think it's a good idea," Elsa replied.

"Why not?" Barry inquired.

"We've gone over that," said Elsa.

"I know, but I'd like to hear it again," Barry responded. "To get a fresh perspective."

"I feel that we've raised our daughter, my daughter, with you as her father, or stepfather, as a family unit, and having this man . . ."

"He's not a 'this man,' " Vidamía said, furious. "He's my father."

"Oh, so you've decided to break your silence," Elsa said.

"Elsa, for crying out loud," Barry said. "You should hear

yourself. Vidamía's right. He's her father. Why shouldn't she be entitled to see him? Please explain that. You're a professional about everything else. What would you advise a client in a situation like this?" Elsa was silent for a moment. When she spoke she explained that it sounded very much like he, Barry, was abrogating his responsibilities as a parent, and she was extremely surprised and hurt that he would be doing so at such a critical juncture in his stepdaughter's development.

"Elsa, Elsa, cut it out," Barry said. "You sound like you're at some damn conference. This is your family. Your daughter has a right to see her father."

"Did you hear what you said?" Elsa snapped, an edge of triumph in her voice. " 'Your daughter.' A clear abdication of responsibility."

"Oh, for pity's sake, Elsie, stop it," he said, smiling and shaking his head, using the diminutive of her name, which should have indicated to Elsa that he didn't wish to fight, that he was on her side, that after six years of marriage he was still crazy about her. "Come on, honey. It's okay. What am I supposed to do? Get jealous? That's not the way I am. Vidamía knows how I feel about her and how proud I am of her."

"Now you're the one that sounds like you're addressing a business luncheon."

"Whatever I sound like, I'm not trying to prevent a child from seeing her family."

"Fine," Elsa said, giving in to the inevitability of the situation. "What you're saying is that I should simply turn her over to barbarians."

"They're not barbarians," Vidamía said. "Grandma Farrell is *not* a barbarian and neither is my father or my brother and sisters."

"That's not what I'm saying and you know it, Elsie," Barry said.

"Fine. What do you suggest?"

"First of all we should talk about it calmly until we reach an agreement about the best course of action. There's no rush. The Christmas vacation's coming up. Why ruin the holidays for everybody? Why can't Vidamía see her father? You know, by law he's entitled to see her."

"He abandoned us," Elsa said and suddenly got a strange look on her face.

"Elsa!" Barry said, his tone one of reprimand, so that Elsa had to admit to herself that the explanation she had given Vidamía was a fiction. She had been honest with Barry and had explained that she hadn't wanted to sacrifice herself like her mother and that she'd told Billy to leave.

"All right, all right," Elsa said. "She can see him. At her grandmother's."

"No, they invited me to their house for dinner around Christmas," Vidamía said. "We're exchanging gifts and then there's a little party."

"When, exactly?"

"The fifteenth of December. It's a Saturday."

"Oh, so it's all set," Elsa said, taken by surprise. "Now you've gone behind my back again and made plans without my permission."

"No, I haven't," Vidamía said, desperately looking toward Barry.

"Elsa, relax," Barry said. "Hear her out."

"I've forbidden her to go there," she said. "My God, Barry, he lives down there where I was raised. That neighborhood's been declining steadily for years. When were you down there, young lady?"

"I haven't been."

"Then how do you know about the party?"

"I talked to him."

"You were told that your telephone privileges were curtailed. Did you call from someone else's house?"

"Yes," Vidamía said, both relieved that she didn't have to continue lying and proud to show her cunning. "I never used the phone here. I called one time and he wasn't there. I talked to his wife. She invited me."

"His wife?"

"Elsie, Elsie."

"Oh, stop with this 'Elsie' stuff, okay, Barry? What do you people want from me? Both of you need a lot of help."

"Stop it, Elsa," Barry finally said, banging on the table. He didn't like growing angry like this, but once in a while he had to, mostly at work when a client wanted impossible things to be done with his books. "What's come over you? All she wants to do is visit her father and her brother and sisters. That isn't a criminal offense. She's entitled to that."

After a few more minutes of bickering it was settled. Elsa suggested that Vidamía call and ask if she could stay at Janet Shapiro's house during the weekend of the fourteenth.

"Barry could drive you to Janet's house Friday night and he can pick you up and take you downtown in a cab."

"He who?" Vidamía asked.

"You know who."

"My father? Sure."

"After the party he can bring you back uptown."

"They invited me to stay over," Vidamía said, disappointed.

"And what did you say?" Elsa said.

"I said I'd have to talk to you guys."

"Well, it's out of the question."

"Why?"

"You're trying my patience, young lady. When the party is over you'll go back to your friend's house."

"Maybe I could stay at *güela*'s."

Elsa, her head down, thought for a moment. Vidamía looked at Barry, who winked at her.

"That's a much better idea," Barry said. "He can pick her

up there. I don't think Doña Ursula's too far from where they live."

"Whatever," Elsa said and got up from the table. "But he has to agree to pick her up."

"Thanks, *mami*. Can I use the phone?" Vidamía asked, truly wishing to mend things between herself and her mother.

"Yes, of course, but don't stay on too long," Elsa said.

Vidamía ran up the stairs, overjoyed with the victory. During the next half hour she made twenty calls, proclaiming her triumph. She also reached Maud at O'Hanlon's to explain what had taken place. Lastly, she called Billy, but he was out. Instead, she spoke to Lurleen and said she would be in the city on December fifteenth for the dinner and party.

Upset that she'd had to capitulate, Elsa rose abruptly from the table, went upstairs to her increasingly inactive marital bed, took a Valium, and lay down. This rage, where did it come from? It was all her daughter's doing, she thought. The girl elicited murderous feelings in her. And then feelings of guilt invaded her again, and she thought about why the issue of Billy Farrell frightened her. Why couldn't she care for her daughter? But why was she asking herself that question? She cared for no one. Once she thought she cared for Barry, but lately she doubted even that.

As she began to feel the effect of the Valium and relax, she thought that perhaps Vidamía's innocence and concern with black people, acquired she didn't know from where, other than from that *Roots* book she'd read a few years before, would eventually unmask her lie that she and her daughter were white people.

And then it dawned on Elsa that Vidamía's establishing contact with Billy Farrell, in spite of his obvious lower-class background, would only validate Vidamía's whiteness and insulate her and her daughter from the stigma of blackness. Giving in to her daughter, she had to agree, was the lesser of two evils.

She had yet to see Billy Farrell, but she imagined that he had found some menial job somewhere and spent his days working at it and his evenings in a stupor from drugs and alcohol, as he had begun to do when they were together. It didn't matter. She would monitor the situation closely. If it got too dangerous, she'd find a way to pull Vidamía back and away from him.

She got out of bed and went down the stairs confidently, fully under the influence of the tranquilizer, her life again in control. She found Vidamía watching television in the den and asked sweetly if she could speak with her.

"Sure," Vidamía said, aware of the change in her mother, hoping it would last.

"Sweetie, can you turn off the TV, please?"

"Sorry, *mami*."

"I'm the one who should be apologizing," Elsa said, sitting across from her daughter and tucking one leg under her as she settled into the stuffed chair.

"I've been positively evil, haven't I?" Elsa added.

"Well . . ." Vidamía said, not sure how to reply, chuckling inwardly because her mother sounded like Joan Crawford in one of her movies. She'd have to read the daughter's book, like Tracy Richardson said. Tracy's mother was a total wacko and had locked Tracy in a closet for a whole day once when she was little. To Tracy, all mothers were the enemy.

"You can speak honestly, baby."

"I've seen you have better days," Vidamía said, smiling diplomatically.

"Anyway, I've been under a lot of pressure and haven't had time to really discuss anything rationally with you concerning the situation with your father. Can I ask you some things? I don't mean to pry, but it would ease my mind to know."

"Sure, if I know the answers."

"You said your father's married?"

"Yes, and he has four other children. Three girls and one boy."

"Have you seen them?"

"No, just pictures at Grandma Farrell's house."

"Really? What do they look like?"

"They're all blond, *mami*," Vidamía said excitedly. "Well, you know how blond Daddy is. Lurleen's also blond, and all the kids are, too."

"My goodness," Elsa said. "Isn't that something? You have blond siblings."

"Yeah, it's kind of weird."

"No, it's fine. Tell me what you have in mind for Christmas presents and we can go into Manhattan next weekend and shop. If you don't want to do that, tell me approximately how much money you'll need so I can give you the cash."

"Really?"

"Sure."

"And that's all you wanted to know? About the kids and the presents?"

"That's right."

"And you're not mad—I mean angry?"

"No, I'm not angry, baby."

"And you mean it, about letting me see Daddy?"

"Sure. As long as you don't neglect your schoolwork and your chores around the house, I have no problem with you seeing him from time to time."

Vidamía had gotten up from the couch and rushed to her mother, throwing her arms around her.

"I love you, *mami*," she said. "Please, please can I stay at their house after the party?"

"Well, okay."

"Thank you, *mami*!"

"You're welcome, darling," Elsa said, patting Vidamía's back with light little motions of her hand, the close contact making her uncomfortable.

On the agreed-upon day, Barry drove Vidamía, carrying a backpack and two bags of presents, down to her grandmother Ursula Santiago's new apartment. The following day, Billy Farrell, accompanied by his son, Cliff, rang the bell, and they brought her to meet Lurleen and Vidamía's sisters. On the way to their place she couldn't keep her eyes off Cliff. He was so blond his hair was nearly white.

They walked down a nearly deserted street to a building that looked like a warehouse. Her father produced keys, unlocked the door, and they went inside and into a huge, beat-up elevator. When they had gone up five floors her father stopped the elevator and opened the doors. On the door across from the elevator there was a big Christmas wreath with a lighted, electric candle within it. Until she was able to return to stay with Billy Farrell and his family for the summer, the memory of walking into their loft remained engraved in her heart as the ideal of what a home should look like during the Christmas holidays. The first thing that hit her were the smells of food, of cinnamon and spices, the warmth, comfort, and disorganized hominess of the place. There were so many details that she wrote them down in her diary. The furniture, the decorations, the musical instruments, the Christmas tree, the homemade ornaments made of tin cans, paper cups and dishes, milk cartons, tinfoil, crepe paper. When she fell asleep that night on her sister Hortense's bed, while Hortense and Fawn shared Fawn's, she was holding the homemade rag doll with a gingham dress and button eyes that Lurleen had given her. Vidamía thought she had never been happier. The following evening after supper, everyone bundled up against the cold, they went out and met friends from a community center. Holding lighted candles, they walked through the housing projects singing Christmas carols: "Good King Wenceslas," "The Twelve Days of Christmas," "Silent Night," "Rudolph the Red

Nosed Reindeer," and "Alegría, Alegría." They all sang beautifully, but her sister Hortense was the best, her voice so pure that it made Vidamía's skin tingle. She joined in as well as she could, but didn't know too many of the words and was forced to hum. At one point Lurleen hugged her. Her father had remained in the loft, and she wondered why. She wanted to ask someone, but thought that her question might be interpreted as rude. When they got back, she wanted to tell her father what they'd done, but Lurleen held her back. Her father was sitting in the semidarkness in his rocker, his back to them, seemingly lost in thought as he looked out into the night at the lights of the city.

13 Families

Elsa recalled being in graduate school and still living on the Lower East Side at her mother's and getting invited to a party on Riverside Drive in one of those large eight- or ten-room apartments with high ceilings and wood paneling. Linda Mushnick's husband, Howard—she and Linda were classmates in graduate school—had just been made a junior partner at the law firm where he worked and they were celebrating the event.

"Just twelve of us," Linda said. "We're shipping the baby off to my mother's in Jersey, so it'll be great. There's someone I want you to meet."

"Who is it?" Elsa said, laughing at Linda's seriousness.

"It's a surprise."

"Is he rich or are you trying to stick me with another one of your cheap friends?"

"Let's say he's very well off."

"I'm getting interested. What time?"

She expected that it would be a Jewish friend of the Mushnicks, a lawyer like Linda's husband, perhaps. Next to dentists and doctors, lawyers made excellent money if they applied themselves and had some ambition, she thought. She had dressed to kill and was all smiles when she kissed Vidamía on the cheek as she sat on the couch, ignoring the Spanish soap opera her grandmother was watching. Her six-year-old daughter looked up from her *Winnie the Pooh* book and literally sighed when she saw her mother.

"Oh, *mami*, you smell so good and you look so beautiful! Are you going on a date?"

"No, baby," she said. "I'm going to dinner at a friend's house."

"Who?"

"My friend Linda from school."

"When I grow up I'm going to go to college like you."

"I know you are, honey," she said, being sweet with Vidamía but not feeling the emotion.

She walked over to Grand Street, enduring the words of the men as she passed them, words about how fine she looked and was it at all possible that she was an angel who'd lost her way and that being the case they'd be very happy to show her heaven, or from the crasser types, comments that as handsome as they were they'd be glad to have her use their face as a seat, all of them sensing or knowing outright that this was an attractive woman with a child, which meant that she knew about sex but had no one to protect her, no husband, no father, no older brother. She went down the stairs to the station, breathing easier now that she was once again escaping the Lower East Side. She took the D train and then changed at Fifty-ninth Street for the Broadway Local, getting off at Seventy-ninth, enjoying the late-summer breezes drifting up from Riverside Park and the Hudson River. When she arrived, Linda kissed her and Howard immediately asked her what she wanted to drink. "A little white wine," she said as she handed Howard the bottle of rosé she'd brought, feeling uncomfortable because she knew little about wines and hoped that she hadn't made a mistake. Linda took her hand and walked her down the hall into the living room. All the men stood up, among them a pale young man with wire-rimmed glasses, a very neat mustache, and thinning black hair. She was introduced to two young couples, one of them a fellow junior partner in Howard's firm and his wife, a very thin young ash-blond woman with a beautiful tan and equally fine manners that set Elsa's nerves on edge.

"Elsa, this is Barry López-Ferrer. Barry, Elsa Santiago," Linda said, introducing her to the young man in the wire-rimmed glasses. "Barry's company handles the books for Howard's firm. Elsa and I are working on our M.A.s at Hunter."

"How do you do?" Barry said, his voice strong and confident.

"Fine," she said, extending her hand. "How are you? I didn't hear your last name."

"López-Ferrer," Howard interrupted, handing her a glass of wine.

"That's López *hyphen* Ferrer?" Elsa asked.

He nodded and smiled. She noted two things immediately about Barry. He was an extremely neat man and he seemed absolutely sure of himself. At the dinner table, Linda's guests were discussing Watergate and the subsequent repercussions of the scandal; Nixon's appearance on the *David Frost Show*, where he admitted that he'd let the American people down; the establishment of Concorde supersonic jet travel between Paris and New York; the bombing of Fraunces Tavern by the FALN four years prior; Larry Flynt, the publisher of *Hustler*, getting convicted for obscenity; the ordination of the first female Episcopal priest in the United States; the Son of Sam case, which had recently ended in a conviction. During a very heated exchange between a man whose name she couldn't recall and the ash-blond woman, who, it turned out, was a staunch feminist, Elsa looked up and caught Barry looking at her in a most intense and admiring way.

She almost pointed at herself to have him reassure her that it was she, Elsa Santiago from the Lower East Side, that he was staring at. She smiled warily at him and he returned the smile easily. They hadn't yet established that he was Puerto Rican, but there could be no doubt about it. The way he looked and spoke were dead giveaways. There was something distinctive about being Puerto Rican. No, it wasn't being Puerto Rican, because she was often fooled by people from the Island. It was being New York Rican, or Nuyorican, as some put it, that set them apart. There was a certain cockiness, and at the same time a reserve, that educated Ricans in New York had.

New York Puerto Ricans were a definite mixture of Italian tough, Irish melancholy, Jewish wisdom, and black jive, all of it blended with whatever it was that Puerto Ricans brought to the mixture. And what was that? It was a strange concoction of wariness, resignation, pride, and a maddeningly roundabout way of getting at the truth, not to mention blind obedience to benevolent authority on the one hand and an almost murderous intolerance for anyone who breached a personal code after due warning had been given. The age, size, or position of the person didn't matter when this violation happened; recklessly, they would throw themselves headlong into battle.

By contrast, Barry didn't seem like what she perceived Puerto Ricans to be and it intrigued her. He was soft-spoken, listened carefully, smiled readily, and didn't seem to have a need to be noticed. He appeared sure of himself but devoid of any arrogance. When the party was starting to break up, he offered to drive her home, but she was ashamed to have him know where she lived. He disarmed her by offering to make a detour past the block where he'd grown up in East Harlem.

"You'll love it. Very scenic—110th between Park and Lex, across from the projects."

"Did Linda tell you where I live?" she asked.

"Yes," he said.

"That rat."

She shrugged her shoulders and said she guessed it didn't matter. They lingered until everyone had gone before saying goodbye to Linda and Howard. She and Barry took the elevator downstairs and walked down the block to his car. He stopped and she nodded approvingly when he produced keys and opened the passenger door to a very shiny, silver Mercedes Benz 220SL. She got into the car, sinking comfortably into the upholstery.

Barry got in, started the car, switched on some lite FM music—Barry Manilow or Neil Sedaka—and off they went. Once they crossed Central Park at Ninety-sixth Street, they continued east to First Avenue. Housing developments forced them to go all the way east before they got to his block. At 111th Street he turned west and continued until he got to Park Avenue and turned left to get on 110th Street. Going down Park Avenue, he explained how he used to help his mother shop at La Marqueta on Saturdays. On 110th Street he pointed to a tenement building.

"Third floor, one twenty-seven," he said, cruising down the block. "My mother and my three sisters. I was the oldest."

"What about your father?" she said.

Barry shrugged his shoulders as he sped up once more, suddenly wary of a group of men walking down the street toward them.

"Went back to P.R.," he said. "We didn't know why. My mother never spoke about him. One Christmas we were expecting him, everybody talking about what Santa Claus was going to bring us, and he never showed up. It was Nochebuena and my mother had made *arroz con gandules, pernil, pasteles*, and everything. Seven o'clock came and no *papi*. My mother said we should wait a little longer, and a half hour passed, and then an hour, and Daisy, the baby, fell asleep, and Marissa, who was five, started crying that she was hungry, so we sat down and ate, except that my mother wouldn't eat. That was the last time I saw him until I tracked him down in Puerto Rico twenty-one years later, about three years ago."

"And?" she asked, as if hearing what he'd done might give her a clue about the sort of feeling she ought to have toward her own father. "Did you ask him to explain his actions?"

"No, I didn't," Barry said. "I just took him for what he was."

"What?" she said, thinking of her own father's philandering and absences.

"A weak man under a lot of pressure," he said. "You should've seen him. He had very poor eyesight to begin with and his glasses were broken. He looked older than his years and was living alone, seemingly, in a little shack up in the mountains halfway between Cacimar and Aguas Buenas. He didn't recognize me and went totally pale when he saw me drive up in this late-model rental car. He thought it was the police."

"But wait," Elsa said. "Your father's from Cacimar? From the town?"

"Not from the town. From the hills. There's a *barrio* up there called Racimo."

"Oh, God," she said.

"What?"

"Your father's a *jíbaro*?"

"Yeah, I guess. Why?"

"So's my mother. Stone hick," she said, using the words that Nuyoricans employ when referring to the people from the mountains—stoic, suspicious, illiterate. "She's from Barrio Flor. That's wild that our parents are from the same town."

"Small island."

"I guess. What did you do? It must've been strange seeing your father after such a long time."

"A little bit."

"So what did you do?"

144

"I hugged him and asked him if he needed anything."

"You did?"

"Sure," Barry said, surprised at her attitude. "What would you do if you hadn't seen your father in more than twenty years?"

"The same, I guess," she lied, fearful that Barry would disapprove of her. "What did he say?"

"He said he was all right, that he was growing all his food and had some goats, a pig, and some chickens and went into Cacimar to do plumbing work once in a while. I gave him a few hundred dollars and said I'd like to stay in touch and he said that would be fine. He asked me about my mother and sisters and I said they were fine. Carmen and Marissa had gotten married and Daisy was in her last year at Queens College." Barry explained that he'd bought his mother a house in Jamaica, Queens, the year Daisy started high school.

"It was the second year of having my own business and we did pretty good."

"Have you seen him again?"

"I went back two months later to get at the truth. I guess I should go back again, but I haven't been able to get myself to do it."

"Why?" she asked, wondering if he had developed the same reluctance toward his father that she had toward hers.

"I don't like talking about this, but I feel I can trust you."

"Thank you," she said, attributing Barry's trust to her skills as a therapist.

"While I was talking with him another man came in. My father introduced his friend Ramón and said proudly I was his son from New York. The man smiled, nodded, and then disappeared into the other room of the shack. I asked my father if Ramón, his friend, lived there with him. My father said the man was mute, that he did live with him, and that he was sorry."

"He was gay?" she said, the words coming out of her without disapproval, but with absolute surprise and amusement. "Really?"

"No, it wasn't anything like that."

"What, then?"

"He said there had been a problem and alluded to something that had happened with his older sister, Josie. I had heard relatives in New York talk around the subject whenever I visited them growing up. I always wondered why my Aunt Josie looked like she did. Everybody said she'd had an accident, but I never believed it. I asked my father if it was about Josie. He nodded, and asked me to go for a walk with him. He told me she had been beaten and he had avenged his sister's assault. No details, except to allude to a crime and mention a man's name. When I got back from Puerto Rico, I talked with some people up in the Bronx. One of them is one of my best friends, Israel Caraballo, a cop who works in narcotics. He told me what he thought happened. He found the file on an unsolved case."

"What do you mean?" she said. "Your father?"

Barry then told her a story about his aunt, Josefina, who was a bit of a party girl. She had been in an after-hours club in the Bronx, and this hood, from one of the gangs that controlled business in the Bronx Terminal Market, took an interest in her. Elsa asked if he was Italian and Barry said no, that he was Puerto Rican and that Puerto Ricans had a fairly well organized underworld, adding that his firm had helped legitimize several such operations. Anyway, this hood came in, got acquainted with Josefina, who was both a beauty and a bit of a loose cannon, very bawdy and demanding, and the two of them left together. The next day they found Josefina wandering around naked on the edge of the Bronx side of the Harlem River, near the old factory buildings by the Third Avenue Bridge. She had so many bruises on her body and her face was so swollen that the police thought she was a black woman. Every tooth in her mouth had been broken and her eyes were swollen shut. Josefina was in the hospital six months. When she came out she looked grotesque, her nose bent, her jaw askew, and her right eye replaced by a glass one. Her larynx had been removed. When she talked she did so through an artificial voice box.

They were now heading downtown and Barry went on, telling Elsa what his father, with a sense of relief and a wish for forgiveness had confided in him on his second visit, when Barry told him the police had discontinued the investigation. When Cipriano López, Barry's father, asked his sister Josefina who had beaten her so brutally, she readily told him and said she didn't care if they killed her, but that he shouldn't say anything because they'd come after him. Cipriano López patiently located the man, Bobby Ramos, and with the stealth of a great cat began stalking him, learning his routine. It just so happened that on that Christmas Eve, while heading home for dinner, he caught up with him by chance when Ramos was a bit tipsy and about to visit a woman on Tiffany Street in the Bronx. Cipriano couldn't pass up this opportunity. It was cold, the sky red, a threat of snow in the air. The street was deserted near the empty lot. Ramos stepped out of his car and took just a few steps before López hit him. The first blow from the two-foot length of inch-and-a-half pipe made a strange thud as Ramos's hat was smashed into the skull, the bone into the brain, knocking him to the ground unconscious. His friend Caraballo had said that the force was so great that the coroner established that Ramos had died instantly. Fear and rage making his heart race, Cipriano looked up and down the street, then pulled Ramos's coat over his head and pounded his skull over and over until he was exhausted. The coroner's report also stated that both of Ramos's eyes had been forced out of their orbital cavities and that there was no discernible difference between one lobe of the brain and the other, the entire mass a liquid miasma that had seeped out of the shattered cranium. Looking through Ramos's pockets, Cipri-

147

ano found the keys to the car and nearly $800. He drove to the deserted riverfront, tossed the pipe into the water, and went on to the airport, purchasing a one-way ticket for the following week since everything was booked for the holidays. He lived in the airport, finding shelter in warehouses, eating in the airport cafeterias, and washing himself in the public bathrooms. Eventually, he got on an airplane and went to Puerto Rico.

Elsa was speechless. She had grown up with street violence but generally the crimes had to do with drugs and money. This was something else. The sheer passion of it unnerved her.

"I was twelve and was hoping to get electric trains," Barry said.

"How did you feel when you found out why he'd left?"

"Confused, just like you felt when I told you," Barry said, pulling onto the FDR Drive at Ninety-sixth Street. "It's not everybody who finds out their father's murdered someone."

"I'm sorry. I didn't mean anything by it."

"I didn't think you had. On the plane back to New York the first time I felt hurt that I had endured the things I did because my father left. I didn't know then what it was, but I could see that whatever crime he had committed had really affected him. It was like he was in permanent shock. I'm sure his friend Ramón hiding out up there in the mountains had done something equally horrible."

"Is that why your name is hyphenated?" she asked.

"Very perceptive," he said. "Exactly. I guess it's a compromise. I didn't want to lose my father's name, but I didn't want it to be how I completely defined myself."

"Did you tell your mother and sisters why your father had to leave?"

"I told Carmen and my mother. Carmen shrugged her shoulders. My mother doesn't believe it."

"And the cops?"

"When I discussed the incident with my friend from the Narcotics Division, he said that I should forget everything. As far as the police were concerned they were glad to be rid of the guy. It hadn't been the first time he'd beaten up a woman, and there had even been a couple of them who hadn't survived the attacks, but they never got anything on the guy. They knew that Ramos's demise had nothing to do with his underworld work because of the manner of the attack. They figured it had to be personal. Ramos's associates had the same idea, and they, too, let matters pass. Both the police and the underworld closed their files on Bobby Ramos and his excesses. My friend said there's at least a hundred cases like that a year in New York," Barry told her. "The papers ignore them. The police archive the files. People forget about the cases."

Elsa was silent a long time as the car moved down the highway. She thought about her own father, who was always leaving and coming back. Over and over again until he finally left the house altogether. Out of the corner of her eye she watched the delicate features of this man who seemed to break all the stereotypes of what Rican men were supposed to be like. Barry drove smoothly, and she felt safe as they wove in and out of traffic, among the lights of the city, the tall buildings and the bridges over the East River to Brooklyn magical in their dark splendor. Suddenly, without warning, her heart felt a lovely tugging and she looked at the man next to her, his suit still unrumpled.

Just then he turned and asked her if he could tell her something. When she said sure, he said that she was a gorgeous, intelligent, delicious-looking woman and that all he'd thought about all night long was marrying her.

"This is a joke, right?" she said. And then she lapsed into street Rican, and told him, "Yo, like *aguanta la yegua* and whatnot"—literally, "Hold the mare." "I've heard some lines before, but that one is very, very special."

"It's not a line, Elsa," he said. "I meant it."

"Like that?" she said. "Just like that? You don't even know me."

"It doesn't matter to me," he said. "I'm willing to wait for you to get to know me, but I definitely don't want this to be the last time we see each other."

"Oh, I didn't mean it like that," she said. "I mean, I'm flattered and everything. You're really nice and I like you, but I have to think about it."

"About seeing me again?"

"No, about the other."

"Marrying me."

"Yes, of course. I have a kid, you know. Did Linda tell you?"

"No, she didn't."

"Are you disappointed?"

"Not at all. Boy or girl?"

"Girl."

"Great. How old?"

"Six."

"How long were you married?"

"I wasn't. I had her when I was sixteen. My mother's helping me raise her."

"What's her name?"

"Vidamía. My mother gave her the name," she lied. "Strange, right?"

"No, not at all. Unusual, but I like it. Anyway, think about it and maybe next weekend we can have dinner and you can get to know me."

He parked the car on Essex Street and they walked the rest of the way, this well-dressed couple at two o'clock in the morning on a summer evening, the people in the street not paying much attention to them. It was common to see people who lived in the tenements dressing up and going out, returning home late from dancing in the Latin clubs. When they got to her building, she stopped and told him she'd invite him up but didn't want to disturb her mother. She reached up and kissed him on the cheek and smiled at him.

"Thank you," she said. "It was nice of you to drive me home."

"My pleasure. When's the best time to call you?"

"I'm always home at night, late," she said. "I'm working as a counselor at the college and taking courses in the evening. Let me give you my number."

He copied down her number and she went inside the door. As she began to let herself into the second door when she suddenly grew fearful that something might happen to him. She ran down the steps, but Barry was already walking away, confidently, at ease in the neighborhood. Back inside the apartment, she knew that something wonderful would happen between her and Barry. As she changed into her nightclothes and then brushed her teeth, she recalled being with her homegirls and, hearing once again the tune, she let it play in her head. *Estoy buscando a Barry, Barry, Barry, estoy buscando a Barry, Barry, dónde está?* As she fell asleep, she imagined herself dressed in a white wedding gown, marching down the aisle.

And that's exactly what happened. The following week they'd gone out on Friday and eaten at a quiet, intimate Italian restaurant in the Village. They ambled through the streets, looking into shopwindows and talking about their lives and their dreams and books and movies, laughing and finding many things in common in their experience of growing up Rican in New York. The week after that he picked her up early in the afternoon, met her mother and Vidamía, and then drove over to the Seventy-ninth Street marina. They boarded his boat, a forty-five-foot cabin cruiser named SUERTE, which he eventually renamed ELSA. He maneuvered the boat expertly down the Hudson River, around the Battery, up the East River, through Hell Gate, and past Riker's Island until they got to City Island, where they docked and went ashore.

He'd called ahead and they were met by his friend Israel Caraballo, the detective. She had expected someone rough and tough, but he was a mild-mannered, gentle Puerto Rican man, about Barry's age. He was very introspective and shy, almost professorial. They went to Israel's home and had a barbecue with his family—Israel's wife, Maritza, a nurse, and their three children, two boys and a girl, ages three to ten. The girl was about Vidamía's age.

The following month they were in Puerto Rico, lying on Esperanza Beach in Vieques. They swam and ate seafood every day and at night lay naked in bed looking at the moon and stars through their mosquito netting after making love. He was a very patient, almost disinterested lover, and in the same way that he drove his car or boat he made love to her, speaking softly about her breasts and lips, describing them with such delicacy that by the end of the week as he was touching her with his fingers she'd had an orgasm. It was the first time in years that she'd felt one so strongly and she clung to him, pushing his hand into herself, and then he was inside her, moving slowly and then more rapidly so that she had another, milder, orgasm, which surprised her because that had never happened with a man inside of her except a few times with Billy Farrell back when she was a crazy little spic. She cried then, recalling Billy Farrell and her supposed cries of ecstasy when he was making desperate love to her and all she could think about was his pain and when it would all be over, her bladder hurting and her breasts tender from his touch.

"Oh, Barry, Barry," she whispered, "I love you."

Afterward, she lay on the bed and wondered if she was being honest about her love for Barry. What was it supposed to feel like? She knew that he was special to her, but there was no overwhelming passion in her heart for him. They got married six months later. Her uncle gave her away. Vidamía was the flower girl. Barry's sisters were beautiful women, very poised and quiet, their children very well behaved. She was equally proud of her own family, although the children, by contrast, were all over the place, during the ceremony and later at the reception. Except for Vidamía, who spent most of the time tagging along with the photographer, peppering him with all sorts of questions about his camera.

They spent that evening at a hotel in Midtown, and the next afternoon they went to the top of the PanAm Building and took a helicopter to Kennedy Airport, where they got an Air Iberia flight to Madrid and changed planes for Sevilla, then rented a car and continued on to the coast. Barry spoke Spanish very slowly and pronounced his R's like they were L's, and by the end of the honeymoon her nerves were completely on edge and she was happy to be back in the United States, where they could return to speaking English. After they had been back a month and were living in the huge, beautiful apartment in Riverdale, she was sitting at the kitchen table, absentmindedly opening the mail one Saturday morning when she opened a badly handwritten letter addressed to Elsie Santiago and in it found a card in Spanish with a corny congratulatory verse and twenty dollars. Below it in an unsteady hand were the words "*Hapi gwedin, yul fadel, Justino.*" The note made her so angry that she banged the table over and over and then ripped up the note and the twenty-dollar bill into little pieces, so that by the time Barry came in from his study she had rendered note, money, and envelope into confetti.

"What's the matter?" Barry had asked.

"I don't want to talk about it," she said, sweeping up the scraps of paper and leaving the kitchen.

She'd gone to the terrace, and, with Barry and Vidamía looking on, she threw the tiny pieces of paper out into the void beyond their twenty-second-story perch. How had her father found out? As she watched the papers fall, she wished, for a moment, to have the courage to follow them. The shock that she could be suicidal sobered her. She returned inside and knew she should have the doctor prescribe something for her nerves. Eventually, she thought, the question of race will come up in their relationship and Barry will know. She had heard Barry make remarks about color. Nothing too revealing, but enough to make her wary.

14 Research

Traveling through the inner workings of subterranean Manhattan, they are nearly impossible to see, owing to their shyness, pulsars or distant stars as they fly in the face of reality, but if you stop and listen you can hear their song, which is crazy, but it's what sixteen-year-old Vidamía Farrell, under the considerable influence of Lurleen Meekins Farrell and her fondness for the universe and its complexities, thought as she banged away at the single string of the washtub bass during The Southern Constellation's rendition of "Sweet Georgia Brown," watching her fourteen-year-old half sister, Hortense McAlpin Farrell, nicked and named "Cookie," for reasons unknown, by her homegirl Gisele Gutiérrez from the projects around Third Street and First Avenue, unhook and set down her tenor saxophone, run her hand over her spiky blond hair, and, affecting that whiskey-laden, throaty sound which their mother had taught her, belt out the song while their brother Cliff, already a virtuoso at the age of thirteen and, like Cookie, scheduled the following year to attend the Fiorello La Guardia High School of Music and Performing Arts, wailed away on his trombone.

This was the first time they were out playing this summer.

With school now behind her, Vidamía looked forward to time away from her mother's house. This was the fourth summer that she spent all of July and half of August with her father's family, returning home for a week of camp followed by a one-week trip to some exotic place with her mother and stepfather. The previous year they had flown to Vancouver, British Columbia, and taken a cruise ship along the Canadian coast until they reached Alaska, the days growing longer and longer as they traveled north until eventually, at midnight, the sun was still out.

Thumping away on her bass, the string vibrating as her left hand moved the stick of the rustic instrument to vary the pitch, keeping up with the steady beat of Fawn's cymbal, Vidamía watched as her father, sitting on the amp, his beard thick and his baby blues far away under his Farmer Jones straw hat, strummed his Gibson, his heartbreaking crab hand crawling sideways across the strings, the rest of him somewhere back in the 1970s, wondering what had gone wrong with his life. Because it had gone wrong, no doubt about it. It began weighing on her mind last Christmas, when she arrived, as she had for the past three years, loaded down with presents for the family, and he'd sat in his rocker throughout the entire celebration, as he did that first Christmas, accepting a cup of eggnog, sipping from it periodically, but, on the whole, merely staring out into the night. Although she had seen this behavior before, her concern expressed itself in a mounting curiosity, but more particularly in a desire to reverse the situation.

She knew that his war experiences had been unimaginably horrible but couldn't fathom exactly what it was that made him so distant. She'd made an effort to read about Vietnam and watched every available cable program on the subject, but she needed to know why his mind seemed to unhinge from reality and hang limply in time, suspended like a psychic rag doll. She asked her mother, and Elsa replied that it was likely her father was suffering from post-traumatic stress disorder, from which soldiers who've been under particularly difficult situations on the battlefield sometimes suffered. She'd asked her mother if she could read something about the ailment and was surprised when she returned one weekend from staying at Fran Nearny's house in Rye and found on her desk a stapled Xerox copy of an article. Paper-clipped to the first sheet was a smaller piece of yellow paper with a note addressed to "Sweetheart," which explained that the material was from the *Diagnostic and Statistical Manual of Mental Disorders*.

Her mother had underlined certain phrases like <u>war veterans</u> and <u>military combat</u>. She had bracketed parts of the long description and highlighted the following part in orange: *In more severe forms, particularly in cases in which the survivor has actually committed acts of violence (as in war veterans), the fear is conscious and pervasive, and the reduced capacity for modulation may express itself in unpredictable explosions of aggressive behavior or an inability to express angry feelings.*

<u>309.89 Post-traumatic Stress Disorder.</u>

The essential feature of this disorder is the development of characteristic symptoms following a psychologically distressing event that is outside the range of usual human experience (i.e., outside the range of such common experiences as simple bereavement, chronic illness, business losses, and marital conflict). The stressor producing this syndrome would be markedly distressing to almost anyone, and is usually experienced with intense fear, terror, and helplessness. The characteristic symptoms involve re-experiencing the traumatic event, avoidance of stimuli associated with the event or numbing of general responsiveness, and increased arousal.

The most common traumata involve either a serious threat to one's life or physical integrity; a serious threat or harm to one's children, spouse, or other close relatives and friends; sudden destruction of one's home or community; or seeing another person who has recently been, or is being, seriously injured or killed as a result of an accident or physical violence.

In more severe forms, particularly in cases in which the survivor has actually committed acts of violence (as in war veterans), the fear is conscious and pervasive, and the reduced capacity for modulation may express itself in unpredictable explosions of aggressive behavior or an inability to express angry feelings.

Thinking about her uncle Joey, whom she never met, Vidamía bracketed and underlined the next sentence and went on reading.

[In the case of a life-threatening trauma shared with others, survivors often describe painful guilt feelings about surviving when others did not, or about the things they had to do in order to survive.]

Vidamía read everything twice and tried to form a profile of a person suffering from post-traumatic stress disorder so she could better understand her father. The most important symptom was that the person reexperienced the horror of the event pretty often. This meant that her father thought about what had happened a lot. His sitting by himself quietly explained the numbness and not moving in order not to think about things. Several items disturbed her:

(4) markedly diminished interest in significant activities
(5) feelings of detachment or estrangement from others
(6) restricted range of affect, e.g., unable to have loving feelings

In another section she found that if at least two of the items persisted, then it was obvious that Billy had to be suffering from what she now called PTSD. She wrote the items down to see if she could detect any of the following "as indicated by at least two of the following": (1) difficulty falling or staying asleep, (2) irritability or outbursts of anger, (3) difficulty concentrating, (4) hypervigilance (which she had to look up in the dictionary), and (5) exaggerated startle response (which she had Elsa explain to her).

She eventually typed the criteria for diagnosing Post-traumatic Stress Disorder into her computer—she was one of the few students in her school, in 1988, who had a computer, courtesy of Barry and his firm. She then printed the information, in the smallest possible size with her dot-matrix printer, trimmed the sheet with scissors, and folded it into her wallet. She could now refer to the salient points of the diagnosis when she needed to. She returned to the dictionary to look up "lability" and "psychogenic," but other than that, after she read the definition a couple of times she understood most of it. From all surface appearances, her father clearly seemed to be suffering from the disorder, except that he was kind and always smiled sadly at you when you addressed him. It was true that he never got angry at anything, even when people yelled at him—like the time the whole troop of them had gone into a diner to get out of the rain and the man said they couldn't stay and called her father a bum and Cookie damn near went after the man with her saxophone case. Lurleen had to hold her back, but her father just smiled and told the man he was very sorry, and they went back out into the rain and stood under a McDonald's awning, Lurleen telling him that it was okay to go in the place, but her father shook his head and stood there stoically, the wind and rain blowing all around and Caitlin sniffling and shivering even with a blanket that Lurleen had put around her. As far as being a threat to the family, there was none of that. Whenever there was anything having to do with war or combat, whether a news item or a film, he always got up and walked away, sometimes leaving the loft completely.

Whenever she asked Cookie, her sister just shrugged her shoulders and said, "That's just the way he is," which Vidamía finally understood, because as long as the children could remember, their father was there but not truly; coming in and out of their consciousness like an image that fades in and out of focus, or like a person observed walking in a partial fog, so that parts of the body appear in startling disassociation from the rest of the human form. So, in truth, Cookie couldn't be blamed for having such a vague notion of her father.

"Does he ever get angry?" she asked, recalling the symptoms, the repressed anger.

"If he does, I've never seen him," Cookie said. "But I bet you one thing. If anybody messed with us, he'd be there to protect us."

"Sure, I believe it."

"No, really," she said, and added that their father really would. "He's not scared of anything. When we were little he'd pick us up at school and drug dealers would just get out of his way. Everybody respects him. He's not gonna hurt us. You scared?"

"Of course not," Vidamía said, not sure that she wasn't. "Does Daddy have a gun?"

"He could if he wanted to. Mama doesn't believe in guns," Cookie said, casually. "Vietnam made him a little weird. That's all. Anyway, he wouldn't hurt a fly."

"Not even himself?" Vidamía said.

"Hurt himself?" Cookie said and gave her a look like she couldn't believe what she'd just heard. "Are you crazy? No way."

"I'm sorry. I didn't mean that."

"He's just a little strange, that's all. The war, Mama says."

"Yeah . . ." Vidamía replied.

Asking her father about his ailment didn't do any good because when he came out of wherever he went, he just smiled and tousled her hair and told her how beautiful she was. He'd tell her that, whatever happened, don't let them get you down, whoever those damn "them" were—the sons of bitches, like her Grandma Maud said.

When she spoke to Lurleen about the problem, Lurleen shook her head and said that he was suffering from a war-related ailment, that he'd gone to the Veterans Hospital a couple of times, but that he functioned pretty well, given what he'd been through. She'd asked what had happened, and Lurleen explained, as best she could, that her father and uncle had been on patrol and had been ambushed by enemy soldiers. She said that as long as they kept him involved in playing simple tunes he was relaxed, and that is why she had thought up the idea of the family band. Vidamía let it go at that, fearful she might precipitate another episode that would cause him discomfort as it had the last time when she'd asked about the piano.

Most days when they played their music in the subway stations there were always forty or fifty people around their band. Cookie was always moving. She'd finish singing and then would once again pick up her saxophone, the string of pearls rattling against the horn where they had seemingly grown. No one in the family understood or questioned how the pearls had cleaved themselves to the instrument, certainly not little Caitlin, almost five years old, who, day after day, sat on Cliff's trombone case, playing her one maraca, always in the same rhythm, no one worrying that she might be an oddity in such a musical family because in a couple of years she would surely pick up an instrument and begin playing as if she had been trained for years, her eyes staring off blankly, like she'd learned the technique of being there but disappearing into space like their father, her gold-blond hair falling in her face.

They stopped playing and her father watched Lurleen fold her accordion—Lurleen, whom Grandpa Sanderson had taken him back to Tennessee to find, and she looked it, all snub-nosed and agrarian, her hair so blond it looked nearly white but washed-out from having the kids and living from hand to mouth down on the Lower East Side; the children talking like they were Southern Puerto Ricans or something, from listening to their mother at home and then going to school and being out in the street with the rest of the kids, the only one oblivious to it all being Fawn, who looked like an ice-cold angel, so beautiful that it hurt you to look at her for too long, her innocence right out there as she stood, not sat, hour after hour behind her drums, perfectly keeping the beat and singing into the mike when it came her turn; effortlessly standing in back of the big ridiculous bass drum on which it said in red circus letters: *THE SOUTH-ERN CONSTELLATION*; standing there in a too-big faded gingham dress that had been taken in after Cookie could no longer wear it.

And now her father, in his I'm-sorry-to-be-disturbing-you manner, said, "Thank you very much" and "God bless you" to the people dropping dollar bills and coins into the bucket and explained that this number was a song of pain and regret and Lurleen counted one-two-three-four and they went into "After You've Gone," Cliff blowing his heart out and Cookie counter-pointing the wah-wah of the trombone with her own brutally lachrymose saxophone and then singing torch and meaning it since she had already lost it, at fourteen, which Vidamía, two years her senior, had not, with her boyfriend from Seward Park High School—Elsa's alma mater, which she now called Sewer Pork, because that's what it was, she said, betraying a bitterness that Vidamía couldn't quite fathom.

15 A Diaphanous Curtain

The whole summer went like that, from ten in the morning till four in the afternoon, three days a week, setting up their underground camp mostly in parts of the Times Square station, where the 1, 2, 3, 7, N, and R lines and the shuttle to Grand Central converge and people stop to buy Latin records or a hot dog. Once in a while they got a treat and their father bought doughnuts, which upset Lurleen and she'd go on a trip about how bad refined sugar was for a person. No, Lurleen didn't waste her college education, explaining to Vidamía once that she'd majored in music with a minor in nutrition, speaking in that slow, wry voice so that Vidamía didn't know if she was being put on, but figured she wasn't since there was no refined sugar anywhere in the house or in the food they ate; if the recipes called for sweets, Lurleen would use natural honey.

Most of the time, however, they ate egg salad or ham-and-cheese on big wedges of homemade whole wheat bread and lemonade sweetened with honey, which Lurleen had Cookie and Vidamía make every night after supper at their big loft down there in East Hellhole, New York City, as Lurleen called it, all the letters scrunched up together and whining so that it sounded like Easheelhol, Kneejerkcitee.

In the evening, before there was a television in the loft, Lurleen would let them all sit at her feet while she sat in a rocker and told them stories, which made Vidamía jealous because her mother never did anything like that; made her so jealous that the first few nights she sat way at the other end of the loft, against the brick wall so that she could hear the droning of the elevator and barely make out Lurleen's voice talking softly about the planetary system, and the children, her half sisters and half brother rapt, their faces gently illumined by the string of bare lightbulbs hanging above like some hastily made constellation of her father's godly invention; sitting there and thinking that it had been a mistake for her to have contacted Grandma Maud and found these Farrell people who were stranger yet than her own; not meaning her own, because these were as much her own as the others, except that they were so strange, all these blond people. But inching closer as Lurleen began talking about being a little girl and going to visit her aunt Vivian who lived in Louisiana and had a beautiful voice; telling them a story about a young man crossing the swamp and being attacked by alligators and finally meeting a beautiful girl and falling in love with her, asking her to marry him but the girl saying no because the one she loved was far away out west and she had sworn to wait for him, and then Lurleen singing:

> O'er swamps and alligators
> I'm on my weary way,
> O'er railroad ties and crossings
> My weary feet did stray;
> Until at close of evening,
> Some higher ground I gained,
> 'Twas there I met with a Creole girl
> On the Lakes of the Pontchartrain.
>
> "Good-eve to you, kind maiden!
> My money does me no good.
> If it were not for the alligators,
> I'd stay out in the wood."
> "Oh, welcome, welcome stranger!
> Altho' our house is plain,
> We never turn a stranger out
> On the Lakes of the Pontchartrain. . . .

On went Lurleen's beautiful, haunting voice, so that all week long Vidamía thought about the story, which wasn't sad or happy but bothered her, the last verse of the song repeating itself insistently in her head:

> At home in social circles
> Our flaming bowls we'll drain,
> And drink to the health of the Creole girl
> On the Lakes of the Pontchartrain.

She finally went to Lurleen that first summer and asked her was she saying "a cruel girl," and was the girl cruel because the man loved her and she didn't love him? Lurleen smiled and reached out and smoothed Vidamía's hair so that it made her feel tickly inside her chest from the happiness of being touched by her, and Lurleen said no, she wasn't a cruel girl but a girl from a Spanish or French family, like herself, but in Louisiana.

"A Creole girl," she said.

"Am I like a Creole girl?" Vidamía said.

"Yes, darling. Very much like a Creole girl."

"Are Creole girls beautiful?" she asked, feeling very small.

"Yes, very beautiful," Lurleen said, hugging her so that Vidamía could smell the sweetness of her breath and her baby milk for Caitlin, and Vidamía felt safe there with her new family.

"You play an instrument?" Cookie had asked that first summer.

"No, I don't, Hortense," Vidamía replied.

"That's okay. We'll teach you. Maybe the tub bass. It's easy, but I gotta ask you to do something, kid. Real special, like," Cookie had said, imitating George Raft or some other movie gangster she'd seen on TV.

"Sure," Vidamía said.

"I don't want you to get uptight, but could you do one little thing for me?"

"What?"

"Don't call me Hortense, okay?"

"Okay, Cookie."

"Thanks, kid. I guess it's a cool enough name down in Turn-and-see, where my moms is from, but here in the neighborhood it sounds like I'm from outer space or something goofy," she said. "You know, like Horton from Dr. Seuss, and whatnot."

Their laughter was raucous and long. They were in the park down by the East River and Cookie went on talking really fast how a tub bass was made, explaining that you had to find a nine-ring washtub, drill a hole for the string, and then you took a broom handle and cut it, then drilled a hole to put the string through, and then put a knot on the string so it didn't slip back out. Depending on the key you're playing in, you shift the stick back and forth across from the middle out to the edge, Cookie explaining that her mother knew how to make and play the homemade instrument.

Cookie then went into a pocket of her bib overalls with the one strap hanging loose and pulled out a rock and flung it way out into the water.

"You see any rats let me know," she said. "I clocked one last week. Knocked it into next year. Right between the fucking eyes. Just signal me the direction with your eyes and don't move an inch. I carry rocks all the time. Practice. Okay?"

"Practice for what?"

"In case boys get fresh and wanna start shit."

"Sure."

"You have hair yet?" Cookie said, turning away from the water.

"Hair? What hair?" Vidamía said.

"On your pussy."

"What? Are you crazy? Don't talk like that, Cookie, please."

Vidamía's face felt hot and she had a terrific desire to either start running or screaming, she couldn't tell which.

"You got titties, so you gotta have hair. Mama says maybe

next year I'll get mine, but I'm only gonna be twelve so I don't know. Mama says she got her period when she was eleven, on her birthday. Fawn says she's never gonna get titties or hair. She's our sister but she's a little weird. Her thing down there is kind of strange and she won't let anybody see her naked."

"Strange?"

"Yeah, I don't know. Mama says we gotta respect her privacy, but nobody gives a damn about mine. I think we're all musical geniuses, and Mama says we ought to have at least five pianos in the loft so that each one of us can practice, including her. She's a Rachmaninoff expert and Papa was what they called an up-and-coming white giant of the jazz piano before the Vietnam War. He jammed with Miles Davis and Wayne Shorter when he was just a kid, fourteen or fifteen. I'll play you some of their shit, too, when we get back. You gotta check out 'Sketches of Spain.' That is some serious music, girl. You have a boyfriend?"

"No, there aren't any boys around where I live," Vidamía lied. "You see them in school, but all they want to do is grab your hand or ask you if you want to do it."

"Yeah, they're pretty disgusting. This one boy in my homeroom, his name's Victor, took his thing out and showed it to me and my girlfriend Myra. It was all red and crooked. I hated it. It didn't have hair all over it, so Myra said maybe it was made out of rubber or something. You know, like a trick thing."

"Yeah, sure."

"So, what about chanting? You like chanting?"

"Chanting?"

"Yeah. It's real cool. My girlfriend Rima does it. She and her mother are gonna take me to a meeting. You wanna come?"

"Sure. What do they do?"

"I don't know. Chant, I guess," she said and began whooping it up and doing a war dance. And then they both broke into an uncontrollable gaggle of giggles, as Lurleen would say. They walked out of the park and up the street with more of the Rican

Spanish coming back to Vidamía from the time she was a little girl and they lived with her grandmother, and the times they visited after moving, everything looking familiar like she had been there all along; and fascinated by the notion that her father had been a pianist, a jazz pianist, whatever that meant, the entire matter sounding very romantic; and wondering why they couldn't just have one piano and take turns; deciding right there and then she'd ask her father why they didn't have one.

She later regretted bringing up the subject of the piano, because all it did was bring tears to his eyes and make him walk out of the loft, into the elevator and down into the dark, which swallowed him up for two straight nights, and when he returned it was like he had aged ten years. All she'd said was, "You know, Daddy, we should get a piano so everyone can play. I'd like to learn." When he didn't return she'd gone to Lurleen and told her she was so sorry, and Lurleen said she shouldn't blame herself because things like that happened with him.

"He'll be all right," she said. "When he's ready he'll come back."

And he did, and she told her father she was sorry, and all he did was tousle her hair and then hug her to him and tell her she was going to be all right, except that she felt like she was the one who should be providing solace for him, her father.

And that's the way it went that first summer, four years before, Vidamía getting to know her family and learning to play the tub bass and to do a few soft-shoe numbers like "Tea for Two," but totally confused about this new door she had opened in her life, so that it felt as if she had stepped into a big room that extended into tomorrow all the way to the Pacific Ocean and up into Alaska, or so it seemed; the room populated by these musical creatures who talked so easily about the universe as if it were their own front lawn, which they didn't have because they lived in harmonious semi-poverty down there in Loisaida, which is what Cookie called the Lower East Side in that second year, explaining just like she was some hybrid Puerto Rican that this poet by the name of Bimbo Rivas, whom she knew personally from readings in Tompkins Square Park and the Nuyorican Poets Cafe, had renamed the neighborhood, and that the name was a combination of a town in P.R. by the name of Loiza and the "Lower East Side."

"Get it? Loisaida."

"Yeah, sure," Vidamía said. "But Bimbo? What kind of náme is that?"

Cookie got all serious and shook her head.

"What do you mean, what kind of name is that? It's a Taino name, that's what we are," she said, stumbling over her words and her identity. "I mean that's what Puerto Ricans are. Tainos. Bimbo means *Guerrero Celestial,* girl."

"Ghe- what?"

"*Guerrero Celestial,*" Cookie said, proudly. "Celestial Warrior in the Taino language. Somebody who fights for the people. I'll introduce you to him next time I see him."

"Yeah, sure," Vidamía said and then Cookie admonished her.

"You better get hip, homegirl," she said. "Get with the program and stop acting like some retard hick, okay? *Míja, ¿qué es lo tuyo?* Are you some kinda *jíbara?*" going back and forth from English to Spanish like she was born to code-switching or Spanglish and whatnot.

And then one day during that first summer, they all agreed Vidamía should play the tub bass, which Lurleen doubled on when she wasn't playing her fiddle. That was when Lurleen got her accordion from the closet and a flowered hat she'd bought at a thrift shop over by SoHo that really made her look like a hayseed, even though she was so smart, teaching them about astronomy and southern constellations like Triangulum Australe, Pavo, Crux, and Volans.

And right there and then, smiling like a lifetime of spring mornings, she broke out a big pan of corn bread and they all sat down and ate it with margarine and clover honey, getting all sticky in their fingers and hair, and that's when Vidamía figured out that, plain and simple, like Lurleen said, she was family to these people and there was no turning back the clock or trying to figure it out. Realizing this made her feel complete and grown up.

She watched Lurleen eat a few little crumbs, lick her fingers, and then get up and take down her dulcimer and sing about maidens who cried the whole night through and trees that bled and magical deer and stones that walked the earth; sitting spell-bound listening to her voice which was sweeter than clover honey, and Vidamía watching her father, Billy the Kid Farrell, knowing she was now responsible for him, and whatever misfortune he had suffered she would share. She was only thirteen that first summer, but decided that since Billy was her father, and since she had gone out of her way to find him, she was up to the task of taking care of him, no matter how much effort or pain that might mean.

16 Meeting Monk

One morose day in August when the skies finally became tired of carrying the clouds, appearing as if they had thrown up their arms in petulant resignation to let the rains crash vertiginously down at a slant from an easterly direction, people hurried through the tunnels beneath Times Square, wet but relieved because the passing of the storm made everything fresh and sweet. Eleven-year-old Fawn Singleton Farrell, observing the scurrying of the people and smelling the clear air which had penetrated the subterranean atmosphere, thought perhaps nature had added fabric softener to the air. She bit into the sugar doughnut her father had bought during a break and let the words form randomly in her head.

> *Aberdeen Gabardine*
> *I'm going to the fair*
> *Don't bring water*
> *But bring talc for*
> *The lady's care.*

She sat very still, repeating the words over and over because then she'd remember them and write them in her secret book when she got home. Because if one looked at these verses, one might get the impression that they were from some old poem or riddle or game dating back to Elizabethan times, but they were her own creation, perhaps induced by some of the songs her mother had sung from the time she was an infant, she lying in a wooden cradle that Billy had found while emptying out an apartment on Clinton Street, and Lurleen singing and playing her dulcimer. So absorbed was Fawn that she appeared to be both chewing and mumbling at the same time.

> *Aberdeen Gabardine*
> *You're the one I trust*
> *Don't bring iron*
> *But bring wood*
> *So that it won't rust.*

> *Aberdeen Gabardine*
> *I will marry thee*
> *Don't bring glass*
> *But bring silver*
> *If your wife I'll be.*

Aberdeen Gabardine
Look out for my heart
Don't bring candles
Bring a goose
In a golden cart.

And who was Aberdeen Gabardine? Maybe Aberdeen was a girl. It sounded like a girl's name. Maybe she was like those women that liked each other. She had seen them in Tompkins Square Park kissing, and sometimes she'd seen others walking down the street with their arms around each other. The thought made her sad and she thought about her thing. Thinking about it usually removed all thought of romance from her head and she went back to repeating the words of her rhyme, enjoying the combination of their sounds and the taste of the doughnut, but thinking about her mama, Lurleen, who was feeling poorly, as she said, and had remained behind. Had she been there she would have been railing at Papa for aiding in the destruction of their teeth and their health by allowing them to eat sugar like that.

So Fawn sat down and savored the doughnut and talked to her big sister Vidamía, who had become her confidante this past year, since Fawn was starting to ask questions about coming of age and it scared her because she had seen Cookie and her mother with their boobs and their hair and their cramps and she wanted no part of it and what was she supposed to do with that thing hanging there like Cliff's, whom she had seen when he was making wee, wanting with all her might to tell Vidamía because she was sure her sister would understand but holding off since her mama had said it was best if no one knew and that soon the matter would be taken care of and she had to just be patient and everything would be all right, which she doubted because she was a freak like they had at freak shows, which she'd

171

read about, belonging with two-headed babies and six-legged pigs.

"Why's it gotta be like that?" she asked Vidamía, her head resting on her sister's left shoulder as she sat on the amp. "It makes no sense why we gotta have boobs."

"They're called primary sexual characteristics," explained Vidamía pedantically, although the word "pedantic" wasn't yet part of her vocabulary. "Primary sexual characteristics determine masculinity in boys and femininity in girls."

"They're awful. Cookie says when you get them, boys want to touch you. Yuck!"

"You don't have to let them touch you."

Fawn was as smart as your proverbial whip and replied immediately that if you didn't have to let them touch your boobs, then you had a choice and you *could* let them touch you if you wanted, and had Vidamía ever let a boy touch her? Vidamía shook her head and felt like a hypocrite because it had happened just the other night with Ricky over in Tompkins Square Park near the bandstand where the light had gone out on the lamppost. She felt herself flush hot, which Fawn didn't notice from being so absorbed in herself.

"Well, has anyone?" Fawn insisted.

"Of course not."

"Has anyone tried?" she asked, licking the sugar from the doughnut off her fingers.

Vidamía was into the lie now and said that plenty of boys had tried but that she always changed the subject and talked about something that was more interesting to them.

Cookie had lost her virginity with some boy by the name of Mario Wong, she'd told Vidamía, describing the utter cuteness of this boy so that Vidamía could see him clearly. Vidamía learned subsequently that young Mario, sixteen years old and aceing every class at Stuyvesant High School—and heading for a perfect 1,600 SAT score—was the product of a Sino–Puerto Rican cultural exchange that took place down on Canal Street, around the corner from Mulberry or Mott, where San Juan and Hong Kong are separated by a diaphanous curtain of Italian pastries and espresso coffee; Cookie promising that Vidamía would meet him soon. "Girl, you have to put a lock on your impatience, *mijita*, cause Mr. Wong ain't going nowhere, baby. He's coming right back to his mama, if you get my meaning," she said, pointing lasciviously at her chest, her eyes sparkling with the double entendre of the Spanish *mamar*, to suck.

Vidamía and Fawn had finished speaking when a thin black man about sixty years of age and carrying an alto saxophone case, stopped in front of them, excused himself, and asked if they had seen Bill Farrell. Vidamía looked up and was at first startled but then began to explain that her father would return in a minute, when Cookie came up and asked the man who he was.

"Alfred Butterworth, a friend," the man said, talking with a rasp in his voice. "I saw him yesterday but wasn't sure it was him. I came back to make sure. You his kid?"

"Yeah, we all are," Cookie said, fanning the area with her arm to include little Caitlin and Cliff as if they were there, which they were not since their papa had gone to find a toilet so they could relieve themselves.

"You play?" she asked, letting him know she was a homegirl, even if she was white and he better not try anything funny, except his eyes had this little smile in them and that was usually something you could trust in people. If it wasn't there, watch it, her mama had said.

"I play a little bit," he said, sweeping his eyes over the blond heads, and then to Vidamía, and wanting to ask if this dark-haired one was Billy's kid, too, but not saying the words.

"Me too," Cookie said. "Tenor. Stick around and you can jam with us."

Butterworth laughed and nodded at this fey little girl who reminded him of Billy, except she was so cocky and sure of herself while Billy had always been so shy and respectful, and he recalled the time he'd brought him to the Five Spot, and Monk had been there that afternoon trying out the piano in preparation for a gig and Billy stood petrified in the dark by the bar and wouldn't come forward to meet Monk until Butterworth dragged him over to the piano and introduced him by telling Monk that Billy was a pianist. When Monk looked up, this squeaky little voice came out of Billy and he said, "Nice meetin' you, Mr. Monk," and Thelonious sent his right hand way up to the high end of the piano and played the same squeaky little greeting, *plin-pliny-plun-pliny-plun*, and laughed and asked Billy if he'd like to sit down, sliding off the bench and Butterworth pushing him down, explaining to Monk that Billy's daddy had been a cop and got shot up a few years back when he walked into a holdup up on Third Avenue in Spanish Harlem.

"The kid takes lessons from Mae Wilkerson up in the Bronx."

"Mae from the colored women's bands?" Monk asked.

"Yeah, you know her," Butterworth said. "Light-skinned heavyset woman."

And Monk said, "Sit down, son." The voice was so imposing that there was no turning back. Billy sat down and looked up at Butterworth, and Butterworth thought the kid'd start crying so he said, "Just do 'Midnight' like you did at Mae's house last week. Go on." And the kid looked at Monk but Monk was looking down, waiting, listening, so Billy went into it, playing the intervals just like he heard them himself, not like Monk but not unlike him, and after a while Monk was humming deep in his chest and when Billy was finished, Monk asked them if they wanted a beer and Billy shook his head, wanting to explain that he was only fifteen years old, although he and his friends had gotten drunk pretty bad the previous St. Patrick's Day.

They'd sat down and talked for a while, mostly Pop Butterworth, because Thelonious didn't say but a few words, and then

Monk said he had to split but to come back that evening, which they did, and Billy sat there spellbound listening to Thelonious play "Straight No Chaser," "Friday the Thirteenth," "Ruby My Dear," "Mysterioso," and many other tunes, including " 'Round Midnight," in the middle of which, while Charlie Rouse was soloing, Monk looked at Billy and, comping with his left hand, touched, ever so subtly, his ear. Billy looked at Butterworth who explained that Monk wanted him to pay attention. He listened as Monk punctuated Charlie Rouse's solo so that Billy had a picture of a painter touching up a canvas. After a while, Charles Mingus came in with a big-breasted white woman and Butterworth introduced him to Mingus, but it wasn't the same and Billy couldn't wait for the next set to hear Monk play.

Cookie, Vidamía, Fawn, and Butterworth had been jamming on "Jealous Love" with Butterworth singing like Louis Armstrong and pretty soon Cliff came back and picked up his trombone and began wailing away behind Butterworth, who stood listening, enraptured by this young boy who looked just like his father, and a crowd formed in a half-circle around the band and dropped coins and bills into the bucket; and then, like they had been playing together forever, they went into "Blues in the Night," the horns crying and the kids letting loose all the pain they didn't yet know they could have; but Butterworth feeling the pain since he had lived it all, including loving Lady Day like he did and not being able to help her; enduring the pain and not saying anything but watching until the end and feeling helpless; always wanting to forget but always playing juke joints and recalling things in his life; especially meeting Buck Sanderson, Billy's grandfather, when Butterworth was just fourteen down there in Memphis and the big white man with the wide smile asking him if he played that thing, meaning his clarinet, and Butterworth nodding but scared stiff because this was a white man talking to him and the white man was walking around in the colored section, down by Beale Street, telling him he was too young to be going into a juke joint but he was just curious to hear him play, going into Bramwell's, where everyone greeted the white man like they liked him a whole lot and was friends for a long time. Buck Sanderson walked over to the piano and from the top of it got his banjo and settled himself on a stool, then Eightball Bramwell, his black bald head shining, sat down at the piano and said, "Go on, boy, if you plays that licorice stick, get with it!" and they'd played "Long Gone John from Bowling Green."

That's when Billy showed up, his Farmer Jones hat pulled down on his forehead and his long blond hair hanging to his shoulders, his beard starting to get gray hairs so that when Butterworth saw him his heart filled with a mixture of emotions—love, pride, regret, pain, and anger. Without being at all aware of Butterworth's presence, so far away did Billy's mind at times go, he picked up his guitar and joined in while Cookie went into *"Hear that lonesome whistle blowin' 'cross the trestle, whooee . . . ,"* Billy strumming pretty good on the Gibson and Butterworth for the first time seeing his three-finger claw hand running sideways across the strings and the sorrow of a thousand men carved into his eyes. Butterworth's alto sax spoke so clearly that you could almost hear it crying "Sweet Jesus, what have they done to this boy! What have they done!"

Butterworth hadn't seen him in all these years, but it wasn't like he hadn't asked about him. No one had seen Billy; some couldn't even remember who he was, and still others, embittered by their own failed lives, had accused Butterworth of chasing after the white man, not understanding that the boy could play and wherever he'd brought him people had praised him. Even Charles Mingus, who was as hard as they came and didn't want to hear about white men and came out with that beautiful *Fables of Faubus* album, angrily attacking Governor Faubus of Arkansas and his racist policies, the music so progressive and fresh so that when you hear it now you think it's been composed recently—even Charles had said the boy could play, for a white boy, which never made any sense to him since he'd heard black folks who could play classical music and receive awards and recognition, who composed scores for motion pictures and knew their instrument and talked about the music like they understood it, but when it came to actually playing didn't have that certain thing that made you want to get up and move or even tap your foot. So that when the real musicians played, you knew there was something going on behind the playing which was personal and new. He'd seen all of them, Charlie Parker, Dexter Gordon, Diz, Monk, Bud Powell, Lennie Tristano, Gerry Mulligan, Stan Getz, Paul Chambers, and Miles, and they all had it. Black or white, they all had that feeling. They could swing. The quality was either present or it wasn't and you couldn't fake it by talking shit.

What a waste! He could still recall that Saturday afternoon in late fall when Billy had come up to his apartment on 145th Street and Riverside Drive while the business with Miles was pending; scared out of his mind and not knowing what he was going to do because he'd been drafted and he'd have to go, talking crazy about how the country needed him and his father would've expected it of him.

"Billy, Billy," he'd said. "Relax a minute and let's think this out."

"I can't, Pop," Billy said, pulling out the draft board envelope. "I gotta do it. If my father was in my shoes that's what he'd do," he added, hitting the letter on the palm of his hand.

"What about the music, son? You're doing so good. Miles really wants you to play with him. Why, in a year or so you could be playing regular and earning a living, cutting your own records. There ain't many like you, son. Even Monk saw it that time at the Five Spot. You could get a deferment, cause you're the only one your mother has. Don't you see that?"

"I couldn't do that, Pop. They need me and I gotta go."

"Why don't you go back one more time and play with Miles, just to see what he says and then make up your mind?"

"I wanna do that, Pop. I really dug playing with him. But it wouldn't be fair, Pop. What am I gonna tell him? Sorry, Mr. Davis, I've been drafted. I better just go down and straighten things out with the army."

And then he walked out of the apartment and the next time Butterworth saw him was four months later just before Christmas. Billy had a crew cut and was wearing his Marine uniform.

Butterworth, playing along with the band, watched Billy and his kids as they finished playing, the little girl, Fawn, coming in at the end, mostly snare and cymbal but showing definite potential, and Butterworth looking over at Billy, and Billy finally recognizing him and going pale and sick in his stomach but leaning the guitar against some McDonald's advertisement stuck on the subway wall and coming over to him and standing in front of him and Butterworth doing the same, the two of them just standing there for the longest time until Butterworth finally took a couple of steps forward, reached out with his open arms and brought Billy against him. But really against his saxophone, so that to the children it seemed as if their father was a small boy and the thin, short black man was bigger and was taking care of him; and they held each other like that for a few minutes. Butterworth let go and held Billy at arm's length.

"How's it going, son?" he said.

And Billy, his eyes a little moist, was nodding and trying to say something. But no words would come out, and he just went on nodding until Butterworth asked him for his address because he wanted to stay in touch and Billy took out paper and pen and wrote it all out, including his phone number, his left hand writing and his claw hand holding the paper on his amp as he wrote. A few minutes later Butterworth had packed up his alto and was gone, and they were back to playing "Bill Bailey, Won't You Please Come Home?" the strains of the music following Butter-worth as he walked away toward the Seventh Avenue train and his trip back to Harlem, remembering how he'd begged Billy not to go into the army; told him it didn't make any sense him going, and if he did he should tell them he was a musician and get on a band—they had things like that where he could use his talent to entertain other soldiers—but Billy'd gone ahead, joined the Marines of all things, never telling them he was a pianist. Buck Sanderson, Billy's grandfather, told him that Billy was at Camp Geiger and that he was going to be a machine gunner, shaking his head, not wanting to utter the fear that sat in his chest like a dark nesting bird that would one day spread its wings and bring him bad news.

> *Won't you come home, Bill Bailey,*
> *Won't you come home?*
> *She moans the whole day long.*
> *I'll do the cookin', darling,*
> *I'll pay the rent . . .*
> *Bill Bailey won't you please*
> *come home?*

Life was sure a harsh thing. Butterworth didn't know any-body who had come out on the winning end. Certainly nobody in the music business—except a few. But for every one of them there were a dozen and a half like him, pushing a broom some-where, tending someone's building, flipping hamburgers on a grill, or, like him, running an elevator eight hours a day, up and down, up and down, locked up in a steel cage like a monkey in a uniform. Somehow white people seemed to come out of the ex-perience all right and found themselves something else to do, but black folks just played the music and the next thing you knew they was being degraded somewhere. But that wasn't fair cause

Billy was white. And then he thought of poor Candy Donovan, crazy flipped out about Bird, then going off to Detroit somewhere and singing in cheap joints, hooking up with some badass nigger auto worker and having six or seven kids by two or three dudes, becoming a drunk and getting her head cracked open one night.

He thought of Billy again, wanting to forget the past and look to tomorrow, to somehow hope that the boy could salvage something of his life, because he, Alfred Butterworth, sure as hell hadn't.

17 Slumming

It is stated in certain writings that the human being is a microcosm of the universe, so that filtered through the contrivances of science and the fashionably opaque lens of popular culture we have come to understand that we are not, as assumed in the past, mere mortals, but grandiosely the stuff of stars. This confusing dictum, as perhaps decanted by *Nova* or some other sound PBS program, led Vidamía Farrell at the susceptible age of nine years, already genetically predisposed to inquiry, to ask her mother, Elsa Santiago López-Ferrer, how this could be, since some people were so ordinary. Her mother looked at her and realized for the first time that perhaps she had on her hands, in the person of her daughter, a bona fide inquiring mind, and although she felt little in the way of maternal stirrings, she decided she ought to cultivate her daughter's considerable capacity for critical thinking, if not for the child's sake, at least for the social value of having an intelligent offspring.

Having trotted through Hunter College in record time to obtain her bachelor's degree, and her master's from City University, Elsa was conversant with IQ tests, Stanford-Binets, and a textbook full of other criteria for measuring intelligence. Yet despite her considerable intellectual training, she made a critical mistake. She corrected Vidamía's attitudes of superiority while believing in them privately. Utilizing her many hours of listening attentively to her professors and beginning to hone her style of addressing the less fortunate, she lectured.

"Honey, you mustn't say that about people," she said. "In any case, the expression 'the stuff of stars' refers to the chemical makeup of the human body. All it means is that the same chemicals that exist in the moon, sun, stars, meteors, comets, and all celestial bodies exist in human beings, therefore we are star stuff. It has nothing to do with Hollywood. Theoretically, all people are equal. As ordinary as people may appear," she went on, "deep inside there is a core of equality which we must respect and help develop in everybody. Do you understand that, sweetie?"

"Everybody?"

"That's right."

"Even if they're like Rosie Slotnick?" she asked.

"Yes," Elsa said, suppressing a desire to laugh, understanding perfectly her daughter's predicament since all that her nine-year-old neighbor wanted Vidamía to do when she went to her house was to play with her vast collection of Barbie dolls and their array of boyfriends, while all Vidamía wanted to do was look at Dr. Slotnick's medical books because the diagrams intrigued her.

"Really, Mommy? Rosie?"

"Especially Rosie," Elsa reiterated, growing serious again.

"All five-point-something billion people?" Vidamía asked.

"I don't know the exact number, but yes," her mother said.

"Okay," Vidamía said and went off skipping across the living room floor, out onto the porch and into the garden, as if the moment had contained just one more adult-manufactured piece of information. As with all things, she thought about it and in time the experience had an impact on her and remained with Vidamía forever, erected in the middle of her being as a monument to be revered. It wasn't so much that her mother's wisdom was necessarily to be respected, but that the notion of everyone's being equal made her feel as if she truly and rightfully belonged in the world. From then on, Vidamía, with a pronounced aristocracy which most people found charming, went out of her way to find commonality with others and in that way fulfilled what she deemed was her responsibility to aid them. By the same token, when she met people of superior intellect she felt neither fear nor shyness, and rather than being dazzled she accepted their brilliance as something quite natural. Out of personal concern for her status Elsa had unwittingly tapped what is perhaps the most natural state of humanity, that of wishing to cooperate and create harmony with others rather than produce strife. Having established that all humans were equal, Vidamía was free to observe more subtle characteristics in the people around her.

Therefore Vidamía, observing her father as she slap-thumped her washtub bass, deduced that Billy's renewal of acquaintance with the small black man must have affected him adversely, and although he appeared calm as he strummed his guitar, he was now more troubled than ever. Suffice it to say that, when it came to her father, Vidamía chose action over theory, so that watching him that day as his friend Alfred Butterworth left, she was convinced, now more than ever, that she must do something.

She had loved her father instantly, the connection to him so natural that subsequently she felt as if she had known him all along and he hadn't been absent from her life those first twelve years. From the time she'd met him at her Grandma Maud's apartment, a bond was created which perhaps wouldn't have been as solid had he raised her and been a party to disciplining her, to disappointing her, to denying her attention when he was in the same room, which all fathers at one time or another do. Whatever the reasons, their relationship was one of mutual admiration. He was dazzled by her beauty and innocence, and she by his melancholy and the utter bulk of his person, both his physical size, but more prominently, and therefore of greater attraction, the psychic baggage he carried wherever he went. She was, after all, in many ways, her mother's daughter, so that the conversations with Elsa's colleagues, who often visited, her exposure to the literature of psychology, to journal articles, and the entire therapeutic nature of her mother's practice all affected her. While in the opinion of some people Vidamía's and Billy's acceptance of each other seemed too perfect, that is how things were between them. Vidamía often thought of asking why he had never attempted to contact her, why he had abandoned them, as her mother had said. But, heeding Lurleen's advice that she not ask too much of him, she was simply grateful for his presence in her life now.

She recalled that first summer with the family, when she had turned thirteen. Elsa and Barry had driven her to the Lower East Side from Tarrytown. Elsa, although more than familiar with the neighborhood, appeared shocked at the contrast between their own comfortable lifestyle and the squalor of the Lower East Side, forgotten images of her youth attacking her senses. With each minute she grew more tense, and eventually resorted to a surreptitiously ingested dosage of tranquilizing pills, later laughing darkly to herself, since she had wanted to get away from the neighborhood because of drugs after seeing her girlfriend Milagros and her boyfriend die of overdoses, the two of them found dead on the floor of his aunt's house.

They parked the silver Mercedes—the new one—and Barry opened the trunk as Elsa stood watching nervously, the whistle on the lanyard around her neck a relic from those years before she'd married Barry, when she'd come home late to her mother's apartment from classes and her full-time job counseling at the college. Getting off the train at Grand Street, she'd walk the deserted winter streets, ever alert for a mugger, the whistle clutched in her hand, thinking that, because of her clothes and her books, in the dark she was just another white person, never conscious that in spite of the people's many faults they instinctively recognized when someone was trying to help himself and was therefore off limits. Nothing had ever happened but she still carried the fear deeply ingrained in her being. She had retrieved the whistle from a drawer in the ironing room of her house in Tarrytown, going to it instinctively when she agreed to allow Vidamía to spend time with Billy.

"Hurry up, Barry," she said sharply as she stood looking up and down the street as if what they were doing was illegal and she needed to be on the lookout for the police.

Vidamía had wandered off to look at the empty lot next to the industrial building where her father's family lived. The weeds in the lot created a fascinating landscape, from which protruded an old refrigerator, discarded tires, and an assortment of trash. In the back of the lot there was a huge ailanthus tree and, like children around a mother, several young saplings. When she heard her mother, an edge of hysteria in her voice, Vidamía returned and stood between them. Her mother was asking Barry where the place could be since the only structure on that side of the street was a factory building and everything on the other side, except for a tenement at the end of the block, was abandoned. Vidamía pointed at the building and said that this one was the place.

"This is one-forty-three," she said. "Daddy said to ring the bell that says Farrell. The fifth floor."

"This place?" Elsa said, supressing her disgust at hearing her daughter refer to Billy Farrell in such filial terms. "Barry, she can't stay here. Look at this block. Can you imagine what it must be like at night? We can't go through with this."

Calmly ignoring her mother's protest, Vidamía went to the metal door and rang the bell, above which had been painted roughly in green letters: FARRELL. Two minutes later, the door opened and out came a blond girl with short, shaggy hair. Billy stood behind her, inside the door, watching nervously. The girl was about the same height as Vidamía, dressed in high-water bib overalls, a T-shirt, and black high-topped sneakers with mis-matched laces, one green and the other pink. She threw the door open, swept her hand to point at her father and said, "Ta-*da*," as if he were about to make an entrance onto a stage. Once Billy had the door, she came forward and kissed Vidamía on the cheek. Vidamía returned the kiss and they hugged. They hadn't seen each other since Christmas, although they must have spent a thousand hours on the phone between December and the be-ginning of their school vacation, nearly six months.

"Looking good, Vee," Cookie said, turning her attention to Elsa. "I'm Hortense McAlpin Farrell," she said. "Friends call me Cookie. You must be Vidamía's mother."

"Cookie?" said Elsa, arching her eyebrows.

"Yeah," Hortense said, looking defiantly at Elsa, so that Elsa nearly took a step back. "Cookie Farrell."

"How you doing, Cookie?" Vidamía said, as if to back up her sister's assertion, looking again at Cookie's eyes, which seemed bluer than she remembered them from her visit at Christmas. "This is my mother, Elsa, and my stepfather, Barry."

Cookie immediately extended her hand to them.

"Please don't be shocked by the neighborhood," she said, as if she could read Elsa's mind. "Everybody's got an attitude, but no-body bothers you as long as you're cool. Hey, that's a nice car. Is it all paid for?" And then, pointing back to Billy, she said, "This is my father, Bill Farrell. Your father too, kid. But I guess you know that. Right, homegirl?" Her father, feeling uncomfortable and squinting in the sunlight, nodded at Elsa and at Barry, his eyes shifting from the car to his shoes and then to the open door of the building. Elsa was more beautiful than he remembered her but he felt no emotion toward her. Perhaps he should but he felt nothing. Elsa, on the other hand, was in a state of shock and didn't want to consider whether she was attracted to Billy. He seemed heavier, but it didn't look like he was drinking much. She avoided his eyes and wanted to be away from him quickly.

When the pause grew too long, Cookie stepped in. "You folks sure look like you could use a glass of lemonade," she said. "Yo, my mama makes the best lemonade east of the Mississippi. Anyway, east of Broadway. You gotta check it out, you know what I'm saying?" she added and grabbed Vidamía's bag. "Damn, girl, what you got in here? You didn't bring your own silverware and cooking pots, did you?"

The profanity didn't go unnoticed by Elsa, who shot Barry a quick look. They followed Billy inside, and, immediately after the door locked behind them, Elsa felt compelled to ask Barry, in a whisper, whether he had remembered to lock the car. Barry said he had and then Billy led them to an industrial elevator big enough to transport several large racks of overcoats, that being its purpose for more than sixty years, until the early 1970s, when the Dorfman Overcoats patriarch, Solomon, became too infirm to supervise the business and none of his sons wanted to run the factory.

The elevator crept up slowly, each creaking inch making Elsa more nervous; she wanting to ask if the mechanism was safe but not daring to open her mouth for fear that the movement might cause an imbalance in the workings and bring about an accident. They arrived at the fifth-floor landing after what seemed an eternity to her, though in fact it had been a mere thirty seconds, the elevator being in perfect working order, serviced periodically by Felix Gutierrez, who worked for the City of New York. Felix took care of elevators in the projects, and his children went to school with the Farrell children. He and Billy had become friends. The two of them had been in Vietnam around the same time. Billy had asked Felix if he had known Joey. Felix said he'd grown up in Brooklyn.

When Billy pulled on the canvas belt to throw open the up-and-down doors of the elevator and they stepped out of the lift and were led through a door, what assaulted Elsa first was the vastness of the world in front of her. It was as if rather than a room she were being shown an indoor park. She rejected the loft outright as cluttered and ill-kempt. For Vidamía, however, the only thing she could compare it to was a castle. She was immediately overwhelmed by memories of Christmas, and tears came to her eyes, much as if she were returning home after a long absence. The walls were bare brick and the floor was wood, polished to an abnormal smoothness by the leather of thousands of shoes shuffling back and forth, day in and day out, of the men and women who sewed fine overcoats. Here and there, as if there were invisible walls, were areas for different family activities: a playroom, a nursery, an area for schoolwork. Along one of the walls, using two-by-fours and drywall, Billy had created rooms so that each of the children had his or her own private place.

At the end of the loft he had built a large bedroom and a platform for a king-sized mattress for himself and Lurleen. Lurleen had made rag quilts for their bed and each of the children's. Each room had a loft bed, and beneath it a desk and a place for storing clothes and other belongings. Since Vidamía's visit at Christmas, Billy had built a room for her. Lurleen had made a quilt for her bed.

"Welcome to the Farrells'," Cookie said. "This is the living room," she added, pointing to an area halfway into the loft. There, placed in the semblance of a living room were two couches and three stuffed chairs, all rescued from sidewalks where they had been discarded because of tears or holes. Each one, however, had been repaired with odd colored patches so that every piece had a personality of its own. Against a plywood wall there was a television set, and here and there were mis-matched tables and lamps.

When the guests were seated, Cookie brought Lurleen over and introduced her.

"This is my mother, Lurleen Meekins Farrell. Everybody, even my dad, calls her Lynn. Fact you can call her most any-thing, 'cept late for lunch. Just joking, folks," she'd said, doing a fair imitation of Lurleen and her fake hayseed routine. Lurleen said how do you do and immediately offered her two guests glasses of lemonade. "You girls can get your own," she said, as Vidamía and Cookie were heading for the kitchen. Lurleen then pointed out Cliff and Fawn and then the blondest little girl sitting in a little yellow rocker holding a blue bear. "That's Caitlin," Lurleen said. "She's going to be two years old," at which the little girl, looking very serious, held up two fingers and everyone laughed.

Elsa, sitting on the edge of one of the stuffed chairs, watched the two girls out of the corner of her eye, gulped her lemonade, and, checking her watch, announced that she and Barry had to leave. She kissed Vidamía hastily, gave her a few whispered in-structions, particularly regarding the matter of calling her every day, and then left the loft, thanking Lurleen for the lemonade, although she felt that it was too tart; again warning Billy as they were going back down on the elevator that if anything happened to Vidamía she would hold him personally responsible. Billy looked at her pityingly and said he'd look after her and she shouldn't worry.

"Well, you can't blame me for worrying," she said. "I can't believe you'd want to live down here. We leave and you people move in. Why? What's the charm? The East Village? I can't be-lieve this. It was the Lower East Side when I lived here. All of a sudden it's the 'East Village' and white people are dying to live here. Why do you want to raise your family in a factory? Unbe-lievable."

"I'm sorry," Billy Farrell said. "But it doesn't cost me anything."

"You're squatting?"

"No, I just take care of the building."

"For who?"

"The Dorfman brothers. Their father had an overcoat business. He died. They keep talking about knocking it down and putting up a high-rise, but I don't think they can get the zoning law changed. A couple of years ago they talked about making apartments out of the floors and renovating the building."

"That's not a bad idea," Barry said, enthusiastically, computing rapidly the number of apartments they could have on each floor and fishing into a pocket to produce his card. "Here's my card. Tell the owners to give me a call if they're interested in financing the plan."

"Are you crazy?" Elsa said to Barry. "Do you actually believe he's going to give the owners your card and do himself out of a place to live?"

"No, I will. I'll tell them to call you," Billy said, taking the card without looking up. "We'll be okay," he added.

Once outside, Billy said goodbye and watched Elsa and Barry drive away. As he returned upstairs he wondered what had happened to Elsa to make her so mean-spirited. She still looked beautiful, but she seemed bitter. He tried to imagine what would have happened if they'd stayed together, then put the thought out of his mind.

As soon as Elsa was gone, Vidamía breathed easier. That first summer, the time spent with them, was the best of her life. Vidamía recalled the evening she and Cookie had met her girlfriend Rima and Rima's mother and they'd taken the train down to City Hall and gone to a loft over on Greenwich Street to someone's by the name of Alice with paintings against the walls, but a nice place. Going up the stairs, they heard what sounded like an engine. When they got inside everybody was sitting on the floor and Cookie said, "Be cool, they're chanting. Just watch Rima and her mother."

You had to take off your shoes but it didn't bother Vidamía because her feet were hot. They sat in the back and pretty soon someone gonged a bell and everybody started reading from a little book, and Rima was showing Cookie how to follow the words and Rima's mother was showing Vidamía, but she still couldn't follow. After about twenty minutes they started chanting, but she couldn't make it out too well, except at the end, when it started to sound like what Rima was saying, which was "*Nam Myoho Renge Kyo.*" What she liked most about the evening was the way they explained that a person could change his destiny; she didn't know whether she believed it or not, but it made her think of her father.

When it came time to ask questions, she raised her hand, just as she did in school.

"Yes," the man sitting up front said.

"Suppose a man," Vidamía asked, "was a fantastic musician, a pianist, and lost a couple of fingers, could he still be as good a pianist if he chanted those words?"

The man, who looked like he worked for an advertising agency because he was wearing a suit and had blue eyes and sandy hair combed neatly, replied that a person could change his karma by practicing this Buddhism. She found it hard to believe. It sounded like magic. However, she read everything she could on the subject. She tried chanting the words, but after a while lost interest and began reading Dostoyevsky, who Lurleen said was a great Russian master of literature and must be read if one wants to understand the depth of the human spirit, which sounded extremely noble to Vidamía.

As she thumped on the string of the bass, Vidamía couldn't remember why the chanting had come to mind, but slowly she recalled the second time she'd gone to the meeting. Someone had spoken of a Buddha that had five sets of eyes. One of those sets of eyes was the capacity to see suffering and be able to remove that suffering from other people. She had prayed fervently, chanting the words over and over, that her father would be able to play the piano again.

She now saw that whatever had been the matter when Mr. Butterworth looked at her father, something beyond the loss of his fingers had made her father suffer. She watched him sitting on the amp, strumming his guitar, his gaze far away, his eyes brilliant in color but also feverish in their intensity. She wanted desperately to ask him what had happened but didn't dare. The entire matter frightened and angered her. And then it dawned on her that her father was hiding. Whatever had taken place had made him take cover, and from his hiding place he was looking out, fearful of emerging, ever watchful that an intruder might come along and flush him out. As their rendition of "Sweet Georgia Brown" came to an end, she felt her wallet stuck in a front pocket of her baggy jeans, placed there at the suggestion of Cookie, who had explained the dangers of not taking precautions.

"Girl, they got pickpockets down in the subway," she said. "I've seen 'em work. They just kinda bump up against you, excuse themselves and the next time you go looking for your *chavos . . . nada. Nacariles del oriente.*"

Cookie talking in Spanish always cracked Vidamía up. If you closed your eyes she sounded like her girlfriends chattering away in both languages. Touching her wallet, within which this year there had developed a plastic safety net, woven finely and connecting her life through her mother to a number of accounts, she decided that she had no choice but to take the next bold step in her plan to help her father come out of whatever place he was hiding. For the first time in her life she saw that the wealth which she was becoming aware of could be put to good use and maybe it wasn't so crazy when she'd gotten the idea at her birthday party, and then, walking around the East Side with Janet Shapiro, they'd seen a showroom with antique pianos, and she'd thought maybe her father could play again.

Second Movement

The Horizon

18 The Offering

What transpired on the evening of July 18, 1988, the day Vidamía Farrell became sixteen years of age, created the impetus
for a further change in Billy Farrell's life. Vidamía's mother, ever
on the lookout for ways of displaying her wealth, made such a
big production out of this milestone, that her husband, the ever
unflappable Barry López-Ferrer, nearly went into cardiac arrest
when, a month later, he received a combined bill of more than
$30,000. Through her considerable managerial abilities, the one-
time Elsa Santiago of the Lower East Side, who on Saturday afternoons years earlier would shop for $12.95 bargain dresses on
Orchard Street, but who now had charge cards for every possible
department store, including Neiman Marcus in Texas where
from time to time she was expected to materialize for confer-
ences on the aberrations of the human mind, shopping not being
one of them, concocted an enormous party with an eight-piece
rock band for Vidamía's friends and cousins her age, who num-
bered in the dozens, some even flown into La Guardia Airport
and limousined to Tarrytown, N.Y. as a demonstration of Elsa's
goodwill, and who came from as far away as Sheboygan, Michigan, and Grand Forks, North Dakota, the Santiago clan and
their conjugal relatives having dispersed to all corners of the
great US of A to drive the good people of the heartland cuckoo
with geographical curiosity. Did you say Costa Rican? No, I
didn't think you had.

For the entertainment of the younger cousins and the sons and daughters of adult friends of the family who had been invited, Elsa hired mimes, a dancing couple on stilts, magicians, face painters, puppeteers, folksingers, and clowns, many of whom performed with great flair, having partaken of large portions of *Cannabis sativa* and other supposed talent enhancers, substances that eighty-five percent of the adult guests present swore on stacks of pancakes, if not Bibles, that they never used, though nearly ninety percent of them found themselves walking leisurely in the woods behind the López-Ferrer property, where they happened to run into someone who offered them a toke, and one has to be sociable, and political correctness is one thing but good manners is something else altogether and what's it going to hurt anyhow, the kids are probably already stoned so let's just relax this one time. Cough, cough.

The grounds of the Santiago López-Ferrer mini-estate with its manicured lawns, tall hedges, and stately trees, purchased four years prior at the cost of $1.2 million, but valued now at nearly $2.5 million, had been festooned with garlands of colored lights shaped like pineapples, bananas, and papayas. All around the terrace there were burning torches set on poles. The theme was Hawaiian, and everyone had been forced to bow their heads to have their necks encircled by one of the 600 leis, which, whenever shed, Elsa forcibly replaced. Everywhere you looked there were discarded little umbrellas and tiny hula-girl swizzle sticks. The rock band was even forced to do a version of the "Hawaiian War Chant," which they totally submerged beneath extremely vigorous drumming, whining guitars, and a bass whose owner was convinced that his responsibility was to emulate the surf. It was the most awful music anyone had ever heard, and even the teenagers, generally tolerant of anyone with an electric guitar, were in total agreement that whatever it was they were playing, it sucked big time. Vidamía took full responsibility for her mother's dubious taste and apologized profusely, instructing the band to ignore her mother for the rest of the evening.

On the spacious grounds behind the house Elsa had a huge candy-striped tent erected and beneath it she had the caterers place tables and chairs where the children and adults, family and friends who came to celebrate this glorious milestone could stuff their faces with broiled shrimp, rib steak cooked on open grills on the spacious back lawn, baked potatoes of nearly epic size, enormous bowls of salad, twelve different dressings, expensive sausages and cured hams, roast pork legs, roasted chickens, ducks, geese, baked turkeys filled with five different varieties of stuffing, including *hayabonga* stuffing made of maize and veni- . son, the latter, according to Elsa, a Native American delicacy concocted circa 1638, although most likely part of some Upper West Side, P.S. 75 myth, from the short time when Elsa had essayed being a student teacher before deciding that psychotherapy was her true calling.

For those with a less adventurous palate there was rice with chicken, rice pilaf, rice with pigeon peas, rice with sausage, and pork fried rice, along with no less than a dozen Chinese dishes, including ginger chicken, beef with broccoli, and egg foo yung. There were also military-size vats of potato salad, macaroni salad, cole slaw, corn on the cob, and, on baking pans and large pots, pastas, or *pasti*, as Elsa referred to them, choosing to employ the Italian plural, necessary in this case since there was lasagna, linguine with white or red clam sauce, meat or cheese ravioli, baked ziti, spaghetti and meat balls, and rigatoni. Of breads, not counting rolls, pita, bread sticks, crackers of 112 varieties, there was nearly 225 yards. Sherbets and ice creams of more than forty flavors were dispensed from a genuine antique soda fountain situated in a gazebo at the north end of the front lawn. Additionally, there were fourteen types of cakes numbering fifty in all, and a hundred pies in ten different flavors to complete the repast.

To liquefy and allow to pass more gently this gastronomic excess through the nearly 500 or so human bodies in attendance, Elsa ordered twenty kegs of beer, one hundred bottles each of red, white, and rosé wine, forty cases of assorted sodas, and a bar so vast that the following morning there were no less than twenty people scattered all over the property in different stages of alcoholic stupor. To handle the egress of this culinary and libational extravaganza, a dozen Port-o-Sans, painted in agreeable pastel colors, had been placed strategically several yards into the wooded periphery of the property.

To add greater drama to an already chaotic situation, a number of children were lost for a time, most serious of all an eight-year-old, one Ralph Maggiore, grandson of a reputed member of the underworld. The boy was later found sleeping comfortably in the den of a neighbor's house a quarter of a mile away, a bottle of scotch whiskey capped but a good quarter of it consumed by him, one had to assume, given the state of disorientation from which Master Maggiore was suffering upon being discovered by the local authorities in the middle of his slumber.

As one might expect, sexual indiscretion was rampant, although generally undetected or ignored. Such was not the case involving Diana Sandoval, Elsa's married cousin from Urbana, Illinois, a runner-up in the Miss Teen Urbana contest a dozen years prior, found panting and in an advanced state of undress with Bobby Renoir, who was the tennis coach at Baldrich Academy, the prestigious prep school in Connecticut. The person who surprised the passionate couple in one of the upstairs bedrooms was none other than Lynn Renoir, who taught history at Baldrich and was Bobby's wife of six months.

But by far the most outrageous occurrence of the evening was the one in which thirty-eight-year-old red-haired Kendra Higgins, heiress to the Lindwell fortune and recently divorced from Dick Higgins, the Washington, D.C., lawyer, first stripped to her birthday suit, except for the plastic lei around her neck, and, drunk, and pathetically roly-poly, having failed miserably Jane Fonda's several attempts to civilize her considerable *avoirdupois*, got on the three-foot diving board of the swimming pool and began doing one cannonball after another until, exhausted, she lay heaving on the diving board, bending the thing in a dangerously moving arc that made it look as if poor Kendra might at any moment be catapulted skyward over the bathhouse of the López-Ferrer property. Fortunately, the *affaire* Higgins took place well past midnight, after all the children had been taken home or put to bed in nearby motels or in the house proper, and only a few dozen people remained awake at the party.

Elsa had called it a coming-of-age party, a turning point in a young woman's life, stressing this over and over so that Vidamía felt as if perhaps she wasn't having a birthday but was about to become part of some ancient ritual like she had read about in a book on the Mayans, who sacrificed virgins, which she still was, and was getting tired of being, but wasn't about to give it up just like that to one of the idiots she went to school with.

Relatives and friends brought presents and kissed her and invariably every third one said the same idiotic thing, "Sweet sixteen and never been kissed." Vidamía kindly gave them her most sincere smile and said thank you and felt like running somewhere and hiding, she was so embarrassed. Bobby Kirkland, who was supposed to be her boyfriend, spent the entire night trying to get her to go with him into the greenhouse so he could feel her breasts. God, he was such a pig. One of the cutest boys in school, but his hands were always sweaty, and whenever he came near her he insisted on pushing his thing against her thigh. And when they were alone, he was always taking her hand and pushing it down on his erections. One time when he was driving her home, he stopped, parked the car, and just like that took it out and took her hand to make her touch it. She refused, and he became rough and began wrestling with her. When she punched him with all her might in the chest, he stopped. That was the last time he'd tried anything like that.

Her birthday had been a nightmare. At one point her mother made an announcement over the loudspeakers, her voice coy and sensual due to her advanced state of inebriation:

"ATTENTION. ATTENTION. SINGING OF HAPPY BIRTHDAY AND CAKE CUTTING. FIVE MINUTES. SINGING OF HAPPY BIRTHDAY AND CAKE CUTTING. FIVE MINUTES. PLEASE BE READY FOR CAKE CUTTING AND SINGING OF HAPPY BIRTHDAY."

Five minutes later, on cue, the hugest cake anyone had ever seen was wheeled out on a Puerto Rican Day Parade float–like structure pulled by a golf cart festooned with more Hawaiian paraphernalia. The cake was in the shape of a volcano, and atop it was a ridiculous-looking Barbie doll–like figure in a corny pink hula skirt, her plastic hips undulating, mechanically or electronically, slightly offbeat, to some sensual Polynesian melody.

Vidamía, seeing at least eight shades of red, was handed a knife. Wishing to perform ritual Japanese disemboweling of her person rather than go on with the profound humiliation which her mother had chosen to inflict on her, she took a deep breath and raised the knife. With a downward swing worthy of a master samurai, she slashed through each of the three tiers, nearly toppling the comfitured structure and, in the process, spraying her mother and a dozen other people with icing.

With her mother whipping the crowd into a frenzy, they all insisted that Vidamía open every present. Some of the stuff was hilarious. At least two negligees. One of them was from Victoria's Secret. She immediately guessed it was from Rita Monteleone, whose mother worked in the boutique. She looked over and Rita just arched her eyebrows, closed her eyes, and pursed her lips, like, who me? She loved Rita, but boy was she wild. She was seventeen, had her own car, and had already had one abortion.

Vidamía must've spent an hour opening presents. Cliff and Cookie had come, and they fit in with the other kids just fine. Cliff was so handsome and tall that the girls wouldn't leave him alone, even though he was only thirteen. Eventually, toward midnight he had come up to Vidamía and pulled her aside behind the gazebo.

"Yo, Vee," he said. "I need a thing, but don't tell Cookie. She gets all plexed about me being too young and whatnot."

"A thing?" Vidamía said. "What thing?"

"You know," Cliff said, not batting an eye. "For protection."

"Oh, oh. A thing thing."

"Yeah," he said. "Use it or lose it."

"You're too much. Who is she?"

"Secret," Cliff said, his smile just on one corner of his lips. "I don't kiss and tell."

"Yeah, I bet," Vidamía said. "Go up to the house, to the third floor. The room next to the bathroom on the left is a guest room. Look in the drawer of the night table."

"Thanks, sis," he said and reached down and pecked her lips.

Eventually, Vidamía found out that he'd taken Clare Gorman, the older sister of her friend Linda and a sophomore at Sarah Lawrence, into the woods and made it with her. Clare, six years older than Cliff, was so taken with him that, whether truth or hyperbole, she made sure that word got around about what a good lover he was. At least three other girls claimed that they'd had relations with Cliff that night. He denied everything, but when Vidamía and Cookie checked the night table the entire box of Trojans that had been there was missing.

But if Cliff was the sexual sensation among the teenage crowd, Cookie made an impressive fashion statement. Dressed in baggy khaki pants, pink Reeboks, and a sleeveless Mets shirt with no bra, she was the ultimate East Village homegirl. When she walked in, her blond hair cut short and spiky and wearing three earrings in her left ear, one on her nose, black lipstick, and cutoff gloves with spikes on them, the other kids couldn't believe it and everyone was whispering how cool she was. When Vidamía introduced Cookie as her sister everybody was overwhelmed and when she crossed her arms over her chest, turned her head to one side, pursed her lips and said things like, "That's really dope, man, but I gotta book," heads nodded in assent and continued to bob as she slid through the crowd like she owned the place.

After everyone danced and ate and drank punch, which had been spiked by Ronnie Goldstein and which her mother overlooked, winking at her as she tasted it, her mother once again made a big announcement. After a drum roll, she called Vidamía up on the bandstand. In front of everybody, Elsa Santiago López-Ferrer, onetime denizen of the lowest circle of Lower East Side society, that of street vendors, presented her daughter, with all good intentions but with as crass a show of materialist arrogance, a gold credit card with a line of credit of $25,000, as she announced proudly. Her face burning with shame while the admiring upper-middle-class coreligionists cheered madly, Vidamía accepted the gift dutifully and as dutifully kissed her mother and stepfather. When she crossed back over enemy lines and got to safety, Cookie saw her expression and inquired.

"Oh, it's this damn card," she said, slamming it down on a table.

"Girl, what you worried about?" Cookie said, picking up the card and examining it. "Yo, now you can really party. Damn, if you wanna go off to a concert in Europe, like in Amsterdam or London, you just book and don't have to be messing around trying to get you a token to get on the subway and whatnot. UnderstandwhatI'msaying?"

"Sure, Cookie," Vidamía said.

Not a second elapsed before Vidamía's chagrin and anger were suddenly replaced by extremely rapid activity within her considerable gray matter. Ever at the ready, these neural cells emitted billions of complex electrical impulses making calculations of a monetary, geographical, and musical nature, and involving such names as Wurlitzer, Baldwin, and Steinway, until extremely quick-moving electrical impulses, traveling from neuron to neuron, produced a perfectly formed mental image of beautifully crafted wood and metal with eighty-eight black and white keys capable of producing entire countries of sound, wars and walls of epic music, choirs of angels, and myriad other magisterial phenomena. In this case, culture, given at times to understatement, has called this invention not a splendid, awesome, breathtaking, gigantic, peachy-keen, magnificent, or monumental but simply a *grand* piano, which Vidamía saw sitting in the corner of the loft where her father often sat, the sunlight streaming in from the windows, Billy lost in tragic contemplation; so that in response to her sister, she said in perfectly cadenced Rican English:

"I hear what you're saying, homegirl. And I'ma think about it," she added, each day feeling more comfortable with the patois of her summer freedom.

"Word," her sister said.

She endured the rest of the birthday party, but something began to gnaw at her. There was something else behind her father's morose nature. Having seen Billy's pain double after seeing Alfred Butterworth, Vidamía's curiosity began scratching insistently at the screen door of her mind. She wondered if perhaps she ought to speak to her great-grandfather, Buck Sanderson, and maybe also to this Mr. Butterworth, to see if they could shed some light on the matter.

19 A Road Less Traveled

The following night, after they recuperated by staying in Tarry-town, sleeping late and helping to clean up, Vidamía, Cookie, and Cliff returned home. After they had eaten supper, having brought with them a duffel bag full of Saran-wrapped whole hams, turkeys, and sundry other uneaten foods, when people were watching television or listening to music and her father had gone over to his corner to read, sitting on his rocker, his head bent over a magazine, Vidamía brought a chair over from the dining room, sat next to him, and began to brush his hair. After a few moments she asked if it was all right for her to ask him a question.

"Go ahead, baby. Ask away."

She asked him how long he'd known Mr. Butterworth. He paused and looked at her, the sadness etched in his eyes, and said warily that he'd known him a long time, and then asked her why she wanted to know.

"He seemed so happy to see you."

"I was happy to see him, too."

"He looked a little sick."

"Yes, he did. He's getting old."

"Is he as old as Grandpa Buck?"

"Grandpa's older. They knew each other down south and came up to New York together."

"Where from?"

"Memphis, Tennessee," he said and then stopped and looked up at her, smiling sort of sadly. "Why are you asking? You writing a book?" feigning the New York question, but not able to pull off the right amount of sarcasm so that she took up the joke where he'd failed.

"Yeah, maybe I am," she said, then changed her tack. "No, I really want to know what happened to you."

"It doesn't do any good to talk about it," he said, shaking his head. "You don't want to know. It was bad. I was in Vietnam. Enough said. It makes me remember, and I don't want to. Me and your uncle were in Nam. He died, I survived. Don't ask me about it, okay, baby?" he said, and began running his hand over his face as if he were trying to erase something from it.

"Sure, Daddy. It's okay."

"Thank you, baby."

"Can I ask Mr. Butterworth about you?"

"I guess so, but I don't think he can tell you much."

"But you don't mind if I ask him?"

"No, I guess not. He gave me his number and the place where he lives."

He got the number, recited it, and she copied it.

"It's up in Harlem, but don't even think of asking to go see him by yourself."

"I'm not, you don't have to worry."

"Good," he said and turned away from her. "I'm going up to the roof for a while. If Mama asks, tell her I'm up there."

"Can I go with you?"

"No, I just want to be by myself," he said. "I'll be okay," he added, but to her it sounded like maybe he wouldn't, and for the briefest moment she wondered if he ever contemplated suicide. She recalled conversations on suicide she'd heard from adults and it frightened her.

"You sure?" she called after him.

"Yeah," he said, and chuckled. "I'll be fine."

She wanted to respond, to say okay, but suddenly, as if she were again peering into that window long ago, when her mother and Barry had stopped off in the desert to get water and she'd looked into the abandoned house and knew that some type of horror had taken place there, she sensed for the first time the depth of her father's agony.

They had been driving through Texas or Arizona, maybe

New Mexico, and they had stopped at an abandoned farmhouse, the land around it barren and flat, three-foot-high tumbleweeds blowing over the dusty ground. She had gotten out of the car while her parents tried to get a water pump in front of the house to work, her stepfather's ever present fear of running out of water in the desert urging him to replenish their reserves at every chance. She had gone around to the back of the house and, through a broken window—one shutter missing, the other hanging from one hinge—she looked into one of the rooms. The room was nearly empty except for an old metal army cot and a chipped porcelain chamber pot lying on its side. In the corner of the room near the cot she saw an animal about the size of a cat, but furrier, scurry by, raising the fine dirt from the floor. Like an arid mist the dust rose in the sunlight streaming into the room so that she was at once frightened and fascinated by the golden particles dancing in the band of sunlight painted against the dark shadows of the room.

The scene, the barrenness and desolation, suddenly frightened her and she ran to the Mercedes, opened the back door, got in, and, as if she were very cold, curled herself up in a corner of the leather-upholstered backseat and closed her eyes against the vision, knowing that something horrible, a murder, or worse, had taken place in that room because it was a room from which every last vestige of humanity had been torn forcibly away, leaving the house bereft, a place absolutely forsaken and without hope of redemption from the sins it had witnessed. When Elsa and Barry returned to the car with water, they sensed something was the matter and asked her. Stoically, she said she was cold, and they turned down the air-conditioning.

Her helplessness at not being able to reach her father angered her. And she knew with increasing certainty that there was more than her uncle's death troubling him. She would have to fight with even more ferocity to rescue him.

Billy turned away from Vidamía, climbed the stairs to the

roof, and sat under the summer sky, the lights of downtown Manhattan like a firmament so that he imagined traveling, if not in space at least in time. He recalled the events of the afternoon a week ago when he had observed the slight black man, carrying his saxophone case, blend into the midday subway crowd, fading from sight and being replaced by images of years past when he was a boy feeling safe with his parents at Christmas or going over to his grandpa's and playing the piano for hours, never getting tired or bored except sometimes in the summer when the Yankees were playing and he'd rush from the piano to turn on the television set. Unable to control his thoughts, he recalled the intrusion of death into his daily life. Often while he sat watching Mantle bat or watched Whitey Ford—to whom he was often compared, being they were both blond and left-handed—pitch, he returned to his father's death, over and over, as if there were within the truncating of that human life a truth to be learned that could only be understood by reliving every aspect of the tragedy.

As he sat, his mind traveled from his father's death to Joey's, back and forth over the same terrain like an animal trapped in a confined space, skipping entire years to fix his glassy-eyed stare upon the two incidents which, when examined, left him powerless. As he did each day, Billy tried to be very still and think about the day's events. He'd heard something like this at a Veterans Administration counseling session, and he thought that by concentrating on the recent past he could somehow replace the horror of the distant past. He had become aware that if he recalled the recent past it would trigger other memories that had nothing to do with the two deaths, and thus he hoped to minimize their power over him.

He returned to the events earlier in the week and attempted to place them in order. He recalled Hortense belting out "Lover Man" in the background and could feel himself chording the changes on the guitar and picking out little riffs in back of the rhythm; he had been hiding in the background of his mind, running to the pleasure of lovemaking, feeling himself growing aroused as he sat playing his guitar and watching the open area of Lurleen's dress beneath her arm as she held the accordion, the curve of her breast making the sensation of his organ grow stronger, so that he pressed down on it with the guitar and immediately felt the same Catholic-school guilt he'd always felt, wondering always what it would feel like to "jack off," like Tollerson and McPherson called it in their southern twang when they were in boot camp.

There were times when he just lay in the dark after making love to Lurleen, lost in her, knowing that he was a lucky man; her body and the texture of her skin the same even after seventeen years; watching her closing in on forty and beginning to age so that she was no longer the pretty little blond girl whom he had gone down home, as his grandfather said, to find in 1973; everything strange then as if he had stepped into another world, the voices of the people sounding like Bobby Hammond except that Bobby was from Arkansas; Bobby had been hit by a sniper; got him in the shoulder, but the bullet traveled downward, deflected off a rib, and went through his heart. He had lain there looking so peaceful that everyone thought he was kidding, but after a few minutes you knew he wasn't, because he had that indefinable look of eternal languor which the dead affect.

He had traveled anxiously but trustingly, with Grandpa Buck Sanderson on the train from New York to Cincinnati and then southward on a bus through Kentucky and into Tennessee, feeling small again, his grandpa telling him how the family had been in central and western Tennessee for hundreds of years. They had then taken another bus, getting off in the middle of a country road, riding in a pickup, and finally going on foot up into the hills, his heart pounding each time he looked out into the distance of the blue and green canopy of the Tennessee forest, the vegetation thick enough so that he had the expectation that choppers would come rising up from the horizon, the persistent beating of the rotor blades like a deathly promise of the firepower they carried, even if it was supposed to be friendly fire, because sometimes the bullets got awfully confused and plumb forgot who was friend or foe, as Tollerson said, but instead of those noises hearing the insistence of ax hitting wood and being able to laugh inwardly at the joke of hearing a different kind of chop-chop sound.

Later on, after the first few nights, relaxing a bit more, and as evening closed in feeling the chill of the night even though it was summer, and smelling the wood smoke, the rivulets rising in the distance from little clearings in the woods, and along with the smoke the smell of cooking, rich and inviting, and as if carried by the wind someone twanging away on a banjo or tuning up a fiddle. Lurleen was a distant cousin, maybe fourth or fifth, related through Grandpa's brother Frazier Sanderson's wife, who was a Meekins, he had been told, as if everyone were not related anyway, they had joked, and laughed good-naturedly.

Time had gone by so quickly, nearly twenty years, and he could still see Joey's face clearly. One minute he was laughing and the next clutching at his chest and then his body suddenly moving wildly and then falling against him, his own mind blacking out for a moment but then coming to and finding that he was sitting in the rice paddy holding Joey's nearly lifeless body. They shouldn't have gone through the clearing at that time of day. Even though the perimeter had been secured and no Viet Cong had been in the area for weeks, he knew better but hadn't listened. This is what he had told Elsa back then when he'd gone looking for Joey's family, and now, almost twenty years later, he still wasn't sure what had actually happened.

Some mornings he woke up convinced that nothing he recalled had occurred and that something quite different had taken place and he was indeed totally responsible for Joey's death.

Not because they had gone in that direction, but as if his part of the responsibility had been more than simply a choice of what path to take in order to get across the clearing. Perhaps he'd had an argument with Joey and had shot him. Whenever he thought of that possibility, he rejected it outright. They were the best of friends. They had met at Camp Pendleton before they went over to Nam; by chance their bunks were next to each other, both assigned to the same "B" Company; liking one another immediately, Joey reminding him of Victor Delgado, who played second base at Hayes and had made two unassisted double plays when Billy was pitching one day against Mount St. Michael's. He'd thrown a four-hitter and the following week in the school newspaper there was a big headline: LEFTY FARRELL SHUTS OUT THE MOUNT. It was the last game he'd pitch, because the following year he just couldn't stay away from the piano, the music pulling him further away from baseball. At school people stopped calling him Lefty.

After the business at Ruby's he forgot totally about baseball and began smoking grass; lingering inside the school under the pretext that he was studying until pretty much everyone had gone home and then crossing the Grand Concourse and going into Franz Siegel Park across from the school and sharing a joint with Matty Halligan and his cousin Sean every day; sitting up there watching Yankee Stadium in the distance and laughing, imagining what it would be like being high and standing up at the plate trying to hit a Goose Gossage fastball. Today Matty Halligan was a junkie and Sean was up in Greenhaven for selling almost a kilo of cocaine to undercover cops. At that time none of them had had much contact with girls. He was sure that was still the case with Sean.

He recalled his first experience with a woman. At first he thought that he should've never asked Pop Butterworth about the place. Butterworth wouldn't discuss it for almost a month, deflecting all inquiries as best he could, until he relented.

"I got urges, Mr. Butterworth," he'd said one time. "Strong ones."

Butterworth laughed.

"Shit, my man's grown up and he want him some pussy. No way, son. Your grampa'd have my neck for sure. It was okay for us to carry on when we was young men down in Memphis, but he wants you on the straight and narrow."

"Please, Mr. Butterworth, I won't tell anyone. Just take me there."

"I guess it can't hurt none," the old man finally said. "You're ready to burst. You got money?"

"I got a hundred from playing the two weddings last weekend."

He'd ended up with a small, very curvy, dark-skinned black girl by the name of Effie Gilliam. She was from Philadelphia and had a deep, smoky voice. She laughed all the time, like everything in life was a joke. He was scared and nervous and shot his load as soon as he was inside. The girl had giggled and he'd said, resolutely, "Again!" He'd paid another twenty-five dollars and she'd excused herself, douched, came back, washed him off and got him ready. This time he'd gone at it, working up a sweat and making the girl grip him in her arms and move her hips to his rhythm, which is what Pop Butterworth said he had to do. "Make them earn their money, son," he'd said. "They whores but they recognize when they being loved by a real man and when it's just somebody jacking off." He went back every week. After a few dozen times he enjoyed walking in and asking Ruby for Effie Gilliam and then going upstairs to her room and going crazy as soon as he saw her, loving the touch of her skin and the chocolate-brown color, day and night yearning for her full lips and sweet tongue, even telling her that he'd go to work on a real job and take her away from the place.

When she was with someone else he'd tried going at it with Petra, who was a tall, olive-skinned, melancholy girl who looked as if she were going to cry. Petra had some kind of accent, and Ruby Broadway advertised her as being from a very respectable family in Europe. She was in fact a Romanian-Polish girl who had been abandoned by her aunt and uncle after her parents died in a fire and had grown up begging around the Bronx; doing little tricks starting at the age of eleven; twenty-five-cent handjobs for high school boys, fifty cents for a blowjob, and a dollar for fucking; sleeping in the horse stables over on Park Avenue in East Harlem in Manhattan and letting the old Italian ragman finger her every night as she fell asleep. Or else Peggy Oppenheimer, an Irish-Jewish girl with blond hair who spoke Yiddish and kept the Sabbath; neither one, nor the other five girls who worked at Ruby Broadway's, including the other black girl or Lucy, the Chinese girl, made him feel the way he felt with Effie Gilliam.

"My God," he once told her, "you're only seventeen years old. You should be in high school, learning things."

"And you're seventeen, so you can't be telling me what to do, white boy," she laughed sweetly, pushing him playfully.

"Please, Effie."

"What? You jealous? You jealous that I be giving my pussy to somebody else?"

Her teasing him made him want her even more.

She drove him crazy, and made him reckless and wild, his playing of the piano so different that it made people stomp their feet and laugh and cheer and want him to do more of the same. He was sure he'd never love anybody ever again. One day, coming home from jamming at a loft in the Village, he told Pop Butterworth all this. His friend and mentor looked at him and shook his head.

"Son, she's a whore. What's the matter with you? That's what she does for a living. You play the piano and she fucks men. She doesn't give one good goddamn what happens to you. All whores are the same when it comes to men. They make you feel good, but that's it. They don't cook, they don't sew, they don't mend, they don't sweep, and they certainly don't take shit from men the way most regular women do. That is, when they're working regular in a house, although if they gotta work the street and got some pimp they love they behave just like most women and carry on like they was honest-to-goodness house-wives bitching and moaning about not having enough money for groceries or some fool nonsense like that."

Billy hadn't said anything, but was angry at Butterworth for nearly a month. It didn't matter, because his mother found out and marched up to the house on MacQuesten Parkway, demanding to see the owner. He had to stop going to the place, being banned and unable to see Effie, feeling ashamed and hating himself for a while; not forgiving his mother for interfering in his life, having then to wake up in the middle of the night to wet dreams. He suspected, and later confirmed, the fact that Butterworth had finally come to Buck, and Buck had gone to his mother. Maud had gone up and raised hell with Ruby Broadway. Of course, that's how they became friends, even though Ruby, her hands on her hips, had told Butterworth at the time, "I'm not going to lie to you, Pop. I was two seconds away from smacking that big-tit white bitch for getting into my business, and telling her to suit herself if she thought it was better for her son to beat his meat." All this Butterworth later confessed.

Thinking back to meeting Joey at Pendleton had made him recall playing baseball at Hayes and those late-spring days when the wind blew from the south and brought the smell of summer. The diamond's grass was new and sweet and his muscles felt strong and taut and his soul invincible. But thinking about good things always triggered the horror of his time in combat. Almost twenty years—1970 to 1988—and he still saw the gaping wound in Joey's chest. It was as if he had no right to feel joy in his life. Seeking respite from the torment, his mind still returned to the raw wounds in Joey's chest and how he had died. There had been some sort of strife, but it hadn't been with Joey. He was positive of that, and yet lately the doubts came more frequently and with greater intensity. As if his life didn't have enough suffering with his missing fingers and Joey's death, he still saw his father's face clearly and saw a picture of him lying on the barroom floor, his body twisted so that his arm looked as if it were part of the barstool. His only release from the agony was the memories of Lurleen when they first met.

It was all so crazy, his life and everything about it; lying there and listening to the music in his mind now that Vidamía was in his life, not quite knowing if the two were connected. She had come in and taken his hand, the ugly hand, the claw, the three-finger monstrosity, had taken it in her own delicate one and walked him slowly but briefly out of the dark. Whenever he ducked back into the tunnel, she'd follow him through the dark fog that was his memories and bring him out again, making him feel safe in the presence of someone kind and good, aware that this precious daughter whom he had somehow created out of his despair understood his life.

This past year she had grown into her womanhood so that he could see in her the stoic strength of her grandmother Ursula, who had remembered him and was happy to see him when he'd gone to pick Vidamía up at her apartment for their first Christmas together four years ago, the old woman, small, weak, and sickly, actually hugging him and crying, saying how glad she was that he and Vidamía had been reunited. She said she wished things had been different when Elsa was carrying Vidamía and he'd gone back to his family, softening the situation for Vidamía's sake, even though back then Elsa had been brutally cruel and gone inside her bedroom to get his things together.

"Elsa should've been more patient," Ursula said. "She should've let you see the baby."

He'd said it was okay, not to worry. The girl also reminded him of the fragility and conviviality of his own mother, Maud, her other grandmother; all of the wonderful qualities of the two women blended into this wonderful child.

Lying on the roof of the building, lost in his musings, he recalled once again meeting Lurleen.

"This here's Lurleen Meekins. Her people are from right here, but she's been going to school to the west over near Claymore, near the Missouri border."

"How do you do?" she'd said, reaching for his hand, which he kept in the pocket of his jacket. Lurleen lowered her head and smiled shyly when he said hello. The attraction had been instantaneous. She was dressed in a simple, silk-like green-and-blue dress with flowers that outlined her small breasts and waist. Below the curve of her waist she had strong hips and buttocks. Her belly was flat except for a slightly rounded part that made him want to touch her so that he immediately could imagine going up into her, which was the first time he had thought of such things in more than a year.

Because after living with Elsa those four months when she was pregnant with Vidamía, there had been no one else except some nights he woke up after a dream and the stuff had come out of him as it did in high school; and now as if inside of his being something had awakened and insisted on being sated he felt a deep hunger for Lurleen, who had graduated from college but looked to be about sixteen, though she turned out to be twenty-three, her nose pugged a little like a fighter's and her lips thick as if she were black, although he knew some black people had thin lips, and her blue eyes large and animal-like, fearful and innocent at the same time, and when she smiled her teeth were perfect, and, a little nervously, she kept pushing her lank, ash-blond hair behind her ears; all of her appearing to him magnetic, drawing him closer to her.

He had remained at his granduncle's home three weeks, walking in the woods day after day with Lurleen; some days going into town and sitting at the soda fountain drinking Cokes; she driving the beat-up pickup; people nodding seriously at them; men and boys carrying shotguns and birds or one or two furry animals slung across their backs—rabbits, coons, possums—grinning at them and pointing at their game and then at their mouths and then at him and themselves as if to say that they'd shot the game special for him.

There were times when he didn't know whether it was possum or coon he was eating, but he ate everything they put in front of him, the cold mountain air making his appetite blossom; the people sometimes stopping on the clay roads and watching them as they walked or drove by; the young girls smiling happily at them because evidently the word had gotten around that cousin Lurleen was engaged to be married to a boy, a cousin from New York, grandnephew to Frazier Sanderson.

"That's right, the banjo maker's brother."

"Harley Sanderson who people say played music with Negroes in Memphis?"

"That's right, Frazier's little brother, Buck, who went to work at the mill in Claymore and then went to Memphis around 1929, '30?"

"Yep, that's him."

"And he brought his grandson to hitch him up with the smart, pretty little Meekins girl?"

"Yep, he sure did."

"Reckon that boy better have his britches on good if he's gonna get hitched to that little gal."

The marriage issue had not yet been decided, but Grandpa

Buck returned to New York after the first week, reassured that his grandson and Lurleen stood more than a good chance of hitting it off and making a go of it. The end of the third week found Billy sitting with Lurleen in a clearing, the two of them bundled up in sweaters and sitting under a blanket even though it was June, watching the sky and its thousand stars and she pointing out to him the different constellations, like Ursa Major and Ursa Minor, Big Bear and Little Bear, though commonly known as the Big and Little Dippers, and focusing on the brightness of Polaris, the North Star, and then others like Cygnus the Swan and Pegasus the Flying Horse, and telling him that if she had a few more years to continue studying she would want to study astronomy, but in the meantime she was reading and studying on her own and did he know that the signs of the zodiac were based on constellations and only Libra wasn't based on a living thing and did he believe in God.

He thought a moment and then said he did and she nodded and in the light of the small fire they had built she said she didn't know what he was going to think of her and she truly didn't know what she believed; that in college she had studied so many wonderful things and had read many books but that there certainly was some sort of order, although she didn't know whether there was a being that had a hand in it all, if he knew what she meant. And he said Creation was a bit confusing to him, but that looking up at the sky it was pretty hard to believe that things just happened.

They went on like that for a few more minutes and then sensing that he was uncomfortable talking about God, she asked him about New York, because her Aunt Crystal told her that he was a wonderful piano player and could he tell her about the clubs because she'd heard records at her aunt's house and wondered about places like the Village Gate and the Village Vanguard and Boomer's and Birdland and the Five Spot. And had he ever seen Sonny Rollins or Miles Davis or Thelonious Monk?

Talking excitedly about the people and places as if she knew their music and histories intimately, Billy finding out later that Lurleen knew more about jazz than most musicians or disk jockeys from reading Crystal Bailey's *Downbeat* magazines.

He thought about the city and said that he no longer played the piano and held up his hand in the light of the fire so that the three-fingered silhouette looked like the head of a snail, and that, sadly, not too many people wanted to listen to jazz anymore. It's all rock and roll now. And rhythm and blues.

And then, as if he had no control, he was in one of his flashbacks that plunged him back into the midst of the horror, and he was suddenly in combat, the automatic fire clicking steadily and his machine gun blasting away at the undergrowth; hearing the bullets crash into the vegetation but never knowing whether his own bullets had torn the flesh and bones of the enemy; dreading going forward later to count and dispose of the dead and tend to the wounded; the voices on the radio calling for air strikes and people yelling for medics and in the background copters and mortar fire and beyond it all as either a memory or an actuality the bombers heading north to strike at the enemy. He tried fighting it, repeating to himself that he was safe in America again, safe in the bosom of his homeland, which he knew and loved and had fought fiercely for, without resentment, knowing that his father would have wanted him to, but the woods and the darkness beyond were an illusion and he was there in the jungle again.

As always, beauty intruded into the ugliness of his life to make things more difficult. He recalled sitting in an English class at Hayes and Brother Cassidy reading in his Irish accent out loud a Robert Frost poem that talked about a well-traveled road. All he could remember were two lines: *Two roads diverged in a yellow wood, And sorry I could not travel both*. Billy never told anyone in the Marines that he had musical training because he was his father's son and had chosen a road less traveled, so instead of playing in the Marine band because he knew several instruments, he went beyond infantryman's training and asked to be assigned to advanced infantry school so that he'd ended up at the front, carrying a machine gun and there would be no doubt about his valor, hearing the bagpipes of his childhood over and over whenever fear threatened to overwhelm him; the pipes, skirling, far away across the sea, in the mist, through the heath, keening their deadly music so that in the marrow of his bones his life urged him forward to his duty. Later, when he returned downstairs to the loft, he found the book of Frost poems and read "The Road Not Taken" again, and understood it clearly, and the sadness of his life overwhelmed him, and he sat in his rocker, frozen, paralyzed, as if by sitting very still he could erase the past.

20 Choices

He had once seen maggots feasting on a dead Viet Cong, the body bloated and the silvery worms making what was once his face alive as they fed, so that he thought, experiencing a high fever, a malarial ailment that still attacked him periodically, that the maggots were making not motion but noise as they quivered in unison, the snarelike rhythm too rapid and complex for him to follow, but definitely a sound rather than movement. And that's how he felt whenever Lurleen or anybody else wanted him to talk about the music. Immediately the maggots began quivering and setting up in his brain a steady buzzing sound which vibrated on some infernal frequency too delicate for a human to follow and yet alluring enough in its brilliance to make him imagine that he could play at that rate, the music and his talent and his knowledge of himself entangled in the quivering of the maggots.

What was there to talk about? He had gone and that was it. And now all his boys were gone. McDougal from Texas was gone as was Bobby Ingram, from Aliquippa, Pennsylvania, who was going back to play football at Pitt, cause he was the baddest mothafucka who ever played cornerback and not only was he gonna be All-American at Pitt, but he'd go in the first round and of course be picked by the Steelers, my man, because they'd traded somebody in order to get that first pick, which was yours truly, Robert J. Ingram. Riddled by machine-gun fire so that his entire chest had caved in, the fatigue shirt shreds. And Joey Santiago gone. All of them, memories. And he with his three fucking fingers, one each, so that every day he'd have to remember his boys. And they wanted him to talk about it. But all Lurleen had asked him about was the jazz clubs and he couldn't understand why that reference had triggered the malady of the flashbacks.

He recalled walking with Mr. Butterworth and the old man talking to him about how good a musician he was and he ought not to waste his life by going in the army and him saying "My mind's made up. I gotta go." So what was poor Butterworth supposed to do? It was what his father would've done. His father had been decorated and he loved his country. Billy would have gone into the army but that didn't seem like much of a commitment, so it was the Marines. Semper Fi. But if he'd gone into the army he wouldn't have met Joey Santiago and perhaps Joey would be alive and his own life might've turned out different. Or would it have? Maybe he'd be dead like his father, but maybe Joey'd be alive. But he wouldn't have met Elsa and there would be no Vidamía. It was all crazy.

His father hadn't shied away from going into that bar and confronting the guys holding up the place. In 1967 Tom Rafferty, his father's partner, had refused to tell him how his father had died, even though he was then seventeen and could handle the knowledge. He'd asked him straight out: "What happened, Tom?" The two of them sitting in a booth at Clancy's out on Long Island, where Rafferty lived, and where he'd taken Billy to get him away from the city. His mother said he was definitely sent back to white school for retraining with Tom Rafferty, working at the marina with Rafferty's brother, Martin, learning all about boats and helping out when they took people fishing out into Long Island Sound. Tom Rafferty even pushed his daughter, Fiona, on him, urging the two of them to go for walks or giving him money for the movies, but pretty as Fiona was, he wasn't interested and neither was she, confiding in him that she liked an Italian boy from New Hyde Park, but that her girl-friend, Christine Toomey, really liked him.

Christine was even prettier, a small girl, with brown hair and brown eyes and a very clear complexion for a girl sixteen years old. The only trouble was that she was a hockey nut who spent most of her time talking about Jean Ratelle and the New York Rangers, but who nevertheless found time on several occasions during that summer to French-kiss with him for long periods of time so that he had blue balls because she always let him play with her breasts and her wonderful Catholic-schoolgirl pussy, the liquid flesh throbbing with each caress that she'd taught him; explaining exactly, almost clinically, how she liked to be touched, and then with uncharacteristic gentleness giving him prolonged, extremely satisfying handjobs as they lay in the summer dark-ness of the Oyster Bay shore, collecting the powerful spurts of his life in delicate little handkerchiefs which she would discard with articulate ceremony, but not before mockingly christening them: Rose, Michael, James, Margaret—good solid, Irish Catholic names she'd say—and told him toward the end of the summer that she'd let him do it to her because she really liked him, but, if she could be permitted some honesty, he'd probably end up on the job, meaning a cop or a fireman, and she wanted to finish high school, go to college, and then law school. And she did.

He had run into Fiona Rafferty about two weeks before Christmas last year when he was coming out of a hardware store on Fourteenth Street. Fiona had gotten heavy. She told him Christine Toomey was an assistant DA in Kansas City. He wanted to know if she'd gotten married and Fiona said she'd married someone in law school but it hadn't worked out. She showed him pictures of Christine looking very professional in a business suit. She was still small and pretty, but Billy couldn't imagine that she would remember their summer together. He felt a longing for the part of his life that had passed into faded memory.

That summer Billy had kept asking Rafferty about his father. "Oh, Billy, what's the use," Tom said one evening, sitting down-stairs in the finished basement with the gun rack, the bowling and softball trophies, and a plaque from the Emerald Society, and the pictures of Rafferty in uniform receiving a citation for bravery from Mayor Lindsay in 1965, and even one of Rafferty with Billy's father, Kevin Farrell, standing on Danny Rafferty's first boat, *Kilkenny*, the two of them smiling as they stood with a shark hanging between them. "Your father was a hell of a man. What's the use talking about it? Don't ask me again, son." Billy persisted, saying he had to know what happened. Rafferty finally said the two of them were riding around in Yorkville, working the 2-3 when a call came about two men with guns trying to hold up the bar on 103rd Street and Third Avenue in East Harlem. This was 1961.

"And off we went, me driving and your father telling me where it was even though I knew where the place was located. 'Turn here and then another hard right and it's right there,' talk-ing like I had just transferred into the precinct. It all happened so fast I didn't even get a chance to turn on the siren, if you know what I mean. Maybe if I had, the cocksuckers woulda taken off," Rafferty said, as if he'd just thought of the idea. "We screeched up to the front of the place and everything was still and you knew something was gonna happen. It was the Estrella Bar on Third Avenue. I think it's a drugstore now. The old precinct was around the corner on 104th Street, so you figured this had to be a couple of hophead yahoos to pull a stickup so close to the precinct. I tried holding your father back. I said, 'Hold on, Kevin, let's wait for backup,' but he was out of the car even before I had stopped. 'Cover me,' he said and he was gone. I got out and he waved me forward and then he went inside the bar. I could hear the squad cars heading for us, but everything happened too quick. I don't think ten seconds went by before I heard four shots and then the two Puerto Rican fellas came out, their guns in their hands. I blasted both of them. One bought it right there and the other one's paralyzed for life, if that's any consolation. Luckily, the ones I got were the ones who shot your father. About ten squad cars showed up fifteen seconds later, their sirens and lights going like crazy."

"I know," Billy said. "I've read the papers a hundred times."

"When I went in, Kevin was still breathing a little bit, but the life was gone out of his eyes," Rafferty said. He ran a hand through his graying hair, his eyes bloodshot from drinking. "God, I hate telling you this. You shouldn't have to hear this stuff, Billy. Let him rest, son. Let him rest. He was a good man and I'm sorry he's gone, but it doesn't do any good for you to know, and I'll probably lose sleep over telling you. I've gone over it a thousand times since it happened, thinking what the hell I could've done to stop him, and I can't think of anything other than maybe if I hadn't gone to work that night, he wouldn't have felt so confident going in like that with me as backup."

He lay on the roof, as he often did in the summer, staring at the black vastness of the sky, and realized that he was in the year

1988, reminding himself that he was in the present. And as he was thinking of this with everything in his mind dark and somber, he recalled standing in his cheap church suit next to his mother and the camera lights going off and the next day in the papers seeing himself on the front page, holding his mother's hand and standing tall like his grandma Brigid had said, but knowing he had wanted to cry, and the headlines saying HERO COP BURIED.

His only respite eventually had been to lose himself in Lurleen, night after night feeling her drawing closer to the core of him; taking his hand and placing it on her breast so that her wish to have him trust her made his heart expand each time and take her deeper into his life until one night, when Cliff was almost six months old, at the mere touch of her softness he was suddenly sobbing violently, this time not for Joey but for his father. She held him and in the darkness he heard himself howling as if he were a wounded animal, hearing a primitive pain emanating from his soul, so that he got a glimpse of himself small and saw young Billy Farrell at age eight, again walking with his father, hand in hand as they entered Yankee Stadium with the crowd; everyone talking and moving purposefully, not shoving but aggressively, as New Yorkers do, not meaning any harm but sometimes getting on your nerves, like Grandpa Buck said; walking up the long ramp and then heading for their seats, entering the walkway to their box seat on the mezzanine and hearing the sharp crack of a bat as it struck the ball, a sound so distinctive that Billy, possessing perfect pitch, heard notes, and eventually he evolved a system that was almost foolproof for determining how hard a ball was hit from the sound it made on the bat—the sharper and higher it was on the scale, the harder and deeper it had been hit—so that later on when coaches found out that besides being able to pitch well he could also hit, they wanted him in the lineup and put him in center field, where he employed his theory with considerable success; later on hearing television commentators talk about Duke Snider, Mickey Mantle, and Willie Mays, and indeed all great center fielders being able to take off after a ball at the crack of the bat. He recalled going up the ramp to their seats and seeing just the sky and then the beautifully trimmed grass and red clay field and the players on it; standing spellbound, yelling, "Daddy, Mickey, Mickey, number seven, Daddy!" so loud that people turned to them and laughed and the great Mantle even looked up and smiled that big Oklahoma-country-boy smile and waved at him so that his father just shook his head and lifted him up and he felt safe and strong in his father's arms as he took off his Yankee cap and waved it at Mantle, who tipped his cap to him.

And then the sobbing subsided and for the first time since he had been wounded in Nam he saw a melody line traveling from his soul, deep inside his being, through his veins, and to his hands and fingers; running around the melody, repeating the phrases up and down the keyboard and far away, his left hand, almost as if it were separate from him, chording the blues, "You was my baby, but you ain't my baby no more; you was my baby, but you ain't my baby no more; you cheated me and left me at the door."

It was like he was walking around dead inside, waiting for death to find him, to call him and say, "Bill, you got to go now. Grab your coat and get your hat, leave your worries on the doorstep." And you saying, "Man, I ain't going yet. Let me play one more tune, man." And death saying, "Shit, man! Quit jiving around and let's go. We sposed to be out the city before dawn." And you sitting down at the piano and playing the first few bars and then running through the changes, letting the piano sing, "It's quarter to three, there's no one in the place except you and me." And death bugging you like you're supposed to listen and you say "Fuck it" and just sit there and play the blues.

Mrs. Wilkerson always told him not to let anybody tell him he couldn't play the blues cause he was white.

"They tell you that, just laugh at them. Just laugh easy like and tell 'em, 'Man, it ain't about if I can play the blues. I be the blues and when you hear me play you gonna wish pain had stayed home and not visited your sorry ass.' You understand what I'm saying, son?"

"Yes, ma'am," he'd say, knowing he could trust her and she wanted him to do well.

But the blues had come, and he just lay there wishing he were not alive; not that he was dead but that he didn't have to face life every day and that he had never gone to Nam and seen all that he saw because now all he could think about was his poor father and Joey, all shot up, the life gone out of them, their bodies broken and useless and there he was, alive but equally useless. And it had been all his fault. There was no getting away from that.

Seeing Butterworth earlier in the week had opened him up even more to remembering. And as he strummed the guitar, and the children and Lurleen were into the music, he recalled being back in the hills in Tennessee again when he'd gone to court Lurleen and he remembered that in the enormous darkness of his despair he understood faintly that Lurleen had been sent to him by God even if she said she didn't believe or wasn't sure about His existence; understood that she was like a safety line to life and he was suddenly kissing her fiercely, passionately wanting her from the depth of his life so that in the cold mountain air she helped him undo his belt and guided him ever so gently, sensing that this first time he would be violent out of his anguish; already caring deeply for him and unconcerned that her first time with a man would be out in the woods under the stars and as a matter of fact being thankful that it had been so romantic so that when they were joined and he was lost in the pleasure, she experienced a strange sort of satisfaction that wasn't sexual but more akin to the maternal emotions she was to feel later on from giving birth to his children. When it was all over and they lay huddled in the cold he thanked her and ran his hand through her hair and then asked her if she'd like to come and live in New York.

"It's real strange but I think you'll like it. It's tough and beautiful, like you," he said sincerely, unaware that his words were clumsy.

That remark made Lurleen laugh and she snuggled closer to him. That was the extent of the proposal. Three days later, with Lurleen's family coming over from Claymore, they were married by a preacher, who was also a cousin; the next day, carrying in two suitcases her clothing and books, and under her arm a dulcimer; and he carrying his own suitcase and a small accordion and a fiddle in its case, which Lurleen also played. His cousin Frank drove them all the way to Chattanooga, where they got on a Trailways bus and began their trek back to New York, staying the first month at his grandparents' and then finding their first little apartment with the bathtub in the kitchen, down on the Lower East Side.

Down there no one bothered him. With his disability check he was able to pay the rent and buy some groceries and once Lurleen was settled in and found out New York City had a shortage of teachers, she went and took her examination and was able to substitute in a junior high school in Brooklyn. After a few weeks returned home crushed by the condition of the children, telling him they had been so damaged that she felt helpless trying to teach them.

"Billy, they hate so much," she'd said. But she hung on for a while, eventually getting transferred to a school in the neighborhood, doing what she loved most, which was teaching music to children, but unable to work too long because Horty was due.

Saturdays they'd ride the subway way up to the Bronx and then cross over into Yonkers to visit Grandpa Buck and Grandma Brigid. His mother, Maud, would come over and they'd have a cookout in the back, and neighbors would visit and

Grandpa got out his banjo and Lurleen her fiddle and he had no choice but to tune up the Gibson and off they'd go playing blue-grass and the neighbors, New Yorkers through and through, laughing, whooping it up, and dancing like they was mountain folk, instinctively recognizing the strains of the pieces from old Irish tunes, their subconscious carrying centuries of ancient music.

He thought again of seeing Butterworth the previous week and knew there was something wrong with him. As the band wound up their rendition of "Bill Bailey," he reached into the front pocket of his bib overalls and removed the address Butterworth had given him and looked at it. He was no longer on 145th and Riverside Drive. He was down near the north end of Central Park, in Harlem. He'd have to go and see him, even if it was dangerous for white people, as everybody said. He hadn't seen him for nearly twenty years and remembered him as old but healthy. The man who had embraced him sounded sick. What-ever it was, it had to be serious for Butterworth's voice to be so raspy.

21 Conjuring

Alfred Butterworth walked feeling two kinds of pain. One was the same dull pain that followed him from the time he rose early in the morning until he could again lie down. He knew the pain was there, but the medication deadened it and he was able to function, to travel downtown and put on his uniform and listen politely as the students and professors and administrators asked for their floors and he delivered them, up and down, listening to them talk about literature, history, philosophy, science, mathematics, psychology, sociology, and anthropology, which made him think of Charlie Parker, who had wanted him to score for him up in Harlem. He'd told him he wasn't going to do it because horse was fucking up Bird's life and Charlie had that young white girl, Candy, who sang a little bit, to score for him. Once in a while the students talked about music, all different kinds of music, but very seldom about jazz. When one did, he'd smile inwardly and look at the young man or the young woman and, if there weren't too many people in the elevator, he'd ask politely if they played music. No was usually the answer, but they said they collected records or tapes and were able to talk about different musicians and their recordings. And then once in a very great while one of the students said he played and if he wanted to come down and hear him jam with the other students, he was welcome to drop in. Twice, by chance, he'd been asked if he played and each time he'd said, "No, I just like listening to the music."

There were times when he'd go to lunch and he'd pass Folk City when it was on Greene Street and there was a blues player appearing there, people like Lightnin' Hopkins or Sonny Terry and Brownie McGhee and he'd tell himself that he'd like to go see them, but at the end of the day he'd get on the train and get back up to Harlem. Once home he didn't feel like going back downtown to watch people listening to music after what happened with Billy Farrell before he went off to the war. He felt responsible for the boy's decision, remembering his subsequent embarrassment and Miles not saying anything, but basically turning his back on him; and then when the record was released, hearing the pianist Miles had finally chosen when Billy didn't show up for rehearsal because it was his duty to serve the country—Chick Corea or Joe Zawinul, he wasn't sure, but both fine pianists who did great work with Miles, but maybe Billy would've been just as good, maybe even a little better. He wanted to explain that Billy had been drafted, but Miles wasn't having any of it, muttering things like "dumb mothafocka" and "white fool" and now Billy's daughter called him up and wanted to know what had happened to her father. She was sure a good-looking girl, sharp, and it was obvious that she loved Billy. She looked a little bit like him around the eyes and mouth, but she wasn't from the same mother as the other ones, that was obvious. She told him that her mother was Puerto Rican, and he'd started telling her about playing down on the island with Machito but figured she wouldn't know what he was talking about. He agreed to meet her, and she got to the school just as he was coming out of the building.

"I'm sorry to take up your time, Mr. Butterworth," she said.

"That's all right, miss."

"Vidamía."

"Oh, yes. Vidamía," he said, savoring the way she pronounced it. "Vidamía Farrell. That's sure a catchy name."

"Thank you. Do you want to sit in the park?"

"That'd be fine," he said, feeling the pain but not wanting to let on and inconvenience her.

They sat on a bench and he told her how talented her father was, how truly impressive he was at playing jazz, but that he was also a very moral young man, very strict about duty and that even though he'd had an opportunity to play with the great Miles Davis, he'd gone into the Marine Corps and had been wounded in Vietnam.

"I know it might be difficult for him to play now, but he could at least teach people," she said, desperately. "He won't even talk about it and gets nervous if even the word 'piano' is mentioned in a film or television. Sometimes he'll hear a piano in a film and just get up from his chair and go out. When Mama— when Lurleen . . . his wife . . ."

"I understand."

"When Mama plays her accordion he refuses to look at the keys. That's what she told me. And I watched him and it's true.

Even pictures of pianos make him nervous. I read somewhere that when somebody's had a shock, things related to the shock trigger memories and flashbacks and it makes the person remember the experience that caused the shock."

"That's what we used to call being shell-shocked."

"They call it post-traumatic stress disorder."

"Sounds more serious than just shell-shocked," he said, honestly.

He apologized for not being able to help her more and said the person she ought to ask was Billy's grandpa, Buck Sanderson. She shook her head and said that he'd been very helpful. Butterworth coughed, feeling the awful rattle in his chest and stood up, almost bending over from the pain. She asked if he was all right and if she could do anything, but he said he was fine and they walked out of the park. He turned to go west to the Sheridan Square station, and she once again thanked him. He nodded and continued walking.

White people had hurt him and disappointed him a whole lot but he didn't hate them, just couldn't understand them real well. Their attitudes made him uncomfortable. Not every white person was this way—certainly not the people around the music. This girl was certainly no problem. Just like Candy Donovan, who was sweet and kind, poor thing. Billy's mother and grandmother were certainly fine white people.

He wondered why he didn't feel rancor against white people as others did. His other pain had to do with his failure in the music that he loved so much, but he couldn't blame white people for that. Thirty years he had worked at the university, running the elevators in the Main Building, seeing students come and go, their faces bright and eager, their eyes filled with that wonderful light of youth. Some even returned and taught there, and others passed into memory.

These days it took him forever to walk from one end of the park to the other, and as he waited for the light he wondered how many years he had left. He should've gone to the hospital before now, and he should've stopped smoking the damn cigarettes and cigars a long time ago.

"How long have you had this cough, Mr. Butterworth?"

"Oh, a week or so," he'd said, lying, not wanting to admit that it had been nearly three months.

"Well, you have a very bad case of bronchitis. I'm going to write out a prescription, but I suggest you quit smoking."

"Not even a cigar, doctor?"

"No, not even a cigar."

He reached into his pocket and lit a cigarette as the light changed.

They all knew him. All the professors and the deans. And each of the presidents.

"Good morning, Dr. Oliva."

"Good morning, Alfred."

"How's it going, Dr. Peters?"

"Very well, Alfred. How are you?"

"Pretty good, sir. Thank you very much."

And none of them knew about his connection to the music. None of them knew that he had played with the greats, had stood with Paul Gonsalves and Clark Terry going over charts at rehearsals with Ellington's band, had played with Lionel Hampton and Count Basie and Fletcher Henderson's band in the thirties. He and Russell Procope and Ben Webster.

And he had known Billie Holiday, and her daddy, Clarence, who played banjo with Fletcher's band back in the thirties. God, he could still see her and often woke up from dreams in which she had been performing and after she was finished, she came to him and time stopped, and there was nobody else except him in her company. But that hadn't been the case and everything had turned out bad for him. He should have stayed with Florence Baines, who loved him and wanted to set up a home with him and didn't care that he was on the road nearly all the time. "I'm just happy working at the hospital and thinking about you," she'd tell him on those hot summer evenings when they sat in Morningside Park, talking about things. Then they'd walk through the tree-lined streets of Harlem brownstones and return to her apartment and she'd give him a glass of lemonade and then they'd make love, her body like silk and her quiet passion filling him with enormous pride in his manhood.

She was a big, kind woman, not very attractive to look at. Folks joked around and said she looked like she was Louis Armstrong's sister. But Florence Baines was warm and generous, and in her eyes he could do no wrong. Even when he'd gone off with some other woman for a while, he was able to come back to her, apologizing for hurting her, and she sitting quietly listening to him, the pain clearly showing in her eyes so that he was reminded of being back down in Alabama when he was a boy and watching the look on his sister Melinda's face when she found her puppy dog ripped open, thinking a coon or a panther had come in the night and done it.

Butterworth recalled his youth once more and thought about making love to Florence Baines. There was something about Florence he remembered vividly and still admired. Her smile was wide, and her even, good strong teeth sparkled. But all he ever did was compare her in his mind to Lady Day, never mentioning Billie, but like a ghostly vision, the sensuality of her face and voice were always there, interfering with his relationship with Florence. More than his failure as a musician, his thwarted love for Billie Holiday made him feel like a failure in jazz. To everyone at the university, he was just an employee of the school who came each morning at seven o'clock and ran the elevator until four in the afternoon, taking periodic breaks for meals and bodily needs. His walks through the Village brought back memories of jazz clubs and the life back then, but he didn't allow the thoughts to take root.

His life at the university became everything. He loved being at the school and basked in the energy of the students, always on the move somewhere, to a class, a laboratory, a tutoring session, a test, a date, a meeting with a professor, or lunch, and he insisted that they all call him Pop. There were mornings when he couldn't wait to get to the job.

"Where would you like Pop to take you, young lady?"

"Fifth floor?"

"Fifth it is."

"Good morning, Mr. Butterworth. How are you doing?"

"Very well, Professor Oliva. Eighth floor? Pop'll take you right up, sir."

Professor Oliva had been there almost as long as he had and people were talking about his being the next president of the school. Who better? Homegrown, and Pop didn't know anybody who loved the school more than Dr. Oliva, except maybe himself.

Back then Butterworth would rise early in the morning, walk up the hill past Broadway and Amsterdam Avenue and then down the hill past Convent Avenue until he got to Saint Nicholas and then had breakfast at the diner near the subway station. Eggs and grits with whole wheat toast. No fried meat. Strong coffee with sugar and milk. No cream. Some days he had wheat cakes with a little syrup. He always bought the *Herald Tribune*, the *Daily Mirror*, and the *Daily News*. Now only the *Daily News* remained. Then he'd head downstairs to the subway platform and wait halfway down the stairs, between the two underground levels, like some people do, waiting for the A or the D to arrive, and either race back up for the one or continue downstairs for the other. More recently, he would wait on the first platform even when the train below was approaching, the effort of going down the stairs too taxing of his strength.

The ride downtown was always a pleasure. Winter or summer, he loved his departure from Harlem to venture out into the city. Leaving the safety of Harlem was like going on an exploration. Often, riding the train he'd hear in his mind Betty Roché singing "Take the A Train" with the Duke Ellington Orchestra. His time with the orchestra had been brief. He'd thought of getting a Walkman and listening to music while he rode the train or walked around, but he knew he'd feel foolish. He was too old for all that nonsense. It didn't matter. He could hear the tunes in his head and hum them and that was enough.

He was nearly to Sheridan Square when he realized that his mind had drifted back to those times when he was a boy back down south. What had made him think of all that? Was it the girl? There was something about her that made her seem familiar. Of course she was Billy Farrell's daughter, but there was something else. Who did she remind him of? That was it, he thought as he began going down into the subway station to wait for the Number 1 local to take him to Ninety-sixth Street, where he could get a seat on the Seventh Avenue express. A few years ago he saw this actress on the *Dick Cavett Show* who said she was black. That her father or mother was black and the other parent had come from Norway or Iceland, someplace up north in Europe. He got closer to the television set to try to figure out if this was a joke, but the young woman was earnest and she talked with a little southern tilt to her words. What was her name? Lana, Lina. Something like that. She had an Irish name. McCarthy. Lina McCarthy. She didn't look any more black than Ava Gardner, who this girl Vidamía looked a little like with her big eyes. But the more he looked at the actress and the more she talked the more he could see that it was possible that the actress's daddy was a Negro. With this other young woman, the Negro was all gone from her looks, but still something was there, and that's how it felt being with Vidamía. And then he recalled why he'd been thinking about being down south again. Just then the train came and he got on and found a seat. He immediately dozed off, not quite sleeping but still remembering his life.

His sister, Melinda, was sixteen years old, but slow and nearly blind, so she couldn't do much to help their mother except husk corn or shuck peas or beans, but not much more. She was eight years older than him, and he loved her because she was so beautiful and kind, her skin smooth and the color of pumpkin pie, but she couldn't read or understand and the only thing that meant anything to her was animals, which she loved to hold and pet. "Let me hold the rabbit, please, Alfred, please. The rabbit, the rabbit, the rabbit," she repeated over and over until he brought her a rabbit and she held it tight to her breast, her eyes closed and her cheek next to it.

He had no memory of his father, Clarence, who died in an accident in Mobile, caught between a barge and a pier on the gulf, his body so crushed that they buried him first and then brought word to the family. He was only a year old when his father died. For his mother it was as if misery had moved into her home. No more than six months after word came that her husband had died, Melinda climbed a tree to look at a bird's nest and fell. Alfred's mother had found Melinda under the tree, out cold in a pool of blood, her head cracked open like a melon and her eyes rolled up into her head, her tongue hanging out like a dead animal's. She picked her up, and, carrying both him and Melinda, walked a half a mile to her sister's house, left both of them there, and ran to town for help.

The year was 1918, and before she was able to convince a doctor to help her, Melinda was nearly dead. She had returned with the doctor three hours later. By this time their aunt Louisa had managed to stop the bleeding, clean up Melinda, and give her a little liquor to keep her heart going. She had fed the girl some soup, which she ate hungrily, and then Melinda closed her eyes and went to sleep.

When the doctor arrived, he asked that the child be woken up immediately. He examined Melinda, shaved the back of her head where she'd been hurt, cleaned out Melinda's scalp wound, and sewed her up. He asked her questions, but Melinda just looked at him and smiled dumbly. The doctor checked her limbs and they all seemed to be functioning. When he examined her eyes, he frowned and then nodded several times. Before leaving he said that there had probably been damage to the brain and that for the next two days she was to be awakened every three hours, no matter what, to make sure she didn't go into a coma. He prescribed some powder for the pain and left.

Aunt Louisa's husband, Buford, put Melinda on the wagon and brought her back home. For the following week her mother watched Melinda, taking care of her, feeding her and making sure she was comfortable, talking to her and asking her questions, but Melinda would simply look at her and smile weakly. The following week she recognized her surroundings and their mother, and even said a few things, but it was obvious that something horrible had happened inside her brain, because she spoke haltingly and as if she were two or three years old. More distressingly, she couldn't see well and for the next six months she banged into furniture and fell as she was going out of the house.

Her mother cried and prayed but Melinda didn't improve. Convinced that there was a curse on her, she began seeking release from the torment by going to a conjure man who went into a trance and said somebody had put a spell on her. What she had to do was first of all find a Blood of Christ plant, mix the roots with sugar, spice, and bluestone and wrap the whole thing in red flannel, wear it around her neck and this would bring her peace of mind and keep everyone safe since whoever this person was wanted to destroy her family. She gathered up the roots, mixed the sugar and spice, and dutifully got herself a small piece of red flannel that her sister Louisa cut from her husband, Buford's, red long johns, putting a patch down on the leg and explaining that he must've ripped them on a nail in the outhouse. The cure worked for a while, as she began to feel tranquillity come into her life. One morning, however, she woke up itching to beat the band. When she opened her eyes there were ants all over her. Yellow jackets, wasps, bumble bees, and a couple of birds were flying around the house, all of them trying to get at the sugar in her pouch. She then went to a roots woman, who said it seemed people were trying to run her life and she should get the leaf from a Ten Fingers plant, measure it with the middle finger of her left hand, then tear the leaf off, wrap it up and keep it in her pocket. This, the woman said, would give her control over anyone she came across. It helped calm her down for a while, but Melinda didn't improve much, and she began once again to despair.

Eventually, she traveled across the border into Mississippi to see a woman that people said could cast out spells. When she arrived at her cousin Rachel's house it was dark. She ate and went to bed but couldn't sleep. The next day after breakfast she and Rachel went down a dusty road, cut through a cornfield, across a fallow stretch and past a few shacks where some Negroes lived, and then entered the woods. Rachel took her through the grove to a house in the darkest part of the forest where the air was cold and the light of the sun barely penetrated the shadows. Inside the house, sitting on a rocker, was the woman.

"Cornelia, this here is Miss Lulu," her cousin Rachel said. "Miss Lulu, this is my cousin Cornelia from Branch, across the border in Alabama."

"Morning," said the old woman.

"Morning," his mother mumbled.

At first sight his mother had been frightened because she thought she'd been brought to see a white woman and she was a witch. She heard of white "granny women" who worked as midwives and did magic and killed babies to feed to the Devil. She protested but Rachel pushed her forward and said not to be afraid. As she got closer she saw that the woman was old and wrinkled, most likely over eighty years of age, but she had clear blue eyes and straight white hair and was indeed whiter than any woman Cornelia Butterworth had ever seen. For a moment her knees buckled and she nearly passed out. And then the woman spoke eight or ten words, but his mother didn't understand them and thought perhaps she was a New Orleans Creole and was speaking French, but Rachel said she was speaking African and Indian magic words and was calling on their spirits to come and help her. His mother's fear was so great that her bladder gave out and she felt the urine running down her leg.

The woman wrinkled up her nose, sniffed the air, and coughed.

"Stop that," she said.

"Yes, ma'am."

"Rachel, take her to the outhouse and let her finish passing water out there. If she's got anything else to pass, let her do it in the outhouse. What is the matter with that child! Didn't nobody ever teach her how to behave with folks."

When she got outside his mother was shaking and wanted to know why Rachel had brought her to a white woman.

"She ain't no white woman," Rachel had said.

"Yes, she is. I ain't blind. I seen her."

"I'm gonna repeat it and I just want you to get ahold of yourself and stop running your mouth like a crazy person. She ain't no white woman. She is Miss Lulu. She is a Negro, just like you and me. What's wrong with you? Why I'd be bringin' you to some foolish ole white woman? Just go in there and finish doing what you gotta do and stop this nonsense. You're in enough trouble as it is."

"But how come she so white?"

"I don't know and I don't care. The woman do roots and cast

out spells and heal people and animals and cure folks of love troubles and lay on hands and everything else you can imagine, and folks round here swear by her. She ain't into no sanctification or pleading with the Almighty, either. She just fix you up as good as new. They bring her people crazy as a crossed goose and they come out meek as a lamb. She's a medicine woman and can cure anything if you'd just shut your mouth and listen."

"Is she a albino?"

"No, she ain't no albino. Has she got red eyes like a bunny rabbit?"

"I ain't never seen no Negro with blue eyes."

"Well, live a few more years, honey, and you'll see a lot more than that. Now go in there and hurry cause I ain't got no time to be standin' around listenin' to foolishness."

When she got back inside she knew she wasn't going to do any such thing because she was shaking worse than before, but at least she didn't feel like she was going to go in her pants.

"Whatcha 'fraid of, child?" Miss Lulu said, in a clear voice.

"Nothing, ma'am," his mother answered.

"Then you's a fool cause they's plenty o' things to be 'fraid of. Whatcha doin' comin' in my house and passin' water on my floor?"

"I'm real sorry, ma'am."

"You wanna know why my skin's so white? Is that what's makin' you so skittery?"

"Yes, ma'am."

"Well, I don't rightly know."

"You don't?"

"No, I don't. My mama was a high yella gal from Louisiana, last name of Breaux, what they call a Creole octoroon, which means that she was one-eighth black. Breaux. That's with an X, but pronounced Bro. Marie Solange Breaux from New Orleans, Louisiana. My daddy's name was Rolando Mendez. He was a gambler, met my mother in the French Quarter and brought her back to Biloxi. Set her up in a fine house in the back bay of the Gulf where there was a colored section. I don't remember him too well because according to my mother he ran off to Texas with James Bowie. Most likely he went chasing after a Mexican woman. He was a handsome, coffee-colored man whose father, Price Mendez, was the son of a Spanish grandee and a beautiful redheaded Irish woman from Atlanta. Some say she was a high-priced lady of the night, but when folks is jealous they'll say any ole thing. His mamma was a high yella gal by the name of Tillie Blake and her mamma's mamma was the daughter of an African Gitchie gal named Delia that come over from Georgia, spoke hardly any English and worked over at the Butterworth plantation."

"Butterworth?"

"That's right. What's the matter now? You look like you ready to pass water again."

"That's my husband's name. My name. Cornelia Butter-worth."

"Then we related."

Cornelia Butterworth had shaken her head over and over again.

"That can't be. You white."

"I can't help that. My daddy's grandmam's name was Eula Mae and when she was born that's the name she got. Butter-worth. From the master of the house, who was probably her daddy anyway cause she was pretty light, but a bit backward. Large, big-breasted, big-haunched woman with a Mandingo nose or maybe crossed with some Cherokee brave from the Car-olinas cause things were pretty wild back then. Folks just run-nin' around in the forest huntin' and trappin' and fornicatin' to their hearts' content any time the urge hit them and the women just dropping the children hither and yon like they was deer in the woods."

The old African white woman then explained that she had

lived part of her life as a white woman. She said that when General Lee was beginning to muster up his Confederate Army she was a sixteen-year-old girl who, because of her beauty and grace, was living at her grandfather Balthazar Mendez's home right there in Mississippi, taking care of his home and doing his books because she had always been excellent with numbers and could read English, French, and some Latin, and also play the piano from sheet music, by ear and from memory.

22 African Antecedents

After her father left, when Lulu was four years old, her mother made ends meet by sewing fine dresses and teaching music and dancing. A beautiful, cultured woman, her mother played the piano, spoke French, and also taught young ladies needlepoint, and manners. Hearing from friends in Biloxi that his colored son, Roland, had married and then abandoned such a woman who had given birth and was raising an equally beautiful young daughter, Balthazar Mendez retained a lawyer and made sure Marie Solange Breaux Mendez was taken care of financially.

During a trip to the Biloxi area to look in on one of his many business ventures on the Gulf, he visited Marie Solange and was utterly charmed by her, telling her that he couldn't imagine why his son would leave such a beautiful woman, hinting that although he was old, he was still virile, and an arrangement could be made if she so wished. Marie Solange said that she greatly respected him and valued his friendship highly and more important, as attractive as his offer was, she looked at him like her father, Henri Breaux, who had been shot helping Andrew Jackson in one of his many disputes. The old man didn't feel in the least rejected. He appreciated Marie Solange's fine intelligence and continued to take care of the young woman and her daughter, Lucinda Bernier Mendez, or Lulu, as her mother called her.

As the South was drawn deeper into the conflict with the North and the economy faltered, Marie Solange, who had several white gentlemen friends helping her, saw both her dressmaking business and the help of her gentlemen friends dwindle. She wrote to Balthazar Mendez, seeking his help, and was relieved to learn that the old man had found a woman to quench his desires, a widow in her forties who owned a property adjacent to his. He wrote back saying that an acquaintance needed someone to manage his home. His name was General Howard Dolcater from Georgia who had come west ten years prior and owned a sizable plantation near Hattiesburg and whose wife suffered from a nervous stomach.

Marie Solange wrote a fine letter to General Dolcater. Some weeks later two wagons arrived to bring her, Lulu, and their possessions to his plantation. Marie Solange was also to serve as private tutor and teach General Dolcater's two daughters, Margaret and Velma, to play the piano, to dance, and to comport themselves like young ladies since, not only had they inherited their mother's nervous disposition, but they were high-strung and ill-mannered. To make matters more difficult, the Misses Dolcater had also been cursed by providence with coarse features and bad complexions. Marie Solange hoped Lulu would befriend the two girls and influence them with her charm.

Two unfortunate things began to reveal themselves no more than a month after Marie Solange and Lulu arrived. One was that she, Lulu, was so stunningly beautiful, and had been so well schooled by her mother, that Margaret and Velma became jealous and so difficult that Marie Solange was forced to send Lulu to live at her grandfather Balthazar Mendez's home in northern Mississippi. The other was that Marie Solange and Howard Dolcater fell in love, and, as was the custom in those days, the master of the house began to cohabit with his mistress, not openly, but with the knowledge of everyone in the household.

Lulu Mendez was fifteen years old, raven-haired and blue-eyed, her skin the color of alabaster—to all appearances, a beautiful young white woman. She became the talk of the area. Her grandfather was proud of her beauty and intelligence and appreciative of her talents as a hostess. He spared no amount of luxury to create an atmosphere of well-being for her. With her consent, he explained that she was his grandniece from Florida whose father was a rich merchant from the Spanish colony of Cuba in the Caribbean Sea, come to help him out in his old age. This wasn't at all so far-fetched a story, as Balthazar Mendez's grandfather had been a sea captain from the port of Cádiz in southern Spain who had settled on the island of Puerto Rico in the eighteenth century and whose oldest son, Felipe, had come north to Florida to help a Spanish settlement fight the Seminoles, eventually traveling west and settling in Mississippi.

Young gentlemen came to call on Lulu Mendez. Many proposed marriage. She would always inform them that she was only fifteen years old and much too young to marry. As the war grew in intensity, the economic situation worsened and the stories of casualties became more horrifying. In time the wealth of the South was depleted and both plantations, the Mendez one, up north near Sardis Lake, not too far from the Tennessee border, and the Dolcater plantation further south fell into disrepair. Daily, there were stories of the atrocities of the Yankees and the treachery of the Negro slaves taking advantage of the deteriorating situation to escape so they could rob and pillage, rape the women, and sell the white children to Yankees as slaves.

"What happened to your mother? Did Negroes rape her thinking she was a white woman?"

"There was no Negroes raping anybody," Miss Lulu said. "That was irresponsible white trash telling stories. Negroes wanted to get away from plantations and white people as fast as they could. You think they was gonna linger there because of some white doxy?"

"So what happened to your mother?"

"She lived happily with General Dolcater for a couple of years. He built a house for her on the plantation, had a new piano brought from New Orleans, and came to see her whenever he had time, which wasn't often, pleased that his daughters, while they hadn't grown beautiful, at least began to act like young women of breeding. In February of '63 he left, and my mother never saw him again."

"Did he run away with another woman?"

"You sure are a mistrustful soul," Miss Lulu said, cackling deep in her chest and throat so that his mother thought that maybe she was a real Negro woman all powdered with talc. "Nah, he got himself killed up in Pennsylvania," Miss Lulu said, pausing as if to refresh her memory.

"Word came that General Dolcater had died in battle. His wife, Marjorie, was a frail woman who had just about enough strength to bear two high-strung daughters, but no more. Overcome by the combination of grief in losing her husband and being unable to manage her affairs, she hanged herself. My mother, Marie Solange Breaux, was left to take care of the house and finish raising Margaret and Velma until they could find husbands since they were not stupid young women. My mother took advantage of the benevolence of the North. She shipped the two daughters off to a college for young women in the City of New York."

"New York?"

"Yes, ma'am. New York City. Margaret married a Jewish gentleman who owned some theaters. She converted to the religion and wrote a book on travel in Europe. Velma married an Episcopalian minister and they lived in Connecticut. They wrote cards and letters to my mother for every occasion and always invited her to come and visit them, but she wouldn't go north, feeling cheated of life and love by the Yankees. She returned to her people in New Orleans and died there."

"And you?"

"Me? When the war was over I took care of my grandfather and then one day a young, very attractive man, a well-mannered Yankee soldier, came to the house and wanted to know if there were still slaves on our land. I said that I didn't believe so, that whoever had stayed on had done so out of their own accord to work the land and live off of it. He said he was working with the Adjutant General's Office of the United States Army and his name was Andrew McAlpin, a lawyer, graduated from the School of Law at Harvard University."

"And you fell in love with him," Cornelia Butterworth said.

"Yes, I did," Miss Lulu replied. "He was the kindest person I've ever met and that's what a woman needs in a man. He wanted to marry me right away," Miss Lulu went on. "I said that I had to speak to my grandfather. He said he could wait and he certainly had no problem asking for my hand. So I told Grandfather Balthazar Mendez that I wanted to marry this young man because I was crazy in love with him, and should I tell him about my African antecedents. He took my hand and said that as far as he was concerned I was his light and joy, Negro blood or not; that there was no need to confuse the young man and that I had his blessing. His attitude was totally different than most white folks. I believe that it was his Spanish upbringing.

"Andrew McAlpin wanted me to go north, but I was firm, child. Very firm. I told him I was duty bound to take care of my grandfather as my mother had charged me and that I could never break that promise. He was moved by my sincerity and said he had only a few more months of service left and then he could set up a law practice there in northern Mississippi. And he did. We had a modest wedding, and lived in the house with my grandfather. That was in '66, when I was twenty-two years of age. We had no honeymoon except to walk in the woods in the spring sunlight just looking at the new flowers and at each other. We had three children. Andrew Jr., who became a lawyer like his father and went west to Colorado. Bernard, who farmed the old Mendez plantation which my grandfather left for us when he died in 1870."

"And the other?"

"Marie Breaux McAlpin."

"Your daughter?"

"Ran off with a hunter from up there. Dirt-poor and sneakier than a polecat. People by the name of Meekins from up near the Sunflower River. They ran off north to Tennessee. Years later she came back to see me and her father and said she was sorry. She looked happy enough and brought a whole houseful of children. But then I moved back down to where I'm living and never heard from her again."

"You said you also lived like a Negro woman. You think that had something to do with it?"

"Yes, when my husband died I left everything behind. It was like I went through a big door into another world. A year later I got word from friends that Bernard had been fishing in the river and a flash storm came up, swamped the boat, and he drowned. He lived alone, didn't like the company of women much and took to staying out in the woods for long periods of time. Andrew lived too far away, and, like I said, I never heard from Marie again. I raised them to be independent and they were."

"That's very sad," his mother had said she told Lulu McAlpin, in recounting the story to Butterworth when he returned home in 1963 for his stepfather the Reverend Lockwood's funeral. He guessed it was his mother's way of telling him that she'd forgiven him for leaving after what he'd done to the reverend, but more important as a way of explaining that perhaps she had been wrong in letting her husband mistreat him. "Very sad."

"It may seem sad to some folks but ya'll got to remember that

Andrew McAlpin and I lived happily for forty-two years," Lulu had said, shooing away her concerns. "The years I spent with him were a lifetime of joy. I was the luckiest woman in the world. One morning I got up out of bed, went to the kitchen to put on water for coffee, came back to wake him, and he was already stiff, his face peaceful. That was 1908. I was sixty-four years old, feeling strong, had all my teeth still, could play the piano and see well enough to thread a needle without using spectacles. I sold some of the land, left the rest in trust for Andrew and Marie's children if they wanted to claim it. I came back down near Biloxi and built this cabin here in the woods."

"To be with Negro folks again?"

"Yes, ma'am. To be with Negro folks again."

"Why did you wanna do that after living as a white woman?"

"I'd done a lot of reading about cures, phrenology, and different things. I've always wanted to help folks and now I had no family. The few times Andrew and I had gone north to his relatives, they seemed distant and cold and you got the feeling that they didn't approve much of him having married a southern woman, which is the way they saw me. Sometimes I think that maybe if they knew I was a Negro they might've taken to me more readily. Yankee folks are that way."

"I wouldn't know, ma'am," his mother had said, chuckling as she told him the story.

"But it went beyond that," Lulu McAlpin said.

"I don't understand."

"Oh, wanting not to lie to myself about who I was."

"That you was a Negro woman."

"No, that wasn't as important as knowing that I had a connection to African people but didn't look like them. Color don't mean a damn thing to most country Negro folks. It's what you got under the skin that counts. What you got in your heart."

"How did folks take to you living here?"

"Oh, they knew who I was so that wasn't a problem. They knew I was Roland Mendez's daughter. One thing African folks have is a memory. Remember, they didn't register the birth of Negro folks so they had to know who was related. They kinda enjoyed me passing all those years and coming back. They wanted to know how it was, so I was constantly in demand to tell stories about living with white folks and they'd just laugh and laugh."

"How was it living as a Negro woman?"

"If you want to know the truth, both got their advantages and both got their disadvantages. Being white helps you live grandly. Big house, servants, a man to provide for your comfort, but your life is too damned ordered and you gotta put up with all sorts of nonsense from folks. You gotta keep up too many appearances. Living as a Negro woman you got more freedom and people don't expect a whole lot from you. On the other hand, the disdain is hard to take and you gotta work like a mule. Menfolks behave a whole lot different."

"But why would whites be prejudiced against you? You look white," Cornelia said.

"It don't matter to them. Crackers is crackers. They're mean as snakes. Once they find out you got one ounce of Negro blood in you, that's it. You're a Negro. You could be white as flour and look like a Hebrew prophet sent special from God and if they found out your great-great-great, back to the time of Noah's ark, was African, then that's it. Right there you're a Negro, no two ways about it.

"I don't want any part of that white world anymore. I'm happy right here. Nobody bothers me and I don't bother nobody. I built me this cabin all by myself, live in it in peace, grow me some vegetables, eat some and can the rest. I have a few chickens for eggs and that's it. Don't eat any meat. Never had a liking for it. Some peanuts once in a while. And lemonade. I love lemonade. No sugar. Never liked it, either. I will eat a melon, however.

The other thing I cannot stand about being a Negro is all this concern with going to Heaven and being in church singing and carrying on. Can't stand it at all."

"They say French people is Catholic," his mother said.

"Marie Solange was raised a Catholic, but she didn't like all their carrying on with incense and plaster saints and folks kneeling and kissing the Pope's ring." Lulu looked at Cornelia. "You feeling better?"

"Yes, ma'am, much better, except I got this chile at home that is awfully sick. My Melinda."

"Just tell Lulu what ails her."

"Miss Lulu, my nine-year-old girl, Melinda, fell outta a tree and cracked her head open. She ain't right and it's like she's a baby again. And last year my husband was killed down in Mobile working on the water. I prayed and prayed, but the chile just babbles on and now that I'm alone with another baby just two years old, I got to run our small farm all by myself cause my girl, Melinda, can't help any. I can't even leave her with the baby. I got a pig, a cow, some chickens, and a field of corn, and a vegetable garden. No money and no nothing. I does a little sewing, but that's it and that don't help any cause things is real bad in Alabama, ma'am."

"Things is bad all over, chile, but you sure got troubles. I can see that," Miss Lulu said. "Come on over here and let me feel your head."

And then Rachel got a squat three-legged stool and placed it in front of Miss Lulu, but his mother wouldn't move and Miss Lulu laughed and Rachel had to sit his mother down.

"No, no," Miss Lulu said, "turn her around. I don't need to see her future, that's bleak as hell. Any fool can see that. I need to see what's in the child's head, feel the bumps on her head. I need to see if there's somethin' in there that can help her get on with her life. Just turn aroun' and let me feel your nappy head, girl."

His mother sat down, her heart beating rapidly and the sweat pouring from her armpits, and then the old woman was touching her head with long, strong fingers, poking and squeezing her shoulders, until she felt real sleepy, and far away she could hear Miss Lulu asking her questions and she heard her voice answering. When it was all over she felt light and as if a great big weight had been lifted off her shoulders and then Miss Lulu was talking to her real slow, her voice sounding like it didn't belong to anybody she'd ever heard, so that later, after it was all over, she knew that Miss Lulu had done some kind of bewitchment on her.

"Now, let me look at you," Miss Lulu said, peering at her face. "You feeling any better?"

"Yes, ma'am. A whole lot better. Thank you."

"Don't mention it. But I got advice for you. Stay away from gambling men and preachers. They'll bring you nothin' but grief."

"Preachers, ma'am?"

"You heard me, girl. You ain't gone deaf on me, have you?"

"No, ma'am."

"Then remember what I told you. No gambling men and no preachers. I examined your head and you ain't got enough room in there for one or the other. Can you remember that?"

"Yes, ma'am."

"Cause if you don't, you're gonna end up in a whole lot of trouble and I don't guarantee that you'll come out of it alive. Do you hear me?"

"Yes, ma'am," she said. She got up quickly from the stool and grinned at the old Negro white woman and then felt foolish.

Rachel paid the woman one silver dollar and went off feeling satisfied that she'd been able to help her cousin from Alabama.

His mother returned home and for a while she thought that Melinda was getting better, but it was just her wishing for it to be so. As she got older, Melinda's body began to change into that of a woman and her female urges became stronger so that she would sit and play with herself without any awareness that there was anything wrong with what she was doing. This distressed his mother, so she took to tying Melinda's hands to a post near the chicken coop like she was one of the animals. Melinda whimpered the first few days but in time got used to it and sat quietly playing in the dirt with her feet. But that was after the Reverend Lockwood had shown up.

Butterworth thought again about his life and decided that he definitely should've stayed with Florence Baines and married her. She had eventually grown tired of him and his absences and infidelities and had gone off with a West Indian man who married her and bought her a house in St. Albans, Queens. One day coming back from Louis Armstrong's house, he'd seen her with her two daughters as they were getting out of a car in a shopping center. She hadn't seen him but it was Florence all right, grown broader and thicker, but still looking trusting and good. He felt a twinge of jealousy, which turned into regret, thinking that the two teenage girls, unusually pretty, could have easily been his daughters had he had more courage instead of wearing his heart on his sleeve over Billie Holiday and her troubled life.

Despite her obvious well-being, Florence still wore a hurt look on her face. The look reminded him of the image of his sister, Melinda, tied to the post. He knew that Billy, too, had that look of defeat hewn into his eyes, as if he had also seen too much futility, too much horror, too much hopelessness. Butterworth was too old and doubted that he could do much about Billy. He had tried, God knows he had tried.

As he was dozing off he heard the conductor announce that the subway train was arriving at the Ninety-sixth Street station. He got up wearily from his seat and reached for his cigarettes, then realized he was still on the train and tried to relax to counteract the pain in his chest, but all he could think about was watching Billie Holiday again, her voice low and throaty like a beautiful fog . . . *"I cover the waterfront, in search of my love."* Thinking about her eased the pain in his chest, but stirred up memories of those days, and then his heart would break for sure.

"I sure wish things could be different between us, Billie."

"They can't, baby."

"Why not?"

"They just can't, Pop. You're like my brother," she'd said.

"But I love you, Billie."

"And I love you too, honey. You're family, baby."

And now she was gone and he was alone, just walking down a long road that went on forever.

23 Banjo Blues

He was not by nature a sentimental man, but the call made him remember his youth. Just a month short of his seventy-sixth birthday, Buck Sanderson was still quite active. While he didn't think much about his past, getting a call from Billy's girl, the Spanish girl, as his wife called her, had excited him.

"Well, sure thing, darling," he'd said. "Your family's coming up for the cookout tomorrow and we can talk about it then. How's that sound? Just be sure it doesn't unsettle your daddy."

"Okay, Grandpa," the girl had said. "Horty and I will be over tomorrow early to help Grandma Brigid. About noon," she added, using Cookie's other nickname to put her great-grandfather at ease. "Bye."

Buck stood by the phone, shaking his head, wishing they'd call that poor girl something other than Hortense. Of all the names Lurleen could've chosen, Hortense was the worst. That was his grandmother's name and never had the Devil spawned a nastier old woman. She smoked a corncob pipe, ran a still, and shot her old man's butt full of buckshot when she caught him with a gal from the next county. And her husband, poor Trent Bailey, sixty-seven years old and worn out, was just talking. It didn't matter none. She was convinced he was up to no good and the minute he had a chance he'd be at that young thang like some ole hound. Hortense McLeish, or the Sheriff, as men called his grandma behind her back, otherwise referring to her as You Bet Miz Bailey Ma'am. His grandmother had once smacked him so hard that whenever he thought about it his head still rang and he saw stars. God, what a nasty woman. But Horty was nothing like that. She was sweet and funny; then again, she was a tough little critter.

He stepped out on the porch, checked the sky for rainy weather as he always did, figuring as soon as storm clouds came, his wife would begin complaining about her rheumatism. He couldn't stand listening to her, but it was worse when he had to look at her wrinkled, sad face and her gnarled and knotted fingers. He lit his pipe, holding it in his mouth in just the right way so that it didn't dislodge his upper plate, puffed on it, smelled the sweet aroma of tobacco, and sat down in his rocker.

At the age of twenty-five, Harley "Buck" Sanderson had liked thinking that sitting in the middle of a jam session down on Beale Street in Memphis, picking on his banjo while the rhythms and melodies of the different instruments were going every which way like strings of party paper falling from the ceiling, was closest in feeling to watching a woman's face when the pleasure was coming on her.

In the beginning there had been dozens of women in his life, both white and black, ladies and whores, young and mature. Eventually he'd come to New York and after a year of drifting from one lonely bed to another, he met his wife, Brigid, and settled down, which he was grateful for, because women left him weak and helpless to deny them their wishes. There were always complications in leaving one for another. His relationship with his wife had also changed, leading him to stray. He didn't like to think about this secret part of his life, his daughter, Maud, being the only one who knew about his transgression, and this quite by accident.

He was a big rawboned man with rugged good looks, his hair once blond turned white, although still thick and luxurious. But it was his eyes that set women's hearts aflutter. Brilliant blue, they looked out at the world from deep-set sockets. In the large, liquid eyes there appeared a constant plea for help, whether a need was there or not. Born in the hills of central Tennessee into perennial poverty among God-fearing people whose only relief from fundamentalist determinism was music and the independence of the forlorn, he escaped his lot in life through sheer will, some luck, and his drive to be within women, finding in them not only solace but profound pleasure.

At the age of seventeen he'd left his home in the hills to come west into the town of Claymore, where he had family, and work at the paper mill. A short time later he made the mistake of getting involved with a young woman by the name of Charlotte Randall, a schoolteacher. Her husband was a state senator who spent a good deal of his time in Nashville. After he had secured a job at the mill, Harley Sanderson rented a room from a widow who ran a rooming house. Each day, on his way home from the mill, he passed Charlotte Randall's house, and he'd see her sitting there reading. Once in a while her husband was with her, but most of the time Charlotte was alone on the porch. As summer passed and the days grew shorter, she spent less and less time on the porch, and not seeing her tore at his heart.

One day she was standing on the porch—he liked to believe waiting for him to come by. When she looked up, he tipped his cloth hat and said, "Evenin', ma'am," but softly, so that the only person who could've heard him was himself, but she nodded her head slightly and the insinuation of a smile crossed her lips. He didn't see her again until a few weeks later, when Jimmy and Bobby Tyrell, who worked at the mill with him, said they were going to be playing some music over at Silas Cummings's house and heard that he played and would he like to join them. He said it would be a pleasure, but he'd have to go by his room, get cleaned up, and pick up his banjo. They said they'd see him at Silas's house, which was a quarter of a mile past the railroad tracks.

He went back to the rooming house, took a bath, spruced himself up, and put on clean jeans, wool socks, and a checked flannel shirt against the chill of fall. He brushed his work boots and combed his blond hair, got the banjo out from under the bed, and made his way back down the street, cutting across the town square with the statue of Major General Winslow P. Claymore, who'd led a regiment of Tennessee volunteers against the Yankees near Vicksburg, Mississippi, toward the end of the war, chasing them deep into the state before being cut off, dying gallantly leading his men in one last charge.

His heart beating desperately and hoping he'd see her, Harley Sanderson hurried up the street that led past Charlotte Randall's house. He saw her sitting on the porch, staring at the dusk, her face beautiful in the light and shadow of the oncoming evening. He slowed down his pace and walked closer to the picket fence to get a better look at her. When he could see her clearly he again tipped his hat and greeted her. She smiled at him and came down from the porch to stand at the picket fence.

"Good evening to you," she said.

She was a good ten years older than his seventeen but she looked no older than he did and her smile filled him with profound joy.

"Evening, ma'am," he replied, stopping in his tracks to admire her. She laughed nervously at his wonder, pleased and dangerously flattered.

She was a tall young woman, with a strong body, pert breasts, and a long waist that descended voluptuously to ample hips, then tapered gently to full thighs and long calves. If there was a flaw to her features, it was that her nose may have been too bony and possessed a small bump halfway down the bridge, but her eyes were large and china blue, deep set, the lashes long and black, so that they seemed to be somnolent and inviting, what he later learned were called "bedroom eyes." Her lips were full and painted in ruby-red lipstick. Her hair was black and thick, tied severely in a French knot. The black hair, more like that of the native Chickasaw Indians, contrasted severely with her white skin, giving her porcelain-like complexion and cheekbones a high sheen. Charlotte was wearing a simple blue dress, a sweater, stockings, and low heels.

"Are you on the way to a dance?"

"No, ma'am. Just some fellas getting together to play a little music over at Silas Cummings's house outside of town."

"My name's Charlotte Randall," she'd said, sticking out her hand over the fence. "I teach over at the school."

"Harley Sanderson. Folks call me Buck."

"You're not from Claymore, are you?"

"No, ma'am. The hills east near Lookout Mountain, but I got folks outside of town. I gotta work to help out my ma and my pa. We got younguns." He didn't want to tell her that his father had been caught making whiskey and was doing time. "There ain't much to do up there, so I'm working at the paper mill."

"I understand."

"You ain't from Claymore either, are you, ma'am?"

"No, I'm not."

"Are you from Chattanooga?"

"No, Dyerburg. Upriver from Memphis."

"No lie," he said, excited by the news and stories he'd heard about the music played in Memphis by blacks. He wanted to ask questions but realized that it was getting dark. "I better go. Don't wanna keep the boys waiting."

"Well, don't stay a stranger, Buck."

"No, ma'am," he said, turning and tipping his hat to her, hearing the music of her voice in his mind and her beauty making him crazy for her. It wasn't anything like Louise up in the hills, kissing him and letting him feel her titties. This was something different, and as he walked he realized that he was hard and his organ was pumping up and down on its own against his jeans. He walked faster, trying not to think of Charlotte Randall. Eventually, as he got closer to Silas Cummings's house, the desire subsided and he was able to play. Everyone praised him for his mastery of the banjo.

Silas Cummings's daughters, Jean and Tillie, were good-looking girls, about fifteen and sixteen like his girl Louise Kincaid, and, like Louise, they kept grinning stupidly at him, their crooked teeth marring otherwise beautiful young faces. They'd whisper things to each other and then snicker into their hands and look his way as if they were talking about him. There were several other young girls there but none of them made the least impression on him.

When he went home that night he went directly to the outhouse, unbuttoned his pants, urinated, then held his organ. Just thinking about Charlotte made him erect. He almost began to button his jeans, but instead grabbed his organ firmly and, blocking out the stink coming at him, pulled on it several times as he imagined lifting up Charlotte's skirt and going inside of her as his brother Frazier had said he'd done to Becky Whitmore and Lynn Thurman. Frazier explained what he had to do, but he couldn't imagine, and he thought about Louise's titties all soft and imagined touching Charlotte's body so that after the fourth time he'd pulled back on his dick the stuff was coming out of him, spurting and spurting and his hips driving forward so that he nearly passed out, almost moaning from the enormous pleasure, ending up banging his organ against the wood of the outhouse. The jolt sobered him up and he quickly tried putting it back in his pants but the damned thing wouldn't go down so he jacked off again.

He laughed now, thinking about Pop Butterworth telling him about this one woman and how all he had to do was take a look at her butt and his dick got "harder than Chinese algebra." That's exactly how it was back then. It was a torment and he was always hard as steel. Billy's girl had said she'd talked to his old friend Butterworth, whom he hadn't seen since Billy came for Christmas before going to Vietnam. That was in 1968, almost twenty years ago. It was good to have friends but this one was worth his weight in gold, and he was forever grateful that Pop had looked after Billy back then after the boy's father had died and poor Maudy was on the verge of joining him. Butterworth had taken him to Mae Wilkerson's and helped him study the music. He missed Pop. The jazz scene had died off, people stopped coming to jam, and time had passed the old players by, Butterworth included. He heard that he'd gone to work running elevators downtown. He guessed not being able to keep Billy from going to war ate at Pop as well. The boy was so close and Pop couldn't convince him to stay and become Miles Davis's pianist.

It had been more than a half century, and just thinking about Charlotte made him want a woman. Why did he have to answer the kid about her father, anyway? He could've said he didn't remember, but he prided himself on his memory, still retaining the ability to play all the songs he'd learned as a boy up in the hills, where his uncle Will taught him to play the banjo. But it still made him ashamed to have to call Ruby and sneak out at night, after his wife was asleep, walking down the hill to his old car and driving over to Mount Vernon to see her. Billy's girl was a persistent little son of a gun. And pretty. God, she was a pretty little thing. What the heck was she, anyway? Billy's daughter. That made her his great-granddaughter.

He reached into his shirt for his ballpoint and on the notebook where he kept track of things that he had to do he subtracted 1929 from 1988. Fifty-nine years. He had to stop thinking about all that nonsense with women or else he'd have to go see Ruby tonight. Maybe it would all pass. It took longer and longer each time and the visits to her were less frequent, but Ruby was so good to him that the pleasure lingered for weeks.

Buck Sanderson still loved his wife, but she did nothing for him and had never been too interested in the whole matter of lovemaking, submitting to him willingly enough, but always uninvolved. The most beautiful body of any woman he had been with, but totally lacking in passion. "Brigid, what do you think about when we're doing it?" "Nothing, Buck," she'd answered. "Something must cross your mind." "I dunno. Mebbe a shopping list, or sometimes I say a Hail Mary, thinking about my poor old mother, dead all these years in Ireland." It was understandable that the girl wanted to know so much about her father. But it was one question after the other and whatever he said she was back to why Billy didn't want to play anymore. She explained that she didn't want to ask him questions because it upset him. And did he think that he would play again if she encouraged him?

Thinking about Billy made Buck Sanderson recall taking the boy down to Tennessee after he'd come back from Vietnam. Being back down there made him recall Charlotte Randall all over again. When he'd come down from the hills to work at the paper mill in Claymore, the president was Hoover, and when he took Billy down home in '73 there was this peckerhead Nixon sitting in the White House. You could tell he was an old-fashioned liar and would sink the country. And his bright, sad boy, the joy of his life, more than a grandson to him since he'd had to raise him after his father's death, but more so because here was the musician he himself would have enjoyed becoming, the boy whose long fingers were able to coax ineffable beauty from a piano no matter how simple the tune, and now he just sat looking out at the world through a curtain of nightmares, his right hand mangled and a piano making him shudder as he went by it, so that eventually Buck had the piano removed from the house after Billy came back from the war and was living with them.

It was a good piano, too, and had been played by Kenny Lyons, Pete Johnson, Sandy Gold, Iggy Marginat, and a few others on those Saturday afternoons when he was still working for the subway system and eventually was the steward of his shop, the union just starting out and the Irish lighting up the city behind the Transit Workers Union. Joe English had gotten him the job at the 207th Street yards as a car repairman after they'd met at a dance he was playing for the Ancient Order of Hibernians and where he'd also met Brigid in 1931. Joe English, Joe Morrison, George Meany, Mike Quill, Billy Burke, Tommy O'Shea, Patrick McHugh, and Serafino Machado, who he guessed was Spanish, and who got arrested with Mike Quill and the rest in 1934 for fighting the injustice against transit workers. All of them tough and smart. But it was Joe English who had helped him the most. He was from South Carolina, and Joe had liked him instantly, taking comfort, he always thought, in his own southern accent. The dreams of playing music continued, but after the children started coming and he had to feed and clothe them, he knew it was over. It was then that he took to inviting his old friends to come out and play, and they'd come up for a cookout in the backyard. The Saturday afternoon and evening music parties during the warm months, from May to September, became a tradition, and people would talk about going up to Yonkers and getting some fresh air up at Buck Sanderson's. They'd jam late into the night and nobody had a care because the Depression was over, and FDR was going to lead them to happy days again. Eventually the Second World War came and everything was somber again and there were blackouts; but as soon as the war was almost over, the jam sessions began again because, hell, all the kids were coming home.

24 Going to School

Of all the fellows who had tickled the ivory on that piano nobody, but nobody, made that instrument sing the way Billy did. Once Pop Butterworth began taking him up to the Bronx to study with Mae Wilkerson after his daddy's death, the boy had blossomed. He'd sit at the piano for hours, doing scales, playing things he'd learned and experimenting with chords so that sometimes Pop just stood admiring him as Billy curled himself over the keyboard, extracting one more ounce of feeling from the notes.

But looking at Billy sitting on the porch of Buck's house after he came back from living with that Spanish girl in Manhattan made him think that perhaps Billy's involvement with her had left him more injured than he was willing to admit. He could always talk to his grandson, but he waited until they were coming back from Shea Stadium after watching the Mets beat the Cubs, or maybe Philadelphia, at the beginning of the 1973 season. The seats were down the right-field line but it was great sitting in the late-afternoon spring sunlight and watching the young men daring time, oblivious to the ravages that awaited their bodies. God, it was a grand game. After women and music, baseball was his third love. On the way home, riding the train from Flushing Meadow, it dawned on him that perhaps he ought to try to find Billy a wife. He said nothing until they were on the commuter train at Grand Central Station and it was moving out of the tunnel on Park Avenue, the light of the afternoon fading behind them.

"How'd you like to take a longer train ride?" he'd said.

"Where to?"

"Tennessee?"

"What for?"

"Get you a wife."

"I don't need a wife, Grandpa," he said, looking out the window as the train began to cross the Harlem River. "I'm okay."

"Think about it."

"Okay."

Two weeks later Buck was reading the newspaper after supper when Billy asked him if he was serious about taking him to Tennessee. He looked at him and said he sure was serious and all he needed to do is give the word and he'd write to his brother Frazier down home and they'd start lining up those fine country gals for him to take a peek at, but if truth be told there was a distant cousin of his, maybe third or fourth, that was very anxious to meet him.

"Bright girl who plays the fiddle, so anytime you're ready we can just hop on the train and ride on down there."

"It can't hurt any, I guess," he said, "but . . ." and his voice trailed off as it always did when he didn't want to mention his hand.

"Whyn'tcha let her decide all that, Billy?" Buck said. "If she can't handle it, then that's that, but it don't do any good worrying about it, does it?"

"No, I guess it doesn't," he had said. "I got a little money saved up so maybe I could get an apartment. I was thinking about moving into the city anyway."

"That'd be fine, although your grandma and I will sure miss you," he said. "But if that's what you want to do, that's fine with us."

"Yeah, I think I'd better," Billy said. "Maybe being on my own won't be so bad."

"I can talk to Brendan Cavanaugh's son about a job with the Transit Authority if you want. You can do track work or even be a conductor and open and close doors."

"No, that's all right. I'll make do, Grandpa."

"Then I'll write to Frazier and see what he says. I believe the girl finished college."

"She went to college?" Billy said, momentarily startled.

"Now wait a minute," he told him. "Don't you go getting spooked by the fact that she's got some schooling. You may not have gone to college, but you've read considerably and you're a very smart young man. I'm sure it'll be just fine. You've been through too much to let a college education make you run in the other direction."

"You're right," Billy'd said. "I'm cool with it. I can handle it."

At the beginning of May, after he had rented an apartment on the Lower East Side, they had gone to Pennsylvania Station and taken the train to Cincinnati, then to Louisville and then a bus to Chattanooga and then on to Wilkins, where they were picked up by Bobby McAlister, a grandson of Buck Sanderson's sister, Sadie. They rode his pickup into the hills to meet Lurleen Meekins and everything had turned out all right.

Riding the train one night with Billy dozing off as they traveled through the flat land of Ohio after crossing the Pennsylvania border, Buck thought again of his youth, wondering how much time he had left on Earth. Whenever he thought of death, thoughts of women entered his mind. He recalled that first true light of love in his life and the passion that had almost driven him crazy. Charlotte Randall had been like a sweet elixir he'd drink and drink from until, intoxicated, he'd drag himself back to the rooming house. But leading up to making love to Charlotte had been pure torture. Day and night his mind turned to images of her, so that he appeared to his coworkers to be distracted. One afternoon at the mill a roll of paper came dangerously close to crushing his foot, making his erection shrink.

Consummation of his love finally took place about two months later. So obsessed was he that he'd taken to going by Charlotte Randall's house after work and then returning every evening after he finished eating his supper. Rain or shine, rather than staying in and reading the newspaper or a magazine or maybe a book at Mrs. Cooper's house, he'd cross the square with General Claymore's statue and walk by Charlotte's house again. Most days she was busy inside, preparing lesson plans. On the days when she happened to be outside, she'd smile or wave and he would wave stupidly back, his heart breaking as he looked at her. The evenings when she wasn't sitting out on the porch or standing by the picket fence, he went back to the rooming house and sat in his room, forlorn, until well into the night, and then, after tossing and turning in disturbed sleep, he would rise reluctantly to face another loveless day. His breakfast, something which he had looked forward to each morning, now tasted like ashes and he hated himself for being so driven to want Charlotte Randall, a married woman. Playing his banjo became a joyless exercise, and rather than go along and play whenever there was an opportunity, he made excuses and turned the invitations down. He thought prayer might help, but all he could think about when he closed his eyes was Charlotte Randall and he'd end up going to the outhouse, always determining that it would be the last time he spilled his seed.

One evening when the air was cold and there was snow on the ground, he was walking with his head down on his way home from work. As he neared her house, Charlotte was crossing the street carrying a great big package and a suitcase. He rushed forward immediately to help her, taking both the package and the suitcase.

"Oh, my," she said, in her sweet voice. "How thoughtful. I was nearly exhausted. Thank you, Harley."

"It's nothing, ma'am," he said as she held the fence gate open, wondering at how she had chosen to call him Harley, as his mother did, and not Buck. How had she remembered his name when he had only spoken it that one time?

She ran daintily ahead, up the porch steps and opened the door for him, motioning for him to follow her into the house. He went in, began to make excuses, about having to go somewhere, about being sweaty and dusty from work, but then, looking at her smiling face, he silently put down the suitcase near a hat tree and placed the package on a small table in front of a mirror with gilded edges and an ornate frame. To the right and left of the mirror were several small portraits, of relatives, he surmised, all of them very stern and handsome, the men as well as the women. He'd never been in a house such as this one, and she later told him he'd stood staring at everything with his mouth open.

"Have you eaten?"

"Well, no, I haven't," he said. "But I was on my way to Mrs. Cooper's, where I live."

"Do you think she'd mind if you had supper here this evening?"

"I reckon she wouldn't."

"Well, good. Please sit down. I've made some meat loaf, mashed potatoes, and fresh peas. It would last me all week. I'll grow tired of it and have to feed it to the neighbor's dogs. I've also baked a pie. All I need to do is heat them up."

"That's sounds fine, ma'am," he said, taking off his hat and sitting down on the edge of a stuffed chair in the living room, worried that he'd brought wood chips or pulp on his clothing. "Thank you. I thought maybe you'd been off on a trip and was coming home," he added, later feeling stupid, since the bus station was the other way.

"No, I took the suitcase to school to bring some things home from the classroom. The package is some fabric I ordered. I had to go to the post office to pick it up. I should've known it would all be too heavy. Come into the kitchen and tell me about work at the mill."

He was awed by his surroundings. The furniture, the curtains, the wallpaper, the pictures of landscapes on the walls, the light fixtures, and the oriental carpet on the floor were all so grand that he imagined that Charlotte must be a very wealthy woman. And then it dawned on him that perhaps her husband was the wealthy one.

At supper she talked about Memphis and her family and asked him about his own family and what life was like up in the hills. He was circumspect, but as always praised his mother and father, who worked very hard to raise their children. Charlotte smiled sweetly at him and urged him to have seconds. The food was delicious. When he was finished with his pie she asked him if he wanted another piece. He nodded. When she returned and reached over his shoulder to put the pie on the table, the front of her dress brushed his shoulder and he took in her fragrance, a mixture of soap, perfume, and her own body, and he closed his eyes in an ecstasy of desperation. She returned to the other end of the table, and when he looked up from his second forkful of pie, she was staring at him. She asked him his age and if he had a girlfriend and what he did with her. He found himself answering Charlotte Randall's questions as if he had no true volition. It was as if anything she wanted he would do. At one point she suggested he go upstairs and take a bath, she'd scrub his back.

"I'd like that a whole lot, but I don't know, ma'am. You being a married lady and all."

"Harley Sanderson, if it will make you feel better I will take my rings off. And please do not worry about my husband. He is right now in the capital, curled up snug as a bug with his mistress. He is the famous Parker Randall, State Senator, with aspirations to the Governor's Mansion. Do you know what a mistress is, Harley?"

"No, ma'am."

"Well, a mistress is a woman who serves as a wife when a man is far from his legally wedded wife, or tired of her. Do you think women should have something similar?"

"I reckon they should, ma'am. Although I couldn't be sure."

"Well, finish your pie, I'll clear the table, begin filling the tub, and we can continue this discussion in a more relaxed setting."

"Yes, ma'am."

She went upstairs, returned shortly to the dining room, and began carrying dishes into the kitchen. He offered to help but she rebuked him playfully, insisting that he was her guest.

"You could put another log in the fire, however," she said and he got up immediately and did as she asked, banking the fire and making sure no embers escaped before putting the screen back up. He returned to his seat at the table and watched her every movement.

She worked rapidly, looking at him and smiling as she went back and forth. Outside, darkness had taken over and he could hear the wind whipping up the branches of the tree outside the window of the dining room. A few moments later Charlotte came out of the kitchen and motioned for him to follow her upstairs. He picked up his hat and climbed the stairs after her, watching her fine figure and legs as he fought the desire in him. The upstairs of the house was equally beautiful, the walls on the staircase and halls covered with delicate, light-yellow wallpaper with tiny bluebells on it and family photographs in their neat wooden frames.

Charlotte pointed to a door and he went in. The bathroom was so large and bright that he stood frozen for a moment, wondering how he had managed to walk into this place. There was a large tub with little feet like an animal, nothing like the tin tub at Mrs. Cooper's or at home. There was also a basin for washing and a toilet bowl like he'd seen in the magazines. The tub was almost filled, so he turned off the water and stuck his hand in it.

The water was comfortably warm. It smelled as if some sort of perfume had been added to it. From outside the bathroom he heard Charlotte ask him if he was in the tub yet. He said he was about to get in and hurried to take off his clothes. He climbed into the tub and minutes later she came in dressed in a bathrobe. He immediately dropped his hands to cover himself and she laughed. She knelt on the floor and began scrubbing his back, not saying anything but touching him gently. And then she asked him if he wanted to touch her, and he was immediately erect.

"I'm really sorry," he said.

She laughed and took his wet hand and placed it inside her bathrobe, and with her right hand reached down into the water and began manipulating him in the most delicious way until his back arched and he came and the stuff was hitting him in the face and she was kissing him and licking it off his eyes and cheeks. When she was done, she kissed his mouth, forcing it open with her tongue, searching for his. When she was finished scrubbing him, he got out of the tub, his organ practically erect again. After wrapping him in a plush bathrobe, she emptied the tub and scrubbed it, then led him to her bedroom. Every curtain had been drawn in the halls as well as in her bedroom. The bedroom was, again, like nothing he'd ever seen except in magazines. The wallpaper, the curtains, the rug on the floor, the four-poster canopied bed, the lamps and furniture bespoke elegance. She asked him if he could wait while she bathed and she would return shortly. He nodded and then she was gone. No more than five minutes later she returned, dressed now in a red silk gown with yellow thread in intricate geometric patterns. He was sitting in an easy chair.

"Take off your robe and lie on the bed. I want to look at you, Harley."

"Yes, ma'am," he said and lay down, looking back at her in the dim yellow light in the room.

She let her robe fall off her shoulders to reveal the magnificence of her body. He almost gasped, and then she said that what she wanted to do might seem a little strange but that she was offering it as a sign of her admiration for him and his boyish beauty and she hoped he wouldn't misunderstand or judge her too harshly, but had he ever heard of a woman taking a man in her mouth? He said that his uncle talked about it once in a while when telling stories about New Orleans. She said the French were very good at that type of thing, but that she wasn't French and just wanted him to experience its pleasure and then tell her if it was something he enjoyed.

"Whatever you feel like, please don't worry," she said. "It will be fine."

"What if I . . . like it happened in the tub?" he said.

"Then go right ahead," she said, understanding. "I won't mind one bit. It will be a new experience for me. I have imagined it and I've always wondered what it would be like."

He nodded and she came to the bed and bent over him and put the head of his organ in her mouth and began to probe with the tip of her tongue up underneath the skin so that he could feel the very tip trying to get into the slit and eventually with her lips she peeled the skin back and began running her tongue around the head and with her right hand she had a hold of him and he couldn't help himself and brought his hands up and grabbed her head and at the same time arched his back and came and could feel her suddenly stiffen and she took his stuff and swallowed it and then she was licking everything off of him and his organ wouldn't go down, so she came up and lay next to him and took his head and made him suck at her nipples, whispering in his ear that he should suck hard and then she put her leg over his thigh and he could feel her wiry hair there and with her hand she began to jack him off until about five minutes later he came and the stuff squirted off and was all over him and her and then she was breathing hard and she was sticking her tongue in his mouth and humping against him and then she sat up in bed and her eyes looked glazed and she asked him if he ever jacked off, except that she said masturbate, and he didn't understand so she took his hand and closed it over his organ as he lay there half hard and made the motion and he blushed and said he sometimes did and she asked him if he would do it in front of her because she had never seen a boy do it and she was just wondering what it was like. He'd shrugged his shoulders and went at it, watching her as she touched herself with her finger down there, the two of them pleasuring themselves, with her sitting on the bed watching until he finally came again and she was next to him grabbing him so that he was surprised at how strong she was, or maybe he was just weakened by all the jacking off, because that's what people said it did, except when he did it he felt stronger and like all the evil in his life was leaving him.

They lay there for about twenty minutes. He was dozing off when he felt her hand on him again. No more than two minutes later he was hard again. This time she climbed up on him like she was on a horse and began moving against him. Ten minutes later she was totally lost in the whole thing and moaning and throwing herself on him and her thing clutching at him so that in later years when he was in Memphis and damn near fucked his brains out he understood that Charlotte Randall had been one of those women who not only enjoyed sex with a man, but loved the enjoyment of a man as much as she enjoyed her own.

The entire matter with Charlotte lasted a little over two months with three weekend interruptions when Parker Randall returned to Claymore. Buck was no longer obsessed with Charlotte and waited patiently until her husband left town once more to visit her, gorging himself, but at the same time learning to control himself so that her pleasure would be prolonged. One evening after they made love and she was lying snuggled up against him under the comforter, he said that someone had made a remark at work.

"What did they say?" she asked, sitting up suddenly.

"That I was sure taking school seriously," he said.

"Well, it is like going to school," she said, sweetly. "I'm learning a lot. Aren't you?"

"Sure, but . . ."

"But what?"

"I think people know what's going on."

She was silent a while and then, as she stroked his chest, she said that perhaps they ought not to see each other for a while. And then she shook her head and said she would go crazy without him, but that it was probably best. She said that her husband was abusive and had even struck her, calling her a "damn squaw." So they went on seeing each other until at some point he had to simply pick up and go.

25 Exiles

Lying in bed with Charlotte Randall, after having made love to her numerous times, Buck Sanderson asked why her husband had called her a squaw. As he lay watching her, sated now but still feeling love for her, Charlotte told him that as white as she was, her great-grandmother had been an Indian woman, a young Cherokee girl by the name of Lydia Spike. Lydia had chosen to remain behind in Tennessee when the tribe was moving west up from Chickamauga on the Tennessee border with Alabama. Feeling proprietary, Buck protested that her husband's abuse of Charlotte was not correct and said he had no right calling her a squaw.

"It doesn't matter. I'm not the least bit ashamed of having Cherokee blood," she said. "Lydia Spike, my grandmother's mother, was a courageous woman who loved her husband. She wasn't your ordinary-type young woman," Charlotte added, sitting up on the bed, her face flushed from lovemaking, a silk stole over her shoulders and her eyes bright and trusting. She went on, telling him that Lydia Spike had gone across the border to Alabama with her husband, who was a doctor, and that in the 1820s and thirties she worked with George Guess—whose Cherokee name was Sequoyah—the inventor of the Cherokee alphabet, helping him with the proofreading of the *Cherokee Phoenix*, a newspaper written and printed in the Cherokee language. "Eventually, they sent the Cherokees and other tribes west to Oklahoma." She went on to explain how the Cherokee, Choctaw, Cree, Chickasaw, and Creek were forced west through the Indian Removal Act of 1830 because gold was found in the area. "My grandmother always talked about her mother, Lydia, and how much she missed her younger brother, Carson Spike, who went west with the other Cherokee and from whom she never heard again. He was only a boy, so there's no telling if he survived the trip. *Nunna daul Tsuny*," Charlotte said, so that it sounded like "none a doll sunny," which made little sense but still saddened him.

"What did you say?" he asked.

"The path where the people cried," she said, breathing deeply.

"What do you mean?"

"It's what our people call the route that brought the Cherokee to Oklahoma," she said. " 'The trail of tears,' in English. In the dead of winter the Cherokee were escorted by the U.S. Cavalry away from their homes. Barefoot, without their possessions or warm clothing they were put on wagons to travel west. About four thousand Cherokee died on the way to the Oklahoma Territory, including Quatie, the wife of Chief John Ross, who gave her coat to a sick child."

Charlotte was silent and then said that perhaps they ought to stop seeing each other.

"We have to think about it, Harley," she said. "We surely do."

He reached across and almost violently held her to him, his heart suddenly beating too fast, like the time he was walking in the woods looking for game in the trees and all of a sudden, no more than fifteen feet ahead, there was a bear sniffing the ground. He had backed away silently, aware that he was downwind from the animal. When he was some distance away he stopped to take aim, but he couldn't see the bear and quit hunting for the day.

"Maybe we can go somewhere," he said, after she settled into his arms.

"No, he'll find us and make everything worse."

"What am I going to do?" said Buck, knowing that the moment he was away from her his body would start yearning to be with her again.

"You won't have any trouble finding girlfriends," she said. "Treat them like you treated me and you'll never want for company."

"It ain't gonna be the same," he said.

"No, I'm sure it won't," she said. "It certainly won't be for me. You are quite the young man, Harley Sanderson. Yes, you are."

There were a few more times with Charlotte, when they made love all evening and then he walked home in the quiet darkness of the town, his mind lost in the wonder of the experience with her, his heart clean and pure and his body relaxed and strong. Then one day after work Bobby Tyrell caught up to him. He smiled at Bobby and said he hadn't forgotten about the dance the upcoming Saturday.

"It ain't that I wanna talk to you about, Buck," Bobby said.

"What, then?" he said, looking puzzled. "What's wrong?"

"I think you better get outta town, Buck," Bobby said.

"What's got into you, Bobby? Get outta town? What for? Somebody after me?"

"You're damn right there is. And the people Parker Randall's gonna send after you don't talk nothing but shotgun. Mean boys that shoot and don't ask questions until you're dead."

"You ain't joshing, are you?"

"You're damn right I ain't joshing. I ain't saying I'm for or against what you've been doing, but damn near everybody in Claymore knows you been going at it with Parker Randall's wife. Can't say that I blame you, but it's sure gonna cost you if you don't get your butt gone."

"Yeah, maybe you're right," he said.

"There's a freight train that stops over in Kenyon to get water about midnight. That's about five miles west. Going north."

"Don't wanna go north."

"Maybe you oughta go on back home to the hills."

"Can't do that, either."

"Then what you gonna do?"

"Take my chances on the river, I reckon."

"The Mississippi's more than thirty miles from here."

"I can walk that."

"Be careful."

"I will, Bobby. Thank you much. Say so long to the boys and tell them I'll send word from Memphis."

"Good luck, bub," Bobby Tyrell said and turned to go.

Although he had appeared cool, Buck's insides were burning with fear and his tongue was dry. He hurried through town, his senses suddenly tuned to everything about him. He didn't know whether the temperature had dropped or it was fear that was making him feel cold. He walked rapidly, each shadow making him alert to upcoming danger. He thought of going through the alleys to the rooming house but decided to cut through the middle of town. If they decided to come at him, let them do so in the open, where he had a chance to fight.

He recalled being nine years old and his father facing down some men who had been passing through. They were at the general store and the men got out of an old jalopy. They were dressed in suits and laced-up boots. One of them tipped his newsboy cap back and wanted directions. He had a strange way of speaking that his father later said was a Chicago-gangster accent. They had approached his father and called him "Mr. Hillbilly." Cradling his shotgun in his arms, his father had looked them in the eye, spit a big stream of tobacco juice in front of their feet, and said, "Let's go, Buck." He turned his back on them and walked out of the store. One of the men hollered, "Hey," but his father kept walking. Yankee fools, his father said as they walked down the street. Thinking about it made Buck Sanderson smile and he knew he'd know what to do if it came to that.

Once inside the rooming house, he announced to Mrs. Cooper that he was leaving, went directly to his room, threw his belongings into the canvas bag, retrieved his banjo from beneath his bed, and counted his money. Nearly eighty dollars, which by all rights he ought to bring home first but now couldn't. He was sure his mother would understand. He put on a sweater, his Mackinaw, and then his long black raincoat. He undid his belt buckle, pulled out his belt, and ran it through the strap of the sheath of his Bowie knife, then placed in its sheath the razor-sharp knife his father used to skin game with and which he had given to him before going to jail. "In case some son of a bitch takes a dislike to you. Go for his neck right away. Anywhere below the jaw's fine." He hoped he wouldn't have to use the knife, but he better keep it handy just in case. When he came down, Mrs. Cooper was waiting for him with some food wrapped in paper and tied with string.

"Thank you, Mrs. Cooper," he said, smiling at the kindly old woman.

"Don't mention it," she said. "You're all paid up and you got one more meal coming."

"I'd sure appreciate it if you only told my folks that I left. Tell them I went to Memphis."

"What folks do ain't none of my business. How you gonna get there?"

"I don't know."

"You think you can get yourself to Ridgely?"

"I reckon I can."

She wrote quickly on a piece of paper and gave it to him.

"That's my nephew's name. He's the postmaster. Just give him the note and tell him where you want to go. He knows people and maybe you can get on a boat going down to Memphis."

"Yes, ma'am. Thank you very much," he said and was gone back out into the night.

In spite of the warning that people would be coming after him, he wanted to go by Charlotte Randall's house; but Ridgely was the other way, and he began walking, leaving the town behind and keeping to the wooded area beside the road. When he had walked for nearly two hours, climbing a couple of hills so that down below the few lights still left on in Claymore seemed like little specks, he stopped and found himself a place in the woods, hoping that he was close enough to town so that animals wouldn't disturb him. It was too cold for bears. He built a small fire, and, wrapped in his long raincoat, he fell asleep quickly. Three hours later he woke up to rustling in the woods. His heart beating rapidly, his hand was immediately on his knife, pulling it out as he sprang to his feet. In the fading light of the fire he saw a pair of eyes glittering in the dark, but they were too low to be a bobcat. He felt around on the ground until he found a rock and flung it at the eyes and heard the yelping of a fox as it scurried away. He tried falling asleep again but sleep wouldn't come. He got up and began walking west again, taking the road now and enjoying the cold night, the starlit sky wondrous, but more so the prospect of his journey. His heart now soared, and, being alone in the dark, he sang about the fox, smiling to himself and hoping he hadn't hurt the animal too badly. People were crazy to expect animals to behave any way but how they were. Foxes behaved like foxes and geese like geese. Only humans could change a little bit of who they were, and not much at that. He sang loudly into the night, knowing no one could hear him.

> *The fox went out on a chilly night,*
> *Prayed to the moon to give him light*
> *For he'd many a mile to go that night*
> *Before he reached the town-o, town-o, town-o,*
> *Before he reached the town-o.*

He walked all night, eating the biscuits and ham Mrs. Cooper had packed for him, wondering what Memphis would be like and what kind of music it was that the blacks played there. Uncle Will said he'd heard some of it down in New Orleans and just couldn't stop tapping his foot. "Just a different rhythm, that's all. Can't explain it." He slept in the woods the following night, after the sun went down. He awoke in the cold of night and began walking. When the first light began to appear behind him he was nearly outside of Ridgely. From the hill above the town he could see the Mississippi River stretching in the distance, wide and dark at this time of morning. His feet hurt, but he couldn't stop thinking about what awaited him.

Once in Ridgely he found a diner, paid fifteen cents for a breakfast of eggs and grits and a big slab of bacon, biscuits, and hot coffee with plenty of milk and sugar, got directions to the post office, where he handed Mrs. Cooper's nephew the note. The nephew, Elmore, said he should make his way to the river and see Tom Clampitt over at the dock. Clampitt could get him on a tug pulling barges on the way to Memphis. And to tell him Elmore Cooper sent him. He did as he was bid, and by midmorning he had located Clampitt.

At four o'clock in the afternoon Buck was on a tug heading downriver, working on the deck and fitting in quite nicely. After supper one of the other deckhands pulled out a harmonica and began playing. Buck listened for a while, then opened his banjo case, tuned the instrument, and picked a few quick runs. He and the harmonica player did some tunes, and then he sang for an hour or so. "Lady Margaret and Sweet William," "Go Tell Aunt Rhody," "The Fox," "Barbara Allen" and about a dozen more tunes. And then Paxton, the boss, said they all ought to turn in because when they reached Bolling on the Arkansas side they'd have to load bales of cotton.

When he asked where he should sleep, Paxton pointed to the deck, saying he had no room for him in the quarters below. He found a place to sleep at the stern of the tug. While he was getting comfortable, a night-black Negro man came over, introduced himself as Charlie Boone and sat on a crate. Boone said he'd enjoyed his playing and offered him tobacco for a smoke. He asked him where he was heading.

"Memphis, I guess," he said.

"Why Memphis? You looking for work?"

"I guess so, but I'm going for the music."

"Beale Street? That's where they got the blues. Is that what you're looking for?"

"Blues?"

"That's right. That's the music. But be careful on Beale Street. You got a knife?"

"Yes, sir."

"Well, just show it to 'em and if they keep coming, gut them. You understand what I'm saying to you? Black or white. Just gut their sorry ass."

"Yes, sir."

"Well, good night to you," Boone said. "I gots to go up front and heave the lead for the cap'n." And off he went. A few minutes later Buck heard the sounding rope hit the water and Boone calling out the depths as they moved out into the channel. *Quarter less twain . . . seven . . .* He thought of Charlotte alone in her bedroom. What would happen to her? She was one beautiful woman. *Mark twain*, he heard Boone shout. Maybe he'd come back to Claymore sometime and see her. That's what he'd do. After he established himself, he'd come back and get her. *Quarter twain* . . . Maybe she'd be gone. She was so sweet. He'd make lots of money in Memphis and buy her a house and they'd just make love and eventually marry . . . *No bottom* . . .

At supper the next day, after they'd loaded the cotton at Bolling, he asked Boone what he'd been saying the previous night. Boone laughed and showed him the rope with the lead pipe filled with chain and lead.

"See this here piece of leather? That's six feet deep. When I gots that in my hand as I'm lowering the rope I calls out 'Quarter less twain six feet.' Piece split in two is mark twain. That's twelve feet. And so on till we hit twenty-four feet and I tell the cap'n, no bottom. All night long till we dock."

"When do you sleep?"

"In the daytime."

Boone was the first Negro he'd had a conversation with and he liked him immediately. Once he reached Memphis he encountered others. He had no idea where the notion came from but he felt a strong kinship with their lifestyle and plight. Whether it was because he was from the hills and had always felt apart from the townspeople or whether it was the pride with which black people lived in spite of the prejudice from most whites, he liked them. Eventually, he decided this affinity with blacks must be due to the music; the music and the fact that he took to the rhythms as if born to them.

In the morning the captain of the barge, Bill Rodham, said he'd heard him play and if he wanted he'd talk to his nephew, who played on a big paddlewheeler downriver and had a band and maybe he could play with them, seeing their banjo player had passed away and he didn't know if they'd found a new one, but if they hadn't he was sure his nephew, Trout, would be mighty glad to hear him play, and who knows? When they got to Memphis the paddlewheeler was docked a few blocks up and, as soon as the cargo was unloaded, Captain Rodham took him over to his nephew, a big redheaded man with freckles. Clearly a happy-go-lucky sort of fellow, Trout greeted his uncle in style, and once he saw Buck Sanderson and his banjo case, he said he'd be right back and went inside a stateroom and came back with his cornet, then introduced himself and asked him if he played New Orleans style. Buck said he didn't rightly know if he did or not. Within an hour or so he was picking up everything there was to know, and Trout Rodham just shook his head and said, "You got the job."

He played for a time with Trout Rodham's band, got to see New Orleans, and fell in love with a Creole girl who reminded him of Charlotte Randall. He didn't learn that the girl was only fifteen years old until it was too late and he nearly got killed by her father, a consumptive Frenchman with pretty bad aim.

Eventually he made it back to Memphis and found work on the docks. By then he was pretty well schooled in the New Orleans style and in the blues, so that when he finally got to Beale Street he could sit in most any night after the clubs closed and the musicians were sitting around unwinding and trying out new things at places like Pee Wee's or Bramwell's. That's how he met Butterworth and the two of them eventually convinced each other they ought to give New York a try.

He smiled and relit his pipe, recalling Alfred Butterworth as a skinny little kid walking around with his clarinet, looking lost and hungry. Time went so fast, he thought, watching the clouds and the failing light of day.

The next day when Vidamía and Horty came over they kissed him and hugged him and made a fuss about him, telling him he looked so strong and handsome.

"Grandpa, everybody says Daddy won't be able to play because of his right hand," Vidamía said, "but I met someone who says he could. What do you think?"

"Well, that remains to be seen, darling," Buck Sanderson said. "I've heard of people with afflictions who made up their minds and played. A few years back there was a young fella by the name of Horace Parlan. Mind you, he didn't have fingers missing, but if I remember correctly he suffered from polio as a child and his right hand wasn't as strong as it could be and he developed a kind of left-hand technique that sounded pretty good. Even recorded and played around New York, I heard. A fine pianist."

"So Daddy could play if he wanted to," Vidamía said.

"If he puts his mind to it I believe he could."

"I think so, too."

"A couple of years back I was down home for my brother Frazier's burial, and my nephew, who was there for the funeral, asked me to come visit him in Missouri. We drove down there where he lives on the Mississippi and went into Cape Girardeau to hear a man play Cajun music. Place called Broussard's down on Main Street. Fine Cajun food. I met the owner, Mr. Baron Broussard. Fine gentleman. I heard recently from my nephew, Dale, that he's opened a couple of more restaurants in St. Louis. Anyway, there was a fella there, I believe his name was Pelletier. Cajun, I guess. Had just thumb and little finger on his left hand. Accident. Chain saw or something like that. It didn't make one bit of difference to him, the man played the piano to beat the band with them two fingers and the five on his right hand. Just like your papa, except that the kid is missing the middle and little finger on his right hand instead of the three on that fella's left hand at Broussard's. But the man played up a storm. About eight o'clock this Cajun fella makes everybody stand up and he plays the "Star-Spangled Banner" and everybody's gotta sing. And then when he's done with that he plays "Dixie" and everybody's got to sing again. Everybody having a good ole time. Black or white, everybody stood up and sang, and when they was finished, the Cajun pianist just went back to playing. After I saw that, I was sure Billy could play again if he put his mind to it. But I ain't one to push folks, especially not Billy."

"Okay, I feel a lot better, Grandpa," Vidamía said.

"Me too," said Horty.

He looked at her and laughed.

"What, Grandpa?"

"Your mama shoulda never named you Hortense," he said. "It ain't right."

"I know," the girl said. "But you can call me Cookie."

"Then that's what I'll call you from now on."

"You hungry, Grandpa?"

"I'm so hungry I could eat the south end of a skunk traveling north," he said.

Both girls made faces, then dashed for the grill to get him some food.

His thoughts again returned to his youth and Charlotte Randall. Maybe after the barbecue he'd go over to Mount Vernon and see how Ruby Broadway was doing.

26 Philosophy

Lurleen Meekins Farrell, who was not one to fill her children's heads with moralistic drivel and ethical dos and don'ts, believed that the reason people can endure things that veer from the norms of human behavior and still go on existing is that there is at the core of humanity—in spite of legal systems, and other imposed social and religious codes—a basic tolerance of itself. This permissiveness, she felt, comes from the awareness that our existence as a species may be unique in the universe and that, therefore, we are alone in its vastness. More to the point, at the formulation of its argument with itself, humanity posits that in the face of such cosmological complexity, the human animal, unable to fly under its own power, swim underwater for more than a few minutes (and rather slowly, at that), move great weights or run very fast, faces life by using—as a prime defense against the awareness of eternal loneliness—its brain, overdeveloped to an outstanding degree but dependent on a steady supply of oxygen, so that deprived of said element for more than a few minutes it shrivels up and dies, but when functioning properly is capable of engendering the assassination of Jack Kennedy, or the elimination of millions by Hitler. But also capable of weaving together a simple folk song like "Greensleeves," or Beethoven's Fifth Symphony.

Lurleen Meekins Farrell often imagined that each human brain was simply a tiny cell within a larger collective brain going back to the beginning of consciousness and that all the information about individual struggles and triumphs was carried in each new cell of this large brain, adding to the knowledge of each generation, so that all that was really occurring when unusual events took place was the wide swing of a pendulum as it oscillated between destruction and creativity. She recalled the afternoon in her senior year of college when she sat rapt, listening to her philosophy professor talk about the ancient Greek concept of *daemon*, that spirit of genius that drove humans forward. Professor Treblehorn spoke eloquently of *eros*, understood popularly as love but representative of the drive to create, and *thanatos*, the death principle, but also the contrasting drive to destroy. She immediately understood why she woke up each morning thinking of how she could help her parents, or how to play a particular tune, or find a better way to keep her clothing from being frayed when it was washed, and why the Parker boys were so mean-spirited and had chopped up an old coon hound belonging to Silas Goins because the dog had run off with a chicken of theirs.

Boyd and Clyde Parker had sneaked into Silas's yard one night, and a few days later, after the hound didn't come home, Silas found the dog's parts hung all over the place; the head over by the outhouse, the tail on the front gate, and the genitals on the porch.

After that last year of reading, studying, and discussing the myriad questions which her curiosity had spawned, she began to look at life without fear, seeing her own part in it as not unimportant but minute, and not separate but part of a larger purpose.

"And what would you say that purpose is, Miss Meekins?" Lloyd Treblehorn had asked as they sat under the large oak tree at the university that spring morning after he had walked into the classroom, shielded his eyes from the sun and announced, "Okay, everyone outside on the lawn, under the oak tree," and they had trooped out, all ten of them registered for the philosophy seminar, sitting around him, awed by his brilliance and kindliness.

Her face had grown hot, but she had said that she believed that the human race was undergoing an enormous trial-and-error experiment in order to help itself evolve.

"Explain," Professor Treblehorn had said, and she had gone on, the words flowing out of her like never before.

"We are attempting to polish ourselves as a species, to perfect our behavior so that we may live in harmony with the universe. I believe that each act, whether violent or creative, whether representative of love or destruction, is a swing of the pendulum and eventually creativity will win out over violence, so that seemingly aberrant behavior is part of a pendular swing, counteracted by the beauty of creativity and goodness of which human beings are capable, and that deep within the recesses of its natural wisdom the human race remains neutral to the swinging of that pendulum," she said.

"Are you saying there is no evil in the universe?"

"Not as such," she had answered. "It's a process that we're going through, Professor Treblehorn. In 1926, right here in Tennessee, over in Dayton, there was a trial in which a man was charged with teaching the theory of evolution. He was defended by a very brave lawyer whose name I cannot recall. There was no good and evil in that case. Simply ignorance and knowledge pitted against one another. Light and dark and folks just trying to figure which way to go in that in-between time between night and day."

"The Scopes trial," Professor Treblehorn said. "Clarence Darrow, 1925."

"Yes, that was the case. The Scopes Monkey Trial," she said.

She went on to explain that overall the human race is a benevolent species, capable of more good than harm, and that this infinite capacity for tolerance is the phenomenon that some people call God, though she attributed it simply to the more profound inner workings of life. Professor Treblehorn ran his fingers through his beard, removed his glasses, wiped them with a handkerchief, and then asked her if she was now postulating that God didn't exist.

She shook her head and said, "No, God exists, if only as an idea." Everyone had nodded, and Professor Treblehorn laughed uproariously, understanding how she had sidestepped the issue, and to prod her immediately challenged her notion of this pendulum.

"Oh, yes," she said. "The human race is basically a creative species. Just like bees produce honey and beavers build dams, human beings produce things of beauty."

"What about the destruction?" Professor Treblehorn asked.

"It's part of the trial and error," she said. "Destruction is inevitable, just like death. Eventually, the destructive aspects of the human being will begin to be employed positively."

"How? A pendulum has to swing both ways."

"It will," she replied. "The destructive swing will do away

with war and illness and all of the things that plague humanity."

"That is a very hopeful outlook," Professor Treblehorn said reverently, and sadly, so that she felt as if he wanted desperately to believe that this was so but was unable to bring himself out of the darkness of his skepticism. They were all very quiet for a long time before someone asked another question and they went on to some other discussion.

At the end of the semester Professor Treblehorn called her into his office, congratulated her, encouraged her to pursue a career in university teaching, and gave her one of his keepsakes, a copy of a typed lecture that Clarence Darrow delivered to the Poetry Club of the University of Chicago. In it Darrow defends pessimism and a healthy skepticism against facile philosophical constructs and the schemes of those in positions of power. "Optimists," Darrow wrote, "are always so disappointed when things don't go well, while pessimists see the world as it is and are never disappointed. It isn't that they look for the bad, but that they know that life is incomprehensible and things happen." Darrow champions simple pleasures and quotes A. E. Housman, whose poetic concern was the fleeting nature of youth.

> *And since to look at things in bloom*
> *Fifty springs are little room,*
> *About the woodlands I will go*
> *To see the cherry hung with snow.*

She treasured the lecture, in which Clarence Darrow used the words of Housman and other poets to support his argument. Her favorite quote from Darrow's lecture remained etched in her mind as a guide in her life. Clarence Darrow said:

That is why I have so little patience with the old preaching to the young. If youth with its quick flowing blood, its strong imagination, its virile feeling; if youth, with its dreams and its hopes and ambitions can go about the woodland to see the cherry hung with snow, why not? Who are the croakers, who have run their race and lived their time, who are they to keep back expression and hope and youth and joy from a world that is almost barren at best.

It has been youth that has kept the world alive; it will, because from the others emotion has fled; and with the fleeing of emotion, through the ossification of the brain, all there is left for them to do is to preach. I hope they have a good time doing that, and I am so glad the young pay no attention to it.

Believing in a vision of life which permitted youth its freedom, she liked to think, caused her children to grow up unfettered by the fear of divine retribution, less confounded by guilt, and, more important, critical of authority. Of all the ideas contained in Clarence Darrow's lecture nothing made more sense than the protection of youth. War, waged by the old and suffered by the young, had robbed Billy Farrell of his love for jazz and his livelihood as a pianist. Such would not be the case with her children. Having come to this environment early on and being eager to fit in, Vidamía understood instinctively that she wouldn't be judged by Lurleen, or her new siblings, and certainly not by their father. For this Lurleen was grateful. But after Billy's initial excitement at meeting his daughter and introducing her to the family, he again withdrew into that world of thought and memory, walking in it with eyes downcast and spirit beaten, his body bending under the weight of whatever demons he endured.

Lurleen had been lucky that her aunt Ida, her grandfather's sister, had seen what was inside of her and begged her parents to let her go to college. Aunt Ida herself had attended the college when it was just a girl's school. Lurleen had met people like Professor Treblehorn and her other professors who took such care to explain things to her and who didn't mock her inquisitiveness. The four years in Jackson had gone so quickly. She loved being on campus and going to her music classes and singing in the choir, which each year went on tour. These excursions had allowed her to meet people in different parts of the South and the Midwest. But she enjoyed the Concert Band most, because there the atmosphere was one of great release and she got to be outdoors. She took the jazz classes but knew she wasn't creative enough to improvise as they did. She also knew that it was a very important music and yearned to visit the places where the music was played.

She wanted her children, and that included Vidamía, because she had grown to love her as if she were her own, to go as far with their dreams as they could. She wanted them to rise each morning as she had, filled with the excitement of what they saw before them, everything clear, not encumbered by fear of failure; and each of their accomplishments adding to the knowledge that would benefit humanity in spite of the sad fact that most people lacked the awareness that they were like bees who, instead of honey, made beauty in each act of goodness. She also knew that even in the sadness of life, as Clarence Darrow had said, there was beauty.

Lurleen had hit on the idea of a family band during a particularly bad time when Billy couldn't find much work, and he'd sit around the house and mope and stare out the windows for hours. When she spoke to him he hardly ever answered her. When he did it was to nod or mumble something. If she pressed him, he walked away or went up on the roof. One winter, when he was gone more than an hour, she had made sure that Cliff, Hortense—not yet called Cookie—and Fawn were occupied watching a television program; then she put on her coat and went up the stairs. She found him wandering around the edge of the roof, pacing back and forth in that stark arctic night, and knew that he was contemplating ending his life.

She approached him slowly, calling to him—"Bill?"—but softly lest she spook him and he jump. When he finally turned, his face was a mask of horror, as if he'd seen death again. At first he didn't recognize her, and then, when he did, he immediately wanted to apologize. She shook her head and walked to him. As he sank down to the tar floor of the roof, she took him in her arms, and then he was weeping and saying over and over that it was his fault. She talked him back to the present and then took him downstairs and put him to bed, telling him sternly that he had no business being up on that roof in shirtsleeves with the temperature in the teens, switching her concern from suicide to his general health.

It was then that she went to the Veterans Administration and demanded to know what had happened to her husband that caused him to act so strangely. On the second day of her quest she was able to track down a psychologist who was familiar with cases similar to Billy's. He'd searched for Billy's file, eventually found it in a cabinet of inactive cases, and sat behind his desk reading it and nodding.

"Cpl. William C. Farrell, U.S. Marine Corps, wounded in action near Da Nang in 1969," the psychologist said and then mumbled something.

"Please go on," Lurleen said.

"It's not our usual procedure to discuss a patient's file," the psychologist said.

"Please," she said. "I feel like he's going to take his life. I don't know what to do," she nearly whimpered when she was finished. "Please."

"Does your husband have a gun?"

"No, he doesn't," she said, regaining her composure. "He just goes up on the roof and it scares me."

"Your husband used to come in for counseling once in a while back in 1971," the psychologist said. "He was basically concerned with having caused his buddy's death. This is not unusual in the profile of combat soldiers. He was also concerned about his marriage and talked about the upcoming birth of your child."

"That far back?" Lurleen said, the curiosity eating her up inside, but never asking him about this other marriage and child; wondering if Billy was a bigamist; eventually asking Maud Farrell but begging her not to tell him she'd been prying. Maud said she'd heard about a kid but didn't know if it was a boy or a girl and reassured her that Billy and the girl never got married.

"Anything else?" Lurleen asked the psychologist.

"No, but he stopped coming after a while. His last visit was in December of 1971. Eventually, the case was closed. I found his records in the inactive files."

"But he talked about the fact that he let his buddy die," she said. "Joey, right?"

"Yes, that's right," the psychologist said. "Not uncommon for combat veterans. Pfc José Manuel Santiago. KIA in the same action as the one in which your husband was wounded."

"I don't believe that's what happened," she'd said. "I don't believe that's what's keeping him from functioning."

"Why do you say that, Mrs. Farrell?"

"I don't know," she'd said, suddenly feeling defensive and as if she'd made a mistake in going to the VA, as if she had admitted something that should remain under wraps. "It's just that he's told me what happened and it doesn't make sense. Sometimes he's in combat and sometimes he's not and when the thing happened I don't think that he was in combat. It sounds like he was in a safe area. He sounds like when a person dreams and the dream doesn't make logical sense. Things get out of sequence and they shift around peculiarly. That's what it's like when he talks about what happened to him in Vietnam."

"Does he know you're here?"

"No, he thinks I'm at work. He'd feel betrayed if he knew that I'd come to look into his problem. It makes him feel ashamed that he can't function as well as he thinks he should—in terms of holding a regular job and earning a living. He's tried everything: security jobs, construction, parking cars, maintenance. Something always happens. He gets depressed and stays in bed or goes into one of his moods where he just sits and no matter what anyone says it's like he doesn't hear them."

"I understand. It's part of post-traumatic stress syndrome. What they used to call battle fatigue. But what makes you think that what he's told you didn't happen?"

"He says that the incident took place near the base camp where he was stationed and that there had been no enemy soldiers near there in months. And he says that there were no mines or booby traps or anything connected with Viet Cong, but he's convinced that it was they who killed his friend and wounded him."

The psychologist hadn't said anything, but had written himself a note and then told her that he'd do his best to look into the situation; that as soon as he found something out he'd call her. She said to please not call her at home and wrote down the number of the school where she taught. She said she would meet him whenever he wanted. The psychologist nodded gravely and said he would do his best. She waited months, but he never called back.

27 The Band

When Lurleen had pretty much given up hope of hearing from the psychologist at the Veterans Administration, she came up with her own plàn to take Billy's mind off his troubles. One afternoon as she sat at her desk during lunch, eating a ham sandwich and an apple she'd brought from home, she began thinking that Fawn, Horty, and Cliff were playing exceptionally well. It would be interesting if the three of them could play together with their father, although Fawn, as good as she was, wasn't interested in the flute, preferring to play with drumsticks, and spent most of the time beating out rhythms wherever she could, her hands moving almost mechanically and her beautifully mournful eyes far away, so that at times she reminded Lurleen of Billy, as if perhaps his melancholy had always been with him.

That evening, after the children were asleep, Lurleen spoke with Billy.

"I think you ought to try and play with the kids once in a while," she said. "Kind of encourage them. They're getting pretty good, you know."

"I don't know," he'd said, looking up from a magazine.

"I think they'd like it, Bill. They've seen you play the guitar. They know you can play and that you understand music better than any of their teachers."

"Not better than you," he said, smiling weakly.

"Yes, even better than me," she replied, frowning. "I may know a great many technical things about music, but I'm not a performer."

"Well, you coulda fooled me, lady," he said, playfully, so that she felt as if she was getting through to him with the idea. "You had me totally bamboozled."

"Please, Billy," she said. "I think we should form a family band. They'll love it."

He said he'd play with the children on one condition—she had to play as well. She hadn't planned on that, but now she had no choice. She got out her fiddle and they all learned to play tunes like "Go Tell Aunt Rhody," "The Fox," "Camptown Races," "Blowin' in the Wind," throwing in things from the Beatles like "Eleanor Rigby" and "Hey Jude," which Hortense insisted on calling "Hey Dude."

Every once in a while somebody came in with a new song like the time Horty said they ought to play the "Que Bonita Bandera" that Pete Seeger sang, about the Puerto Rican flag and independence for the island, so they learned how to play it and Hortense sang it. It became a big hit when they played in Tompkins Square Park on spring and summer afternoons. They learned to play "Alegría, Alegría" and "De las Montañas Venimos," which are both Puerto Rican Christmas songs. Playing these songs in the middle of the summer produced great mirth in the Ricans who came to see them, especially the older people, who would then talk about *las navidades* and eating *pasteles* and clapped with total delight at the hippies, the five of them blond and raggedy: Billy on guitar, Horty on sax, Cliff on trombone, Lurleen with her fiddle, and Fawn with a snare drum strapped in a harness Billy had made for her, so she looked like a little Revolutionary War drummer boy, which somebody said, and which she promptly corrected. "Oh, no, I'm a drummer *girl*. A drummer *girl*," she'd repeated several times, making Horty and Cliff uncomfortable, because they knew nothing at that time about Fawn and her condition. They all became lost in playing, oblivious to everything except the music. People dropped coins and dollar bills into Billy's guitar case, on which Cliff had written out different funny messages like: LOST OUR PASSPORTS AND MONEY, or NEED PLANE FARE TO GET BACK HOME TO RIVINGTON STREET, or WE ARE BOAT PEOPLE FROM STATEN ISLAND.

But the band sounded weird. It was confirmed when the family went up to Grandpa Buck Sanderson's house on the Fourth of July, and they played and Buck tried joining in. He ended up shaking his head, saying they ought to consider making some changes to their repertoire. After they ate—broiled hamburgers and hot dogs in the backyard—they all played bluegrass, with the old man on banjo, Billy the guitar, Horty the sweet potato, Cliff the mandolin, Fawn the harmonica, and Lurleen her fiddle, the music just flowing out of her like the times when she was back home playing with her own family and friends and people had stood around openmouthed that a little girl could handle a fiddle like she did at ten years of age. At one point she looked across at Billy and he truly seemed to be enjoying the experience.

After they finished playing, Grandpa Buck told Hortense and Cliff to get their regular instruments, and the kids came back with the sax and trombone, and Grandpa got out a bunch of sheet music and handed it out, explaining how Cliff and Horty should transpose it. After that afternoon they felt more like a family band. Coming home on the subway that night, Fawn asleep against Lurleen, and Horty and Cliff snuggled against their father, their instruments under their legs, Lurleen recalled Buck Sanderson—who was her uncle's cousin or something, she couldn't keep track of her connection to him and just called him Grandpa Buck—telling them that they ought to play old standards from the twenties like "Sweet Georgia Brown," "Hard-Hearted Hannah," "Carolina in the Morning," "I'm Just Wild About Harry," "California Here I Come," "Bill Bailey," "Birth of the Blues," "Ain't She Sweet," "Let's Do It," which was "Let's Fall in Love," and a dozen more, because they were upbeat melodies and the kids could get a chance to solo and improvise, which they could learn to do real easy, he said, if they listened.

After that, they began playing the old songs, and she put a little extra money aside and bought Fawn a trap set with one cymbal and a pretty good-sized bass drum. Again it was Horty who came up with a name for the band. The Southern Constellation Family Band, she said, and Billy took the drum over to Sixth Street, where one of his buddies, Boyd Perkins, from around Baton Rouge, Louisiana, who painted portraits and lived in a storefront, wrote out, on the face of the drum, the name of the band in red circus letters. In time she heard about getting a permit to play in the subways. And that is what they did. It was the only thing that saved Billy, she thought. His life perked up, and he began getting more jobs in the neighborhood, writing in a little notebook to keep track of them.

A few years later they added a tub bass, which Lurleen played from time to time when she wasn't playing the fiddle. When Vidamía joined them, Lurleen brought out her accordion from the closet, expecting fully for Billy to have an odd reaction to the keyboard. She had given up playing the instrument after observing, over the years, what happened to Billy whenever he saw a keyboard. But the accordion didn't affect him at all now, so that it wasn't the black and white pattern of the keys, but actually the piano itself which caused the reaction in him. She was convinced that the band had saved Billy and brought him closer to the children, helping him to understand how much they relied on him.

On summer days when they weren't playing music in the subways, time seemed to stop for her. After the children had gone off to summer camp and Billy to do his odd jobs, repairing one thing or another in the neighborhood—a busted pipe, replacing a window, or fixing the railing on a staircase—she would sit in his rocker and knit or embroider, walking about her mind, stopping in a meadow of memories, wishing to get respite from her quest to understand life. She had tried meditation, chanting mantras, study, but couldn't control her thirst to make sense of the mystery of existence. It was an ever-present concern, part of her mind for as long as she had been conscious that, in her own community of decent but small minds, there was something wrong in teaching folks that there was a supreme being who sat in judgment on individuals. The notion of a creator reduced life and its complexities to a fairy tale and kept the human race at an infantile stage in its development.

She had always loved the symmetry and the cold exactitude

that seemed to be the universe, awed by its magnificence. As a young girl she would stand for hours on the back porch of her parents' house a half-mile from town, transfixed as she watched the night sky, the outline of the hills a shadow on the horizon; above her, in the breathtaking blackness, a thousand stars. Every once in a while a shooting star streaked across the firmament, burning itself out, making her think that perhaps it was a rocket ship traveling from one planet to another. At some point her mother broke gently into her trance and brought her, shivering, inside, rubbing her arms through her sweater and bringing her a cup of sweet cocoa, which she held in her two hands, feeling alternately the warmth of the cup and the sweet liquid within her. She'd ask her mother about the stars, and her mother would say that it was all God's doing. Lurleen was later disappointed when she understood the scientific explanation of shooting stars.

These days she was lucky if, going up on the roof of the old factory building, she was able to see even a few stars. In the winter, when arctic weather descended on Manhattan, enveloping everything in its frigid winds and ten-and-twenty-degree temperatures, she bundled up after the children were in bed and climbed the stairs to stand there again, awed by the beauty of the night sky. If she concentrated she was able to block out the lights of the city and let her mind drift away in search of an answer to the mystery.

She sat in the rocker, moving slowly and letting the motion relax her. Everything she'd seen, from the snake handlers of her childhood to the more sophisticated Christian denominations, was superstition. Everything else, every kind of ism that relied on blind faith, robbed people of reason, and therefore freedom. Whatever provided sublime and humble feelings and at the same time lifted the spirit of exaltation, served the same purpose as religion. This convinced her more than ever that in America music was the religion of young people, and it was in this primitive form of celebration that black and white, rich and poor, worshiped. The more she thought about it the more convinced she was that she was correct. People came alive when they heard music that was consonant with their lives. There was never superstition where music was concerned, although there were people afraid of certain music. She'd read in some conservative journal put out by Lyndon Larouche's people that jazz wasn't truly music, that it was a plot between blacks and Jews to distort people's sense of spiritual structure and destroy classical music. The article cited Gershwin as one of the culprits.

Most nights, when she finally was able to relax, she'd think about the vastness of the universe and let her mind wander in the utter loneliness of individual human life. If Billy wasn't feeling amorous, she'd drift off, traveling through her knowledge of the galaxy, naming the constellations until she was asleep. "Amorous," she thought, was a curious word since all Billy did was get into bed totally naked and like a child snuggle up to her, reaching a hand to her breast and resting his bearded face on her shoulder, seemingly making himself smaller, and then she would reach down gingerly as if it were a game, her hand creeping barely below his stomach and always thrilled by the hardness and the heat as if she could feel his heart beating down there and then he'd touch her with the index finger of his clawed hand until she was gasping and sucking at his mouth and he was inside of her and she was lost in him because she loved him so much and he was so damaged by the war.

Sitting in the rocker made her drowsy and sensual, so she stopped, went to the kitchen, and poured herself a glass of water before returning to her musings. These days, between Fawn and Bill she didn't know which way to turn and was certain that her mind was being affected like crazy Woodrow Rayburn's, who was the brother of Aunt Sarah's husband, Wilbur Rayburn, back in those Tennessee hills when she was a little girl. Crazy Woodrow Rayburn stole Bibles. When everyone else was sleeping, he was sneaking around in the woods and crawling into people's homes, stealing their Bibles and burying them in the ground. But he wasn't totally crazy, because he didn't steal the family Bibles where they kept the births of people; he only stole their personal Bibles. Nor did he bury all of them. He saved some and used the pages for wiping himself in the outhouse, claiming that it was no big thing since it wasn't the word of the Lord, anyhow.

"Just some crazy-ass scribbling by Jews," he'd say. "And if you listen to Jews, who killed Jesus, then you're headed for eternal damnation and the fires of hell, because the word of God is revealed to people in dreams and not through some damn Jew writing."

If God existed, Lurleen was sure, He would have punished Woodrow Rayburn. But He had not, choosing instead to let him live on year after year so that at the age of seventy-four he was still cussing and carrying on, healthy as a horse, and had even taken a new wife, a little black-haired, mean-looking teenage girl from East Arkansas, or "Arkansaw," as they all pronounced it, who pleasured him with her mouth, almost toothless from eating candy, and who helped unearth Bibles all up and down the hills so that he could read sarcastically out loud Deuteronomy or Romans or Corinthians or Acts, farting and shitting while he sat in that latrine rain or shine, massaging that big ugly horse dick which he liked showing young girls and which she had seen. Her cousin, Willa Bailey, said she watched him beating his daughter, Doreen, and then stripping her naked and driving his nasty old thing into her and the girl just ten years old, so that she began going crazy after that and eventually wandered off into the woods and people say bears ate her, but most likely her father killed her to shut her up about what he'd done and then buried her along with the Bibles. Lurleen had run to her grandpa, crying about what Willa had told her she'd seen, because Willa was too scared to tell anybody, even though she was already fifteen years old.

"You gotta do something, Grandpa," she said. "Willa saw him, Grandpa."

Her grandfather shook his head and told her he felt real bad about young Doreen, but he couldn't rightly interfere in the business of another man's family, but one thing was sure. She needn't worry about Woodrow.

"Lurleen, if he ever tells you anything, just tell him you're Otis Meekins's granddaughter and that he'd rather kiss a rattlesnake than mess with a West Tennessee Meekins. Ole Woodrow's just the spawn of one of those trashy ole Rayburn boys that come up from Mississippi chasing a hound dog after the war."

"The war Daddy was in?"

"No, darlin', the war a long time ago. Against the Yankees."

"Are Yankees bad, Grandpa?"

"Naw, they're just folks. It ain't got nothin' to do with you. You're a smart young girl and shouldn't be botherin' with all that nonsense. But I'll tell you one thing, if that son of a bitch Woodrow Rayburn says anything to you just let me know. Only good that ever came out of those folks was his brother, Wilbur, that married your aunt. As for the rest of them Rayburns, they're all trash, every one of them. All they was ever good for was beating their women and laying around drinking whiskey they stole from other people's stills. Mean and ornery coots. Only thing they understand's a 12-gauge aimed dead at their noggin. So don't fret none, Lurleen, darlin', cause if he as much as lays a finger on you I'm gonna make that ole woman of his a widder."

As she sat, she recalled arriving in New York, coming off the bus over at the Port Authority Terminal, her heart beating with anticipation because she'd read about how grand things were and how large and fast everything was in New York City. She had fallen asleep in Pennsylvania somewhere reading Pearl Buck's *The Good Earth*, and she had dreamt of stepping out of a house in the middle of Central Park. She was wearing a bonnet and there were millions of small, yellow butterflies and every one of them that came near her kissed her gently on the face and some rode on her bonnet as she walked. She was so happy in the dream. She sat up, awakened to the blinding sunlight beating on her as she lay on Billy's shoulder, his good left hand resting perfectly on her left breast as she slept, even in his own dream world insatiable in his need for her. As the bus got closer to the entrance of the Lincoln Tunnel, which connected the United States to Manhattan Island, she saw the Hudson River and across it, like some distant fantasyland that she had only imagined, the majesty of the New York City skyline.

She couldn't wait to ride the subways and go to the top of the Empire State Building. She wanted to visit Rockefeller Center, see the Statue of Liberty, the lights of Broadway, Yankee Stadium, the Museum of Natural History, the Metropolitan Museum, Carnegie Hall. She'd even heard of the Russian Tea Room and '21' and El Morocco, and was disappointed when she learned that the latter was no longer open. Everything she knew was acquired through reading novels. *Breakfast at Tiffany's*, *Butterfield 8*, *Call It Sleep*. And the authors of other novels: Ayn Rand, Henry Miller, James Baldwin, J. D. Salinger, all of them painting New York so that every sight of the city evoked for her some memory from her reading.

They had gone outside of the bus terminal with all their bags and instrument cases and Billy waved and up came a big yellow Checker cab. She had pointed at the jump seats resting on the floor and asked what they were and Billy'd laughed and pulled one up. She sat in it, facing him as they sped across town.

"Thank you, Billy Farrell," she said. "I love you."

"And I love you," he said, unashamedly. "God bless you."

He sat shaking his head and two big tears appeared in his eyes, so that she'd always remember him that way. He was a great big, blond boy with a broken heart and she was going to mend it. She had sat on his lap and kissed him deeply, feeling him instantly erect beneath her so that she pressed herself against him, hugging him desperately to herself until she couldn't breathe and got off his lap and looked at the city as it sped by on the East River Drive, pointing at the bridges in the distance and asking where they led.

He explained that on the other side of the river was Brooklyn. Oh, yes, she said. *A Tree Grows in Brooklyn*, *A View from the Bridge*, and Thomas Wolfe's story "Only the Dead Know Brooklyn." And he said "What?" and she laughed and said never mind and asked if they could go to Brooklyn sometime, surprising him by saying that she wanted to go to Coney Island and the Botanical Gardens and maybe Ebbetts Field. She knew the Dodgers had moved to Los Angeles but was disappointed when he told her the old Dodger ballpark had been torn down. She said her favorite team was the St. Louis Cardinals.

"Stan Musial, Enos Slaughter, Red Schoendienst, Marty Marion, and then Bob Gibson and Mike Shannon. Tim McCarver, their catcher, is from Tennessee. Yes he is, and he is a lovely-looking man like you. He was my favorite and I had his baseball card."

"Well, maybe we can go to Shea Stadium when the Cardinals come into town to play the Mets."

"Okay," she said, as the cab approached Houston Street. "We're almost there, aren't we?"

"How can you tell?"

"I don't know," she replied. "I just feel it. The way you described the neighborhood. Look, there's a synagogue."

"You're too much," he said.

She was taken a little aback by the odd-looking apartment, one room lined up after the other, and the bathtub in the kitchen, but within a month she'd scrubbed and cleaned and sewn and mended and by the time she was through, the place

302

looked so pretty that her friend Brenda Torres whom she'd met at the supermarket, said she should go into interior decorating. She read an article in a magazine about utilization of space and drew up a plan for building a loft bed in their bedroom so that she could set up a little desk underneath where she could read, plan meals, work out budgets, and write letters to her mother and father and Aunt Ida.

They had so little money and Billy was so incapable of earning sufficiently to supplement his disability check that in time she began inquiring and eventually was able to get work teaching music in, of all places, Brooklyn. She had been disappointed by the poverty she found there. All the children seemed as if they had been consistently beaten and ridiculed, their sullenness and pain oozing from them. Eventually, she'd managed to get herself transferred closer to home, and that's where she remained for nearly fifteen years—except for the times that she took off to have the children and take care of them—getting to know the people well enough so that she always found someone to care for them while she was teaching and they were not yet ready for play school. But as the children grew up, she worried about what was to happen to Billy. At noon she got up from the rocker and made herself a sandwich, thinking that they had never gone to see the Cardinals at Shea Stadium, but Tim McCarver was doing the Mets games, and that pleased her. She went to the TV, turned it on, and switched it to the game, listening to him, the announcer's voice reminding her of home as she cut vegetables.

28 Of Promises and Leprechauns

One day toward the end of that summer of 1988, her fourth year of spending July and most of August with her father's family,

Vidamía, by now nearly obsessed with the notion of restoring her father to some semblance of normalcy, asked Lurleen why Billy had such a fear of playing the piano. Lurleen explained that because of a wound to his head in the war he couldn't recall much music. She said that maybe not being able to recall the tunes was too painful and it caused him to fear the piano, but she didn't actually know, because Billy wouldn't talk about it, the questions always driving him deeper and deeper into himself. Vidamía said he didn't seem to have any problem playing the guitar. Lurleen explained that it wasn't the same. The kind of music he'd played was a lot more complex and required the player to improvise within the tune, at times deviating from it and reinventing an even more complex structure than the original. And it would appear from the little that Billy had explained to her that all of that was gone and he was no longer able to improvise.

"Knowing that you could do something and then not being able to do it can be frightening."

"Improvise? Making it up as you go?" Vidamía asked.

"Yes, but within a certain structure," Lurleen replied. "Like 'My Favorite Things.' Did you ever hear John Coltrane play that tune?"

Vidamía shook her head and Lurleen went over to the sound system and cued up Coltrane's "My Favorite Things" and asked her if she recognized the tune. Vidamía nodded.

"The movie with Julie Andrews. *The Sound of Music*. I remember now."

"That's right, but listen," Lurleen said. "Coltrane did some amazing things with the tune."

She went on to explain the technical aspects of how John Coltrane reinvented the music and added his virtuosity to a fairly uncomplicated tune. When they were finished listening to the music Vidamía said she felt as if she had been spinning around for a while, except that she didn't feel dizzy, but as if she had been lifted up in the air and was floating.

"And Daddy could do that?"

"That's what I hear," Lurleen said. "He was amazing in the same way. Billy had an opportunity to play with Miles Davis."

"But Daddy doesn't remember the tunes?"

"It's complicated but, yes, something like that. Then there's the problem of his fingers. The technique requires pretty fluid and rapid movement of the right hand on the piano."

Vidamía explained what she'd found out when she stayed overnight for a weekend the previous winter at her friend Elizabeth Reich's house in Tarrytown and her sister Frances, who was twenty and studied the cello at Juilliard, had overheard them talking about Billy's inability to play the piano because of his missing fingers from an accident in the war. Elizabeth had told her of a three-fingered technique for playing the harpsichord that dated back to the sixteenth century. She asked Vidamía which fingers Billy was missing. Vidamía tucked in the middle and pinkie fingers on her right hand with her left, so that her own looked similar to her father's. Elizabeth tucked in the ring and pinkie fingers and moved her three other fingers rapidly and said that maybe Billy could play in a similar way.

She told the story now to Lurleen, who smiled kindly at her and nodded, refreshed by Vidamía's enthusiasm to bring Billy out of his misery. She asked what she had in mind.

"Well, I thought maybe I could talk to him," she said. "He trusts me."

"It wouldn't hurt to try, but don't be disappointed if he doesn't respond."

"Thank you," Vidamía said and reached forward and kissed Lurleen.

To understand the burgeoning of Vidamía's new idea, we must look at her great desire to see her father happy. Like a well-seasoned and simmering stew, the idea of helping Billy had been distilling slowly in Vidamía for a number of years, the ingredients softening and blending with each other, the sauce growing thicker and its fragrances more tantalizing.

Irish stew is a staple and whether concocted in the factories of Dinty Moore or Mrs. Meehan's kitchen, it warms the heart and lets one go forth to battle the effings, as does the Rican *sancocho*, or *salcocho*, as it is called in different parts of the Island of Enchantment, meaning *Borinquen*. This tropical stew contains not beef, potatoes, and carrots with a bit of celery, but pork, *yautía*, plantains, corn, green bananas, and the appropriate condiments, including salt, pepper, onion, garlic, sweet peppers, and cilantro, or coriander, which sounds like some sort of bird or maybe a French weapon. But whether Rican or Irish, be it in Kilkenny or Caguas, Cork or Camuy, Donegal or Dorado, Belfast or Bayamón, Ulster or Utuado, Mayo or Mayagüez, Galway or Guayama, Connemara or Cacimar, this concoction must cook slowly, to allow all the ingredients to mix with each other, draw from each other flavor and strength, boil and simmer and settle before it can be served. Sometimes, it tastes better on the second or even the third day, depending on how large a stew has been initially prepared.

A similar process began when Vidamía realized that in her wallet she held the final ingredient for helping her father. She didn't know how she would accomplish this, but it seemed to her as if the idea of purchasing the piano, which began to form during her sixteenth-birthday party, now created a new urgency in her.

She fell asleep that night thinking of how she would approach her father and explain that she'd like to help him try to play the piano again. She hoped it wouldn't frighten him, but she had to make an attempt. If he was that good, and if that was what he loved doing, then perhaps his avoidance of the music was making him withdrawn. Great-grandpa Buck and Great-grandma Brigid had said he could play. Grandma Maud said it was a waste that he wasn't playing. Mr. Butterworth had said that back before the war there weren't too many who could play as well as Billy.

Vidamía woke up with the same concerns. She dressed in jeans and a floppy shirt buttoned to the top and put on orange socks and her black high-top sneakers. When she came into the kitchen Lurleen was already making breakfast. Her father was sitting at the kitchen table drinking coffee and reading the paper.

"Good morning, Mama," she said.

"Morning, darling," Lurleen said. "You want some coffee?"

"Yes, please," she said, sitting on a chair across from her father. "Good morning, Daddy."

"Good morning, honey," Billy said, looking up from the paper. "How you doing? We ain't playing today. Why are you up so early?"

"I wanted to talk to you."

"I gotta go and empty out an apartment," he said, returning to the paper.

"Can I go with you? I can help you."

Billy sipped his coffee, ran a hand through his beard and then his hair and shook his head.

"Naw, that's the last thing I need. Your mother coming down on me cause I got you working emptying apartments and selling the stuff and then cleaning out the place."

"I'm not going to tell her. Please, Daddy."

He thought a moment, relented by nodding his assent, and went back to reading the paper until Lurleen brought him eggs, grits, and bacon with four pieces of toast and more coffee. Vidamía had eggs and toast and some juice and around eight o'clock she put her Yankees baseball cap on backward. They took the elevator and walked the few blocks to Ludlow Street. Although she had walked these blocks many times, as they crossed the street she noticed, as if for the first time, the piano store. She was going to wait until it was time to come back to the loft for lunch to talk to her father about it, but there it was. It was like an omen, like it was meant to be. Like Rima had talked about karma—like it was her karma to want to do this and have the piano store be there on the way to this job.

They spent the better part of the morning putting the place in order, separating clothes, books, dishes, glasses, and anything else salvageable into boxes. The furniture was useless and Billy spent the next hour carrying the heavier pieces down from the second-floor apartment to the sidewalk. She tried thinking of ways to bring up the subject of his playing the piano, but he was totally absorbed in what he was doing and it wasn't right to disturb him. Around noon Billy said they'd go back and eat lunch and that he really appreciated her helping, but now he had to bring the boxes with the books and glasses down the street to see if he could sell the stuff, and he'd feel ashamed to have her see him doing this.

"I won't feel ashamed, Daddy," she said. "I don't care what you do. I'd never be ashamed of you. You're my father. If you just worked at this and nothing else I wouldn't be ashamed."

He nodded and looked at her, his eyes hurt and his left hand rubbing his beard.

"This is all I do, baby," he said.

"You play music, Daddy," she said. "That makes people happy. You should look up and see their faces once in a while. All those people that come by when we're playing. They're just regular people. Some of them are going back to their jobs after lunch, maybe some of them just got fired; or maybe they're out looking for work, or going in to quit work; or maybe they're coming from visiting someone in the hospital. Whatever they're doing they stop because they wanna take a break from their lives, and when we play it makes them forget what they have to go and do. If it wasn't for you they wouldn't be able to do that."

"Naw," Billy said, turning and looking out of the window to the other tenements. "That was all Lurleen's idea. She's the one who thought of it."

"Yeah, but if you didn't play music and go with all of us we couldn't go out there and play. When you're with us we feel like we can go anywhere and nothing can happen to us. We feel safe when we go with you. And we love playing music with you. We all play because we like playing, but we also do it to make you happy. Because we know that you like to see us happy."

When Billy turned there were tears in his eyes. He couldn't say anything but stood there, his eyes to the ceiling, the tears running down his cheeks and his head nodding slowly. He sat down on the windowsill and took a bandanna and wiped his eyes.

"Sometimes when we're playing," he said, looking down at the worn linoleum floor, "I get so much into the music that I forget you're my kids and I think I'm with my parents and you and Cliff and the girls and Lurleen are my brother and sisters." He looked up, his eyes helpless, pleading. "That's crazy, ain't it? I shouldn't even be telling you stuff like that."

"No, it's beautiful," she said, and before she could think how she should put it, she asked, "Could you try playing again, Daddy, please?"

There was a momentary panic in his face as if he understood her request perfectly, and immediately he disappeared behind the curtain of fear from which he peeked out at the world. She grabbed his face and made him look at her, pleading with him not to go away.

"Please," she said. "Please, Daddy. Don't, please. I'm not asking you anything terrible. Please, could you try?"

"Try what, baby?"

"Don't," she said. "You know what I'm asking you."

"I don't, baby."

"Try playing the piano again."

At the mention of the word his eyes grew dark and he turned away to look out of the window, shaking his head violently. At one point he started to go outside, but she blocked his way and told him not to. And then she was sobbing uncontrollably from the emotion of the request, as if in asking she had been drawn into the vortex of her father's horror, so that she felt as if at any moment she would faint from the effort. She felt as if within the room there was a force of tremendous magnitude, fighting against her and pressing on her chest, and a voice telling her that she had gone too far and she'd have to answer for her boldness.

"You can't do this," she said. "I don't know everything that happened but you can't keep this up. We love you and we see what not playing does to you. You gotta try, Daddy."

"I'm sorry," he said, holding her desperately to him, smoothing her hair as she nestled into him, and she, feeling his beard and his hair and the tobacco and sweat of him. "Please don't cry. Please don't," he was saying over and over.

She began to relax and he let her go and was again shaking his head.

"I can't, baby," he said, holding up his hand. "You need five fingers to play the piano."

"That's not true," she said. "I talked to my girlfriend's sister, Frances Reich, who studies cello at Juilliard and she said there's a way you can play the piano with three fingers. It was a technique they used for the harpsichord."

"You're too much," he said, shaking his head and mussing up her hair. "Too much. With the first two fingers and the thumb, right?"

"Yeah," she said, momentarily deflated.

"That's not the same."

"It doesn't matter, because you haven't tried, and you should."

"Honey, let's go eat lunch."

"No, you have to promise you'll try."

"What am I gonna do with you? Just thinking about it gives

me a headache and makes me wanna go for a long walk off a short pier."

"Very funny," she said, not grasping the allusion. "I'll go with you."

He looked at her and frowned, for a moment unsure if she understood and was willing to die with him, but worried now that she was truly serious about what she was saying.

"Why does it bother you so much?" he said, his voice adult but not at all fatherly, inquisitive as to her motives, not suspicious but truly wanting to know what she thought.

"You really want to know?"

"Yeah, I really want to know," he said, a small smile crossing his lips at her boldness.

"Can I speak and not feel like I'm gonna hurt your feelings?"

"Yeah, sure," he said. "Go ahead."

"You wanna know what kids think is really important about their parents?"

He shook his head, helplessly, afraid to tell her that it didn't matter because whatever it was he couldn't fulfill her expectations. He was lost and whatever had taken place in his life it was too dark and deep for her to penetrate, for he had allowed someone who trusted him with his life to die, and therefore whatever trust she had in him was false, something she had made up but which had nothing to do with him.

"I'm not too good at that kind of thing, baby," he said. "Let's go eat lunch. Okay?"

"No way," she said, strongly. "Your family loves you."

"I know that."

"Well, it hurts them to see you like this."

"I can't help it, baby."

"Yes, you can. You know what we love about you? That you haven't given up. With everything that's happened to you in your life, losing your father and then the thing with Uncle Joey, you still hold your head high. And everybody says you're a fantastic piano player. I've spoken to everybody, Daddy. Grandpa Buck, Grandma Brigid, Grandma Maud, and Mr. Butterworth. They all say it. 'He was a great piano player.' They say that when you were seventeen there were famous men who just stood around watching you play and shaking their heads about how much feeling you could put into the music. I don't know much about jazz, but what I've heard from Cookie and Cliff and the little that Mama explained, you gotta be pretty good to get that kind of praise from people. I know that if you tried, you could play, Daddy. I know it."

"But I can't, baby," he said, stopping in midsentence. "Most of the time I'm hiding."

She was stunned and looked at him in the early-afternoon light coming in through the unwashed glass of the window. He had finally admitted it. She had been right and it struck her as significant that he was using the very same words she had thought. He had been hiding, but now he realized it. She knew enough about psychology to know that this was a significant moment. He thought a few seconds and knew that he had spoken accurately, but he couldn't say what in fact it was that he was hiding from. He knew it had to do with Joey, but . . . what?

After a while he stood up and with his arm around her said that they should go and get some lunch, suggesting that rather than going home they should go to Katz's and get a hotdog or a kasha knish and a root beer soda. She said that was fine but that she wasn't moving unless he gave her his word that he'd try playing again.

"Sure," he said. "Whatever you say, boss."

He was kidding with her, trying to avoid the subject. He locked the door of the apartment and they walked north on Ludlow Street, her step bouncy and her heart soaring as she imagined telling Cookie about it. Her smile was so wide that people looked at her and couldn't help smiling. As they got halfway down the block between Rivington and Stanton Streets she saw the piano shop and immediately ran across the street and motioned him to come over.

"It's an omen, Daddy," she said. "Look at them. Pianos. All kinds. New ones, used ones. Wow! Of all places! Right under our noses!" She looked up and remarked on the fact that here they were, on Ludlow Street, almost on the corner of Stanton Street. "This is very strange. A definite omen."

He came over tentatively and stood on the sidewalk, looking at the pianos inside the store, waiting for his head to begin hurting, but nothing happened. She took his right hand and held it tight, making the knuckles of his missing fingers tingle. He didn't feel the pain in his head, but inside of him everything was racing and wanting to get away from the front of the store as soon as possible.

"Let's go, baby," he said.

"Promise?"

"Promise what?" he said, angrily. "Stop it, okay?" He tore away from her and continued down the street, crossing and heading toward Katz's. She followed him and when she caught up, she matched him stride for stride until they were inside the restaurant and had taken their tickets and gone to the counter. After they got their food and sat down, he said he was sorry for being angry.

"Forget it," she said. "You got plenty to be angry about." And then she surprised him and herself. "If it was me I'd be so pissed, I'd be punching people every other fucking day."

"No, that's not right. It wasn't anybody's fault."

"That may be, but I'd be pretty angry, so I don't blame you," she said, noting that he had softened up considerably. "That doesn't mean I'm gonna let up on you," she added.

"What's that supposed to mean?"

"That I'm gonna keep bugging you about playing the piano."

"You're too much," he said. "You know who you remind me of?"

"Grandma Maud."

"Nope."

"Who?"

"My old man," he said. "Kevin Farrell. Your grandpa." And then his eyes clouded over and filled with tears. "He woulda loved you, and you woulda loved him. You're just like him." And then he was talking to her openly about being with his father, recalling a time when they had gone sledding and he'd fallen off his sled on the way down the hill and didn't want to do it anymore, but his father just stayed on him, not mean or anything, but talking to him about how he was the greatest kid any father ever had and the best sledder in the whole state of New York—no, the whole United States—no, the whole world—no, the whole universe. On and on, until he was delirious with laughter and back on the sled, flying down the hill and had totally forgotten the spill, unafraid and free, so that when he got down below all he could see was his father standing above silhouetted against the snow, smiling at him, his fist up in the air in triumph so that he had no choice but to do the same. And then right in the middle of the restaurant he was laughing uproariously, crazily, his eyes crinkled and his face suddenly red, laughing like she'd never seen him, so that at first it frightened her, then after a while she was laughing right along with him while people in the restaurant looked at them. After a while he stopped himself and his jaw hurt, as if muscles long unused had been strained to their limit.

"I just figured something out," he said. "The reason that you remind me of him is that you both have the same gift of blarney."

"What?" she said. "Blarney?"

"Yeah, the gift of talking," he said, looking at her so admiringly that she was slightly embarrassed, and a little frightened by his intensity. "It comes from a stone in a castle in Cork back in Ireland. You have to hang upside down and if you kiss the stone you develop the gift for talking smooth like you do. It's the first time I've realized how Irish you are. I always thought of you as this beautiful Puerto Rican girl, but you're Irish. I mean, you're both, but I now recognize you. You're more like my cousins Rose and Deidre and the girls I grew up with than you are like your mother. You know what my old man used to say to me?"

"What?"

"May the Lord keep you in His hand and never close His fist too tight on you," he said, raising his bottle of root beer soda so that she had no choice but to raise her orange soda and clink his. "That's what he'd say whenever we were drinking a soda. And then he'd tell me stories that my grandfather, Seamus Farrell, had told him."

"About what?"

"About fairies and leprechauns," he said, leaning over to her conspiratorially. "Leprechauns have bags of gold, and if you catch one they have to give them to you. I had a leprechaun friend. His name was Mr. McQuinlan. He was a black leprechaun."

"Black?"

"Yeah, black. Very well dressed. I always talked to him before I played music. The piano. This is too much! You remind me of my dad. Oh, man, he could praise you, my father. And you're the same. After a while you find yourself caught up in the words."

"That's the same thing Mr. Butterworth said about your playing," she said.

"See, there you go again," he said.

"No, honest."

"Yeah, yeah," he said. "You know who you are?"

"Who?"

"Beara," he said, except it sounded like Beohrrah to her.

"Who's that?" she said, scrunching up her face.

"She was the daughter of the king of Spain."

"Spain?"

"Oh, Spain and Ireland have a long history together. Study it and you'll see. Anyway, it was told in a prophecy that she'd find her husband in the river Eibhear. Some people say that's the Ebro River in Spain. Anyway, a salmon showed up in shining armor. It was the salmon of wisdom. Beara took him as her husband and she was able to know everything that was going to happen in Ireland. It's just a story that my grandfather Seamus Farrell used to tell. But that could be you. My grandma Caitlin swore it was the truth."

They continued eating, and, scarred for life or not, Billy was suddenly talking about things he had buried in his childhood. Whenever she attempted to talk about his life as a young man, with as much gift for gab as he accused her of having, he steered the conversation away from that part of his life and talked about his childhood and the times he'd spent with his father and mother prior to his father's death.

29 Blind Walking

When Billy and Vidamía were done eating, they went back to the apartment and finished clearing it. She then accompanied him while he sold the items of value which he'd found. Around two in the afternoon they returned to the loft with nearly a hundred dollars. More important, she had obtained a promise that he'd go with her and try to play the piano at a dance studio one evening that week. Her end of the bargain was that she was not to tell Lurleen or the kids about it, nor about his talking as he had, and certainly not about his laughing. She asked why, and he said that he didn't want them to think that he would be like that all the time and he didn't want them to be disappointed. She said that maybe he would be, but his eyes were far away again and he nodded patiently, pleading silently with her. She agreed and said it would be their secret. On their way home she asked him if she was really like his father, Kevin Farrell. He said she sure reminded him of his father and she asked if he believed in reincarnation.

"Like when people come back as something else?" he asked.

"Yeah," she said. "Buddhists believe in reincarnation. I went to a meeting a few years ago and they talked about that."

He thought a moment and said that he didn't think so, and that he never saw it happen, but monks in Vietnam had burned themselves alive to protest the war.

"They poured gasoline over themselves and lit a match," he said. "I guess they believe in that kind of stuff. They figured they were going to come back, so why worry, right?"

"At the meeting they said that human life was the most important thing in the world. Once a human, always a human, but you come back a different person. So maybe this time around, even though I'm a girl, deep inside I'm your father," she said.

"Yeah," he chuckled. "Maybe you're right. Except you're bossier than he was."

The thought intrigued her and she said nothing more, thinking about her resolve to take care of him. She wondered if she was up to the task. The idea frightened her a little bit.

Three days later Vidamía explained to Lurleen that she had made plans to meet her friend Rosalind to help her with her summer-school math course. She'd be back no later than ten. Lurleen saw no problem with that, knowing that Vidamía was up to something and that it had to do with Billy and the discussion she and Vidamía had had about Billy's being able to play again and her friend Elizabeth, who had a sister at Juilliard. Vidamía left at seven o'clock and waited for Billy near the Grand

Street subway station, watching the hustle and bustle of early evening. It was hot and muggy and each waiting minute made her more anxious. A couple of guys around twenty came by and eyed her. Another tried to start a conversation, but she turned away, took a file out of her pocketbook and began filing her fingernails as Cookie had said she should do. "They get real scared when you pull out the nail file," she said. "Like you're gonna stab them in the eyes. Which is what you gotta do if they try to, like, do something to you." The guy shrugged his shoulders and went off, saying something like there's other fish in the sea.

About ten minutes later she saw her father walking up the street, his head down and his hands in his pockets, his fatigue jacket on, even in the heat. When he saw her he smiled, nodded his head, and said let's go. She had never seen him so frightened, but she steeled herself to whatever was to happen. They went down the stairs into the subway. She was certain her father would have turned around and gone back had the train not come right away. They rode up to Fiftieth Street, in the Theater District. The subway car was air-conditioned, and most people sat comfortably. He, on the other hand, was nearly shivering, hugging himself against some perceived cold. When they emerged into the street the sun had gone down and the bright lights of Broadway made him flinch and shrink back for a moment, his eyes opened wide. He pointed at a topless bar but said nothing. She asked him what was the matter, but he just shook his head, having recalled that the place, which now advertised a cure for lonely men, had once been the most famous of all jazz clubs, Birdland, named after the legendary Charlie Parker. He wanted to tell her that Pop Butterworth had brought him to the club in 1964 to hear Miles Davis rehearse. He was only fourteen years old, but he was big and so withdrawn that, wearing his suit and tie, he looked like another one of the musicians. But the words couldn't come out because if he started talking, then he'd have to tell her about not wanting to play and record with Miles and his quintet, and then his head would hurt worse than it was hurting at that moment.

"I know about Birdland," she said.

"You do? Who told you?"

"Mr. Butterworth."

"Did he tell you anything else?"

"Lots of things."

"What things?"

"He told me how great you were and how you could've played with Miles Davis," she said resolutely, unafraid, certain that the truth would win out.

"I wish he hadn't," he said.

"It doesn't matter," she said. "You could try again."

"But—"

"You promised, Daddy," she said. "It's nothing but straight ahead now," she added, borrowing Buck Sanderson's phrase.

He recognized the phrase, and the fact that the music—be-bop—was also called that. The music he loved was also called "straight ahead," and he had promised. But the fear was no less, and he tried bearing it as he had walking through the jungle, his machine gun on his shoulder, hearing the bugs and the birds, aware that the enemy was out there, tightening up so that he wouldn't pee in his pants.

They continued walking until they came to a building. She then pulled on the sleeve of his jacket for him to stop. Taking a slip of paper out of her jeans, she checked it and went inside. Rosalind Louden, whose mother owned the dance studio, had assured Vidamía that there would be no one there. She had handed her the keys, shrugging her shoulders and saying they could stay as long as they wanted and told her exactly where the lights were so that when they got out of the elevator on the third floor Vidamía guided herself with her right hand on the wall until she found the door. With her left she held on to her father's hand, feeling his nervousness and sweat and his heart pounding from fear. She let go of his hand and found the lights exactly where Rosalind had said, switching them on so that the big studio with its mirrors and barre were illuminated brightly and, at the far end, like a dark shadow, like some primeval beast, its maw opened and ready to swallow its prey, sat the grand piano in all its splendor.

Vidamía took his hand again but it was like cold stone, his body frozen to the spot where he had stopped, his eyes unseeing and the fear burning forth from them. She pulled at him and he came forward reluctantly, the weight of him, not his size but the heavy pain he was carrying, making her struggle so that before long she was sweating and finding it hard to breathe, such was the effort. When they finally got to the piano she was exhausted and simply pointed to the bench for him to sit down. But he was unseeing and simply stared out into the night to the theater and neon lights of Broadway.

"What's the matter?" she said.

"We should go," he replied without turning.

"Please sit down. You have to try, please."

He took a big breath and saw himself in the mirror and closed his eyes at the shock of his image. He hardly ever looked into a mirror. It was one of the reasons he never shaved. Whenever he had to wash up, brush his teeth, or comb his hair he avoided the mirror, but now everywhere he looked he saw himself. His head was bursting, the pain unbearable, so that even his face hurt, and his eyes were tearing from the effort he was making not to scream and bolt. He felt the flashback coming. Suddenly he was there again, the automatic fire coming in spurts, the thudding of the mortars dull as they whooshed and then hit, and overhead the choppers blasting away, beyond them the screaming of the jets as they dove and whined to drop their napalm and rise once more into the sky.

"I can't, baby," he said. "Let's go."

And then she hit on an idea. She went to the light switches, turned them off and asked him to close his eyes. He insisted that they should go, but she asked him again to close his eyes.

"Just make believe you're blind," she said, taking him by the arm.

"Blind?"

"Yes, blind. Like Ray Charles."

He shook his head but did as she told him, letting the warm darkness envelop him so that he was traveling away from the war into some other place where he'd never been. Even his step seemed oddly buoyant as she held his arm and walked him to what he imagined was his eventual destination, which was the piano. But they walked and walked and never got there, going round and round the dance studio, Billy wanting to open his eyes but in spite of himself enjoying the effect the enforced blindness had on him. She didn't know where the idea had come from; perhaps she had read it in a book, or overheard it in a conversation between her mother and a colleague; perhaps from a television program, but it didn't matter.

After five minutes they had not yet reached the piano. Guided by the lights outside, she walked him around the perimeter of the room, avoiding the triangle of half of the room where the piano sat, tracing a trajectory along the opposite three sides of the make-believe triangle, asking him if he smelled anything. He laughed and said he could smell nothing. She insisted and after a while he said he could smell her perfume.

"What else?" she said.

"They mopped the floor."

"What do you smell?"

"Floor wax. I don't know. Soap."

"What else?"

"Leather. Sweat."

"Do you smell the piano?"

"The piano?"

"Yes, the piano. Can you smell it?"

"I don't think so."

"What does a piano smell like?"

"I never thought about it . . ." he said, his voice trailing off. He wanted to open his eyes, but he felt good walking as he did. "Oil . . . brass . . . wood . . ."

"Did you play with your eyes closed?" she asked.

They had stopped and she felt him suddenly relax.

"Yes, with my eyes closed," he said.

"Good," she said. "Don't open your eyes, and take me to the piano. I'm closing my eyes, too," she said.

He kept his eyes closed as Vidamía had asked, more out of a need to shut out the moment than a willingness to participate in his daughter's experiment. He stood rooted to the spot where he was standing. She said nothing and he waited, swaying a little. Surprisingly, his headache was gone and he began drifting off as if he were in a dream. With his right hand out, sniffing the air, he took about six steps, found the piano, felt along the keyboard, found the leather-covered bench, and sat down, guiding her until she was sitting next to him.

The keys felt cold to the touch, but as if his fingers were filled with iron filaments and the black-and-white keyboard were a magnet, he felt drawn uncannily to hear its tone. He played a few chords and was surprised at the clarity of the sound that emerged from the piano.

Vidamía stood up and asked him to play something for her.

"What?" he asked, recalling that at one time he had known over three hundred and fifty tunes from memory.

"I don't know," she said. "Something you like."

And then he was once again a boy and he was sitting at the piano at Grandpa Sanderson's house and it was his father's birthday and he was asked to play and he'd said what? and his father had said please play "Danny Boy" and he'd played and his father had sung the song in a surprisingly beautiful tenor voice:

> Oh Danny Boy the pipes,
> The pipes are calling.
> From glen to glen
> And down the mountain side.
>
> The summer's gone
> And all the flowers are falling.
> 'Tis you, 'tis you
> Must go and I must bide.
>
> But come ye back
> When summer's in the meadow
> Or when the valley's hushed
> And white with snow . . .

He was surprised that he'd found the melody with his right hand. She asked him what the song was, because it was so sad and beautiful, and he told her, and she asked if it had words.

"It has words."

"How do they go?"

He recited the words and she said they were beautiful.

"Could you play it again? Please."

He played it again and she hummed, her voice finding the notes easily. He was pleased that she could hear the music as well as she did. When he finished he said that they should go, and he opened his eyes. They were in the dark. Outside the window the lights of Broadway were shining inside the dance studio, making long shadows of the barre and the piano, the images reflected in the mirrors. Although he still felt quite anxious, he felt oddly relieved, literally as if a great weight had been removed from his shoulders. In its place, however, the dreaded thought that he'd caused Joey Santiago's death had grown larger. Why did the idea persist? What had really happened? More important, what had been his part in it?

In order to please her, he went back to the studio with her a few more times, but then summer came to an end and she went back to school in Tarrytown and he went back to his routine, promising her that he'd find a place in the neighborhood to practice but never doing so. Even though the idea of a piano no longer induced in him the same panic as before, the notion that he could actually play as he once had, made him consider dreams, and at this juncture in his life that was the worst possible thing that could happen. He wanted no dreams, no future, no expectations of tomorrows or ambitions of glory or goals to attain. Silence and solitude were his aims, and nothing would stand in his way of achieving them.

But she was relentless. In November she came down to the city, met Butterworth and the two of them went to the loft. She was now a woman proper, looking much older than she did during the summer when she went around in jeans; now wearing a skirt and sweater and heels and a long leather coat, her hair cut in a blunt style, her makeup perfect, her green eyes huge and confident.

"Daddy, Mr. Butterworth says you can go over and practice at NYU. Not officially, but there won't be any problem. I know you haven't been able to find a place to practice, so I spoke to him. You can use one of the practice rooms there. No problem at all. Okay?"

He looked at Pop Butterworth and his old friend nodded.

"That's right, son," he said. He gave Billy the address and said, "Just come in, go upstairs, and take one of the practice rooms."

"Yeah, sure, I guess," Billy said, grateful for their caring.

She spent Thanksgiving with her father and his family.

Billy'd gone and practiced at the university, enjoying walking in and taking the elevator and being alone in the soundproof cubicle, acquainting himself once again with the piano. There was always a bit of panic, but it passed quickly, and he was able to recall old standards, mostly ballads, which he would play in long, lugubrious improvisations, but staying away from the more upbeat, hard-driving jazz tunes that would force him to reach into his life. He actually felt grateful that Vidamía had been so persistent, because he knew now that the piano presented no threat. This knowledge, however, did nothing to banish his recurring doubts about how Joey Santiago had died. Why had he said all these years that it had been Viet Cong? There had been none in the area for months, and no one ever found traces of them afterward.

By Christmastime, when Vidamía came down to celebrate the holidays, he was practicing three or four times a week, at times for three hours at a stretch, the music drawing him as if the piano possessed a magnet that pulled consistently at him, its power growing stronger. She asked if she could go with him one day and had stood spellbound, watching him, the music transporting her to another level of awareness where she forgot that the person bent over the piano was her father. She knew then that she was helping him come out of himself and felt intense satisfaction. She wanted to share this with her mother when she returned home, but the opportunity never came up and she had to be content with discussing her elation with her grandmother Maud. Her grandmother, with typical Irish pessimism, having experienced a lifetime of disappointments, cautioned her about becoming too hopeful. Vidamía nodded patiently, hugged and kissed her, and, as was her style in reassuring the adults around her, said that she shouldn't worry.

30 The Idea

As the spring of 1989 rolled around, it became apparent that the upcoming summer would be different from previous ones. Both Cliff and Cookie, whether out of teen rebellion proper or because playing in the subways would be too embarrassing for them if any of their classmates saw them, announced one day that they didn't want to play in the family band anymore.

They had spoken to Lurleen and that was fine with her. Cookie was already waiting tables at a Tex-Mex restaurant called Sometimes down in SoHo, having obtained identification that listed her as eighteen years old. She managed to charm the owner, Pam Morgan, a tough Texas cowgirl, or so she described herself, who had worked on Madison Avenue as a copywriter, dabbled in the stock market, got lucky, and eventually, in the mid-eighties, went to school and became a chef. Within a week of working there, Cookie was able to get Cliff a job bussing tables. A couple of evenings a week they worked at the restaurant. Within a month Pam Morgan promised both of them steady employment during the summer. Cookie asked Vidamía if she wanted to work there during the summer.

"We can work together, Vee," she said. "Check it out, it'll be cool. Maybe you'll meet somebody. All kinds of people come in there. Movie stars and everything. There's some cute guys who wait tables. I'm sure you could meet somebody."

Vidamía replied that she wasn't interested in meeting anyone since she was going out with Taylor Breitenbach, a very nice young man studying at Yale who wrote her very nice letters.

"He's studying classics and wants to become an Egyptologist. When he comes home, we spend a lot of time talking and he doesn't have his hands all over me every second."

It occurred to Vidamía at that moment that things in her family were changing rapidly and everyone was growing up quickly. She had to take the SATs the following year and had to do better than she had in her PSATs—at least break 1,500. She'd have to take advanced placement tests in all the sciences, plus history and English. She was determined to go to Harvard, or even join Taylor at Yale. If neither of those schools accepted her, she'd go to Cornell or Brown, but she definitely wanted to be out of New York and away from home.

Whenever Taylor came in, he would pick her up in his car and they'd take long drives or else park somewhere and talk and look at the Hudson River. Sometimes when they kissed, she began to feel extremely strong sexual urges, but the more passionate she became, the more distant Taylor grew. He would break off the embrace and in the most charming way he would begin telling her about sarcophagus construction or the different methods of embalming used in ancient Egypt. His all-consuming passion was antiquity, and, as brilliant a conversationalist as he was, she began to feel that she was risking nothing with him, that she had chosen him precisely because he wouldn't go beyond a certain point.

Her seventeenth birthday was nothing like the extravaganza of the previous year. Her friends came to the small party and gave her books and tapes. Elsa, with great ceremony, gave her a gold bracelet, pendant, and matching earrings, each holding a tiny ruby. Barry gave her a leather bag that had a dozen small pockets inside where she could place books, papers, pens and pencils, calendar, stapler, and other school supplies. The leather was soft but sturdy and, as with everything in their lives, expensive-looking. Inside was a very delicate envelope with a note saying that whatever college she chose, he would handle all the fees, and that she would be assured the use of her gold card without limitation for personal expenses, including living off campus if she so wished. Mrs. Alvarez gave her a poncho from the mountains of Colombia which she said was called a *ruana*. Her grandmother gave her Maja talc and face soap from Spain.

Two days after her birthday she went into New York to meet Cookie on a Saturday. Cookie gave her a new Madonna tape as a present and they talked about how trashy she was. Secretly they both admired the singer's style and cool. They were both attired beautifully in layers of mismatched clothing, mostly silk things they had picked up in thrift shops around lower Manhattan. Each wore high heels, carried big bags, and featured heavy earrings and bracelets. Lurleen said they looked like "high-fashion gypsies." They were done up to emulate Madonna's style, the heavily painted eyebrows, dark lipsticks, fifties-type hairdos, and very pale makeup. Cookie, who was almost sixteen, was already on the pill. She was becoming voluptuous and confident so that when she played her saxophone nobody could focus on the music, only on her beautiful haughty face and her shapely body.

Vidamía and Cookie chose an Italian restaurant near Bleecker Street in the Village, and ordered salads and linguine with seafood. They also ordered a bottle of white wine and got thoroughly plastered. No one questioned them regarding their age since they had mastered, particularly Cookie, the art of acting older. When the check came, Vidamía placed her gold card on the tray with the bill and through the alcoholic haze asked Cookie if she thought their father was going to be all right not having the band.

"I mean, do you think he can handle it?" she said.

"Oh, yeah," Cookie replied. "He's cool with it. He goes over to NYU almost every day and practices. Something's up with him. I don't know what it is, but he's cool."

"Whatta you mean, 'something's up'?"

"Oh, the other day we were bringing groceries up and this cab came too close to us when we were crossing the street and he began yelling at the cabdriver."

"Yelling at him? Daddy?"

"Yeah, Daddy. Shocked the hell outta me, too."

"Yelling?"

"Yeah, yelling. 'Son of a bitch,' and 'stupid mothafucka',' " Cookie whispered and giggled. "Are we drunk?" she asked.

"I think you are," Vidamía said. "I'm not."

"Oh, sure," Cookie said, and they both giggled.

The waiter came over, asked for the fourth time if everything was all right, and Cookie, playing the sophisticate, said, "Quite all right, thank you." It was as Vidamía began slipping the card back in her wallet that the idea finally burst forth and began to wiggle and turn in the sunlight. When the waiter went away, they both looked at each other and began giggling again. And then all at once Vidamía was very serious and Cookie looked at her.

"What's the matter?" she said.

"I was thinking maybe I'll get him a piano."

"Get who a piano? Daddy?"

"Yeah, for his birthday."

"A piano? Are you fucking crazy?" Cookie said, loud enough so that a number of people looked in their direction and frowned. "Sorry, folks," she said. "This girl wants me to go home with her and we just met. I mean it's okay being a lesbian, but be cool, right?"

"Cookie!"

"The hell with them," Cookie said. "They want a show, I'll give 'em one. Come on, let's get outta here."

"Yeah, let's go downtown and get dessert and coffee," Vidamía said.

"Whatever," Cookie said, and, slinging her scarf back over her shoulder so that it flared out and came to rest perfectly on her other shoulder, darted a look of disdain at a table of very stately people, gave her blond hair a delicate shake, turned her head away theatrically, and made the grandest exit the restaurant had seen since Sophia Loren visited the place back in 1960 after she'd finished filming *The Black Orchid* with Anthony Quinn.

Arm in arm, their balance a bit awry, they managed to make it to Houston Street, where they hailed a cab, got in, and told the driver to take them to Little Italy. In the cab, Cookie ascertained that Vidamía was serious about purchasing a piano for their father.

"You're not kidding, are you?"

"No, of course not."

"Girl, you're crazy. *Más tostá que una bolsa 'e maní, mamita.*"

"What? What's that supposed to mean? I'm more toasted than a bag of . . . what?"

"Peanuts, mama. More roasted than a bag of peanuts. Your brains are fried, honey. A piano? Girl, get real, okay? Where you gonna get ahold of that kind of money?"

"How much can it cost?" Vidamía said.

"Don't even think about it. We better talk to Mama when we get back."

"No way. I don't want her to know. You gotta promise. When it's done we'll tell her."

"No good, Vee. We gotta tell her. She knows about shit like that. I mean, a piano, a good one could cost as much as twenty-five thousand bucks. If you get a piece of junk, it won't do him any good. You gotta figure all kinds of things. You seen the way he plays. Even with those eight fingers, the piano's gonna take a beating. He can be *très* lyrical on ballads but, honey, on up-tempo shit the man goes crazy. Brubeck and his vertical style is a summer breeze compared to Daddy."

"Like what? How much?"

"Oh, I don't know. That's why we gotta talk to her. You gotta make sure the frame's in good shape, that the mechanism is okay, and the keyboard is balanced. It's a lot of work. Why don't you just forget it. He's doing good going over to NYU. Ever since you came down before Thanksgiving and hooked him up, he goes over there almost every afternoon. With Mr. Butterworth being over there and everything, he's cool. He's been acting a little weird the last few days, like I said, but you know. He's a moody guy."

"Yeah, I know, I know," Vidamía said, with considerable annoyance. "Could we get one for, like, under ten thousand?"

"Oh, shoot the messenger time, will you? Relax, girl. Ten thousand? You're gonna spend ten thousand on a piano? How?"

"I'll put it on my card," Vidamía said, patting her pocketbook. "The same way I paid for dinner. I've been thinking about it. If we're not gonna have the band, then that's what I'd like to do. You have to help me, Cookie. Maybe Fawn could learn how to play, too."

"You're crazier than I thought, honey," Cookie said, the alcohol no longer a factor. "Maybe your mother was right. She should've never let you come down here. You're getting like some of my homegirls, totally in the clouds about things. You have to be more practical about stuff."

"Oh, excuse me," Vidamía said with considerable attitude.

"What now, Ms. Cranky, I'm having a bad day and whatnot?"

"You're getting like Taylor," Vidamía said, haughtily. "Very uptight and conservative."

"Bitch," Cookie said, laughing.

"Takes one to call one," Vidamía said, wanting to laugh but maintaining her posture and looking at Cookie like they were in the playground and some badass *jeba* walked in and was trying to intimidate them, her lips pursed and her head turned like get outta my face.

"*Tu madre,*" Cookie said, as if to say go take that attitude to your mother, knowing that to every Rican, the mention of their mom in that way is a big insult.

"*La tuya que es mi comadre,*" Vidamía said, employing the traditional retort in which you turn the insult back to the other person's mother, a type of dozens, a oneupmanship game.

The bantering escalated. Cookie told Vidamía where she could go with her harebrained idea.

"*Vete pa'l carajo*," she said.

"*Contigo abajo*," Vidamía replied, the two of them laughing and pushing at each other, enjoying this bit of male-oriented cursing.

"Fine," Cookie said, accepting the latest insult, feigning hurt and looking out the window of the cab.

"Does that mean you're gonna help?" Vidamía said.

"Only if Mama's involved," she said without turning from the window.

"Okay, Mama's involved."

Cookie now turned back, shook her head, and smiled lovingly at Vidamía.

"You're such a crazy girl, you know," she said. "Half the time I don't know why you do stuff. You got such a big heart that I worry about people taking advantage of you sometimes."

"I love you too, you dope," Vidamía said. "You still up for dessert?"

"Yeah, let's get fat, honey," Cookie said as the cab arrived at their destination. "That boy Mario wears me out."

Cookie paid and they got out of the cab and headed for Ferrara's, where they sat for the next hour discussing their plans. They each had *baba au rhum* and espresso, all the while smoking cigarettes, which they didn't inhale but which they held with considerable style, Cookie even sporting a cigarette holder and producing the cigarettes out of a silver case she'd found in an antique store in the East Village. Every man, young or old, looked in their direction admiringly.

"We'll talk to Mama, see if she has any suggestions," Vidamía said. "Maybe get her to come with us and we'll start the process, okay?"

"Process, right," Cookie said, arching her eyebrows mockingly.

"What's the matter now?"

"Nothing."

"No, come on. Tell me."

"You talk funny."

"What? What?"

"Why can't we just get a fucking piano. Why we gotta get a *process* going?"

"No, c'mon. Seriously. What's the matter?"

"Nothing! I like making fun of you. You gotta tell Taylor Breitenfrog, or whatever, to get his ass someplace else. You're starting to sound like the Bride of Frankendemia, girl. Oh, God, remember when we had that fight about how you were always correcting people?"

"Yeah, you made me cry," Vidamía said. "You're right about Taylor. I have never seen such a dull cute boy in my life."

"There you go, girl. He is so white bread. No soul at all," she said, and suddenly brightened.

"What?"

"There's this party next Saturday and I really wanna go and knowing you, you're going to be totally obsessed with this piano thing and I'll get dragged into it and miss the party. I dig parties and whatnot, but this is really special. And I really want you to come."

"Why? What's the big deal?"

"It's up on the West Side, and my friend Dina's brother who went to Harvard is throwing the party, and he's invited a whole bunch of friends from the school who live in New York. There's gonna be some good jazz musicians there. Older cats, but really cool people. She says she wants me to meet some of them and maybe we'll jam. You should come with me."

"Cats, huh?" Vidamía said, using the opportunity to poke fun at Cookie.

"What?"

"You talk funny."

"Oh, shut up, you virgin *puta*. You gotta go with me, Vee."

"Okay, okay, but I wanna get this other thing done."

"We will, don't worry. We won't party Friday night, and we'll get up early and go piano hunting. There's gotta be stores open on Saturdays."

When they finished their coffees, Cookie took the little bit of lemon rind between her lips so that one of the Italian waiters nodded approvingly. She batted her eyelashes at him and then shrugged her shoulders as if to say, "I know I'm gorgeous."

Vidamía paid the bill and they walked the eight or ten blocks past Italian restaurants and Chinese noodle joints, through deserted streets, their high heels clicking on the sidewalk, prompting Cookie to exclaim that chances were if anybody drove by they'd probably think the two of them were hookers.

That Saturday they began trying to find the right piano for their father. In the evening Vidamía and Cookie went to the party, impressively attired. Vidamía met someone there and suddenly began to look at her life from a different perspective. The attraction wasn't immediate, but the curiosity was immense. He asked her if he could see her again and she said that they had mutual friends and probably would see each other if he was going to be in the city. Could she give him her phone number? She wrote out the Farrells' number.

"Okay," he'd said, looking at her and smiling so that later she recalled the feeling of ease she felt in looking at Wyndell Ross.

They had stood there in the warm summer night just looking at one another, feeling as if they knew each other, which was crazy because they had just met. She wanted to tell him about her father and getting a piano for him, wishing for him to understand how much it meant to her to do this for Billy. She wanted to hear her father play, to understand more about jazz, which meant so much to him, and to her life now.

31 Hanging Out

That first summer Cookie took her everywhere and introduced her as "my sister, Vidamía"; not half sister, but sister, sometimes even saying "my big sister," letting the pride speak for itself, because it validated her existence among her friends whose pedigree originated in Puerto Rico, that Island of Enchantment which in her eyes produced a firmament of dazzling language and music, and whose bloodlines were those of Spanish and French corsairs, Andalusian gypsies, Catalonian poets, African drummers, and Taino Indian warriors. A tie to this tanner, darker-haired being confirmed that in spite of her own blond hair, blue eyes, and white skin she was truly part of her Rican crew. Whether they were in the Pitt Street Pool or Henry Street Settlement for their summer-camp program or went over to Tompkins Square Park or the playground hanging out with her homegirls, Cookie now felt she truly belonged in her world. Unlike Elsa, who wanted to legitimize her whiteness by having Vidamía connected to her blond siblings, Cookie wanted validation of her Ricanness.

"Yo, Cookie, who's your friend, huh?"

"Ain't you gonna introduce us, homegirl?"

"Yo, like, I'm sorry, Nydia. This is my sister, Vidamía. Vee, this is Nydia Torres and the bad one over there's Patria Nuñez. S'appenin', Patria?"

"Your sister?"

"Yeah, my sister."

"Yo, she don't look like you?"

"Yes, she does. Look at her nose. We got the same nose."

Talking like that and Vidamía watching everything as if it were going three times the regular speed, the language flying from English to Spanish, and her sister, Cookie, staying with it so that she couldn't believe she'd say things like: "So, like we went up to the roof, right? *El rufo* over on Avenue C. And we was up there scopin' on Rafael cause sometimes *se baña* with the window open. Yo, *velando*, right? *Ligando*, up there and whatnot. And me and Laurie Quintana are up there and, check it out, right? *Ahí viene. Esnú*, baby, totally without any clothes and his *coso* hanging down real thick and long. Yo, me and Laurie fell out laughing and Laurie almost slipped and *por poco se cae del rufo, coño*. She almost fell off the roof, girl. It was awesome, honey. *De película*, like in the movies, if you get my meaning. Full frontal, mama."

Vidamía was amazed at her sister's freedom, running around the neighborhood and talking to everybody—crazy people, drug addicts, drunks, homeless people, cops, and boys of all ages, some of them saying all kinds of things to her, and she laughing and telling them things back. Like they'd say: "Looking good, mama," and she'd just roll her eyes or answer them with "You got it, *loco*, but you can't get it." And the boys would laugh and slap each other five and whistle and walk after her with their tongues flapping like they were dogs.

They often went into the Odessa Restaurant across from Tompkins Square Park and ordered potato pancakes with apple sauce and Cokes with the money they'd earned baby-sitting or running errands, being enterprising and offering to do shopping for elderly people for a dollar or two. Or they went to Kiev or Theresa's over on Second Avenue and ate big kielbasa breakfasts on Saturday mornings after sleeping late, trying on their independence at thirteen and eleven respectively, self-conscious of their figures and their budding womanhood, aware that they were being looked at by grown men and feeling odd because, although everyone independently said they were beautiful, they didn't yet understand their appeal and simply imagined that they hadn't dressed properly, or that a blemish on their face was marring their appearance.

Later, when they were older and Cookie and Mario were really hot for each other even though they weren't doing it yet, Cookie explaining that she wanted to wait until she was at least fifteen, they went down to Chinatown with Mario and some of his Chinese friends and ate Chinese food. It was fun watching Mario go back and forth from English to Spanish to Cantonese and even a little Mandarin. Sometimes he'd get mad at his Puerto Rican mother, and she'd be talking in Spanish to him, and he'd be answering in Chinese and then she'd say, "Speak English, *condenao chino*, you're worse than your father," calling him a "damn Chinaman," while his younger sister, Carmen, translated from Chinese to Spanish to spite him. And Mario would refuse to listen and kept talking in Cantonese, which he'd picked up while staying at Lily Wong's, his aunt from Hong Kong, when his mother went to work at the factory after Henry Wong stopped coming around and she heard that he'd found some Hong Kong floozy whose father owned a restaurant in Queens and he was going to marry her. Lily Wong consoled Mario's mother and said she was her sister and apologized for her brother, who thought he was a movie star from the cheap Chinese movies they had over on Chrystie Street and the Bowery and could go around breaking young girls' hearts. Lily couldn't understand why he would behave that way since they were brought up in a nice Christian home and were taught by missionaries.

So Mario grew up going back and forth from his aunt Lily Wong's above the Castle and Dragon Restaurant owned by Mr. Leong, Lily Wong's lover, and his grandmother Marina Rios's house over near Delancey Street, talking Spanish in one and Cantonese in the other and in school English and taking it all in and not seeing his father for a long time until he showed up and took him to a hockey game because he was crazy about the Langels and Jean Latelle.

After going with Mario, Vidamía and Cookie went to Chinatown on their own and sat in noodle restaurants and dim sum houses like they were older than fifteen and thirteen, and ate, and lit cigarettes, not inhaling but blowing out the smoke in long, sophisticated plumes, at times suppressing coughs discreetly. They talked about movies, crazy about Michael J. Fox and Richard Gere, telling themselves they hated Sean Penn, but secretly admiring him and blaming Madonna totally for their breakup; shifting easily to music and the different clubs that the older girls went to, rock clubs or Latin clubs, and did Vidamía know how to dance Latin?

"No? I'll teach you. We'll go up to my homegirl Nancy Almodovar's house."

And on the way there Cookie'd tell her all about her friend. "Her *mami*'s got this awesome stereo and all kinds of tapes of great Latin music and we can dance. Nancy's mother's the coolest lady. Her name's Josie. She dances topless in New Jersey. Nancy's father got killed in a drug deal last year. And it wasn't like Josie didn't beg him to stop running with those idiots. But, like, he didn't listen, right? Yo, what was she supposed to do, huh, mama?" (Cookie called her mama, like her homegirls called each other; either that or *mami* or *mamita*, assigning parental authority to each other, which had always seemed odd to Vidamía, since her grandma Ursula called her *mamita* for as long as she could remember.)

They would eventually call this tradition FIAT or "Feminine Indoctrination and Training," and laugh at the irony years later, because if any culture was a matriarchy, bar none, it was the Puerto Rican one and for all the *macho* nonsense the *gringos* laid on the culture, the women knew what they were doing calling the boys *papi* and *papito* and spoiling them rotten so that they went around strutting and posturing with their *cositos* in their hands waving them at pretty women; and these same women calling the girls *mami* and *mamita* and giving them responsibility and toughening them up for their hard lives ahead, but definitely handing down the reins of power to them.

"Anyway, Nancy's gotta take care of her two little brothers when her mother goes off to work, and she gets lonely," Cookie explained. "She doesn't have a boyfriend yet, so we can keep her company. Would you dance topless? No? I wouldn't either. I don't have much as jugs go yet, but I wouldn't want them bouncing around. We gotta take a shower together, cause I wanna see yours. Mama's are pointy." Day after day, Vidamía got one shock after the other until, by the end of that summer of 1988, being with her sister was the most natural thing.

At home, of course, it was another story because there Cookie was almost a different person, addressing her mother as Mama and responding with "yes, ma'am" and "no, ma'am." Always very polite and speaking English very properly like her mother, with lilting southern intonations, but if she was around Grandpa Buck she'd start talking like she was from Central Tennessee. And Vidamía had seen her talking to the Polish waitresses at the Odessa and, without meaning to, imitating their accent innocently. In Chinatown or at Aunt Lily Wong's she would talk English with a Chinese accent. Cookie denied doing anything of the sort, and Vidamía said she'd point it out to her the next time she did it.

A month later Grandma Brigid had asked her to begin setting the table.

"Hortense, could you be getting the crockery for dinner?" Grandma Brigid asked.

"Gran, would you be wanting the blue crockery or the flowered?" Cookie said most naturally, her voice dropping and then rising as if she'd been raised in Ireland.

"The flowered," Grandma said, from the kitchen.

"See?" Vidamía said. "You just did it. Why did you talk like Grandma Brigid?"

"Oh, shit," Cookie said.

"Did you say something, Hortense?" Grandma Brigid said, peeking into the dining room.

"No, ma'am. Nothing. I stubbed me toe," Cookie said, and slapped herself. "My toe."

They both laughed and pointed at each other.

"You do accents," Vidamía said. "I've seen you imitate Grandma Ursula and Mario's aunt and everybody. You're like Peter Sellers, you minkey. Maybe you should be an actress."

"Nah, I'm gonna be like Dexter Gordon or John Coltrane. Mama said she was getting me a soprano sax. I'm learning the solo from 'My Favorite Things.' The whole thing by heart. Acting is phony. I want to be a great tenor girl."

For Vidamía each summer spent away from her mother's house was one of learning, primarily about her father and his family, but in a way learning about herself and her puertoricanness, if there was such a thing, absorbing details about the neighborhood and sharpening her understanding of the code of behavior of the street: who not to stare at or play with and who took no offense when you joked with them, knowing which situations to steer clear of and which offered no danger, learning that when men played dominoes girls shouldn't stand around them. Cookie wasn't able to explain why, but reassured her that it wasn't done, thus establishing how attuned she was to the neighborhood.

"*Tu hermanita americana tiene razón*," Ursula Santiago would say, nodding whenever Cookie explained some fine point of behavior. If comportment among Puerto Ricans was complex, home was a haven of simplicity. Lurleen had three rules: no foul language, respect for the opinions of others, and orderliness. If you removed something from a common place, put it back where you found it; if you used dishes, wash them; if you bathed, clean up after yourself; don't leave your junk around, pick up after yourself, always, cause other folks are busy just like you.

They were required to be punctual for meals, especially the evening meal, which was served at six. On weekday nights they had to be back home no later than eleven, and one o'clock on the weekend. And no going uptown on the subway unless it was to a specific place, like a movie theater or a museum. But there were no subjects they couldn't discuss, nor books they couldn't read, nor things they couldn't explore openly so that it wasn't unusual, although it shocked Vidamía, when Cookie asked her mother how often she and her father had sexual relations. Lurleen hadn't even looked up from her embroidering.

"Two or three times a week," she'd said.

"And do you always have an orgasm?" Cookie asked.

"Not always," Lurleen replied.

"Why?"

"My mind's not in it sometimes. Or I don't need to."

"Like Papa wants to do it and you don't?"

"Yes, something like that."

"When I get old enough I want to do it. How old should I be?"

"I can't tell you that, but I would think that you have plenty of time to decide. Whatever you do, you must be careful and make sure you know where the person has been, because there are many illnesses that you can get from sexual contact."

Going on like that, like they were talking about making sandwiches or picking out a dress.

Vidamía couldn't imagine her mother talking with her about such things, but hearing Cookie talk about them made her even more curious about boys. Cookie was younger than she was but was so much more sophisticated about such issues. On the other hand, whenever Vidamía told her about credit cards, or Club Med, or going on vacation to Europe and riding the Talgo train from Sevilla to Barcelona or going to certain beaches in Europe and seeing women walking around without their bikini tops, for example, Cookie was like a five-year-old, lost in thinking about it. "I've never even been on an airplane. Is it scary? I don't think I'd be scared, though." Or whenever she spoke of shopping at Cartier or Bergdorf Goodman or the time she took her to Ham-

macher Schlemmer and then to FAO Schwarz, Cookie had literally stood with her mouth open, saying things like "Gaw" and
staring at everything like she had been dropped into the middle
of a jungle and was in shock.

"What are you gonna do after junior high?" Vidamía asked
one day.

"I'm gonna audition for Performing Arts High School,"
Cookie said. "Music."

Vidamía'd asked her to explain more and Cookie said that
her mother had told her about Performing Arts and it was
something to think about, and that they'd done a movie about it
called *Fame*.

"Yeah, it's a real cool place. Liza Minnelli and Suzanne Vega
went there," Cookie had said. "They have dance, acting, music,
and art. You have to audition to get in. I'm gonna play a classical
piece, and then 'Sergeant Pepper's Lonely Hearts' Club Band.'
It's my own arrangement. I'll play it for you when we get back.
I'd do Coltrane's 'Things,' but they're real stuffy and it'd blow
their minds and they'd think that I was making mistakes."

At the end of each subsequent summer, Vidamía returned to
Tarrytown filled with an increased sense of power, each year her
sense of self growing and making her want to dare to do more
and more. For Cookie, however, her sister's absence filled her
with longing, and for the first month of September, when she
should have been getting back into the rhythm of school and the
days grew shorter, she'd mope around and look for her big sister,
and the void was too great. By October, though, she was back
into her schoolwork. During the rest of the year, Vidamía and
Cookie were in contact almost daily, telling each other things
that had happened to them and laughing on the phone for no apparent reason, everything either being the trigger for hilarity or
else magnifying the most innocent intrigue into an occurrence of
tragic proportions.

In time, Cookie realized that in spite of her sophistication and apparent adult grasp of the world around her, her world was limited to life in the neighborhood, and as smart as she was about the neighborhood where she lived, when she ventured north of Fourteenth Street by herself, she was totally lost. There were certain social conventions which were totally foreign to her so that just as she had served as guide and interpreter to Vidamía during that first summer, Vidamía was now in a position to return the favor.

Whenever Vidamía was invited to one of her friends' parties in Manhattan, or a few times in Tarrytown, she asked Cookie to come, and if there was any hesitation on Cookie's part, Vidamía insisted until she was persuaded. Heidi, this is my sister Cookie. Cookie, this is Heidi Rubinstein. And Cookie, awed by the opulence of the Greenwich Village town house or the Sutton Place triplex or the twelve-room apartment on Park Avenue, would do gauche things like flop down on a couch without being asked, or use the wrong fork at lunch, or pick up food with her hands. She knew that she had done stupid things because it always got back to her mother, and Lurleen would gently explain how things were done. Not once did Vidamía criticize her about her behavior, but like Lurleen she was gentle and loving.

The two sisters were both eager pupils and understanding teachers so that there was hardly ever any friction between them and each grew to love and appreciate the other with an almost blind loyalty. Once, however, Vidamía had a pretty heated argument with Cookie about the way people spoke English in the neighborhood. Vidamía had corrected a girlfriend of Cookie's who pronounced the word "tests" as "tesses" and who consistently said that "she stood at her house" when she meant "stayed." Cookie said she had no right to correct people. They were in the loft and got into it pretty heavily, Lurleen watching them.

"Mama, all Nilsa said was that her teacher gave hard tesses. This one," she said, pointing at Vidamía, "had to correct her and explain that the plural of 'test' is 'tests.' "

"That's right," Vidamía said, defending her position.

"Well, you made her feel real bad and that's also true. You knew what she was trying to say, Vee. You're smart, but sometimes you act like a retard when it comes to people. You don't do it to me, and I make plenty of mistakes."

They went at it a while. It was at this point that Lurleen stepped in and told them to please sit down so they could discuss the matter calmly, and perhaps they might want to split a piece of lemon meringue pie that was left over from supper. She then explained that although Vidamía was correct, she had to consider that in the United States alone there were probably a hundred different accents and that people pronounced words differently from one region to the next.

Vidamía realized that she often behaved like Elsa, and it bothered her. She promised not to correct people again, but couldn't help reminding Cookie of one of her own questionable habits.

"Well, you imitate people's accents."

"No, I don't."

"Oh, no. What about that time at Grandma Brigid's or at Mario's mother's house. It probably makes them uncomfortable."

"No, it doesn't. It makes them feel like I'm one of them."

"I still think you should be an actress."

"I'm a musician."

And so it went from year to year, Cookie putting one foot in front of the other and things happening and she absorbing things and being totally crazy about Mario and kissing him up on the roof and getting very wet and having to do it to herself and seeing his face so clearly; having to stifle her orgasms they were so sweet. She couldn't imagine then what it must be like with him in her and then he had touched her one time and she came immediately and he was so scared and then she did him with her hand. She liked him because he wasn't big and long like that guy she saw from the roof, but he was very hard and she wondered if it would hurt.

She had done it with Mario and it wasn't such a big deal. He enjoyed it and she did sometimes but not that often and she'd asked her mother and Lurleen said that she was still too young but that she should just enjoy her life and not get pregnant because that would certainly tie her down, and she agreed and was very careful and she went with Lurleen and got contraceptive pills and made Mario swear that he wasn't seeing anyone else and he swore and she believed him because he was so crazy about her and all he did was go to Stuyvesant High School and study and play handball with his Chinese friends over at the Essex Street playground, and nobody could tell he was part Rican because other Chinese had curly hair and their skin was a little dark.

Vidamía was totally out of control and now she wanted to buy their father a piano and that was totally crazy. But *she*, Cookie Farrell, would see what their mama would say. She was sure Vidamía wasn't going to tell her own mother and have all hell break loose. And there was no telling what the blazes would happen when her father saw a piano in their loft. No telling whether he'd flip out or not.

32 Just One of Those Things

When Billy's girl, as he sometimes called Vidamía, had called him last year with her worries about getting her father to play again, Buck was flattered that she had wanted his advice. Maud said Vidamía had now finally convinced Billy to start playing. Although he had yet to hear Billy, Buck was proud of his part in it. Now Maud said Billy's girl was getting ready to purchase a piano for her father. Still strong and mentally agile at seventy-six, Buck resented the way most people treated him. But Billy's girl didn't seem to take age into consideration. Last year the two girls came up early for the Fourth of July, before the rest of the family showed up. They talked with him and then helped Brigid and Maud set up for the barbecue. That turned out to be Brigid's last Fourth of July. She came down with the flu in September, pneumonia developed, she went into the hospital, and passed away a week later. The priest came and performed the last rites. Brigid never uttered a word of complaint, but she looked frightened as she clutched her rosary. Buck was asleep at home when she died. The doctor said that there had been no pain, and that she looked peaceful in her death. Buck remembered their youth together, and the rare moments when she permitted herself laughter and hope.

And here it was, a year later, and the two girls were even more grown up, young women now, beautiful and confident. With Brigid gone it was now Maud who took charge and they'd come up early to help. They kissed him and sat with him for a few minutes, and then were gone, their fine figures making him recall his youth once more. He'd asked them their ages. Vidamía was almost seventeen years old and Granny, his name for Cookie, was almost sixteen. He had always been able to tell when a girl had had a man be at her. He was sure Granny was now a woman. There was still a naïveté to her sister, even though she was older.

After Vidamía and Cookie left the porch to help Maud with the grilling, Buck sat down on the steps and lit his pipe. He wondered how many more Fourth of Julys he'd see. Born in 1912, he'd turn seventy-seven in November. The house was empty now. Even as he walked through it, he could hear Brigid's ghost.

He didn't believe in such things, but at night in the winter, the house, contracting from the cold, creaked and groaned as if someone were walking down a corridor.

He felt bad now that as they had grown older their marriage had turned loveless. He felt desire from time to time, but not for her, not for a long time. Her beautiful body had turned fat, thick veins bulged out on her legs, the skin became pasty white and scaly in places. Her once reddish blond hair had grown white and thin, and she was balding. The long delicate bridge of her nose had turned downward to give her a witchy look, the always suspicious eyes filled now with regret and anger. She must have known that he'd stopped loving her long ago, remaining married because he didn't want to create disorder in her Catholic world. But he had strayed anyway and was certain she had known.

How old had he been when he'd gone off with Candy Donovan? She began coming up to the house in 1950, when she was twenty-two years old, so he was already thirty-seven. Maudie was sixteen, and had dropped out of high school. He remembered Brigid coming to him to tell him about Maudie's beau, as she called him. One day, about four or five days before Christmas, Maud brought Kevin Farrell in to see him. He was a big strapping fellow, his eyes very serious and respectful. He came forward and extended his hand. They spoke for a while and then Buck asked him about his father. Kevin said his father, Seamus Farrell, had come from Ireland when he was eighteen years old. He became a fireman the following year. He had liked Kevin, and Maud had never been so happy, and then Kevin was killed and Billy was orphaned. Luckily he and Alfred Butterworth had been able to help. Between the two of them they had taken care of Billy. He didn't know what had made the kid go off and join the Marines and go to Vietnam. He figured Billy was lucky to be alive, if that were a consolation. He was eager to hear him play again. Thinking back, he was certain Billy would've taken his place with the big guys. He had everything they had. Miles Davis had wanted him to play and he'd gone off to war. What a waste. He thought again of Candy Donovan and he felt even sadder.

She had come up one summer afternoon with Iggy Marginat, who'd met her on the West Side of Manhattan, up above Columbia University, where there was an Irish enclave bordering Harlem, and told him the girl could sing. Iggy sat at the piano and she sang "It's Only a Paper Moon," "I Get a Kick Out of You," and "Just One of Those Things." It was while she was singing that last song that he looked up from his banjo and saw that she was singing to him, focusing on him, as singers do when they're close up to an audience, her attention innocent, but so direct that he felt himself erect against his banjo.

> *It was just one of those things,*
> *Just one of those crazy flings,*
> *One of those bells that now and then rings,*
> *Just one of those things.*
>
> *It was just one of those nights,*
> *Just one of those fabulous flights,*
> *A trip to the moon on gossamer wings,*
> *Just one of those things.*
>
> *If we'd thought a bit*
> *Of the end of it*
> *When we started painting the town,*
> *We'd have been aware*
> *That our love affair*
> *Was too hot not to cool down. . . .*

He'd smiled at her and she shrugged her shoulders and, between verses, said, "I can't help it," and that had been it. The following Friday he called home after he finished work and told Brigid that he had to go downtown on union business. He got on the elevated train, got off at the 125th Street station, went down the stairs, and waited for Candy Donovan. At seven o'clock she finally came down the stairs in her high heels and nylons, her legs long and her dress clinging to her fine figure. She turned up the street, saw him, and nearly ran to embrace him, her face beaming with excitement.

"I knew you'd come," she said. "I'm so happy to see you."

"How are you?" he said. "You look so pretty."

"Thank you. Can we go for a walk?"

"Sure," he said.

They went up the hill on Broadway, with students walking past them, the males looking at her and the females glancing at him. Turning west, they continued past Riverside Church and into the park, going down to the edge, near the river, to watch the sun set over the Hudson.

"Candy Donovan," he said. "Is it Candace?"

"No, it isn't, and don't I wish," she said.

"What, then?"

"You don't want to know. It's some dumb mick name."

"Sure I do. Please, tell me."

"Cliona," she said. "Can you beat that? My old man fancies himself an Irish poet, the drunken son of a bitch."

"It's a beautiful name."

"He's always threatening to kick me outta the house because I won't go to mass and I like jazz music. With him it's Ireland this and Ireland that. Why doesn't he go back to the damn place? He drives everyone crazy with the stuff. I mean, we're in America. It's great here. What did he have over there? A sod house, a friggin' shillelagh, and two potatoes, and one of them was rotten. Jesus, Mary, and Joseph, he's one dumb mick. And he's not content with giving his children adequate Christian names. John, Catherine, Brigid. Oh, no. With him it's *Erin go*

Bragh until you drop dead. Connaire, Fergus, Siobhan, Padraic, and yours truly, Cliona."

"I shouldn't be here," he said, hearing Candy mention his wife's name as an example. Although he was sure it was merely a coincidence, it made him uncomfortable.

"Where should you be?"

"Home, I reckon," he said, rattled by her. "I guess, I mean."

"I like 'reckon' better," she said.

She turned from the river to face him and he saw how truly beautiful she was. Her eyes were light brown, almost a light chocolate color, and her hair was golden. She had a wide face with high cheekbones, the skin of her nose peeling from being out in the sun during the summer. Time had stopped and he was again a young man back in central Tennessee, and then farther west, in the flatter country, and then in Memphis. He felt enormous desire such as he had once felt, and was now deadened, for Brigid.

"Do you feel as strong about me as I feel about you?" she asked, as if she could read his mind, already displaying how attuned she was to him.

"I'd be a liar if I said I didn't."

"That's all that matters. When we're old and gray, that's all we're gonna remember."

"It's that just now hearing you talk about your father made me think about my family. My oldest girl Maud is already married and is due this month. I'm gonna be a grandfather."

"Age doesn't matter," she said. "I'm not going to lie to you. I'm twenty-two years old, but I'm not a virgin. I'm a big girl. I've been with three men. Two of them were Negroes and the other was Cuban. Did Iggy tell you?"

"No, he just said you were a singer."

"Does it matter?"

"What? The other men?"

"Yes."

"No, of course not," he said.

"I don't like white men much," she said brashly. "With you it's different. Even before I walked into your house I could feel you, and as soon as I saw you I wanted to kiss you. Did you like how I sang?"

"You sang great."

"That's what I wanna do. I think I could really do it, and make records and everything."

"I'm sure you could," he said, looking out over the river. "It's getting late. We should go."

"Do you really want to?"

"No, I don't."

She leaned against him and they kissed gently, admitting that what was happening was inevitable. They stood for a while silently, watching as the sun settled into the woods over New Jersey. She was small and only her personality made her seem bigger. Before he knew it he had his arms around her and was kissing her desperately, the sweetness of her mouth making him drunk. In the failing light they walked down a grassy embankment near the river where there was a thicket of trees and there they laid down and made love, her passion making him gasp for wanting her. She was a fierce lover, totally open and generous in her desire. When he was spent and she was lying against him he heard her say, "I love you, Buck, but I don't remember your last name. Iggy told me, but I can't remember."

"Sanderson," he said.

"Do you love me?" she said.

"Yes, I do," he answered, and he recalled Charlotte Randall and knew that he loved Candy Donovan because he felt exactly as he had with Charlotte more than twenty years ago.

He walked her back to her apartment building, going through the park, the late-summer air clean and fresh so that he could smell the grass and feel the dampness of the dew and was lost in her as he held her around the waist, her body fitted to his, their pace uniform, synchronized, rhythmical as if they had been made for each other. In the darkness the fireflies traced odd green patterns as they sought their mates, their phosphorescence magical. When they were in front of her building, she kissed him and then ran inside, leaving him feeling abandoned so that he was more convinced than ever that he loved her.

The following weekend she came up again and sang, but she was discreet, avoiding looking at him. They continued to meet during the fall and winter and into early spring. They usually went to her sister Siobhan's apartment in Hell's Kitchen, where Candy had moved the month after they began seeing each other. While her sister, whom she called Sally, and her husband, Harry, were down on Wall Street cleaning offices in the evening, the two of them made love desperately. Candy was an uncompromising lover, her heart served up whole and her body totally in tune with his needs, arousing him when he couldn't imagine how he could become erect again. More than any other woman, Candy Donovan had awakened in him a desire which he had imagined was over, because of his loveless marriage to Brigid. Candy was strong and loving and often bruised him, her fingernails marking him with her passion.

She was extremely loyal and like a tigress in warding off potential rivals. The only women from whom she felt no threat were Brigid and his daughters. For Brigid she felt pity, since she was sharing her husband. And yet Brigid was eventually the one she grew to resent the most. One evening when they finished making love, she asked him what was going to happen.

"I don't know," he said. "I really don't know."

"I wanna have a kid," she said, sitting up on her elbow, her breasts beautiful in the light coming in from the kitchen.

"Are you pregnant?" he said, sitting up suddenly.

"Would it matter if I was?"

"No, but I already have six kids. Are you?"

"No, I'm not, but I'd like to be. Maybe I could get my own

place. I'm doing good working at the restaurant. Mr. O'Bannon says he's gonna open another restaurant in the Village and I can help manage it. I asked him if we could have music and he said he didn't think it'd be a problem. I could sing there. You could get a little band together. They have beautiful garden apartments in the Village. Fifteen or twenty dollars a month. I can pay that. You wouldn't have to spend any money at all. I want you to go with me and pick it out."

"I don't know," he said, lying back down on the bed and putting his arm over his eyes.

"It doesn't matter that you're married," she went on, making plans and telling him how important he was to her. "You being married doesn't matter because I know that you truly love me and there's nobody else. I don't mind if we see each other a few times a week. Please, Buck. I'm not asking you to leave Brigid. You have your children, but we should be together."

"I'll have to think about it," he said.

She turned away and he knew that she was crying and he felt her leaving him, going away from him, the distance widening as he lay on the bed, his eyes closed, his mind drifting off into sleep. After a while he heard her ask if he wanted a cup of tea and woke up startled, thinking that it was morning and he had spent the night, immediately wondering what Brigid must've thought and worried about being late for work. He quickly understood that it was still late afternoon and he was on vacation. He sat up, and she was in the kitchen, dressed. He tried to explain why he thought it wouldn't work out, but she stopped him and shook her head, again on the verge of tears.

"It's not that I don't love you, Candy," he said. "It's not that at all."

"I know. You'd feel like a bigamist, wouldn't you?"

"Yeah," he said, but immediately he could tell she was being sarcastic and closed to him. "It would be like we were married."

"Sure," she said.

They sat in silence for an hour or so and then he left, knowing he'd never be with her again. As quickly as it had begun, it was over, although she still came up on summer weekends for the next four or five years. She seemed happy enough and she remained friendly toward him, always in good spirits, except that she was smoking and drinking a lot, and the nightlife was starting to get to her. And then she met Charlie Parker, and that was it. She became obsessed with him and the stories began to circulate. It was like Bird was this bright flame of a candle, his music burning everything around him with its brilliance, and Candy was a moth that couldn't help itself and was drawn to the light, not feeling the heat until it was too late.

Buck had remained celibate nearly a year, stunned by the absence of Candy's love and the contrast of his life with his wife. Brigid didn't question his lack of intimacy. In a way she was relieved. Eventually, he had returned to Brigid's bed, often recalling their first years together when merely touching her silken skin was enough to make him want her. In those days she had laughed with embarrassment at his ardor, taking extra care to look pretty on weekends when he wasn't so tired. Slowly, as childrearing and its attending duties took its toll on her, she grew less and less drawn to intimacy.

Years passed. The children left to get married and he was again alone with Brigid. One day before he retired from the Transit Authority, he was returning from Maud's house in Mount Vernon, walking on MacQuesten Parkway, above the railroad tracks, when he saw a black woman wielding a broom and waving it at a couple of white youngsters, running down the steps of her house.

"Aw, you're nothing but a nigger whore," one of them said, once he was outside the gate.

"Your mother's the whore, you fey little mothafucka," the black woman said, threatening to come off the porch with the broom.

Their hands supporting them as they leaned out the windows, a few girls observed the scene with interest. He didn't notice it then but recalled later that a couple of them were black and the others were white. One of the two young men, neither one of them over eighteen years of age, now picked up a rock and threw it at the black woman, barely missing her. It was then that he stepped forward and grabbed the boy and shook him.

"Why don't you cut that out and go home," he said.

"Fuck you, old man," the first one said.

"Yeah, grandpa, mind your own business," said the other, making a threatening move.

He was close to sixty, still working, and strong. Before he realized it he'd grabbed the first youngster by his shirt, brought him forward against his body, and then shoved him back several feet so that he landed in a ditch. Buck began to move toward the other one, but he ran off and the one in the ditch got up and, limping and cursing, followed his friend. He'd heard about the house from people on the job but had never been that curious about it.

That was how he'd gotten to know Ruby Broadway and how he ended up going there, every couple of weeks at first, paying his money and making love to Ruby, who in 1972 was around forty. Ruby liked him and after the first year told him to forget the money, but then he brought her presents or asked if she needed any repairs done on the house. There was always something to do, so he went there almost every day, if only for a few minutes. He felt sorry for the girls and wondered if they had fathers. All of them called him Mr. Sanderson and none of them ever made the least lewd remark to him. He imagined that Ruby must've told them how respectful they must be. For a while he worried word would get around, but even if gossip reached Maud's ears, she would pay little attention to it, preferring to sweep any unpleasantness under the rug of her conventions. He often saw men he knew—cops, firemen, trainmen, shop owners.

They would nod to him and he would return their dour greetings, their recognition an acceptance of their illicit compact with each other.

When he told Pop Butterworth, they'd go together, and Pop, who was younger, lay up with one of the girls and Buck sat with Ruby in the parlor and they talked about Mr. Eisenhower and Mr. Kennedy and the Reverend Martin Luther King, Jr., and communism and Marilyn Monroe and Dorothy Dandridge and he would tell her she was just as beautiful and she would say, "Go on, you smooth-talking southern man. You think I ain't heard that kind of stuff before?"

"Well, it's true, Miss Broadway, ma'am," feeling so comfortable with her that his accent surfaced.

"Were you a dancer in shows down in New York?" he once asked her, wondering how she'd come to the name Broadway.

She laughed good-naturedly and slapped his arm as they sat drinking hot cocoa one winter afternoon with the snow falling in great big flakes that looked like cotton balls. Ruby explained that it was nothing as exciting as that.

"I liked boys a whole lot and was carrying on from the time I was eleven, wanting to touch them and getting touched and touching myself and just interested in johnsons in general. You know how some people have a love of things. I loved dick. All kinds. Little ones, big ones, white ones, black ones, thick, thin. It didn't matter—it gave me pleasure to look at them and touch them and get them all excited and have them go up into me. I read it could become a sickness, but it always made me real happy and healthy and I always slept like a baby and didn't feel like the Devil was gonna come knocking on the door any day. One day I was fourteen years old and the Reverend Mr. Wilson began preaching about the straight and narrow and keeping to the ways of the Lord, and right there and then I start giggling, and my mama pinches me real hard so that tears come to my eyes. My friend Livonia asked me later what the heck I was laughing about and I said I was going to Little Rock and from there to Saint Louis and that from then on she should refer to me as Miss Ruby Broad Way, cause I wasn't cut out for the straight and narrow. So I became Ruby Broadway."

He'd nodded and said that was certainly as good an explanation as a man could wish to hear, but what was her real name?

"Ruby Broadway," she said, looking at him in dead earnest, her eyes narrow and deadly, just like Buddy Whelan's eyes, who lived with his mother in Hell's Kitchen and who did jobs for the fellas on the docks and they said he'd killed so many people that, had he been working for the IRA, Ireland would be by now united and free of the British. He found out later that Ruby herself had killed a man once, in Saint Louis. "Had to shoot him," she said. "He was coming at me with a knife. I put a little hole to the left of the nose. It was sad, cause I loved him. He gave me the clap and it got so bad that they had to take everything outta me. See, I was planning to retire from the business and find me a good man and have children and everything."

So he never pushed her about the name, or anything else, and just enjoyed her company. Sometimes, he'd fall asleep when she left the room and only woke up when the sun had gone down and then he'd wait for the bus back to Yonkers and once he was home Brigid would ask him where he had been and he'd make up a story, something he heard at a bar, like he'd run across Mike Flanagan and he was telling him about a nephew of his that had been jailed by the British and accused of a shooting in Ireland. And she'd mumble something about the IRA being ultimately the end of Ireland and go on about her business.

Brigid was gone now and in spite of all the emptiness that he'd felt with her, it was worse without her. He couldn't get over how the girl had gotten Billy to play the piano again. The two of them, Vidamía and Granny, had promised to bring him down to the city so he could hear Billy play, but he didn't know if he was up to it. They were little she-devils, the two of them. He thought about how they'd gotten Billy to come up to the house in August, under the pretext that it needed repairs, while they moved the piano into the loft. He'd gone along with the deception, caught up in their daring and enthusiasm.

What a life he'd had. What a long and wonderful life. How much longer would it last? Last time he had spoken to him Billy said Butterworth wasn't doing too good. He wished he could go see him, but didn't want to take a chance driving his car. Ernie Witkowski, an old friend from the Transit Authority, had had a heart attack while he was driving on the highway and his car struck a station wagon with a family of eight. Killed four of the kids and the mother. He didn't want that on his conscience. Even though the doctor said he was still healthy, you never knew. If it wasn't too cold tomorrow, he'd take the bus across to Mount Vernon and look in on Ruby. Fall was approaching, and then winter. He sat back in his rocker, lit his pipe, and when the tobacco was glowing he closed his eyes and he thought about Ruby's body, the still taut skin that drew him to her. And then he once again recalled Candy Donovan and the lyrics of the song. *It was just one of those things, just one of those crazy flings* . . . He still wasn't sure if he had done right by Candy.

33 Ruby Broadway

Maud Farrell sat across the diner booth from Ruby Broadway and, after they'd ordered lunch and it was brought to them, told her that Vidamía had gotten her boy to start playing the piano again and that now the girl had come up with another idea but she didn't know quite what to make of it, and Billy's wife had called and asked her what she thought of the scheme.

"What scheme, woman?" Ruby said.

"She's gonna get him a piano," Maud said.

"She's gonna do what?"

"Yeah, she's going to buy it."

"What's it made out of, cardboard?"

"No, a regular grand piano. Used, but a real one."

"Where she gonna get the money?"

"She's got one of them gold cards."

"Say what? You saw it?"

"I sure did."

"And it's got her name on it?"

"That's right, Vidamía Farrell."

"Looky, looky," said Ruby. "Whyntcha talk to that child and see if she take us shopping. Ruby could use her a fur coat or some sort of girlish trinket. Her mama's rich, ain't she? No, it's her stepdaddy's got the bucks. It don't matter none to me if he ain't good-looking."

"What do you mean?"

"The song."

"What song?"

" 'Summertime.' Her daddy's rich, and her ma is good-looking."

"Oh, right," Maud said, cutting into her open roast beef sandwich.

"You know something, girl?"

"What?"

"You're too blond. Where do you go in your mind when you get like this?"

"Oh, stop it, you old witch," Maud said, brandishing the knife at Ruby.

"Oh, scary white lady with a dull knife," Ruby said, shrinking back in mock horror. And then becoming serious again: "You worried about this piano thing, ain't ya?"

"Yeah, she says that it might cause problems when her mother finds out. She wants me to go with her."

"To get the piano? You going?"

"I don't think I've got a choice. She's got her sister on the case and if this one is smart, the other one is twice as cunning and can talk you out of your last dime."

"I know, honey. I seen her. You're one lucky grandma having those girls. I gotta tell you something, though."

"What?"

"Whoever named that child had no consideration. Your daddy's right, that is one ugly name. I mean colored folks will make a blunder from time to time, calling a girl Velveeta or Linguina, but white people got some serious problems when it come to naming children. Hortense? Look out! Here come Hortense. Name sound like a threat and whatnot."

"A threat?"

"Yeah, I'ma put a serious Hortense to you," Ruby said and laughed, explaining that's the way people up in the hills in Arkansas, where she came from, talked. "So's you can hardly understand them. But that's one ugly name, child."

Maud laughed uproariously, nearly choking on her food.

"I don't like it too much either, but everybody calls her Cookie or Horty."

"I like Cookie, but what she gonna do when she grows up?"

"I guess she'll deal with that when she gets to that point," Maud said as the waitress asked if they wanted dessert. Both chose cherry pie.

"Anyway," Ruby said, "the reason I wanted to talk to you was that I'm worried about your father."

"Me too," Maud said.

"Business's dropped off considerably the last couple of years, with AIDS and everything. My girls have always been clean, but to tell you the truth the kinds of young ladies applying for employment these days shouldn't be trusted very much, if you ask me. So I've officially retired. At the end of the summer I gave the girls their bonuses. Right before I went to see my sister, Pearl, in North Carolina. To this day Pearl still thinks I been running a rooming house."

"Well, it *was* sort of a rooming house, wasn't it? People roomed for short periods of time."

"No, it wasn't. The place was a genuine, no-nonsense ho house," Ruby said, pointing her knife at Maud. "Just shush for a moment and let me tell you about your dad."

"Okay, I'm sorry I interrupted you."

"That's okay, just eat your vegetables and listen. Your father came by the other day," Ruby said and paused, letting her statement hang enigmatically.

"And?" Maud said, knowing something else was coming.

"Shush! He just sat on the porch and talked about how tired he was, except he looked fine. I knew something was up."

"It's Mom being gone, I think," Maud said.

"No, it don't have nothing to do with your mom being gone."

"What, then?"

"Well, I'm thinking I don't need a great big house like that," Ruby said, her tone unsure, uncharacteristic for her. "I'm selling it and I'm going to get me one of those condominium-type apartments. And then again, I don't know."

"What are you getting at, Ruby?" Maud finally said. "You sound like some teenage girl. Condominiums, my father, selling your house. You have to know that I know all about you and my father all these years so it can't be about that."

"Well, it is and it isn't," Ruby said.

"I see," Maud replied, turning her eyes up to the ceiling in exasperation. "That really explains a whole bunch."

"Well, I was thinking that if you don't mind, I'd keep him company, permanent like. If you don't mind, that is. You being a white lady and your father being a white gentleman, I thought I better discuss it with you and kind of get your view on it."

"You gotta be joking. Tell me I'm not hearing right."

"Well, you never can tell with white folks."

"Ruby Robinson," Maud said, warning her friend. "You insult me one more time and I'm never gonna talk to you again."

"Watch it, girl," Ruby said, relieved that color wasn't an issue between Maud and herself. It had been for a while during the business with Billy, but that had passed. "Just cause I told you my last name don't mean you can go using it in public places."

"Didn't you tell me you were officially retired?"

"Yes, I did."

"Well?"

"Okay, okay. You are permitted the honor of addressing me as Miss Robinson."

"Thank you, ma'am," Maud said, and looked up at her friend. "Ms. Robinson."

"Girl, don't you call me that. I am a Miss. That Ms. stuff sounds like some ole bumblebee's loose on the lot. *Miz* this and *Miz* that. No wonder those gals look so unhappy, their faces all scrunched up like prunes and like a bee done stung them."

"Well, I'm sure they'd have a whole lot to say about you and your line of work all these years. You being underprivileged and everything and exploiting young girls for your gain."

"I've never exploited nobody and you know it," Ruby said, genuinely affronted. "Every one of those girls was out in the street giving it away for nothing, getting bounced off walls by their pimps and catching everything there was to catch except the right bus. I took them in, gave them a home, clothed them, fed them, taught them about the world, and most important taught them about stocks and bonds so that at some point they could relocate to some place where nobody knew them and start over again."

She went into her pocketbook and extracted a letter and pushed it across the table to Maud. "Grace Pinder just wrote to me from La Puente in California. Open it up and take a look at the picture. That's her home and that's her husband and her two children. She does word processing right now. What was she doing when Nicki Braverman brought her in? Working at McDonald's and turning fifty-dollar tricks for some pimp on the Upper East Side to keep herself high on drugs. Go ahead and open it up."

Maud opened the envelope, looked at the picture of the plain-looking, matronly woman and her balding husband and the two teenage kids in front of a ranch-style home. She nodded and then opened the rose-colored paper and shook her head. The letter opened with the words "Dear Mom." Tears came to Maud's eyes, and she said she was sorry she'd said anything.

"They didn't all turn out okay, but nothing and nobody ever does," Ruby said. "Look at that Effie that your boy took a liking to. Sneaky little cuss. Do you know that she'd go to Philadelphia some weekends to visit relatives and turn tricks. She never infected anyone in my house, but she could've. She went one Christmas and never came back. A friend of mine in Philly said she's doing time for stabbing a john."

"Yeah, I remember you telling me. About Dad?"

"Yes," Ruby said, not sure again of Maud's response.

"I think that would be fine if Dad's willing," she said.

"We already talked and he's all for it," Ruby said, coyly.

"You really like my old man, don't you?"

"He's always been a sweet and kind man," Ruby said. "And he don't have hang-ups about color. He just loves a woman like no man I've known. We're like candy to him."

"Candy?" Maud said, wondering if Ruby knew about Candy Donovan.

"Yeah, sugar pops and bonbons," Ruby said, innocently.

"Well, I'm glad for the two of you. I don't have to call you Mom, do I?" Maud said.

"Oh, you dingbat, shut up and eat."

Matters once again on an even keel between them, the two women returned to their meal. While they were having their dessert, Ruby looked up from her cherry pie and had an expression on her face that Maud had only seen on the faces of young girls. She recognized it because she recalled how she looked in the mirror when she thought of Kevin, after their first date. They'd stood there on the porch after the long walk from the train station and she finally thanked him. Not knowing what to do, she reached up, kissed him, and held him for a moment, then broke away from the embrace and ran inside. Once inside, she stood by the window, parting the curtains slightly to watch him go down the steps. In the light from the porch she saw him again raise his hands in triumph. She took off her coat and in the big oval mirror by the coat tree looked at herself and couldn't help smiling, and that is how Ruby looked.

"What now?" Maud said.

"You're not gonna laugh, are you?" Ruby replied.

"That depends, and wipe that silly grin off your face. You have cherry pie all over your teeth."

"Don't laugh. Promise."

"I promise," Maud said.

"Well, it's like this," Ruby said. "Your father sings a special song to me," she added.

"That's nice," Maud said, touched by Ruby's tenderness.

"It's our song. It's kind of personal. He sings it real soft and then I sing it with him. I never thought I could sing much. Yell real loud, but never sing. But I sing it with him. He says when he dies y'all should get someone to sing it at his wake. Maybe Granny, your blond-headed grand, who has a fine voice."

"Cookie."

"Yeah, Cookie. You know what the song is?"

"After that buildup, I think you better tell me."

"I don't even know the title, but it says 'For love's sweet dy-

ing ember,' ", and Ruby hummed the tune in a really tiny voice
that contradicted the bigness of her person.

The tough madam, who by her own admission had let lie between her legs close to three thousand men, had managed the
lives of two hundred girls as they plied their whoring trade, was
now reduced to being a young girl in love again even though the
wrinkles at the corners of her eyes betrayed her true age. Her
eyes sparkled and were liquid with that look that signalled love.

"You're in love," Maud said, her own eyes moist. "You're
very lucky."

"Yes, I am," Ruby said.

"And you know what, Miss Ruby Robinson?"

"What?"

"You're still a silly old broad."

"Shut up, Maud Farrell."

They now laughed and carried on and ordered more coffee.

34 Consequences

Elsa knew something was up. She was a hundred percent sure
something was brewing, but she couldn't figure out what it was.
How Vidamía managed to keep up her grades with so many
trips into the city, she didn't know. If she wasn't on the phone
with her sister she was in a huddle with Mrs. Alvarez. Barry was
no help at all. The company was expanding and opening up offices in Florida and Puerto Rico, which required him to be away
most of the time. On top of that, he and a business associate decided to form a partnership and launch a tax-preparation company. During the past year the new business had flourished
beyond their expectations.

At first Barry and his new partner, John Marrero, a Cuban

M.B.A. and lawyer, with his many contacts in the Cuban community, thought of simply providing services in Florida and the New York metropolitan area. But after they did a marketing survey of the entire country, they found they could easily provide the services nationwide and give H&R Block a run for its money. They wanted to call the operation Latitax, but Elsa asked them to please reconsider the name since it sounded so much like Latex that people might think it was a paint store.

"I agree with you, Elsa," John said, before dinner at the Marreros' apartment in Trump Towers. "We would have been the laughingstock of the business community. What would you say if we called the company Spantax?"

"That's certainly an improvement," Barbara Marrero said.

"Spantax," Barry said, opening up his arms as if he were holding a banner. "We speak your language. Remember, we're on your side."

"What do you think?" John said.

"I like it," Barbara said. "It's a play on words. 'Spanish' and 'tax.' If the advertising is handled correctly it could catch on."

"Spantax," Elsa said. "Like Spandex."

"Spandex?" Barbara said, with a questioning tone in her voice, even though she was intimately familiar with the material from her exercise classes.

"You know," Elsa said. "Spandex stretches. We'll *stretch* your dollar."

"Oh," Barbara said, slightly annoyed, while Barry and John looked at each other and considered Elsa's observation as if she were being frivolous.

"I think it's perfect," Elsa said, stretching her arms outward. "Spantax, we'll stretch your dollar," she chirped happily, then realized that the humor was lost on them. She was slightly embarrassed. "You have to understand," she quickly added, unfazed by their lack of enthusiasm, "Spantax is much better than Latitax because the word 'Latino' has the wrong connotation for a serious business enterprise. People are going to be entrusting you with their personal finances. See, when you hear about something Latino, you picture tropical music, maracas and congas, tawdry women in bright clothes with flowers in their hair and men with thin mustaches and pointy shoes and everybody dancing, talking real loud and fast in some sort of corrupted Spanish. Gangs, drive-by shootings, drugs, crimes, infidelity, macho behavior. Those people are Latinos. But when you hear 'Hispanic,' it's literature, fine music, painting, subdued tastes, intelligence, and culture."

John and Barbara Marrero were now nodding their agreement. Barry was looking at her admiringly. Her clear, straightforward analysis had returned Elsa once again to her position of "equal" among the Marreros of the world, meaning the wealthy Cuban exiles, completely white and adapted to the United States. Everyone had nodded, but suddenly she felt stupid and left out again. Who was she kidding? She was a Latina. Look where she'd come from. She was sure the Marreros held it against her that she had African blood. When she returned home, she had to take two sleeping pills to fall asleep.

All she could think about was being at Hunter College and reading *La Vida* by Oscar Lewis and being furious that the book had been printed at all. In it the author describes La Esmeralda, a slum by the sea inhabited by the worst kinds of people. But it was all a deception because Oscar Lewis was talking about La Perla, one of the worst slums in all of Latin America and all of it in the shadows of El Morro Castle, that great symbol of Puerto Rican culture. She read the book and she was preoccupied for weeks as if she were rearranging her childhood memories. It was like she was reading about her father's family, the African shadow pursuing her. She recalled visiting Puerto Rico as a little girl, before her father left, descending into La Perla and walking on the narrow streets with houses built on stilts above the seashore and waves pounding constantly at the wood so that the houses seemed to rock.

"*Esta es tu abuelita, Chela,*" her father had said, introducing her to his mother, who was very dark and had frizzy white hair. "*Mami, te presento a Elsa, tu nieta.*"

"*Un besito pa' güelita,*" the woman had said, picking her up.

The toothless old woman had wanted a little kiss, and she had dutifully kissed her. Her grandmother smelled sweet to her, and then she realized that she had been making *dulce de coco*, and shortly afterward Elsa had been given a big wedge of coconut candy, which she loved. Güela Chela, which her grandmother insisted the children call her, was the color of a *caldero*, the black cast-iron pot in which Puerto Ricans cooked rice. All little Elsa could do was stare at her, mute. They had stayed in the little house that night, sleeping on canvas sacks on the floor, and her mother and father talked with her grandmother by a kerosene lamp, the sea pounding the shore and the cool breezes making her feel strangely happy. But her father had deceived her and when they returned to New York she'd asked her father why his mother was so black. Her father had insisted that his mother was *trigueña*, which she later learned was the euphemism for dark and really came from the word *trigo*, which meant wheat.

In a Puerto Rican Studies class at Hunter one day the professor began lecturing on the Negroid tradition of poetry in Puerto Rico, and for the next week she had to endure a discussion of race, which she hated hearing about. Eventually, the professor assigned a poem which she had tried to forget over the years but which still turned up in her recollections. Written in the black Puerto Rican patois, just like what her grandmother spoke, the poem angered her. What the hell was the writer trying to prove by spelling words that way? He had written a whole book of poems in that style. What was the name of it? It bothered her that she couldn't remember, and she suspected she was unconsciously repressing the title.

368

And now, about a week after the Marrero dinner, Elsa happened to be in the library in their house and saw that Vidamía had brought that very book home and had written a translation of the poem. There it was, *Dinga y mandinga* by Fortunato Vizcarrondo. She opened the book, saw that it was first published in 1946, and then as she turned the pages, out fell a sheet covered with Vidamía's handwriting. She had copied the verses and then attempted to translate the poem. It was a rough translation, but the impact was still there in English and she wanted to take the sheet of paper and tear it into little pieces. *¿Y tu agüela aonde ejtá?* the African pronunciation thick, instead of the normal Spanish *¿Y tu abuela dónde está?* "And your grandma, where is she?" She felt pride that Vidamía was so diligent, but in the next instant, an intense hatred replaced that feeling. Vidamía had crossed out "where is she?" and had translated it in the black vernacular as "where she at?"

> *And Your Grandma, Where She At?*
>
> *Yesterday you called me black*
> *And today I'm going to answer*
> *My mother sits in the living room.*
> *And your grandma, where she at?*
>
> *I have hair like steel wool*
> *Yours is nothing but silk*
> *Your father's is very straight*
> *And your grandma, where she at?*
>
> *Your color came out white*
> *And your cheeks a rosy red*
> *Your lips are very thin*
> *And your grandma, where she at?*

You tell me I got big lips
And that my hair is nappy red
But tell me for goodness sake
And your grandma, where she at?

Cauze you have a white kid
You show her off all the time
And me wanting to yell at you
And your grandma, where she at?

You like dancing the foxtrot
And I dance the plena with style
You're passing as if you're white
And your grandma, where she at?

You're a white only in name
Rubbing elbows with the rich
Fearing people will know
The one your mama calls ma.

Here, whoever doesn't have dinga
Has some mandinga . . . Ha, Ha,
And that's why I ask you
And your grandma, where she at?

Yesterday you called me black
Trying to make me feel ashamed
My grandma comes to the living room
And yours is hidden in the back.

The poor woman is dying
Knowing you treat her so bad
That even your dog barks at her
If to the living room she comes.

I know her well, I'll have you know
They call her Siña Tatá
Cause there's no doubt
That she's really very black.

When Elsa had read *La Vida* she'd felt as if the author had been following her family around, recording everything they said. As for her grandmother, she felt bad that, years after her visit, her house had collapsed into the sea during a storm and she was never found. It was ironic that if anyone asked about her grandmother, she could extract enormous sympathy by telling the story, but that each time she told it, the only thing that emerged inside of her being was resentment at having to confront her grandmother's negritude.

Her thoughts returned to Barry and she once again admired her husband's capacity for success. One quarter, the marketing survey; the following quarter, the business plan; and the next one, the real estate and staffing. After intensive local advertising campaigns on Spanish-language as well as English-language television and radio stations, they opened offices in Miami, Sarasota, Tampa, and St. Petersburg.

The following month they opened six offices in California, and one each in Phoenix, Tucson, Albuquerque, Dallas, San Antonio, and Houston. By the beginning of March, when people were scurrying around to beat the IRS's April 15 deadline, they were at full operational capacity in Illinois, New York, New Jersey, Pennsylvania, Connecticut, Michigan, and Indiana. From concept to providing tax services, in less than a year.

She had looked at one of their marketing packages and was truly proud of what Barry and John had accomplished. She leafed through the booklet with the simple Spantax logo and motto, color pictures of bright offices and smiling Hispanic people, all the models very light-skinned and Caucasoid, here and there the slightest hint of Indian blood—for the benefit of the

Mexican Americans and Central Americans. It was a good idea. They had found people with already established insurance or travel offices, offered to set them up in business, train a staff for tax preparation, and provide them with advertising and technical support. When the rush of the tax season was over, the staff was trained to sell insurance, arrange home mortgages, and handle other financial services. Everything was computerized, and new software had been developed especially for them by a company in Oregon.

But the tax-preparation operation was a thing of beauty. The offices were attractive and new, everything following a standard design, so that if one walked into a Spantax office, whether you were in Newark, New Jersey, Gary, Indiana, or Dallas, Texas, you felt at home in the warm, adobe-like rooms with palm trees and bright prints of figurative art in scenes reminiscent of the ideal places your parents and grandparents talked about. Walking into a Spantax office was like walking into the home of a trusted relative. In middle-class and staid communities, where there was crossover business from white or black Americans, soft music reminiscent of a Spanish garden played imperceptibly and very well-groomed and courteous Hispanic people spoke to you, offering to help you with any tax problem you might have. No *salsa* here, no *merengue*, or *cumbia* or *corridos*. This was serious business, and you didn't want to be arrogant and loud with Uncle Sam. Respect. Always respect. You just sat at their desks and the neatly groomed clerks keyed in the information you provided them and in a matter of minutes your taxes were being processed. In working-class neighborhoods where the pace was more hectic and the people didn't yet have a firm grasp of why they were being taxed, many worried about their legal status in the country and their bogus social security numbers and identities as they sat nervously in the upscale offices. Whether you ate *pastelas* in the Bronx, *arepas* in Queens, or *tamales* in Corpus Christi, the staff worked diligently without a sweat, until, softly in the background, a Hewlett-Packard laser printer produced flawless IRS forms with all your information on them.

"For another twenty-five dollars we will transmit your return electronically to the Internal Revenue, *señora*. This will ensure that your return will arrive sooner. Yes? Very good. A very wise decision, *señora*."

Barry was happy, and Elsa liked Barbara Marrero, a Vassar grad who was a Spanish medievalist and had done graduate work in Spain. She did volunteer work for the Metropolitan Museum, drove a cherry-red BMW, was a gym rat, looked totally fit, and dressed impeccably. Her father was in banking in Miami and was connected through different business arrangements to the powerful Puerto Rican Ferré family, one of whom, Luis Ferré, had been governor of the island. After the Puerto Rican offices of Barry's accounting firm were inaugurated in May and the Spantax promotional campaign had been a success there as well, John and Barbara Marrero invited Elsa and Barry to go island-hopping with them for two weeks on a yacht belonging to Barbara's father. They had helicoptered from the airport to the nearby marina, and after a light lunch they had set sail for St. Thomas.

Elsa and Barbara lay on deck chairs in their very brief bikinis, the sea breezes and salt air instigating their sensuality. Elsa felt proud that she was still young and her body was firm. The Marreros' two boys, Roger and Doug, both gorgeous—the one attending Carson Academy, in his last year, and the other finishing his second year at Princeton—came along and on more than one occasion she had caught them looking at her admiringly. She'd smiled openly so that the young one had blushed. Doug was accompanied by his blond girlfriend from Virginia, while Roger, who was the handsomer of the two, athletic and very polite, was by himself. Elsa had introduced the Marrero boys to Vidamía when the Marreros had visited their home and Roger and Doug had both seemed friendly.

Elsa made a serious attempt to invite Vidamía to come sailing with them, but Vidamía said that this was a pivotal year in her family's life and that she wanted to devote as much time as possible to being with them. "Pivotal," she'd said. The word didn't belong in her daughter's vocabulary, although she had to admit that there was something quite different about Vidamía lately. A tinge of jealousy crossed Elsa's heart, again mixed with an odd, confusing pride. Vidamía was a beautiful young woman, svelte and strong and remarkably sensual, her body perfectly sculpted. Her face, however, was truly stunning, the large green eyes and high cheekbones emphasized to a greater degree now that she was using makeup. Her nose was a little bony but it validated her whiteness. And yet it was her confidence, her poise, her sense of personhood that made her appear older, more in command.

Elsa was sure Vidamía was already having sex, although she couldn't imagine her involved sexually with the Breitenbach boy. Vidamía's birthday at least had been uneventful, and she seemed genuinely grateful for the present. Two thousand eight hundred dollars the ruby jewelry had cost. She hoped her relationship with her daughter would never change. She genuinely admired her. The girl was smart and mature, and although Elsa didn't like the influences she was acquiring down on the Lower East Side during the summers, she was proud that instead of becoming more American Vidamía was able to retain her Puerto Rican culture. Rather than Billy Farrell's family molding her daughter into just another tasteless white girl, the neighborhood had turned the tables on him. It was Cookie who had been converted into a Puerto Rican dittybop, *una jebita loca*. God, she couldn't believe the girl and the way she talked. She was just like Elsa's own homegirls back when she was growing up. The victory over Billy Farrell gave her profound satisfaction, but she knew better than to get too comfortable.

There were other matters that caused her even more concern. One was the fact that on the sailing trip in the Caribbean, Barry began to make overtures to her about having a child. He said he had spoken to his doctor and that there was a definite possibility that his vasectomy could be reversed. The idea of being pregnant again, as romantic as it sounded, didn't appeal to her. She was still only thirty-four, so the idea didn't seem that far-fetched. She'd wait and see what the doctors said.

35 Confrontation

In June, when Vidamía's classes were all but over, Taylor Breitenbach came home and gave her a ring to express his wish for a commitment, pointing out that it wasn't an engagement ring or anything like that, but that he wanted her to know that he had no desire to see anyone else but her; he hoped she felt the same way. The next time they saw each other, however, she returned the ring and told him that maybe it would be better if they were just friends and didn't date anymore. He asked if she'd met someone else. Without thinking, she said, "Yes, I did. Down in the city." Taylor simply nodded and said that maybe it was all for the best. He wished her luck and added that if Yale accepted her and she decided to attend, he'd see her in New Haven and maybe they could have lunch sometime. She said that would be fine and when he dropped her off in front of her house, he actually put out his hand and they shook hands stiffly.

It rained and rained that night, and, unable to sleep, Vidamía sat in the window seat of her room, watching the lightning and listening to the thunder. She thought about Wyndell Ross and was certain he wouldn't call and that if he did she wouldn't go out with him. She didn't know why, but it didn't seem right. And then she thought about her mother and knew it had to do with her and recalled once again Kunta Kinte and knew that her reluctance had to do with Wyndell's being black. She felt confused and was afraid that Wyndell would call her. Deep in her chest she felt a horrible loneliness and hugged herself against the realization that she was alone in the world. That as much as she loved her family and her friends, and as much as that love was returned, she was alone. For the first time in her life she understood the word "melancholy" and knew that other people in the world must feel the same. She didn't know where her awareness came from, whether she had read something or heard it in school or perhaps talked about it with Lurleen, but she knew that human beings spent a good deal of time warding off loneliness and often clung to each other and to things and ideas in order not to feel the despair of this awareness.

The loneliness made her feel vulnerable, but she stepped fully into it, unafraid, knowing that perhaps if she wasn't afraid of it she might learn something profound about herself. The thought of being brave made her recall the time she'd thought about being a drummer boy in the Revolutionary War and about Fawn and her insistence that she was a drummer girl. What would happen to Fawn without the band? Perhaps she needed the band as much as her father did. Vidamía began thinking about how she could help Fawn. Suddenly she felt very drowsy and lay down. She was asleep almost instantly. During the night she woke up in a sweat after having a dream in which she was running, carrying two babies in her arms. She was in a field of heather and there was a very large, hairy dog running alongside of her. She wasn't afraid of the dog. In the distance she saw smoke coming from the chimney of a stone house sitting on a bluff. Below the cliffs she heard the sea pounding the rocks. It began to drizzle and she went into the house and made a fire. She fed the babies and then began singing, and although she couldn't discern the words, she was certain that she was singing in the Irish tongue. When she got up in the morning she was as confused about Wyndell as before.

Toward the end of summer, Elsa's problems with Vidamía grew in intensity. One weekend afternoon as she worked at preparing a paper for a conference of Hispanic psychologists at a university in Michigan later in 1989, Barry came into her study and dropped a credit-card statement on her desk. The amount $8,578 was circled in red and above it was the name of her darling daughter, the ingrate and social barbarian, who was lately driving her crazy with her behavior and speech. Elsa was suddenly blinded with rage. Standing up with the paper in her hand she shook it at the Heavens. Her feelings for her daughter were so incongruous. One minute she admired her and the next she wanted to strangle her.

"Jesus Christ, what in the hell cost eight thousand dollars?" she said. "What did she do now—buy a car for those people? Did she put a down payment on a co-op for herself? She's been threatening to move out, you know."

"Just read it," Barry said, patiently.

Elsa looked at the statement and then slammed the paper down on her desk.

"The Greene Piano Company on Ludlow Street?"

"That's what it says."

"Who in the hell plays the piano in that godforsaken neighborhood for there to be a piano company there? She bought a piano?"

"It looks that way."

"We already have a piano. Why does she want another one? Nobody ever plays the damn thing anyway. When are they going to deliver it? Maybe you can call them up and cancel the order. No, it's Saturday. Okay, Monday you call them up and cancel it."

Barry directed her once more to the statement and explained that the purchase had been made at the beginning of August.

"I'm sure it's been paid for and delivered."

"Her father," she said, the awful truth slapping her awake.

"She bought it for her father. I'm going to kill her when she gets home. Where is she?"

Just minutes later, Vidamía walked in after having jogged several miles. She raced immediately upstairs to shower and was about to enter her room when she heard the familiar "Young lady!" followed by a stern request that she report immediately downstairs. When Vidamía reached the bottom of the stairs, Elsa was looking away in her best I've-had-it-with-you pose, her right arm extended and the long coral pink fingernail of her index finger pointing to the library.

"March," she said.

"March?" Vidamía said, snottily. "How butch!"

"What!" Elsa shouted. "What did you say?"

"I said, 'How butch,'" she replied, staring defiantly at her mother. "You know, how macho."

"Macho? Are you accusing me of some sort of sexual aberration? Butch? That's a derogatory term used by homosexuals. What did you mean?"

Vidamía laughed as she walked into the library. Without removing her running shoes, she tucked a leg under her and plopped into one of the big leather chairs. When Elsa reminded her that her shoes were on the furniture, Vidamía ignored her. Barry was sitting across from her, his head down and his spectacles in his right hand, in which he also held several pieces of paper. He looked pained and uncomfortable. Elsa continued her attack on Vidamía. Barry finally told Elsa to calm down. Fuming, Elsa sat on the leather couch between the two chairs.

"Just relax a minute," Barry said, putting his glasses back on.

Vidamía felt a little sad for Barry. He worked so hard and demanded so little. Perhaps he didn't want to admit it, but her love for her father had affected her relationship to Barry, and each subsequent year he seemed more and more subdued in manner. He now avoided her more than he had previously. Although she wasn't supposed to know it, doctors had been unable to reverse his vasectomy, and his wish to have a child of his own now weighed heavily on him. He was still cordial and answered her questions with patience, once in a while making a thoughtful suggestion. He was still the same impersonal male who smiled at her accomplishments and tolerated her faults, never judging or praising her. And yet since she had found her true father, Barry's status in her life had shifted. For the first time she realized how deeply hurt he was that he no longer commanded the position of most important male in her life.

"Well, are you going to tell her or do I?" Elsa said.

"Elsa, please," Barry replied. "Just relax."

"She doesn't have the right to do as she pleases."

"The credit-card bill came, right?" Vidamía said.

"Oh, so you know exactly what this is about?" Elsa said, shifting forward. "Incredible. First she does it and then she brazenly defends it."

"Defends it? I'm not defending anything. You gave me a credit card for my birthday last year. It had a twenty-five-thousand dollar credit line on it and I used some of it."

"Some of it? Some of it? Almost nine thousand dollars, young lady."

"What's the big deal? We've got money to burn."

"That's not the point," Elsa replied.

"What is the point, then? When I was a little kid and we moved into this house, I thought it was great. Getting driven to school by a chauffeur, pampered by Mrs. Alvarez, huge Christmas and birthday presents; trips to Puerto Rico, to Cancún, to Spain, to Portugal, to Holland. Even to Japan. How many girls eleven years old have a special guide take them through the Louvre for the afternoon while their mother goes shopping for clothes in Paris? Mademoiselle, over here we have the Fwench impwessionist Monet. Monsieur Monet was known for his paintings of . . . Blasé, blasé, blasé. Everything first class. I thought all airplane seats were the same size until I talked to some girl in junior high school and she said she was all cramped in her seat and I thought maybe the girl had some sort of eating disorder because she didn't look that overweight. And then we flew to Boston on the shuttle to visit Titi Hilda after she moved there. Right away I realized that seats for regular people were smaller than the first-class seats. All of this excessive wealth before I was twelve years old."

"Of all the ungrateful . . ." Elsa started to say and looked to Barry for support.

"No, wait," Vidamía said, shifting agilely on the chair so that she was now kneeling on the cushion, her arms gesticulating in her best home-girl imitation, the body language aggressive, challenging. "Look at this house. Eighteen rooms. The wealthiest section of Tarrytown. Last year I asked Billy Horn, whose father has a real estate office in Mount Kisko, how much he thought our house was worth? He said that he'd ask his father. The following week he came back and said that with the land that it's on it was now worth about 3.2 million dollars."

"You're a very lucky young lady," Elsa said, feigning hurt. "You just happen to have very little appreciation for it."

"C'mon, *mami*. You gave me the card. What was I supposed to do with a twenty-five-thousand-dollar credit line, buy records and clothes? How much did I spend all together since you gave me the card last year? Not even a thousand dollars. You must think I'm an idiot. I hear people talking at parties and at dinners. I mean, Babs Marrero . . ."

"Mrs. Marrero to you," Elsa interjected.

"Yeah, yeah, whatever," Vidamía snapped. "Anyway, Mrs. I-hang-out-with-Ivanna-in-the-sauna Marrero can't stop talking about the success of Spantax and swears that her husband, Mr. I'll-kick-that-damn-Castro-out-of-Cuba-myself Marrero, will be on the cover of *Time* by Christmas. Give me a break, okay? Does 'Spantax netted twenty-five million dollars' sound like we're getting on line for the welfare cheese Grandma Ursula talks about?" she inquired of Elsa, and at the same time happened to look at Barry, who was subtly enjoying her awareness of how well his enterprises were doing. "And that doesn't even count what Barry's company makes now that it's expanded to Florida and Puerto Rico. Damn it. We're rich."

"So what!" Elsa said. "That doesn't give you the right to squander money on your whims."

"We're rich."

"Dammit, your stepfather works very hard, and in my own small way I contribute quite handsomely to our income. We're not spendthrifts. Our expenditures are for necessities."

"Necessities? We have two Jacuzzis in this place, one in the pool house and one in the guest house. And now you're having a second swimming pool built. What necessities? Oh, and my sweet sixteen party was a real necessity."

"I'm talking about when we were starting out."

"Right, so why are you making such a big deal about me buying a piano for my family?"

"Your family?" Elsa shouted. "What are we?"

"You're my family, too," Vidamía said, tears coming to her eyes. "I'm sorry, *mami*. You know I didn't mean it that way."

"She knows that," Barry said.

"Wait a minute, Barry," Elsa interrupted. "I want an explanation."

Barry was firm.

"As far as I'm concerned she doesn't have to explain anything," he said. "All I want is for Vidamía to learn how important it is to handle money wisely. She's right, the amount is small if we consider our overall wealth." He turned to Vidamía and asked her if she understood.

For the first time Vidamía saw a profound tenderness in Barry and understood why her mother clung to him, seeking what she hadn't been able to find in another male. It was obvious Barry adored her mother, but she had never seen how it was possible for her mother to feel the same for him, although she was constantly praising him. Perhaps it was all a show on her mother's part. Vidamía's heart felt strangely pained, and then she realized that deep inside she also loved Barry. Not in the same way that she loved Billy Farrell, but with respect and admiration and a kind of awe.

"I'm sorry, Barry," she said. "I thought I was doing a good thing."

"A good thing?" Elsa said.

"Maybe you were," Barry said, ignoring Elsa. "But I wish you had consulted us first."

"I thought she'd say no," Vidamía said, gesturing with her chin toward Elsa.

"Maybe she would've, but I think you realize that you have a responsibility."

"I know," she said, her head bowed. And then she looked up proudly. "I'll pay it back."

"Oh, sure," Elsa said. "Eight thousand . . ." and she reached for the paper, ". . . five hundred and seventy-eight dollars. Fat chance."

"I will," Vidamía said, defiantly. "Wait and see."

"I don't think it's necessary for you to pay the money back," Barry said. "You're absolutely right. It was your credit card to do whatever you wanted and you did. I don't want to belabor the point of accountability and the need for consultation and advice."

"Oh, Barry, stop trying to pacify her. You sound like an accountant."

"Basically, that's what I am," he said, injured, his words falling with a thud and causing him to rise and leave the room.

"I've got homework, *mami*," Vidamía said.

"I think you know that I'm going to have to curtail your privileges, young lady."

"This is a joke, right?" Vidamía said.

"It's no joke. You should be grateful that your stepfather is so lenient," Elsa said.

"I am."

"Well, then, why are you abusing your privileges?"

"I'm really sorry you want to see it that way, Mom," Vidamía said, employing the English, instead of the Spanish, *mami*, which to her way of thinking represented a harsher stand. "I really trusted that the card was a gift, that it wasn't just for show."

"It wasn't. It was given to help you develop the capacity to manage your life."

"Well?"

"Don't get snotty with me, sweetie pie."

"I'm not, but, *coño, mami* . . ."

"Don't you talk to me like that . . ."

"Fine, try and control me. I said I was going to pay the money back and that's exactly what I'm going to do. Like I said, I've got homework and SATs, Regents, advanced placement tests, essays to write, and a whole bunch of shit that I'm about to say fuck it to. You know, fuck graduating and fuck college. I'm about to tell the whole system to kiss my royal mick-spic ass."

"Young lady, I will not have you talk that way in this house."

"Fine, I'll move out. I'll start packing."

"I'm canceling the card."

"What is your problem, lady?" Vidamía said. "I'm seventeen years old. You give me a gold card for my sixteenth birthday, I use it, and it pisses you off. Great. Cancel it. See if I care."

" 'Lady'? 'Pisses me off'? Is that the way you're going to talk to your mother?"

"Yeah, that's the way I'm going to talk to my so-called mother," Vidamía shouted, her hand on her hip and her shoulder thrust out like she'd seen Cookie's homegirls do.

Elsa recognized the chip-on-the-shoulder gesture immediately and totally lost it. *El palito*, they called it, because in Puerto Rico kids put a twig on their shoulder and dared someone to knock it off. In an instant she was back on the Lower East Side again, back when she was fifteen years old, before the whole thing started with Joey's death and her involvement with Billy.

"Girl, let me tell you something," she said in her best Afro-Rican accent, squaring off at her daughter. "Honey, you're in deep trouble if you start messing with me."

"Oh, please," Vidamía said, turning her face in disdain.

"Please? Check this little bitch out! What in the fuck is it with you? You think you're the only one that can act all bad and come up in somebody's face selling tickets? Well, let me tell you something, homegirl. You better get your shit together big time. I mean, who in the fuck do you think you are? You think you're some grown-up, big-time Lower East Side homegirl that's gonna walk all over her mama? Is that what you think, bitch? Yeah? Well, fuck you!"

Vidamía looked at Elsa and suddenly saw through her act, knowing that she was still like one of Cookie's friends, putting up a front and inside she was scared stiff. Her parting words tore at her mother's heart, wounding her at her most vulnerable.

"Yo, mama, whyntcha chill?" she said. "It's no big thing. I told you I was gonna pay back the money and that's what I'ma do. I got shit to do. Bye-bye, Mommie dearest."

Elsa stood there glued to the spot as she watched Vidamía heading up the stairs. She finally turned away and went looking for Barry to confront him about his lack of support.

Vidamía immediately called Cookie to report what had happened with her mother, alerting her that quite possibly she'd be coming down to live with her and the rest of the family permanently. Cookie's response was that this was the coolest and most encouraging news she'd heard because she and Mario'd had a big argument at his mother's house and of course she's a cool lady and took her side and that pissed Mario off even more and he said he was sorry to have such a traitor of a Puerto Rican mother who loved his crazy girlfriend more than him because she spoke Spanish and listened to her stupid stories about the stupid island because that's all they had down there were stupid coconut-headed people and maybe he'd go and stay with his father in Queens and work for him in his restaurant and the hell with going to college and then he'd called both of them a bunch of stuff in Chinese, including *noiy yun*, which she knew meant women. And then under his breath as he went out the door, *so po*, which was said to stupid women. When Vidamía asked what he'd done Cookie said Mario did the same thing that he always did when he got mad.

"He just walked over to Canal Street real fast and then all the way to the West Side Highway and came back. By the time he got back he was okay, but he wouldn't talk to me."

"What are you gonna do?"

"Wait till he calls."

"You're not gonna call him."

"No way, honey. What am I, some love-starved *pendeja* that's gonna chase after this ungrateful-ass Chino-Rican? He don't know how good he got it. A hundred-percent-passion-and-no-nonsense kind of gal. That's what he's got. So I ain't calling. Not me, mama. And when he calls he better be Super Mario nice."

They both laughed and Cookie asked her how her love life was proceeding up in the northern territory. Vidamía said that Wyndell had called and they were supposed to get together.

"You're ready to lose it, ain't you?"

"Don't, Cookie," Vidamía said, feeling weepy.

"You really like him, don't you?"

"Yeah, he's really nice."

"Well, honey, I don't blame you. The nigger is one fine-looking *moreno*, girl."

"Cookie?"

"Yeah?"

"Could you please stop using that word."

"Word? What word? Oh, right. I'm sorry. Just a habit from

being with the homegirls. It doesn't mean anything. I mean, you seen them. They be talking about me and saying nigger this and nigger that and pointing my way, and I'm whiter than God."

"How do you know God is white?"

"More important, like Mama says, how do you know God *is*?"

"Yeah, well . . ."

"C'mon, baby. Cheer up. I'ma have to go up there and slap you and whatnot."

"Stop joking, Cookie," she said. "I gotta figure out how I'm gonna pay back this money."

"Maybe you could get a job as a go-go dancer in New Jersey," Cookie said.

"Be serious, okay?" Vidamía replied.

"Honey, you got the body."

"Cookie!"

"I'm kidding, mama. Don't bug, okay, girl?"

"I'm not, but this is serious shit."

"I know, and I'ma think about it. When you coming down?"

"I better chill for a couple of weeks, but I'll let you know."

They said goodbye with the promise to talk the following day. They spoke every day for the next three weeks, discussing schemes for Vidamía to make some money. Selling Avon, going to work for McDonald's, selling magazine subscriptions were all vetoed by Elsa, so that Vidamía began to suspect that her mother would do everything in her power to keep her from having money of her own. Although her card had not been revoked, her purchases, few as they were, were checked and rechecked by Elsa for signs of further abuse of privileges.

All dreams, if they are to benefit the dreamer, must be hopelessly complex and barely retrievable, but most of all they must be incongruous. Upon hearing of a dream, someone other than the dreamer may complain of the implausibility of the psychic concoction or the incongruity of its structure, or else remark that it bears little connection to the exterior reality of the dreamer. Such critiques do not matter, since the dreamer is the person responsible for the genesis of the dream and stands to gain the most from its occurrence. That being understood, it becomes incumbent upon us all to accept that there were times when Charlie Parker or Coleman Hawkins, or Benny Carter or Dexter Gordon, or John Coltrane or Charlie Rouse or Lester Young, smelling of aftershave, a slight aroma of expensive scotch hanging in the air, came and sat on the edge of the bed of little Wyndell Ross with their saxophones and practiced scales for hours; once in a while essaying a tune, folding the melody in inverted fashion and then improvising upon on it so that it sounded lyrically fresh and like something no one had ever heard. There were times, however, when the tempo was so accelerated that, through the somnolence produced by the dream, an observer would attest, with hand resting upon an accumulation of divine scriptures, that Mr. Gordon or Mr. Parker each possessed not ten but twenty, or perhaps thirty, fingers, such was their virtuosity.

They didn't come every night, and sometimes they didn't sit down on the side of the bed, like the time Charlie Rouse came and stood over by the closet so that little Wyndell Ross could see him and his image in the mirror as he played "Darn That Dream," the tenor at first in the low register and the music hanging in the air like colored clouds so that little Wyndell Ross could see every note clearly. Little Wyndell Ross would listen intently and could then figure out exactly how Bird and Trane were producing their wondrous music—insisting that little Wyndell Ross call them by those names, Trane and Bird and the Hawk; playing and taking one small part of the melody and extending threads of music from the phrase; first one way and then the other, making circles and triangles in the air as if they were drawing with the music.

There were times when they showed up late at night, their jackets open and their ties pulled down. Some wore porkpie hats and others sported berets. They brought drummers and bassists, and always a pianist, like Monk or Bud Powell. The pianist looked all around the room, pushed at doors, looking for a piano, and they'd look at Bird or one of the others and say, "Man, why'd you bring me all the way here if there's no piano?"

And Bird would say, "Man, hold off and don't get so cantankerous. There's a piano. My man Wyndell's going to lead us to the instrument. Do you understand what I am relating to you?" And off they'd go, looking for the piano, which wasn't difficult to find downstairs in the living room, but so as not to wake up the other members of the family it was necessary to climb down into the basement to his father's den and there find the other piano on which his father played when his friends came over to jam, but which was just as good.

Because of his dreams there were times when his parents or an older sister, Garlande or Davina, found Wyndell in the basement of their home at four or five in the morning, reincarnating those days at Minton's Playhouse when folks like Dizzy Gillespie, Bird, Monk, and Kenny Clarke were busy in the laboratory of the mind, inventing bebop; little Wyndell Ross shivering in his pajamas, his eyes absolutely closed, playing on his own tenor saxophone the most musical and progressive improvisations, at times counting as he traded eight bars with some imagined partner, so that his father, Dr. Barkley Ross, Denver pediatrician and amateur jazz pianist, was reduced to tears of joy though at the same time experienced trepidation when he heard his young and beautiful son, who at the age of ten understood the music instinctively, and although his intellect told him he should encourage his son to study medicine, he had no choice but to let his heart rule and help the boy achieve whatever he chose.

There were times when Dr. Barkley Ross thought of sitting at the piano and joining his son, but instead opened a linen closet, found a blanket and unfolding it placed it on his son's shoulders and sat down to listen to Wyndell's solo, noting, although he couldn't prove it, but later told his friend Lawrence Stanton, whom he had known at Howard University and who was now a fine surgeon practicing in Atlanta, that he was certain that his son Wyndell had been playing with jazz greats in back of him, such was his feel for time and so precise was his phrasing, perhaps a rhythm section of Philly Joe Jones, Paul Chambers, and Red Garland from the old Miles Davis Quintet.

And years later, when Wyndell would stand on the stages of jazz clubs and play a tune, his eyes closed and his fingers working the keys of his tenor in rapid-fire sequences, daring a rhythm section to match his virtuosity, he recalled the séance-like feelings of those dream sessions with the great masters and couldn't truly tell where the music from his horn was emanating; certainly not all of it was his, for it was as if he were simply a conduit and the music was being passed from the others across to him and he was being asked to interpret it.

There were moments, after he had become a man, that would become unforgettable for Wyndell. Like the time in L.A. when he was with the Sonny Pointer Quintet and they were being recorded live. The club was Catalina's, and Sonny Pointer was on piano, Mike Arnold on bass, Pete Manfredi on drums, and the Swedish trumpet player, Lars Andriessen, whom his sister Davina had said was a friend of her old man's and nobody thought the Swede could play until they began rehearsing and Lars had literally blown them away with his virtuosity and his incredible knowledge of the music, playing standards as well as obscure charts back to Fats Waller and forward to some of Charles Mingus's most complex orchestrations.

But they were up there in the middle of "Cherokee," literally in cuisinic rejoicing, when Wyndell, into about his fourth chorus, all of a sudden heard the horses' hooves and saw the braves galloping in the open plain, the cloud of dust flying behind them and their feathers fluttering in the wind, their lances with their totems carried effortlessly at their side, and all at once he heard a totally different musical language and played it so that later on in the liner notes of the album, *Pointer View*, the jazz critic Martin Froelich would write:

> While the young quintet's blend of virtuosity and technical brilliance is unquestionable, particular attention must be paid to the remarkable inventiveness of Wyndell Ross, whose tenor saxophone's phrasing is nothing short of spectacular. In an impassioned rendition of "Cherokee" Mr. Ross takes us away from the commonality of the well-known standard and into another dimension which evokes in its totality the American Indian at his most noble, punctuating each note with the staccato of hooves and the plaintive cries of exultation of the Plains Indians.

Wyndell had a big laugh when he read this. When he went home for Thanksgiving that year, his father played the tape and proudly read the liner notes out loud. During dinner his grandmother had informed everyone that the critic was mistaken. Genetic and cultural heir to a rich Afro-Amerindian tradition, the octogenarian Mimi Ross, in regal attendance, her high cheekbones and large eyes watching hawklike the proceedings, her gray hair pulled back and well oiled, noted that the Cherokee Nation, which was native to Georgia, Tennessee, and the Carolinas, had been forced to resettle in Oklahoma when gold was found in Georgia, and that therefore they were not technically Plains Indians.

"Yeah, Gran," Wyndell said, "but was it true what the man said about my playing?"

"I don't know if it was true," Mimi Ross, his grandma, replied, "but it was sure pretty."

"Yes, it was, son," his mother said.

"Yes, thank you," his father said. "It was truly an outstandingly gifted performance."

"Let's not get melodramatic," Garlande said, "we still got dessert to serve."

After Thanksgiving, Wyndell returned to the West Coast and did some club dates but mostly played rhythm-and-blues gigs, backup work on rock albums, score work on soundtracks for motion pictures, all of which paid the rent, but he found that more and more he was drifting away from the music, playing gigs that paid well but sapped his energies because of the restrictions of what he was being asked to play. He began to feel as if he existed in a cage, as if he were an exotic animal and everyone was watching him; like a male dancer in a cultural striptease joint.

Women constantly came on to him, and although they were invariably of the gorgeous variety, he was growing jaded by the games he had to play and the persistent worry that in spite of protection he was endangering his life. One night white, the next time black, or Latin, or even Asian. He was left empty and without any sense of being. But the money was good. Good enough for him to purchase a Mercedes and live in a spacious beachfront apartment in Santa Monica. He even went so far as to be swayed by the availability of drugs, experimenting again with cocaine as he had when he was at Berklee and his friend Rebecca Feliciano had scolded him for his folly. She played piano like she was trying to destroy the instrument except that each chord she played opened up like a brilliant musical sunburst and nothing but beautiful sounds came forth.

She had heard about his using blow and marched into his room one Saturday morning and, indignant as all hell in her invented badass Puerto Rican persona from the ghetto, which wasn't at all the case since she was very wealthy and her mother had a town house on Riverside Drive, told him sincerely in somewhat affected bebop jive language that he was one crazy mothafucka and that if he was planning to fuck himself up with junk and end up dead by the time he was thirty-five, to inform her so she could disassociate herself from him because talented as he was if he was going to turn into a junkie, then there was no hope for the country.

"Oh, man, cut it out," he said.

"Like I shouldn't give a fuck, right?" she said.

"No, Becky," he replied. "It ain't like that, man."

"Don't 'Becky' me, mothafucka," she said.

"Sorry, Rebecca."

"Right, but forget that shit about my name right now. The thing is you gotta stop putting shit up your nose. You got a responsibility, man. An artistic responsibility. This country ain't shit without the music, and you're the one that's gonna set all this jive straight and play and compose and make the thing go forward again, and never mind all this funk, fusion, and electric mothafuckin' bullshit these people are trying to sell folks. Or are you another of these self-destructive brothers that gotta throw their life away?"

Wyndell looked at her in her baggy pants and her butch haircut, no makeup, and bad beautiful self, and wished for all the world Rebecca wasn't into women, because there was no telling what would have happened. After graduation he'd lost touch with her for nearly a year, but then he'd heard she was still living in Boston, found her number in the directory, called her up, and a week later he was driving up there, mostly out of boredom.

She was giggin' at a small club. She and a bassist and drummer. She now affected a derby, which she wore even when she was playing. He sat in, and even without rehearsal, after a couple of tunes they fell into a groove and people who'd been drinking and talking began listening. After the last set they went out to eat and Rebecca began to tell him about how great things were between herself and Meredith, her lover, a small delicate blond girl, who was becoming a respected poet.

Later, she invited him to the house, and they sat around talking. Meredith smiled tenderly at him when Rebecca introduced her to Wyndell. She served them drinks and returned to her studio. An hour or so later she came back and said good night, kissing them both good night like a dutiful child. Wyndell and Rebecca stayed up, catching up with each other. Around three in the morning she showed him to his room and they'd said goodnight. He couldn't fall asleep and knew it was because of Rebecca, and the feelings he'd always had for her. But Rebecca acted more married than most of his married friends, male or female.

As she slid into bed with Meredith, Rebecca was still thinking about Wyndell. To her he represented jazz and its promise, but also its pain. Wyndell Ross's message on her answering machine had unearthed once again the feelings she had buried concerning the last days of her father's life. Her only consolation was that she had loved her father. She wondered whether she loved Wyn as a man. She let herself imagine herself naked with him and the thought made her feel cold and frightened. She decided she loved Wyn because he was about jazz and not because he was a man. But she had loved her father. And of course she had loved her Grandpa Iggy as much as her father, perhaps more since she'd spent more time with him. During her childhood, her father was gone for long periods at a time. Whenever she asked, her mother replied that her father was at the hospital. "In surgery," she said. Not until she was seven did she fully understand that her father was performing the operations, and not being operated on. She still recalled sitting at the piano with her grandfather, not being tall enough to reach the pedals, knowing even then the difference in sound between when her grandfather used them and when she played the same melody, without them. Where had they gone, her father, her grandfather? She had never held much hope in religion and the promise of seeing loved ones again. She had no family other than her mother. Her father's mother, her *abuelita*, had returned to Puerto Rico, up in the mountains to a place called Cacimar, which made no sense since it wasn't near the sea. With Puerto Ricans, even though she considered herself one, things were always weird. Later she learned that the name had nothing to do with the sea, and *casi mar*, which meant "almost to the sea," was two words; and Cacimar was spelled differently, and it was one word, and was the name of an Indian chief.

She couldn't fall asleep and didn't want to wake Meredith up. She recalled that in her second year at Berklee, when she had become quite proficient at playing jazz piano and her technique was beginning to develop, able now to play fast and coherently, the choruses coming whole and her improvisations extending fluidly, her left hand chording and her right hand flawless in its runs, fear set in and Rebecca Feliciano became convinced that she would never be good enough to play the music. Her grandfather had died years before, so she couldn't speak to him, but she recalled sitting on Iggy Marginat's lap as a little girl, listening to him talk about music.

"I knew all the great ones," he said.

"Like who, Grandpa?" she said.

"Oh, like Diz and Bird and Thelonious Monk," Iggy Marginat said.

"The loneliest monk, Grandpa?" she asked, puzzled.

"No, no," he laughed and tickled her. "Thelonious." He spelled the name, then set her on the floor and went to the record rack. From it he extracted an LP, which he placed on the turntable. "Listen carefully," he said. When the record was over he said, "Can you dig it?"

"I can dig it," she said and her grandpa would put out his hand for her to slap. She slapped it and said, "I can't play like that. My hands are too little."

"You definitely can play, so don't worry about anything. You just play. You'll grow up and your hands are going to be real strong. You'll see. You just keep playing. At least you won't have to worry about where your next meal's going to come from. Life is rough if you want to play jazz. You won't have those problems. You'll always be taken care of."

And then her grandfather said that for most people, playing jazz is a difficult thing, financially. And back then when things were rough during the Depression, he'd bring the fellows home to eat.

"The house was always full of jazz musicians. Your grandmother didn't like it too much."

"Who else, Grandpa?" she said.

"Musicians who just loved the music like me."

"Who?"

"Oh, Pop Butterworth, Pete Carroll, Bobby Russo, Candy Donovan," he said, sadly. "They never became great. They were like me, they just loved the music. Sometimes we'd go up to Buck Sanderson's house in Yonkers and jam and have cookouts," he said, his mind back in those days.

"Jam, Grandpa?"

"Yeah, jam . . ." he said and then explained.

Those memories sustained her through her doubts until she began to feel her confidence returning. And then each day she'd sit for three or four hours at a time just chording and playing melodies against their chord structures, trying out new things, complicated runs and imagining others soloing and she laying out and just comping, working on her rhythm and time and then imagining herself coming in and soloing, playing chorus after chorus, letting the music at times explode from her so she could feel the piano shivering with excitement. This drove her to experiment with her strength in a greater and greater desire to play well. She began listening to Charlie and Eddie Palmieri, Cal Tjader and Ray Baretto, Dizzy Gillespie and the Latin influence on jazz, and began evolving an especially percussive style of playing the piano.

She also recalled speaking Spanish with her grandfather, learning things about his life as a little boy in Puerto Rico. He taught her games. *"Ambos a dos," "Aserrín, Asserán,"* and *"A la limón."* Her father, Dr. Paul Feliciano, had once told her, after he revealed to her the truth about his own private life, that her grandfather, till the end of his life, was also very proud of the fact that he spoke Spanish well. He told her that during that same period of time when Iggy Marginat went into Harlem, around 1929 or 1930, her grandfather met a young man from southern Spain whom he always referred to as "Federico, the poet." The young man was a writer in residence at Columbia University during those years. The two men became friends and often Ignacio Marginat traveled to the university, picked up his friend Federico, and they walked down the hill on Broadway, across 125th Street, and entered that wondrous world of Harlem.

Rebecca's father, Paul Feliciano, first told her the story of her grandfather's friendship with the young Spanish poet the evening they returned from their second Gay Pride Day parade down Fifth Avenue. The first time he'd marched with her in support, but the second time he was doing it for himself. They had bought Chinese food and returned to the house and that's when he told her he'd marched for himself. "I thought so," she said, and he laughed. That's when he told her about her grandfather. Paul Feliciano said he had often asked his father-in-law, Ignacio Marginat, whether he was talking about García Lorca. "Your grandfather said that was a secret, but admitted that his friend, the Spanish poet, had visited the house and written about his time spent in New York.

"Pick up García Lorca's *Poet in New York*. I can't be sure, but I've always believed they were lovers," her father told her—this when he had already begun losing weight and there was no longer a doubt that the HIV virus was affecting his immune system.

"Grandpa was gay?"

"Yes. Closeted, I suppose."

"Three generations?" she said. "That's like a tradition."

She was serious, but he laughed uproariously, his eyes suddenly blazing with health.

"I guess it is," Paul Feliciano said. "There were times when I'd kid myself and think that I was bisexual, but of all my sexual and emotional experiences, my gay ones were the most intense."

"That takes a lot of courage to admit," she said, taking his hand. "I love you, Daddy."

"I love you, too," he said, and she hugged him.

He asked her if she wanted to go with him to Sevilla in the summer. They could go to Andalucía and see Córdoba and Granada and swim on the Costa del Sol. She said she would if Meredith could come along. He said he had no problem with it, if Meredith didn't mind seeing him wasting away. A month later, after classes were over, they flew to Madrid, traveled by train to Sevilla, and then rented a car, which Rebecca and Meredith alternated driving, stopping often to examine the sights, the girls listening patiently as Paul Feliciano told them about the Moors and their conquest of Spain. "The Catholic kings were very foolish to kick the Moors and the Jews out of Spain in the fifteenth century," he said on more than one occasion. Arranged ahead of time Paul Feliciano had rented a small, two-story house outside of Málaga with a spectacular view of the Mediterranean, and there Rebecca and Meredith took care of him as best they could. He had taken a leave of absence from his duties at the hospital six months prior and closed his private practice, certain that he wouldn't survive too long. To all appearances, her father still seemed healthy. Thin, but in good health. Yet to Rebecca, who had known him as strong and decisive, it was obvious that the most minor exertion pained him now, the effort making him tentative, unsure of himself.

They returned to New York and no more than a month later he began dying in earnest. For three months, she came from Boston twice a week to endure the pain and horror and disgust of watching him wither and ooze before her, his cavernous eyes pleading for one last expression of love, which she could produce only with her presence and her words.

Meredith moaned in her sleep and turned toward her, seeking her out. She placed an arm under her blond head and like a child the smaller woman snuggled against her. Soon Rebecca felt sleep coming on. Out of the despair of losing her father, and her grandfather before that, and feeling alone, a ray of hope, brilliant as the sun of those Andalusian mornings a year prior, again emerged as Rebecca thought of Meredith next to her and their love for each other. So much had happened in the past five years. She had graduated from Berklee, taught piano privately for a while, and then began gigging regularly up and down the East Coast, avoiding New York for no other reason than that she didn't want to be reminded of her father.

She thought of Wyndell often, keeping in touch through cards and telephone calls. Once in a while he came to Boston and they went out to dinner like the first time he had come to her house and met Meredith and slept over. On those occasions they found other musicians and jammed. There was no doubt that

Wyndell was becoming stronger, fighting his demons. She was certain he would win.

It was now the late summer of 1990 and Wyndell had called her, left a phone message in which he sounded a bit desperate and wanted to know if she would come to New York. She'd have to return his call and see what was up. Jazz was a trip in more ways than one.

37 Going Home

Back then when they were students at Berklee, Wyndell had promised Rebecca Feliciano that he wasn't going to use cocaine anymore, and that had been the case until two years after graduation, when he was at a party in Beverly Hills after some gig at some stupid-ass movie star's house and stupid-ass, guitar-playing, blues-singing Willie Jones had accepted, as partial payment, some blow. Wyndell had ended up with some young blonde from UCLA, who hadn't taken her baby blues away from him, alternately looking at his eyes, his crotch, and his ax from the time they were setting up to the time they stopped playing, and whose family were members of some country club in Hilton Head, South Carolina, or Augusta, Georgia, since '86, meaning 1886, and after they'd had some blow she had properly sheathed him with her own supply of contraceptives, using not one but two "rubber duckies" as she called them and mounted him as they lay behind the bushes, down by the swimming pool. After they were done and she had nearly torn him up with her gyrations she boldly told him that she had been determined to make love to a black man that month and she sure was glad it had been him because she'd never forget him even when she was married and balling her old man. Wyndell felt totally useless and like his life was eroding from within. Later that night, after driving back to his apartment in Santa Monica, he thought more carefully about his life and what awaited him. He wasn't playing jazz and he wondered whether he ever would really be able to do so, given the meager demand for the music.

He recalled graduating from high school and spending that summer studying at the university in St. Louis, staying at the home of the trombonist Glenn Briscoe, who was a friend of his father's and taught in the music department; Wyndell sitting in with professional musicians and learning more about the music; at the end of the summer, flying to Boston with his mother to register at Berklee, being brave but feeling lonely and a little bit afraid after his mother left because in spite of his size and his musical confidence he was only seventeen years old. The first time it snowed it wasn't anything like Denver. There was a sadness in the weather, the sky was low and dark and the architecture and landscape looked old and tired.

In time, however, he grew used to the rhythm of the school, and of Cambridge and Boston and the T and the accent and the absolutely collegiate climate of the city, plus the respect with which he was treated by everyone connected with the music. There was, everywhere he went in the school, a sense that they were part of a very serious endeavor whose consequences would be felt for hundreds of years.

His first friend there was Rebecca Feliciano. By definition a piano is a percussion instrument, but Rebecca Feliciano attacked the instrument as if it were a long drum. And it was understandable, because the first time he'd shaken hands with her it was like shaking hands with his dad's friend Wilfred Atkinson who had played tackle at Bethune-Cookman College, or Alcorn State, and now coached at a little college in Arkansas after he had tried out for the Los Angeles Rams and torn up his knee so badly on a kickoff return during the exhibition season that he could never play again. But that was what Rebecca's hand felt like when she gripped his, not like some men who loved squeezing the life out of you, but like the entirety of Rebecca's hand had swallowed his.

His life had become a nightmare in Los Angeles and in the midst of a profound depression, in which for the first time in his life he considered suicide, he decided he had to get away. He was involved with Leslie Alton, a senior at USC and a former finalist for Miss Black Teenage America, whose father made snide remarks about musicians and was a partner in an extremely prestigious entertainment law firm in Los Angeles. Leslie, on the other hand, praised him for his love of jazz but, too often to be ignored, talked about his going back to school and getting something besides a musical education, something more in line with Dr. Ross, as she referred deferentially to the man she considered her future father-in-law, even though she had yet to meet him. She was sure Wyndell could become a fine lawyer and play on weekends like his dad, and were they going to Denver for Thanksgiving like he'd said?

He said they were on, but three weeks before Thanksgiving of 1988 he packed his ax, his tapes, and his clothes, and called up Teddy Banks, his technician buddy at KSRF, and told him he could have anything in his apartment, that the keys were downstairs in Lily Dunn's crib. He was going up to San Francisco to see if he could play up there. If that didn't work out he was going home to Denver, or wherever, but that Teddy wasn't to tell anyone where he'd gone. And off he went, leaving about three in the afternoon, regretting everything about himself and not really knowing what his life would become, his eyes moisting and blurring his vision as he drove; hoping his life and talent didn't extinguish itself in some horrible car crash like trumpeter Clifford Brown's, or disappear in a haze of alcohol and drugs like Bird's.

When he was away from Los Angeles and traveling up the coast on 101, the sea on one side and the mountains on the other and the music going on the radio, mostly fusion and idiotic stuff from guys just about his age whose music had no feeling but who were already household names, he began to calm down a little. He read the highway signs and cursed the sameness of American highways, everything so impersonal and antiseptic; names and distances. From Santa Monica he sped north along the Pacific Coast Highway, flying through Malibu, where he'd gone to parties in expensive beachfront homes and had his fill of beautiful women and exotic drugs, and, before getting to Oxnard, passing the exit to Camarillo, where they'd held Charlie Parker, working on his mental health, convincing him that he was just another crazy, worthless Negro and ought to straighten out his life and accept that it's one thing to be a genius if you're white but something else altogether if you're black, and it's not supposed to hurt to be unappreciated and unrecognized.

He was zoned in now, the machinery beneath him responding to his touch in much the same way as the tenor saxophone. He felt that strange power he always experienced while he was playing. He drove fast and devoured the highway; flying past Ventura, Carpinteria, Santa Barbara, heading inland at Gaviota and then up to Los Alamos, Santa Maria, and San Luis Obispo. With the sun setting, he stopped to get gas and something to eat, and then got back into the Mercedes and, rather than continuing on 101, veered off and kept to the coast road. It was as if somehow he needed to feel the edge of America, the last frontier, seeing the Pacific Ocean ahead of him and to his left, its vastness, like the infinite reaches of space, dark, foreboding.

His theory teacher at Berklee, who knew the West Coast and had jammed at Bob Cooper's Lighthouse, the Drift Inn, and Shelly's Manhole in the early sixties, and knew all the sidemen from Stan Kenton's orchestra—Pete and Conte Candoli, Charlie Mariano, Bob Holloman, Shorty Rogers, Maynard Ferguson, Boots Mussilli, Charlie Ventura, Lee Konitz, and Hank Levy, who had arranged some of the Kenton orchestra's charts in the seventies—and the rest of the musicians who were involved in the West Coast jazz movement, told him that West Coast jazz was the outgrowth of a Miles Davis innovation. He had played a record for Wyndell. It was a little scratchy but the freshness of the music had totally knocked him out: *Birth of the Cool*, with Lee Konitz, Gerry Mulligan, J. J. Johnson, and Kai Winding alternating on certain cuts, and the same thing being true for Kenny Clarke and Max Roach on drums. "Move," "Jeru," "Budo," "Boplicity," and a bunch of other tunes in which you heard, besides the regular instruments, tuba and French horn.

"When do you think they recorded this?" the teacher asked him.

"It sounds pretty modern, so I'd say maybe 1965," Wyndell had said. "Around there."

"Nope," the teacher said. "Recorded in 1949 and 1950 in New York City. And that's not all. John Lewis played piano on some of the cuts. The Modern Jazz Quartet's style and musicality emerged from the refinement that Miles created out of his time with Charlie Parker's quintet. In many ways the MJQ, because of its coolness and involvement with classical music, began to bring jazz into a more acceptable consciousness."

Wyndell Ross turned off the radio as he was approaching Morro Bay and slid in the tape of *Birth of the Cool* and settled into listening and watching the moonlight shimmering on the water below. He stopped in Monterrey to stretch his legs and to check everything, oil, water, tires, and fill up before going on again. To Santa Cruz, and then, choosing to stay close to the coast, to the end of America, its precipice, wanting to go as far as he could before falling off, he thought, up Highway 1 to Pebble

Beach, Half Moon Bay, Pacifica, Daly City, before turning inland once more, to San Francisco proper. Then, before getting on the Oakland Bay Bridge, calling up Sue McCallister to make sure she was home.

She had written to him last year, reminding him that he had once shown her Berklee and it was time for her to return the favor and show him Berkeley. After getting back into the car he drove across the bridge, loving the lights and the magnificence of the structure, recalling Sonny Rollins's composition, "The Bridge." Man was a daring being, he thought, and began thinking of how he could orchestrate his own composition, "Pacific Rim." He thought that of all the instruments the French horn had the most potential to illustrate the vastness of the ocean. He wanted to make sure, when it was played, that the soloist, someone like Julius Watkins, had the freedom to stretch out.

When he arrived at Sue McCallister's in Berkeley, where she now taught in the English department, she and her husband, Martin Travis, who taught in the history department, greeted him warmly and made him feel at home. Martin said that he was welcome to stay as long as he needed to. The house was a beautiful modern structure on a hill overlooking the city. There was a hot tub, and he luxuriated in it, talking art, music, and literature with Sue and her husband. That evening they had supper and then talked some more, and about ten o'clock he began to doze off and went to his room. Before he fell asleep he wondered if he'd ever be able to make any money from his music. Sue's father was the CEO of some plastics company that had its hands into everything from dishware to parts for the space program. He'd met her walking along the Charles River one spring afternoon. She was with her friend Lee Harwell from Atlanta.

He had been at Berklee a year and Sue and Lee were seniors at Harvard, Sue very blond and WASPish and Lee very black and revolutionary, but so close as friends that to listen to them it was hard to tell that they hadn't been raised in the same household. Lee's father was a judge in Atlanta and she was headed for Harvard Law after graduation. God, she had ended up working in Thurgood Marshall's office in Washington one summer. Sue had written recently and said that Lee was going to run for the State Legislature in Georgia. Wyndell and Lee had gone on a couple of exploratory dates, but Lee reminded him of Garlande and Davina, his sisters, and that took the romance out of it.

Things didn't work out in San Francisco. He met some musicians, they jammed, but they all said the same thing. "You're crazy leaving L.A., man. That's where all the movie and television and advertising money is. You wanna starve, stay up here. What you gonna do, teach?"

Wyndell remained and continued trying, calling people and making contacts, but there was no work. In the evening he would return and sit at Sue's piano, working out the orchestration for "Pacific Rim" and playing passages from it for Sue and her husband. He explained that it was part of a series of compositions on the U.S. "Not quite Dvořák's *New World* Symphony, or Ferde Grofé's work, but not unlike it," he said, invoking two composers who wrote of America. He played the familiar, lilting passage from Dvořák's work, which has formed the thematic structure for those lighthearted lilts in westerns. "Ambitious, but not pretentious," he'd added, self-deprecatingly. They laughed, and Sue's husband poured more wine.

Two weeks later he said goodbye to Sue and Martin and packed his car, the feeling of bitterness making his mouth taste as if he were sick and would never recover.

"Don't be defeated," she said. "I know you're very proud, but if it gets to be too much, please come back. You can stay here as long as you want. I want you to finish 'Pacific Rim.' "

He thanked her and then with all his gear back in the car, now freshly washed, he got in and left, driving through the beautiful Berkeley hills, the homes expensive and neat, every-thing exclaiming the greatness of the country. He sped up and got on the freeway, concentrating now on the steady flow of traf-fic, finding his way to U.S. 80 heading for Sacramento. From Sacramento it was a little over a hundred miles to Reno. The city seemed like a woman who is used to clubs—beautiful at night, but in the daytime glaringly unhealthy-looking. Recalling his nightlife in Los Angeles, he sped through Reno and headed still farther inland, away from the edge, seeking the comfort of his soul. Wadsworth, Lovelock, Winnemucca, Battle Mountain, and then Elko, where in 1883 his great-grandfather Ingram Ross had gone on a cattle drive as a young cowboy soon after he married his Cherokee wife, Rowena Spike. The drive got caught in a freak spring blizzard and he and the other cowboys had used the cows as cover from the snow. They'd gathered the horses to-gether in the middle of the herd, taken their horse blankets, hooked them onto the cattle's horns and stretched them to make a shelter, taking turns all night dumping the snow off the blan-kets and keeping an opening in the drifts created by the huddled cattle. When the storm was over the cows on the periphery of the circle facing the storm were frozen solid. When they finally gathered what was left of the herd and began moving south, the frozen cows looked like someone had sculpted larger than usual cattle. Ingram Ross had lost a couple of toes to frostbite and walked with a limp, but he still rode in all the rodeos and worked on his ranch until the age of seventy-seven, when he went riding one afternoon and on his way back had a heart at-tack and just slumped over the neck of his horse. The horse made its way back to the ranch but Ingram Ross was dead. "Talk about dying in the saddle," his grandmother, Mimi Ross, said whenever she told the story of her father.

She told other stories, too. He especially liked hearing the stories about the Cherokee. He couldn't recall ever seeing his grandmother in a bad mood. Even when Grandpa Henry died, she sat quietly, humming something which his father said was a prayer, but there was a slight smile on her face as if she knew that Grandpa Henry was safe and happy somewhere. She and her husband were second cousins, with both Ross and Spike relatives, their families going back to the Trail of Tears migration of the Cherokee.

Whenever he spent time at her house outside of Denver, she joked with him and told him of the Nunnehi, the little people, who were responsible for everything that happened. If a stroke of good luck came her way, it was the Nunnehi; if something was misplaced, it was the Nunnehi at it again, playing a trick on her. The Nunnehi men had beards, long gray hair, and hairy toes, and they lived in bushes and rocks. The Nunnehi women were very beautiful. All the Nunnehi were Cherokee and they spoke the language. His grandmother would sometimes point out of her kitchen window as she stirred a pot of stew and tell him she'd seen a Nunnehi. He'd climb up on the counter and look out the window into the pines and bushes, peering with all his might.

"Where, Grandma?"

"There, behind the tree," she'd say. "Concentrate. But don't look at the girls too long."

"Why, Grandma?"

"They'll bewitch you and you'll fall in love and go off with them to live in the woods."

He'd get down off the counter and his grandmother would give him a gingerbread cookie and tell him that he mustn't let anyone know that he'd seen the Nunnehi.

"Why, Grandma? I saw them."

"Oh, they don't want anyone to know that they're there, because then they'd be blamed for everything. Please take them a cookie. The little people love cookies. Go."

And he'd go out into the backyard, feeling the coming of winter in the air and he'd place the cookie behind a pine tree and come back into the house. The next day he went behind the pine tree and the gingerbread cookie was gone.

"They ate the cookie, Grandma."

"Of course they did. The little people wouldn't pass up a gingerbread cookie. You want another one?"

"Yes, Grandma. Thank you."

He was six years old and the following year his father's friends came over to play music in the den and left their instruments there while they went upstairs to eat and he'd tried playing Mr. Pearson's tenor saxophone which smelled of tobacco because he smoked so much. He'd removed the mouthpiece guard, picked up the instrument from the table, and blown into it. He was startled at the big sound, but he'd liked it and tried to play a tune but couldn't figure out how to do so. He kept trying different things until his sister Garlande came to get him. When he wouldn't listen his father came down and asked him if he liked the saxophone. He'd nodded, and his father asked him if he wanted to learn how to play it. He smiled and his father said he'd get him a clarinet first. He could start on that, and maybe he'd take him over to Mr. Pearson's to learn.

Thinking about his childhood made him want to be home and he sped up as he neared the Utah border, watching the sun set behind him so that in his rearview mirror it was light and ahead of him approaching darkness. Beyond the darkness he could see the silhouettes of the Wasatch Mountain Range of Utah, and Wyndell Ross's soul began slowly to mend itself. He went up and down the high plateau road heading toward Salt Lake City, and then drove the rest of the way through the Salt Flats, listening to the car's tape deck and stereo system surround him with *Miles Ahead*, *The Modern Jazz Quartet with the Stuttgart Symphony directed by Gunther Schuller*, *Charlie Parker with Strings*, and *The Thelonious Monk Orchestra at Town Hall*, with Charlie Rouse on tenor and Phil Woods on alto discoursing eloquently on "Friday the Thirteenth" and "Little Rootie Tootie," so that as each hour passed, rather than making him drowsy, the music filled him with greater determination to complete the journey and perhaps not give up on his dreams.

In Salt Lake City he checked into a motel, carrying his suitcase and his ax from the car, endured the disapproval of the clerk and went into his room. If you were black you had to be up to no good. Something as simple as getting some rest turned into high drama. He showered and changed and went out to eat. When he returned to the motel, it was eleven o'clock. He dialed the desk and asked for a seven-o'clock wake-up call, stripped naked, got into bed, and was asleep within seconds.

Five hours later, however, he was wide awake and eager to go. He washed, dressed, and packed everything back up. He wasn't hungry now but bought juice and prepacked sandwiches. He sat and mapped out the trip, tracing a meandering line with his pen. When he was done he had the gas tank filled. Once again inside the car, he looked at the map and decided against taking U.S. 80 into Cheyenne, Wyoming, and U.S. 25 to Greeley and then home to Denver. He chose instead the narrower U.S. 40, which had less traffic and gave him a chance to travel a part of Colorado he didn't know, even though he'd be driving through it during the night. He felt intense pride in his citizenship in the state. It had its problems, but it was his home and as his father and mother insisted, "It's our country," meaning the United States, "and it's our state, and we have a history here. It's up to us to change it. In spite of prejudice and small-mindedness, it's up to us."

He moved down the road again, crossing into Colorado at Dinosaur, with Miles's muted trumpet talking to him, making him laugh and say damn; Paul Chambers's bass beating inside of him as if it were his heart; at times unable to help himself and singing as Miles played "If I Were a Bell," going "ding-dong-ding-dong-ding" and feeling enormous joy in his heart. Blue Mountain, Elk Springs, Maybell, Lay, places that probably never had blacks living in them, maybe never even passing through them, except perhaps his great-grandfather Ingram and his great-grandmother Rowena. Rowena Spike, the Cherokee's daughter, had talked about other black Cherokee cowboys in that part of the country and how she had fallen in love with the handsome Ingram Ross and followed him, traveling from her parents' home in the Oklahoma panhandle, which shares a border with Colorado.

Wyndell changed tapes and listened to *Charlie Parker with Strings*, the engine humming and he alone in a time capsule traveling through the darkness of his land, because it was his as much as anyone's. An hour later the sun began surfacing in the east, the orange-and-gray dull haze quickly giving way to full sunlight. Hayden, Milner, Steamboat Springs, and then south through Arapaho National Forest to Kremmling.

His grandmother Mimi had said once that one of her father's sisters, Blossom Spike, had taken up with an Arapaho in the late 1850s. Blossom had died with her children at a place called Sand Creek, to the north of the Arkansas River, up near Fort Lyon. He'd asked what had happened. She shook her head and said that's all she knew. Her grandfather Sandford Ross, who'd been a blacksmith at the army fort, had told her father, Ingram, the cowboy, about it.

He continued to ask questions, writing home to his father to urge him, much as Lee Harwell—to whom he'd sent a fifty-dollar check, for her campaign to become part of the Georgia legislature—was urging him, to look into his family's background. He'd asked his grandmother so many questions at Thanksgiving that Mimi Ross took to locking the door to her room whenever he came into the house. When he came home for Christmas, one of his presents from his father was *Atlas of the North American Indian*, by Carl Waldman. The book had considerable information and maps on every tribe.

Wyndell read about the Sand Creek Massacre, the anger rising slowly in him until he was shaking. He became obsessed and returned to those pages time and time again, reading with shocked fascination, so that from then on he couldn't watch a film depicting Indians without an overwhelming feeling of rage. He read the book overnight, devouring each page and finally getting to the place that no doubt held the history of his grandmother's aunt.

In the course of the next outbreak of violence—sometimes referred to as the Cheyenne-Arapaho War or the Colorado War of 1864–65—a tragedy occurred that served to unite many of the Plains tribes in their distrust and hatred of whites. Because of the rapid growth of mining interests in Colorado after the Pikes Peak Gold Rush, Governor John Evans sought to open up Cheyenne and Arapaho hunting grounds to white development. The tribes, however, refused to sell their lands and settle on reservations. Evans decided therefore to force the issue through war and, using isolated incidents of violence as a pretext, ordered troops into the field under the ambitious, Indian-hating territorial military commander Colonel John Chivington.

In the spring of 1864, while the Civil War raged in the east, Chivington launched a campaign of violence against the Cheyenne and their allies, his troops attacking any and all Indians and razing their villages. The Cheyenne, joined by neighboring Arapahos, Sioux, Comanches, and Kiowas in both Colorado and Kansas, went on the defensive warpath. Evans and Chivington reinforced their militia, raising the Third Colorado Cavalry of short-term volunteers who referred to themselves as "Hundred Dazers." After a summer of scattered small raids and clashes, Indian and white representatives met at Camp Weld outside Denver on September 18. No firm agreements were reached, but the Indians were led to believe that by reporting to and camping near army posts, they would be declaring peace and accepting sanctuary. A Cheyenne chief by the name of Black Kettle, long a proponent of peace, led his band of about 600 Cheyenne and some Arapahos to a camping place along Sand Creek, about 40 miles from Fort Lyon, and informed the garrison of their presence.

Shortly afterward, Chivington rode into the fort with a force of about 700, including the Third Cavalry, and gave the garrison notice of his plans for an attack on the Indian encampment. Although he was informed that Black Kettle had already surrendered, Chivington pressed on with what he considered a perfect opportunity to further the cause of Indian extinction. On November 29, he led his troops, many of them drinking heavily, to Sand Creek and positioned them, along with their four howitzers, around the Indian camp. Black Kettle, evertrusting, raised both the American flag and a white flag over his tepee. In response, Chivington raised his arm for the attack. With army rifles and cannons pounding them, the Indians scattered in panic. Then the soldiers charged. A few warriors managed to fight back briefly from behind the high bank of the stream, and others, including Black Kettle, escaped over the plains. But by the end of the quick and brutal massacre, as many as 200 Indians, more than half of them women and children, had died. Chivington's policy was one of no prisoner taking, and his Colorado volunteers had been happy to oblige. Chivington was later denounced in a congressional investigation and forced to resign. Yet an after-the-fact reprimand of the colonel meant nothing to the Indians. As word of the massacre spread among them via refugees, Indians of the southern and northern plains stiffened in their resolve to resist white encroachment. Cheyenne and Arapahos stepped up their raids and, on January 7 and again on February 18, they stormed the town and freight station at Julesburg along the South Platte River, on the overland route from the Oregon Trail to Denver, forcing its abandonment. The final and most intense phase of the war for the Plains had begun. It would take another massacre at Wounded Knee a quarter of a century later to end it.

As the sun climbed higher, Wyndell donned his sunglasses, ate a sandwich, and drank some orange juice, reducing his speed and watching the landscape grow brighter with the new day. He finished his meal and, driving as if he were racing to meet the sun head-on, he listened once again to Thelonious Monk with Milt Jackson. Kremmling, Hot Sulphur Springs, Granby, through Berthoud Pass to Idaho Springs, and then he was almost home. He opened the window on the passenger's side of the car and breathed in, filling his lungs with cold mountain air until his chest hurt and he felt light-headed and a smile began to surface in his heart.

After arriving home, he spent hours talking with his mother, confiding in her as he always had, trusting her and basking in her love. For several weeks he slept late and read and gained four pounds from her pampering. His father looked worried most of the time, but never once talked about career changes or any similar subjects. The day before he left again, Wyndell sat in the living room with his father and explained that he was going to New York.

"Are you all right?" his father had asked.

"Yeah, I'm okay. I've gone through it," he said. "I know what I have to do now."

Whether because of his tone of voice or because indeed something had changed in Wyndell, his father smiled and suddenly the worry was gone from his face and he knew he'd made the right choice in letting his son seek a life in jazz.

And now he was free from the life in Los Angeles and was working in New York. At first he played Monday nights in the jam sessions at Visiones, meeting different musicians and being asked to sit in, still having to earn money playing dances and weddings and every so often commercials for TV or radio (which now, with their electronic rigs, didn't even have to use live musicians), but once in a while playing on a video and then watching it and even appearing in one, which he secretly dug doing; always going back to the music, jamming late at night with other young guys like himself, all of them committed to the music; constantly tuned into WBGO, the New York City metropolitan area's jazz station, at all hours of the night, the station like a beacon somewhere in the darkness, the brilliance of all his heroes sending out musical rays, every one producing dazzling light to guide him. Jazz 88.

On the lonely days and nights when he felt like returning home or seeking employment somewhere, the disk jockeys kept him company. He relied on them like close friends or even family. Rhonda Hamilton. James Browne. Gary Walker. Charlie Ventura, Jr. Alfredo Cruz on Sundays with his Latin Jazz Cruise program. Michael Bourne. Larry D'Albero. Michael Anderson. Marian McPartland's *Piano Jazz*, and *Jazz from the Archives* with Dan Morgenstern, or Ed Berger from the Institute for Jazz Studies at Rutgers University.

He'd subscribed during a membership drive and felt as if he owned part of the station. Even when he was just puttering around the house, he had BGO on, listening to the enthusiasm and intelligence of the programs' hosts, their humor and humility in having accepted the responsibility as guardians of the music, and at the same time feeling the immense pride they had in their work. Once, late at night, he'd heard *Pointer View* and stood transfixed by his solo on "Cherokee," not sure that it

was him playing, the purity dazzling him and making him rede-
termine to continue making attempts to play jazz.

From time to time he'd go to hear well-known musicians
play, and he'd sit enraptured by the music and their virtuosity,
knowing he could do as well, hating that he had to be patient.
One night when he was wandering around downtown he
walked into the Village Vanguard and listened to Larry Coryell
play. Larry had looked straight at him and nodded like he knew
him. Although he was familiar with and admired Coryell's music, he had never met him. When the set was over, Coryell rested
his guitar on its stand, bounded down off the stage, all gray-
haired and intellectual-looking in his big tortoiseshell glasses,
and, smiling, put out his hand.

"Hey, man, how you doing? You're Wyndell Ross, right?
You play tenor."

"Yeah, man," Wyndell had said. "How did you know who I
was?"

"I was in L.A. on my way back from a gig in Japan and heard
you playing at Catalina's. With Sonny Pointer if I'm not mistaken."

"Right. For the recording."

"Right, right. *Pointer View*. Excellent. How about a drink,
amigo?"

"A drink would be fine, man," Wyndell replied, feeling good
that a musician of Coryell's stature had recognized him.

They walked over to the bar. The bassist came over and
Larry introduced him.

"Wyndell, this is my good friend, Buster Williams. Buster,
this is Wyndell Ross. He plays tenor. Excellently, I might add."

"How you doing, man?" Williams said, and with great dignity the bassist nodded and extended his hand.

"Pretty good," Wyndell said, smiling and nodding.

He had to admit it. Wyndell Ross was on top of the world,
especially now that he was convinced without a shred of a

doubt that he was hopelessly in love with Vidamía Farrell, who, though she might well have African blood, the product of Irish and southern white folks and Puerto Ricans, looked whiter than a lot of white folks, and that could be a problem. He guessed he'd have to deal with it by and by. The thing that concerned him most was that Vidamía seemed obsessed with getting her father to play the piano again. He had yet to hear Billy Farrell play, and doubted that he could. Not only was the man disabled, but he seemed extremely distant, removed from normal life.

38 Drums

Vidamía came to a conclusion a few months short of graduation from high school. She had spent an entire hour thinking and looking alternately at the soft rain falling in the garden of Wyndell Ross's apartment and at the lovely sculpted black face and naked body of this man she loved, as the song said, as he slept, beautifully, like a child, one arm tucked under his head and his body turned so that his thing lay helplessly on the sheet, dormant now and not excited and wanting to devour her, as she liked to think of it.

He often spoke about children, sensing that she, as he did, probably thought about what their children would look like, should they have some. Once, when they passed a very pregnant woman in the street, he said he'd like to see her that way someday.

"Oh no you don't," she said, because he had that look on his face like, right there, as they were walking by the planetarium in the early summer, before she turned eighteen, they were going to go at it. And she had no idea why, but once or twice she had thought she'd stop taking the pill and get pregnant just to see what their baby would look like. It was crazy. She always came to her senses, but it was like something inside of her was calling out for her to get pregnant. It was like standing on the edge of a cliff and knowing it wasn't good to jump off, but also wanting to.

"Don't even think of it, you nut," she said to him.

And as he always did, he put his head down and looked shy and innocent and told her he wasn't implying anything of the kind, and she called him a liar, and eventually he "fessed up," like his grandma Mimi would say, and said yes, the thought had entered his mind on occasion.

"You'd like Grandma Mimi," he said. "Her mama was Cherokee. My great-grandma Rowena Spike. Grew up in Oklahoma on a ranch and came to Colorado following her husband on a cattle drive, my great-grandpa Ingram Ross, who also had a Cherokee grandfather and was a black cowboy."

"A black cowboy?" Vidamía said, as they entered Central Park. "Stop putting me on."

"No kidding," he said. "I'm not putting you on, girl."

"Yes, you are, you big faker," she said, spinning away from him and leaping in the air, feeling beautiful and light and then coming back to leap at him so that he caught her and put his hands around her waist, which he said was the smallest of any girl in the entire United States and therefore gave her an even more magnificent bunky. He lifted her up in the air and on the way down she wrapped her legs around him and unashamedly kissed him, enjoying with enormous delight the taste of him and the way she melted inside from his touching her lips with his tongue, feeling her nipples stiffening against his body and letting go because, as she told Cookie, she would have gone off right there in the park, with her clothes on and everything. "You're putting me on about your cowboy grandpa, right?"

"No way, Vee," he said. "Maybe I ought to take you to Denver next time I go home. You can see for yourself. Right there in my dad's den you can see all the pictures you want. And he's got the saddles, ropes, chaps, and hats. He's even got Great-grandpa's guns."

"Guns?" Vidamía said, opening her eyes. "Really?"

"Yeah, really," Wyndell said. "Guns. Pearl-handled, silver-plated forty-fours in their tooled Spanish-leather holsters, everything shiny, but with a few cracks from age. There's a picture of Grandpa Ross with a big mustache, big hat and guns, standing by a buckboard."

Vidamía couldn't help laughing. He was too much. A black cowboy great-grandpa.

"I guess I have to believe you," she said. "Otherwise you're going to kidnap me, take me to Colorado and subject me to all sorts of western sexual indignities, right?"

"Only if you're good," he said and ducked back as she aimed a punch at him.

Perhaps Wyndell was right. As she did with all matters of logic, Vidamía wondered if she was indeed denying that part of herself which was black. All this cerebral activity and speculation concerning her racial makeup was based on his vague assumption that her background was somehow connected to the continent of Africa. The idea excited her. She also felt trepidation because if her mother ever found out that he was black and was six years older than she was, she would have a heart attack. More to the point, if she knew the things they did when they were alone she would have two heart attacks. As if her mother hadn't, when she was younger, done the same things with her father, Billy Farrell.

And then she was recalling that first time she saw Wyndell up on the bandstand, so proud and dignified, his eyes closed and the tenor saxophone emitting those beautiful sounds, low and sweet, playing his interpretation of the song and in the middle of it opening his eyes and looking straight at her as she was sipping from her Perrier and without missing a beat playing a quote from another song, which he later said was: "You Go to My Head," singing the words in this little-boy's voice which was the loveliest thing she'd ever heard any human being do so that it made her giggle because she was absolutely charmed by this big *moreno*, as Becky Polanco, her sister Cookie's Puerto Rican girlfriend from Avenue D, had called him at the party, not hiding her disdain for blacks. *You go to my head . . . Like the bubbles in a glass of champagne.*

But it hadn't mattered what Becky said because it was at that party, in late July, right after her seventeenth birthday, as she was standing out on the penthouse terrace of Dina Wilton's father's apartment overlooking Central Park, talking to Cookie and Dina, who were best friends at Performing Arts and who had invited her and Becky Polanco, who also went to PA and was in the dance department, that she had met Wyndell. The crowd was college age and older, like Dina's brother, Ken, who had gone to Harvard and was working down on Wall Street.

Ken Wilton was by far the handsomest of the young men at the party, so handsome in fact that Cookie later told Vidamía that she strongly considered being unfaithful to Mario Wong when they walked in and he greeted them. She was quickly dissuaded from attempting such a move when Dina, observing Cookie's predatory glances, revealed to them that her brother was gay even though he had played club hockey in school. That was when Ken, accompanied by a tall, elegantly dressed, handsome young black man, came out on the terrace. Both Vidamía and Cookie assumed he was also gay.

"Dina, this is my friend, Wyndell Ross," he said. "He is an absolutely fabulous tenor saxophone player. We met at a party in Boston when I was seeing Peter Lloyd, who played piano and was studying at Berklee. Wyn, this is my sister, Dina. These are her friends—I'm sorry but I've forgotten your names."

Dina extended her hand and Wyndell shook it gently, smiling easily at the three of them. Dina then introduced Cookie and

Vidamía, pointing out that they were sisters. They talked for a while and eventually Ken was summoned inside about a lack of ice or club soda and Dina went with him. A young Wall Street type asked Cookie if she wanted to dance and off she went, the music of Madonna spilling out from the large room within. Vidamía wanted to return inside as well, but thought it would be rude to leave the young man alone out on the terrace. Gay people were rejected enough, she thought, and he was black, which meant that he probably suffered even more rejection.

"What did you say your name was?" he said.

"Vidamía," she answered, smiling at him easily, never suspecting that her smile might be interpreted sexually. "Vidamía Farrell."

"Mine is Wyndell . . ."

"Ross, right?"

"Pretty good. Are you Spanish? The name sounds Spanish. Your first name, I mean."

"My mother's Puerto Rican. She was born here, but her parents are from P.R."

"P.R.?"

"Yeah, that's what we call it. You know, the initials. Like U.S."

"Right, right. I follow. You always hear 'P.R.' for 'public relations.' Oh, never mind. I had a friend at Berklee, you know, where I went to school, whose family was from Puerto Rico. I think her grandfather or her father, maybe both. Her last name was Feliciano. Like José Feliciano, the singer."

"That's nice," she said, beginning to grow uncomfortable.

"*C'mon baby, light my fire,*" Wyndell sang.

"What?" Vidamía said.

"That was one of his songs," he said. "Also 'California Dreaming.' "

"Oh, José Feliciano. Yeah, I know," she said, looking out over the park, the lamps along the paths making little pockets of light.

420

There was a long silence and then she asked him if he'd ever read James Baldwin. He said he had and asked her why.

"I was just wondering," she replied. "Did you read *Giovanni's Room*?"

"Yes, I did," he said and then burst out laughing, understanding immediately her concern. It wasn't a gentle laugh, but a raucous belly laugh that made her also laugh, although hers was more a laugh of nerves than mirth. "That's funny. Wait until I tell Ken. That's really charming."

"Well . . ." she said, sheepishly.

"That's very touching. You were actually trying to make me feel at ease, weren't you?"

"There's nothing wrong with that," Vidamía said, a bit off balance.

He was resting his arm on the wall, looking down at her, his eyes bright and smiling, his perfect teeth matching the smile. He was clean-shaven and his skin was so smooth that she wanted to touch it. He wasn't gay, and all of a sudden she felt ten times more uncomfortable.

"What kind of music do you play?" she said.

"All kinds. Rhythm and blues, rock, show tunes, TV scores. I'll read anything."

"Jazz?"

He was suddenly still and looked at her, puzzled.

"You like jazz?"

"Yes, the little I know about it."

"Well, I do play jazz," he said. "It's what I love doing best," he added, openly, sincerely, so that she felt as if suddenly a barrier had been removed and they could talk more freely. He said that it was funny that she should ask him this question, since he had decided not too long ago to try and make a go of it just playing jazz, which was very difficult.

And then she told him about the members of her family, all of whom were musicians.

"We used to have a family band and played down in the subway."

He asked what she meant by "we" and she explained that they had taught her how to play the tub bass. He laughed and made a hillbilly kind of gesture, bowing his legs, hunching over and making a slapping motion against an imaginary string. She said that it was just like that and she mimicked the action. She said they no longer played but that she had gotten her father to play the piano again and explained about his disability.

"We're going to chip in and buy him a piano for his birthday but it's a secret," she said, knowing it would be only her putting up the money, even then feeling apprehension about doing so because Lurleen said it might prove to be expensive.

"When he was young, my sister told me—"

"The blond girl?"

"Yeah. Anyway, Cookie said that our father jammed with Miles Davis and Wayne Shorter and had even played for Thelenos Monk. Not with him, but to show him he could play."

"Thelonious."

"Yeah, sorry. Thelonious."

"That's pretty hip," he said. "Far out. I mean, about your dad."

"Yeah, my mother . . . well, she's like my mother. I don't like to say 'stepmother' because that sounds like there's a distance, and that's not the case. Cookie's mother, my sister's mother, or whatever, says that jazz is the only true art form that the United States has given to the world."

"Some people would say that movies were also developed in the United States and constitute as important a contribution."

"Movies were developed simultaneously in Europe," she said, suddenly feeling pedantic.

"Yeah, maybe you're right," he said. "I guess if you consider its roots."

"The blues, right? Blind Lemon Jefferson. Leadbelly."

"Right," he said and laughed. "The blues. I guess you've been instructed well."

"My family talks about music about eighty percent of the time."

They had returned inside and she'd gotten involved in talking with other people and dancing and eating junk food and drinking beer, which made her a little tipsy, and then Wyndell had asked for her phone number and she'd given it to him.

He eventually called and asked her if she'd like to come and hear him play. Without even considering it she said, "Yeah, sure," and she was going no matter what because she was fascinated by the way he talked, not bragging like Gordon Walker, the big football star up at school, whose father was a state assemblyman. Everything with Gordon was black this and black that. Everybody was scared of him because he was a football star and was always threatening to punch somebody. He even told Todd Sasso that he didn't care how many Mafia uncles he had, if he had to get a gun and shoot one of them, he would. Todd had looked at him like he was crazy and later told Bobby Winthers that he wished he had a couple of Mafia uncles, but that all he had were these two uncles who made stringed instruments in Milwaukee, and Bobby Winthers said maybe they could get a couple of the bigger guys to get dressed up in dark suits and walk up to Gordon with a couple of violin cases. They laughed and then went to biology class.

But Wyndell was nothing like any black person Vidamía had ever met, and the next day she asked Lurleen was it okay for her to go out on a date with him. Lurleen said she was seventeen years old and as long as he was a good person and treated her with respect, she saw no reason that she shouldn't see him. Vidamía then asked what Lurleen meant. Lurleen explained that she was on safe ground as long as he didn't try to get her to do anything she didn't want to do. Lurleen smiled and pushed her lank hair back behind her ears as she always did.

Vidamía dressed demurely in a modest black dress, stockings, half-inch pumps, and a small black bag. She sat in the club and watched as Wyndell played way up-tempo things, like he was running a race but beautifully, the ideas coming out of the music so that she felt as if he were delivering a wonderful speech to the audience and then stopping and letting the trumpet and the piano and the bass play, and then alternating playing with the trumpet and then the piano, which he explained later was "trading fours or eights," Vidamía not quite understanding and he explaining it so gently that she knew this was a very special person.

He explained what he'd done during the lovely, sad song, which he said was a ballad that he'd written called "Amanda," which was his mother's name. The sound seemed so deep that Vidamía knew instinctively that his mother was someone he loved and respected. She listened to him playing the melody and then his own improvisation as he had explained: the pianist, the bassist, and the drummer drawing little figures of music behind him and the drums, just the brushes whispering behind his playing, the notes linking themselves to one another, not in a linear way, but as if they were part of finely woven cloth, one part of the pattern even, symmetrical, and another abstract and new.

After he finished the set and they left the club and he was walking her to the Farrells' loft, they got on the topic of a man hurting a woman because maybe she mentioned Becky's aunt who had gotten beaten up by her husband and spent two weeks in the hospital. Vidamía said she would never allow anyone to lay a hand on her, that she would die before letting anyone do that to her. They hadn't even kissed or anything yet, this being the first time since the party that they had seen each other. There was a great big pause and then Wyndell said he would never ever hurt her. His words went through her chest and lodged in her heart as if she'd been pierced by a long feather.

Neither of them said anything for about ten blocks, from

Sheridan Square all the way through Washington Square Park and a few blocks beyond. They eventually crossed Broadway and Lafayette and were standing next to the black cube on the Astor Place island across from Cooper Union when all of a sudden Wyndell Ross put his tenor case up against the base of the cube and, solemnly, as if he were introducing a composition of great importance, said, "Check this out"—

If the Drum Is a Woman

If the drum is a woman
why are you pounding your drum into an insane
babble
why are you pistol whipping your drum at dawn
why are you shooting through the head of your drum
and making a drum tragedy of drums
if the drum is a woman
don't abuse your drum don't abuse your drum
don't abuse your drum
I know the night is full of displaced persons
I see skins striped with flames
I know the ugly dispositions of underpaid clerks
they constantly menstruate through the eyes
I know bitterness embedded in flesh
the itching alone can drive you crazy
I know that this is America
and chickens are coming home to roost
on the MX missile
But if the drum is a woman
why are you choking your drum
why are you raping your drum
why are you saying disrespectful things
to your mother drum your sister drum
your wife drum and your infant daughter drum

If the drum is a woman
then understand your drum
your drum is not docile
your drum is not invisible
your drum is not inferior to you
your drum is a woman
so don't reject your drum
don't try to dominate your drum
don't become weak and cold and desert your drum
don't be forced into the position
as an oppressor of drums
and make a tragedy of drums
if the drum is a woman
don't abuse your drum
don't abuse your drum
don't abuse your drum

Wyndell finished and picked up his instrument and got ready to continue walking, but Vidamía was spellbound, watching this tall black person who made her heart feel strange, listening to his voice which was strong and fragile at the same time so that, when Wyndell asked her what was the matter, she wanted to know if he had created the poem.

"No, that was a poem by Jayne Cortez," he laughed and shook his head.

"Cortez? Is she Puerto Rican or Cuban?"

"I don't know. She's African-American. A poet. She's a friend of my mother's. She came to our house in Denver and there was a reading. I remember looking at this beautiful woman and she had an enormous dignity, reciting this poem about a drum, with my father playing this intricate melody on the piano, not interfering with the words but sort of like a background. Something from Ellington. He's a composer. And then the next morning I asked my mother about the poem and what it meant and she went and got the book which was signed by her friend and read it to me while I ate my Wheaties, and it's always stayed with me. I mean, I liked it so much that I memorized it. Hearing my mother read it, I suddenly understood that maybe some men hit women. I know now that it happens but back then it never entered my mind."

. "That's a song," she said, nervously, feeling stupid, knowing something wonderful was happening and suddenly wanting him to like her.

"What?"

"It never entered my mind. It's a song."

"Oh . . . yeah," he said, absently. "Yeah, I know."

"I'm sorry, I interrupted you," she said.

"I was twelve, maybe thirteen."

"Did your parents ever hit you?" Vidamía asked.

"No. Yours?"

"Oh, I think my mother probably gave me a swat once in a while when I was little, but nothing heavy. If I ever hit a child I'd feel awful and would regret it all of my life."

And then they kept walking, and when they turned south at Tompkins Square Park, Wyndell took her hand. When she looked up at him he had this shy look on his face like maybe he shouldn't have done it, but she smiled and let her own hand fit into his and he gave a great big sigh and hanging on to the saxophone case let it come flying up in the air like he was cheering and he said, "Great, that makes me feel a whole lot better." And she said, "What?" And he said, "Nothing," and then, "Wow!"

So as she watched the rain she recalled all of that and the next two months of going everywhere with him, worrying, in spite of her identification with the characters in *Roots*, what other people would think of her going around with this black person. After a while she forgot that he was black and just enjoyed the way he made her feel, how adult she felt because he always asked her what she thought of things and was very open about everything she asked him.

39 Photo Album

When Vidamía returned to school at the end of the summer of 1989, after she'd met Wyndell, it took her nearly the entire month of September to get used to not being in his company. Most days she moped around the school, recalling the times with him, replaying conversations in her head and smiling inwardly at their secrets, their intimacies. In class there was a languor about her that made her teachers concerned. Eventually she began to discipline herself and spoke to him briefly two days a week, forcing herself to be strict. On weekends she came into the city and spent long hours with him when it was possible. Often she simply sat and listened to his life and his dreams, prodding him, hungry to know more about his family. He would then elaborate on his father, the pediatrician in Denver who played jazz on weekends, no, not saxophone but piano; and on his mother, who ran her own small art gallery. He told her about his two older sisters, Garlande, who taught cultural anthropology at a college in Washington State, and Davina, who was a painter and lived in Paris with her twin sons by a Swedish trombone player.

"Jazz?" she asked, when Wyndell mentioned his brother-in-law.

"No, with the Stockholm Philharmonic. She and the children go back and forth from Paris to Stockholm."

"Are they separated?" she asked.

"No, but their work is very important to them. Davina wants to paint in Paris. He needs to be in Stockholm."

"Do they love each other?" she asked timorously.

"Yes," he answered. "One thing has nothing to do with the other. And you should see the children," he said. "They're really beautiful."

"I'm sure they are," she said.

A few weeks later, during the weekend before Thanksgiving, when she came to see him at his apartment over by Sheridan Square, he made her sit on the couch and close her eyes. He then placed a huge leather-bound photo album on her lap and told her to open her eyes. She looked at the album, touched the leather gingerly, fearful for a moment of what she was to find inside, suddenly feeling as if by opening the album and looking at the photographs she was signing a compact to be a part of Wyndell's life.

Slowly she opened the photo album and took in the photographs, allowing Wyndell's history to enter her, seeing the family resemblances and immediately loving the dignity of the people, the naturalness with which they seemed to be living. The rooms of the houses were elegant and bright and well furnished and the people dressed with enormous good taste so that she felt as if somehow, through some magical and exciting device, she was in the company of regal people, except that everything that came through spoke about what she'd read about white America, and these people were black.

She recalled reading *Roots* and suddenly she needed desperately to believe that beneath the color of their skin Americans, black and white, were the same people. Her need to believe was enormous, and whether it was true or not, she wanted it to be so. They were the same, she thought. Perhaps there were exceptions, but for the most part there were more similarities than differences. If one took the time to examine deeply, to go beyond appearances, in attitudes and beliefs they were the same. Only their skin was different.

"They're beautiful, Wyn," she said, tears forming at the corners of her eyes.

"The photos? Oh, yeah. I called my mom and she Fed-Ex'd me the album," he said.

"No, your relatives," she said. "They're beautiful."

"Oh, I'm sorry. Yes."

"I want to meet them," she said.

And then he knelt in front of her and told her he loved her. It was the first time he'd said such a thing to a woman and meant it. She leaned forward and took his face and brought it to her breast and held him there, kissing very gently his eyes, misted now by his own tears. Quite naturally one thing led to another and they made love and she cried, not sure whether she had done the right thing but feeling her heart expand and accept how much she loved him.

She didn't like to think of her virginity in terms of losing or surrendering it to Wyndell. Instead, she felt as if Wyndell had helped her to cross a mythical barrier into adulthood. Whether her decision had been based on an impulse caused by Wyndell's sharing his life with her or peer pressure no longer mattered. It was done and that was the end of the discussion. She often heard her parents' friends talk in Spanish about women giving themselves. It was nonsense. In her mind the woman was in control and the man cooperated in the defloration ritual.

In the unusually warm air there had been a breeze of jasmines and geraniums wafting over her from the garden as her head floated pleasantly from two glasses of wine. She had finally done it, at the age of seventeen years and four months. Not crying at first, as she had read in a novel, but surprised by her curiosity and the almost cold and calculated interest she had taken in the process; concentrating solely on how Wyndell behaved; letting him do whatever he pleased and moving this way or that;

letting him open her legs and lift her thighs, kissing him and enjoying it, but having no idea what she was supposed to do until he was touching her with his fingers and she was sucking at his tongue and breathing so heavily that a few times a moan of pleasure escaped her and then his fingers were in her and she was moving involuntarily; desperately wanting to touch him and explore the hardness she felt against her legs, but not daring for fear that this wasn't done at this point in the lovemaking because it wasn't the same as with the dopey boys that had wanted handjobs, which she had never done, rejecting their needs, and merely listening to the excited discourse of girls who had manually satisfied their boyfriends.

And then he asked her to wait. She watched him fit himself with a condom and then they were kissing again and a short time later he was inside of her, his organ forcing her open seemingly but then sliding in and out smoothly; wondering if there was much blood because she had read that sometimes there was; Wyn moving slowly at first and she concentrating on what he was doing; forgetting now her own sensations until he was moving violently against her and then pounding at her pelvis, driving her into the bed and his hands beneath her buttocks squeezing her to him and then he was finished and she cried and was confused but he held her and she relaxed and it was wonderful to be with him.

She remembered thinking after looking at Wyn's album again that Elsa Santiago and Billy Farrell must have had a similar scene. Knowing her mother and her theatrics, she must have uttered some words of supposed passion. And then she knew that it had happened exactly that way. Her mother had called her father *vida mía*, my life, my darling, my beloved, and whether genuine or insincere the emotion had been there to at least wish to create theater; enough for her father to have picked up on the core of the feeling and inquire about the phrase. *Vida mía*, she thought. She was probably the only person in the entire world with such a name. My life. She played with the words in English. Mylife. Melife. She tried the little French that she knew. *Ma vie.* No, that was no good. In French it sounded like the drink she had liked so much in Puerto Rico. She always asked her grandmother to buy it when she visited her on the Lower East Side in the summer.

Mabí. She recalled seeing the word once and running downstairs and into the library. After about ten minutes of looking on the shelves she found Augusto Malaret's *Vocabulario de Puerto Rico,* which had all sorts of words common to the island, words that had Indian or African roots. She looked up *mabí* and there in the middle of the definition was: *"Arbol pequeño de corteza de sabor amargo con la que se hace la bebida de este nombre,"* describing as bitter the bark of the tree from which the drink was made. *"Colubrina reclinata,"* explaining that it was sometimes written *maví* and that some people thought that it was written this way because its origins were in the French *ma vie,* my life. Why? She replaced the book on the shelf and went looking for a French–English dictionary. When she found it she looked up the word bitter. *Amer.* It was like the Spanish *amargo.* So maybe when the French found the bark, they tasted it and one of them said, *"C'est comme ma vie, amère."* It's like my life, bitter. She was proud that she had been able to come up with a possible explanation for the origin of the name of that drink. Her life was nothing like that. Vidamía. She loved her name, and her life was not bitter at all.

The following weekend she reciprocated and brought her own albums and Wyndell pored over them, asking her questions about Puerto Ricans and their different shades of colors, and he said that his family was quite similar in that skin tone varied and he had cousins who were as light as she was and could pass as whites if they wanted; white Cherokee, anyway, he said, and that Puerto Ricans were similar in that regard. She said he was right and then he said jokingly that maybe she had African blood. "Yeah," she said, innocently, liking the idea; thinking that if that were the case she would now feel closer to Kunta Kinte, Kizzy, Chicken George, and the rest of the people in *Roots*.

Upon her return to Tarrytown at the end of the Christmas holidays, spurred by Wyndell's idea that she might have a connection to Africa, she broached the subject of black relatives with her mother. Elsa went bananas on her, going on about how the whole thing of race was an irrelevancy since weren't we, after all, she and her stepfather Barry López-Ferrer and Vidamía, first and foremost Puerto Rican and didn't concern ourselves with color.

But Vidamía wasn't having it and said, "That's all well and good, but could you please tell me if we have black relatives, because you have somewhat curly hair, and sometimes I look at myself in the mirror and, even though my skin is white and I have freckles and green eyes and my father is Irish and has blond hair, I can see a little bit of my friend Charisse Robinson, maybe around the eyes or the lips, so I'm wondering if I have black relatives."

"Sometimes you are impossible," Elsa said. "What difference would it make?"

"None," Vidamía said. "I just want to know. But if you're ashamed that we have black relatives, then forget it."

Elsa had raised her hand but hadn't slapped her. Vidamía hadn't even flinched, knowing more than ever that her mother was no longer a force in her life. For some reason, which she quickly identified as rebellion, she recalled the first time she and Wyndell had made love. She now looked at her mother and smiled, relishing the fact that her mother couldn't know what she was presently thinking. The feeling of power was enormous.

Needing to find out about herself, she took the "big train" into Grand Central Station and then took the "little train," the subway, the Number 6, to be exact, getting off as always at Astor Place rather than on Bleecker, which was closer to the Farrell loft, but needing to immerse herself each time in the rhythm of the neighborhood; walking down St. Mark's and into the East Village, which was now her turf, homegirl; needing to walk the fifteen or so blocks to measure herself against the harshness of the neighborhood; bopping like she was attitudinally bad when she walked the street cause then nobody messed with her; people thinking there goes one crazy-ass Puerto Rican girl, with her baggy jeans and brogans and her leather jacket and blunt haircut and dark lipstick on some kind of mission so don't mess with her or she'll get her posse after you and whatnot; watching the tough white girls emulating us, as she now liked to think of herself belonging to the P.R.s, this urban tribe of incomprehensible cultural savages.

So visceral was her need that she'd gone and visited her grandmother, Ursula Santiago, threatening never to go back to her mother's house in Tarrytown unless her grandma, her *abuela*, told her what was going on with everybody about *los negros*. Her grandmother had gotten all emotional and said don't say *negros* but *gente de color*, which literally meant people of color, which to Vidamía sounded horrible. Her grandmother sat down in the kitchen and said that her grandfather, Tino Santiago, was dark-skinned, not black mind you, not really.

"You know, *trigueño*," she said. "Justino, but they called him Tino."

"Where's he live, *güela*?" Vidamía asked.

"In the Bronx, *mamita*," Ursula said. "I don't know. I lost touch with him a long time ago, six or seven years after your *mami* was born. That was almost thirty years ago, baby."

"Does *mami* know him?"

"No, he was never home. Always playing somewhere with the other musicians."

"He was a musician?" Vidamía said, unbelieving.

"Yeah, *un conguero*."

"*Conguero*," said Vidamía nodding her head happily, allowing the Spanish to take over, wondering where all these musicians in her life were coming from, and she with not a musical bone in her body, except for slapping that "funny-ass" tub bass with her family's band.

"They used to call him Tumba."

"Tuba, güela? I thought you said his name was Tino? Tuba, like oom-pa-pa?" Vidamía said, making like she was holding a big ole sousaphone, puffing up her cheeks and rocking from side to side, so that her grandmother slapped her arm playfully.

"Not tuba, boba," she said, calling her silly. "Tumba."

"Like a tomb?" Vidamía said, earnestly. "Where they bury people?"

"Not like that and not like the Tombs, where they send the junkies and thieves to jail," replied her grandmother. "Tumba, tumbadora, like the big conga drum. That's what it's called, the bass one—tumbadora."

"Oh," Vidamía said, "a drum. And they called Grandpa that?"

"That's right. Tumba Santiago. That was his name."

She had gone back up to Tarrytown armed with enough ammunition to blow anything her mother said about not having black relatives totally out of the water. Right after the Christmas holidays, which she spent in New York with the Farrells while her mother and Barry went off to Puerto Rico with friends, everything exploded like never before. The blowup was brought on by Ursula telling Elsa innocently that Vidamía had been asking about her grandfather.

"What did you tell her?" Elsa asked.

"I said he left us a long time ago," her mother said. "That's all. That he was a musician."

"Anything else?"

"No, nothing else," Ursula Santiago said and felt bad for lying. It didn't make sense to tell Elsa that Vidamía had been asking whether any of her relatives were black. And since Elsa hadn't asked, she wasn't going to provide any extra information.

"Did she seem like she wanted to go and find him?"

"I don't think so," Ursula said.

Elsa forgot about the issue until one evening after supper Vidamía brought up the subject of her grandfather, stating that she was going to begin looking for him. Elsa sighed patiently.

"Why?" Elsa said. "He's probably remarried and doesn't want to be bothered."

"I'm not going to bother him," Vidamía said. "I just want to meet him."

"Why? Are you still on this *Roots* kick?" she asked, knowing that she'd slipped up in bringing up the issue of color, which Vidamía immediately picked up on.

"Mom, for God's sake, you sound like such a racist."

"I'm not a racist. You have no right to make such accusations."

"I didn't say you were. I said you sounded like one."

"I was only talking about your wanting to know about your relatives. That's what I meant about that book. That's what it's about. That has nothing to do with race."

"Fine, but you sounded so paranoid."

"That's enough, young lady. You know very little about psychology, and labeling people because of their concerns is extremely dangerous."

"Forget it, okay? I'm just curious. It's not like I have all kinds of grandfathers, you know. As a matter of fact, I only have one. My other was a cop and got killed. Did you know that?"

"Yes, I'm aware of that."

"And your father might as well be dead, too."

"Right, and I forbid you to spend any time trying to find him."

"You have to be joking, okay?"

"I mean it."

"What are you going to do?"

"Never you mind," Elsa said and got up from the table.

Vidamía looked at Barry, who shrugged his shoulders. For Vidamía the matter was a moot point since she didn't have enough time to begin looking for her grandfather in the middle of the school year. For Elsa, however, the issue took on a completely different meaning.

While there are always a few detective shows on television, some new ones and others in rerun, and there are at least a dozen films a year dealing with detectives, in actuality there are many more private investigators than one would imagine. Few of them are as glamorous as Magnum or Mike Hammer, or as interesting as Columbo, but all you need to do is open the Manhattan Yellow Pages and look under "Investigators" and you'll find over four pages of ads. *Are your phones bugged? Matrimonial. A Team of Former Federal & Local Law Professionals. Confidential Private Investigators. Problems Discreetly Handled. Full Service Security Professionals. Difficult and Unusual Cases. Know the Truth for Peace of Mind.*

So, at the beginning of April 1990, when she knew her daughter would be spending her Easter break on the Lower East Side, Elsa, sitting in her office after finishing with her last patient that morning, dialed the number of the agency she had settled on and asked for an appointment. At three that afternoon she went in, and, impressed by the professional way in which she was treated by ex–New York City police detective Richard Flanagan and his partner, Walter Pavese, himself a retiree from the Connecticut State Police, she explained her situation.

"It's just a matter of safety," she explained to Flanagan. "I'm worried about my daughter."

"Do you think she's involved with drugs?"

"It's always a concern these days," Elsa said. "It would just ease my mind if I knew where she was spending her time. She comes into the city almost every weekend. Her father lives down in the East Village, and she spends quite a bit of time there. I'd like to know if she's hanging around undesirable people. She has threatened to make contact with her grandfather."

"What's wrong with her grandfather?"

Elsa had put her head down and looked pained.

"It's pretty difficult for me to talk about him."

"He's your father?" Flanagan had asked.

Elsa nodded and dabbed at the corners of her eyes, pretending to be troubled.

"Yes, but I don't want you to turn him over to the police," she said, feigning panic.

"That's not our job. But we have to know the extent of the criminal activity, if there's any."

"I think he's involved up in the Bronx," she lied, relishing casting her father in that light and being purposefully vague.

"I see," said Flanagan, nodding. "Do you have a photograph of your daughter?"

From her briefcase Elsa produced several pictures. Flanagan said that they could create a surveillance routine for a period of a month and write up a report if she was able to provide approximate times when her daughter came in the city. Flanagan quoted his fee, which seemed quite reasonable to Elsa, who would have agreed to twice the amount. Flanagan then explained that for a slightly higher fee they could provide a photographic record. Elsa said she didn't think it would be necessary, and then thought another instant and changed her mind.

"Yes, maybe that would be the best thing," she said, nodding.

"If anything were to happen after we were off the case, at least you'd have the photographs. By the way, you can count on us to testify in any court proceedings."

She wrote out a check, shook hands with Flanagan, and left, her mind going in a dozen different directions. The photos were a good idea. Although she had no desire to ever be in the company of her father again, she would welcome seeing how age had ravished him, wanted to see how poverty had subverted his spirit and defeated him, the black bastard. Ultimately, she needed to see proof of Vidamía's disobedience, even if it meant having to deal with the issue of blackness.

40 The Music

The first time in twenty years that Billy Farrell played Thelonious Sphere Monk's tune "Straight No Chaser" all the way through on the piano, he was alone in a practice room at New York University around one in the afternoon a week after Thanksgiving in 1988. The previous night he had lain in bed, restless and unable to sleep, thinking again about Joey Santiago's death and imagining things like being a Marine again and sitting in a barracks in Beirut and suddenly flying through the air in a confusion of sound, blinding light and flying debris, watching, in slow motion, limbs and heads flying by him, until, as if a dawn were breaking on a new day, he saw "Straight No Chaser" clearly, and, on its tail, other tunes like "Friday the Thirteenth," "Little Rootie Tootie," and "Epistrophy." He had previously avoided those compositions, fearing that he wouldn't be able to play them without his two fingers.

All he thought about the entire morning as he walked the twenty or so blocks to New York University was Monk's austerity. Was this what he was doing? Isolating himself in order to emulate the great pianist? He entered the Main Building hoping to see Pop Butterworth, but his elevator had just gone up. When he arrived at the practice room that day he went in, closed the door of the soundproofed room, and sat down hesitantly at the piano. At first he had watched his hand, playing an improvisational sequence against the chord structure of a blues, noting that the speed at which he was able to play had increased dramatically. It was exactly as Lurleen had explained learning curves. For a while there appeared to be little progress, then suddenly there was a huge leap forward. All at once he realized that he was playing in a totally different way than he had ever known. His left hand was as strong as ever, its capacity to span three keys over an octave and still sound coherent pleased him and he watched now, independent of his playing, what his right hand was doing.

What he observed pleased him even more, and he saw that when he attempted to play a tune like "My Funny Valentine," the melody line was merely insinuated, as if his conscious mind were attempting to play the tune but the missing middle and pinkie fingers couldn't hit the required notes so that his left hand was now compensating for the lack, producing contrapuntal chords that, when played up-tempo, sounded new and unlike anything he had ever heard. He also found that this method sounded better on the lower part of the piano. The melodies he was creating reminded him of Monk's chording—except in his case the missing notes were created by his attempts to play the melodies.

He chuckled once when he held back his left hand and played the melody with the three fingers of his right hand and it sounded like *M— Fun— va——tine —eet com— val——ine,* or something like that. He hummed the melody, suppressing his right hand and playing the chords, and, indeed, where the spaces were in the melody, he had employed a perfect complimentary chord, so that as a ballad the tune sounded odd, but quite pleasing. He tried it with "Autumn in New York" and then "April in Paris." In each instance the result was the same. For some reason the tunes sounded as if Monk were playing them sideways. The notion made him smile and talk to himself and say things like "Go ahead, man. Play it. Work" or "That's some deep shit, man.

That's some nasty mothafuckin' stuff. Where you been hidin' all that music?"

And he'd answer himself, mumbling: "Oh, man, get outta my face. You just trying to figure out what I'm doing so you can get over and not have to think for yourself." Holding dialogues with himself like he was talking again to Mr. McQuinlan, the black leprechaun of his youth. It was then that he tried playing "Straight No Chaser," carefully at first, and then with increasing confidence, opening up the tune to a variety of interpretations, first going in one direction and then exploring another, the trails filled with a landscape of ideas, each one branching off into other tunes that, unlike some of the bop exponents, he wouldn't play but leave open, so that while playing an improvisational chorus he would get to a certain place where he could've easily played "How Are Things in Glockamora" as a little joke but instead left the tune implied and under it played its chord structure.

After that day he spent three days a week from November 1988 till well into August of 1989 playing melodies and their chord structures, going up and down the keyboard doing scales, exploring the changes of a tune, trying out riffs and improvisational variations, but always plumbing the depths and the wealth of material of Thelonious Monk, the pianist he most admired, and the hundreds of tunes by other musicians and composers which formed part of his large repertoire.

Students as well as faculty came by and stood spellbound outside the closed door, listening to him play variations on tunes, the virtuosity obvious, the intensity apparent, his up-tempo runs reminiscent of the most accomplished bop pianists, particularly the breathless abandon of Bud Powell and Lennie Tristano, needing to fly, to give himself totally to the music and on its wings to soar beyond any level he'd ever known, each time pushing the boundaries of his capacity, daring himself, as he imagined instinctively every great artist must, to go beyond the commonplace and stand courageously, to face the storm and relish its fury. At this point he didn't know yet that it was the shrinking from this stand, this daring of destiny, that had brought him to the life he now led.

There were times when he played on beyond his allotted time, but no one ever bothered him, and eventually someone would get word to Pop Butterworth, who people in the Jazz and Contemporary Music Program at the school knew was responsible for getting Billy the practice time. Butterworth would come upstairs to the practice rooms when he got off work at five, listen to him for a few minutes, and then open the door, go over and put his hand on Billy's shoulder, and tell him it was time to go.

"You sound real good, son," he'd say.

"Thank you, Pop," Billy would say. "I played some more Monk today."

"That's great. You gonna be ready to get back into it soon."

"I don't know about that," Billy would reply, feeling suddenly cold and frightened and then surprisingly angry and then slamming the lid on the keyboard. Butterworth didn't even ask him what was the matter but just walked him out. He waited until the elevator came and once downstairs and out in the street walked with him until they were back in the neighborhood when Billy would start snapping out of his fear-induced haze. He would then smile with embarrassment and ask Pop if he wanted to come up and have supper and Butterworth would hesitate, but Billy would insist and Pop would go up, the children always happy to see him, as if they somehow knew without being told that he was very close to their daddy. One evening it snowed heavily and they made a bed for him in the living room so he could spend the night. That winter morning in 1988 Butterworth woke up to find five-year-old Caitlin, dressed in her slipper pajamas, sitting on the floor, watching him as he slept.

"Good morning there," he said to Caitlin as he opened his eyes.

"Mr. Butterworth, you make noises when you sleep," she said by way of returning the greeting. "It's like growling. Why?"

"To keep the bears away," he said, noticing the stuffed toy in her arms.

"Oh, I'm sorry," she said, holding up her teddy bear. "He won't hurt you. He's a toy bear."

"That makes me feel a whole lot better," Butterworth said, his voice still hoarse with sleep.

"You want some granola?" Caitlin said. "Mama doesn't want us eating sugar."

"That sounds like a good idea," Butterworth replied, smiling and shaking his head.

"You'll have to get up, though. Mama doesn't want people eating on the couch."

"You start getting everything ready and I'll be right there," Butterworth said, grateful that Billy had managed to live through the war to father such bright children.

Now, almost a year after Billy began practicing at NYU, while he was playing "Straight No Chaser," he noticed that when he played Monk's tunes they had a totally different dimension. Rather than the absence of notes, he'd discovered a different lyrical quality in the music so that he found himself slowing down the tempo of a tune like "Friday the Thirteenth" and filling in, for example, a riff after the first seven notes, making the twelve-bar blues ballad-like. The melodies he was now improvising were filled with a tremulous melancholy which he played soulfully, bravely, and each day with more conviction and gratitude for being able to play the piano again.

And yet as soon as he finished he could feel the anger in him raging as if it were an animal too long caged, a soul too long enslaved. Images of destruction filled his mind, creating a band of crimson wrath across his eyes. Through it, as if filtered, he saw the damage that he could do. More significantly, he found himself becoming short with Lurleen and the children, even Vidamía, whom to a great extent he still treated as a guest, a respected acquaintance and not quite family, except that he truly loved her, just as much as he loved the other children and Lurleen and his mother, grandfather, and grandmother, may she rest in peace, all of them meaning a great deal to him.

Most of the time he held back his rage. In the street, however, whenever anyone crossed him he would talk back to them, and yell at drivers who ventured too close to him when he was crossing the street. His attitude worried him and he thought that perhaps Lurleen was right and he ought to contact the veterans group she had mentioned. When she first gave him the telephone number he put it away without any intention of calling, but then, two weeks before Christmas, he almost slapped Cliff when he told Billy that he needed a new pair of sneakers.

"What are you trying to tell me?" he snapped. "You need new sneakers? I ain't got no money. Who told you to quit your job, stupid! Tell me that! You think I got money for new shoes? I ain't got shit. I ain't got a pot to piss in. You know that, goddammit. Why in the fuck are you asking me? The two of you are in that damn video store, day and night. You were all excited when you quit your job and now the store isn't making as much money as you thought and you want a new pair of sneakers. Tough tittie, pal."

"Lighten up, man," Cliff said, talking to his father as he always did, not worried, trusting him, joking around and treating him like a friend. "I'm not asking you for money. I got money. I get paid for working at the store. Not as much as I did in the restaurant, but enough so that I don't have to ask you for money. I give Mama half of it for expenses. At least we don't have to be down in the subway playing for nickels and dimes and people staring at us like we're homeless and whatnot."

"Hey," Billy said, standing up from the rocking chair. "Who in the fuck are you talking to? Your mother put that band together and you should be fucking grateful, man. She put that band together to help us out and all you can do is put it down."

"Wow, man, what's wrong? Take it easy."

"You think you're too good to work in a restaurant? That was a good job. Not for you. Right? Now you got this faggoty job punching a computer and looking up films and finding them on the shelves, and that's called working. Give me a fucking break, will you?"

"No, man, I just like the store better. It's closer, I can do my homework there and I see my friends. That's all."

"That's not good enough. You're supposed to be studying music. I never hear you practice anymore."

"We practice in school."

"We?"

"Yeah, Cookie and me."

"Oh, yeah? Forget your sister. What the hell is she doing? Acting? Who in the hell is she kidding? She should be studying the flute, so she can get a job with an orchestra or something."

"Dad, you should talk to her about that."

"Shut up. How are you gonna do anything in music if you don't practice?"

"I told you, I practice in school."

"And I told you to shut up," he screamed, coming forward so that Cliff took a step back, confused. His father was totally out of control. Cliff had never seen him like that—he looked like the guys on crack.

"Yo, just lighten up, Dad," he said, putting up his hands in front of him.

"Don't 'yo' me, you little punk. Just shut the fuck up, you little mick bastard. Are you fucking deaf? Is that your fucking problem, Marine? Is it, shithead?"

Billy heard himself say it, but couldn't believe it and all he saw was the red film of rage across his eyes and through the crimson haziness he saw his drill instructor at Parris Island, Sergeant Parker, his bronzed skin like leather and his steely-gray eyes filled with intense, killing hatred, his mouth no more than a few inches from Billy's face so that he could feel the spray of spittle as he called him scum, a mick fairy, and a worthless, New York Irish cocksucker, no more a Marine than some long-haired Bob Dylan pansy, making Billy wonder if the drill instructor had found out he played music and he wouldn't be allowed to be an infantryman. He had stuck it out, clenching his teeth and responding: "No, sir. Twenty push-ups? Yes, sir. Ten laps? Yes, sir! Clean the head? Yes, sir."

"Marine?" Cliff said, confused.

And that's when Billy raised his left hand and Cliff backed off another step, wanting to run but his dignity not allowing him as he watched his father grimace and the upper part of his body shift from right to left. Billy's hand was coming forward from the left side of his body as if he were going to throw a pitch sidearm, he thought later, like that kid on the Mets, David Cone, and his Laredo pitch, except that Cone was a right-hander. At the last moment Billy held up as if the umpire had called time. Days later he reflected and tried to make a joke about it, explaining the whole baseball comparison to Cliff as he attempted to apologize. It was too late. The trust that had been in the boy's eyes for such a long time had turned to a mixture of anger, suspicion, and pity.

"I'm sorry, Daddy," the boy had said as he covered up to ward off the blow. "I didn't mean anything by it. I didn't mind working in the restaurant, but now that the store's open and it's doing good, I like going there better. I'm just glad we don't have to worry about money so much. I liked going to play with the family when I was little, but after a while, I didn't like it as much. I'm sorry. All I was saying is that I was glad we were doing better and we don't even have to go and play in the subway. That's all, Dad. I'm sorry."

"It's okay. Forget it," he said, but hated himself for frightening Cliff and making him back down, knowing there was nothing else the boy could do. Cliff was nearly as tall as his father, but still, at fifteen, innocent and trusting of him, and he'd gone and scared the boy. Billy wanted to reach out and hold him in his arms as he had when he was little and he'd fallen and hurt himself and come to him for comfort. He looked into Cliff's eyes and saw uncertainty and the same frightened look Joey had as he held him in his arms, the awful truth dawning on him that his life was nearly over.

Before the week was out, Cliff realized that he had done nothing wrong and that a human being who had been very important in his life had erred and was no longer that infallible being he'd wanted to believe in; that the man who was his father and ruled absolutely from that position, at times benevolently, at times with little concern, was himself frightened by something, and whatever was going on, it had nothing to do with anything he'd said or done. When Billy saw that Cliff had changed and was now aloof from him, almost avoiding him, he finally called the veterans group and started attending the meetings, listening to the other soldiers' sad stories and identifying with their suffering.

Outside the loft, the snow fell silently in large, wet flakes that hit the ground and quickly melted away. As Billy played he watched the flakes descend, and, as effortlessly, he played the music, realizing that each note had the same quality of impermanence as the flakes, yet the overall effect of the tune remained with a person, just as the quality of the falling snow created a sort of peace over the landscape. As the echo of the last note faded into the emptiness of the day, and sunlight began to break through the scattered snowflakes to bathe the loft in a soft, early-afternoon winter light, Billy sat on the piano bench and examined his mind, wondering where the music could have come from after being away so long. Safe in his own home after the surprise of the piano, he wondered at how much he had been able to regain in his ability to play.

His capacity for learning tunes quickly and being able to play them with fluidity and up-tempo when it was required was what had attracted Miles Davis to his playing and the reason he'd been asked to join the quintet, Pop Butterworth had told him back then. He'd gone and played with Miles that second time, looking at the charts a couple of times, running through them effortlessly, looking up a couple of times and having Miles tell him that Tony, the drummer, would be speeding up there and he'd better be ready to up the tempo, and he'd nod, and when they went to playing he'd hear the rapid fire of the sticks on the drums and then on the first beat of the cymbal he'd come in exactly on cue, playing all out.

The whole thing was for *Filles de Kilimanjaro* and he was going to replace Herbie Hancock, who was leaving the quintet to get married, Butterworth had said. They had a rehearsal and he played the tunes and it was totally different from anything he'd done before. Miles had talked with the other musicians about using an electric piano and playing outside the chord structure and about things he'd never heard of so that by the end of the afternoon he felt an enormous challenge. That evening when he got home his mother handed him an envelope. He opened the letter absentmindedly, read it, and told his mother he'd been drafted.

Now as he sat at the piano he couldn't recall if his decision had been instantaneous or if he'd thought it over, but by the end of the week he'd enlisted in the Marines, thinking that his father would be proud of him up in heaven. He couldn't imagine how drastically different his life would have been had he not been drafted. They didn't have a draft now. Going into the Marines had seemed the right thing to do at the time. Even if he'd wanted to stay and play with Miles, he couldn't have because of the draft notice. Though maybe he could've stayed out of the war altogether. All of it was speculation now, Monday-morning quarterbacking, hindsight. He reflected on his life and then for a fraction of a second he saw that everything might really turn out okay, and a ray of hope appeared like a single beam of light from his heart and he delighted in the pleasure of sitting at his beautiful piano in his own home with the possibility of playing with other jazz musicians again.

41 The Piano

It had now been nearly a year since he had gone up to Yonkers to help his grandfather Buck get the storm windows back on his house. August had seemed a bit early to be doing so, but his grandfather had insisted and he'd gone up early in the morning on the subway and worked all day, with his grandfather, as always, telling him stories about growing up in Tennessee. Lurleen told him that she had promised Fawn and Caitlin a trip to the zoo, Cliff was working at his job bussing dishes at a restaurant in Tribeca, and Cookie and Vidamía had gone to the beach with their friends. When he was finished hanging the storm windows, his grandfather had insisted he eat again so he sat down and had some potato salad, a sandwich, and a beer before leaving to get back on the subway.

Back home after helping his grandfather, Billy came out of the elevator, walked into the loft, and, his head down, went into the bathroom to urinate. He took the strapless watch out of his pocket and noted that it was twenty minutes past six, but apparently no one was home yet. As he walked out of the bathroom and was heading for his rocker by the windows, he saw the large, dark shape and froze for an instant—its size and form didn't fit the reality of any known mammalian being—before he realized it was a piano.

Sitting with its tail pointed in the direction of their dining area, the keyboard facing the windows, and the wing of its top open as if poised for flight, the instrument appeared enormous, its surface polished to a high sheen and the black and white keys shimmering in the afternoon light. Running several times around it from top to bottom, the thick red ribbon with the bow made its presence even more incongruous so that he suddenly felt a sensation of light-headedness and a slight nausea. He wanted to go to it, to at least touch its surface to convince himself that it wasn't an apparition, for often things seemed to appear from his past, and he had to shake the memory away before it became too powerful and got hold of his mind.

He couldn't imagine why the piano had a red ribbon and bow around it and finally turned away from it as if, indeed, this monstrosity were a figment of his imagination. It was then, as he turned, that he saw all of them, and heard the instruments playing "Happy Birthday," and Caitlin, of all people, singing the song in a clear, pure voice. They were all there—Lurleen playing the fiddle, Vidamía the tub bass, Cookie her sax, Cliff the trombone, and Fawn the harmonica. All he could do was stand and shake his head, the pain so deep in his chest that he thought he'd split open. Caitlin sang two more choruses of "Happy Birthday," each time faster and then they stopped playing the instruments and all of them sang the birthday challenge, the "Happy Birthday" tune but with the words changed. Each member of the family was duty-bound to answer on his or her birthday, no matter how old they were. As if she were doing magic, Caitlin came forward with a big birthday cake and not a bunch of candles but two of them with the numbers 3 and 9.

How old are you now?
How old are you now?
How old are you, Daddy?
How old are you now?

Then they began playing again, and, with tears streaming down his face and his head shaking in disbelief, but the feeling of hurt leaving him, replaced now by the love that he felt for all of them, he nodded over and over again. Summoning up all the courage that was left in him, and feeling as if the shadow of death were stalking him, he sang mournfully:

I am thirty-nine years old.
I am thirty-nine years old.
I am thirty-nine years old.
I am thirty-nine years old.

Everyone clapped and came over and hugged him, and each one of them had an individual present, including Vidamía, who gave him a beautiful new wallet since he'd lost his the previous week repairing a pipe on the roof of one of the buildings where he did odd jobs. Caitlin had made him a small quilted rabbit, the pattern of which she had cut roughly and which Lurleen had helped her put together and sew. He didn't ask about the piano, knowing that the only one who could afford something like this was Elsa, but he couldn't imagine that she had a hand in it, so most likely the person responsible was Vidamía. Eventually, they made him go to the piano, and inside on the strings he found a card which read "*To Daddy, from your family, with love.*" It was signed by all of them.

"Well, thank you very much," he said, nodding. "That's a pretty hip present. The biggest one I've ever gotten. It's a good thing Santa didn't have to bring it on his sled," he added, picking up Caitlin. "What would have happened to the reindeer?" he asked.

"They would've gone on strike," Caitlin said, giggling and making everybody laugh, since her answers to questions were always so off the wall. "Right, Daddy?"

"Definitely," he said. "Woulda walked right out if they had to haul something like that."

"Yeah," Caitlin said.

"Come and get it," Cookie had announced. Billy set Caitlin at her place at the long table, and after everyone was seated, he said grace, the one compromise to religion Lurleen permitted since it taught the children gratitude. Lurleen had made his favorite foods: ham steaks with lima beans, scalloped potatoes, a crawfish gumbo, corn bread with honey, and a large pan of blueberry cobbler with large crispy biscuits into which the sweet juice from the blueberries had seeped. Afterward Lurleen brought him herbal tea and with ritualistic insistence his vitamins and digestive enzymes for his nervous stomach. As if he hadn't had enough, they insisted that he eat at least one slice of the cake. Cookie had baked it, and it was a delicious carrot cake with pieces of pineapple. They brought him a large piece with a big scoop of ice cream and slowly he had also eaten it, feeling a different kind of light-headedness and patting his stomach, which in the past year had begun acquiring a bit of a paunch.

While they were eating, the chatter and banter went as always, with great raucous laughter about all their activities, Mario and Cookie, Wyndell and Vidamía, Fawn getting ready to audition for Performing Arts in the spring of 1990, Cliff and his many girlfriends and how snooty they were, which meant they were totally deficient socially, Caitlin's upcoming sixth-birthday party in September and whether she was going to make a speech as she had last year. They had yet to figure out why Caitlin liked making speeches. They sounded like political speeches, so perhaps she was influenced by the television, although they didn't think so, being that politicians on TV were generally subdued, so they figured she must have heard one of those neighborhood sound trucks during a political campaign, because for no apparent reason in the middle of playing with her dolls or tea sets, she'd stand up and start talking about the oppression of the bears or some weird thing. They spoke about Lurleen's orchestra at the junior high school and the upcoming concert, and then, since they were talking about music, speculated on the chance that their father would at some point start to play with other musicians. They had finished eating, and all at once Caitlin jumped up and got a tambourine and Cliff the washboard Lurleen had brought back the last time she'd gone home to visit her mother, used now when they played Cajun music for friends. Cliff slung the washboard over his shoulders and began scratching and setting up a beat. On the required beat Caitlin hit the tambourine, her lips pursed and her head turned to one side like a real live homegirl.

Cookie stood up, did a spin, put on a serious attitude, and went into her piano rap, which included the names of over forty piano companies. At the end Caitlin gave her critical appraisal of the composition, declaring that it didn't sound so much like rap, but like "Dr. Zeus and Ice-T go Christmas caroling," which cracked everybody up and earned Caitlin a mild nuggy and a wrestling match with tickling from Cookie.

> *Petrof, Samick, Sängler & Söhne,*
> *Jasper America,*
> *and Shafer & Sons.*
> *Those are some pianos*
> *we played just for fun.*
> *Just to check them out*
> *for feel and for tone.*
>
> *On Sauter, on Brentwood,*
> *on Fandrich, on Kimball,*
> *on Grothrian, on Blüthner,*

on Baldwin and Schimmel.
We sat and we played,
like Santa was waiting
but needed the slade.

"Slade?" Cliff said, right on cue and with just the right amount of sarcasm, which gave Cookie the opportunity to talk "Tennessee," as she called it, meaning a Southern accent.

Slade's, what I sade
and definitely mean it.
We tried Studios and Grands,
and Consoles and Spinets.
We went and we sat
and we tested each key.
We played us some tunes,
using the ole do-re-mi.

"Word, nothing's too good for Billy Farrell," Cliff said, putting aside the rejection of his father, which had grown since his run-in with him before Christmas, joining in the African-American–accented talk, which to them had nothing to do with black and white but with music and relaxing, which now provided Cookie with an opportunity to do a few more spins and get down on the floor and jump up again like a blond gazelle, her gold hair flying.

And check out this shit—
the trip was terrific.
Cause some pianos we played
were from the Pacific.
Yamaha, Tadashi,
Hyundai, and Kawai.

Right here in New York
and not in Hawaii.

And so it went until she got to the last verse:

So there you have it, Daddy,
a beautiful piano so you'll entertain
and knock them all out
like you were playing with Trane.
We hope you'll continue
to play and bring hope.
Even with just eight
we know you can cope.
Word.

Everyone clapped and came over to him and hugged and kissed him. After a while, someone, he didn't recall who, suggested that he play the piano. Even though he'd been practicing at New York University for months, he suddenly felt panic and he momentarily swooned and felt as if all the lights had dimmed and he was about to pass out. Vidamía was immediately near him, smoothing his hair and helping him to his feet.

"It's okay," she said. "Come on," and she took his good hand, brought him over to the piano, and sat him down as Cookie and Lurleen removed the ribbon from it.

The piano was breathtaking in its beauty, exuding awesome power, reminding him of a magnificent racehorse. Billy recalled the times he'd gone with his father and uncle to Aqueduct Race Track, where, holding his father's hand, they'd gone to the stables and spoken to his uncle Charlie's father-in-law, Mickey Finnegan, who was a horse trainer. Billy'd stood looking at the beautiful sleek animals, admiring their power and strength and their delicate legs, wondering how they could go so fast on such thin legs. Once they had been watching a race and a horse stumbled and fell, sending the rider over the railing. The horse tried to get up but couldn't. Billy turned to his father for an explanation, but his father just shook his head. "Mickey's gonna have to put him down," he said. Soon there were a number of men around the horse. Billy didn't understand. He and his father left the grandstand and went back to the stables. On the way there he heard the muffled sound of a gunshot. When they reached the track level, the horse's body was being dragged back to the paddock. His father pointed at the shattered leg, the thin area around the ankle twisted grotesquely. "He's dead, isn't he?" Billy asked, hoping his father would tell him the horse was just sleeping. "Yes, he's dead." "Why?" he asked. "They can't fix his leg. The body's too big for the leg to hold the weight." What always remained with Billy was the size of the horse's large and dreamy eyes, the long eyelashes, making the face of the animal delicate. He recalled also how startled the animals sometimes looked. On some complex level the horses reminded him of women. He wasn't sure whether it was their eyes or the shape of their haunches, because the curvature of that part of the equine anatomy made him think of women's thighs and buttocks; perhaps it was both the dreamy eyes and the haunches.

The piano possessed some of the same qualities, its color and curves resembling racehorses, and therefore women, and suddenly he was alive and saw his hands move to the keys and without knowing what action the keys had he hit a chord with his two hands and let his right hand slide easily over the melody as he had relearned it. Without thinking, he was into "Thanks for the Memory," playing with ease the introduction, the melody, the bridge, and then a simple improvisation that gave him an opportunity to test the middle six octaves of the piano.

No more than two minutes elapsed before his left hand was actively working and there was a definite swing to the music, so that before the end of his next chorus he heard behind him Cliff, perfectly on key, blowing a series of extremely well-placed and harmonious blasts from the trombone, signaling that he'd like to join in. Billy nodded, played once more the basic chord structure, and heard plainly his son's unmistakable virtuosity. Eventually, Fawn was on her drums and set up a nice little rhythm. Cookie came in beneath the chording part of the melody on her tenor saxophone, Lurleen on the fiddle, and Vidamía on the tub bass, instinctively creating enough harmony to fit in with the rest, although she had never heard the tune.

As he played he recalled going with Pop Butterworth to a loft in Brooklyn for a jam session. The two piano players they were expecting hadn't arrived and everybody was beginning to grow impatient when Pop pointed to Billy and told the musicians that here was a pianist. He wasn't as scared as he'd been that first time with Miles, so he sat down, and John Coltrane asked him if he knew "Body and Soul" or "April in Paris" or maybe "I Cover the Waterfront," and he said, "What key?" and all the musicians, who were black, laughed and slapped hands and Trane had said, "Right. 'Waterfront' in F," and counted and Billy took the intro and off they went, and then one of the other pianists came in and John Coltrane thanked Billy, but he couldn't stop grinning and shaking his head. That was in 1966 when he was sixteen. The following year, just before he turned seventeen, Butterworth called the house and told him John Coltrane had died. He was forty. Next year, Billy thought now, he'd be forty.

He and Lurleen and the children went through ten or twelve tunes, even taking a shot at John Coltrane's rendition of "My Favorite Things," one of Billy's favorite tunes, with Cookie on her soprano sax, which, admittedly, would have made Trane turn over in his grave—but "Knowing him," Pop Butterworth had said later when Billy told him about it, "Trane probably would have laughed and said, 'Yeah, something like that.'"

Billy had been at it over a year, at first secretly resenting Vidamía's insistence that he had to play again. She had made him listen to a tape Butterworth had given her. It was him playing solo down at the Village Vanguard on Seventh Avenue. One night, after Kenny Barron—or Cedar Walton, he couldn't remember who—finished performing and all the musicians had left and the place was being swept, Billy'd sat at the piano at Butterworth's urging and played a lugubrious "Darn That Dream," followed by "My Funny Valentine" and a few other ballads, each of them measured in their melancholy so that he felt whole, and from the darkness he heard applause. It was Max Gordon, the owner. He stopped playing, said he was sorry, but Mr. Gordon told him to keep going, that he sounded real good. Butterworth had been carrying a large, reel-to-reel tape recorder, had plugged it in, and was taping him. And now he'd gone and transferred the large tape to a cassette and given it to Vidamía. Deep in his heart Billy felt the sadness of the past, accepting unquestioningly just how fused he was to the dead.

Unconsciously, the tribulation of his spirit served as a background to his best memories, so that his father remained alive, his face bright, his blue eyes smiling and friendly, making Billy feel innocent and small again, wishing to kiss his ruddy cheek and muss up his da's sandy hair as his father had done to him, wanting to be just like him. And he wondered if he was having the same effect on his children and then, realizing that he must be, he sat up and, as if a large electric shock had been shot into him, he came suddenly awake and decided that whatever it was the children and Lurleen wanted him to do, he would do it. He wouldn't make the same mistake twice. Back then he thought it was right to go into the Marines, but it hadn't turned out right. He should have listened more closely to his heart. Maybe if he listened to his heart he would be okay now. And yet he was much better off than he had been in a long time and for that at least he was grateful.

But there were times when his memories attacked him and,

no matter what he played or thought about, the feeling overwhelmed him and he knew that nothing he could do would ease
his mind, because Joey's death had definitely been his fault. The
obsession would not leave him. He recalled once again walking
on the edge of the rice field, knowing they shouldn't have gone
in that direction, but reassuring Joey that they could get back
easily enough, and in any case they were close to the base and the
perimeter had been secure now for two weeks, the Cong driven
from the area.

What had they been talking about? Baseball? Music? Most
likely music, since Joey was always talking about Latin music.
Machito, Charlie and Eddie Palmieri, the Fania All Stars, and
Joe Cuba. It had to be music but he couldn't recall the tune or
the group they were talking about. It didn't matter. One minute
they were walking and the next there was the sound of automatic fire, punctuated by the explosion of a grenade. Joey had
turned to go in the direction they had come from but Billy had
called him back and then the two of them were running for the
cover of the trees, knowing that once there they could return to
the base safely. But it had been the wrong move. As soon as they
began running they knew it was a mistake.

The decision had been instantaneous and irreversible. In a
matter of seconds the water around him was exploding with
death, the air alive with flying steel, as if it were raining, except
this rain was coming from unexpected directions. He'd lost consciousness, everything going black, and didn't know how much
time had transpired between the explosion and his waking to the
dull pain in his head. He looked for his wristwatch to ascertain
the time and saw the damaged wristband, the glass on the face of
the watch shattered, the watch itself twisted on his wrist. He
then reached with his right hand to straighten the timepiece and
saw his bloody fingers, not comprehending at first that his middle and pinkie fingers were missing; thinking only how strange

his hand would look in a glove, or gripping a bat when he played softball; the notion that he might never again play music not yet entering his mind.

Instead a sudden, terrible panic hit him when he thought about Joey, calling him and turning around as he sat in the rice paddy; his eyes finally seeing Joey's helmet behind him and his body half-submerged; going to the place and not bothering to retrieve his own helmet; calling Joey's name and hoping that, like himself, Joey had simply been knocked out by the blast; knowing, even as he splashed toward him that it would be useless since Joey was facedown in the water.

When he got there he stood looking at the bloodstained water and the wound below Joey's left shoulder, the slight wound creating in him some hope that death hadn't intruded so personally into his life again. Kneeling in the rice paddy, he turned Joey Santiago's body over and after the water poured away he saw the intestines, red and blue, trail the body, noting that the entire front of Joey's body, from sternum to pubic area, was torn open, exposed, and inside his torso, like a sloppily put together display in a butcher shop, his organs lay in spectacular disorganization, everything raw and seemingly without life. Somehow Joey was still alive and recognized him, and the fact that he was dying. The scene caused Billy no repugnance. Instinctively he grabbed the limp body and, in spite of his own shock, or perhaps because of it, hastily scooped everything that could be salvaged of Joey's visceral disorganization and replaced it inside the body cavity and, ripping off his fatigue shirt, he hopelessly packed the wound as if with patches from a medical kit, and then he sat in that rice paddy.

He imagined later that from the time of the attack until he turned Joey over it couldn't have been more than thirty seconds since Joey was still alive. He wished it had been longer, because then Joey would've drowned and wouldn't have had to go through the torture of however long it took him to die. After packing the abdomen with his shirt, Billy Farrell then took his friend in his arms and rocked him as he would a sleepless child, in the way his father had held him, and in the same manner that he would one day hold his own children, as Joey drifted in and out of delirium, still barely alive, until at the end, like a wisp of smoke from a burnt-out match, Joey's life disappeared into the ether of memory. Why hadn't he called for the medic? Why hadn't he returned fire? At times he thought that he had called out, "Doc, Doc, we've been hit! Hit bad, Doc!" Other times he was certain that he hadn't called for help and wondered why.

Shortly before the medevac helicopter landed, the platoon had arrived at the edge of the woods and laid down a blanket of fire and mortar shells at the grassland beyond the rice paddy, a few of the soldiers skirting the perimeter of the area and patrolling where they thought the attack had come from, but they found no activity and everyone was puzzled by this. All around Billy and Joey Santiago, now dead, bullets were flying and Billy could hear the voices of the fellows in the platoon that had come out of the woods, aiming their weapons across the rice paddy, the automatic fire sounding odd, as if they were shooting at ghosts. McKenzie, Florio, and Tony Fuentes, the medic, were the first ones to get there, and beyond them Hitchcock, Palucci, and Bobby Miranda, staring at him hard like they always did with everybody, the mistrust a result of their running a little dope operation.

Maybe the fellas in the group at the VA were right and he ought to talk about the whole thing. The idea that he was responsible for Joey's death had lingered far too long, and Rogers, who was a psychologist, suggested that maybe it was just a cover-up for something else. If Billy understood him correctly, Rogers was saying that Billy was afraid of something deeper and so was focusing on Joey's death so that he wouldn't have to face this other thing. Now that Wyndell had set up the gig and asked him to play, he'd have to face whatever it was that was making him re-live his life in Nam every day. The gig was in five weeks. Maybe the fear would surface again. He suspected that, just like twenty years ago, it was the feeling that he had no business aspiring to play jazz, now less than ever.

He'd gotten the piano last year and his birthday was coming up again and perhaps after all this time he could put the night-mare of the past twenty years behind him. He thought of his father's friend Mike Cunningham who had hit a man with a baseball bat. The man died. Mike was nineteen at the time. The man had been making lewd remarks to Mike's girlfriend, Peggy Lyons, at a softball game in Central Park. Mike was playing for an insurance company where he worked as a clerk. He had been making plans to take the test to go into the police force, and they sent him to jail for fifteen years. After he did his time, Mike Cunningham had come to their house, looking for Billy's father. His mother had opened the door.

"Hi, Maud," Mike said. "I just got out and came over to see Kevin."

"Kevin died five years ago, Michael," his mother had said.

"Jesus, Mary, and Joseph, nobody told me," Mike Cunning-ham replied. "I'm sorry."

His mother invited him in, gave him coffee and a sandwich. She asked him if he'd seen his mother yet. Mike shook his head, said he was going down to the Bronx to see her that night. Billy noticed that Mike still seemed young, even though he looked like he'd gone through hell. In spite of his youth, Mike reminded Billy of an old man in the way he moved and did everything carefully, as if something might suddenly fall and break. His mother began to say something but changed her mind. Perhaps she was about to tell Mike that Peggy Lyons had gotten married and moved to Boston, but maybe he knew, and if he didn't she didn't want to be the one to give him any more bad news.

462

Billy wondered if he behaved that way, if the last twenty years of remaining locked up in his memories had caused him to age the way Mike Cunningham had. Billy also wondered if Mike had felt the same rage and regret and sadness of life which haunted him, and which, it seemed, would always remain with him.

42 Faceless Shadows

Like all whom the nightmare calls as it gallops madly in the pale moonlight, Fawn Singleton Farrell wrote secretly, living each day in resignation as she wandered through a labyrinth of interminable sorrow, fear and despair her only companions. She loved desperately and without hope, much like a caged bird that yearns to give itself to flight but, unable to, cries mournfully through the day. There was no specific person whose love she sought, or whom she wished to grace with hers. Still, within her heart there existed a need to nurture and give comfort, much as a child will feel pity for a wet, hungry kitten, or, having found a broken-winged bird, will pick it up gingerly, observing its naked uncertainty, hoping to assuage the quivering bird's instinctive dread that its benefactor may be a predator. Having picked up the wounded bird and smoothed its feathers, the child sets out to find some understanding adult who will help with the bird. And thus each day she sought an answer to her life, desperately but shyly, undemanding and alone.

Juxtaposed against her protective instincts there was within her another side seething with rage, seeking to obliterate that which threatened; wishing, at least in fantasy, destruction of the miscreant, rendering him to a fine powder that would drift away in the wind forever—*him*, because she never thought of women

463

as harmful, having received from her mother and her sisters and Grandma Maud loving care and affection, but from her father, in her perception, hardly a glance, his distance and inaccessibility monumental in her eyes, even though he felt exactly the same distance from his other children. Inside the cauldron of emotion that consistently boiled within her, the notion existed that no matter what took place in her life, she couldn't be happy.

But all of this life of contradictions, of violets and daggers, of violence and goodness, all of it remained within her, struggling to express itself, so that at times she would feel violent spasms of pain within her chest and her face would contort horribly, disfiguring her generally kindly and innocent features so that if observed closely one could see previewed a wizened old hag of eighty or ninety, the fine nose grown bony and hooked, the skin around the eyes creased with wrinkles, the smooth, rose-tinted porcelain skin gray and warted. Even when she stood behind the drums keeping the beat for the family, inside her there raged this battle, and despite her best efforts at dissimulation, every once in a while the smooth exterior of emotions was interrupted by the facial contortions, which for the most part went unnoticed, except when she had to solo, and then she put her head way down over the snare and let the thick blond hair fall over her face to cover the horror. But there was no band now, so it didn't matter. Lately the dread that lived within her had become intensified in response to her father's own rage; the horror within her centered around a distorted view of herself, which her mother, Lurleen, with love and understanding, had tried to ease by explaining her condition.

"I know, Mama, but am I a girl?" she had cried out once when she was eleven.

"Of course you are, darling," Lurleen had replied, holding her to her bosom and smoothing her hair. "A beautiful, lovely, talented girl whose mama loves her very, very much."

"Then why do I have to have that yinandyango hanging

down offa me like Cliff?" calling the horrific appendage the funny name Lurleen had given her brother's infant organ.

Billy had once asked Lurleen why she called Cliff's thing a yin-andyango while she called his own a "big red baby," like the times after the children were asleep when she'd come and sit on his left side on the sofa and with her right hand reach down and massage him and whisper throatily, "Honey, whynatcha let me borrow your big red baby so's I can have some fun," and he'd sort of smile, his eyes veiled and he'd reach his lips down to try and find her nipples.

She explained that she had an uncle, Luke, in Minnesota who was married to a Swedish gal named Hannah and she had spent two summers with them up near Rush City, where there was a large Swedish community, and this Hannah, who had eight sons, called their thing a "ninganango."

Lurleen had imagined it was the name that Swedish mothers used, just like some mothers called their little boy's organ a peepee or a winkle. Except years later when Lurleen was in college she'd met a girl who did yoga and meditated and was into herbal cures and acupuncture. Around her neck on a silver chain she wore an amulet which was a perfect circle with what seemed to be the inside part of an S with one side of it black and the other white, onyx and mother-of-pearl, and within each side a black dot on the top of the white side and a white dot on the bottom of the black side. Valerie called it a yin-yang and said that it explained the duality of all things.

One day she and Billy were making love and she was lying atop him with his organ completely in her. She began moving gently, letting her pelvis massage itself against him, and after a few moments the sensation was so strong that she felt as if his organ was attached to her and she was within *him*, and then it dawned on her that perhaps what Hannah might have been saying was "yin-yang," so she began calling Cliff's penis his "yin-andyango," imagining that it was both male and female and belonged to both the man and the woman since it gave so much pleasure to both when used the right way, and Billy, in spite of everything that troubled him, sure knew how to use his yin-andyango.

But Fawn knew nothing of this. What she did know is that she had once stood, fully clothed, watching her mother giving her brother a bath and had wanted to take off her clothes and get into the bathtub with Cliff, but knew that she couldn't. Her mother had said she must always dress and bathe privately. And now it was worse, because she had hair down there and the thing had grown over or out of it, it seemed, all weird, so that it felt like a finger without any bones. So when she asked about her odd appendage, which hung over her own place where she peed from, serving no purpose and looking more each day like those awful, wrinkled-up, red things that hang from a turkey's head, Lurleen's heart nearly broke.

"Oh, you poor baby," Lurleen said, and then explained that the doctor had said that this type of condition took place in nature from time to time. "It also happens in animals: cows and goats, pigs and horses, you know. It ain't as serious as it looks, sugar. You just have to trust me and the doctors and everything will be all right."

Although Lurleen hadn't explained it then, eventually she told Fawn that what she had was a type of pseudo-hermaphrodism. There were cases in which the person "presented," as the doctor had said, complete male genitals but upon reaching puberty, this person who had grown up as a boy began to grow breasts and widen at the hips and the pelvis began rotating downward. After a few examinations, doctors could tell the person had a set of ovaries, fallopian tubes, a uterus, and a vaginal canal.

In those cases the false penis and testicles had to be surgically removed and a vaginal canal opened in order for the person, now a woman, to be able to bear children, though in fact they

466

were seldom able to. Lurleen didn't go into it with Fawn, but recalled listening to the doctor tell her that in the beginning only the vaginal canal was opened. But this was not the case with Fawn.

When Fawn was born, the doctors had discussed the tiny penis-like growth and the almost imperceptible vagina below it, explaining to Lurleen that Fawn would have to be examined periodically.

"We could remove the pseudopenis now, but we don't yet know the psychic disposition of the child as it develops. From all appearances your infant may be intersexual. It is probably best if we do further tests and wait until she's gone through puberty to see what happens then. We'll monitor how she develops and what gender choices she makes."

Although Billy was aware of Fawn's condition, he didn't feel comfortable in dealing with it. Lurleen brought Fawn home and did the best she could. Every six months she would take Fawn to the doctor for examinations. On one of those early visits Lurleen asked the doctor if he had any books she could read about the condition. The doctor took her address and a few weeks later she received a manila envelope with photocopies of a section from a medical book. In a chapter called Intersexuality, in section 4, "Principles in Management of Intersexuals," she underlined the passage to which the doctor had alluded. "There are two prevailing periods in the life of intersexual patients when a choice has to be made: shortly after birth and at the age of puberty." She put the article away in the bottom of a suitcase with her other important papers. Fawn was definitely a girl socially and sexually, but Lurleen was still advised to wait until Fawn had finished developing before making any decisions. If, after puberty, Fawn continued growing as a female, the surgery would be performed.

On her way home from seeing the doctor the last time, having decided to go ahead with the operation, Lurleen worried about the impact this would have on Fawn. While Fawn had reluctantly agreed to the surgery, it was obvious that she was frightened. She still seemed unsure of her sexuality. But she had always been a girl, except for the growth, which had no reproductive purpose. She'd be fine. If she asked questions, Lurleen would answer them honestly, as she always did.

There were times when Lurleen wanted to explain to Fawn about the sexual duality of all human beings. Every man had a bit of woman in him and every woman was in part male. This was common knowledge, but with Fawn one had to proceed slowly. If not, she might become confused and, like a frightened colt, bolt away. One could harness both sides of his or her sexuality and use either element, masculine or feminine, to enhance one's life.

Maybe it wouldn't be so bad, Fawn thought. Her mama had explained that except for the yinandyango, she had a vagina and a clitoris and could have babies someday, although Fawn couldn't imagine that she could take the pain of childbirth or even wanted a boy touching her, like Cookie, who was so fresh, said she would, letting Mario do it, and also Vee with Wyn, and her mama and her papa and everybody else, Cliff with different girls and maybe with his new, rich, stuck-up girlfriend, Phillipa Ralston, all of them doing it. But if she chose she could have babies, and maybe having a boy in her *would* feel good like Cookie and Vee said. She didn't know.

She sat alone in her room, watching the rain outside as it streaked the bridges to Brooklyn in silver and gray, listening to Willie Nelson singing "On the Road Again," "Uncloudy Day," and "Me and Bobby McGee," and imagining that this Bobby McGee was neither a boy nor a girl, and she got out her harmonica, which was by far her favorite instrument, and played mournfully along with the music. Although she enjoyed playing with her family, it was this music that seemed more of a mystery to her because California and Louisiana, Kentucky and Texas, Minnesota and Missouri, North Dakota and Georgia were places she had never been, though she knew if she went there she could find Bobby McGee whom she loved desperately and then they'd go everywhere together, singing and playing the harmonica, just like it said in the song, except that Willie Nelson called it a harpoon, which was weird because that's how she felt having the thing down there.

Sometimes she felt happy, like when everybody had agreed that it was okay to do "Me and Bobby McGee" when they played down in the subways, and Lurleen had gotten her a harmonica holder so she could continue to play the drums and also play her harpoon, and they had rehearsed and everything and it sounded so good that she could actually see herself traveling throughout the land which her great-grandpa Buck said was the best and most beautiful land in the world; traveling all over with Bobby McGee, from the gulf-stream waters to the redwood forests, hitching rides and sometimes sleeping under the stars next to Bobby McGee. And Bobby wasn't white, and he wasn't black or brown, or yellow or red. He was just a person and her friend who loved her and whom she loved with all her true and loyal heart. She listened once again to the song, trying to understand what the words meant: *"Freedom's just another word for nothing left to lose."*

As she lay on her bed, listening to the characters on *Sesame Street* who kept Caitlin company, she allowed her mind to drift away. She loved everyone in her family, but most of all Vidamía, who was so honest with her and told her everything she wanted to know. She had loved playing with them down in the subways or out in the street, but all of that had stopped now with the video store doing so well and she just sitting around listening to music and wondering what was going to become of her life. She hadn't been accepted at Performing Arts, and she was glad because she didn't know if she could handle some of the things that Cookie and Cliff talked about, the jealousy and phoniness of some of the people, or even just the size of the place.

She figured maybe she played too loud or maybe she wasn't creative enough in her playing or maybe her face had started twitching and she'd looked weird or maybe they could tell about her thing through the pants and she should've worn a skirt but that would've looked even stranger, a girl playing drums in a skirt. It didn't matter. She was glad. She guessed she'd go to Seward Park like everybody else was doing. She loved singing the songs and playing the drums, but most of all she loved it when the family was at home and they played bluegrass tunes. Then she could play the harmonica and sing her heart out and let the pain come out of her soul, "somebody robbed the Glendale train," listening to Cliff pick at the banjo and imagining being up in the hills of Tennessee or Missouri, lost in the woods and living with the deer and the other animals, a wild girl who needed no one. She tried to imagine sex, but the subject frightened her. Sometimes when she thought about certain things like Cookie and Mario, or Vee and Wyn, she got wet and her turkey thing got hard and she had thought of maybe bending it and putting it in herself but was afraid and never tried it. Maybe women had to have men's things inside of them and she should do it and then she wouldn't have to depend on a man, because there was no way she'd let anyone touch her.

When she was alone and wasn't thinking, she sat down and wrote, letting her mind go and inventing words, letting the images and the sounds come to her unbidden, as if in a dream. That big boy had looked at her the other day. His look was direct and it made her uncomfortable. She remembered him from the fourth grade, but he was with the other boys and they were scary and loud and kept laughing and pushing each other. She didn't know whether he remembered her, but she remembered him because he was cross-eyed and always kept his head down, like she did, ashamed of his deficiency and fearful that someone would see him.

She wanted to tell her mother or Vidamía about the boy looking at her and how funny it made her feel, but changed her mind, since they were all so busy. God, she couldn't believe her father played the way he did. It was awesome, the things he could do. He was still very strange and hardly ever said anything and when he did he was generally angry these days, but when he sat down at the piano, you couldn't believe he didn't have those two fingers. He played so fast and yet every note was so clear that it gave her goose bumps. He'd asked her if she wanted to learn and she'd nodded and he patted the piano bench and she sat next to him. He had just finished working and he had a real strong smell and all she could think about was that maybe all men smelled like that and it would be awful to let them get too close. But she made herself concentrate and learned to do some things on the piano that she really liked. "Just make believe you're playing a conga," her father said, "or the drums." And she could do it. She tried playing a salsa tune and it came out pretty good and she laughed, but got up because of her father's smell. She went into the bathroom, locked the door, and, without looking at herself, took a shower and changed her underwear and clothes.

Everything was happening too quickly. Vidamía and Cookie were like two crazy girls these days, on the phone all the time and talking about doing a million and one things and still keeping the store going, and at night they'd come in with the money and Lurleen filled out the slips for the bank and in the morning she'd go with them and deposit the cash, and from the checkbook they'd pay the bills for the store. It was a separate checkbook from the one her mama paid the regular bills from.

One day in the beginning of June, Vidamía came in with Cookie and announced that they had been over in the Village and went by this place and they had jazz and they'd gone in and asked the owner if their father could play there. Lurleen wanted to know what kind of place.

"It's a restaurant," Cookie said.

"What's the name of it?" Lurleen asked.

"I don't know," Cookie said. "What was the name of it, Vee?"

"The Cornelia Street Café," Vidamía said. "On Cornelia Street."

"Boring," Cookie said. "Where's it gonna be? Thompson Street?"

"Chill, okay, Cookie?" Vidamía said. "Anyway, I asked this guy if Daddy could play there and he said it depends. When I asked him what it depended on, he said he had to be able to play jazz and he and his partners had to hear him. I told him no problem."

"I think you should've waited and talked to him first," Lurleen said.

"See, I told you, Agent Ho," Cookie said.

"I'm gonna talk to him," Vidamía said and closed her eyes at her sister dismissively. "If he doesn't wanna do it, that's fine. No harm done."

Cookie and Vidamía went back and forth, insulting each other and laughing and pushing each other, and Vidamía said Cookie was a good one to talk about Agent Ho since she was banging Mario Wong, her Chino-Rican boyfriend, and *her* name was Fortune Cookie Ho, and silliness like that. Their father had gone and auditioned and they said he could play. That had been okay because he continued to practice for hours at home and played once a week and brought home a little money, but he was still sullen most of the time and he had almost hit Cliff and Cliff said he was going to move out and he and his girlfriend were going to get an apartment. It wasn't fair. But it hadn't stopped there. Wyndell had gotten a gig at some club and Vee said why didn't he give their father a chance and they'd gone and set up a band and left her out. She didn't know much about it but she heard Vee talking and Wyn had said no way and Vee insisted that he hear him play or let him sit in on a jam session and Billy had blown them away with his virtuosity and Wyn had finally said yes.

Now that they were going to play the gig, they spent the whole day cleaning out the sixth floor and the next day they painted the place white and put in new lights and they rolled the piano out and put it upstairs and they rehearsed almost every night. At first they had let her play drums but now they'd brought a friend of Cliff's from school. "Fawn, this is David Weinstein. David, this is my sister Fawn. She plays the drums, too." David said "hi," but you could tell he felt embarrassed, like he'd taken over her job. Anyway, she liked playing the drums, but she couldn't keep up with the things her father was doing, and although he didn't say anything you could tell he was uncomfortable with her playing. She liked Wyndell. He was always nice and made her feel like she was older than thirteen. She thought David was cute, but Cookie had said he was gay. Maybe she was both. Maybe when you didn't like boys or girls it was really like that because you liked both and couldn't decide.

She hated them all now because they had this gig and didn't need her. It wasn't fair. None of it. First the family band stopped playing and now Wyn had gone and gotten a real gig together at the Village Gate of all places, which her father said was a really great club. A real jazz-playing job with Wyn and Cliff and a bassist. Someone should have said something, anything, even just "Sorry, Fawn, your drum playing is real nice, but we need someone older," but nobody did, and now she felt that her drumming sucked and that was the reason. Maybe it wasn't true but that's how it felt.

Maybe she'd just run away and go looking for Bobby McGee. Maybe she'd just go out with her harmonica one day and just start hitchhiking and go to Tennessee and hide up in the hills,

473

like her mama talked about, deep in the woods, so that no one could find her ever again and then they'd be sorry. Or maybe she'd get a boyfriend, even if she hated the idea. Maybe she'd be real bad and take her yinandyango and do it to herself; maybe she'd jerk off, like the boys said, and then put it in herself. She thought that perhaps she could give herself a baby, but the notion was so strange it frightened her. In any case she thought that would be impossible because her thing wasn't hollow and her mother had said boys' things were hollow and that urine and sperm came out of it and her urine came from inside her peepee.

She didn't like looking at herself now that she had hair and breasts. Whenever she had to dry herself, she closed her eyes and then got dressed quickly so she didn't have to look at her body. She had seen herself a few times and had felt ashamed and her face had gotten real hot and she had hit herself with her fist for being bad. She went into her room, opened her desk and from the very bottom of the drawer she pulled out her book and wrote in it.

Faceless shadows walk with me
dark shadows
emerging each night out of
the depth of the asphalt,
rising like
waves of summer heat,
waiting to torture me
with their wicked tenderness,
waiting for me to succumb
to their siren song,
waiting for me to surrender
myself to the pleasure
of their deceit,
waiting for me . . .

She read this, shook her head, and ran the pen over it several times diagonally in X fashion, so that later, when she was gone, or in jail, and people saw her notebook, they'd know she had been angry, because the ballpoint pen had ripped through several pages of the notebook. She returned the notebook to the desk and went upstairs to the roof. As she passed the sixth floor she heard them rehearsing, her father playing soulfully, way up on the piano, the notes like heavy drops falling to the floor and the bass painting beautiful dark swatches of music beneath the brushes of the drums, where she wished to be, so that it made her cry.

Nobody loved her, nobody. She was a freak and nobody loved her, and nobody ever would. Her mother had to say she loved her because mothers were expected to say such things, but she couldn't love her. How could she let them break up the band? It was awful. They didn't even play bluegrass anymore. Everything was jazz and her father was so mean lately, yelling and screaming and wanting to know where everybody was going.

Sometimes there was a little noise and he'd jump up and start looking around, muttering that somebody was trying to get in. Vidamía had also betrayed her. She hated them all, and maybe she'd stop eating like the TV program about the girl singer, something Carpenter. Maybe that's what she'd do. Just stop eating. When she got to the roof, she sat watching the buildings of the city, wondering how many people felt as she did. Probably many, but thinking this didn't take the ache away and she sat quietly on one of the benches and cried. She thought that maybe she'd sit on the edge of the roof like she'd seen her father do and maybe close her eyes and just drift off, but the idea of hitting the ground frightened her. She would have to be brave and not open her eyes. Once she hit the concrete below, things would be over.

She watched a flock of pigeons circle above and then head

home to their coop several blocks south. To the west the sun began to set, into New Jersey it seemed, and she tried to think positive thoughts, but couldn't. She was a freak, like Angela with her harelip was a freak. The two of them were freaks, except no one knew about her problem. She was a secret freak, and even after the doctors did the operation, in her mind she would always have the thing hanging there between her legs swinging back and forth, so that she could feel it slapping against her thighs like some live thing trying to invade her.

Once, when she was alone in the house, she had lain in bed and taken the spongy organ in her fingers and caressed it, feeling it grow and then bending it so that its fingertip point was touching her clitoris, which Cookie said felt good if you rubbed it. She had done exactly as Cookie said until she was almost in a dream world, and from far away she could hear herself gasping and the yinandyango fighting against her, wanting to go inside and she keeping it under control until she could no longer stand the pleasure and pushed down on the yinandyango and heard herself scream and her face began to twitch and then everything was black and she fell asleep so that when she woke up she was sweating, her whole body ached, and she felt damp between her legs.

She had gotten up out of bed, gotten dressed, and come out into the loft, but nobody had returned, and for a moment she thought that perhaps her family had gone away forever and left her behind, abandoned her. She felt indescribable loneliness and then a wild rage which made her scratch her face. She knew the yinandyango had been trying to get into her during her sleep, trying to fuck her. Don't fuck me, she thought. She repeated the phrase over and over and pounded herself in the groin until she was twice as sore and then through her jeans she grasped the appendage and squeezed it with all her might, her nails digging into it so that she imagined that she was making it bleed, reducing it to nothingness until in a final gasp of agony she fell to the floor and was overcome by one of her attacks, her face contorting itself into a hundred hag grimaces, the witch of a thousand nightmares rising up to curse her life over and over, spitting venom from her sulfur-filled mouth, the teeth like a viper's and the eyes like red-hot coals.

As Fawn sat on the roof, she again saw the visions of horror that at times threatened to choke her and she again reached down and squeezed the cursed yinandyango, wanting to kill it, disintegrate the power which kept her at all times focused on its ugliness, on its spongy redness; its image ever present except when she was playing music, and now that was impossible because everyone was going one way and she wasn't included; everybody had somebody who loved them, and even Caitlin, caught up in the game, talked about her boyfriend Ricky in school, while she was utterly alone, her only companion the yinandyango. As the visions of hell and burning grew in intensity, she again thought of going to the edge of the roof but thought better of it and sat gripping the bench with her hands at her sides. And when the visions began to ebb away she lay on the planking of the roof garden which she had helped construct, the failing light shrouding her despair, and again cried quietly and more profoundly, knowing she could never be happy.

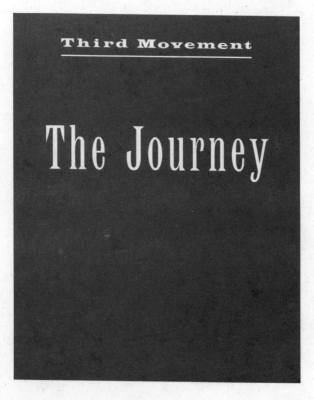

Third Movement

The Journey

43 The Four Horsemen of Avenue B

If you ever saw them together, which people in Alphabet City couldn't help doing, since the four spent every waking hour and some sleeping ones in each other's company, you would come to the incontrovertible conclusion that in their case civilization had gone astray in its socialization process and, having deviated so drastically, perhaps ought to have stopped by the side of the road to make amends and give them, as would a benevolent welfare system, rudimentary instructions on behavior among members of the human race. Ranging in age from fourteen to twenty-two, they were called Papo, Pepe, Pipo, and Pupi. You could as easily call them Famine, Pestilence, Destruction, and Death or Faminapo, Pestilenpe, Destructipo, and Deafpi, since the LC (linguistically correct) pronunciation of the Ricans in this part of the planet isn't *death* but *def*, just as *health* becomes *helf*, and *breath* becomes *bref*, as in: "Man, I jumped into the pool and held my bref almost two minutes before I came up." Rejoinder: "Man, you're one crazy mothafucka. That ain't helfy, bro."

It is generally accepted that the quantification of cerebral capacity isn't always the most productive measure of intelligence. Most tests of this nature do not take into consideration cunning, criminality, Machiavellian design, and other demonstrations of evil. In the case of the four horsemen of Avenue B, it is safe to say that their individual intelligence quotients averaged about 80, a score reflective of low-level rote learning and perhaps some expertise on the comings and goings of Bullwinkle Moose. When together for the purposes of evil, however, said young men became dangerous, capable of mayhem and cold-blooded murder, an activity in which they had indulged on at least one occasion.

The leader of the four was unquestionably Pipo, an eighteen-year-old the size of an underfed poodle-terrier mix with a heart so cold that rather than ventricles his *corazón* had ice-cube trays. His eyes, veiled by an ever-present anger, had lost all semblance of trust or any glimmer of hope. This condition came about at the age of four, when his mother's boyfriend, Big Yuyo, a bi-coastal type, pried Pipo's mouth open for the express purpose of introducing him to the pleasures of fellatio, thus making him his special *puto*. When Pipo reacted negatively to Yuyo's advances, Yuyo convinced his recruit otherwise with an assortment of well-placed blows to the face and head.

Big Yuyo was eventually shot in a bad drug deal, but the experience of being violated left Pipo with a sense of outrage concerning the human race. The outrage took the form of a seething anger which kept his own meager and underdeveloped organ erect and in miniature priapic splendor, yearning for release.

Eventually, his alcoholic mother became the recipient of this rage, for he had intuited subconsciously that she had, albeit unwittingly, condoned his violation. One Christmas Eve, after a pugilistic encounter in which she had gone fifteen brilliant rounds with Kid Bacardi, only to be KO'd in the last round when she could have at least salvaged a draw by staying on her feet, the fun began. A couple of friends had brought Awilda upstairs and deposited her on the bed. Morning came and thirteen-year-old Pipo had risen to a urinary erection and had seen his mother, Awilda, pantyless, skirt hiked up over her hips and legs spread in pink and black splendor, left in that condition by her girlfriend Petra's husband who had come back up to "make sure she was all right."

Pipo tried waking his mother but she had been seduced by inebriation and caught in a dream in which she was traveling back and forth from a soap opera to the welfare building in a pink subway shuttle staffed by blond American stewardesses and so couldn't hear her son and didn't respond. Availing himself of the sexual training he had acquired from porno movies and magazines provided to him as his birthright, which all citizens of a democratic society must defend lest we lose all our other liberties, he essayed his first encounter with pubic reality.

As was and forever would be his fate, being that he suffered from promptness in this endeavor, he'd thrust harmlessly one or two times into his mother so that you couldn't even truly accuse him of attempting a return to the womb before he was spent. Somewhat physically satisfied, he was once again angry and erect and once again genuflected at the shrine of the Blessed Mother of Bacardi. Luckily, Pipo was incapable of producing any life-giving fluids; knowing nothing had ever emerged from him in his manual explorations but accepting this fact in accordance with his belief that such ejaculations occurred only in the company and within the confines of the female anatomy since now whenever he was finished he was wet; learning eventually that this information was erroneous when he came home one day and wishing to emulate some large-membered screen stud with whom he identified, being that his every waking moment he was pursued by the image of Big Yuyo's enormity in his face, he entered, thrust, withdrew, grabbed his minute, erect member and tried to spray his mother's belly and face while she traveled comfortably through the suburbs of oblivion. Observing a string of zeros appear rapidly from his M&M-size glans, he became angry, released his Pee Wee Herman, and, making a fist of his right hand, pummeled his mother about the cheeks and eyes, causing contusions and welts to appear on her already ravaged face.

Now, at all hours of the day and night as she lay in torporific repose he'd separate her thighs and quickly drive his infantile but erect member into his besotted mater, often combining this pseudo-conjugal activity with the dual enjoyment of a classic "Sylvester the Cat" or "Roadrunner" adventure on television. When his mother, Awilda, became aware that her own son was playing feed the bear on her person, her maternal instincts protested, and while he was out she had a lock put on her bedroom. This action truly enraged Pipo, who now resorted to even more masculine strategies, walking in one day to confront his mother and demand to know who in the fuck she thought she was, scabby bitch that she be, and no more his mother than any other whore in the street, shit.

And with that opening salvo he delivered a perfect right cross to her temple, which stunned her. Grabbing her by the hair, he drove her into her unlocked room and proceeded to rip her clothing until she was naked before him, cowering, and reduced to a whimpering mess of tears, snot, urine, and feces, such was her fear. One would think that such a sight would produce, if not compassion, at least disgust in young Pipo, but nothing could stand before his rage, and, staring at her with lifeless eyes, he ordered his mother to hit the bed and spread. She pleaded for the dignity to be allowed to first cleanse herself, but he insisted on his rights immediately and she complied; shutting her eyes and wishing for death; conflicted as he lay atop her and within her, her maternal circuits awry since she wished to comfort her son but knew that her arms about him were tantamount to approval of this violation and she would have no part of it.

Down at the Sixth Precinct they knew Awilda as a drunk and a whore so that when she complained that her son was beating her up and raping her, the officers laughed and said, "Yeah, yeah, Awilda" and "That's a good one, Awilda." So that oftentimes she wandered the streets, hungry and cold, fearful of going home because of the humiliation and pain that awaited her; after a time growing used to the sexual abuse, but weary of the blows which rained upon her for the most minor of infractions; wondering, of all her sins, what particular offense she had committed to cause God to punish her in this way.

This use and misuse of his mother was kept a secret from Pipo's partners. If they knew they would've found a way to rationalize it, much as they rationalized their own brutality and heartlessness, but Pipo didn't reveal his secret to the others, because they would have wanted to have a go at her, too, and what person in his right mind was going to allow somebody to fuck his mother? That would've been too much. In any case, he was sure they would rather spend their time by recalling films they'd seen up on Forty-second Street, or programs they'd seen on television, particularly cartoons. Sometimes they remembered an especially horrifying experience, laughing and slapping hands at the details of the adventure.

They still recalled the time last summer when they picked out, at random, a fifty-seven-year-old expert in the preparation of egg foo young, sweet and sour pork, and moo goo gai pan who worked at the Golden Dragon Restaurant on Mott Street, and trailed him as he made his way up from his place of employment, across the Bowery and up Chrystie, carrying the ubiquitous translucent pink plastic bag, which held food for his cancerous wife, Mai Ling, whom nightly he would feed and console, telling her he wasn't ashamed of their childless marriage, recalling their miserable life in Hong Kong, but here at least they had been happy, even if they lived in such a small place. Poor Huang, hurrying through the night, knowing fate followed him, but little could be done, headed home to his second-floor apartment and sad, delicate Mai Ling, who had been a true beauty in her youth. It didn't matter that she had no fortune with children, though he knew she would have been wonderful with them. He moved with little steps, his legs hurting from standing all day.

Two more blocks and he'd be home—and then they were upon him, silent and mean, their arms around his neck so that he couldn't breathe; the Cantonese words of outrage and violation pouring out of his brain, but no sounds coming from his mouth, as Papo, who was the youngest but the biggest of the four, his left eye slightly crossed, squeezed his larynx with his forearm, bending his head back so that if one were watching this on celluloid, one would've held his breath hoping the actor upon whom this outrage was being perpetrated would be able to walk away unharmed since the back of Huang's head was nearly touching his back. The other three had already gone through his pockets, removing forty-five dollars, two lottery tickets, some change, and his keys. But Papo, fourteen and wishing to prove himself among his partners in crime, felt a great desire to learn whether what he had seen in that spy movie was really true and was it possible to have this trashy-smelling *chino* acquire a permanently damaged spinal cord by forcing his head back as far as it could go. No more than thirty seconds elapsed from the time the pack struck until Papo's desired effect took place and he heard the neck snap as if he were breaking a brittle stick across his raised knee. Huang's body went immediately into spasmodic shock and his bladder and intestines began to emit their contents, causing Papo to immediately drop him and, at the urging of the others, take flight, hearing Pupi or Pipo or Pepe yelling not to forget the food.

Later, when they had run along Houston, splitting up as they hit First Avenue and meeting up again in Tompkins Square Park to partake of Mai Ling's dinner, slandering dead Huang because there was no pork fried rice or ribs, which was the extent of their knowledge of Chinese cuisine, they decided in a 4–0 landmark decision that "Da fuckin' *chino* deserved it, even if Papo had kilt him, and whatnot."

They were genuinely mean, these four. To this day, Marcos, who saw the four defiling Pupi's seventeen-year-old retarded cousin, Sandra, cannot talk about the experience without shuddering and cursing them. Marcos had been hit by a car while crossing Houston Street when he was nine years old. He was now forty and existed seated in a wheelchair, reading detective and science-fiction novels, the formulaic sameness of the fare narcotizing to his mind. Beneath mundane propriety Marcos lived a secret life of self-provided pleasure. Ugly and loveless, he contented himself with watching other apartments from his bedroom at his sister Lucy's fourteenth-floor projects apartment near Thirteenth Street and Avenue D. Seated in his wheelchair, he used powerful binoculars mounted on a tripod to study the human condition, in particular, the goings and most certainly the comings in nearby Stuyvesant Town, which, having been built in the forties, was not wired for air-conditioning, such that in the summertime, residents do whatever they can to stay cool, often parading themselves in denuded splendor.

Although a great many of the residents were too elderly to draw even the slightest glance from Marcos, there were young women and couples who, unaware of this distant but persistent observer, pleasured themselves and each other, allowing Marcos to find satisfaction in the expert use of various thick lumberjack socks filled with Noxzema—which he diligently washed and hung up nightly—no fewer than twelve to fifteen times in a twenty-four-hour period.

Marcos didn't limit his rounds to Stuyvesant Town, for he had access to a number of tenements in the area. Most of the time it wasn't worth the bother, since the people in the area guarded their privacy and lowered the shades. Once in a while there was some crazy, drugged-up, white hippie girl who walked around naked, and that was cool. Most of the time it was dull as hell, except when there was a family dispute, and then he'd shift his binoculars from one room of the watched apartment to another, observing as a child was chased by a parent or a wife by a husband; enjoying the action and the culmination of the drama as the parent or husband cornered his or her prey and struck without mercy.

One spring day around one in the afternoon he was making a cursory sweep through the tenements when he observed four young dudes undressing a girl. This was going to be a classic gang bang, something he had yet to observe in nearly twenty years of patient reconnoitering. Although the scene caused him to become thoroughly excited, what took place next made him nauseous.

What transpired was that Pupi's aunt Gertrudis had to go to Puerto Rico because her grandmother was sick, and so she left her oldest daughter, Marta, to take care of her sister Sandra, who was retarded. Marta, who worked at the Con Edison offices on Fourteenth Street, saw no problem with this. It was simple. Marta would come back to the apartment on her lunch hour to check on Sandra. She did this the first couple of days, but then her girlfriend Conchi, who worked for Citibank, said that this guy Robert at work really liked her, and she really liked Frank, who was the assistant manager, so why didn't the four of them and Lillian Pacheco, who was engaged to her Italian guy, who worked for the cable company in their accounting department, go over to one of those cute restaurants on Irving Place? Anyway, Robert was cute and he looked like he was from P.R. even though he was from Chile or Peru or one of those weird South American countries where they rode around on them giraffe-looking animals and wore pointy hats with the strings hanging from them. Since her cousin Pupi was just hanging out and not going to school, she asked him if he could kind of keep an eye on Sandra and gave him a set of keys, and started hanging out with Conchi and her crew at lunch time, never suspecting that Pupi was part of this twisted quartet of perverted junior executives of evil.

Sandra was retarded but she wasn't no Mongolian *boba*, as the double-negative parlance of the people went. She was just slow, couldn't read, and always wanted to talk about dopey things like songs, singing a couple of lines, then going on to something else, repeating things like "Michael Landon is so cute" or "Kojak *es muy feo*. He's too ugly." She could take a bath, comb her hair, get dressed, and fix herself cold cereal, except that she put too much sugar in the cereal and her teeth were rotting because she didn't like brushing them; and she could make sandwiches and pour herself a glass of soda, but beyond that she was useless, barely able to remember anything from one minute to the next. If you told her to clear the dishes from the table and put them in the sink, she would put one dish in the sink and when you turned around she was looking out the window, or turning the pages of a magazine. One thing she liked doing was playing games, especially made-up games that didn't have too many rules and didn't require her to remember much, like "Let's pretend we're a train, so put your hands on my hips and here we go."

Cross-eyed Papo's brother, who dealt a little bit of *coca*, had a Doberman to watch the house, but since he was up half the night hanging out, he slept in the daytime and paid Papo twenty dollars every day to walk Simbad twice, because if Simbad wasn't walked he wouldn't go in the apartment, but he would bark and bark until you took him outside. Simbad was a monster Dobie, not mean but big and crazy-looking, so that just to see him coming in your general direction made you scared.

So one day the homeboys were hanging out on the stoop of Pupi's aunt Gertrudis's building when here comes Papo with Simbad and they all start messing around and talking about the flick they had seen with this guy that came all over the chick's face and:

"Wasn't that a bitch?"

"All in her face and whatnot."

High-five, high-five, high-five, slap-slap-slap-slap, goof, goof, goof, slap-slap-slap.

"Man, all in her face and shit."

"Word, man."

So talking about all this stuff and remembering the film made the four horny. As usual, they talked about sticking it to that one or the other, but since none of them had ever done it with a woman, except for Pipo, who hit on his mother regularly, the only thing they did was brag about having done it, which they individually knew was bull while collectively they upheld having made it with at least a hundred bitches each.

When Pupi saw Simbad resting on the sidewalk, his tongue hanging out and his pointy pink *pingo* sticking out, he said he had heard about horses doing it to women.

"You crazy, man," Pipo said. "What da fuck are you talking about? A horse? Did you ever see a horse's dick? I was up by Central Park one time with my cousin, Agustín, looking to bust somebody and get some cash for shit, and these bitches were riding horses and they got off and this horse took a piss and he had a *pingo* da size of your arm. How in da fuck is a horse gonna do it to some bitch, homeboy? Da shit come out of da bitch's mouth and whatnot, man."

"Some dude tole me," Pupi said. "It was a little horse, not them big police mothafuckas."

"Oh, you fulla shit, homeboy," Papo said. "No woman can take a big ole horse's *pingo*. They be having trouble with mine, man, so how they gonna fuck a horse?"

They kept arguing and getting more excited till one thing led to another and who knows which of the four thought of it but they ended up in Pupi's aunt Gertrudis's apartment, and Sandra was there eating Sugar Pops with gobs of sugar and she said, "Hi, boys," and asked if that was their dog, even though she had seen Simbad a hundred times. They laughed and said yeah, this was their dog and did she want to play a game.

Sandra said yeah and glommed the last of her Sugar Pops and stood up. She said she was ready, so they told her she should come out into the living room. When she got there Pupi explained to his cousin Sandra that they had to play like babies and they had to take their clothes off. Sandra shook her head, but Pupi said if she didn't want to play then they'd have to go. Sandra got all sad and said okay but not in the living room because people don't get undressed in the living room. They asked where and she said the bedroom. So in they went, and when she was undressed they scoped on her and she was fine and whatnot with big *tetas* and her *bollo*, her *crica* all hairy and black and shiny and they all wanted to touch her but there was something that kept them from doing so.

Finally one thing led to another and Papo, Pepe, and Pipo agreed that since Sandra was Pupi's cousin, he was the one that's got to get Simbad ready. Pupi said no fucking way, so Pipo, who knew what was going to happen when the whole thing got started and he wasn't about to take out his own *pingo* for these mothafuckas to laugh at when nothing came out, said they was punk faggots and he'd do it and he grabbed Simbad down there and started stroking and Simbad's *pingo* got tremendous and it had a *güevo*, a knot, in it. When Sandra saw this she started to laugh and asked if the dog had two tongues. They said it was like a lollipop and did she want to lick it. She shook her head. But then they told her that Simbad liked playing horsey and did she want to play that. She said yeah, so they held Simbad and she got on him and they held her up and they walked her around with her titties bouncing around and everything.

This went on for a little bit and then they said that Simbad wanted to play horsey and could he get on her, so she got down on her knees and put her hands on the floor and they helped Simbad up on her and before you knew it Pipo had Simbad's thing in Sandra and now Simbad was going at it and poor, retarded Sandra, felt what was going on but she was having so much fun watching the other three boys with their red things out like the doggie and going back and forth over them with their hands and then they were over her and she could feel stuff falling on her face and on her back and then the doggie was really grabbing her and she felt this pain in her stomach that made tears come to her eyes but she wasn't crying.

When they were done they made her take a shower and get dressed and said it was all part of the game. They mopped everything up and everything was fine except for the fact that Simbad's thing wouldn't go down and it just hung there and Simbad looked all confused and whatnot so Pipo said he heard that it took a dog's *pingo* about two hours to go down so they turned on the television and watched cartoons on cable and Sandra came out of the shower and got dressed and ate some more cereal and then came and sat down with them to watch cartoons until Simbad's *pingo* went down.

Marcos watched the whole thing, but even he couldn't enjoy what he had seen. Worse off, he didn't know what to do about it. He thought he should call the police, but he was ashamed of having them find out he was a peeping Tom. He also recognized one of the boys and knew that his brother was a drug dealer and there was no telling what they would do to him if he ratted them out. It wasn't like the time the man had been threatening a woman with a knife. He had called the police then, but by the time the police came the guy had calmed down and nothing happened.

When Simbad was back to normal, the *Posse of the Pingo*, as they would now call themselves, went back downstairs like nothing happened. When Papo brought Simbad back, his brother, Frankie Cabeza, who had a really big head, thus the name, was up and feeling nasty as a mothertrucker. He did a line, fixed himself some *café con leche* and bread and butter, and began calling his boys on the cellular. Cabeza, when he saw Papo walk in with Simbad, wanted to know where the fuck you been, you fucking retard. It's four o'clock in the afternoon. And Papo said that Simbad didn't want to go, so he'd had to walk him all the way down to Houston and the Drive. Simbad went and sniffed around his food dish, drank water from the toilet bowl, and then sat on the couch, licking his red, pointy *pingo*.

So this was the nature of these four, except that not having a go at a real woman was beginning to annoy them, and one day as they were roaming the neighborhood, Papo, the young man who had snapped Huang's neck, spotted Fawn Singleton Farrell, now blossoming into a delicate young woman, too shy and frightened of herself, and recalled that he had been in the fourth grade with her and she lived down by Eldridge in some big old factory building where hippie white people lived and wasn't she a fine-looking little bitch.

44 Economics

One afternoon, exhausted by the problem of her credit-card debt, and her resolve to find a way of repaying it, which in the end was a matter of pride more than necessity, Vidamía stepped away from the obsession and called her sister to ask what else was going on. Cookie was relieved that Vidamía had stopped focusing on the problem. She told Vidamía she didn't even feel like going to school anymore since she had announced to everybody at the school that she was going to reaudition to get into the drama department but hadn't made it, and now going to school every day and having to face them all felt like hell. Vidamía said she was sure the drama department had made one huge mistake in turning her down.

Cookie said she was taking acting classes right there in the East Village, at a place called Medicine Show on Second Street. They had workshops and maybe she'd do a small part as a mermaid in this thing they were putting together about a nun and a clown. It was super funny and very sexy. The role called for her to seduce the main character, who had this big *coso* that whistled.

"She's a mermaid. *Una sirena.* And that's like an omen. Cause you know I'm gonna become a movie siren. I'ma make me some movies."

"Are you really serious about acting?"

"Damn right I'm serious."

"I'm glad you changed your mind. What about your music?"

"I can keep doing that, but I wanna be an actress. I know I can do it. I met someone who has a cousin at NYU Film School and he's gonna ask the guy if he has a part for me."

They went on talking a little longer and then said goodbye. After Vidamía hung up the phone, she turned the radio back up, lay back on the bed, closed her eyes, and listened to the lyrics of Bruce Springsteen's "Born in the U.S.A." What was made in the U.S.A.? The people? He? Mr. Fox, her history teacher, said the U.S. had fallen back in almost every aspect of manufacturing and that the Japanese had an edge in automobile and electronic-equipment manufacturing because the people cared about their work. Valerie Perkins, whose father was a lawyer down on Wall Street, backed up the teacher and said the U.S. was in decline because it had been built on the basis of crisis and that in its history of 213 years, from 1776 to the present, it had engaged in over 160 wars, conflicts, and skirmishes within and without its own borders and that whenever there was war the U.S. did fine, but that it didn't seem to handle a peace economy too well. Valerie's mother was an antiwar activist and had chained herself to a fence when they began building nuclear submarines in Groton, Connecticut, when she was a student at Smith.

When Springsteen's song was over, Vidamía turned off the radio and sat up. What was it about that discussion of products made in the U.S.A. that kept bothering her? She went downstairs, put on her down jacket, retrieved a flashlight from the pantry, and told Mrs. Alvarez that she was going for a walk.

Mrs. Alvarez told her she shouldn't go far. Vidamía said she was just going to walk to the edge of the property and back. She zipped up her jacket and let herself out by the back door with Beanbag, the family's golden retriever, following her.

It was cold for September. Her hands stuck deep into her pockets, she walked down the path away from the backyard to the small replica of the house which her mother had a carpenter build for Vidamía, explaining that well-off families in Puerto Rico built such structures on the property for the young daughters to play in. She went there whenever she needed to think things out. These days she could reach the top of the roof if she stood on tiptoes. Inside it was just one room with a little table and chairs where she and her friends used to play. She opened the door, heard a bit of scurrying, and thought perhaps she was disturbing a chipmunk or a squirrel family nesting there. She shined the light into the house and sat on one of the small chairs. Beanbag sniffed around and lay down next to her. She had played office with her friends. She wouldn't permit them to play house. And no boys were ever allowed in her office. She was very silent, listening to the early evening.

Then suddenly an idea hit her. She realized that the United States' best export was its culture, especially its music and movies. Nathan Davenport, whose father was a film editor—she saw his name in film credits from time to time—had brought up the point. So sudden was her movement and departure from the little house that Beanbag barked loudly several times and tried jumping on her, excited by whatever it was that Vidamía was feeling. That was it, she thought, as she ran back to the house and up the stairs to her room, Beanbag panting as he followed her. She had to call Cookie.

She could hardly talk when Cliff answered the phone and said he was on the other line. She told him to have Cookie call her back.

"Tell her it's urgent, Cliff," pleaded Vidamía.

"I can hang up and call my friend later."

"No, no. Everything's okay. Just tell Cookie I gotta talk to her, please."

For the next twenty minutes she paced up and down her room, went downstairs three times, drank water, ate carrot sticks, turned on the radio, turned off the radio, tried reading, but nothing could take her mind off the subject. Movies. That was it. After the one on Delancey Street had collapsed, the only movie theater left on the Lower East Side was on Grand Street. When Cookie finally called back, Vidamía blurted out some question about video that Cookie didn't understand.

"Girl, what language are you talking?" Cookie said. "Slow down, mama."

"A video store, Cookie? Is there one in the neighborhood?"

"A video store?"

"Yeah, yeah. Is there one in the neighborhood?"

"Around here? I don't think so."

"How about over in Alphabet City?"

"I don't know. I can't remember. Is that why you called me?"

"Yeah. I wanna know if there's one around there."

"Why do you wanna know? You want me to check out a movie?"

"No, I think I got an idea for opening up a store."

"A video store?"

"Yeah."

"How? With what money, girl?"

"I don't know. I'll figure it out. I don't know how but I'll be there late Friday afternoon."

"Good, cause I was gonna call you about a thing on Saturday."

"Put me on the list."

"Okay, I gotta go. Lover boy is telling me my time's up. He's got this hot thing going with some *pendeja* Barbie doll in the drama department. Your brother, and I stress *your* brother, because I don't claim him anymore, has turned out to be a class-A traitor. He dares to date some airhead in the drama department of the La Guardia High School for the Disgusting Arts."

Vidamía laughed as she heard Cookie and Cliff scuffling like they were still little.

On Friday, after she got home from school, she packed a bag, called a cab, wrote a note for her mother, kissed Mrs. Alvarez goodbye, and left for New York. She spent the weekend going into video rental stores in Manhattan, bugging the managers regarding inventory, rental fees, cards, and the minimum capital needed to open a store from scratch. Anywhere from $15,000 to $25,000 for a moderate place with an inventory of maybe 2,000 films, which, one guy told her, was not a lot of films. "You want at least five thousand films, plus someone who can get you the latest films right away," the man said. "Clean copies, not pirated ones." She and Cookie met Mario and Wyndell and they had Japanese food at New Tokyo on University Place. The three agreed that Vidamía seemed abstracted and wasn't being very pleasant or communicative.

Wyndell was going out of town, and once he realized that she was still concerned about paying the money back, he hugged her and told her not to worry, that she'd figure it out. He kissed her almost like a big brother, so that when she was on the train heading back to Tarrytown on Sunday afternoon, she worried that he'd drift away from her. He was so beautiful and open and he really liked her. But the problem of the money bothered her. What was she going to do? She already owed nine thousand dollars and in order to open the store she was going to need about twenty. She wasn't even eighteen and she was going to be $30,000 in debt. By the time she got home she was totally depressed. When she got out of the cab, she looked in her bag for her keys to the front door and couldn't find them. She rang the doorbell but apparently everyone had gone off somewhere. Beanbag whined at the front door and then came out through his door in the kitchen and banged himself against her leg happily. She petted his head, went around to the back, found the key to the kitchen door in the garage, and let herself in. As she turned on the light in the hall outside the kitchen, she tripped on a pile of newspapers and went tumbling, with Beanbag all over her, licking her face and bouncing up against her. She wrestled with him, feeling his hot breath as he growled and licked her face. "Oh, you're so tough, aren't you? Tough guy, right? Beanbag the gangster dog." They were rolling around on the newspapers when she saw it next to her face: BUSINESS OPPORTUNITIES. "Stop, stop," she pawed at Beanbag with her hands. Beanbag thought it was part of the game until she stood up and yelled at him to stop, which startled the dog. "Sorry, Beanbag," she said, and the *New York Times* classifieds section in hand, she dashed upstairs.

She went up and down the column several times until her eyes fixed on a certain little ad. "Entire inventory of video rental store, $10,000. Computer already programmed with inventory; 4,000 titles, shelves, etc." And a telephone number somewhere on Long Island. Her heart was pounding violently. There it was. This was their store. But how?

Two weeks went by and she was going crazy trying to figure out how she was going to pull this off. And then on Monday of the third week as she was walking from social studies, where they had been discussing the economic system of capitalist countries, to go to English, it hit her. Barry. She'd get a loan from Barry or maybe ask him to go into business with her until she could pay all the money back. That night she waited until her mother had gone to bed and Barry was still downstairs watching a television program.

"I'm sorry to disturb you, Barry. I have to ask you something."

"That's okay," he said.

"Barry, could I come and see you tomorrow in your office?"

"Is everything all right?"

"Yeah, fine. I just need to talk to you. But not in the house."

"I can't this week. I'm going out of town. I'll be back Sunday evening late. But next week is fine. Let me check." He went to his desk and looked at his calendar and nodded. "Tuesday is fine. Sure, come on down. Around twelve. We can have lunch."

"Please don't tell *mami*, okay? I'll have to miss school."

The weekend that Barry was away she came down to Billy and Lurleen's, and during Saturday and part of Sunday before she returned home, she and Cookie spent nearly the entire time looking at storefronts in the East Village and calling numbers to speak to brokers and landlords. Cookie was not convinced that opening a store was a good idea. After a while, seeing Vidamía's determination, she began to feel the same enthusiasm, but they came up with nothing. On Monday, Cookie called early in the morning and said she'd found a place and could she skip school to come and see it. Cookie suggested they meet at the Odessa on Avenue A, at around ten a.m. When Vidamía was dropped off by Elsa at school, she waited until her mother was gone, placed her books in her locker, left school, and took the train into Manhattan. They looked at the store on Avenue C. It was perfect. It had been a clothing store that went nearly eighty feet from front to back.

The following morning, Barry and Elsa were gone by seven-thirty and Vidamía was to be picked up by a friend. She called her friend and told her she wasn't feeling well. Instead of going to school, she called a cab and got on the train. She was at Barry's office around eleven-thirty, dressed very elegantly in a pants suit and a long black coat with matching black shoes and bag. To the unstudied eye she could have been an executive in her early twenties. Her voice was strong but her manner extremely polite, firm without being demanding and seductive without being sexual.

When she walked into Barry's new offices she told the receptionist her name and said she was there to see her father. As she waited for the okay to go in, she hoped she'd be able to explain her idea clearly. The young woman smiled and said, "Please go in, Mr. López-Ferrer is waiting for you." She opened the door and stepped inside. His office was huge, the view overlooking Midtown Manhattan from the forty-fifth floor spectacular. To the west, she could see the Hudson River and its piers. In the distance, the anchored ships looked like toy boats. One wall of the office was covered with awards and plaques. Another wall was devoted to pictures of Barry with Governor Cuomo, Mayor Koch, and one where he stood flanked by Bronx Borough President Fernando Ferrer on one side and Congressman José Serrano on the other. There were pictures with Ruben Blades, Reggie Jackson, Gloria Estefan, Andy García, and a dozen other celebrities, all of them personally autographed to him.

On another wall there were pictures of his family depicting different scenes from her childhood: birthday parties; trips on the cabin cruiser; camping in Canada; bullfights in Sevilla; riding bicycles in the Netherlands.

"You look great, Vidamía," he said, standing up as she entered.

"Thank you," she replied, smiling at him and going back behind the desk to kiss him.

They ate lunch at a Spanish restaurant in the fifties. She ordered shrimp and a salad and had mineral water, speaking Spanish very correctly as her mother and Mrs. Alvarez had taught her, not imitating Spaniards, but pronouncing all her R's. She explained the idea to Barry, showed him the ad for the video-store equipment; it had appeared again that past Sunday. She said that they could open the store right away and Cookie and Cliff could begin working there after school. When summer came they'd work extra hard and the way she figured it, they could pay the nine thousand dollars within a year and the other ten from the loan the following year.

"I heard you say once at dinner that if you made adequate

preparations, had a good product, advertised, and subsequently worked hard, anybody could be a success, and that's what we're determined to do."

"Do you have a place?" Barry inquired.

"Yes, and the owner says he can hold it for us for a month. The rent's only a thousand, but we have to do the renovation. Mickey Fuentes's father said he could do all the work—the floor and everything—for less than a thousand, including materials. All he's really gotta do is put up a wall and cover the other walls with masonite. That's what he said. Mickey's one of Cookie's girlfriends. An investment," she said, calmly. "You put up the capital and share the profits."

"I'm the major investor," he said, slightly amused by the conversation.

"That's correct," she said.

"My initial outlay is going to be twenty thousand dollars."

"We only need ten."

"By the time we get certificates, permits, fire and theft insurance, and create the business it'll be twenty, maybe a little more. But what are you offering me besides a tax write-off?"

"Does that mean, if the business fails, you get to declare a loss?"

"Exactly."

"Well, it won't," she said, firmly, smiling at him. "Cookie and I talked about it and you can have fifty percent of all profits after expenses."

"Fifty?" Barry said, laughing.

"That's not enough?" she said nervously.

"No, no," Barry said, putting up his hands. "I'll take the fifty. Whose name will the store be under? You're too young."

"Cookie's mother's," Vidamía said quickly.

"Have you discussed it with her?" Barry asked.

"Oh, yeah," Vidamía said confidently, lying through her teeth.

"Where do we have to go to get the equipment?" Barry said, chuckling.

"New Hyde Park on Long Island," she said, showing him the ad again.

"Okay, I'll call him up and set something up for next Saturday. I'll have to invent something for your mother, but you have to promise to be nice to her. She's a wreck these days. She's got a lot on her mind."

"You have my word, Barry," she said.

"Good. You make your plans. I'll announce that I'm going in, and you ask for a ride. We'll go to Long Island and look at the stock, and then check out the place in the East Village. I have a friend who knows about this kind of equipment so he can help us out."

She went back to Tarrytown on a cloud and that night called Cookie to tell her it was done.

"Get ready for the big time, homeslice," she said. "We're gonna do it."

Everything went according to schedule, except that one of Barry's friends told him that the entire stock was worth at best six thousand dollars and not the ten the owner was asking. Barry offered five. The guy said forget it, that they were trying to rob him. Barry looked at him, put out his hand and said he was sorry to have taken up his time. He turned to go and the guy said seven. Barry stopped and came back.

"Listen, you seem pretty honest," he said. "I'll give you fifty-seven hundred and that's it."

"C'mon, buddy. You're ripping out my heart. Six thousand."

Barry said he should prepare a bill of sale. He wrote a check to be cashed in thirty days.

"By that time we'll have the place ready. We'll come up and get the items," Barry said, extending his hand. "It could be sooner. If so, we'll call you. I can write you out a new check."

They returned to New York, looked at the prospective store,

Barry spoke with Mickey Fuentes's father, Ray, and explained what he should do, telling him he wanted nothing but the best materials and a new floor put in, pointing out a couple of places that needed reinforcement.

"I don't want any lawsuits," Barry said.

"No lawsuits," Ray Fuentes said. "Who's gonna run the store?" he asked.

"My daughter," Barry said, pointing his chin at Vidamía and winking at her.

"Oh, yeah," Ray said. "She's friends with my kid, Migdalia—Mickey. She and the blond kid. That's her half sister, right?"

"Yeah, something like that," Barry said.

When they were done with the details for the store's renovation, they went to a diner. Vidamía called Cookie at work, told her where she and Barry were. As they were ordering, Cookie, who'd gotten off from work, came in. The girls kissed and embraced and high-fived and squealed. Cookie was ecstatic and thanked Barry effusively, throwing her arms around him and kissing him, leaving a big red imprint of her lips on his cheek.

"We're going to make you proud of us," she said.

"I hope so," Barry said.

"Don't worry. There isn't a video store for blocks and people are going to come to the place cause everybody's gonna know our store."

"Do you have a name?" Barry asked.

"Yeah, but it's a secret," Vidamía said. "When you come to the opening you'll see."

"I need to know for the official paperwork," Barry said.

"Okay, okay, but it's a secret," Cookie said, and told him.

They explained that they had two names, one that began with Vidamía's name and the other with Cookie's, and then they told him what they were.

"Why not use them both?" he said.

"Vidco Comía?" Vidamía said.

"No, the other way around," Barry said.

"Comía Vidco," Cookie said. "I get it. It sounds like a place you go to eat. *Comía*, like we say down here, even though it's *comida*. Food. Wow."

"Wait, wait," Vidamía said. "Couldn't we put soda machines and one of those machines for selling potato chips and peanuts?"

"Sure," Barry said. "You could also put in game machines. They can bring in cash."

So it was done. In early November, they opened the store. Vidamía and Cookie cut the ribbon, and Barry was in attendance. He even brought one of the New York Giants football players, and although everybody made a big deal out of his being there, Vidamía had no idea who he was. There were two photographers taking pictures.

The sign above the store was tremendous—bright colors in the day and well illuminated at night. *Comía Vidco*. Cookie and Vidamía. Vidamía and Cookie.

"It sounds like a video-store restaurant," Gloria Marcano had said when Cookie asked her to paint the blank sign sitting inside the store two weeks before it opened.

"Draw a real deft homegirl watching TV and eating, mama."

"I don't know," Gloria said.

"How much we paying Gloria, Vee?"

Vidamía held up two fingers, shook her head, then held up three.

"Three hundred *cocos*, mama. I'm sure you can paint us a real heavy sign for three bills. It ain't like you Frida Kahlo yet. And I ain't saying you ain't gonna be the most incredible artist ever. Notice I didn't say nothing about woman artist. Or Rican artist. We ain't trying to exploit your talent and whatnot. You down, mama?"

"I guess so," Gloria said, smiling sheepishly.

Gloria went to work and quickly made a preliminary sketch. She spent most of the day painting so that not until the light began to disappear did she step back to admire her work. In very brilliant blues, yellows, oranges, and greens she had painted this busty Rican homegirl watching TV and eating an enormous plate of rice and beans with *chuletas y tostones*. The TV screen had a good cartoon likeness of Cookie and Vidamía handing the viewer a videotape. Mickey drew up a flyer, which they got printed at a copy store for another fifty dollars and then paid a couple of squatters to paste up all over the neighborhood.

For the next two weeks, as Thanksgiving approached, both sisters poured themselves into the work. When it was obvious that the business was taking off, Cookie quit her waitressing job and with some of her friends from the neighborhood helping her, began to spend more time at the store. They worked long hours and people were constantly in and out, renting videos. So exhausting was the routine that, after finishing Thanksgiving dinner, when she lay on the floor to watch television at the Farrells', Vidamía fell asleep and didn't wake up until ten in the evening. She ate a slice of pumpkin pie, drank a glass of milk, brushed her teeth, and went to bed. It was like she had been hit on the head. Within seconds she was asleep again.

45 Tumba Santiago

Vidamía visited her grandmother before Palm Sunday and brought her a beautiful bonnet and matching handbag, "just in case you want to march in the parade next Sunday, *güela*." Observing her thin white face and high cheekbones, which her mother said she had inherited, for the first time in her life she mentally classified Ursula as a white Puerto Rican instead of simply her grandmother. The awareness disturbed her. Granted, being with Wyndell had made her even more conscious of

African-Americans, but she was certain that she was being negatively affected by her heightened awareness of the black-white issue. Up to now she had barely focused on people's skin color, but now she was too conscious of the differences and it bothered her. She was also certain, however, that in spite of her mother's attitudes and fears, it would make no difference to her if she had black relatives. In fact, the more she thought about it, the more she hoped she had dozens. It was confusing because she was certain that her mother had hang-ups about race, and she wanted to confront her with the truth. Nothing would give her greater pleasure than to be able to say to her mother that they were both related to Mr. Haley's ancestors, and to other great black Americans such as Harriet Tubman, Sojourner Truth, Martin Luther King, Jr., Frederick Douglass, and hundreds more. She was aware that she was being idealistic, even romantic, but that is how she felt. She knew that she had to find her own link to Africa, and from all indications, her grandfather, Tumba Santiago, seemed to be it. The stuff with the drums was too much of a coincidence for her to ignore. Last year there was Wyndell with his mother's friend's poem, and now this stranger who was related to her and who she suspected was not white and was a drummer, a *conguero*, a *tumbadero* or *tumbero*, this Puerto Rican grandfather who would finally prove whether Mr. Wyndell Ross was right or wrong.

One would imagine that with not much to go on, frustration would set in and Vidamía's mind would begin to unravel. But we aren't talking about your garden-variety *señorita* full of fuzzy-headed notions regarding the comings and goings of fate and destiny. Instead we are referring to a no-nonsense kind of young gal, full of gumption, get-up-and-go, and many super-accelerating gray cells sprinting back and forth in her brain, all of them energized by hybrid vigor, which is a genuine biological phenomenon that comes about when vastly different gene pools combine to produce an individual of superior capacities, the exact opposite of the theory proposed by Herr Adolf Schickelgruber and other racial extremists. In fact, if one had the guts to examine the scientific documentation, one could propound it freely at cocktail parties and church socials and give neo-Nazi lunatics a few more sleepless nights. Because you may think that Herr Schickelgruber is dead, but he is still around, lurking in the shadows of the heads of addle-brained people who live in fear that the white race is going to be wiped out.

Vidamía, being inquisitive, began looking for her grandfather in the best way she could. She asked relatives for photographs of him, but none were forthcoming except for an old faded photo her grandmother showed her. The two people in the photo were young. Ursula Santiago looking nothing like she did now, forty years later. The same thing had to hold true for her grandfather. So Vidamía asked her grandmother for a description and was told that he had dark skin and bad hair. She figured if her grandpa, Tumba Santiago, was a *conguero*, there was no sense looking for him down on Wall Street, or in housewares at Macy's. She decided that her best bet was to ask around in Loisaida. If she asked enough folks, they would tell her where the Latin clubs were, and then she could find out where Tumba Santiago played, and maybe even where he lived. So she made a deal with Lurleen and Cliff to do double shifts at the store for a week while she and Cookie searched for her grandfather.

Vidamía concentrated on moving as fast as possible to find Tumba Santiago. The first thing Vidamía and Cookie did was to go over and visit their friends Yvette Contreras and Christina Texidor on Avenue C. Faced with the question of how to find such a person as her grandfather, they replied that the one person who might shed light on the subject was Yvette's aunt.

Yvette and Christina took Vidamía to see Yvette's aunt, Blanca Contreras, who was about Elsa Santiago's age and checked coats at the Tropicoro. The three of them sat in Blanca's kitchen while Blanca, high as a kite on reefer, chain-smoked Salems and drank Diet Pepsi and told them she had never heard of Tumba Santiago but that the musicians at the clubs might have. And then Blanca reeled off the names of a bunch of clubs, names like El Tropical, Siboney, and Club 96, which Vidamía dutifully wrote down in a small notebook, in her neat script, the address below the club and below that an annotation for the subway line and the stop nearest the club. "You gotta bring ID, and you can't go there looking cheap, cause then they figure you be there hustling like some of these homegirls who don't wanna work for a living and be hanging out at after-hours joints."

"Damn, Titi Blanca!" Yvette said. "What chu think she is?"

"What chu say your name was, honey?" Blanca said, ignoring her niece.

"*Coño*, Titi Blanca," Yvette said. "She tole you already, shit. Her name's Vidamía."

"You don't gotta get nasty, girl," Blanca said, her eyes rolling up into her head as she blew a big cloud of smoke from her pursed lips. "You may be my sister's kid, but that don't give you no right to be getting nasty. What's Josie teaching you?"

"Don't be talking about *mami*, okay?" Yvette shot back.

"Anyways, I was talking to the girl and not to you," Blanca said.

"Dig her," Yvette said, turning to Christina for support. "Just cause Ruben Blades came into the club and kissed her on the cheek one night, she think she a celebrity and whatnot. You must be high," she added, stating the obvious and reminding her aunt that she was aware of her weakness, because, no matter what anyone on the outside thought, not every Puerto Rican in the neighborhood stayed high like her aunt, who maybe had an excuse because her old man was up in Attica doing a bit for blowing away some dudes up in the Bronx, and her kid Felix had died of spinal meningitis.

"Anyways, what did you say, honey?" Blanca asked, leaning over the dinette table and staring through hooded eyes at Vidamía.

"Vidamía Farrell," she answered.

"Vidamía?" Blanca said. And then, it was like a flash went off and her eyes opened up. "Oh, shit, you're Elsa's kid from Rivington, right? Your father was this American dude who was in Vietnam with Joey. You all moved out and we never saw your mother again. How is she?"

"She's fine, thank you," Vidamía said. "I'll tell her you said hello."

"Yeah, tell her I miss her," Blanca said, obviously moved. "You're one gorgeous homegirl. Stand up and let me look at you. Go ahead, don't be shy."

"She ain't no homegirl, Titi Blanca," Yvette said, and she and Christina giggled.

"Go ahead, homegirl," said Christina to Vidamía, "do your shit and whatnot."

Christina and Yvette gave each other high fives and Vidamía stood up, feeling self-conscious because she thought her butt was too big, even though a minute didn't go by that Wyndell wasn't talking about how fine she looked from behind.

"Oh, my God, honey," Blanca said. "You're too much, baby. What a body! *Un cuerpo divino, mamita.* Your waist ain't no bigger than most women's thighs. You should think about modeling or something. God bless you. Your *mami* and me was homegirls together back at Seward Park about fifteen years ago."

"Almost twenty," Yvette said, "cause Vidamía is eighteen, right, Vee?"

"That's right," Vidamía said.

"Let's book, Vee," Yvette said. "C'mon, Christina. Bye, Titi Blanca."

"You gotta go?" Blanca said, disappointed.

"Yeah, I tole *mami* we was gonna be back before six," Yvette said. "See you," she added as she headed out of the kitchen.

"No kiss for your Titi?" Blanca said, her eyes misting. "I'm still your aunt."

"Right," Yvette said and went over and painfully kissed her aunt's cheek and allowed herself to be pecked noisily. "I'm sorry about what I said," Yvette added, half meaning it.

"That's nothing," Blanca said and reached into her pocketbook and gave Yvette a ten-dollar bill. "Buy yourself some ice cream or something down on Mulberry Street."

"Thank you, Titi Blanca," Yvette said, feeling ashamed about how she'd treated her aunt.

It was the beginning of the summer, and for the next three days, Vidamía, accompanied by Yvette and Mickey, the three of them dressed for partying in tight, shiny, low-cut, short dresses and spiked heels, made up delicately but expertly by a cousin of Yvette's who "did hair and paint" for photo shoots, and armed with fake identification and Vidamía's credit cards, traveled from club to club, dancing and sipping mixed drinks, allowing men to dance with them, and generally enjoying the evenings, though getting back down to Loisaida no later than two a.m., as Lurleen had requested of Vidamía. On Saturday, Cookie insisted on going, dressing up in a red party dress and red high heels and pocketbook, her blond hair done up in cornrows. After applying makeup, she adopted a haughty look, cocked her head to the side as if she couldn't be bothered, and turned away from the mirror.

So the four of them went up to Club 96 and walked in and the band almost stopped playing because in walked this tremendous-looking blonde in a red dress and, to a man, they all swore she was some big-time movie star. Being she was only sixteen, and already had a boyfriend, Mario, to whom she was super-loyal, whenever any dude hit on her, the attitude came out and she'd say, "No thank you," or "Thank you very much," but if the guy insisted, she'd say things in this perfect Loisaida patois, "Man, whyntcha get outta my face, okay? Like, I done tole you, right? *Coño!* What *is* with this dude, homegirl?" she'd say, turning to Vidamía or the other two. "Just book, okay, man?" she'd say, turning back to the guy who was by now totally flustered at having this "American" girl not only dissing him terribly but talking "like she been raised by people from P.R., man—from Cataño or Villa Palmeras, or some fucking place like that, shit!"

So eventually, going from one club to the next, Vidamía met a young trumpet player by the name of Tony Betancourt. When there was a break she went over to him and asked him where he went to school and he said he'd studied up in Boston.

"Berklee?" she said, feeling knowledgeable.

"Right," Tony said. "How did you know?"

"Friend of mine," she replied. "Maybe you know him. Wyndell Ross."

"Yeah," he said, smiling real big. "We took classes together. Tenor sax. From out west."

"Denver."

"Yeah, right. I met his pop once. Doctor. Played piano. We jammed together."

They talked for a while, and Vidamía promised to tell Wyndell that they'd met and Tony gave her his number for Wyndell, and then Yvette came over, and right away it was obvious that she and Tony dug each other, but before anything could happen Vidamía got in between them.

"Oh, before I forget," she said, "do you know Tumba Santiago?"

"I don't think so," he said. "Oh, wait. Milton might know. Is he a conga player?" he added, recognizing that if his name was Tumba, it probably came from *tumbadora*, the bass conga drum.

"Yeah," Vidamía said. "He's my grandfather."

"Yo, Milton," Tony said, waving at someone up on the band-stand. "Come here, bro."

A light-skinned Latin young man came over and Tony asked him if it hadn't been a dude named Tumba who had taught him to play. Milton nodded as he eyed the women.

"Yeah, sure, Tumba Santiago," he said, bringing his taped fingers to his nose and pushing it from side to side like it itched. "Lives up on Longwood, if he hasn't moved. Between Fox and Beck. Nine-ninety Longwood, I think. Second floor in front. You know him?"

"Yeah, he's my grandfather," Vidamía said, feeling uncom-fortable, as she always did around people who were heavily into drugs. She took out her notebook and wrote the address down.

"Your grandfather, huh? That's really cool. He's a beautiful dude."

"What train?" Vidamía said.

"Take the six to Longwood Avenue and walk up Longwood. But you should get someone to go with you. I can meet you, if you want."

"No, that's all right," Vidamía said. "I'll get my boyfriend to go with me. Thanks, man."

She went back to working in the store, and the next time she saw Wyndell she told him about finding her grandfather and asked him to go with her to see him. The following Saturday af-ternoon they headed for the Bronx to find Tumba Santiago. It seemed to Vidamía that Wyndell was more nervous about what awaited them than she was. When she wanted to know why he was bringing his saxophone, he snapped at her before explaining that he'd just come from a recording session for a video and didn't want to go back downtown. He apologized immediately and said he felt ashamed that he still had to earn his money from doing dumb videos for crappy songs.

When they got to Longwood Avenue they followed the di-rections Tony Betancourt's friend had provided for her. Once they reached the building there was no way of telling where her grandfather lived. Although there were mailboxes in the lobby, none of them had names on them. There were over thirty apartments in the building.

"What now?" Wyndell said.

"Let's ask at the *bodega*," she said, bounding off the stoop and heading for a small grocery store on the corner, where she asked if anyone knew Tumba Santiago. One very black man who was just leaving the store came back in and addressed her in Spanish.

"Who wants to know?" he said, trying his best to act fierce.

"I do," Vidamía said, answering in Spanish. "I'm his granddaughter. I gotta find him."

"How do I know you're really his granddaughter? What's your mother's name?"

"Elsa."

"And your grandmother?"

"Doña Ursula."

The black man pursed his lips and nodded his head.

"Okay, okay," he said, in a thick accent. "I'm Flaco. Tumba's friend."

Vidamía introduced Wyndell, and Flaco extended his hand. She noted that Flaco was blacker than Wyndell, the skin of his face almost blue. Before they got up to the third floor of the apartment building where Tumba Santiago lived, Flaco was calling out his name and announcing that he was bringing him a surprise. When Tumba Santiago opened the door, he was grinning widely, his gold tooth gleaming on his cocoa–colored face. He was wearing bright red polyester pants, white shoes, and a yellow long-sleeved *guayabera*. He had recently showered and changed and there were several fragrances competing with each other for dominance on his person. Vidamía introduced herself as his granddaughter. The old man nodded approvingly. She then introduced her grandfather to Wyn. Unlike the scene with her father, it almost seemed as if her grandfather had been expecting her. Not once did he question her about her reasons for finding him.

Tumba Santiago ushered them inside, calling behind him to his lady, Panchita. Vidamía walked down the long hall to the living room with the plastic covers and the plaster figurines on the walls and on shelves cheap knickknacks similar to those she'd seen at her girlfriends' apartments in the East Village. Panchita came in and was introduced to everyone. She looked to be about thirty-five years of age, some thirty years younger than Tumba Santiago. Panchita was the color of pumpkin pie, her hair blond, peroxided and processed, her face pretty, if chubby. Her body, also tending toward excess, seemed poured into green slacks that ended a few inches above her ankles and only accentuated her chubbiness. She wore a loose blouse and high heels and was made up heavily. From her earlobes hung enormous, elaborate earrings resembling crystal chandeliers. On either wrist she wore brightly colored bracelets. Over this ensemble she wore an apron.

"You Millie's daughter?" he asked once Vidamía was sitting in an easy chair.

"No, Titi Milagros is my aunt. I'm Elsa's daughter," she said.

"*La americanita*," Panchita said, wiping her hands on the apron, retrieving a handkerchief and wiping the sweat from her forehead. "The one you told me about, Tumba."

"*Sí, sí, pero ella habla español*," her grandfather said, explaining proudly that she spoke Spanish, and, looking at Vidamía, hoped she would prove him right. "*Verdad que sí?*" he said, asking for her assent.

"*Sí, claro que sí. Desde que era chiquita*," Vidamía said, confidently explaining that she'd spoken the language ever since she was a little girl.

"How's your mother?" Tumba asked. "Is she still nervous?"

"Yeah, still nervous, and on top of that, she doesn't know I'm here. Worst than that, she doesn't know that I have a *moreno* boyfriend."

"*Novio*," her grandfather said, offering up the correct word for "boyfriend" in Spanish. He then reassured her that her secret was safe with him.

Vidamía shook her head and said that *novio* sounded like they were getting married. Wyn looked a little lost as they spoke Spanish. Her grandfather smiled proudly, and pointed at Vidamía enthusiastically.

"*Soy muy joven pa' casarme, güelo,*" she said, telling him that she was too young to get married. He laughed and nodded and said he didn't know about that, because she was very *guapa*, very attractive.

"*Tú, güelo. Tú eres el guapo,*" she said, telling him that he was the handsome one.

"You see, Panchita," Tumba said proudly, urging his lady to take notice. "She's not American. She's Puerto Rican. Listen to her," he added, directing Panchita back into the kitchen to finish cooking. A few moments later, Tumba Santiago was talking with his friend Flaco, the two of them arguing in Spanish about which was a better team, the Mets or the Yankees, and pretty much ignoring Vidamía and Wyndell, who watched in amazement as the two men argued and laughed. About twenty minutes later, Panchita came back into the room and announced that dinner was served. On the dinette table Panchita had set big plates of rice, beans, *tostones*, pork chops, lettuce and tomato salad, and plenty of soda and beer. With only four chairs at the kitchen dinette table, Flaco, Wyndell, Vidamía, and Tumba Santiago sat around the table, while Panchita stood eating near the stove. Wyndell got up to give her a seat, but Tumba Santiago ordered him back in his chair.

The dinner was loud and the chattering constant, all of them trying to teach Wyndell how to pronounce various words and phrases, and laughing when instead of *chuletas* he kept calling the pork chops *chulitas*. This caused such hilarity that Flaco nearly choked and Tumba Santiago had to get up and hit him on the back, because, as they explained, *chulitas* are "sexy girls," and you better be careful when eating *chulitas*.

After the meal they returned to the living room, and Vidamía said that her grandmother had told her that he'd gotten the nickname Tumba because he played congas. At the mention of Ursula Santiago, her grandfather got a funny look on his face and, shifting his eyes toward the kitchen, put a finger to his lips and urged her not to mention her grandmother. Vidamía nodded, then said she wanted to hear him play.

Her grandfather went into another room and Flaco followed. When they returned they brought three different-sized congas, the heads of the drums aged and dark where they had been played. Flaco held two cylindrical pieces of wood. Vidamía watched Tumba Santiago's dark, thickly veined, and powerful hands as he brought a chair from the kitchen into the living room and sat down behind the drums. His fingers barely touching the skins of the drums, the instruments immediately responded with several tones which lingered in the air. Vidamía had once attempted to play Sammy Polanco's conga in the park, but all that had come out of the drum were dull thuds. Her grandfather seemed to caress the head of each drum, and immediately the air was filled with resonance, a resonance that felt like speech, like a greeting of some sort, so that later on, when Wyndell had gotten over his dark mood, she discussed it with him. He explained that Africans used drums to communicate with each other, and perhaps her grandfather was saying something to her, to see if she understood.

46 *Clave*

Her grandfather, Tumba Santiago, had been warming up with little flourishes of rhythms. Suddenly he was playing full out, his head turned to the side and his face producing a number of expressions which to her looked like the African masks she had seen in the museum. Before too long, Flaco began to hit the sticks together, setting up a steady rhythm over which her grandfather played his congas, making the room fill up with the sounds. There was a texture to the rhythms, the simplicity of the clacking of the sticks—which Flaco explained as *clave* and let her try the sticks, instructing her—one-two-three (pause), one-two, over and over, the rhythm invading her soul until she recognized it from dancing salsa and then she was totally into it and playing with her grandfather, standing up and moving naturally as they played together, the subtle but strong thuds of fingers and palms upon the drumheads weaving a palpable fabric of musicality, so that deep within the rhythms she could hear a melody. She couldn't help moving to the rhythms and watched Wyndell thoughtfully nodding and tapping his foot gently on the linoleum floor. When her grandfather was finished, his face was glistening with perspiration and he was laughing.

"You play Latin?" Tumba Santiago said with a heavy Spanish accent, looking first down at the case of Wyndell's tenor sax and then up at him.

"I can play some things. Caribbean things."

"Like what?"

" 'St. Thomas.' "

"Never heard of it."

Wyndell scatted the tune and Tumba Santiago played the melody back to him on the smallest of the drums. Wyndell recalled his father's friend Howard Dryer, a musicologist who had studied African rhythms in Nigeria, describing the relationship between rhythm, melody, and the spoken word. Howard had said that some of the languages could be played on drums exactly as one heard the words, so that there was no difference between the beats of the drums and a person's speech. "Go ahead and play it," Tumba said.

As Wyndell removed the guard from the mouthpiece, the old man sat in front of the congas and with his eyes told Flaco to begin. Flaco, holding the two rounded pieces of wood, one cradled in the palm of his left hand and the other poised above it, nodded, his lower lip turning down and showing pink on his black face. In another second the room was filled with the sharp wooden sound of the *clave*: ONE-TWO-THREE, ONE-TWO. ONE-TWO-THREE, ONE-TWO. ONE-TWO-THREE, ONE-TWO. Over and over, about ten times, until Tumba Santiago came in on the congas: PACATUN-PATUN. PACATUN-PATUN. PACATUN-PATUN. PACATUN-PATUN. PACATUN-PATUN. PACATUN-PATUN. ONE-TWO-THREE, ONE-TWO. ONE-TWO-THREE, ONE-TWO. And then Wyndell joined in, playing the tune easily and thinking the words in his head: *"I came to St. Thomas but I ain't going back. I came to St. Thomas but I ain't going back going back. You can yell, you can shout, you can do your stuff, but you can't kick me out."* They played together for about ten minutes with Wyndell improvising on the melody and making it swing, Tumba Santiago keeping the tempo even when Wyndell became more intricate in his playing and then trading fours with the old man on the smaller of the congas, which he explained later was the *quinto* and actually carried the melody, with the *tumbadora*, the bass one, and the medium-sized drum, making up the rhythm. The old man's virtuosity surprised Wyndell. Tumba Santiago knew exactly what he was doing and the smaller drum had sounded unlike a percussion instrument, perhaps a bass flute.

When they were done playing, Wyndell bowed his saxophone to the old man and Tumba Santiago nodded slightly and turned to Flaco, who was nodding. He asked him in Spanish if he liked what he'd heard and Flaco, his face becoming thoughtful, said he sounded a little like Dexter Gordon, except that he pronounced it "Destel Goldon," but it was close enough for Wyndell to think he heard the name. He was dismantling the horn in order to put it back in its case, but stopped himself and grabbed Vidamía's arm.

"What did he say?" he whispered to her.

"Who?"

"Your grandfather's friend. I think he said Dexter Gordon."

"Ask him."

"They were speaking Spanish."

"Yeah, but they understand English."

"Yeah, right," Wyndell said, as he finished putting the saxophone away and closed the case. "Excuse me."

"Sure," Tumba said.

"Your friend, Mr. Flaco . . ." Wyndell began, and the two old men began laughing and slapping their thighs. "What's the matter?"

"You call him Mr. Flaco," Tumba said.

"That's right," Flaco said. "I'm Mr. Flaco from now on. No more of this 'Flaco' stuff."

"What's so funny?" Wyndell said, embarrassed and looking back and forth, from the two men to Vidamía, who now had a mischievous look in her eyes and was about to burst out laughing herself. "What?"

"Nothing," Vidamía said and collapsed laughing on the couch.

Tumba and Flaco were now poking at each other.

"You gotta call me Mr. Flaco."

"Then you gotta call me Mr. Tumba."

Vidamía finally stopped laughing long enough to explain that Flaco was her grandfather's friend's nickname and all it meant was "skinny" in Spanish.

"His name's Pascual Quintana," Tumba Santiago said. "My name is Justino Santiago."

"Oh," Wyndell said. "Anyway, did he mention Dexter Gordon?"

"Ask him," Vidamía said, "or are you going to act like some sort of American *jíbaro*?"

"I ain't no HEEbaro," Wyndell said. "Whatever that is."

He was about to address Flaco when Tumba Santiago said that his friend Flaco had said he sounded a little like Dexter Gordon. Wyndell then asked if they knew Dexter Gordon, and they both nodded their heads and said yes, but just from listening to records and hearing him in clubs down in the Village when they were young men. They then began to talk about the old days and it became obvious that Tumba Santiago had played with many of the big bands of the forties, fifties, and sixties. Miguelito Valdez, Machito, Perez Prado, Tito Puente.

And then they lapsed totally into extremely complicated, rapidly spoken Spanish with the peculiar lilt of the Puerto Ricans, flavored by the New York ambiance and garnished with the musical patois of their experiences and a perfect example of linguistic *salsa*, so that even Vidamía had a difficult time understanding.

They reminisced like that until it got dark and Vidamía said she had to go and she and Wyndell got up and began getting ready. Vidamía threw her arms around Tumba Santiago and kissed him on the cheek. She was nearly a head taller than him and for the first time she realized how small and old he really was. Tumba laughed and said she should come back and see him from time to time. She asked for his telephone number and he called Panchita and she gave Vidamía the number.

When she and Wyndell were back on the subway she snuggled against him, aware that people were looking at them, this supposedly white girl with this beautiful *moreno*. She closed her eyes and gave herself up to the pleasure of being with him as the train rumbled through the Bronx and then Manhattan, until they changed at Forty-second Street to continue downtown to his apartment.

Once there she fell into bed and allowed him to undress her, feeling sleepy and warm. As she drifted in and out of sleep while Wyndell caressed her body, she saw once again her grandfather's dark face. The notion of being related to him gave her an unusual, almost sexual pleasure. She knew she was being romantic, but she felt brave and as if she were now part of a wonderful history that connected her to all the African people who had struggled in the United States. Wyndell went into her fiercely. When she protested he apologized, and then he was going in and out of her slowly, gently, the length of him nearly coming out of her before once again entering her so that she began feeling more and more and grasped him to her, wanting him with greater urgency until in his desperation he came and she held him as he shuddered. After he fell asleep she got up and eventually left.

As she walked home across Houston Street she felt as if she had crossed into another world. She had finally met her grandfather and although she couldn't think of him as a *moreno*, because he spoke Spanish, he was certainly dark and African enough to qualify as one. Did his presence in her life make her an African-American? The notion appeared ludicrous and she worried that others would ridicule her for it. The feeling of pride in her grandfather turned to confusion interspersed with anger. What was she now, she thought as she turned the key to enter the loft.

She came in, greeted everyone, and started to go into her room when the phone rang. Lurleen called out that it was for her.

"Who is it, Mama?"

"Wyn." Lurleen smiled across at her.

"Okay, I'll take it in the back."

She made her way to the back room which served as a kind of library and quiet place where family members went when they wanted privacy but didn't want to be in their room. As she walked by, she saw her father staring at the television screen, shaking his head and mumbling. She picked up the phone and told Lurleen she could hang up. Later on she asked Lurleen what her father had been shaking his head about and Lurleen said that he was worried that the United States would go to war in the Middle East.

"Wyn?"

"Yeah, hi."

"You okay?"

"Yeah, sure. Why did you leave?"

"I don't know," she said. "I guess I wanted to think and be alone. Kind of sort things out about my grandfather. Did you like him?"

"Oh, yeah, he's great. Listen, I got great news."

"What? Tell me, tell me," she said, suddenly excited.

"I got the gig at the Village Gate."

"Oh, Wyn, that's great. When?"

"August twenty-third, -fourth, and -fifth. Friday, Saturday, and Sunday. It's part of the Summer Jazz Festival. It was set up to give new musicians a chance. I left the CD and they called me back. Now all I gotta do is get myself the rest of the musicians. What's today's date? Wait, I got a calendar."

"It's July thirtieth," she said. "Almost the thirty-first."

"That's just three weeks away. I told them I had a quintet."

"Wyn, please ask my father. Please."

"I don't know. We can talk about it."

"No, really. He's ready. You have to hear him. Maybe we can go to the Cornelia Street Café and hear him next Tuesday."

"We'll see."

"Please, Wyn. It's really important."

"I know it is, Vee, but I gotta figure everything out. Give me a couple of days."

"And Cliff."

"I was thinking of a trumpet. Tony Betancourt called me. I went to school with him."

"I know, Wyn. But Cliff's great. Everybody says so."

"He's a kid, Vee. I don't even know if they'll let him play down there."

"They can make an exception."

"We'll see, baby. Just slow down a little. I just wanted to call you to let you know. You're the first person I called. What time is it?"

"It's almost midnight."

"Good, let me call home and tell my folks. I'll call you tomorrow. Okay?"

"Yeah, I'll be at the store in the afternoon. I love you, hunk."

"Did you say 'hung'?"

"Go to hell, you conceited creep."

"Hey, I love you too, morning star."

"What? What did you call me?"

"Morning star."

"Why?"

"I don't know, but I love you a whole lot."

"I know you do, you crazy man. I love you, too. See you tomorrow."

She hung up the phone, feeling dreamy and weepy and wanting to curl up right there on the worn couch with all the books around her and the prints on the bare brick walls, framed carefully by Lurleen and hung carefully by her father at her behest. He did everything Lurleen asked, obediently, following all her directions like a dutiful child, trusting her totally or as much as one human being could trust another. Inside her now, as she roused herself from the oncoming somnolence, there emerged a powerful determination to convince Wyn that her father was capable of playing the piano with him, and that it would be beneficial for Wyndell as well as for her father.

She fell asleep visualizing the bandstand with her father sitting at the piano, hunched over it, humming as he did, his hands working the keys in rapid-fire progressions of color and sound, the music flowing as if by magic, his hands barely seeming to touch the keys. It was the same sensation she had experienced with her grandfather, who seemed merely to wave his hands over the drums and the mere energy of the fingertips coaxed wonderful rhythms from the taut skins. Inside her there burned a fierce wish to see her father play again publicly, as she had heard Mr. Butterworth describe. Lurleen had explained it to her.

"Playing the piano," she said, "is a skill like any other."

"It seems like a lot more than just skill."

"You're right, it is more than skill. Playing jazz piano takes strength, stamina, willpower, a great memory for tunes, a whole bunch of creativity, and something else that some people call temperament and makes you go forward. Like a scientist or an explorer. These people come along once in a lifetime."

"Does Daddy have all those things?"

"He sure does, honey." Lurleen had nodded seriously. "He's got all of them and then some. Please believe me, little girl, your daddy's one in a million."

Vidamía had never wished for anything so much in her life. Her father would play with Wyn. She knew it had to happen, but didn't know how. She fell asleep imagining her father and her lover playing music together and she dreamed that at some point they began to blend into one, the black and white skin making stripes like chocolate and vanilla ice cream melting on the same dish, and then she was naked and dancing, her skin smooth and in stripes like ice cream, and the sound of the *clave* repeated within the music. She was dancing wildly, the beat of the drums insistent and her life bursting forth like a large flower.

Later, she looked in the big Spanish dictionary and had seen that *clave* meant the treble clef, and that it also meant key as in a code. So she had found the key and her life was now opening up to all possibilities. The feeling made her spirit soar.

47 The Return

After nearly forty years, Alfred Butterworth had come home that Christmas of 1963, the year that President Kennedy was shot, summoned there not because of his stepfather's death a month prior, but because his mother had fallen down and broken her arm. The old house the Reverend Lockwood had built still looked impressive, although badly in need of painting. The trees had grown taller, shading the house and garden and the hedges were nearly six feet high. Butterworth felt the same tensions he'd always felt going down south, but this time it was different. This time there was an edge of frustrated anger that he couldn't decipher. It seemed like the black people finally understood that they had been mistreated and were angry. And whites, realizing that they could no longer afford to treat blacks as they had, were equally upset. It wasn't until he began to factor in Martin Luther King Jr.'s impact on the country and the inspiration that blacks were getting from him and people like Malcolm X that he understood the new tensions that he experienced in going home. Dr. King himself had been arrested in Birmingham earlier in the year.

When he stepped up on the porch and said, "Hi, Mama, I'm Alfred," Cornelia Butterworth Lockwood just looked at him, hardly able to believe her eyes, because in spite of letters and photos he'd sent over the years, it wasn't the same as having someone right in front of you. Here was her son, now grown and a man, dressed in a suit, looking quite handsome, if still a little frail of body, and evidently doing well. The letters and pictures always went to her sister's and were kept a secret from her husband, Reverend Lockwood, all those years for fear that he'd set the police after Alfred because of what he'd done.

Butterworth had brought her yards of cloth, recalling how much she enjoyed sewing. That week they traveled to Mobile and he bought her a brand-new Singer electric sewing machine. His job at the university paid well enough and he was a thrifty man. The expense of the trip and the gifts hardly made a dent in his savings. At one point he asked again about Melinda and his mother explained, as she had in her letters back then, that she'd passed on in 1946, drowned in the lake, but most likely somebody took a liking to her, forced himself on the poor girl, and then killed her. He'd wanted to ask if she suspected anyone and was the person black or white, but thought better of it. What difference did it make? His sister was dead.

Alfred Butterworth wanted to apologize to his mother for running away, but didn't want to unearth those memories. He still didn't know what had come over him that day. His best explanation had always been that he'd grown tired of being beaten and humiliated. But he'd had another reason, and he had a need to find out if he had been justified. He inquired about his aunt Louisa and was told that she still lived down the road. One morning he walked the two miles down to his aunt's house, noticing that many new houses had sprung up along the still unpaved road, the dust rising from it, the countryside wilted in the winter sun. When he got there he saw that, as in the case of his mother's house, rooms had been added and there were electrical appliances scattered about: television set, toaster, fans, and even an electric blanket in his aunt's bedroom, which she proudly showed off.

Butterworth told his aunt he'd felt bad about running away

after what he'd done. His aunt replied there was no need to apologize. Maybe the Reverend Lockwood had it coming to him.

"The man had two sides. No different than most folks, but in him it was glaring, since he was supposed to be bringing everyone the word of God, and while there isn't a body alive who can claim perfection, a preacher has to set an example and Reverend Lockwood often fell short of that, if truth be told."

She explained, in rather convoluted language, how Reverend Lockwood had at one point also attempted to romance her.

"I never told your mother," his aunt said. "It would've broken her heart, with everything that has happened in her life, but I warned him that if he got out of line again, not only your mother but the entire community would hear from me."

"I guess he didn't pay you no mind," he said.

"Folks like him can't help themselves, I guess. But your mother's got to share the blame for ever taking up with him," his aunt said and went on to explain.

Because it wasn't as if his mother hadn't been forewarned by the conjure woman in Mississippi to whom cousin Rachel had taken her. Around a year later a man rode up to the house on a mule and dismounted. He was dressed in black and carried a Bible and very politely announced that he was the Reverend Isaiah Lockwood from Atlanta, Georgia. By that time his mother had forgotten everything Miss Lulu McAlpin had said, and as busy as her life was her heart gave three skips and two jumps. She was utterly and helplessly charmed by the Reverend Lockwood, who dismounted from his mule, saw that God had set in front of him a fairly young, pliable woman in need of assistance, and who could know except the good Lord what might come of a situation such as this one.

The first thing Isaiah Lockwood did was ask to speak to her husband. His mother told the Reverend of her husband's death. Reverend Lockwood closed his eyes solemnly and mumbled a prayer about the Lord keep him and then asked if it was too much trouble if he gave the mule some water, and since it was near dark could he let the mule graze nearby. Also given that he was a stranger, he shouldn't be traveling the countryside that late, and could he rest the night over in the shed by the well.

His mother said that would be no problem and that they didn't have much in the way of food, but if he was willing to say grace for them, he could join in. "Tain't much," his mother said. "Just some yams, a little okra, and parsnip greens in fatback. We also got a pan of cornbread, and some buttermilk if you don't mind it thick," she said.

"Simpering like a young fool over the man," his aunt recounted. The Reverend, according to his aunt, ate like the twelve lost tribes, burped, excused himself, and the next morning he was up bright and early chopping wood, milking the cow, collecting eggs, drawing water, and generally making himself useful so that his mother was sincerely grateful that God had chosen to reward her suffering.

A week passed and the Reverend Lockwood was still making himself useful and making Cornelia Butterworth's heart flutter for he was a fine specimen of a man, his skin black and smooth and, although his teeth were already long and yellow, being he was in his fifties, he was lean and strong. Going into town to purchase goods, he was eventually able to trade for a wagon for his mule to pull. They began to plant more vegetables and sell them. On his trips into town he was also able to learn that, although there was a church in Pinckney, there was no black preacher around, the last one having passed away. The Reverend Lockwood went into the church, chased the bats and mice out, and, with saw and hammer, water and soap, got the church in shape and began to preach on Sundays. With great determination, smiling sometimes, chiding at others, he was soon able to convey to the congregation the importance of tithing.

"Why did they think white folks owned the entire earth and

half the sky? There is no reason other than they tithe. Yes, sir. They don't look up and say, I'm sorry, Lord, I can only give you one percent of the money my crop brought this year. No, sir. White folks are grateful that their harvest is bountiful and they turn over ten percent of their earnings to the work of the Lord. So if you want to see your riches grow, brothers and sisters, tithe."

Soon after, Reverend Lockwood had little tithing envelopes printed. The envelopes said in beautiful gothic lettering:

EBENEZER BAPTIST CHURCH

PINCKNEY, ALABAMA

REV. ISAIAH LOCKWOOD, PASTOR

"Just like they do in the African Zion Baptist in Atlanta!" said one of the sisters in the Ladies Aid. "My cousin Bertha lives there and that's exactly what she told me."

Overnight, the members of the church began to deliver into the collection plates dollars and coins. Whether out of desperation or the fact that they now had to work harder, people actually began to prosper and soon the church was filled every Sunday. From the meager offerings of the sharecroppers and the folks in the town, Reverend Lockwood was able to purchase wood from the mill and began to build, with Cornelia Butterworth's permission, an extension to her small two-room house.

"One moonlit night, six months after the Reverend Lockwood's arrival, when the weather was too hot to sleep, your mother came out to the kitchen porch after you and Melinda were asleep, and the Reverend Lockwood came and sat next to her," his aunt continued. "One thing led to another and before the night was over they had been intimate, and before the week was out they were living together as man and wife." Knowing he would gain greater respect from the congregation as a true, God-fearing man, the Reverend suggested to Cornelia that they be properly married. One weekend three-year-old Alfred and his sister, Melinda, were brought to their aunt Louisa's house, and his mother and the Reverend Lockwood went into Mobile to be married.

"When they returned, your mother was the happiest she'd ever been," Aunt Louisa said.

The Reverend Lockwood worked hard at the farm, and in time, with the use of his mule, he plowed a good piece of the land behind the house, leasing it from the owners, the Pritchards, whose mansion sat in white splendor in the distance. With the money brought in by the corn, beans, and watermelons that the Reverend and Cornelia planted, they were able to buy pigs, and within two or three years they had a healthy boar and two sows and began raising pigs. Some of the pigs they sold, others they slaughtered. The Reverend Lockwood even built a smokehouse where they began curing hams and shoulders and pickling feet and knuckles, and making chitterlings, and soon business was so good that, at the urging of Malcolm Pritchard, who recognized a good business opportunity when he saw one, the Reverend Lockwood and his bride built a spacious new wing on the house and a store next to it. Now people, black and white, came from all over the county to buy pork products from the Lockwoods.

Over the next five years Cornelia Lockwood gave birth to three more children: Nathan, Luke, and Miriam Lockwood. By the time Alfred Butterworth was eight years old the Reverend had expanded the store, from which he now also sold dry and canned goods, clothing, and household items.

"Isaiah Lockwood was like King Midas. Everything he touched turned to gold. But he was a man driven in odd directions. Easily tempted by the flesh," Butterworth's aunt said.

As the haze of his memories began to lift, Butterworth recalled being in the store as a young boy when a man about the age of thirty came in and said he had to feed his family but things hadn't gone well on his recent selling trip and he was wondering whether the Reverend could give him some items of food on credit.

"I'm from up near Bessemer, but my wife's mamma's from down here. We came to stay a spell till things get better. Me and my Lizzie got two little ones and I'd be indebted to you if you could do that for us."

"What do you sell, young man?" the Reverend Lockwood had said.

"Musical instruments. Brass and wind, both. For a company in Memphis, Tennessee. Also sheet music and if you have a pianola, I can get the latest rolls for you."

"You don't say?" Reverend Lockwood exclaimed. "And are you a musician?"

"Yes, sir, I certainly am. My daddy was from New Orleans and he taught all of us."

"And can you teach music?"

"Yes, sir. I certainly can."

"Well, I'm very happy to hear that. How would you like to help me start a colored folks' band right here in this town? You're welcome to charge five cents per lesson."

"Yes, sir, I would like that very much."

Alfred Butterworth was looking through his aunt's lace curtains into the yard, recalling again those days when he was beginning to explore his life. He closed his eyes for a moment, turned to Louisa Blake, his aunt, and said that things were coming back to him.

"Nathan Winslow St. Charles was a neatly dressed, meticulous man with very long, slender fingers and a great love for music. He suggested the clarinet for you, I believe," his aunt said.

Butterworth nodded again and recalled that he had liked the instrument instantly. It was different from the others. And when Mr. St. Charles played, it had sent shivers through him. In no time he learned to read music and was playing simple classical pieces and some Stephen Foster tunes like "Old Black Joe," "Massa's in the Cold, Cold Ground," and "Camptown Races." One joyful aspect of the music and the subsequent formation of the band was that it provided so much pleasure for Melinda. Butterworth loved to see Melinda smile when she heard the music, her mind attempting to decipher how it was produced and her eyes blind.

By the time he was twelve he was playing pieces by Mozart and Beethoven easily, Mr. St. Charles telling him that he was a very talented musician and that in time he would do everything that he could to aid him in finding a good conservatory, perhaps up north, in New York or Boston. Inspired by Mr. St. Charles's praise, young Alfred Butterworth began helping teach the younger children of the congregation. But the harder he worked, the more dissatisfied his stepfather became, the Reverend demanding that he devote more time to the store, the farm, and the smokehouse. When young Alfred protested, his stepfather went into a blinding rage in which he struck the boy repeatedly with a razor strop. More punishment followed, over the most minor of infractions. He was often left dazed and bleeding after a beating when an errant blow caught him near the face. In time the beatings became a daily occurrence. He went to his mother, but she said that what the Reverend Lockwood was doing hurt him more than he could ever imagine. "He just wants you to learn the value of hard work," his mother said.

One afternoon, about three weeks after his thirteenth birthday, he came in late because he had stopped to talk with May Thigpen, who was fifteen years old, very pretty, and learning the flute. It seemed to him that she was kind of sweet on him from the way she looked at him. They had walked leisurely to her house, the two of them carrying their instruments in their cases, stretching the time as much as possible and talking mostly about geography and different songbirds. When he showed up at the store, the Reverend Lockwood was fuming and spitting. He told young Alfred to go into the back and pull down his trousers.

Butterworth shook his head over and over, feeling his bladder starting to go, as it always did during a beating, so that invariably he felt the urine coursing down his leg and later hated himself and beat his own head with his fist for allowing himself to be humiliated.

"It ain't right, Daddy," he said. "I ain't done nothing wrong."

"Then where were you?"

"I was just walking May to her house. I'm sorry I'm late. It's just a few minutes. I'll stay longer and clean up and work all day tomorrow."

"May Thigpen?"

"Yes, sir."

"She's a hussy, and her father's a blasphemer. On top of that, he makes moonshine whiskey. An abomination in the eyes of the Lord."

"May's not a hussy, Daddy. She's a wonderful girl."

"Don't you sass me, boy," Isaiah Lockwood said, towering over the slightly built Alfred. "Just go in the back and drop your britches."

"It ain't right," he said, and immediately felt the slap, the large hand knocking him down and disorienting his mind.

In an instant his stepfather was on him, kicking him, so that he could do nothing but scurry on all fours to the back of the store. Time stopped then and he steeled himself for the beating, but he wouldn't remove his trousers and refused to stand up. He curled up and covered his head until the Reverend Lockwood had spent himself and he was panting as if he had been running. The bell on the door clanged and his stepfather left him lying against a flour sack. Alfred Butterworth could taste the salt of his tears and the mucus running from his nose, but he hadn't wet his pants. He stood and went out to the back, drew water from the pump, and poured it over himself, needing to wash away whatever of the humiliation still stuck to him.

He couldn't go back into the store, couldn't face his stepfather because if he did he would want to kill him and then God would punish him further. Where was his own father? Was he in Heaven? "Help me, Daddy," he thought. "God, help me, please," he prayed, his eyes closed momentarily. He walked away, moving aimlessly as the sun set and the crickets and frogs took over the night. When he finally returned home his mother said that his stepfather was very upset with him and he ought to eat his supper, do his prayers, go to bed, and in the morning ask the Reverend Lockwood's forgiveness.

"Yes, Mama," he said.

He did exactly as his mother had asked and went back to his routine. Mr. St. Charles, however, could tell immediately that something had happened to him. It was as if his spirit had been damaged and he no longer wished to learn or know anything about music. May Thigpen waited for him on Friday after rehearsal, but he shook his head and said he couldn't talk to her. She grabbed his arm and very sternly said, "Alfred Butterworth, I ain't done nothing to you for you to just push me away like I was some old rag. I know he beat you. My daddy told me."

They talked for a while and then he went over to Blue Thigpen's house and ate supper with them. Blue Thigpen was the most menacing-looking man he'd ever seen. Blue hardly ever spoke. He nodded and every once in a while you'd hear a yep or a nope, but other than that he said nothing. After supper Blue sat out on the porch smoking his corncob pipe and cleaning a shotgun. When Alfred Butterworth got ready to leave, he stepped off the porch, thanked Mrs. Thigpen, said goodbye to May, and began to say good night to Blue Thigpen.

"Ho, there," Blue said.

"Yes, sir, Mr. Thigpen."

"You best get yourself on outta that house, heah?" said Blue

Thigpen. "That man ain't gonna rest till he kill you. And then it's gonna be too late, unless you's one of these fools that believe in ghosts?"

"Yes, sir. I mean, no, sir. Thank you, sir," he said, walking backward away from the porch, turning and running through the yard, hearing the sounds of the approaching evening.

When he got home it was dark and way past bedtime. All the lamps were off, but he heard rustling coming from the barn. He figured maybe a fox or some other animal had gotten caught inside and was trying to get out, but the dogs were sleeping, and usually when there was an intruder, human or animal, they'd be up and about, barking and carrying on. He let himself into the barn slowly and edged himself along the side, silently, making sure the horses and cows didn't stir. One of the dogs came up and sidled against him. He reached down and petted it. And then he saw his stepfather bending over Melinda. He only saw the outline of the two bodies, but Isaiah Lockwood was spreading her legs and he was letting himself down on his sister. He'd wanted to scream for him to stop, but knew that his stepfather would kill him and his sister. Unable to do anything to stop it, he left and went into the house and climbed into bed with his clothes on. He couldn't fall asleep, his being racked by the new anger. After a while he heard his stepfather and Melinda when they returned to the house.

A week later he decided to leave. He knew where the house money was kept, and, after packing some clothes in a paisley bag, he got his clarinet in its case and placed everything under his bed. In the middle of the night he got up, dressed, set his bag and case outside on the porch, and returned inside to the kitchen. In one of the drawers of the hutch, he fished around until he found his mother's sewing basket. Beneath a pin cushion he found the folded bills. He took two tens and a few one-dollar bills and went back outside. He hadn't taken ten steps past the barn before an overwhelming spasm of anger came over him.

He set his bag and clarinet case near the barn, went inside, and found an ax handle. His heart pounding and his hands sweating, the cold perspiration making him ill, he went back into the house and let himself into his stepfather's bedroom, where he slept alone. Taking a deep breath, he raised the ax handle over his head and with all the strength he could muster swung down on the Reverend Lockwood's head as he snored. All he heard was a groan.

And then he was gone, walking all night, and toward morning finding the railroad tracks and following them until he crossed into Mississippi. He walked pretty much the entire day, except when he stopped to eat from the cornbread and smoked ham hocks he'd managed to wrap in a kerchief. He chewed on the ham hocks whenever he got hungry, letting the tough skin become soft and pliable before swallowing it. By that time the hunger had passed and he was able to press on. In Biloxi he found the black section of town and was able to buy some crackers and dried meat before going on to the train station, where he purchased a ticket north to Memphis.

All of that had been such a long time ago. Memphis had been hell at first. He swept floors at a whorehouse and worked for an undertaker, helping the owner pick up the dead, and carrying out the entrails in preparation for the embalmer, the smell of formaldehyde staying on him. There were musical bands but when they asked his age and he told them he was thirteen nobody wanted anything to do with him. A couple of times they wanted a cornet player. It wasn't until Buck Sanderson found him wandering around Beale Street and took him to Bramwell's one afternoon that he began playing again.

By the time Alfred Butterworth had returned to New York after his visit in 1963, you could tell that the president's death had affected everyone and the country would never be the same again. And now Buck's grandson, Billy Farrell, was coming to visit him, to look after him. He and Buck Sanderson had been young men together and now his grandson who already had grown children was coming to visit him again after all these years. He didn't quite know if he was up to it.

48 Memories

Alfred Butterworth worked all morning to get the apartment ready for Billy Farrell's visit, sweeping, dusting, changing the sheets on the bed and generally getting the place spiffed up. He had to work slowly, but the anticipation of Billy coming to see him lessened the pain. It was a three-room railroad apartment with living room, bedroom, bathroom, and kitchen lined up one after the other and a narrow hall running from living room to kitchen, and the bathroom and bedroom off the hall. The apartment was small and neat, a place for everything and everything in its place. Sunlight came in and settled gently on the furniture and walls at different times of the day. But there was a sadness to the rooms, as if everyone who had ever resided in the apartment, who had come and gone, who had made love and cried, who had gorged themselves on food and slept long hours, who had drunk and vomited and eventually died in their sleep or dropped dead from strokes and heart attacks for the hundred years that the building had stood there, beginning with the Irish and Germans and Jews who had come to Harlem before the blacks, had left their pain within the narrow walls of these rooms.

By the time Alfred Butterworth was done, he was exhausted and the pains came with greater frequency, threatening to choke him. He wanted to lie down but fought the urge and set the kettle on the two-burner electric hot plate. When the water boiled, he poured himself a cup of tea, put lemon and honey in it, and sat back down by the kitchen window, where the sunlight was coming in and the apartment was warmest. He knew the tea would do very little because whatever was ailing him, it wasn't a cold. It was something awful raking at his throat, and he felt like taking a spoon or a fork to try and extract whatever it was that impeded his swallowing. He'd lost ten pounds and about all that he could eat was a little oatmeal. He'd have to go to the hospital at some point, but he was certain that it was already too late and no treatment would do any good. The time had come for him to go. He was certain of this.

He guessed he had the same damn thing that Iggy Marginat ended up with. He'd kept in touch with Iggy over the years, but he disappeared and Butterworth stopped seeing him except one time down near Riverside Park. "The Cuban kid," they called him—a serious, rich Spanish kid who was a very good piano player, classically trained. He lived in a rich man's house over on Riverside Drive. When things got bad during the Depression, he'd have a bunch of musicians over and feed everybody and then they'd go back to Harlem and jam till all hours of the morning and then Iggy would take them all out to breakfast and tell everybody not to worry because his old man owned over a hundred buildings. He'd talk about taking all of them to Puerto Rico someday, telling them that's where he was from, but everybody called him "the Cuban kid" because nobody knew much about Puerto Ricans.

Later on, after things got better, some of them went down and played with bands on the islands. "No big deal," fellows said. "Easy charts, no problems. Plenty of rum, good-looking women of all colors, and nice friendly people who liked to dance." He'd gone to Puerto Rico and played with Machito's band, and spent an entire winter season living in an apartment in Santurce with Brady Rivers, the trumpet player. He'd met a beautiful mulatto girl by the name of Ileana who took him places where all the people were black and they played rhythms he'd never heard before and the people laughed as if their color were not an issue.

Butterworth sat in the chair by the window, holding the teacup in his two hands, staring out at the garbage-strewn lot below his third-floor apartment. The lot reminded him of his life, as if his life, along with a number of other people's lives, had been declared worthless and discarded. It didn't matter what field it was: sports, acting, the law, medicine, and of course music. You reach a certain level and there's a few that go on but the majority get left behind. For black folks it was worse. It was as if somewhere in that thing called life there was a Harlem, and that Harlem was a huge empty lot full of discarded black people.

He sipped again and recalled sitting around with Charlie Parker, Dizzy Gillespie, and Monk toward the beginning of the Second World War, and Dizzy was saying, "Charles, listen to this," and then bringing the horn to his lips, puffing out his cheeks and blowing a strange, rapid-fire series of notes that sounded like *betupiadippitty*, *bittibitty*, *biattibittybop*, and Monk laughing up a storm and saying, "Ain't that a bitch," and Bird becoming all serious and, hooking up his ax, he blew something very similar, but Diz shook his head and said, "No, no, listen, listen," and he played it again. Bird got a funny look on his face and said, "Man, what the fuck are you doing? You played that shit backward." And Diz said, "So what!" And right then Kenny Clarke, who'd been in the bathroom, listening, sits down at the drums and plays something similar on the traps, and Monk hits a hellacious chord on the piano and they all laughed and Diz says, "Let's do 'How High the Moon.'" And Bird said, "Come on, Alfred," and Butterworth picked up his clarinet and Diz counted and they played the tune and then Diz came in blowing some of the weirdest stuff anybody'd ever heard, it sounded all discombobulated, and Monk is chording weirder stuff yet, and then after about eight choruses from Diz, Bird comes in for about ten choruses of even more amazing stuff, everything up-tempo and so fast that Bird's fingers were a blur, but through it all the beat and harmony intact, and Monk and Oscar Pettiford, if he remembered correctly, staying with Bird as he literally flew through the tune, taking it apart and putting it back together. This happened at Minton's. It could've been Small's. He couldn't remember exactly. Time had become a fog.

And then they looked to him and Butterworth played a simple improvisation of the tune with some flourishes but it sounded totally out of place and Monk finally bailed him out and came in, the music strong and supple, but insinuating rather than actually playing the melody, his time perfect and the music definitely swinging. They were all very understanding but no matter how hard he tried he couldn't figure out what they were doing. He switched to the alto to see if he could imitate Bird. He watched him incessantly but couldn't get it.

By about 1950, when he'd made sense of what they were doing, what everybody was calling bop, he recognized that not only were they playing in a new way, but that central to it was some extremely fast playing, and he knew there was no way he could keep up with them. He began drifting then. He went on the road for a few years, but whenever he ran into Diz or the others, although they were never disrespectful, you could tell that he'd been left behind. The way they talked with each other, the jokes they shared, the places they'd been—Paris, Stockholm, Copenhagen, Rome, London, Cairo—made them look and feel bigger than they were, and he was just somebody they had known back when they were all starting out. And then younger musicians came around and they dug what was going on. Miles Davis and John Coltrane, and even white cats like Gil Evans and Gerry Mulligan, nineteen and twenty years old, and they knew what Bird was doing and would get up on the bandstand and stay with him, but he couldn't, and he felt worthless, like whatever his contribution had been to the music, it had meant nothing.

And then he'd gone up to Buck Sanderson's in Yonkers whenever the old gang got together for a celebration and had heard Billy play and knew the boy was one of a kind and told Buck he ought to let him study the music. Buck said there was nobody around to teach him. Butterworth suggested Mae Wilkerson.

Billy was shy, a little withdrawn, but he had great big strong hands. As soon as Mae saw him she took his hands and asked his name.

"Billy Farrell," he'd said, almost so you couldn't hear him.

"And how old are you, Billy Farrell?"

"Eleven."

"Well, Billy, do you play the piano?"

"Yes."

"Do you read music, Billy?"

Billy nodded and Mae Wilkerson brought him over to an upright and asked him to pick something out from the book. He flipped through a book of 1920s songs sitting up against the stand, found "Ain't She Sweet," and played a lilting rendition of it, flipping the pages when it came time without missing a beat or a note. Halfway through the song, Mae was moving and singing along with his playing. When Billy was finished she clapped her hands. "And can you play something from memory?" Mae Wilkerson asked.

Billy nodded and remembered that there was a song that Bobby Darin had recorded the previous year, "Bill Bailey, Won't You Please Come Home?" In the middle of it was a lilting piano solo that had kind of a boogie-woogie sound, his grandpa Buck had said. Over a few afternoons of listening to the record, Billy had learned how to play it by ear on the piano and he and his grandfather, on the banjo, would do the tune together. He played it now singing the song to himself as he went, so that he sounded as if he were humming.

"Looky, looky," Mae Wilkerson said. "You sure can tickle the ivories, but Mae's going to teach you to really play. Would you like that?"

"Yes," Billy said, his eyes dreamy.

"You sure like that song, don't you," she said.

Billy nodded, his head down and his hands caressing the keys, hoping they'd ask him to play something else.

The way Butterworth saw it, for whatever reason, Billy felt comfortable at Mae's. It was like he was sure enough coming home because that's where the music was and he was definitely of the music. He always suspected that Billy getting involved with the little whore up at Ruby's was a culmination of being taught by Mae and having that woman shower all kinds of love on him, as if he were the son she never had.

The day that Butterworth told her about Billy and how his father had been shot, Mae cried, recalling the loss of her husband, Raymond, who had been a fighter pilot with the Tuskegee airmen. She always talked about General Benjamin Davis, who commanded the 332nd Fighter Group and how brave they all were, fighting for America. Lieutenant Raymond Wilkerson had been her true love and hero and she had a room in the house devoted to his pictures, her husband looking debonair sitting in his airplane, his flight cap on and his goggles perched just above the forehead, a white scarf flying in the wind; or else standing next to his aircraft with his flying buddies, looking like Bill Robinson, but handsomer, so that she could never again see Bojangles Robinson in films or in photographs without being reminded of her husband. She still had his medals and flight jacket and uniforms in the closet of that room and there were also pictures of the two of them, she slim and beautiful and he tall and handsome.

"He was shot down on a mission over Italy," Mae Wilkerson once told Butterworth. "When I heard about it we were playing USO dates all over the United States and like a trouper I went on playing, knowing it was going to hit me later on that night.

We were someplace in Indiana. Terre Haute. Maybe Gary. I don't know. We finished the set, packed everything up and headed for the train station, and I was still holding on. All the other girls knew I'd lost my husband and finally on the train outside Kansas City my whole world collapsed, Alfred."

It was the name she always used when speaking with him, abhorring the nickname by which Butterworth was known, just as she didn't like calling her husband Skip, as he was known at home and as the other flyers referred to him. Skip Wilkerson.

"Kansas City, Missouri. That's where Raymond was from. I asked the band to replace me and I went and saw Raymond's mother and stayed there for the next two months or so."

Butterworth and Mae Wilkerson tried to keep company in 1949 when she was still young, but she picked up right away on his obsession with Billie Holiday and asked him to get himself straightened out and when he did she'd be more than happy to open her heart to him. He hadn't been able to get Lady Day out of his mind and had blown his chance of happiness with Mae as well.

Mae recognized Billy's grief immediately, but in a way, the solemnity of that room, that museum devoted to her husband's memory, may later have inspired Billy to the duty he felt he had to fulfill. Mae told Butterworth that when Billy finished his lessons, he'd often go up and sit in the room for hours, and had once told her that he'd built a model P-51, just like the one her husband had flown.

What a shame it all was, Butterworth thought. It never ended. The pain just kept on coming as if there was an endless supply. It would all be over soon, he thought, and closed his eyes, feeling the warm afternoon sun on his face. But he recalled the tunes all right, so maybe he'd get better and be able to play again. As he dozed off in the sunlight he again saw Billy's family and the young girl singing while she stood behind the drum, tap-tap-tapping the cymbal.

Won't you come home, Bill Bailey,
Won't you come home?
She moans the whole day long.
I'll do the cookin', darling
I'll pay the rent.
I know I've done you wrong . . .
Bill Bailey won't you please come home.

And now he was sitting in his apartment, awaiting Billy's visit. Maybe he was a sentimental old fool, but he felt as if his own son were about to visit him. He was definitely an old fool, pretending that this white man was his son. That's how it had felt when the boy had gone off to Vietnam and he couldn't do anything to stop him. It was like something had been torn from his heart. The feeling of helplessness now was no different than it had been back then. He didn't know how Billy had found out that he wasn't feeling well, but he had, and now he was coming uptown to see him. He sounded excited on the phone, showing some of that quiet enthusiasm he'd possessed as a youngster. He had told Butterworth that he was getting a group together to play at the Village Gate in a couple of weeks. At least that part of his life was in order. Somehow, Billy Farrell was going to play the music again. He'd get better and go and see him play.

He rose with difficulty and walked across the floor to look out the front window of the apartment to make sure Billy made it safely inside. There was no telling what would happen with the crackheads all over the place. What had happened? Cocaine had been a nothing drug back then. He watched for a few minutes, but even though it was summer the apartment was too cool and too damp and he returned to the kitchen and the warmth of the sun. He dozed off for about five minutes, until he heard the doorbell and rose to answer it. Alfred Butterworth moved slowly, for the moment unaware of the pain. He threw the door open and for a second didn't recognize the man standing there, and then he recalled the younger Billy Farrell. He now had a blond mustache and his hair was trimmed.

Billy, for his part, was saddened by how much Butterworth's health had deteriorated since he'd last seen him.

49 A Day in Harlem

Billy went up to Harlem one Sunday afternoon in mid-August of 1990. He had stopped cleaning out apartments but was still called on to fix broken pipes, repair loose steps on staircases, caulk bathrooms, tar roofs, and putty up windows while the weather was still warm. In the past he'd approached each job with intensity, working diligently and looking forward to nothing more than sitting in the loft, reading the newspapers and magazines that he collected on his rounds. Now he hurried through each repair so that he could return home and go to the sixth floor of the building, where the piano had been moved. Once there he played for long hours, lost in the music until one of the kids came to get him to eat supper. On rehearsal days he returned and continued practicing until the other musicians showed up.

One afternoon he'd gone by NYU to tell Butterworth about the upcoming gig at the Village Gate and was told that the old man was out sick. Billy called him and Butterworth sounded bad. Billy said he was coming to see him on Sunday. He took the 6 at Spring Street, changed to the shuttle to Times Square, where he had played with the family band during the previous summer, and then took the 2 until he reached 110th Street on the North End of Central Park, worlds apart from Central Park South at the other end, which boasts the St. Moritz Hotel, the New York Athletic Club, and huge, luxurious apartments with breathtaking views of the city. He'd never visited those places but had heard about them from Pop Butterworth who, back when Billy was sixteen, worked for a caterer on weekends and would tell him about the parties, pulling things wrapped in tinfoil out of his pocket and saying, "Try this, son," his big friendly grin and bright eyes illuminating his life.

"What is it?" Billy'd ask.

"It's caviar, son. Go ahead and taste it, and if it's a little strange, get used to it, because the way you play, you're gonna perform for royalty, and they always serve this kind of thing."

He trusted Pop Butterworth and ate the stuff on the cracker, eyeing the round little marble-like globules suspiciously but liking the taste immediately; asking him what it was, and Butterworth laughing at him and telling him it was fish eggs. He nodded and took a handful of crackers and dipped them in the caviar and ate them. They'd sat down and eaten nearly a quarter of a pound of caviar and had champagne and he'd felt blessed and strong, like nothing would ever happen to him and the whole world would hear him play.

Billy was grateful for his neighborhood jobs, since they provided extra money, even though now with the store the children didn't seem to need much. Still, he enjoyed giving them gifts for their birthdays and at Christmas. They were good kids and he loved them. He had no idea how he and Lurleen had ended up with them all. He recalled those days in that first apartment when he and Lurleen made love three or four times a day, his body hungering for her like she was some life-giving essence without which he'd perish. In time he knew he was addicted to her, as much as he was to smoking pot, which he did with as much regularity. She had tried it a few times, and liked it, but she began reading about the effects and one day said she never wanted to smoke dope again and that he had to stop, too, and that if he didn't stop she would have a very difficult time explaining to the children that no matter how you cut it, if they were called drugs, it meant that whoever used them had to be sick. "Sick from what?" he'd said. And she said that she didn't know, but sure enough if people used drugs they had to be sick of something. "I don't want drug use in my house, and I don't want my children exposed to them, especially from their father. I want them to be healthy and learn from our example. I hope you can respect that, Billy. No drugs and no guns. You've had plenty of both."

It didn't dawn on him for another half hour that she was telling him, in a roundabout way, that she was expecting their first child. When he finally asked her, she said she thought so, but that she'd have to see the doctor to be sure. The idea of having a kid with Lurleen was unbelievable. He didn't say much, but inside he was churning. For a while he snuck around, copping a smoke here and there, always outside the house. After a while, however, the knowledge that he was lying to Lurleen ruined the experience. He quit smoking weed and eventually stopped taking pills, and only had a beer once in a while. But then all the stuff about Joey got worse, and all he could do was want to go and find cover.

It all happened very quickly with the kids, except for Caitlin—that had been an accident. One day he was walking down the street, carrying Cliff with his right arm, Horty holding on to his left hand, and Lurleen pushing the carriage with Fawn in it, and it sort of woke him up that he had three kids. Four really, except that he never expected to see the other one, the one he'd had with Elsa. And now there she was, beautiful and mysterious and so smart that he could hardly believe it, although he'd always thought Elsa was pretty smart. He imagined where he'd be if things had worked out with her, if they had stayed together and maybe had other kids. It was always weird to think about those things, because it meant that he never would've known Cliff and the girls. He thought about Cliff and wondered how he'd turn out. What would he do if Cliff came to him and said he wanted to join the Marines? But he wouldn't. He was growing up big and strong, but he had no interest in proving himself. He was a good athlete, but sports didn't interest him much. "That's cool," he'd told a friend, when he was warned that he'd be cut from the basketball team if he didn't show up for practice. "I gotta study and rehearse." Cliff was totally unlike him. Even at thirteen he had seemed in command of his own life. It was especially apparent in the way women treated him. Even older women complied with his wishes without his having to ask. The only ones he seemed to have little power over were Cookie and Vidamía. And with them he'd state what he wanted in a nonchalant, take-it-or-leave-it way and off he'd go, leaving them to throw things at him or call him names. Billy wished he hadn't been so rough on him.

The week before he'd called the number and spoken to Pop Butterworth briefly, telling him that he was coming to see him. So he went up to Harlem, his mind on the music, oblivious that he was a white dude, and feeling, but without any arrogance, as if he belonged because he played the music and it was his life, hundreds of tunes coursing through his body and, as if the history of the music were alive in him, loving the life and what it meant to him. As he walked in Harlem he imagined that he was going to have his picture taken with all the greats in front of the stoop of a brownstone, kidding around with Monk and Diz, he one of the few white cats, so his fantasy went. Pop Butterworth had shown him that photograph in *Life* magazine, the one titled "A Great Day in Harlem," that featured over fifty jazz musicians. Pop Butterworth wasn't in it and said he didn't belong in the photo, and the rest of the cats must have agreed because no one had called him to let him know about it.

As soon as Billy saw Butterworth he shook his head. Entering the apartment he could smell death, just as he had smelled it in Nam. Blood had a particular too-sweet smell to it, and when there was enough of the smell, death was usually at hand. Death also had its own brand of silence, and that is what he felt walking into Pop Butterworth's apartment. He took one look at the old man and knew there was something drastically wrong. He was much thinner than the last time he'd seen him and his movements were too deliberate, as if any more effort would cause him pain.

"How you doing, Pop?" he said, putting his arms around the old man and patting his back. "You hanging in there?"

"Yeah, trying to, son," Butterworth rasped, his voice worse than ever. "Sit down over here and tell me all about the gig."

Billy sat down on one of the chairs in the kitchen, observing the unhealthy, grayish tint of Butterworth's skin.

"You know Wyndell Ross, don't you, Pop?"

"Yes, I do. He's that colored boy that sees your daughter. Fine tenor saxophone," he said and coughed.

"Anyway, he went and talked with Art D'Lugoff down at the Gate and got himself a gig. It looks like I'll be playing with him."

"Who else?"

"My boy Cliff, on trombone."

"Another J. J. Johnson," Butterworth said proudly.

"A friend of his on drums. Real young, but he's like Philly Joe Jones."

"White boy?"

"Yeah, but he can swing."

"Bass?"

"Buster Williams."

"No kidding? Fine style. Fine musician. He and some fellas used to play Monk's music."

"Sphere with Charlie Rouse."

"Right, Charlie, before he passed. My memory's slipping."

"Yeah, with Kenny Barron and Ben Riley. Wyndell met Buster through Larry Coryell."

"The guitar player?"

"Yeah."

"Heard him a couple of times at the Gate. Brilliant musician."

"Yeah, a beautiful cat. Anyway, I guess Wyn asked Buster. He's gonna be in town so it's set up. Wyn and me was talking and we figured maybe you could sit in for a few tunes."

Billy saw the pain in Butterworth's eyes and regretted making the suggestion. It was a poor attempt to make him feel better. He was about to apologize when Pop spoke up.

"Thanks, son," he said. "But I'm real sick. I went to the hospital."

"I'm sorry, Pop."

"It ain't your fault. I shoulda left the cigarettes alone a long time ago."

"Bad?"

"Bad as it can get. Throat cancer, son."

"Can they do anything?"

"Oh, they're talking about going in and removing the voice box and giving me one of those numbers to talk through."

"Sure, I've seen them. The important thing's to hang in there, Pop. You can't be checking out without seeing me play again."

"I don't know, son," Butterworth said, his voice sounding defeated by the illness. "It don't seem worth it to go to all the trouble."

"I ain't having none of it, man," Billy said. "Whatever you gotta go through it'll be worth it. They got real fine treatment these days. When did they say you had to go in?"

"I gotta go up to Harlem Hospital for some tests and observation tomorrow."

"What time?"

"I gotta be there at ten."

"I'll be here at nine to pick you up."

"You don't have to, Billy. It's okay. You got things to do. I don't want you to go to any trouble on account of me."

"I ain't hearing it, man," Billy said. "If you wanna lock the door on me, that's fine, but I'll be here nine o'clock sharp."

"That's real kind of you, son. I'll be ready."

"How long they want you in the hospital for?"

"About a week. They wanna see if it's spread anywhere else."

"Good. The gig's the twenty-third of this month. Thursday. Today's the twelfth. Tomorrow's Monday the thirteenth. In a week it's the twentieth and you'll be out, and that Thursday we'll come and get you and you can sit up front with Lurleen. It'll be great. How's that sound?"

"Sounds great," Butterworth rasped. He reached over and took Billy's hand. "Real great."

He'd never seen Billy sound so good. Even back when he was in high school he'd sounded sad most of the time, but now he seemed excited. It was as if he had learned something about life which up to that moment had been hidden from him. They spoke a little more and then Billy said that he had to get back. There was a rehearsal that evening. He asked if Butterworth needed anything, but the old man shook his head.

Billy said goodbye, but, true to his word, there he was the next morning. He helped Butterworth pack a few things to take to the hospital. And then Butterworth asked that Billy bring down a cardboard box from the closet.

"Open it," Butterworth said when Billy had set the box on the bed.

Billy opened the box. It was full of photographs of Butterworth with other jazz musicians. Monk, Bud Powell, Charlie Parker, Dizzy Gillespie, and dozens more.

"What do you want me to do with them?" Billy asked.

"Keep them for me," Butterworth said. "All except Lady Day's picture. Take that one out and put it with my stuff."

"We'll put the pictures in albums," Billy said, recalling Albert T. Zorich's suitcase full of pictures which nobody had ever bothered to care for. "We'll organize them and make albums and write under the pictures who the people are. If we don't know somebody, you'll tell us, okay?"

"That'd be good, son. Thank you."

He went into the box and took out a framed, glass-covered picture of Billie Holiday, with a gardenia in her hair. It was signed: *To Alfred—With my greatest affection, Billie.* He placed the picture between the layers of pajamas, bathrobe, and underwear, and closed the beat-up suitcase which Alfred Butterworth had taken on the road when he had traveled with different orchestras.

Outside, Billy hailed a gypsy cab and felt proud that he could pay the fare with money he'd earned at the Cornelia Street Café, where he'd been playing the last couple of weeks. Butterworth protested when Billy paid the driver, but Billy explained that he had a little extra money.

"I got a steady gig, Pop," he said proudly.

"Where?"

"Place called the Cornelia Street Café."

"Say what?" Butterworth said, his voice suddenly stronger for a moment. "Cornelia?"

"Yeah, on Cornelia Street in the Village. Why? You know the place?"

"No, but that was my mama's name."

"Cornelia?"

"Yeah, Cornelia Butterworth," he said, omitting the Lockwood. He tried laughing, but instead began coughing. "That's a real good sign," he said when he stopped coughing.

At the hospital, Billy helped Butterworth check in and signed several papers. A nurse helped the old man into a wheelchair. Billy was standing behind him. When asked if he and Butterworth were related, he nodded. The black nurse laughed.

"Oh, yeah? How?" she asked.

Butterworth started to answer, but Billy interrupted him.

"He's my father," Billy said, his voice serious, as he squeezed Butterworth's shoulder gently. Butterworth reached up and touched his hand.

"Oh," the nurse said. "I didn't mean to laugh. Sign here, Mr. Farrell."

Once they were in his ward and they had dressed him in his pajamas, Alfred Butterworth looked at Billy and shook his head. Beneath the illness, there was a great satisfaction that made Butterworth grin a nearly toothless smile.

"That was real kind, son," he said.

"It's the truth, Pop," Billy said. "I'll come and see you tomorrow. And you do everything they tell you so you can get out of this place right away and hear us play."

"I'll do my best, Billy," he said.

Two nurses came now and settled him again into the wheelchair. Billy watched as they wheeled him down the hall, recalling the hospitals he'd been in after getting wounded in Vietnam. Each hospital had a distinctive atmosphere. The one in Japan was the neatest, and yet the three months he'd spent there had been the loneliest, the period during which he'd begun to fully understand his loss of Joey, as well as his own tragedy. He wanted desperately for Butterworth to improve, but he had already smelled death on him and he knew that soon he'd have to mourn his passing. The pain never ended, he thought.

50 First Date

Fawn Singleton Farrell lived in a dense fog day and night, waking or sleeping, secure in a gauze of thought about circles and cycles and repetitions, just like the drums she played. Everything seemed circular—like orbiting stars in a universe totally ordered, except it wasn't at all like that and they had finally grown and they weren't just the two little pink cones that had appeared last year. They were big, like on the chests of her sisters Cookie and Vee, but bigger still, so that her mother said she'd have to start wearing a bra and they had gone to the store and the one she had to wear was a 36C. Her mother said she was going to be like Grandma Maud and that she had a lovely body, extremely well-shaped and she would be fine after the operation. The doctor said she would be just like any other girl.

"It won't be painful and no one will even notice after," Lurleen had said. "Not even your boyfriend or husband."

"I don't know," Fawn said. "I'm scared. And, anyway, I'm never gonna have a boyfriend."

"Sure you are, honey. You're a beautiful and talented girl."

"Not like Cookie and Vee," she'd said.

"Yes, exactly like the two of them because you not only have great physical beauty, but you have talent like Cookie and brains like Vidamía. That's not to say your sister Hortense isn't smart, but we all know she has a few academic problems. You don't." And then her mother looked to the side, as if she were talking to other people in the room. "This here girl is smart, folks," she said, pointing at her. "You cain't tell no blonde jokes about her, heah?"

Fawn smiled and put her head down, not wanting to look at her mother.

"Really?" she said. "Like Cookie and Vidamía?"

"Yep, cross my heart and hope to die," her mother said.

"Nothing's going to happen, darling," her mother added, hugging her so that she felt little again, except she could feel her breasts getting mushed and hurting, so that she said ouch and her mother pulled away and asked her if she noticed Angela's lip where they did the operation.

"No," she said. "She's my friend."

"But do other people?"

"No, nobody pays attention."

Lurleen helped Fawn remember how she'd come home crying from school when she was seven because some boys had made fun of Angela. Fawn nodded and said the boys had said that Angela looked like a rabbit and Fawn had thrown a bottle at them and they'd hit her with a magazine and pushed her down. Lurleen asked her if she recalled that during the summer they'd gone and visited Angela's parents to encourage them to take her to the hospital to have her lip repaired because she'd been born at home in Puerto Rico up in the mountains, and there was no hospital nearby.

"I remember. We took Cookie to speak Spanish."

"Angela had her operation and she came back and you were so happy for her and she grew up beautiful and everything, though she's still a little shy. So you'll have your operation, and we're the only one's who'll know about it, except for your daddy and the doctor and nurses."

"I know that, Mama. You're the best mother and I love you."

"I love you, too. You're going to be all right. Yessiree Bob. Thank you very much. Before school starts you'll go into the hospital, they'll do the operation, and in a couple of days you'll be out and getting ready for high school. Are you sorry you won't be going up to Performing Arts with Cookie and Cliff?"

"No, Mama, it's too far. I wanna stay with my friends, anyway. I'll go to Seward Park. Angela and Margie are going there, and they have music at the school."

"Maybe after high school you can go to Juilliard. It's pretty around there, with Lincoln Center and everything. Remember when we went to see *The Nutcracker*?"

"I remember," she said, but all she could think about was having the things on her chest. Two of them right in front just like her mama and Cookie and Vee and the rest of the girls and she with that other thing so that she didn't know which way she should be. She wanted to ask her mother if they could make the things smaller, like she was just a young girl again.

Ever since the business with the Doberman, they watched the blond girl day and night as she went from school to her home or to the store for her mother. When summer came, she sometimes walked with the two girls: "the blonde, the little stuck-up bitch who said hello to everybody"— except them—"and the other one with brown hair cut like some butch *cachapera* lesbian, but with a fine *culo*, which she was probably handing out left and right cause they'd seen her with some big *moreno* musician and those *morenos* could fuck you up just like that, man, so you had to watch yourself at all times when they were around. *Morenos* all carried pieces and they'd blow you up for nothing so you had to be fucking careful, man."

One afternoon toward the end of summer when things began to get real boring, the four of them were loping like a pack of wild dogs, their tongues hanging out, smacking each other five as they went, stopping over by Houston Street in the playground to "light up some erf and get stoned and maybe go to the hangout in the basement and light up the pipe and get really good wif some rock," when they saw her, "all blond and her titties sticking up big from the T-shirt and whatnot." She was all alone, without her sisters that they heard were called Cookie and Vidamía, "like she was P.R. and whatnot," which they didn't believe, "not because she was white, because there were plenty of white Puerto Ricans, blondes and redheads like the family over by Norfolk Street that all the kids had red hair and whatnot."

"And shit, you can't get no whiter than Papo wif his green eyes, even though he's all *bizco*, cross-eyed and whatnot."

"Oh, goof, man, gimme five, bro, daniggah be buggin' out. One eye be goin' one way and da otha goin' da otha way."

"Niggah, fuck you, it's your mother that's *bizca* from takin' all that *daga* in her *crica*, bro."

"Hey, niggah, don't be dissin' my moms, okay, faggot? Whatcha think your motha is, a burgen, like Madonna?"

"Oh, shit, daniggah call your motha Madonna. I be buggin' if some dude call my moms Madonna. That bitch take a lotta dick. Julio and Davey from Avenue C said they fuck her in her limo and whatnot."

"Oh, shut up, you retard mothafucka. Madonna ain't no burgen. You gotta a GQ of about twenty-two and can't read or write you so stupid."

"Oh, fuck you, niggah. Your GQ about twelve. You buggin' cause you got your eagle all indaway whendaniggah said your motha was Madonna, who be fucking niggahs all up and down Avenue C in her limo."

"Niggah, suck my dick. Youdaone that's plexed up, cause you got serious eagle problems and should be goin' over to Bellevue regular to see a shink."

"Your motha should be going to see a shink since she's so crazy that she had you, cause you gotta be totally bugged out to have a niggah like you in her family."

So it was obvious that the girl that was always with them couldn't be Rican even if her name was Vidamía, which wasn't even a Rican name anyhow, even though her name sounded like it cause they heard her talking and she talked "like she was on television, right, bro?"

"Yeah, like a ankle woman," Pipo said.

"A what?" Pupi inquired.

"A ankle woman," Pipo replied. "Them bitches that giveda-news on TV, man."

"Oh, yeah, like that Michelle Fifa on Channel 2, or that chink bitch Connie Yingyang on CBS," Pupi said. "They all fine bitches."

"So like what'sdabitch's name?" Pipo said.

"I tole you, niggah," Papo said. "Fun. She was in school wif me."

"Phone? Wha kine o' name is that?" Pepe inquired.

"Not Phone, you dumb mothafucka," Papo said. "Fun, like we gonna have us some fun."

"That's a fucked-up name," Pupi said. "How you gonna name a baby Fun?"

"Man, American people name their kids all kinds of weird shit," Papo said. "Her name's Fun Farrot. Somethin' like that."

"Parrot?" Pepe said. "Like a bird? My grandmotha gots two parakeets. They fly all around da house and sit on her shoulders. She had three but one landed ondafrying pan when she was frying pork chops and got fried. My uncle Ricky ate it."

"Forget you, okay, Pepe?" Pipo said. "You got a fucked-up head and trying to get niggahs to watch another one of them science-friction movies. Whyncha chill?"

"No, it's true, man," Pepe protested. "It ain't no science friction."

"Shut up, homeboy," Papo said. "And it ain't science friction. It's science fixin, cause they always be trying to fix shit like they be doin' on *Star Trek* and whatnot. You always seeing 'em trying to fix something some monster broke. Anyway, da bitch's name is Fun."

"Yo, how you spell that?" Pipo asked.

"Man, whatcha wanna know for?" Pupi said, crossing his arms in front of him and pursing his lips, his head turned so that the peak of his baseball cap, already askew, was facing Pipo.

"You ain't gonna remember da mothafucka, so whatcha wanna know for?"

"Word," Papo said. "You another re-tard."

"Niggah, fuck you," Pipo said.

"Oh, man, suck my dick," Papo said, grabbing his crotch.

"Chill, fellas," Pupi said. "I betcha we could get us some pussy offa that girl."

"Yeah?" Pipo said.

"Hell yeah, man," Papo replied. "I tole you I was in da fourf grade wif her. She's fine, ain't she? I know she likes me."

"Yeah, I bet she got them serious blond *pendejos* down there and her pussy's all pink and whatnot," Pipo said.

"Damn, homeboy," Pupi said. "Stop talkin' about that shit. My dick's getting so hard it's gonna rip my pants. I'ma go lookin' for that fine *mami*."

"We gonna fuck 'er, Pupi?" Pepe said, finally catching on to what they were talking about.

"Yeah, but we gotta go slow," Pupi said.

So, their brains, which didn't function too well when it came to ordinary problems but went into high gear when it came to the production of criminality, ascertained that the best course of action was to have Papo, who knew her, begin *haciéndole el cuento* and *comiéndole el celebro*. Not *cerebro*, as all other Spanish-speaking people said, but *celebro*, which anyone with enough Latin or even a rudimentary science education can figure out since it refers to your thinking *sombrero*—using phrases which their predecessors had used, but which still served them when talking about women, because things hadn't changed that much since it had been tribally and traditionally established that women weren't all there. When you talked to women about love, when you gave them a story, or *the story* to be precise, *el cuento,* their *pantaletas* immediately needed about three-quarters of an hour to dry after you had eaten up their brain, so that the only conclusion one could come to regarding the amorous discourse of Latin men to their women is that their words had a corrosive effect on the cerebral cortex and rendered the women unable to think and triggered some mechanism in their brain which was connected to their vaginas and which caused their underpants to fly off them and their legs to spring open in grateful anticipation.

So Papo began his conquest of his lady fair, not with the childish intent of your average male who wishes to reenact some idiotic pageant of courtship in order to entice an unsuspecting maiden to her sexual doom, but with the intent of getting the *Posse of the Pingo* finally laid properly instead of manipulating their *morcillas*.

They didn't even talk about how to proceed, but instinctively knew it was required that they separate from each other until the proper time. Although they periodically got together in the evening to hang out and smoke erf and some rock and talk about things, they generally spent most of the day occupied by their own responsibilities, nefarious as they were. Pipo, his mother having escaped to Puerto Rico, managed to remain in the apartment by selling small amounts of crack. Pepe spent most of his time at his grandmother's house watching Spanish soap operas with her, being told to shut up, and getting smacked on the head so that his grandmother could concentrate. He liked getting hit on the head. It was almost like getting high. His grandmother hit hard.

Pupi was the envy of the other three because he had the most prestigious job. Pupi, through his uncle Mike, who raised pit bulls and fought them, was helping him to train them. Every day he had to bring one of the dogs down to the park on the other side of the FDR Drive, near the Baruch Projects, throw the training rope over a tree branch and bait the dog until he grasped the other end of the rope. The dog's end of the rope had a knot which the dog grabbed in its massive and powerful jaws and refused to let go. In order to strengthen the dog's jaw, it was Pupi's job to pull on the rope until the dog was off the ground. Such was the fighting spirit and determination of the dogs that it was virtually impossible for them to let go once they had locked in on their prey. Sometimes, he tied his end of the rope to a bench and watched the animal hang by his jaws for an hour or so, incapable of letting go. When he'd let the dog down, the animal would stand on unsteady legs, the knot still clutched in its jaws. That is how Pipo would bring the dog back home, the animal still clutching the knot until he got him to the kennels in the basement of the building on Avenue D and gave the dog water.

Pupi also had responsibility for cleaning up after his uncle's dogs, walking them, and making sure they had food and water. For his efforts his uncle paid him fifty dollars a day and had let him pick a puppy from a litter one of his bitches had whelped the year before. Pupi named the puppy Macho Man—"in case some crazy-ass homeboy wanna fuck wif me." The puppy was a brindle color with red gums and strong, bowed legs. Eventually, it grew to be a magnificently large and powerful dog, trained to attack on command.

Once, in the park, he had cornered a fairly large stray and ten minutes later the other dog lay dying in spasms of horrible pain as Macho Man bit deeper and deeper into its throat, crushing the larynx so that even in its death throes the victimized dog, attempting to bark, did little more than emit small, wheezing sounds that resembled escaping gas. So magnificent was Macho Man that his uncle Mike offered Pupi five hundred dollars for him. Pupi shook his head, but, knowing that his uncle could take the dog if he really wanted to, he told Mike that he could breed Macho Man whenever he wanted and could keep all the puppies. His uncle laughed and said, "Word," and told him that wasn't a bad deal and pulled out a big roll of hundred-dollar bills and gave him a couple and threw a nickel bag of grass his way. Pupi's affection for his dog was the closest thing to love that he would ever feel for another living thing.

Papo now became a lone wolf and got himself pretty straight, so that he was only smoking grass a couple times a day, and even got himself a little job, helping the vegetable man at the super-market. He avoided hanging out with his homeboys except late at night when they'd get together up on some roof and he'd report on the progress of his hunt. His romantic pursuit of Fawn Farrell was minimal until one day when it was pouring rain and he caught sight of Fawn running through the wind-driven downpour and ducking into the pizza shop over on Houston Street, around the corner from Katz's on Ludlow Street. Papo went in carrying his umbrella.

"Yo, how you doin?" he said, and stood by the door shaking the rain out of his *sombrilla*.

Fawn immediately blushed and looked down at her shoes. The chill of the rain was making goose bumps on her arms. The big boy, his cap turned all the way back, his green eyes boring into her, made her feel more awkward than usual. Unable to speak, she was on the verge of dashing from the store and running home in the rain to get away from the discomfort.

"We useta be in school together, right?" Papo said.

"I don't know," Fawn replied.

"Yeah, in da fourf grade wif Miss Gold."

"Oh, yeah," Fawn said, suddenly recalling him. "Your name is Carlos, right?"

"Yeah, right, Carlos Marcano," he said. "Papo."

And then she saw him in the picture: back row, standing to the left of her; his hair falling a little to the side and his eyes clear like hers, but a little crossed, so that she always felt sorry for him. His skin was white and not like the other boys and girls, who were dark.

"I remember now," she said. "Did you move away?"

"Yeah, we moved up to Harlem and whatnot," he said, posturing, his hands turned inward toward the middle of his body and then going forward to either side as if he were giving a safe sign as he explained, his gesticulations perfectly timed to the rhythm of his words, mesmerizing her. "My moms got a project up there, but I don't like it wif so many niggahs so I come down here and stay wif my aunt over on Avenue B. You're Fun, right?"

"What?" she said, confused. She guessed she could be if she tried, but this was too scary.

"I mean, your name's Fun," Papo said.

"Oh, yeah," she said shyly, looking up and sweeping her hair behind her ears, finally catching on. "Fawn Farrell." She made sure he heard her name correctly.

"Oh, I like that. It's a pretty name," Papo said. "I always liketed it. You wanna pizza?"

Fawn shook her head but then Papo smiled at her and he was really cute, his hair cut nice and his eyes smiling at her even though he was still cross-eyed, which made her feel bad for him because she was sure people made fun of him, like they had with Angela and her lip. He asked her again. She finally nodded and said okay, so he pointed to a booth and she sat down and he asked her what kind of soda she wanted and she said Pepsi and he went up and got them pizza and sodas and they sat down and she kept thinking, even though her clothes and hair were all wet, that she was on a date like Vee and Cookie and Cliff. Her heart sort of gave a little jump and then she was frightened and began thinking that maybe he'd want to touch her or kiss her and her left eye began twitching a little bit like it always did when she got nervous. She immediately was afraid she'd start making the ugly faces that came on her sometimes, but everything passed. And then he was asking her about what she was doing during the summer and she said that she sometimes helped out at the video store over on Avenue C and she was reading a book about horses.

Papo said he liked horses, but all he was thinking about "was being in Central Park that day and watching the big horse dick," and then he felt his own dick getting harder as he watched "the little bitch all wet and her skin rosy and her big *tetas* all sticking out through the wet T-shirt so you could see her nippers all outlined on the clof," as he said in reporting to his homeboys, so that all he felt like doing was "whipping out my dick right there and *haciendo me la puñeta* under da table so that it shot right at her jeans, bro. One big blast that smash up against her and burned her mothafuckin pussy," he said to them. Instead, his "eagle" mediated the dispute between his "lid" and his "super eagle," as they would have called it had they had full awareness of this Freudian concept.

"I got a serious pit," Papo said.

"A pit bull?"

"Yeah, a big one. Macho Man. That's what I call him. You like pits?"

"Yeah, they're cute," she said, lying, as even sophisticated adults will do on dates.

"Yeah, they be chomping on your leg and they just shake till it come off and whatnot."

When they were done eating the pizza and drinking their sodas, it was still raining, but she said she had to go and he told her he'd walk her home and she shook her head. He insisted, telling her she'd get all wet and maybe catch a cold and he sounded like he was worried about her and all at once she was thinking about the song and about Bobby McGee. The end of the song said, "Good enough for me and my Bobby McGee." Fawn didn't want to be there with this boy. She wanted to be with Bobby McGee. She and Bobby McGee were running in the rain outside of Baton Rouge and they were happy. The thought relaxed her for the moment, so she said okay and when they got outside he opened up the big umbrella and she got under it and they began walking south on Allen, crossing Rivington and then Delancey and then when they were near the loft she said she had to go and he asked where she lived and she pointed at the big factory building and he said, "Yeah?" like he didn't know.

Fawn nodded and started to go but he held her back, his large hand grasping her arm and his veiled, sleepy eyes boring into her, so that she felt trapped and shook her head but no words came out of her mouth. She could feel the power of his strong right arm—the same arm that had snapped Huang's neck—coursing through her blood and she began to hyperventilate and her face contorted horribly and he let her go.

"What's the matter?" he said.

"Nothing, I gotta go."

"Maybe we can go to da moobies."

She shook her head, turned, and ran the half block to the door of the loft, all the while searching for her keys in the little bag that she carried. When the keys were finally out, she stuck the key in the lock, turned it rapidly, opened the door and nearly tumbled inside, pulling the door behind her and standing in the semi-darkness. Her breathing was labored and her face moved uncontrollably until all she could do to stop herself from shaking was to pull her own hair until it hurt so much that she cried. She then sat down on an old milk crate, put her head down between her legs, and vomited, feeling the acidy taste of the tomato sauce and the sugar from the soda mixing and making her gag worse so that she continued to dry-heave for several minutes. Oh, she hated him, just hated him, and couldn't stand how he'd held her so that she couldn't move.

She took a deep breath and pushed the elevator button. When she heard it commence its creaky descent, she hunted for a broom and swept the vomit from the concrete floor, spreading it here and there so that in a few minutes the floor would be dry again. She'd have to tell her mother and then come back with a bucket of water and some Lysol and clean it up.

She hated herself so much because what she should've done

was not accept the pizza and simply run home in the rain and not sit there with him as if he really liked her. When the elevator came, she got in, pushed the number five on the panel, and, as the elevator climbed, she began to relax once more and even considered that perhaps Carlos "Papo" Marcano really liked her. She then asked herself whether she liked him and her heart gave an unnatural tug and she saw his face once more, his green eyes behind the heavy lids toying with her and she smiled slightly, the only awareness of the event in a vast and complex universe being her own private witnessing. It was like she'd had her first date, but she wasn't going to tell anybody. She blushed deep red and shook her head in chiding disapproval of her folly. Deep within her, however, she felt satisfaction at her conquest.

51 Threats

Elsa Santiago's rage was monumental as she sat alone on the train speeding out of the 125th Street Station, the station situated, ironically, in Harlem. She once again opened her briefcase and stared at the eight-by-ten glossy photographs of Vidamía leaning against the young black man, her eyes closed as they rode the subway; the two of them holding hands as they walked in the park or lay on the grass, kissing unashamedly; them sitting at an outdoor café in the Village, staring into each other's eyes; him feeding her daughter sushi with chopsticks in a Japanese restaurant. There were other photos of them simply walking down the street, her arm through his as he carried his saxophone case.

Elsa's jealousy was overwhelming as she took in her daughter's radiance, her face shining with love for this "Wyndell Ross," so named in the report, which also gave his address and the time she'd spent in his apartment—indicating that on at least six occasions during that month of April, Vidamía had spent the night in his home, most likely cohabitating although this couldn't be ascertained. For a slightly higher fee the detective agency would attempt to plant a bug in the apartment, and for a somewhat higher fee they could photograph the lovers in the act, although this was generally restricted to infidelity and divorce cases. Elsa shook her head violently and insisted that neither the phone conversations nor the explicit photos were necessary.

She was going crazy, she thought, because she was now fantasizing about watching Vidamía make love to Wyndell, imagining an enormous black organ swollen, pulsating and entering her daughter who was writhing with delight beneath him.

That night she made love to Barry wildly, devouring his mouth with such ardor that, although he enjoyed himself, he wondered what had come over his wife. She rode him violently and when her orgasm took over she bit him and pounded his arms and chest with such force that he grabbed her and shook her until she was crying, and then he raped her brutally. He apologized but she was lost in her world. He got up, turned on the lights, and asked her what was the matter.

Elsa got out of bed, not bothering to dress, her body still lithe and well-formed, still appealing to Barry, although for the moment all he felt was soreness, both on his member and throughout his body. She walked over to a chest of drawers and from it extracted the report and photographs. She took everything out of the manila envelope and spread the pictures on the bed.

"A black man," Elsa said.

"Handsome," Barry said. "A cross between Denzel Washington and that football player for Minnesota who married Bill Cosby's wife in the show. Mrs. Huxstable. Ahmad Rashad."

"Stop it, Barry," Elsa had said through gritted teeth. "This is serious."

"Give me a break, Elsa. All I said is that he's handsome. Are you going to deny this?"

"Yes, I am," Elsa said, pulling a nightshirt over her head as if the young black man could see her from the photos. "I don't think he's that handsome," she lied. "He's ugly, in fact."

"Because he's black?"

"Barry! Dammit, whose side are you on?"

"Nobody's side. But I have to tell you something. You're going to lose your daughter. And when you do, you're going to regret it."

"What's that supposed to mean?"

"Just what I said. She's going to get fed up with your trips and disappear from your life. She's too smart and has too much dignity to put up with this kind of harassment. And let me tell you something else. She has a tremendous amount of character. Threatening to cut her off financially isn't going to affect her one bit. Look at how she's managed to pay that money back. She's helped her father's family set up a video store, and it's turned out to be very profitable. At her age I had nowhere near her business acumen."

"Well, she had a pretty good consultant," Elsa said, sarcastically.

"It was her idea all the way. All I did was set up her books."

"Oh, sure. Take a look at the rest of the pictures," Elsa said, pointing at the photos on the bed. "There are pictures of their operation and a detailed account of the undesirable characters that go in and out of the store. Drug dealers, prostitutes, pimps, thieves."

"Hey, since when did participating in illegal activities disqualify a person from renting and watching a videotape in their own home?"

"That's not the point and you know it."

"No, I don't. You're saying that in a neighborhood that is mostly Puerto Rican, everybody is some sort of social deviant. You know that's not true, and saying so is a gross generalization."

"She probably borrowed the money from drug dealers to set up that store."

"Wrong again," Barry said, perhaps a little too smugly.

"Oh, really?" she said. "And where did she get it? From you?"

"That's right," Barry said, standing up and reaching for one of his infrequent cigarettes. Elsa was stunned. She turned away and looked out into the night. "She came to me with a business proposal and I had no choice but to accept it."

"Just her books? You are a liar, just like her," she said. "Just get the hell out of here."

The next day she canceled all of her appointments. She remained in the house, pacing, and eventually took her silver Porsche out, heading north, driving very fast, until she was nearly a hundred miles from her home, somewhere in Connecticut, before she turned around and came back. On her way home, the rage no longer threatening to consume her, she knew she had no recourse but to go to the authorities with the case. Her daughter was, after all, a minor. She'd be eighteen in three months, but for the time being she was a minor, and if she understood the law correctly, Mr. Wyndell Ross, whatever his charm, and whatever his attraction to an unbalanced young woman, was guilty of statutory rape.

She didn't move immediately to formulate a plan for punishing the deviant, cradle-snatching Mr. Wyndell Ross, who almost nightly appeared in her dreams, as if in a motion picture, once dressed in a vampire outfit, like Morgan Freeman as the Count on *The Electric Company*, announcing himself boastfully and then counting the times he had ravaged her daughter, except that he was pointing at her, at Elsa. Another time Wyndell Ross was dressed in white tails and tap shoes, his black skin shimmering like polished ebony, while she, not her daughter, wore a beautiful black gown, her skin alabaster white and equally shimmering, and the two of them joined for an elaborate dance number similar to those made famous by Fred Astaire and Ginger Rogers, spinning and twirling in wide arcs across the glistening glass-like dance floor of a mansion, the columns rising to an ornate ceiling, a crystal chandelier above them, the musical production of Hollywood proportions, the two of them spinning madly, tap-dancing, and she, smiling sensuously at him. Often she woke up sweating, her vagina wishing to be entered, causing her to masturbate in her now lonely bed. When she didn't dream, she woke up in a bad mood and cursed her rift with Barry and her now loveless life, insisting still that he sleep in one of the guest rooms at the other end of the house.

Two weeks later, understanding that she had been foolish, Elsa phoned Barry at work and asked if they could meet somewhere in the city. He agreed, and they went to dinner at a French restaurant in Midtown and then went dancing at a club in Tribeca. At two in the morning she said it didn't make sense to go home, and they ended up staying at the Waldorf and making love in a huge suite of rooms, the two of them drunk and angry, he cursing at her and she crying and accepting the abuse as though she deserved it, although she knew that she was partly acting, to induce a catharsis, if you will. In the morning, over their room-service breakfast, she told him about her plan to have Wyndell prosecuted.

"She'll hate you for the rest of your life, Elsie," he said. "I understand how you feel, but you don't know the guy. Just cause he's black doesn't mean he's some sort of undesirable."

"It's not that he's black," she said, sheepishly.

"Okay, then. Leave it alone."

"What are the Marreros going to think?" she said, almost in a whisper.

"The hell with the Marreros, baby," Barry said. "I'm thinking of selling my part of Spantax and moving on. Someone was telling me about the Internet and how it's going to explode in the next ten years. I'm not so sure, but I'm watching things closely."

She nodded and snuggled against him. They kissed tenderly and then made love slowly, and for the first time in a while she felt safe again with Barry. They eventually got up, made phone calls, and before eleven they were back to the routine of their lives.

Elsa, however, couldn't leave the issue of Wyndell alone and one evening about a week later, feeling edgy, she coaxed Vidamía into the library and began to ask about her college plans, congratulating her once more on her acceptance into Harvard and the other colleges, wondering if she ought to look at the other schools before finally deciding.

"No, I went up to Harvard and I loved the campus and Cambridge and everything. Really, it doesn't make sense to go running around, wasting time and money."

"As long as you're not going to regret it later," Elsa said, nodding thoughtfully.

"I won't, *mami*," Vidamía said. "Don't worry."

"So, how's your love life?" Elsa then said, matter-of-factly, almost jokingly.

"Oh, there's this girl that I've been seeing, but it's not serious," Vidamía said, mischievously.

"What?" Elsa said, momentarily off balance, then realizing she was being put on. "That's all I need," she said, feigning relief.

"No, really, there's nobody special. I've been on a couple of dates, but that's all."

"You wouldn't lie to me, would you?" Elsa said, looking into her eyes.

"I'm capable of it," Vidamía said, with as much aplomb. "But I'm not."

"My friend Amelia Boswell said she thought she saw you with someone in Central Park."

"Really? That's possible. A musician?"

Elsa couldn't believe she could be so cool and lie so expertly.

"Yes, she thought so."

"Oh, that's Wyn, a friend of Cookie's."

"Is he black?"

"He certainly is. His father's a doctor. Not like you. I mean, he's not a Ph.D., he's an M.D. By the way, I've pretty much made up my mind that I'm going to go into pediatric medicine."

Elsa could no longer stand what she perceived as Vidamía's arrogance. She stared out through the opened French doors, through the sliding screen door, and into the garden, the fragrance of the spring night wafting in to intoxicate her fury.

"You're lying to me," she said, as if she were speaking to the night. "He's *your* friend."

"What if he is? That's none of your business."

"Well?" Elsa said, facing her.

"Well, what?"

"Is he your friend or your lover?"

"What are you talking about? I don't wanna go on with this. I've got things to do."

"I have a right to know these things. I'm your mother."

"You're my mother but you don't have a right to pry into my life. If I were going out with him, I'd tell you. I don't have your kind of hang-ups about race."

"You're a liar," Elsa said, the rage now boiling over. She reached behind her to a reading table and from a large atlas she removed the folder with the photographs, the report having been safely locked away, and slapped the folder on the table. "What's this about?"

Vidamía came over and looked at the photographs and shook her head. She laughed sarcastically and looked at her mother with intense hatred.

"Well?" Elsa said.

"Well, nothing," Vidamía said. "You've been snooping around, and about the only thing I can say to you is that if I trusted you, I would have come and told you about it."

"You lied to me."

"So?"

"I'm your mother."

"And I'm your daughter."

"What's that supposed to mean?"

"You lied to me for twelve years."

"I did nothing of the kind."

"Yes, you did. About my father. Whenever I asked you about him, you evaded the question so that I had to go find him myself. You even told me that he had abandoned us, which is a huge lie. Or have you forgotten that?"

"Is that how you met this Wyndell Ross of yours?" Elsa said, avoiding the challenge.

Hearing Wyndell's name shook Vidamía violently. She was ready to ask how she'd learned his name, but knew that Elsa had either been following her, checking up on her, or had hired someone to do so. She went rapidly through the photos, recalling each instance, but unable to remember whether she'd seen someone with a camera. They must have used a miniature for the shots in the subway. She wanted to scream at her mother, to tear the pictures up, but thought better of it. She had to remain calm to best her mother. She smiled smugly and with immense pride addressed Elsa.

"Isn't he beautiful?"

"Beautiful? You call that Harlem or Bedford Stuyvesant deviant beautiful?"

"Oh, yes, very beautiful. And you don't have to worry about all those esoteric psychopathologies that you're so familiar with, *Doctora*. He's so straight he comes pretty close to being boring sometimes. Very well-off family in Denver, Colorado. Father physician. Mother owns an art gallery. One sister is a college professor and the other a painter who lives in Paris and is married to a Swedish musician in the Stockholm Philharmonic. They made all their money the old-fashioned way, they earned it. No drug deals, no bank holdups, no underworld hits. Actually, my boy-friend's family is the only black family in the United States that doesn't earn their money from drugs or crime. The only one."

"Stop the sarcasm, dammit."

"Only one nondysfunctional black family in the entire coun-try and your daughter happens to be involved with their son. You should be very proud."

"Oh, so you admit it."

"Admit what?"

"That you're screwing him."

"Regularly and with passionate abandon. He even gives me head to hasten my orgasms."

Elsa felt slightly nauseous and she banged her fist on the table.

"Stop it," she said. "How can you talk like that?"

"On occasion I reciprocate and it drives him absolutely wild. His penis is sort of a purple color. Get it? The color purple. Like a large grape and just as sweet."

"Stop it."

"Cut the bullshit, Mom," Vidamía said. "What kind of a fucking hypocrite are you?"

"Don't talk to me like that, young lady."

"Young lady, nothing. When the hell are you gonna get off this young lady crap? I have a name. Vidamía. Grandma told me what happened. You wanted to call me Katherine or Samantha or some bullshit name like that. I asked Lurleen about my name and she told me what my father said. He said you had called out "*vida mía*" or something like that when you were, pardon me, *screwing*."

"Stop it right this minute."

"I'm assuming this outpouring of passion didn't take place while you were decorating my Lower East Side nursery, but in a moment of supposed ecstasy in which you were playing the lead in some imagined soap opera and you thought it would sound cool to utter "*vida mía*." Believe me, it doesn't matter. In fact, I love the name. It's so unique I'm thinking of having a large neon sign made in multicolored letters, like Fruit Loops, and getting a harness and carrying the whole fucking thing wherever I go. The name blinking on and off. What do you think?"

"I think you're having a nervous breakdown and you need help."

"Bullshit. You're the disturbed one, snooping around on her daughter."

"Fine, treat the whole matter of my concern with disdain."

"Disdain? I don't feel disdain. I'm actually pissed off and ready to fucking kill, I'm so angry. You didn't have any right to do what you did. He and I are in love with each other."

"Oh, that's lovely," Elsa said, sensing Vidamía retreating from the argument. "The two of you may be in love, but I'm seriously thinking of turning the case over to the authorities. Whether you know it or not it's been established that you spent time in his apartment and by your own admission the two of you have been sexually intimate. That's considered statutory rape. You look shocked. That's right. Having sex with a minor is statutory rape. Whether that minor gives her consent or not, the law treats the case as rape. Remember, sweetie, you're not yet eighteen. Three more months, so all of this took place prior to your birthday."

Vidamía was suddenly seized by an attack of panic. She vaguely recalled a case such as the one her mother was describing. She knew that Elsa was sufficiently driven to do as she threatened. Her mind was suddenly flooded with images of Wyndell standing before a judge, having his career ruined and possibly having to serve time in jail. And then a cold, slicing swath of illumination cut through the building despair and she smiled kindly at her mother.

"Do you know what I'm going to do if you even raise the subject of Wyn and statutory rape again? I'm going to go upstairs, pack some clothes, go directly to Manhattan, and tell him what you're up to. We will immediately take a plane and go somewhere and get married. How's that?"

"Are you threatening me?"

"Ayep, ma'am, I guess I am," she said, hooking her thumbs into the loops of her jeans.

"You would, wouldn't you?"

"I'm your daughter, ain't I?"

"Unfortunately," Elsa said icily as she gathered the photos.

"The feeling is mutual," Vidamía said. "It's your loss, you know. I'm sure you would've found Wyn fascinating. And you have to admit, Wyn and Vee make an outstanding couple. We are so fucking photogenic. We are like Ellen Barkin and Laurence Fishburne sucking face. Or like Wesley Snipes and Annabella Sciorra in *Jungle Fever*. We be two boogies. We be two niggahs, one black and the other white," adding this last in her most extreme black English.

Elsa looked at her daughter with the deadliest expression Vidamía had ever seen on anyone's face. It was as if whatever drove her mother had been sucked out of her life and what remained was spiritually skeletal, the vestiges of a damned soul, which by her second year of college she could assign specifically to a circle in the infernal literary convolutions of Dante Alighieri. For now, however, she was reminded of the boys around Avenue B who stood glaring at her and from time to time made lewd suggestions when she walked by on her way to the video store. Their eyes had no life to them, no mirth, no compassion. Whatever traces of humanity had at one time existed in them had become extinguished and only mistrust and hatred were now there. Her mother's eyes looked very much like that.

Meeting her grandfather, Justino "Tumba" Santiago, master *conguero*, raconteur, bon vivant, Latino good-time Charlie, skirt-loving *guaguancosero*, and *hombre del basilón*, threw Vidamía Farrell for a humongous loop. This thin, dark, impish man—with skin the color of cordovan leather, an infectious smile that featured a dazzling gold tooth, and the sparkling eyes of someone who has seen the world in all its splendor and degradation and has distilled the experience into a most relaxed attitude—appeared to treat the entire matter of existence, without any philosophical basis or words to articulate such, as a great cosmic joke. And, to ward off any pretense that death will look the other way when it comes calling, he seemed to have decided that one must always keep uppermost in one's mind the truly important things in life: first and foremost, one must learn of those places where good-looking *muchachas* perch their glorious *nalga*s and what threads to wear when standing skintight-close to their magical flesh, conveying to them how truly unique a flower they are in this vast garden of life; or who's bringing the rum; or whether to choose red, pink, kidney, black, or white beans, pigeon peas, *petitpois*, or chickpeas to go with the rice. Because, after all, he seemed to say, besides the music and those things, what the hell was there?

Listening to Justino Santiago talk made the core of Vidamía's cells become itchy to know where he had truly come from. Puerto Rico, yes, she knew that. But she needed to know the interior of his life and how he existed and what it was about him that drew her to come back to see him and ask him questions about this Puerto Rican thing that seemed different from what her mother talked about.

As she saw it, the problem was that her mother wanted to pretend that the Puerto Rican thing was only a matter of language, history, politics, and culture, with a great deal of rhetorical justification, rather than the indefinable quality that her grandfather possessed. Her mother and Barry and their friends sounded as if they were trying to convince themselves of how wonderful it was to be Puerto Rican, and that someday when Puerto Rico was free, they would rest from their labors of preaching its greatness, in spite of being ravaged these many years by Yanqui imperialism, and go back. But she doubted that they truly would. Her grandmother and most of the people of her generation talked longingly about returning to their homeland. Few that Vidamía knew, perhaps because they lacked the financial resources, ever did so. The younger generation, the people who had been born in the United States and were under forty, had little desire to go back, yet insisted that they were Puerto Rican, and proud.

Her grandfather's attitude puzzled her for it was totally different. He showed no zeal for going back, nor any sense of resignation about staying, no resentment of the United States, nor any great flag-waving concerning the island. Tumba Santiago took everything in stride and, whenever she asked him about Puerto Rico, he'd smile and tell her a story about playing at the Escambrón Beach Club with Noro Morales and his orchestra, or traveling with Bobby Capó or going to Ponce to play at society dances, adding how beautiful the women were, but always telling her that none were as beautiful as she was; telling her that there had never been a Puerto Rican girl as beautiful as Vidamía Faro, as he pronounced her name, saying those things about her in such an honest way that it made her believe it more than when Wyn would shake his head and marvel at her.

Vidamía Faro. She had looked in the dictionary for the word and found that *faro* meant lighthouse. This reading of her name made her laugh. She was Mylife Lighthouse. You light up my life. C'mona my house, which her mother sang and said that it was by Rosemary Clooney, who had been married to José Ferrer, who was Puerto Rican, even though some people thought of him as a Spaniard who happened to be born in Puerto Rico. This angered her mother and she explained that this was the way the society looked at Puerto Ricans. If the person achieved something great then it must be because he was from Spain. If the person had accomplished little or had done something bad, then the person was Puerto Rican. Her mother was always throwing famous Puerto Rican names at her. But unlike her mother, Vidamía didn't have a Puerto Rican name. Her last name was Farrell, and not Faro.

She knew she was an attractive person, better than average-looking, she thought, but never took it further than that. She also realized that her sister, Cookie, was brutally honest and couldn't be hypocritical if her life depended on it and, if she had said that she was very beautiful, then there had to be some truth to it. Wyn had said the same thing, but she knew he was blinded by love. But when her grandfather said it, it was different because underneath he knew something and that something was Puerto Rican so that everything he said had a hidden meaning, an *indirecta* which told you a truth without spelling it out.

If it wasn't the *indirectas*, there was always some kind of joke going on, the language so convoluted that Vidamía needed an explanation most of the time. She often imagined they had to be talking about sex, since her grandfather just laughed at her, pointed at Flaco or his other friend, Baltazar, who had African features, reddish processed hair and pale, white skin with freckles, and who had one brown eye and one blue eye, which, her grandfather explained another time, when Baltazar was sitting at the table and they were eating crabs Baltazar had caught in the river in East Harlem where he lived, was a problem that he, Justino, also had.

"No, grandpa," she'd argued. "*Tus ojos son negros.* You have black eyes, *güelo.*"

"Oh, no, *negrita,*" he'd said, calling her "my little black one," which she liked hearing because it had so much tenderness in it; using the term of endearment her grandmother and all of Cookie's friends and their relatives used no matter how white the person was, but which she never heard from her mother. "*Yo tengo un ojo negro y otro azulado.*"

Vidamía shook her head and then took his face in both her hands, smelling the traces of cigar smoke and the lingering sweet taste of rum, and, peering closely at his eyes, challenged his contention that one of his eyes was black and the other bluish.

To which he replied, pointing to one eye and then the other, "*Uno negro y otro a su lado.* See the other one, next to it? *A su lado.* Not *azulado.* I guess you heard me wrong, *negrita,*" he chided her, speaking English much better than she'd thought he was able.

"Oh, *güelo,* I'm going to strangle you."

"I got you again," he'd said with total delight, hugging her, and his face now smelling of aftershave lotion and his body of baby powder, traces of which you could notice around his neck, so that the skin there was dusky with a fine layer of talc.

"You're so bad," she'd said, hugging him back, "but I love you. You're my *güelito.*"

And he'd laugh and tell her little rhyming puzzles like "*Plata no es, oro no es, abre la cortina y verás lo que es.*" To which she'd say that if it wasn't silver and it wasn't gold, why bother to open the curtain because she wouldn't be able to guess, and he'd laugh some more and say, "*Plátano, plátano, boba,*" calling her silly and telling her that behind the curtain was a plantain. But if she asked him something complex, such as what he thought of the lack of opportunities for Puerto Rican people on the island and in New York, he'd say no more than "I love Puerto Rico and I love the United States."

As much as she loved her grandfather, she had to admit that he wasn't much help, because she had so many questions and most people she asked didn't know what she was talking about.

She wanted to find out what had happened to the Taino Indians or how African slaves had gotten to the island. Had the same thing happened to Puerto Ricans that happened to the people in *Roots*? Why had so many Puerto Ricans come up to the United States, and why were so many of them so poor? Why was it that practically every girl she'd met who was a friend of Cookie's, in the six years she'd gone to spend summers with her father, had a brother or a sister, cousin, uncle, aunt, father, or mother in jail, addicted to drugs, or murdered?

Needing answers to these questions, she spoke with Elsa, with whom she had fashioned an uncomfortable truce after her threat to marry Wyndell. Two weeks later, Vidamía spoke with Barry about Wyn. He reassured her that he'd had nothing to do with the photos, though he did express his concern over the difficulties that a mixed relationship still had in this society.

"I mean, if you really like the guy, there's nobody in the world that can give you advice. Your mother worries about you. I suppose like every mother she doesn't want to see you hurt."

"All she worries about is how she's gonna look to other people."

"Deep inside, that's not the way she is," Barry said.

"I don't know . . ." she replied.

"You ought to be open with her," Barry had said. "I really think she'd appreciate that."

"I don't know if it's a good idea. I met my grandfather. Her father. I went to see him."

"Then you ought to tell her. I don't feel right revealing a confidence to you regarding your mother, but I'm going to and hope that it'll stay between us."

"I'm not going to tell her."

"Anyway, hiring someone to keep an eye on you had nothing to do with your boyfriend. Your mother was afraid of you establishing contact with her father."

"She was afraid?"

"Yes, that's the reason she did it. It's too bad she got different results, but in the long run it's probably for the best that it's out in the open. I'm sure you feel relieved."

"You're right. But you think I ought to tell her that I went to see *abuelo*?"

"Yes, I do."

"His name is Justino and he is *so* cool," she said, enthusiastically, jumping up and down.

"Good, but you should tell her."

She nodded and that weekend, when Elsa returned from one of her trips, Vidamía decided to sit with her mother and explain what she had done. Ostensibly, Vidamía came back to Tarrytown to begin packing the things she would eventually take to Harvard. It was the beginning of August and things were moving very rapidly toward Wyn's gig. Nervously, she approached her mother, who was sitting on the second-floor terrace outside her bedroom.

"May I speak with you, *mami*?" she said, returning to the more tender form of address she had for her mother, and using the more proper "may I," which she knew Elsa would appreciate.

"Sure," Elsa said, removing her sunglasses.

"I've met Grandpa Justino," she said, taking a seat in one of the patio chairs.

"I see," Elsa said, tensing up immediately.

"I tracked him down and went to see him. He lives up in the Bronx."

"When did you go up there?"

The tone of Elsa's voice annoyed her, but she kept calm, deciding to ignore the inquisitorial attitude behind the question.

"In the middle of July," she said. "A couple of weeks ago."

"I see," Elsa said. "And do you want to invite him here?"

"Oh, no, it's nothing like that. I just wanted you to know. Do you *want* me to?"

"Not particularly," Elsa said, rising, and, as she did when things became difficult, turning her back and speaking out into the expanse of lawn below the terrace, her arms crossed in front of her. "This may sound cruel, or perhaps detached, but I was never too close to him. With the years, I've distanced myself from any emotions that may have remained as vestiges of child-parent bonding. You understand, don't you?"

Vidamía wanted to tell Elsa that all she was doing was de-fending herself from being hurt, from having to identify with a man who lived life simply and without a need for pretense, a man who was sophisticated neither in his view of life nor in the subtlety of his emotions.

"Sure," she said, diplomatically. "Things happen. People become estranged," she added, enjoying the word, infusing what she was saying with sincerity and understanding for her mother's plight. "But wasn't it difficult growing up without him?" Vidamía asked. "I mean, you knew he was around but he never came to see you. Didn't it bother you? Didn't you want a connection to him? He's your father."

"It was difficult, but something I had to do," Elsa said, and turned to face her.

"Had to do?"

"To cut myself off from him. I asked about him from time to time but didn't want him involved in my life."

"Why not? He seems really nice and respectful," Vidamía said, wanting to reach her mother, to make her see she wasn't be-ing fair. "He asks about everyone and feels bad that he wasn't able to be there." Elsa began to respond, but shook her head. As she did, Vidamía saw the sadness in her mother, saw how painful it must have been for Elsa to create the separation be-tween father and daughter.

"He asked me how you were," Vidamía said.

"Really?" Elsa said, uncomfortably. "What did you say?"

"I said you were fine. I told him you were married and I

described our house. He asked me if you were rich and I told him no. I thought he'd feel bad if I said we were. I said you lived comfortably, and then he asked me if I thought you were happy."

"And what did you say?" Elsa asked, the anxiety in her voice betraying her concern for how her father would see her.

"I said you were very happy."

Elsa smiled wanly, sat back down and put on her sunglasses.

"Thank you," she said, softly.

Vidamía was certain there were tears behind her dark glasses.

"Anyway, I asked him about Puerto Rico. You know, the culture and politics, but mostly the history. That's what I'm interested in. He doesn't know. All he could tell me about was playing in different clubs with different orchestras. I want to know about the Tainos. How come they were wiped out? Cookie said that they were. I want to know why. I don't know why I do, but I want to know about everything."

Elsa's spirits were suddenly alive again and she said that she was very happy to hear that Vidamía was interested in finding out more about their culture. She said it was one of the happiest days of her life, to hear that her daughter was finally interested in Puerto Rico. What Elsa really meant was that perhaps in studying about Puerto Rico Vidamía would eventually get rid of her obsession with black culture.

"I've been waiting for this moment a long time," Elsa said.

"Really?" Vidamía said, somewhat surprised by Elsa's reaction. "Why?"

"Sure, I always worried that raising you like I did, you'd forget that you're basically Puerto Rican. I mean you're white, but you're Puerto Rican. When people say blacks, whites, Puerto Ricans, they're forgetting something. Puerto Rican isn't a color. We come in all sorts of colors. I'm sure you're very much aware of that. Finding out just now that you're getting interested in P.R. culture is, I don't know. Really cool."

Elsa went on chattering happily about the relationship between learning about one's culture and developing into a healthy adult, as always, referring to her own field of expertise.

"I was hoping you could suggest some books," Vidamía said. "Maybe they're even downstairs in the library."

"Oh, sure," Elsa replied. "I'm sure there are some. Start there. Whenever you can't find a book I'll refer you to other people and they can help you. I have colleagues all over. Vassar, City College, Hunter, and Princeton. I'll send you to my friend Dr. López Adorno at Hunter, and he can get you a pass to the Center for Puerto Rican Studies. Whatever we don't have here you can get there."

Vidamía thanked her mother, kissed her cheek, and returned downstairs. After talking to her mother Vidamía was left with an odd sensation that something was still amiss in her mother's enthusiasm. Why would Elsa all of a sudden be all smiles when she had just told her that she had seen her grandfather? She was sure it had to do with the business of color, but she couldn't figure out what it could be.

Being a reader of gargantuan capacities Vidamía Farrell availed herself of the opportunity to go up to Hunter College, where she did enough reading in the next two weeks to write a fairly decent thesis. She read that in colonial times the Taino Indians had fought the Spaniards. When they could no longer fight, they clasped their children to their breasts and leapt into the sea, thus setting in motion a strain of self-destruction rather than capitulation in Puerto Ricans. She also understood that race was swept under the rug, and everyone acted as if it didn't matter.

She saw then that her grandfather and her grandmother and even her mother were all suffering from this malady, this ailment that made them act as if nothing were truly the matter. Her mother dealt with the issue of race by pretending that someday the island would be free, and then differences of skin color and hair and features wouldn't matter. Her grandfather and grandmother dealt with it by ignoring it and yet at times making pronouncements that revealed their inbred racism. She heard them both, speaking in Spanish, stating in all innocence that soand-so was black but was one of the good ones. *Sí, él es negro, pero de los buenos.*

Racism was racism, but it seemed to come in different forms. Some was overt and some was subtle, but it was always racism. With the knowledge that she was dealing with a particularly subtle strain of racism in her mother, Vidamía now felt as if she had to completely reexamine her view concerning her own identity. Without question she was an American, but all this Puerto Rican stuff was too powerful to ignore. What was she? On her last day at the Center's library she ran across a small history of the island by José Luis Vivas. In the back she found a collection of brief biographies and drawings of illustrious Puerto Ricans. One of them caught her attention because of his name. It was Ramón Power, and he had been born in San Juan in 1772. He was a naval captain who died very young. The name Power intrigued her. It was Irish, but both of Ramón Power's parents were Spanish-born. She decided that there had been an Irishman involved somewhere in the lineage of Ramón Power, so there was a precedent for Puerto Ricans with Irish last names. She recalled her father talking about the link between Spain and Ireland. Vidamía Farrell wasn't such a strange name for a Puerto Rican, then. She was definitely Puerto Rican, but was she then black, as Wyn had insinuated? Standing in front of the mirror, she examined her face and skin, looking for traces of Africa, and was disappointed to find little to connect her in appearance to black people. She thought of her grandfather and knew that her connection was through him and that was the important thing.

Whatever her mother's hang-ups she'd have to deal with them. She couldn't wait to tell Wyn about her insight concerning her grandfather, but he wouldn't be back for a week.

And yet, for the first time in her life the notion of color wasn't a curiosity but a burden and she didn't like it. Was she in denial like her mother? Was it true that she must now consider herself black? What happened to her Irish background, her American background? What was she to her father, her grandma, her great-grandfather? While she relished her connection to Africa she didn't understand the notion that in the United States if you had a certain percentage of African blood you were considered black by both blacks and whites. The entire thing felt uncomfortable. She recalled Wyn talking about Dizzy Gillespie and the Afro-Cuban influence in jazz. Was she an Afro-Rican? Was that an apt description of who she was? What advantage was there to being called black when your skin was white and there was hardly any trace of Africa on your face? This was a new problem, and it angered her to have to think about it.

53　Group Therapy

The afternoon Billy began to decipher what had happened to him in Vietnam, he was sitting with his group at the VA hospital. All the men were veterans of the Vietnam War, all of them still suffering the agony of their battlefield experiences more than twenty years later. The group was mostly army and Marine, but also one navy man who had seen a friend decapitated by the hurtling landing gear of a jet on their carrier and had stood helplessly by as two of their deck crew exploded in flames before his eyes from leaking fuel and the spark of an engine. In the therapy group there was also a guy named Rupert, a Mohawk Indian from upstate New York, who had been in an air force special counterinsurgency and intelligence unit and had seen his entire group of about a dozen men, plus about forty Rahde montagnards, wiped out by the Khmer Rouge near the Cambodian border toward the end of the war.

Simms, a black paratrooper sitting in a wheelchair, finished talking about being shot in the spine getting out of a chopper. "Sniper got me," he said. He told the story and then talked about how he felt, the injustices of racism, of wearing his uniform and having to hear the word "nigger," of having young guys taunt and threaten to push his chair into the subway tracks; cursing his bad luck and the fact that as much as he wanted to fuck he couldn't because he had no sexual feeling, the tears coming into his eyes so that it made some of the other guys pound their fists into their hands and attempt to cry, but all that came out was more and more anger.

And then Conroy turned to Billy.

"What about you, Farrell?" he said. "Two months in the group and all you've told us is your name, rank, and serial number. What happened to you? What's your story?"

"I'm not too clear, man," Billy said. "Sometimes it feels like I'm making the whole thing up, and then I get flashbacks and I'm right there. I had this buddy, right? This Puerto Rican guy. Joey Santiago. We met at Pendleton before we went over. Bunked next to each other and everything and we became tight. We were both from the New York area and found out we'd been at Parris Island about the same time in boot. But we didn't know each other then. He was like a brother to me, and me to him. I was with him when he got it. I saw him die, man. It was heavy, man. I could see his heart and everything. Still beating, man."

"Is that how you lost your fingers?" Simms, the black paratrooper, said.

"It sure was, my man," Billy said. "They put a plate in my

head, too," he added, smoothing his hair. "Right there. It was a definite mothafucka, brotha. I saw a lot of shit over there but nothing like this. Maybe because me an Joey was so tight."

"I hear you," Simms said.

Everybody nodded and some guys said "shit" and "oh, man," and Billy went on talking, recalling all the good times he and Joey had, the raps they used to have about music, girls, baseball, football, basketball, martial arts, comics, television, movies, food, and especially New York; talking about the time when they'd come home and how they'd visit each other.

"He was a righteous dude, man," he said. "Bravest fuckin' dude I ever met. You never had to worry about your back. You dig what I'm saying? It fucks me up to talk about the shit."

"Yeah, but it's better if you get it out in the open so we can look at it," said Tony Bracco, who'd been a mortar man in the Corps and had lost his right arm almost to the shoulder, always making jokes about how he was connected and was having to learn to shoot left-handed, but really he was married with three kids and working for his father-in-law as a dispatcher for a fleet of cars; and coaching a Little League team, and inspired now by the success of Jim Abbott, the one-armed pitcher of the U.S. Olympic Baseball Team and a member of the California Angels. "That's what the Yankees need. A kid like that. Fucking guys on that team have no guts. Ever since Thurman Munson got killed and George sent Reggie packing, the Yankees are dead." Talking a mile a minute, his eyes bright with anger and hope at the same time, laughing one minute and cursing the next. "So just let it out, man. Semper Fi. Semper Fi. I'm right here, baby. Just like we were in-country again. I got your back now."

"I hear you, man," Billy said. "But it's a bitch."

Everybody nodded and he told them that the attack had come rapidly and was over as quickly, so that he never knew whether it had truly been the Viet Cong or simply a fragging by three malcontents from an army unit. "Nothing personal against you army guys," he clarified. "See, they were bad-mouthing Ricans."

Billy remembered how the subject of Puerto Ricans created considerable touchiness in Joey Santiago. Upon hearing the three bravos utter epithets such as "spic," "greaser," and "wetback," referring not to Puerto Ricans but to Mexicans, Joey had taken up the fight and informed the three Chicago white boys that they had better lay off talking shit about Puerto Ricans and Spanish-speaking people in general if they knew what was good for them. To which one of the bad boys said, "Fuck you and your mother, you spic faggot," which made Joey crazy, and, unstrapping his web belt with the bayonet and .45 and canteen, and flipping off his helmet, he began to systematically beat the three with an assortment of well-placed kicks and punches from his more than four years of training with Willie Chung at the Tae-Kwan-Do Center down by Pike Street near the Manhattan Bridge. Joey never talked about his black belt, remaining quiet and inscrutable and always speaking reverentially of his sensei. That day he left the three loudmouths bloody, sore, and embarrassed, so that Billy thought that it might have been them that killed Joey. But it wasn't them, because he subsequently learned that they had been transferred out months before. He said that Viet Cong had been in the area, but had all been captured, so that there was doubt that it had been Viet Cong who had ripped Joey's body apart.

"It's never made sense to me," he said.

"How come?"

"I don't know," he replied, and as if a curtain of darkness had descended on his mind, he shut off. Conroy's voice and that of the others receded as if he were on a chopper and were watching the ground fly away from him, the hooches and trees, the equipment and figures growing progressively smaller until they were dots and squares with no definition and no substance. Billy listened to the other men, trying to pay attention to their stories, wanting to contribute something, but he was gone, flat, seeing but not seeing, hearing but not hearing, there but not there, existing and dead at the same time, staring at a future with no landscape, no next moment, no tomorrows. He knew that he had to fight the condition and wondered whether it would last as long as it had previously when he'd spent days staring off into space.

When the session was over Conroy called him into his office and introduced him to someone by the name of Johnny Castillo. At first Billy didn't recognize Castillo, but he began putting things together and finally he nodded, and they threw their arms around each other and sat down and talked for a while. Castillo told him what he'd heard had happened with Joey back in Nam. Billy listened, not quite taking in the whole thing. Everything Castillo said made sense but the knowledge made him feel queasy and unbalanced. He said goodbye to Castillo and then Conroy stuck out his hand and told him he had done great that day.

"You're beginning to put your life back together, Farrell. That's great. You're playing music again, and that's what you wanted to do all along, right?"

"Yeah, man. Thanks," he said.

Billy went outside and walked in the late-afternoon light. He headed west along Twenty-third Street until he got to Broadway and turned downtown to go and pick up some forms for Pop Butterworth to sign at the hospital. He couldn't help admiring the pretty young girls looking so confident. Just like Cookie and Vidamía, he thought. Something had happened with this generation of girls, but he couldn't yet understand what it was. They seemed more sure of themselves, braver, less prone to going around trying to get boys to say they were okay. They seemed to know they were all right, and if their attitude didn't sit well with somebody, too bad. He worried about Fawn, but he guessed she'd come around.

He stopped and watched people setting up their trucks for the next day's farmers' market in Union Square Park, ran into a fellow he knew who asked him if he wanted to go and chant *nam myoho renge kyo* at the Buddhist center nearby. Billy shook his head and said he was cool. "Maybe some other time," he said. The guy said: "That's what you always say, man. Why don't you come up. It can't hurt. You need to change your karma." "You're probably right, man," Billy said. "I'll check it out one of these days." He thanked the young man and went on. On University Place he bought a slice of pizza and a Coke and then continued walking to Washington Square Park, where he sat on a bench and watched people roller-skating, playing Frisbee, juggling, playing the guitar and singing. Some guys were making like they were playing soccer with a little beanbag-type ball, bouncing it off their feet over and over again. After he finished eating he lit a cigarette and smoked for a while before picking up the forms at the administrative offices.

Watching the students outside of NYU and recalling the year he'd spent going there sometimes two or three afternoons a week to practice the piano for hours, he wondered what it would have been like if he'd gone to school like Pop Butterworth had suggested back then when Pop was working and had gotten Wayne Shorter to see if Miles would hear him play. Now Pop Butterworth was in the hospital with throat cancer and the doctors were telling him that it was starting to spread to his brain. Thinking about it began to work on Billy's mind and he told himself to be positive, to think about the things he had to do, about what he was going to play the following night at the Cornelia Street Café. He had even heard his name announced on WBGO's Jazz Calendar. "At the Cornelia Street Café, Billy Farrell solo piano." He smiled but his mind kept returning to what Castillo had said.

He walked down St. Marks Place to Tompkins Square Park and then through it, looking at the makeshift shelters of the homeless, identifying with them and feeling like they, too, were victims of the Vietnam War. Kevin Tracy, who had been a clerk and hadn't been up front much was almost finished with his Ph.D. in history at Fordham, but he still suffered from recurring nightmares and chemical poisoning, and had said the war had cost the United States nearly five hundred billion dollars. "That money could have provided jobs and could have housed, fed, educated, and kept millions of people under doctors' care for a long time," Kevin had said.

Billy turned south on Avenue B, his mind working, turning things over. On Sixth Street he turned east, and when he got to Avenue C he stopped by the store and said hello to Cookie and Vidamía. He couldn't believe that they had pulled off this stunt. When they'd told him the whole story he couldn't stop shaking his head. And the sign above the store window, COMÍA VIDCO, which Cookie's friend had painted with the Rican girl eating in front of the TV set, made him laugh each time he saw it. Vidamía and Cookie had both come out and draped themselves over him as they always did. God, they were gorgeous, he thought, admiringly. And inseparable.

"You gonna play tomorrow, right, Daddy?" Cookie said.

"On Cornelia Street? Sure, baby."

"We were gonna come, but I'm trying out for a part as a mermaid in a play. Anyway, I gotta go. When I get the part you have to see it, Daddy."

"Sure, let me know."

"We'll come hear you play next week," Vidamía said. "I gotta close up the store tonight."

He said he had to go, and just wanted to stop by to see if they were all right. They said they were and pointed to the activity in the store, which had a couple of game machines and the usual crowd of kids hanging around, talking music and movies and joking around, but keeping the place too busy for anyone to get strange. If anyone did, all they had to do was go and talk to Julio at the candy store. He ran a numbers operation, so he wanted things nice and quiet on the block.

Billy continued walking, his mind far away, going over the events, seeing Joey ripped open again but now feeling disconnected from the emotions. By the time he got home, he felt disoriented, as if something were not quite right. He ate supper in virtual silence. Cliff came in, said hello, and hurried through supper before running out to relieve Cookie, so she could go to her rehearsal. After Cliff left, Billy finished eating and then went to his rocker and sat looking out at the Manhattan skyline, the setting sun making the buildings shimmer silver in the distance.

When darkness fell once again on the city, Lurleen came over with the newspapers and the mail and turned on the lamp. Billy read until he fell asleep. He dreamt that he was sitting atop a hill of the greenest grass one could imagine. Below the hill there was a valley of equally green splendor, and here and there he could see stone huts with smoke rising from the chimneys and sheep grazing in the fields. He heard a flute playing an Irish tune, and then he was near a stream, his hand half-submerged in the clear, cool water. And then he saw the tiny chocolate-dark man dancing to the music of the flute, his dark suit and vest spotless and the creases of his trousers like razors, the red carnation in his buttonhole matching the red tie behind the matching vest of his suit. His shoes were shiny and he was chomping on half of an unlit stogie. The tiny man was wearing a derby which he removed to reveal shiny, patent-leather-like processed hair, parted neatly.

"You gonna sleep the rest of your life or you gonna get with it?" said the impish little man.

It was Mr. McQuinlan, the black leprechaun. He skipped up and landed next to Billy. Billy sat up quickly on his knees.

"Watch it, man," Mr. McQuinlan said. "You trying to mess up my threads?"

"No, Mr. McQuinlan," he said. "Where have you been?"

"Traveling," Mr. McQuinlan said haughtily. "You didn't expect me to stick around while you was crying in your beer, did you?"

"No, I'm sorry. I've been looking for you. I'm playing again."

"Well, it's about time, cause I'd about given up on your sorry butt."

"How do you like my playing, then?"

"Fair to middling, but you're getting there."

"Thank you. My kids got me a piano."

"I saw that. Well, time's a wasting. I'll see you around."

"Can I call you?"

"Sure, kid, anytime," Mr. McQuinlan said, reaching into his vest pocket. "Here's my card. No collect calls."

"Same one for fax?"

"No fax."

"Why not?"

"You know how some people don't believe in leprechauns?" Mr. McQuinlan said.

"Yeah . . ." Billy said.

"Well, I don't believe in faxes," said the leprechaun, laughing, then he donned his derby and patted it with his cane. "Be seeing you, my man."

Billy reached for the card but the card turned into a gold shamrock and then a dove flew away with it and he woke up yawning in his chair. He asked what time it was. Lurleen said it was nearly eleven. He got up and went to the kitchen for a glass of water, and drank it and then another before returning to his rocker. So Mr. McQuinlan was back. He wondered if that was good or bad, but the dream had been strangely pleasant, not like the nightmares he was used to. Caitlin and Fawn came to say goodnight and he kissed them both and hugged them, looking at their faces as if for the first time. He felt like telling them that they had grown so much, but he knew that was stupid. He must have looked strange because Caitlin asked him what the matter was.

"Nothing," he said. "Why?"

The girl shrugged her shoulders and laughed nervously. After they said goodnight, Billy went to the corner of the loft where the piano had been before they moved it upstairs and stood looking at the night. He then sat next to Lurleen on the couch, where she was watching a film. He sat looking at the TV, but she knew he wasn't really paying attention to the film and was instead deep in his mind, torturing himself. He waited until the credits began to roll and was pretty sure that Fawn and Caitlin were asleep and said he had to speak to her, but that they ought to go up on the roof.

"No, Billy," she said, sensing that something wasn't quite right. "You have that strange look on your face. I don't want to go up there if you're going to start going off. I'm still heartsick with all that stuff, baby. Something's wrong, isn't it?"

"No, honey, there's nothing wrong. I ain't gonna do nothing," he said. "I'm okay. I just gotta talk to you. It's, like, heavy and everything. I don't want it around the kids. That's all."

"Then let's go for a walk. We can go over to SoHo and sit and have a drink if you want."

"That'd be okay," he said. "But I don't want nobody to hear me. So maybe we could just sit on a bench over by the Pitt Street Pool or something."

"That's fine, but we have to wait until Vidamía and Cookie and Cliff get in before we go out. Is that okay, baby?"

"That's cool," he said.

It hurt that she didn't trust him about the roof, but, hell, he'd given her plenty of reasons for mistrusting him. It was like an illness that lingered and made the body uncomfortable with pain and twinges of aching, like an agony that invaded the muscles and made them lethargic for fear that motion could only be a precursor to further torture. Sitting still at least provided some respite from the onslaught of the affliction. And yet the pain wasn't your ordinary kind of pain, neither with its chronic lingering nor its sharp intrusion into consciousness. It was more akin to being in the dark and suspecting that somewhere within the darkness there was a beast waiting to slash deeply with its claws into your flesh. He could feel the darkness coming, and he once again saw Joey's life ebbing away and saw his own hand, where the empty places were, the flesh torn and bloody and the fingers missing.

54 Back from the Jungle

He sat next to Lurleen and relaxed, waiting for the children to get home before he and Lurleen could leave. Some days were better than others, but still, every once in a while he would sit for hours absolutely motionless, his mind fixed upon an object and wishing that there was some way for him to quit existing without causing Lurleen and the children trouble. The doctors called it depression, but he knew it was a curse for letting Joey die. There had been times when he had gone up on the roof and stood, seven stories above the city, on the narrow wall, rocking in the wind, unable to step back onto the roof or let himself fall forward into the void. Other times, he had walked along the wall, each step daringly carefree, as if he were walking on a sidewalk or in a park and not on twelve inches of concrete a hundred feet above the pavement. He'd read about something like that in a book by Norman Mailer, something about a man doing the same thing as a test of his courage. His wasn't a test of courage, he thought, since he couldn't decide to end his life. There were times when he closed his eyes and walked a few steps as in a trance before seeing Fawn or Caitlin at his funeral, and himself laid out in his one suit, his eyes closed forever. But perhaps he'd be too smashed up and the casket would be closed, as it must have been with Joey when they shipped him back, and they'd never see him again. And maybe that was the best thing that could happen, because he wasn't doing them any good. He couldn't earn enough money to provide for them other than getting them together and playing music, and even that had been Lurleen's doing.

Once, about three years before, as he walked on the ledge, eyes closed, he stumbled, falling onto the tar-covered roof, where he banged his head on a fallen television antenna, opening up a gash on his cheek. He'd touched his face and upon seeing the blood saw Joey's entrails spilling out of him as he held him, and he banged his fist on the roof and then on his head until he could no longer feel the pain, the blows making his head ring as he tried to drive the images away. As his rage subsided he lay on the roof and cried silently, not for Joey but for his own life, and for his children.

About an hour later, when the agony had subsided, he'd gone to the edge of the roof where he had stumbled and found a knob of concrete where a brick had been shoddily replaced. He noted that it was three bricks away from the corner of the roof. Had he not stumbled, his next step would have been taken in a void and he would fallen to his death. The thought sobered him, and he never again tried walking on the edge, with his eyes closed *or* open. A few weeks later he told Lurleen about what he'd done and felt worse when she told him she'd watched his entire dance with death.

"Just that one time?"

"No," she'd said. "Four or five times. The first time, I came up to talk to you about what the doctor said about Fawn's condition. When I got up to the roof you were already on the wall."

"Why didn't you say anything?" he'd asked, helplessly.

"I didn't think saying anything would help. I thought you'd be angrier and then you might really do it."

"Then why did you follow me up to the roof the other times?"

"It's stupid, but I thought if I was near I could pull you back with my love," she said and burst out crying, the sobs making her chest heave and her skin turn blotchy.

"Maybe you did," he said, almost inaudibly, abstracted from the moment, his mind already racing away from the situation. He'd said he was sorry and held her against him, smoothing her hair.

But he still thought of taking his life. Walking across Houston Street once he had an overwhelming desire to lie down in the path of the oncoming traffic. Oftentimes he'd walk across the Williamsburg Bridge with the express intention of climbing over the edge and letting himself fall into the river. Something always held him back, and he thought that maybe it was God's doing— that if he hadn't died in Vietnam, then God must have a purpose for him and therefore he should remain alive.

And yet God didn't interfere in that manner. He knew enough about religion to recognize that God had given human beings free will. At times he felt no desire to remain alive and yet each time he'd wanted to end his life, he'd been unable to. Something other than free will or God's design was at work in preventing him from taking the plunge, but he couldn't imagine what it was. If it wasn't God pulling him back, and it wasn't his own doing, what was it? He imagined the flight through the air. He'd read about the suicides of people who had jumped from New York bridges. Some people had come out of the experience alive, and he worried that he'd be one of those. But there wasn't much chance of survival if he let his body float freely and made no attempt to dive into the water. He'd heard that hitting the water from that height was just like hitting concrete.

On the other hand, he might fall in such a way that he entered the water cleanly and perhaps would be knocked out and regain consciousness when his body was too deep to be able to surface. So he would drown. He imagined the sensation and held his breath until he nearly fainted, which reminded him of diving into the sea when he'd go swimming out on Long Island Sound and he'd keep going down until he had hardly any breath left and then tried making it back to the surface, his lungs straining, pulling one more bit of oxygen from the depth of his life in order to survive, the exercise leaving him frightened and drained, but strangely alive.

All this speculation amounted to little, for there was something tugging at him and he didn't know its origin. And for the past year, each morning when he woke up and came out of his room, the first thing he saw was that enormous grand piano sitting in the corner of the loft like a leviathan figure, daring him to sit down again and attempt to make music. Why had Vidamía done it? After the novelty of the birthday party and that evening of playing and celebration, he had begged her to have them take the piano away. But all the children had insisted that he had to keep the piano, and there was no reasoning with them.

The day after he told Vidamía that she should send the piano back, or sell it, Cookie and Vidamía met him at the elevator as he was stepping out of it, and they begged him to please keep the piano, the two of them hanging on to him, their arms through each of his, making him go back into the elevator, and then Cookie closed the doors and took him up to the roof. Back then, the roof was still an ordinary New York City tar roof. They had now fixed it up with the extra money from the store, getting thick planks for a floor and making benches and bringing up potted trees, even a coconut palm, which was doing quite well, its fronds opening and the trunk thickening so that it was now nearly four feet tall. He still couldn't believe that Vidamía had spent nearly nine thousand dollars on the piano and that she and

Cookie had then hit on the idea of opening up a video store. Even kids could do things like that, while he went on day after day doing odd jobs and earning just about enough money to take care of himself.

He was now glad they had prevailed upon him to keep the piano. One day, about three weeks after it arrived, when Lurleen and the kids had gone back to their school routine and Vidamía had gone home to Tarrytown, he had walked by the piano and, as if the instrument possessed a magnet, was pulled to it. He lifted the lid off the keyboard, slid onto the bench, and began playing, losing himself in the pleasure of the music. He played a blues progression and then improvised on it, finding that in the simplicity of the tune he could let his left hand walk freely as it always did while his right could play the melody without too much of an effort. The only snags came when he had to hit some chords. But he found that he was able to solve the problem by playing more rapidly and imagining that all he was doing was avoiding playing with the middle and pinkie finger of his right hand. Very much as Vidamía had said, he began to develop a three-fingered technique for playing the right hand.

He had sat down at the piano that morning at 8:15 a.m., shortly after Lurleen left for school, and he played the entire morning before taking a break for lunch. He was still sitting there at 3:45, when Fawn, Cookie, and Cliff walked in. Coming up on the elevator, they heard the piano and knew it was their father playing a variation of "Wonderful, Wonderful Copenhagen," and Cookie said, "Listen! He's playing. Don't make noise." They had let themselves silently into the loft and stood transfixed, listening to Billy Farrell play, his eyes closed and his body bent over the keyboard.

Cookie motioned for them to sit on the floor of their library room and listen to their father. She then went to the phone in the kitchen and called up Vidamía in Tarrytown. It was Monday and Vidamía wasn't due in the city until the weekend, but

Cookie held the phone for Vidamía to listen. "Vee, he's playing, listen," she said. About a minute later she asked her sister if she could hear him. Vidamía was on the other end, crying.

"That's beautiful, Cookie," Vidamía said. After Cookie hung up the phone, she and Cliff and Fawn sat on the floor of the library until Lurleen returned at 4:30, after picking up Caitlin from the day-care center when she finished work at school. Unbeknownst to Billy, he had treated them to over an hour of his virtuosity. Accomplished musicians themselves, they were left awed by their father's brilliance.

"He played everything so beautifully, Mama," Cookie had said. "Like ' 'Round Midnight,' 'Autumn in New York,' 'Speak Low,' 'Every Time We Say Goodbye,' and a whole bunch of other stuff. I didn't know he knew so many songs from memory."

Lurleen nodded and said that their father was a remarkable musician.

"One of a kind," she'd said.

It was one o'clock in the morning when Vidamía, Cliff, and Cookie walked in, dutifully on time, and went immediately to the refrigerator. They turned on the television and switched it immediately to MTV. It was as if they were programmed to eat and watch videos, Lurleen thought as she accepted kisses from them.

"Your father and I are going out for a walk," Lurleen said, as they started for the door. "Don't stay up too late."

"Mama!" Cookie said.

"I just don't want you to get careless at the store tomorrow."

"We'll be fine, Mama," Vidamía said as the door closed.

Billy and Lurleen walked several blocks, until they got to Delancey Street, and then continued along until they reached the Williamsburg Bridge. They went up on the walk, ambling along quietly in the warm summer night, the air fresh and the city lights magnificent as they went farther up on the bridge. Above them, the full moon illuminated the river far below, making the surface of the East River shimmer as if minute stars had been dropped into the water. They stopped and he pointed to a sailboat in the distance. It looked like a ghost, since the boat itself wasn't visible from their vantage point and all they could see was its tiny wake trailing beneath the sail like a small playful marine animal. He placed an arm around her and kissed her. Lurleen knew there was something the matter because his mouth had the bitter, burnt-out taste it took on when he was truly worried. The taste disappeared only when they were in bed and he was able to relax.

"I'd like to have a boat," he said. "I'd just get in it and go around the Battery and then up the Hudson to the beginning of the river. We could all go on the boat and have a picnic and sail it up the East River into Long Island Sound and go swimming there."

"That sounds like a fine idea, Bill."

"My dad's partner, Tom Rafferty, had a boat," he said, sadly. "One summer I worked on it. We took people fishing out on the Sound. My mother called and said he had a heart attack and has to have a bypass operation. I should go see him sometime."

She thought this odd, since he never talked about his father, avoiding the issue whenever it surfaced. That he would want to establish contact with his father's partner seemed contrary to everything she knew about him. Perhaps he thought that this was expected of him, but she quickly discarded that notion. She knew him too well; it had to mean something else. He'd go because it was his duty.

He didn't say anything more for a while and just held her, her back to him, getting harder as he played with her breasts. She felt herself stir but didn't let herself go beyond that, sensing that something wasn't right. An airplane flew by overhead, perhaps heading for Kennedy Airport. The sailboat was no longer visible. She had always been in tune with him. Her pregnancies had announced themselves and she had known the following morning that life would soon stir in her, her body tuned totally to his. As she knew then, she now knew that something dramatic was to take place and she tried to relax. She had to be absolutely patient and not frighten him back into himself.

Ultimately the urgency of the moment got the better of her. She decided to take a chance, though she knew it was like reaching out over a precipice to try and help him back up before he plunged down forever.

"Did something happen at the VA today?" Lurleen asked, easing herself out of his embrace and facing him.

"Sort of, I guess. I ran into this guy, Castillo," Billy said calmly.

"From your outfit?" she said, letting out a sigh of relief.

"Yeah, he was in another platoon," he said. "He said there were no Viet Cong or regular North Vietnamese Army people in the area when Joey got it."

"But you knew that," she said.

"Yeah, but not for sure."

She knew it was difficult for him to say "Viet Cong" instead of "gooks," because that's how everyone around him referred to them.

"How did he find out?"

"He said after Joey got it and they took me away, they swept the perimeter looking for VC, but there was no one around. That wasn't surprising, because they came and went, but they didn't find any trace of their having been there for a while. I'd always thought the area was pretty secure. We had gone back to a safe area and were waiting reassignment to go in-country one last time. Castillo told me today that word came back that the fragments they took out of Joey were ours, so they knew that it was our own guys that did it."

"Why?"

"I don't know. I can't imagine why they'd want to get Joey. We were just gonna go get some smoke. He was friends with everybody. Other than the three guys from Chicago I told you about, everybody was cool with Joey. Nobody had a grudge against him. Nobody. Anyway, Castillo said that after I came back to the States something similar happened, except that it got botched up and the dude saw who it was that was trying to get him."

"Who was it?"

"These dudes that ran a drug operation over there. It was super-organized, like the Mafia. Man, you couldn't believe these guys. They bought heroin big time in Saigon and distributed it like they do here. Anyway, they got caught, and one of them ratted on the others to get a deal."

"And that guy said that they had been responsible for Joey's death?"

"Yep."

"Well, at least you know it wasn't the Viet Cong."

"Yeah, but I still feel responsible. I didn't have to cross the rice paddy there. I was just in a hurry cause we'd run out of smoke and I needed some. A dude told Joey that we could get the smoke real cheap from some dudes cause they had to unload it quick, so I told him let's go, and he wanted to go around the rice paddy, and I said it didn't matter because the area was secure, and there was a path that divided the rice paddy, I told him. I was smoking ten or twelve times a day. Sometimes, when we were in-country I was totally fucked up. 'Let's go on through it and save time,' I said. 'Suppose the gooks sneak up on us?' he said. 'No, man. Forget the gooks,' I said. 'It's secure. Let's go, man.' Joey shrugged his shoulders and followed me. We could see the guys on the other side waiting for us. It wasn't the guys that was gonna sell us smoke. It came from the woods on the side. Bam, just like that."

"And you're sure it wasn't them."

"Yeah, I'm sure. These guys just sold smoke and didn't get involved in shit like that. Castillo said that the dudes selling smack copped to it."

"Did he say if the fellow explained why they were trying to get Joey?"

"Yeah, but it doesn't make any sense, honey."

"What did he say?"

"That it was an accident."

"An accident?"

"Yeah, that they got the wrong dude."

"Joey?"

"Yeah."

"Who were they after? You?"

"No, not me. At least I don't think so. They gave some other dude's name, but Castillo said that didn't make any sense because the dude's name they gave was this guy Meléndez from the West Coast. A Chicano dude—and he'd gotten it about two months before. But the brass bought the story, and that was the end of the shit. I figured the guy trying to cut a deal when he ratted on his buddies threw them a bone and covered up for somebody else."

"And you're still wondering why it happened?"

"Yeah, like they got the wrong guy, but it wasn't who the dude said. It's really messed up, what they did."

"You think he was protecting someone else?"

"Yeah, maybe. But it doesn't matter. I still feel it was my fault, but I don't know why. I'm kind of getting used to the idea that it could've happened anyway, while we were fighting Viet Cong, because whether we'd been there or someplace else, they would have tried doing us. But now that I find out that it was these dudes maybe if we had been going along the woods they would've seen that it was us and wouldn't have fired. It was a rifle grenade, Castillo said. I'd thought it was mortar but it was a rifle grenade."

"How do you feel?" she said.

"I don't know," he replied. "You wanna walk to Brooklyn? I feel like walking. I can take you back if you want."

She said it was all right, they could walk to Brooklyn. It was a nice night and she didn't mind. They walked some more, their arms around each other, the moon now higher and brighter, illuminating the Brooklyn docks. When they were almost in Brooklyn, he stopped and stood shaking his head. She asked him what was the matter, but she knew instinctively that he was finally going to emerge from his nightmare. There, in the middle of this beautiful summer night, Billy Farrell, her own true love, her pain-filled man, his brave heart broken, was going to come back from in-country, back from the jungle to be safe with her.

55 The Lie

Billy Farrell, his mind wandering through the corridors of his memory, the clock of his life inexorably marking time and his awareness becoming lost in a fog of denial, recalled once more the question Conroy had asked him at the VA. It was as if Conroy already knew the answer but wouldn't tell him. He hated sitting with him, hated his smugness, his glass eye staring at him and not seeing him behind the thick glasses. Conroy's right eye had been gouged out on a loose nail on the wall of an obstacle course in basic training, and so he never made it to Vietnam. Conroy had been discharged with full disability, gone on to college, majored in psychology and had gotten a master's degree in counseling, which enabled him to work with returning fucked-up dudes like himself. He talked about Nam like he'd been there, but always a little self-consciously. He'd say things like, "When the Third Marines were in Da Nang . . ." or "One day at Tan Son Nhut Air Force Base, the tower handled over one thousand landings and takeoffs in a twenty-four-hour period . . ." and then he'd add that he wasn't in Nam but he'd heard enough about it to write a book. It was like he wanted to draw everything out of them to give himself a sense that he'd been there.

As they walked back to Manhattan, Billy explained to Lurleen what had taken place earlier that afternoon at the VA:

"So what really went down, man?" Conroy had said.

"I told you. The Cong did my buddy. Ambushed us. The whole area was secure, but they snuck in like they always did. Could've been a couple of kids or some girls for all I know."

"Kids?"

"You know, they sent kids sometimes."

"Yeah, I know. It's just the way you said it."

"The way I said what?"

"Kids. The way you said 'kids.' It's like that's the first thing you thought of."

"No, man. You took it the wrong way. I also said it coulda been a couple of girls."

"But first you said 'kids.' "

The rest of the fellows around the circle were nodding and Billy was starting to feel uncomfortable.

"Yeah, okay. I said 'kids,' " he replied. "What are you getting at, Conroy?"

"Don't get uptight," Conroy said. "I'm just asking you a question."

"Go ahead."

"Did you ever have to do a girl?" Conroy said.

"No, but I heard of guys that did. They said the girls had guns. They didn't give a fuck, the Cong women. They were just as tough as the guys. I don't know if I could've. The whole thing was fucked-up over there, man."

"Were you ever present when shit went down and they shot a girl?"

His head was hurting and it felt like the little plate in his skull was being hit by a hammer so that he heard, and felt, the clanking behind his eyes.

"Leave me the fuck alone, mothafucka!" he screamed at the top of his lungs. "I told you. No! What the fuck do you want from me, man? I don't wanna talk about this shit."

"Are you sure it was gooks?"

He hated when people used names for other people. Bobby Frazier from Atlanta was a nigger, Tim Kittrige from Little Rock was a cracker, Nick Ameruso from Boston was a guinea, Sean Quinlivan from Philadelphia was a mick, Frank Wojtasik from Chicago was a Polack, Kevin Kishimoto from Los Angeles was a Jap, Jimmy Eng from Sacramento was a Chink, George Breitig from Milwaukee was a kraut, Eddie Nielsen from Fargo was a squarehead, Marty Spiegel from Cleveland was a kike, and Joey Santiago from the Lower East Side was a spic. He was a mick, but he knew that. Yeah, Billy Farrell was a mick, a harp, a Paddy.

Everybody had to have a fucking tag on his name, on his existence, as if just living wasn't hard enough. On top of your pain you had to carry the pain that your people had brought with them to the country, and you had to wear the indignity—all the time.

He recalled coming back to the city after Elsa had the baby, and talking to a few fellas who had been in Vietnam. They smoked pot, talked about women, drank beer, and told him there was this group called Veterans Against the War and that he should check it out and maybe demonstrate against the war, and he said maybe they were right. He joined the Veterans

Against the War and went to a couple of demonstrations where they burned the flag and chicks were coming up to him offering to fuck him because they knew the kind of deprivation he'd gone through in the war and it was really brave what he was doing, protesting the war.

He took one of them up on it, and they ended up in an apartment up on the West Side that she shared with about a half-dozen people. There was graffiti painted on the walls, and Chianti bottles holding candles. No furniture to speak of. People slept on mattresses on the floor and sat on cushions. There were posters from antiwar marches, pictures of Mao Tse-tung, Ho Chi Minh, Bobby Seale, and Huey Newton. Huey Newton reminded him of Rick Mallory, this guy from Port Arthur, Texas. Rick had tripped a wire and blown himself up, himself and three of his buddies. But he looked like the Black Panther leader. Light-skinned and handsome. Billy didn't know him well, but they'd spoken about music. His father was a blues guitar player and had known Leadbelly. Rick Mallory said his father always called him Mr. Ledbetter.

As he recalled it now, he thought the girl's name was Gina, a pretty Italian girl from Bensonhurst who was studying political science at Brooklyn College. They had burnt incense, smoked grass, and gotten very high. She was giving him a massage, her strong hands kneading his shoulders as he lay on the mattress and she was astride him, her buttocks moving against his. Eventually, he felt very sleepy. As he relaxed, she turned him over and finished undressing him. She kissed him very gently and went down his chest and belly. She took him in her mouth and ran her tongue around the head of his dick until he couldn't help himself any longer, sat up and went up into her like an animal. She kept repeating that he should do it harder. But he came, and she was disappointed, got dressed and left him to sleep. In the morning he woke up with some other girl next to him. Gina was nowhere to be found. Someone said she'd gone to work. He didn't even ask where she worked. He came around to the demonstrations a few more times, but after a month or so he stopped showing up, because all he could think about was Joey lying in his arms, the life in his eyes fading, the whites of the eyes becoming a bluish yellow and his skin grayish and deathly, devoid of life.

Conroy was calling his name, but he was locked in his mind and couldn't respond. The walls had come up and he was in a bamboo cage that had been dropped into a hole in the ground; his body barely able to move, his knees to his chin, his arms grasping his tucked-up legs. The fellas talked about tiger cages, but those were different from the bamboo cages. He'd never seen a tiger cage, but he'd heard about them from a navy flyer they'd picked up in the bush. His carrier plane was shot down, and he and his navigator bailed out. The flyer had managed to parachute safely and hide but his navigator's chute had gotten entangled in a tree, and the Viet Cong had captured him. The flyer watched helplessly as the captors put his buddy in a bamboo cage and carried him off. Billy heard later that tiger cages were concrete bunkers in the ground, but the image of the bamboo cage remained fixed in his mind as the true tiger cage. The Viet Cong must have assumed the plane had only one crewman, because they didn't come looking for him. He hid in the tall elephant grass, and when night came he began traveling along the river, using his compass until one day he heard the chatter of an American outfit as they sat in a little wooded area before they marched down the road toward a village. Billy was out on patrol with his platoon and they rescued the navy flyer.

They'd radioed their outfit, and about an hour later a chopper came and whisked the flyer away. Before the chopper arrived, they'd given him rations and cigarettes and he told them he'd been on the move for two weeks, mostly at night, eating grass and a little fruit after his rations ran out. He told them that he'd gone to school with Carl Yastrzemski, and then he told them about the tiger cage. When Billy Farrell got back to New

York he'd wanted to look up the pilot, but was afraid he hadn't survived the war, that he'd gone back to his carrier and had eventually been downed again and hadn't made it back a second time.

Sitting at the VA now, he felt as if he were in a cage, unable to move, and Conroy's question pushing his head farther down until it was being driven between his knees and the pain in his head was threatening to crack his forehead open. He wanted to pound his head, but he'd been warned that he could injure himself badly by jarring the plate, and although he'd often wanted to end his life, he didn't want to incapacitate himself and put an added burden on Lurleen and the children.

They wanted him to talk about it, but there was nothing to talk about. He'd fucked up, fucked up like he always did. He had no business trying to play the piano, or getting married, or having kids, and he definitely shouldn't have gone into the Corps. What the fuck good was he, anyway, if he had caused a buddy's death. Because it had been his fault. He guessed Conroy was right and he'd been blocking it out all this time. But the last thing he needed was to talk about it. He didn't believe it would do any good. What he'd told Elsa and her mother had been a lie, something to make himself feel good. Coming to the group and hearing others talk about their experiences made him recall the whole painful thing with Joey. Now Conroy wanted him to spill his guts, so he could make himself feel better about not having been in Nam.

Conroy was crazy. Why in the hell would anyone in his right mind feel left out about going to war? Especially Nam. Everybody said it was the craziest fuckin' war ever fought. You could as easily get killed by your own people as by the enemy. You could be in the middle of a fire-fight, having a protected position and an advantage in numbers and then you'd hear them screaming in the distance and before you knew it the shells were exploding all around you and the great big 20-millimeters from the

Skyraider or Skyhawk jets' machine guns were ripping into men right next to you. That had happened to a regular army outfit. Wiped out a whole platoon in a village that they had just taken. Or else a couple of outfits from the same brigade would surprise each other in the bush and some nut would panic and open fire and before everybody got a grip you had casualties on both sides. Friendly fire, they called it.

Or else somebody didn't like somebody else's attitude, ambushed the poor bastard and blew him away. Fragging was one thing, but guys actually walked up and did a dude right there. He wasn't going to talk about it. What was past was past and that was it. Why the hell had he gone into the Marines anyway? Butterworth was right. He had no business going in. And maybe Conroy was right about his attitude, maybe he *was* self-destructive. Conroy was like a vulture.

"You know what's underneath all my shit, Lynn? I'm a coward. I've always been a coward. I don't wanna go to Brooklyn. Let's go back to Manhattan. I want to tell you there."

"All right," she said, her heart beating twice as fast, knowing it was coming now. The tension she felt was similar to that of his climaxes, which were powerful, violent, emotional spasms, except that what was coming was enormous, much greater. He was quiet for a long time until they were once again in the middle of the bridge and heading back to Manhattan.

Billy shook his head and raised his arms to the heavens and said, "I'm gonna be all right, Lynn." And then it was like a torrent, the words coming out, at times garbled, other times so rapidly that she couldn't keep up with everything he was saying; talking first about the reasons he'd joined the Marines, and then about what really happened to Joey. He was like a different person, like the person she imagined he'd be if he hadn't been damaged by the war.

"And I knew it all along so that the thing with Joey helped me cover it up. Do you understand what I'm saying to you?"

"I think so."

He talked about being scared because he'd been a very good musician, asking her to corroborate what was obvious when she heard him play. Even with his missing fingers he was a superb pianist. His left hand was genius, its capacity for rhythm and velocity outstanding. She heard him talk about being afraid that he wasn't good enough and not knowing what scared him, that he was supposed to start playing in a club with a bassist and a drummer, just the three of them, and that they had even made a tape and studios were listening and all along he was dreading having to prove himself.

"Why?"

"At first I thought it was because I was white, but it wasn't that. It was just thinking that I wouldn't be able to play like all the greats. You know, feeling like, who the fuck am I? Some punk white kid from Mount Vernon, New York, wanting to be like Thelonious Monk or Bud Powell or pianists like that. It was like because I wasn't black I wasn't entitled. I guess the way I figured it, at least if you're black you can let everything hang out and since black people get messed with so much, they don't care and just play. That's the way I wanted to be, because being around black people, I used to hear all kinds of stuff about the way people were treated. Crazy shit, like tar and feathering people, whipping them until their skin was raw flesh. This one cat showed me his back where some rednecks in Georgia had caught him coming home from school and had beat him with their belt buckles. He made me touch the scars and the skin. The skin was raised in big ugly welts. And lynchings. You know that song by Billie Holiday, 'Strange Fruit'?"

"Yes, it's about a lynching."

"Pop Butterworth says that people think that Billie Holiday wrote the song, but she didn't. She just sang it. He says it was a

Jewish guy in the Bronx. He told me about it. But, you know—shit like that."

"I understand," Lurleen said.

"So I got it into my head that it wasn't enough that my old man had gotten killed when I was eleven years old. Hell, that shit happened to Irish cops all the time. That's nothing compared to what happened to black people. I told myself that my old man would've wanted me to go and defend this country. I'm not kidding. And it wasn't only that my old man would've wanted me to go. It was like the priests and nuns and everybody around me expected me to go."

"Your mother?"

"No, no way. Forget it. Not her. She went crazy and even threatened to get a gun and shoot me in the legs. And my grandfather said he understood how I felt but that I ought to think it over, being I could probably get a deferment or something because I was the only son my mother had and her husband had been killed. I said that my mind was made up and I enlisted in the Marines. I was totally fucked up, Lynn."

"Oh, honey," Lurleen said, hugging him as they walked. "It must have been awful."

"The worst part of it is that all I was doing was hiding from having to find out if I could really cut it out there. I mean Dave Brubeck and Bill Evans and a whole bunch of other white pianists had made it, but that didn't mean shit to me. The man I wanted to sit next to was Monk. When they lined up the great pianists they'd have to say: Waller, Monk, Powell, Farrell. You know, shit like that. And it could've been different if fear hadn't taken over. It hit me this afternoon on the way home from the VA group, Lynn."

They came off the bridge and walked east along Delancey Street, turned north on Pitt Street to Houston and east again until they reached East River Park. The awareness of his lie stunned him and made him feel nauseous. He sat on the park bench with Lurleen patting his arm. Had he gone into the Marines hoping that he'd be killed and never have to face playing jazz? Why did it have to be that way? Why couldn't he just play music and not have to measure himself up against others? How could anyone equal Bud Powell or Thelonious Monk? But maybe he wasn't even good enough to compete with any of the lesser ones. They had something he lacked although he couldn't say what it was; he'd proven to himself that he could play better than some black pianists and even black musicians preferred him to their own.

God, Miles Davis had wanted him to play with him. It may have been that when Miles began exploring alternatives to straight-ahead jazz, he'd wanted a white kid with a connection to rock in order to create a fusion between rock and jazz, which he eventually did. But Miles's reasons shouldn't have mattered. Ladies and gentlemen, the Miles Davis Quintet, with David Holland, electric bass; Tony Williams, drums; Wayne Shorter, tenor saxophone; Billy Farrell, piano; and Miles Davis on trumpet. Ladies and gentlemen, the Miles Davis Quintet. It wasn't about color, because both Chick Corea and Joe Zawinul had played with Miles. And it wasn't technique, because he had that. And it wasn't lack of a repertoire because he had always remembered everything he ever read or heard. All he'd have to do was look at the music a couple of times and he'd remember. And it wasn't the capacity to improvise, because the music always flowed into his mind easily, coming up from inside of him like there was an inexhaustible, sweet fountain of melodies and harmonies in his soul.

He tried recalling those days back in 1968, after he turned eighteen and graduated from high school. It was as if everything then was happening to him and he was just walking in this fine mist, enjoying the moistness on his skin, his mind almost nonexistent. Each moment felt as if he and the events in his life were inseparable, and he was at the mercy of some force. He felt as if

God had a hand in the matter, and he went slowly with what he felt were deeper feelings. He wanted to set aside his selfishness and like Christ give himself up for others, but it had all been a lie.

He looked up and smiled at Lurleen. Later, in telling her friend Gloria Myers at school, she described his face as one of total purity and innocence, like she recalled her son when he was totally and absolutely trusting of her, before he began to question the world around him.

"Lynn, as long as I thought that I had let Joey die I didn't have to face my hang-ups about making it in jazz. All I did was cover that up all these years."

"You could've played with anybody. I've always felt you could. I talked to your ma and she said growing up there were always musicians at her parents' house. She said she'd heard a hundred different pianists, but that you were special. And not because she was your mother, but because it was obvious. That it was as if you became transformed when you went near a piano. She said that as your mother she always saw you as her little boy, even when you had grown up and were in high school, before you went into the Marines. But that when you were sitting at the piano, you seemed grown-up, complete, a man. She said it was the only time she didn't worry about you because it was then that you reminded her of your daddy."

"I didn't know that," Billy said. "I guess I fucked up, didn't I?"

"Don't think of it that way, baby," she said gently. "Stuff happens. The important thing is what's happening now. I mean, I don't know where these girls get their ideas, but having that piano, practicing the way you do, and getting that gig on Cornelia Street, you'll be playing full-time before you know it. It's gonna be great."

"We should go back," he said. "You have to get up early."

"I'm fine," she said. "I'll leave a note for the kids. I told them

617

I'd get up and fix them breakfast before they leave for the store. They'll be fine. How do you feel?"

"I'm okay, I guess," he said.

They sat in the semidarkness, the lights from the lamp-posts in the park hidden by the foliage of the trees. At three in the morning the park was still populated by young lovers and groups of seemingly parentless children playing their games, their English-Spanish chatter like a background melody to Billy Farrell's decanting of his misery and lost youth. He was quiet a moment and then knew that there was still doubt in him, that the most important person in his life didn't know how truly cowardly he'd been. And then, painfully, he began telling her about coming back and speaking with Pop Butterworth after the first rehearsal with Miles and the other musicians, when it was almost certain that he'd be playing with them on the album.

"Pop, he wants somebody to play electric piano."

"You'll do fine on electric piano."

"I didn't like it. The music sounds funny. It doesn't seem right."

"You'll get used to it. There's nothing wrong with it. You'll be playing with Miles and Wayne Shorter, son. That's the important thing."

"Pop, they play like I never heard anybody play. They don't stay in the changes."

"I know, but you'll pick up on that. The times you did it, it sounded fine, and Miles liked it. That's why he asked you back. He explained how it works and you understood it."

"It's like I'm too young, like they know so much more."

"Don't worry about being too young. That don't mean nothing. Sure, you're eighteen, but you got the talent and the capacity to play with anyone. I ain't never seen somebody that could retain a tune as good as you. And when you start digging into the changes, you come up with stuff that makes a person wanna cry with joy. You're good, Billy. Real good. Miles can see that. All the good ones had it when they were young. You can keep learning as you go along. You've heard Miles when he first started. He didn't sound nothing like he does now. He was eighteen years old when he hooked up with Bird. And look at Herbie. He was playing with Miles when he was just a little bit older than you."

"I can't, Pop. I can't do it."

"Well, fine. It breaks my heart to see you turn down such an opportunity, but whatever you do, don't go in the army. Go to Canada and wait out the war. Plenty of American boys are doing that."

"That's wrong."

"Billy, Billy. What are you talking about? What did you tell me a few months ago when they fined Muhammad Ali and sentenced him to five years? Didn't you tell me how much you respected Ali for what he did?"

"Yes, I did, but this is different."

"I know some people that can take you up to Canada in no time. You can play up there. There's plenty of good jazz folks that'd help you out. Please, Billy."

"I can't. I'd feel like I was betraying everybody. Like my father died for nothing."

When he finished telling Lurleen about his conversation with Butterworth, he had his head down in his hands and was stiff with tension. She leaned up against him and told him everything was going to be all right.

"It's over now, honey," she said. "We're done with that. Finished, baby. It's going to be great from now on. I can feel it. Just wait and see. You wanna go back and make it? I do."

He pulled her up to him and held her before he kissed her, feeling again how sweet she still was to his taste. For a brief moment he couldn't tell whether he was himself or had blended into Lurleen, or whether the two of them had drifted off into a wonderful ether that was the night and memories of other times when they had made love. Their arms around each other, they walked back to their home and then quietly, in their bedroom at the end of the loft with the open summer sky pouring into their window, they made love, slowly, until they were both spent, and slept until nearly ten the following morning.

When they got up Cookie, Vidamía, and Cliff had all left, and Fawn informed them that there was a note on the kitchen table. Caitlin was watching television and eating cold cereal. The note poked fun at their middle-age folly of trying to recapture their youth and questioned how seriously they took their parental responsibilities. They knew the note had been written by Cookie because the word "responsibilities" looked like a fruit salad of letters—"respansonblitys," or something like that. It was signed "with love, from the Video Crew." Billy and Lurleen both laughed. Lurleen said they should eat something and he insisted on making blueberry pancakes and serving her breakfast. Caitlin wanted to know if he was okay. He said he was fine and she wanted to know why. "I don't know, I just am," he said. Caitlin shook her head and said she would never understand grown-ups, but that when she grew up she was going to make sure they were locked up. She talked like that. Off-the-wall Caitlin, Cookie had started calling her. That, or else she called her Cuckoo Puffs.

56 Race

As things got closer to the day of the gig, tempers became frayed, and little brushfires of hurt feelings sprang up everywhere. Wyn felt that the rhythm section was always either playing too fast or dragging its feet. Cliff, after a great deal of pouting, confessed that he felt he wasn't being given enough opportunities to solo. From time to time Billy would get so lost in an improvisation that Buster Williams had to stop him and explain that in that particular piece he and Cliff and Wyndell were supposed to be trading fours. The tension spilled over to the people not connected with the gig. Cliff ended up yelling at Cookie and Lurleen. Billy nearly spanked Caitlin because she filled an ice-cube tray with oatmeal and when they were frozen she set the cubes on a bookshelf to see how they would melt.

One afternoon when Wyndell and Vidamía were returning from the Bronx, where they'd gone to ask Tumba if he wanted to sit in on a couple of numbers, they once more got on the subject of race. In the past, they had never argued about it, but Wyndell had mentioned the likelihood of her having an African heritage. She had had no problem with the idea. Wyndell had been in New York a while and had seen plenty of Puerto Ricans, so it was obvious to him that many had African ancestry. In the past they had laughed about it, but now something was up. Maybe he was annoyed because most of the conversation at her grandfather's had been in Spanish. Wyndell had wanted to know what her grandfather was talking about when the three of them—that is, she and her grandfather and his friend Flaco—were laughing so much.

"Was it a joke?"

"Flaco and my grandpa don't really get the deeper meaning of the joke, about the self-destructiveness of Puerto Ricans. Or any other oppressed people. But the joke is funny to them. You want to hear it?"

"I guess."

"Anyway, this Dominican, this Cuban, and this Puerto Rican are walking in the jungle, and this tribe of cannibals captures them, right? So they tell the three of them that they're going to throw them in a big kettle of boiling water, peel their skin off, make canoes with their skin, and then eat their flesh, but that they each have one wish before they die. So they point at the Dominican and the Dominican says he wants to hear some *merengue* music. The cannibals get up a *merengue* band, and after the Dominican has danced about an hour, they strip off his clothes, throw him into the boiling water, he screams, dies, they peel off his skin and start eating his flesh and making the first canoe. Okay, so the next day they point to the Cuban and he says he wants to hear "Guantanamera," so the cannibals get up a band and a chorus and they sing "Guantanamera" until the Cuban is in tears. The same thing, and they start making the second canoe and feasting on the Cuban. Okay, so the next day they point to the Puerto Rican and they say, '*Qué queriendo último deseo?*' "

"The cannibals spoke Spanish, right?"

"Stop, okay. I don't know if they spoke Spanish. Maybe they did. Anyway the joke's in Spanish, and that's what my grandfather said. So . . . they asked the Puerto Rican what he wanted for his last wish and he said he wanted a fork. They asked him if he wanted food with the fork, but the Rican shook his head and said, 'Yo, I told you. Just bring me a fork.' So the cannibals brought him a fork and he grabs it and starts stabbing himself in the chest and stomach and saying, '*P'al carajo con sus canoas, p'al carajo con sus canoas,*' " Vidamía said, dissolving into laughter, catching herself and realizing she had been speaking in Spanish. "Oh, sorry. So, anyway, he's stabbing himself with the fork and saying, 'Fuck your canoes, fuck your canoes, fuck your canoes,' " she said and was laughing again as she pushed against him. When she looked up, Wyndell had a look of disapproval on his face.

"What's the matter?" she said. "You understood the joke, didn't you?"

"I didn't think it was that funny," he said.

"See, the Rican was saying that he'd rather put holes in his skin than let them make a canoe out of him," she said, doing the same thing her grandfather had done in explaining the joke.

"Yeah, so?" Wyndell had said, dismissively.

"What's the matter now?"

"Cannibals, right?"

"Yeah, cannibals. That's how my grandfather told it."

"In Africa, right?" Wyndell said.

"Hey, I don't know where they were," Vidamía snapped. "Maybe they were in the middle of some shopping mall in San Juan. Maybe standing on a street in Nairobi. What's the matter with you? What difference does it make?"

"A lot of difference. Whenever people talk about cannibals it's always Africa."

"God, you're sensitive, Wyn," Vidamía said, slamming herself against him playfully.

"Cartoons have big-lipped black cannibals throwing a white man into a kettle."

"Oh, my God, Wyn," Vidamía said. "Maybe idiots think like that, but anyone who's studied knows that the eating of human flesh was practiced everywhere at some time or another."

"Europe?"

"You're damn right, Europe. My mother said there are anthropological records of cannibalism in the British Isles as late as the fifth century A.D."

"I don't believe it," Wyndell said, looking like he was being put on. "That's bull."

"No it isn't," Vidamía said, and then she got serious and told him that attitudes like his were the ones that were perpetuating the African cannibal myth. "Maybe some white people believe that, but so do you."

"I still don't believe you," Wyndell said. "I have to go to the West Coast to record, and I'll ask my sister. She's an anthropologist. England, right?"

"Yeah, the British Isles. Ask her. She'll tell you it's true, and that it's pretty common knowledge."

"Great! And now just because I'm black I'm supposed to know this shit?"

"I didn't say that it had anything to do with being black. I said it was common knowledge. I know about it and I'm not black," she said.

"You're not?"

"No, I'm not," Vidamía said, outraged and turning her head away.

"Even after seeing your grandfather?"

"Yeah, even after that," she said, turning back to him, her face fighting the anger. "I mean, what is your problem with wanting me to be black? You've insinuated it before."

"Are you telling me that even after you saw your grandfather, you consider yourself white?"

"I never said I was white. I told you all that stuff is bull. I have a white father and a Rican mother, who has a father who defines himself as a man, a musician, a father, a grandfather, a husband, lover, Puerto Rican, and maybe once in a while thinks about color. I don't know. Maybe he does, but he sure doesn't go around obsessed with the thing."

"And how do you define yourself?" he said, a little too arrogantly in her opinion.

"I don't want to discuss this right now," she replied, aware of people staring at them.

"Fine," he said, pursing his lips and looking away, so that they rode back in silence. At Grand Central, where he should have changed to go west to his apartment, he stayed on and tried to talk to her, but she was impassive. At Fourteenth Street she got off to take the Number 6 and he followed her. She got off at Astor Place, and again he followed her, up into the street. He said goodbye. She said whatever. She walked east on St. Marks Place, still seething. At one point she looked back at the black cube where that night they'd stopped and he'd recited the drum poem. Still standing there by the cube, he put his left pinkie and thumb up close to his face and pointed at her to indicate that he'd call her. She turned angrily and continued down St. Marks Place, toward the store.

She walked fast now, ignoring everything around her, her head boiling over with thoughts. Who did he think he was, imposing his values on her? Didn't she have a culture of her own? Granted, it included a partial African heritage, but why did she have to go along with the notion that even if you had one ounce of black blood you had to be black, or at least Afro-American. She knew Wyndell hadn't said those exact words, but that's what he was implying, and so did American culture insist. It was nonsense, and it wasn't fair. But Puerto Ricans were the same way, weren't they? No matter who they married, the kids were Puerto Rican. Or the Jews. If the mother was Jewish, the kids were Jewish—even if the woman married an Eskimo. Barry had mentioned reading a book about a Puerto Rican Eskimo, but she'd assumed he was putting her mother on because she hadn't believed him. He'd gone out of the room and returned from the library with the book. Vidamía hadn't read it, but she would have to at some point, since Barry said it was fascinating, and pretty funny. Puerto Rican Eskimos. What about Jewish Eskimos? And then she began smiling as she remembered the seder she'd gone to at her friend Linda Gould's house on Long Island, except that the seder she was imagining now took place inside an igloo, and, imagining everyone wearing parkas and asking why this night was different from all other nights, she began to relax. And then she wondered if whale blubber was kosher and cracked herself up. And in the next beat she asked herself if she loved Wyndell, and the answer came back, absolutely, and she almost turned back to try and find him, but she knew that she was expected at the store to relieve Cookie. Her mirth and good humor lasted only a block, and then she was again thinking about the subject of race.

Meeting Justino Santiago was both a blessing and a curse, for now there was no denying that she had African blood. She wondered if she was now considered a black person. As she walked the anger subsided, but the question remained, gnawing at her.

Was she now a black person? Were all Puerto Ricans who shared an African background black? She had been to North Africa and the people there were mixed. In Morocco and Algeria the people looked a lot like Puerto Ricans, and that made sense, because the Moors had been on the Iberian peninsula for centuries. It would be difficult to make Arabs believe that they were black because they had Negroid ancestors, which many across Northern Africa obviously did. Was it because being black was a bad thing? Was it something to be ashamed of? Was she ashamed? Were black people ashamed? Was the bravado, the attitude all a protective device because they were ashamed of being black? As she went over the subject she shook her head. But the doubt remained, interfering with everything else she thought. Was she looking at things from a white or a black perspective? How would a black person feel about it? How did she feel about it? Did the way she feel have to do with the blackness? She felt like such a phony, with all that Kunta Kinte stuff.

When she got to the store the usual crowd was hanging around, talking and listening to raps on a boom box outside. Not too loud because they knew it hurt business. Inside, a couple of homeboys were playing the Super Mario and one of the other machines they recently had installed. As soon as Cookie saw her, she knew something was the matter. Vidamía went into the back of the store and collapsed in a chair. The tears flowed from her in a combination of anger and regret about how she'd treated Wyndell. There was no doubt that the subject of his blackness was important. She had been insensitive. She was such a hypocrite. All her liberal crap about respecting the dignity of all people, and she was setting herself apart from the person she loved.

Cookie called her friend Gloria, who was standing just inside the door of the store, and asked her to come behind the counter and take people's orders. It was about six on Saturday and people were coming in from shopping to rent movies. Fridays and Saturdays at this time were the busiest. When Gloria went behind the counter, Cookie immediately rushed into the back and found Vidamía with her head turned to the wall.

"What happened, Vee?" she said. "Was it those slimy lowlifes again?"

She was referring to the four homeboys from Avenue B who had followed them home a couple of weeks back. They were really nasty until Billy, walking up the street, saw what was happening and crossed the street and the four homeboys turned off at Rivington and kept going, goofing and slapping hands, their caps askew and their baggy pants low on their hips. Their father had asked them what had happened, but they'd said it was nothing. "Just stupid boys," Cookie had said. Their father had nodded and opened the door to the building and they went up on the elevator, agreeing later that they didn't want to worry him.

"I can get a posse on them," Cookie said. "Raymond told me he'll get his brother Miguel from the Wald Projects and he and his homeboys'll straighten them out."

"It wasn't them, Cookie," Vidamía said. "I had a big fight with Wyn. My fault, I think."

"What about?"

"About that whole thing with me supposedly being black and whatnot."

"Girl, *qué es lo d'él*? What's the matter with that man? What's he want you to do, frizz up your hair and wear dark makeup and shit? He wants you to be like that chick Eddie Murphy talks about in that show. Right? You have to put a bone through your nose and ride around on a fuckin' zebra and whatnot? Gaw! He is too much, child."

"No, nothing like that," Vidamía said, laughing through her tears at her white sister who could talk Afro-Rican better than anybody she knew. "Anyway, I'm sorry I'm late, baby."

"That's all right, *mami*. Don't worry about it. Take your time. Mario's not due here until seven. I'll take him with me when I go change. He can hear me in the shower and know that I'm in there *esnua*, homegirl. Totally nekked, like they say down home. You gotta keep them under your power. Cliff's late, too, so don't worry."

"I should've been more understanding," Vidamía repeated.

Cookie sat down and made her dry her tears and go and wash up, and then while Vidamía was in the bathroom, she talked about how she and Mario had at least one big fight each month, but always made up, and wondered if maybe Wyn was worried about his decision not to pick up phony gigs anymore and make a commitment to only playing jazz.

After Vidamía came out of the bathroom, Cookie sent Gloria for pizza and sodas and then Mario Wong came in with his friend Gilbert Montoya and his girl, Nicole, and the four of them left. Two minutes later, Cliff walked in, trailed by his girl from Performing Arts.

The rest of the evening went quickly, and at nine-thirty they began to clean up and get ready to close the store. At ten o'clock Vidamía and Cliff counted up the receipts, put them in a bag, called Tito Delgado, who was a cop, and he came over with his car and drove them back home. They paid him his fifty-dollar fee and he waited until they were inside the building and the door was locked. Vidamía walked in and immediately went to Lurleen, gave her the bag, and reported on the sales for the day. She kissed her father, who was sitting in his rocker, reading the newspaper and listening to music with the headphones on. He looked relaxed, his face placid, as he kept time by nodding his head lightly as he looked at the paper through his reading glasses.

Vidamía fixed herself something to eat and sat with Fawn and Caitlin while they watched television. Caitlin was her usual unconcerned self, but Fawn looked uncommonly sad. She moved closer to her and smoothed her hair. Fawn stiffened at the touch, but eventually leaned into her and put her head on Vidamía's shoulder. Vidamía asked her if she was all right. Fawn nodded, whispering that she'd gotten her period. Vidamía said she understood and wondered what Fawn's thing looked like. Whenever Fawn wore pants there didn't seem to be a bulge in her jeans, but then again they were generally baggy, so it was hard to tell. She wondered if Fawn knew that Cookie had told her about it. Of course, Cookie'd only seen it once, back when Fawn was seven years old. Vidamía couldn't imagine how it would feel to have both organs.

After Cliff and his girlfriend went back out, she felt the urge to call Wyndell, but she decided that Cookie was right and he should make the first move. He was leaving in a few days and maybe he'd crash or something would happen to him and she'd have regrets. She decided to take her chances. She wanted to discuss the issue with Lurleen, but she was reading and Vidamía didn't want to disturb her. She went to her room, came back out in her bathrobe, took a shower, letting the fine spray of warm water relax her body. She tried not to think of the times she and Wyndell had taken showers together and how fascinated she still was at the contrast between the color of their skins, at the patterns they formed when they held each other. Lying in bed together with him gave her a sensual rush and she often thought that if she were a painter she would do many poses of the two of them in different types of light at different times of the day, both of them nude. She washed her hair, stayed under the water a long time and then came out of the shower, put on her thick terry-cloth bathrobe, and sat on the toilet seat to blow-dry her hair. When she was finished she dried herself again, put on deodorant, powdered her body, and put on clean underpants and her cotton nightgown.

She thought the shower would make her sleepy, but she was as wide-awake as she had been when she walked into the apartment. Her mind was flitting back and forth between the argument with Wyndell and her concern with how she was to identify herself when she was asked what she was. It had been so easy when she was young. She was American. She was Puerto Rican–American. But that wasn't good enough, because there was no such thing. It wasn't like Italian-Americans or Polish-Americans who had come here as immigrants. Puerto Ricans were American citizens, whether they were in the United States or back in Puerto Rico. Barry and her mother had said this over and over, never talking like other people did about "the island" and "the mainland." By saying "mainland," Barry had said, we're admitting that P.R. is part of the U.S., and that's just capitulating and not upholding its right to independence. But they were. They couldn't help it, they were Americans. Did she want Puerto Rico to be a state? No, it was wrong. If it became a state it could never be a country. Puerto Rico should be free, just as Quebec and Northern Ireland and everyone who had a distinct culture should be free.

What was she? She tried reading a book of classic American short stories. There were stories by Steinbeck, Hemingway, Welty, Faulkner, O'Henry, and many others. She began reading Faulkner's "Barn Burning," reread the first two paragraphs over and over, but could retain nothing as a basis for going on. Her mind was focused totally on herself and her confusion. How could she have been so moved by Alex Haley's book and yet resent Wyndell's contention that she was black? She looked at her arms and legs, then got up from the bed and looked at herself in the mirror. Around the eyes there were similarities between herself and some of her black friends, but that was understandable. She had African blood, and that was fine. But the way that it was being presented to her by Wyn, it meant that all the other aspects of her background, the Irish part and the southern white part, no longer counted. That Africa was part of her background was without question, but why did she have to wear a badge that announced to the world I AM BLACK. *Was* she black? Weren't those the rules of the race game? The slightest trace of African heritage and you were black. It wasn't fair. Her silent plea angered her, for in the desire for personal justice, for a need to have the issue adjudicated in her favor, she was admitting that to be black in the United States meant a sentence of suffering, of pain and rejection, of a perpetual shroud of slavery, which she was not willing to wear.

The thought filled her eyes with tears, and in a moment she had turned to the wall and was sobbing quietly. If she believed that everyone was equal, why couldn't she give herself up to being black? What was the difference, white or black? If she truly believed that deep inside there was no difference, why couldn't she choose? Wyndell was absolutely right. She pounded her pillow several times in anger, then sat up and stared at the wall of her room. Even the poster on her wall—the African savanna extending to the horizon with Mount Kilimanjaro in the distance, a pride of lions in the foreground—made her feel shame, for in her stance she was also rejecting the essence of that beauty.

To the right of the poster there was a picture of Wyndell, holding his tenor saxophone just as tenderly as he held her. It was the same photograph due to appear the following week in the *Village Voice* to announce the gig at the Village Gate. She thought then of a folk song's lyrics in which a girl is asking to be held like a baby that will not fall asleep. Above her desk, on the bulletin board, there were pictures of the two of them. Written with Magic Marker on the bulletin board was the innocent *Vidamía loves Wyndell 4 Ever*, the letters curleycued within a heart. In every photograph you could see how much Wyndell admired her. At least a dozen photos, each of them showing how in love they were: at the Central Park Zoo near the Polar Bear pool, at Jones Beach, under the arch at Washington Square Park, eating at a sidewalk café on the Upper West Side, and dozens more.

On the desk there was a mug from Harvard University. To the right of the bulletin board there was a pennant from the school. She had been accepted, had gone up for a summer weekend to get acquainted with the campus and in the fall, in little more than a month, she'd be attending the school. The only other person accepted to Harvard from her graduating class was Todd Carey, whose father was a graduate. People said it was the Kennedy influence, that Harvard favored the Irish. She'd felt pride when they referred to her as Irish. And she *was* that, too, wasn't she? These thoughts plunged her once again into an agitated state. Her Irish was up. No, it was her Latin temper. Or maybe it was the savage African blood in her. For the first time in her life she didn't want to be herself.

She got up out of bed, turned off the light in her room, went to the refrigerator and cut herself an enormous slice of chocolate cake from the half left over from dinner, put about four spoonfuls of strawberry ice cream on the cake and poured herself a large glass of milk. When she came back to the living room, Fawn and Caitlin said good night and went off to sleep. She asked Lurleen if she minded her turning on the TV again, and Lurleen shook her head without looking up. She was reading a book about space. Vidamía turned on the television and switched to MTV and mindlessly ate the cake and ice cream and drank the milk, knowing she'd have an awful stomachache in a while. She would become a fat pig, and then she wouldn't have to deal with the whole business of color. When you saw fat people the first thing that struck you about them was their size, not their color. No one would care what she was when they saw her. She would just be a fat chick, a fat broad, a fat cunt, a fat cocksucker, a fat bitch; but then people would get to know her and find out that she was a fat Irish Puerto Rican black bitch. So it didn't matter. She felt nauseous and thought that maybe she'd become bulimic like Pam Ashley, who didn't break a thousand on her SATs and said she was going to kill herself because her mother had gone to Vassar and so had her grandmother, and they had turned her down and she'd have to go to some state school or maybe community college. She turned off the TV, got up, went to the sink, rinsed out the glass and dish, came back to the living room, and told Lurleen she was going up on the roof.

"At this time of night?" Lurleen said, and then looked up and knew immediately there was something the matter. "What happened?"

"Wyn, Mama," she said, standing in her long nightgown, feeling foolish. "We had a big fight. Ever since he got back from the West Coast he's been on my case."

"You feel like talking about it?"

She nodded and at that moment her father came over, leaned down, kissed Lurleen, and then came over and kissed Vidamía and told her not to let stuff get to her. When he was gone, the tears came back. Lurleen asked her if she wanted some chocolate cake.

"No, I had some already," Vidamía said, and laughed ironically. "It was good, but I ate too much and my stomach hurts."

"Poor baby. What did you argue about?"

She told Lurleen the entire story and said she felt worse because she was a hypocrite.

"I don't know what it all means, Mama," Vidamía said. "I've been going up to see my grandfather, and, like I told you, he's dark, but he looks like my mother. He's not *black*. I mean, you can tell he's African. But not like Wyn, you know. He behaves totally relaxed. He's not uptight all the time. It's cultural. It's like African people in the U.S. and African people everywhere else behave differently."

"Well, I'm gonna tell you something," Lurleen said, pushing back her lank hair. "I don't know what *we* all are, either."

"You and Daddy and the kids and all of us?"

"Just me and the kids. Let's go up on the roof."

They took the elevator to the seventh floor. Lurleen turned on the light to the roof and they went up the stairs. The night sky was high and cloudless and there was a breeze blowing in from the south bringing with it a blend of tropical air and the sea.

They sat across from each other at the picnic table and then Lurleen asked for her hands. When she placed her hands on the table, Lurleen took both of them and said that whatever she told her she must promise never to discuss with anyone. She almost thought that Lurleen was going to tell her about Fawn, but Lurleen began talking about being a young girl in Tennessee and learning how to play the accordion, and later the fiddle.

And then she talked about the time in 1963 when she was thirteen and her aunt April Sanderson got married to a young man down near the Gulf, but inland from Biloxi, and they had all gotten into her uncle Bobby Meekins's car, all scrunched up in the back with her cousins Mel and Lloyd and her brother Morgan and her sister Laurel and their mother, and up front her uncle Bobby, his wife, Clara, and her own daddy, Donald Meekins, who had a bad leg from being in the war and couldn't hear and got terrible headaches all the time. And they drove all day, it seemed, stopping off to pee at gas stations and eat at diners, until they got down to a little town called Surrender, Mississippi, and this big farm where a whole bunch of tables had been set up for the wedding reception.

Lurleen told her how they'd all piled back up into the car and found a motel and each family rented a room and they'd all slept in the same bed, her mother and father in the middle and she and her sister Laurel on her mother's side and Morgan on his father's side. The next day, they woke up early in the morning, got dressed up, and went to the church, which was painted bright white and was in this grove of pine trees with sandy soil and little patches of grass growing out of it. There were blue jays and crows squawking and squirrels and chipmunks running around in the trees. It was hot and uncomfortable in the church, and she kept thinking about her fiddle and maybe they'd let her play someone's, but then she thought that maybe all she really wanted to do was show off.

57 Passing

The wedding was pretty, and her aunt April looked beautiful dressed all in white. The groom was tall and not bad-looking, although he did looked frightened. He had red hair and his ears stuck out a little bit, but she figured her aunt must love him very much. All the women cried, and while people were standing around getting ready to go back to the reception, she and Laurel and another cousin, Glenda, giggled and poked each other with their elbows and made jokes about the wedding night because they all knew what happened then and thinking about it made them giggle even more and whisper to each other whether they thought she'd take her wedding dress off first and maybe she didn't have bloomers under the dress to make it easier, until her mother snuck up behind them and heard what they were saying and grabbed Laurel, who was fifteen, and pinched her arm, took her off, and gave her a good talking to.

"When she came back, my mama said we ought to be ashamed of ourselves spoiling Aunt April's wedding, and if we kept it up God had some very unfortunate things in store for us."

By noon they were back at the farm and there was a barbecue since the groom's father was originally from Texas and they'd set up great big grills and placed huge flanks of steak on them. There were also hamburgers, wieners, potato salad, fried chicken, corn bread, hush puppies, coleslaw, all kinds of pies, and the wedding cake with homemade ice cream.

At about three o'clock the musicians began to play. They

were doing things from the Kingston Trio. It sounded pretty good. After about an hour they switched to bluegrass music, and she went up to where they were performing and kept looking at this thin, red-faced man with a straw hat who was playing the fiddle, and she knew that if she stood there long enough he'd kind of point both fiddle and bow at her and ask her if she wanted to play, like people did, and then he'd be real surprised because she'd say you bet and take that old fiddle and show those folks what fiddling was all about. She was standing there when her mother took her arm and said that she ought to stop being rude and quit staring at folks that way. She made her come in the house to dry dishes, and she kept thinking how she could've played and then everyone would have seen how good she was. She was so annoyed that after she finished drying the dishes, she'd wandered off into the woods in back of the house, walking on a little trail, thinking that she'd walk until she could no longer hear the music, and then she'd wait there until it was dark and come back. If they were worried, too bad, because they had no right to boss her around and make her life miserable.

She followed the trail into the pine trees until she could no longer hear the music and then it began to grow dark, not from the sun setting but from the denseness of the forest, and then, as hot as it had been, all at once she felt chilled and the air seemed charged and smelled like a storm was approaching. She came to a clearing and through it she could see a field, a couple of hundred yards wide, with a half-dozen cows and, off by itself, a mule. Beyond the field there was a hill and to the side of it another grove of trees. The sky had turned ugly, the dark clouds menacingly angry. The smell in the air frightened her and she decided she ought to return and was worried that she'd lose her way and not be able to get back to the wedding reception. As she turned to go, the sky beyond the hills was suddenly streaked with lightning and seconds later thunder exploded above, the huge clap driving her to the ground with fear.

She stood up and brushed the pine needles off her dress and stockings; then another thunderclap boomed closer, followed by three more in quick succession, and then, seconds later, came an awful rumbling and a sprinkling of rain, the drops thick and cold. There was no use running back into the woods because it was as likely that lightning would hit in the forest as not. Her father had told her that running under trees in a lightning storm was the worst thing a person could do, so she began running across the field. Before she was halfway across, she felt the chunks of ice hitting her shoulders and then her head, pelting her so that she covered herself with her arms and continued running, the rain and hail blinding her until, her lungs burning, she reached the other side and then she saw it: a cabin, the wood weather-beaten as if it had never been painted, the pathetic brick chimney black and nearly falling in on itself.

Out of breath, she knocked on the door, but no one answered. She pushed at the rough wood and was surprised at how easily the door gave. It didn't occur to her that there might be a dog or perhaps an evil person lying in ambush for her. She was cold and frightened and needed someplace to sit until the storm passed. She went in, closed the door, and stood shivering against it, listening to the hailstones hitting the roof and the trees and the ground outside. It sounded like the icy pellets were the size of golf balls now and she wondered how the folks at the reception were doing with the storm. As her eyes got used to the dark she saw that she was in someone's home. There was an old table with a checkered tablecloth on it—forever after when she went into a restaurant and saw a similar tablecloth, all she could think about was the moment she escaped the hailstorm and stepped into the strange world behind the door of that shack.

"Who's there?" a rough voice said. "I can't see real good, but this shotgun will scatter buckshot fifteen feet either side of that door, and I got it aimed right at the middle of it."

She couldn't tell who the voice belonged to, whether it was a man or a woman's voice. One thing was certain, whoever owned the voice was old and not too pleased with the intrusion. As hard as she tried she couldn't help it and began crying and saying that she was sorry, that it was hailing outside and she was just a poor, lost girl who didn't mean no harm and wasn't looking to cause trouble.

"Quit sniveling and explain why you nosing around an old Negro shack in the woods."

"I'm lost and it got cold, ma'am."

"Gal, you best not be trying to fool ole Lulu, heah?"

"Lulu, ma'am?"

"Yeah, Lulu. You deaf too? Lulu McAlpin," the voice growled.

"No, ma'am. I ain't. Honest I ain't. I got lost and it was hailing, ma'am."

"I hear it," the voice said. "I don't see too good anymore, but my hearing's just fine, thank you. You know how to light a lamp?"

"Yes, ma'am."

"You know how to make a fire?"

"Yes, ma'am."

"Then go on and light the lamp and then when you can see where you're going so you don't end up banging your fool self knocking into this and that, light the fire and come over here and let me take a look at you. There's matches right there on the table if you open your eyes."

"Yes, ma'am," she said and went about doing as she was told.

She lit the kerosene lamp and then built a fire. She saw that she was in a one-room house with a couple of small windows, none bigger than a large book. When the fire was going, the woman said there was some chicory coffee on the stove that she could heat, and if she was hungry to open the pantry, because she was sure to find a biscuit or two in there. The old woman said if she was wet she should take off her dress and in the chest of drawers over on the other side of the room, in the bottom drawer, she could find a frock that would fit her just fine and she could even keep it if she wanted. If she wanted anything else she was out of luck. She thanked the woman and said she wasn't hungry, that she was fine exactly as she was. She had been standing, staring at the fire, trying to warm herself.

"And what's your name, child?" the old woman said. "Come on over here."

"Lurleen, ma'am," she said, going over to the rocker. "Lurleen Meekins."

When she was close enough, the old woman peered into her eyes and then touched her face, going over it as if she were blind, but squinting her eyes in the light of the kerosene lamp. The woman's skin was white and her eyes had once been blue, but were now sort of cloudy.

"Meekins?" she said.

"Yes, ma'am."

"You related to the Meekinses up near the Sunflower River?"

"No, ma'am. I don't think so."

"Then where you from?"

"Tennessee, ma'am. Wilkins, Tennessee."

"Who's your daddy?"

"Donny Meekins, ma'am."

"And his daddy? Your grandpa?"

"Will Meekins, ma'am."

"What was his mama's name?"

"Marie Meekins. She lives in Cape Girardeau, Missouri. She's real old."

"I reckon she would be."

"You know her?"

"Now, I didn't say that, did I?"

"No, ma'am."

"Then don't go jumping to conclusions, young lady."

"No, ma'am."

"You got any McAlpins in your family?"

"Yes, ma'am. My sister is Laurel McAlpin Meekins. We have McAlpins on my mama's side of the family."

"You don't say?" the woman cackled. "Well, I'll be. Come a little closer and let me take a look at you again." When she was close enough the woman laughed and touched her face. "Yep. Sure could be," she said.

"Could be what, ma'am?"

"Could be the storm's passed and you better get going before it gets too dark."

"It's already dark, ma'am, and it's raining worse than ever."

"Then I reckon you better bed down on the floor," the old woman said. "You'll find a quilt over in that chest. It'll keep you warm enough. There's an ole coon comes sniffing around the cabin, but he ain't gonna get in here to harm you none. Just ignore him."

"Yes, ma'am. An ole coon don't scare me none. I shot plenty of 'em," she lied.

The old woman harrumphed and snorted.

They talked a little more, and about an hour later the woman said she was going to sleep and Lurleen ought to put the lamp out and go to sleep herself. She did as she was told. She got the quilt out, made herself a bed, and curled up with the quilt around her. In the morning, the sun shining through one of the windows and the birds chirping, she awoke to see the woman cooking breakfast in the fireplace. She got up, asked where she could pee, and then went outside to use the outhouse.

"There's a barrel of rainwater outside. Draw water and wash your face," Lulu said.

After she came back in, Lulu fed her eggs and bacon, biscuits, and black coffee with sugar. Around eight in the morning, after they'd eaten, the old woman took her outside and showed her how to get back to the Burrells'. That was when she heard dogs barking and voices coming her way. Five minutes later there were a dozen men and three bloodhounds sniffing around. The red-faced man who'd been fiddling was now wearing a sheriff's badge. Her uncle Bobby was with them.

She said goodbye to Lulu McAlpin and the men took her with them. When she was back in the house, she got a good thrashing from her mother, who talked about how worried everyone had been and how she had managed to spoil her aunt April's beautiful wedding.

"I'm sorry, Mama," she said.

"Sorry ain't good enough. And you ended up in an old Negro's house."

"She wasn't a Negro, Mama," she said.

"Don't you sass me."

"She certainly is a Negro," said an older woman. "She may look white, but she's a Negro. Crazy as a bedbug. Living all by herself like that for years. Eating grass and bugs, I reckon."

On the drive back to Tennessee, all they did was talk about her getting lost in the woods and ending up in an old Negro's shack. She fell asleep, and when they woke her up it was time to eat. Her mother was still talking about it. In the diner where they stopped to eat Lurleen spoke up. She said the old woman's name was Lulu McAlpin and that since Laurel's middle name was McAlpin maybe they were related, and that's when she felt her face sting. Her mother had slapped her and told her to eat and keep her mouth shut.

She said nothing else for the rest of the trip, but when she got back she went and saw her grandfather, William Meekins, and asked him about his own grandmother. He said her name was Lulu McAlpin. She asked if Lulu was a Negro.

"No, she wasn't, darling," her grandfather laughed. "She was white, just like you and me. Had big china-blue eyes. I recall going down and visiting her and my grandpa Andrew when I was a little boy. They lived in a great big house down near the Sun-flower River in Mississippi. She was a beautiful white woman who played the piano."

She asked when he was born and when his mother was born. He said he was born in 1893 and his mother, Marie, he believed, in 1872 and added that it was the year Susan B. Anthony tried to vote. She next asked about his grandma and he didn't know, maybe 1845. She thanked him. He wanted to know why she was asking and she said she was just curious.

And then Lurleen looked at Vidamía more directly, her eyes burning fiercely, and made her promise again to keep what she was about to hear to herself. Vidamía nodded several times and was silent, thinking of how to ask what seemed an obvious question.

"Did you mean to say that the old Negro woman in the shack and you were related?"

"That's the way it's always seemed to me," Lurleen said. "That was my great-great-grandmother I met. My mother was having none of it and said it wasn't unusual for whites and blacks to have the same name down south and that everyone she had spoken to reassured her this was a Negro woman. White or black, she was a Negro woman."

"How old was she?"

"I don't know. This was back in 1963. If she was born in 1845, she'd have been almost a hundred and twenty when I met her."

"How long did she live?"

"I don't know," Lurleen said. "I meant to go down there when I was in college, but I never did. I don't know. You know how you get vibes about people. For me it's like she's still alive."

"Maybe she is."

"She'd have to be a hundred and forty-five years old."

"People have lived that long."

"I guess."

"You can't be sure she was your great-great-grandmother," Vidamía said.

"I'm pretty sure. Before my great-grandmother Marie Meekins died, I visited her in Cape Girardeau in Missouri and asked her about it. I was in my first year of college. She was in her nineties, but still pretty lucid."

"Did you ask her if her mother was black?" Vidamía asked.

"Not in so many words. She said there was talk about it. That her husband had talked to people up around where he was from and they said Lulu McAlpin had returned to the Biloxi area and was living with Negroes off in the woods, but that they just treated her as a crazy old white woman. People had insinuated that the crazy old woman was the daughter of a New Orleans octoroon and how as a girl, Lulu, my great-grandmother's mother, had passed as white sometime back around the Civil War."

"So you knew the woman you met was your great-great-grandmother."

"Yes siree Bob," Lurleen said, suddenly amused. "Although I didn't know it then."

"What's it mean? Does that mean you have African blood?"

"I guess it does," Lurleen said.

"How much?"

"I don't know. I've written to friends in that part of Mississippi to have them look up birth records but a lot of information was lost during the Civil War. As far as I can tell from family records and photographs, maybe Lulu was one-eighth, maybe one-sixteenth. I've seen pictures of her when she was a young woman and there's no way you can detect any African blood in her. She looks Spanish or Italian. She could be anything. Even English."

"So what does that make you? What does that make Cookie and the kids? Daddy?"

"Oh, your daddy doesn't enter into this. We're related through my papa's side of the family. The Sandersons. Anyway, if Lulu McAlpin was one-eighth, then I'm about one one-hundred-and-twenty-eighth African, and the kids are one two-hundred-and-fifty-sixth African."

"That's ridiculous," Vidamía said. "Does that make all of you black?"

"I don't know, but it sure confuses things. It shouldn't make any difference, but it does."

"To you?"

"No, not to me. I don't want the kids confused. When they grow up, I guess I'll tell them at some point. It's not gonna matter much to them. They don't have those kinds of hang-ups."

"No, but I do."

"Well, you shouldn't. We're your family and what color you are or where you came from doesn't matter because we love you and that's the important thing."

Vidamía was quiet awhile, absorbing further what Lurleen had said, feeling how fortunate she was to have someone like her stepmother in her life. She looked closely at her, but there was no trace of any African features, except perhaps the fact that she had full lips, something which all the children, including Cliff, shared. Having full lips was almost required now in the modeling industry. And they all had them. Cookie was simply gorgeous. Like Kelly McGillis, or somebody like that. She'd read that some models and actresses had collagen injected into their lips to make them fuller. As she thought about this she began getting sleepy and they went back downstairs and said good night.

When she was in bed with the lights out she tried to picture what a white black would look like. She imagined a very white person with African features, but that didn't work because there were all sorts of different African people. Some had thinner lips and thinner noses than Scandinavians. In fact, when she had

644

traveled with her parents in Denmark, Norway, and Sweden she had seen people with full lips and some with kinky hair. Some blacks in the U.S. were every different color imaginable and some were the color of ebony and had clear, almost translucent eyes. Maybe the whole country was black. The notion amused her and she thought that perhaps she would call Wyndell in the morning and tell him what she thought about the issue. She knew that she couldn't tell him about Lurleen and the kids, but she sure would like to be able to challenge him with Lurleen's story and ask him what he thought. Were her sisters and her brother black? Cookie, Cliff, Fawn, Caitlin, and Lurleen were all blond and blue-eyed, but by Wyndell Ross's standards they were now supposed to call each other black. No wonder the country was so confused. She fell asleep thinking of this.

58 People of Color

The following day, before Vidamía had an opportunity to call Wyndell, he phoned, apologized, and explained that he was under a lot of pressure and had been thoughtless. She was equally contrite and told him she understood. They chose a place where they could have lunch, and a little after twelve they were sitting outside a restaurant in SoHo. He said he hadn't yet had breakfast and ordered a huge brunch. She loved to watch him eat. He had perfect manners but ate vast amounts of food.

His body, however, remained slim and taut, muscular without the need for much exercise. He often joked that she was all the exercise he needed. Looking at him, she felt a desire to be naked, feeling him growing aroused. She ordered a salad and a Bloody Mary, and as they ate she reminded him that they were due the following day at Alan Flusser's to try on suits. It was her birthday present for him. She wanted him looking sharp and elegant for his official New York debut on the jazz scene. His response was that he felt like a kept man.

"Well, you are," she quipped. "I'm keeping you all to myself."

When lunch was over they jumped into a cab and headed for his apartment. In the cab all she did was lean against him for him to be fully erect. While looking at the rearview mirror from the backseat to make sure the driver wasn't spying on them, she reached down between Wyndell's legs, massaged the hardness, kneading the flesh, and reached up to kiss him. She felt daringly free and sexual and couldn't imagine what it was going to be like to be away from him when she went off to school. Once in the apartment they made love desperately. She wasn't as aroused as he was, but she was happy that he had been so passionate. During the lovemaking he called her *negrita*. "I love you, *negrita*," he'd said.

When they were done she asked him why he'd used that word. He replied that he was using *negrita* as a term of endearment, as she had explained. She told him that she didn't think he was using the word as intended. He said she was paranoid, and she said he was still on a black-white kick. They argued about race and identity and prejudice until they were both angry and hurt again.

"The word describes who you are. Aren't you a *negrita*?"

"That's not the way Puerto Ricans use it," she said. "We don't use it to identify someone's race. That's the way *you're* using it. And you don't have the right to demand that of me, Wyn."

He accused her of wanting to be white and fooling herself about it. She denied wanting to be white. As she slipped into her jeans she explained that being white meant little to her.

"Then how come you have problems thinking of yourself as black?"

"Because I'm not, okay?" she said. "I'm American, not Irish-American or Puerto Rican–American. Anyway, if I had to choose an ethnic identity I'd have to pick Puerto Rican." A little too stridently she explained that Puerto Rico had a history, a culture, a literature, painting and musical traditions, and a language that makes it distinct from other Latin cultures. "Don't ask me why a little island a hundred miles long has created all that, but it has. The truth is that people in the United States can't deal with it, and you're a reflection of that."

"Maybe we don't have to deal with it," Wyndell said. "Maybe it's not a big deal to the United States. Maybe the whole thing of Puerto Rico is insignificant. Another West Indian island."

"Be smug and reduce seven million people to a neat little stereotype of cute brown people who talk fast, smoke pot, dance well, and carry boom boxes so you can deal with all of them. Because there's no question about it. They can be very unruly, unmanageable, and ungrateful. And attitude? You want attitude? P.R.s invented the thing. So now, just because you can't deal with it, everybody becomes black. I bet it bugs the hell out of you when we speak Spanish."

"Well, it is kind of rude," Wyndell said.

"That's right. Seven million Puerto Rican spics talking all at once and waving their hands. A gang of seven million people. One of them is the Surgeon General of the United States and the rest are welfare mothers and dope fiends. Seven million. Half here and half down there. Are you telling me that because this country has a hang-up about race, all seven million Puerto Ricans suddenly become black?"

"You think white people care about what ya'll think? They take a look at most Puerto Ricans and you know what they say? There goes a bunch of Spanish-speaking niggers."

"So what! That's their problem. Some people in Puerto Rico are white and others are not. Look at my stepfather."

"So if they're not white, what are they?"

"We're an ethnic group, a nationality, a culture with very different rules about race."

"No, but the ones who aren't white, what are they?"

"I don't know, some of them are black."

"What about the in-betweens? The ones that have both."

"They have both, that's all."

"So, what's that make them?"

"I don't know. They're just people. Why do they have to be black or white?"

"They are persons of color," he said, smugly.

"Say what?" Vidamía said, staring at him. She had heard the expression but had never heard someone use it directly in a conversation. "Colored people?"

"I didn't say colored people," Wyndell said, getting up from the bed and getting dressed. "I said people of color. Native Americans, Orientals, African people are all people of color."

"Asians."

"What?"

"Asians, not Orientals," she said. "Is this your concession to me?" Vidamía said. "I don't have to be black but I can be a colored person like in South Africa? That is really great."

"Vee, a colored person and a person of color are not the same thing," he said.

"Well, you could've fooled me. It sure sounds like the same thing to me."

"It isn't the same. It's a way for all nonwhite people to unite against racism."

"Well, Puerto Ricans have all kinds of different people so what you're saying is that because blacks in the United States were oppressed, all the other people who aren't from Europe have to adapt to this misguided black agenda, this people-of-color crap? I'm not going to deny that P.R.s have been oppressed, but it's a little more complex than just color."

648

"It's a call for unity."

"So everyone can be oppressed as blacks have been?"

"So you see black people as simply 'being oppressed'?" Wyndell said.

"Hello? Earth to Wyndell," Vidamía said, getting attitudinal. "Aren't black people oppressed? In fact, they are so oppressed that they cannot rid themselves of this hang-up with color and now they want to lay it on everyone else. You know what? You're saying that color is more important than culture. Europeans got homogenized into whites. Africans into blacks and their culture was obliterated. And now 'people of color.' Why don't you solve the problem of color by calling everybody People of Crayola. Crayola even has a white crayon."

"Cute, make jokes. You're big with the jokes."

"Wyn, color is a conspiracy between rich blacks and rich whites to keep everybody confused. And now you want Ricans to join in the confusion. Well, honey, I'm clear about what I am. I have Irish ancestry and I love it. And I have Rican ancestry, and I love that, too. But I'm Rican. If I go to Dublin or Belfast and they see that my name is Farrell and they say I'm one of them, I'm down with it too."

"I'm not getting through to you about racism in this country. And I didn't say anything about your ancestry not being important."

"You don't have to. It's all implied in wanting me to say I'm black. It sounds like you're saying that folks can't define who they are according to their reality. You're saying that because this country is so powerful, Puerto Ricans have to play by the rules a bunch of evil people created to oppress blacks, and that blacks, out of fear, went along with it and whoever's not white has to say that he's black, or now, to make it more palatable, a person of color. It's wack, Wyn. I vote for People of Crayola. That's what you're saying, and it's bullshit!" she said, reaching behind to hook her bra and then putting on her blouse. "If I have to pick something to be I'm gonna choose Puerto Rican, because that's how I was raised. Nobody was going around saying he's black and she's white. Everybody was Puerto Rican. Real clear.

"The way we look at certain things is totally Puerto Rican. The way we look at friendship or family or the things we do for Christmas, the lullabies we sing our babies, our jokes are Puerto Rican. And you know what? I wouldn't trade any of it. I'm just like every other Puerto Rican. Deep inside, like Cookie says, *Yo tengo a Puerto Rico en mi corazón*. I have Puerto Rico in my heart. I don't know why, I just do. There," Vidamía said and put her fist to her heart. "Tattooed to my heart is a big Puerto Rican flag. If you want ethnic, I'll give you ethnic. Don't ask me how it happened. Maybe it comes with the rice and beans. Not beans and rice, like y'all say. But rice, mostly white rice, and beans in salsa on top. And then we mix it all up. White rice and red beans. White rice and black beans. White rice and yellow chickpeas. White rice and pinto beans. Even white rice with white beans. No hang-ups, just good eats, honey. So why do I have to go and pretend that I'm something I'm not?"

"That's pretty impressive," Wyndell said, not wanting to sound too sarcastic, but not pleased. "But from where I'm standing, it still sounds like you're saying that you're white," Wyndell added.

"I don't believe I'm having no impact on you!" she said, her hands on her hips. "You're just as prejudiced as the worst white supremacist."

"What?"

"I'm totally convinced that underneath the color of their skin all American people are prejudiced. Black or white. Prejudiced and hung up on color."

She had finished getting dressed and, slipping into her sandals, walked into the living room to get her bag and leave. She came back into the bedroom, stepped into the bathroom, quickly put on lipstick, ran the brush through her hair, and returned to the living room. Wyndell came out of the bedroom wearing jeans, his chest still glistening with perspiration.

"What are you talking about, woman? What in the hell are you talking about? You sound like a crazy person."

"Listen to me," Vidamía said. "And don't call me crazy. I'm not crazy. I'm good and pissed, but I'm not crazy. And if you keep it up, I'ma go upside your head with a fucking stick."

"Lookee, lookee. Miz Vee's talking herself some honest-to-goodness, down-home Negro talk. Ahz sorry. I didn't mean to call you crazee. I jes doan know what debilment got into me."

"Shut up, you asshole," she said, picking up an ashtray and brandishing it at him. "You just wanna play the fool. You'd rather remain stuck in your little Afrocentric cocoon."

"Oh, oh, that's it, bitch," Wyn said, feigning seriousness. "Who you calling a coon?"

Vidamía stopped dead in her tracks, took aim and let fly with the ashtray so that it traveled dangerously close to Wyndell's head, thudded against the books in the floor-to-ceiling bookcase, and bounced harmlessly on the couch.

"You gonna keep it up?"

"Okay, okay," he said. "Lighten up."

"Don't tell me what to do."

"Okay, I'm sorry, but relax. Oops. Sorry. Whatever. See, I'm sitting and I'm going to listen," he said, picking up the ashtray. "Can I put on BGO?"

"No, not now, dammit," she said. "I know what you're doing. You'll put on the music, something deep will come on, Coltrane or Monk, and you'll feel compelled to tell some story about getting up at night and playing your ax, just to illustrate how gifted you are. Forget it."

She sat down and looked away. Beyond the humming of the air conditioner there was no other sound in the room. Her breath was coming in quick spurts and her head felt light, her forehead hot, the sweat running from her armpits.

"So?" he said, after a few moments of watching her.

"Just hold on," she said.

"All right," Wyndell said. "But I think I understand what you're saying. That it's not fair to be forced to call yourself black, because you have different types of backgrounds."

"Yeah, but that's not what I'm talking about," Vidamía replied.

"What, then?"

"I don't know. I don't wanna argue. I just think people would be better off if folks cut out all this black and white stuff," she said and took a deep breath. "Something doesn't make sense. If you're not supposed to look at difficult things in life in terms of black and white, why is the race issue seen that way?"

"Because it *is* a black-white issue," he replied.

"Bullshit, Wyn," she snapped, growing angry again, tears beginning to form in her eyes.

"It isn't?" he said.

"No, it isn't," she said. "People call themselves black and white, but it's a sickness. What about the people with one white parent and one black parent? What the fuck are they supposed to do? Being half black and half white makes you black? That's crazy! God, Lurleen told me of small towns in Louisiana where every person, black and white, is related by blood to each other and yet they go on referring to this one as white and that one as black."

"Well?" Wyndell said, smugly.

"Well, what? That makes sense to you?"

"Yeah, it makes sense."

She was dying to tell him about Lulu McAlpin, but had sworn to Lurleen that she wouldn't discuss it with anyone. Knowing that Lurleen and Cookie and the girls and Cliff had African ancestry gave her a certain kind of power, because they couldn't be whiter. And yet that kind of thinking had to be eradicated from her heart.

"The race thing makes the country crazy," she said. "Can't you see that?"

"The country's crazy because of all the hatred of white people toward black people," Wyndell said. "That's what makes the country crazy."

"Wrong. The country's crazy because of hatred. White hatred. Black hatred. All kinds of hatred."

"Wait a minute, girl . . ."

"Don't 'girl' me, okay?"

"Sorry. Anyway, now you're gonna start blaming black people for the troubles of the country?"

"Don't twist my words, Wyn. You know I'm not blaming black people for anything. But there's just as much black prejudice as there is white in the fabric of the country."

" 'Fabric'?" Wyn had said, smirking but unsure of what would next surface from Vidamía.

"Fine, make fun of me. I'm eighteen years old, so I have to act like a retard and behave like some Westchester County valley girl, right? Like I have nothing but air between my ears," Vidamía said, jumping up and making a megaphone out of her hands. "Step right up, ladies and gentlemen, and see the amazing girl chump. She oohs, she aahs, she bats her eyelashes, and no matter how dumb it sounds, things get by her." She turned her face to the window and kept talking as she watched the street. "Anyway, the thing that holds the country together, that's the fabric. I'm sorry if the metaphor offends you."

She returned to the couch and sat down.

Wyndell got up and stood over her, this time seriously demanding a better explanation.

"White people have fucked with blacks, messed over their dignity, and stolen everything they had, and now you're telling me that we ought to relax because blacks are just as prejudiced as whites, right?"

"First of all, sit your butt down and stop playing at being

menacing, it doesn't impress me," Vidamía said. "And I didn't say everyone black was prejudiced."

"You might as well have."

"You're trying to confuse things so you don't have to look at your own prejudice."

"On the contrary. I'm trying to get you to see yourself."

"And you're failing miserably at it," Vidamía said. "You can't force people into things."

"Oh, yeah?"

"Yeah, otherwise people are going to make decisions just for appearances. Just like people behaved during slavery. 'Yes, massa. I be the best house Nigra you could hab,' " she mocked him, and immediately hated herself for it. "I'm sorry," she said. "I don't wanna argue, Wyn, but you know there are blacks making life miserable for each other over how black they are or are not. Black people, especially kids, are gonna go along with messed-up ideas because they're afraid they're gonna be pushed away. I've seen it in my school. Black girls who were friends with white girls breaking off friendships that went back to grammar school just because other black girls ran a trip on them. That's messed up, Wyn. Excluding people because of their color. There's no way you can figure out how many people in the U.S. Congress are racist because they're too slick. I bet you eighty percent of black people who spout a lot of militant stuff do it because it's expected of them. It's the same everywhere. Maybe it isn't true of your parents, but I know of black people whose parents would go through the roof if they found that their daughter or son was going out with a white person."

"They have rights like anybody else."

"To be prejudiced?"

"No, to their opinion."

"Even if they haven't met the person? Just because the person is another color? Forget it. That's prejudice. But wait. Wait. Suppose that it was me, all white and green-eyed, and a black man said, 'Mama, this is Vee, she's black.' Then they'd be over-joyed, wouldn't they? You'd be improving the race, and the children might even end up with 'good hair.' It's the same with P.R.s."

"Forget it, Vee," Wyndell said. "That's an old argument. White people have a right to their likes and dislikes, but when a black person does it, it's wrong."

"I gotta tell you something, Wyn," Vidamía said. "You're probably a genius at playing the tenor saxophone, but you can't think worth a damn."

"Forget it," he repeated angrily. "Like I don't have enough to do with this gig and now you're trying to fuck my head up. Your own head's fucked about race and you're trying to fuck mine up."

She was on her feet immediately, demanding that he apologize. He turned away from her and when she grabbed his arm he pulled away roughly, the force nearly knocking her down. She was now seething with anger and headed for the door, slamming it on her way out. Let him go to the West Coast and find himself some other fool. That was it. She was through with him.

59 ● An American Boy

Garlande had recently moved in with her lover. They lived in a huge, modern condominium apartment overlooking the city and the water. There were Romare Beardens, Richard Mayhews, Elizabeth Catletts, and Jean-Michel Basquiat originals all over the apartment, and here and there were artifacts and masks from Garlande's time with the Kikuyu in Africa during her field studies. She spoke Kikuyu, Swahili, Xhosa, and other Bantu languages fluently. In one of the rooms there was a full array of

African drums, masks, utensils, shields, spears, costumes, and other artifacts. Along one wall there were framed photographs of Garlande with tribesmen and women: sitting in front of huts, working in the fields, dancing in tribal costume.

Wyndell's recording had gone well in Los Angeles, and being in Seattle with his sister Garlande again helped him deal with his blowup with Vidamía. He had told Garlande about it and she was understanding. At dinner she and Carl had discussed natural selection and the advantages of a darker skin on a planet that was losing its ozone layer. In New Zealand children had to go to school covered from head to toe because otherwise they'd develop skin cancer. They tried to convince him that there was no advantage in fighting about race. He stood on the balcony, looking out at the night, again on the rim of what was America, the Pacific vastness in the distance. Both Carl and Garlande called him to come in for dessert. They noticed that he was on the edge of depression and they both encouraged him to look to the future and his upcoming gig.

When they were seated and Carl had cut the pie and dished out the ice cream, Garlande talked about music being the history of the United States, and jazz the heart of that music. At times she was so passionate that it embarrassed him. "I'm not much of a musician, but I know enough from listening to Dad talk about it." She said that it was in the complexity of jazz that you could truly see what this country was about; that in the other forms of American music you get a glimpse, but it's more like traveling through a landscape in a speeding car. You get images. "With jazz, and I shouldn't be telling you this because you know it as well as anybody, once you learn to listen you understand what the United States is really about, because it is a dialogue. Jazz is an ongoing dialogue that forces you to listen intently to the nuances of its language. And you're gonna throw it all away by turning into a zealot about race. What you told me about your argument with your girlfriend sounds a little extreme on your part."

"Oh, come on, Garlande. What do you want from me?" Wyndell said.

"I don't want you to give up."

"I'm not giving up, but everything you're throwing at me is part of some Eurocentric reality that destroys my identity as a black man."

"Wyn, you sound like you've been programmed. If you look at it logically, Afrocentrism does the same thing as Eurocentrism. Don't you see that?"

Garlande took a deep breath and her tone became conciliatory again as she explained that he had to understand that the United States was the only place where both European and African ideas and ways of being have had a chance to flourish. Here. Not in Europe and not in Africa or India or any place else where Europeans went and colonized the people. And it's because of the music," she said to him. "Because the blues rose out of the experience of slavery. The blues is what survived the African holocaust that took place in the United States. I don't want to get corny, but the blues is our Afro-American phoenix. It rose from that holocaust."

"Holocaust, huh?" he said, sarcastically.

"Please be quiet and listen, because that's *exactly* what it was," she said quietly. "A cultural holocaust. And it's here where the experiment is taking place. Here, man. This is the place," she added, stressing that if they didn't make it work here, then it wasn't going to work anywhere. "Just like the blues developed and gave birth to different music, the same thing could happen in other areas. Black people have more influence on the culture than you and other African-Americans take credit for. I know this isn't going to sit too well with you, but I'm convinced that the United States is an African country."

"Oh, great. The great anthropologist Dr. Garlande Ross has flipped out. You sound more and more like a black apologist for whites."

"Be open-minded. Let's say for the sake of argument that the U.S. is an African country in its soul. Because of slavery, because of the influence of Africans on the language, on the culture, on its music it can't help itself and it is an African country."

"Okay, let's say that's the case."

"Okay, who's supposed to teach the people of this country to be African? Who knows the most about being African? And I'm not talking about geography or language or other elements of the African continent, but the courage and dignity of struggling like African people have. *We* do. Instead, you spend half your life pushing white people away, talking nasty about them and creating your own kind of separatism. Afrocentrism this and Afrocentrism that."

"There's nothing wrong with Afrocentrism."

"Of course there is. Just like Eurocentrism gives preeminence to European things, Afrocentrism wants to exclude valuable things that come from Europe, and some that come from the United States."

"Like what?"

"Like democracy."

"There were and are democratic governments in Africa."

"C'mon, Wyn. I've been there. I've lived with the people. There's nothing like this anywhere in the world. Nothing this complex, with so many kinds of different types of people trying to get along."

"That's white propaganda, Garlande," Wyndell said. "What are we supposed to do, go around adopting white people and teaching them how to act?"

"It's not propaganda. And, yes, that's exactly what people with an African background should do."

"My lady included?"

"Sure, if she wants to. Has she ever said that she doesn't share an African background?"

"No, she loves her grandfather, and read *Roots* when she was about ten years old. She's always on a kick about black people being mistreated. You should hear her."

"She sounds wonderful, Wyn. You're very lucky."

"Sure, but I say she's a person of color and she jumps all over me. 'See, there you go again with this color shit,' she says. And then she tells me that color's a trick. She says instead of people of color it should be People of Crayola because there's even a white crayon."

"That's cute," Garlande said. "I like it."

"Caribbean people, especially in places like Puerto Rico, have different notions about color," Carl said, offering him more coffee.

"Maybe it *is* a trick," Garlande said.

"What is?" Wyndell said.

"People of color," Garlande replied. "The United States has a real tough time dealing with differences. Just like whites couldn't deal with the fact that there were Mandinke or Ibo or Fulani running around speaking their own languages and made them all speak English in order to homogenize them. The masters raped the slaves and African women had half-white children, and to control them, whites started lumping all the different shades together as colored people. Maybe the African descendants of those folks have fallen into the same trick bag. The country has no problem homogenizing most Europeans. We're doing the same thing with this 'people of color' nonsense, Wyn. Culture, language. Wiped out. One generation here and people forget their parents' language. I mean speaking more than one language isn't a liability anyplace in the world except in the United States."

"I'm not denying that," Wyndell said. "Whites wanted to control their slaves. No African languages, no drums."

"Right," Garlande replied. "And everybody that they wanted to control became 'colored.' The more people they could control, the better. What better way of messing with people than branding them? Even if they have one sixty-fourth of a degree of African ancestry, they're black. Does that make sense to you?"

"Maybe those people with the African blood want to be black," Wyndell said, getting up and looking out over the terrace from twenty floors above the city. "Maybe they identify with black values."

"Maybe they do," Garlande replied, following him. "And I'm not saying there's anything wrong with doing so. But it shouldn't be because there's pressure to conform or because their life depends on it."

"Discrimination against black people doesn't concern white people."

"Wrong," Garlande said. "Racism has always been a problem and there have always been white people trying to combat it. On a lighter note, I've even heard there are white kids who think it's cool to be black."

"That's bull," Wyndell said, turning around to face Garlande.

"It's not bullshit, Wyn. You're so caught up with your own thing that you're losing touch with what's going on around you. I hope you don't get upset with me and don't think I'm pulling some big-sister trip, but it's like, you're twenty-five years old but belong to some old-man's group that stopped thinking thirty years ago. I'm surprised you're not talking about 'the good old days.' Man, later on this year, right in your own backyard, I think in December, there's gonna be a concert at the Apollo. A rap group called Young Black Teenagers made up of white kids is opening for Public Enemy."

"Yeah, show business. Schtick."

"No, it's not just schtick, Wyn. Something else is happening. Look at what kind of music kids all over the United States are listening to," she said. "Rap, rhythm and blues, rock, hip-hop, dance music, salsa. All of it has an African beat, doesn't it? I don't care where you go. Even the sons of good ole boys driving their pickups are listening to rap music."

"Yeah, probably some white rappers."

"What do you care? That's my point exactly. The subjects and lyrics may be different, but the gestures and the beat are going to be that of black homeboys, of Africans. The moves they make are so genuine that it's like I'm back in Africa, sitting around watching people dance. White kids have the same moves, and we transmit that to them. And how do people talk and act? Is the high five, low five, and all that other hand-shaking jive folks do in sports restricted to black people? Why do people want to go to the beach and get darker? Why are models with full lips more in demand? Is having an attitude and talking black a bad thing? People really want in on what we have as African people and all you can do is be rejecting. These people live in an African country, support African music, and all so-called blacks can do is play hard to get. And now that black people have a little power, they're going to reject other people. I talk to people all over the United States and they say that colleges are more segregated than ever and the ones behind the segregation are black student groups."

"What are you getting at?"

"What I'm getting at is that rather than try to deal with the differences between groups of people—Asians, Latinos, Native Americans, whatever—blacks are now going to call everybody people of color. Just drop everyone in there and let them homogenize. I'd say that's a major trick bag. Your girl is right. Eventually, instead of progress, what we're going to do is get more colored people. Right back where we started. Let's demean the African experience. And don't tell me it doesn't make you squirm when people start talking about colored people."

"Well . . . it's better than . . ."

"C'mon, Wyn. Admit it. Defining people by color is limiting. There are Europeans—Sicilians, Spaniards, Portuguese, and French—who are darker than some people we call black. There are people from different tribes in India who are blacker than the darkest Africans. They're considered Caucasians. Color doesn't explain anything. It's a nightmare to refer to people as blacks and it doesn't help matters any when you start talking about people of color."

"What you're saying is pretty dangerous, Garlande," Wyndell said. "It borders on some sort of cultural genocide. It sounds like you're advocating destroying black identity."

"You know that I would never do that, Wyn. That something might get destroyed I don't doubt. What I do doubt is that it will be the soul of the United States. And the soul of the United States is African. I spent years in Africa, Wyn. You know that. What I'm telling you is based on observation. I've sat in on tribal meetings. I've talked to thousands of people in their own languages. Believe me, the United States is an African country."

"You're gonna get lynched talking about the U.S. being African, sis," Wyndell said.

"Everybody's gotta wake up. Just because something is European doesn't mean it's evil and black people should get rid of it."

"Oh, no? Folks should lay back and get raped intellectually and emotionally."

"Stop it, Wyn," Garlande said. "That's beneath you. Do you admire Miles Davis?"

"Yeah, he's done some hip things."

"*Sketches of Spain?*"

"Yeah."

"The music was based in part on the work of European composers."

Garlande motioned him back inside. She went over to the sound system and the rack where the CDs were kept in the living room. She searched for a few moments and then pulled out *Sketches of Spain* and removed the liner notes. "Listen."

"I know," Wyndell said.

"Just listen, okay?"

"Okay, okay."

"No, really listen."

"I know, I know. Arranged by Gil Evans, a white man. Is that what you're getting at?"

"Let me read you the liner notes, Wyn. The album came about because when Miles was out here on the West Coast early in 1959, in California, 'a friend played him a recording of *Concierto de Aranjuez* for guitar and orchestra by the contemporary Spanish composer Joaquin Rodrigo.' And . . . here, listen to this," she said, flipping the booklet. " 'Among the music he'—meaning Gil Evans—'he and Miles listened to in preparation for the album was Manuel de Falla's 1915 ballet score *El Amor Brujo*.' So there you have it, even Miles Davis recognized the contribution that European music could make to jazz."

"Yeah, but that was Spanish," Wyndell said.

"What difference does that make?" she asked.

"Spain was run by Moors for hundreds of years," he said. "Where do you think Moors are from? They're Arabs from North Africa."

"So what."

"Most of Spain is African."

"You tell them, okay? Southern Spain has a Moorish influence, but also a Jewish one. And up in the northwest they have bagpipes like they do in Scotland and Ireland. But be like every arrogant American and tell people with a rich tradition what they are. In any case, the music is definitely European, and Miles Davis made it even more beautiful. Good stuff, isn't it?"

"Excellent. He's a genius."

"Even when he veered away from straight-ahead jazz and

began experimenting with electronic music and did *Bitches Brew* and all that stuff?"

"Yeah, it was still improvisational music," Wyn said. "High-quality shit."

"Well, maybe that's what Miles Davis saw?"

"What?"

"That he wanted to reach a bigger audience and still be able to be an artist?"

"Are you saying I oughta do the same thing?"

"No, baby, what I'm saying is that Miles Davis never compromised his integrity. And more than that, he freed a lot of people from the constraints and prejudices of just playing straight-ahead jazz."

"You don't like straight-ahead jazz?"

"I love it. That's what Daddy raised us on. Love and straight-ahead jazz and Mommy's love of art and her cooking and dry humor. Remember when Dexter Gordon came to the house for dinner and jammed with Daddy and his friends?"

"I think so," Wyndell Ross said, feeling soft inside, not defeated but thoughtful and sad and missing being back in New York with Vidamía.

"Her old man's a jazz musician," he said. "White cat."

"Your girl?"

"Yeah."

"Any good?"

"Pretty fair. Pianist," he said and thought of Billy Farrell's right hand, those three fingers blurring as he played complicated runs on the piano when he was soloing and trading. "No, that's not true, Garlande. Not fair. He's a jazz musician, and in that he's a brother. Billy Farrell is brilliant. That's his name. He's my pianist for the gig at the Gate. He's got two fingers missing. A very simple cat, but a brilliant pianist. Had a chance to play with Miles at one time. But that's another story."

"That's great. Not every white person can play jazz," Garlande said. "Just love her, Wyn. Enjoy your life with her. She sounds like a treasure. Next time you come out, bring her."

"Okay," Wyn said, nodding, basking now in his big sister's love for him. "I will."

He slept soundly and then the next morning he left to fly back to New York.

Back home in New York, WBGO was playing "Love for Sale" with Cannonball Adderley and Miles Davis, the horn wailing mournfully. He listened carefully and recalled being back in Los Angeles recording with Sonny Pointer again and all the feelings the experience had dredged up. He recalled driving up to San Francisco and staying at Sue McCallister's house and how kind and concerned she'd been about him, how supportive she and her husband had been. He shook his head and knew it would hurt Sue to hear him spouting black and white stuff. With them that had never mattered. He poured himself another shot of whiskey and then heard the key turn in the door and knew she was coming back to him.

"I'm sorry," Vidamía said, coming over and sitting down. "I shouldn't have run out."

"No, no," Wyndell said, getting up and feeling the effects of the whiskey. "I didn't mean to hit you. I promised that first time, and I just lost it . . ."

"You didn't hit me," she said. "I was off balance and almost fell."

And then she was overcome by all the emotion and she was crying and curling up on the leather chair by the window. Wyndell let her cry and then came over and picked her up in his arms and brought her over to the couch.

"I'm sorry," he said, kissing her forehead. "I really am. I missed you so much."

"I never wanted to see you again. All week long while you

were gone I kept thinking about us and I couldn't figure anything out. It was this big lump of hurt inside of me. And then I started thinking, and maybe I figured it out. I was thinking about you and Daddy," she said.

"About the gig?" Wyn said. "No matter what happens, we're going to do it. I can't wait to get back to rehearsing. I called everyone."

"No, it's not that," Vidamía said, breaking away from him so she could face him. "It's like every time you start with this race stuff, it's like you're asking me to choose between the two of you. I could never do that. I love you both so much. Can't you understand that?"

"I understand," he said. "I was just pissed."

"About what?"

"You and me. I mean, you're a white chick. It cracks people up when I tell them you have African blood. I get so much fucking heat from people. Especially sisters. I tell them you're Puerto Rican and they just laugh in my face. They act all nice in front of you, but deep inside they can't take me and you feeling the way we do about each other. I was never into this black and white thing until I came to New York."

"Bitches!" Vidamía said. "Which ones?"

"I'm not gonna tell you. I'm sure you'd kill at least two of them. No jail for you."

Vidamía laughed, looked at her watch, jumped up from the couch, and ran into the bathroom to wash the redness out of her eyes. When she came back out she kissed Wyndell quickly and said she had to be at the store. He asked her if everything was going to be all right. She nodded happily and reminded him that he had rehearsal at the loft that evening.

"I know," he said. "You want to get together afterward? Let's have dinner late and just walk like we used to."

"Okay," she said. "I love you."

"And I love you," he said.

Wyndell closed his eyes and knew something was happening in his life that had never happened before. He didn't feel cynical now and couldn't understand why he had behaved as he did. The black and white issue was confusing and he couldn't really say that he felt totally convinced that Garlande or Carl or Vidamía was right. He thought of all the white friends he'd had over the years, people who respected him and even loved him. And he thought of the black people who ridiculed him and disliked him immensely.

Maybe they were right. Maybe he had to begin forgetting about skin color and concentrate on the way he'd been raised. And then he recalled sitting on the floor of his mother's gallery as she placed small plastic plaques next to the paintings for an upcoming exhibition. He couldn't have been any more than seven or eight years old. Amanda Creighton Ross, who had studied art history in Rome and Paris, was beautiful, and she was his mother. She had never once told him any horror stories about Europe.

One summer he had traveled with the family to Paris and they'd gone through Germany and up into Denmark, crossing the sea on a big ferry that the railroad cars traveled on. They went by train through the Danish countryside, the fields yellow with mustard flowers, and in Copenhagen they took another big ferry to Sweden.

Everyone they met was pleasant and relaxed. His father's friend Gerald Grayson, who was black and an architect, was married to a blond woman who was a violinist. They had two children, and their family lived in a beautiful house near a lake with hardly any other homes near. Wyn and his family returned to Paris and spent time with friends and he got to stay up late and they let him drink a little wine. He always watched his mother to learn what he must do. There was nothing that made him prouder than his mother. He recalled watching her figure, the legs long and shapely, the high heels accentuating the muscles, the hem of her dress just above the knees, and then her shape, which was round at the hips, narrow at her waist, and then widening out again to full breasts. Her neck was long and elegant, her face sculpted—high cheekbones, her nose narrow at the bridge and wide at the base, like the sculptured masks in Garlande's house.

They were the same color, he and his mother. His father and his sisters were lighter, but his mother's skin was dark and smooth, the color of the mahogany furniture in his parents' bedroom. Perhaps his father and mother had fashioned him from parts of the furniture, he thought one day when he was six years old. He laughed to himself and thought of Pinocchio, another wooden boy. But he wasn't a wooden boy. And then, as he sat on the floor of the gallery, alternately drawing geometric patterns on his Etch-a-Sketch and watching his mother work, the aromas of her womanhood and perfume wafting to him, he thought of what the man in the car had shouted to him when he was walking home from school the previous week.

"Mama?"

"Yes, darling," she'd said, her back to him.

"Am I a nigger?"

"No, you're Wyndell Ross," she'd said, turning and smiling at him from above. Her face was radiant with love for him. "Wyndell Ross, an American boy who lives in Denver, Colorado. That's who you are. Could you please get me the rest of the plaques from my desk?"

"Yes, Mama," he'd said.

He'd gone for the little plastic signs with the data identifying each painting—artist's name, title, materials. As he walked back he kept thinking of his own name and who he was. He had not yet begun playing music, but his father and mother were always talking about people in jazz. Wyndell Ross. The name sounded like Charlie Parker. Like Miles Davis. Like Thelonious Monk. Like Dexter Gordon. Wyndell Ross. An American boy living in

Denver, Colorado. Wyndell Ross. An American man trying to make sense of things. And Vidamía had the same right as anybody, he thought. Vidamía Farrell. An American girl living in New York City. He shook his head and promised himself that he'd listen more carefully to his heart. God, she was beautiful, and bright, and he loved her and didn't care what color she was, and that was the truth.

6O Sermon

The week beginning with Sunday the twelfth of August, 1990, was like three weeks crammed into one for Vidamía. On Monday she took Wyndell to Alan Flusser's to pick out his suit. Flusser himself took care of them. He was dressed impeccably and reminded them of David Niven without the mustache, so suave was he. Vidamía offered to take Cliff as well, but Cliff said he knew what he wanted to wear and his girlfriend Phillipa was working on something. Billy went up to see Pop Butterworth and returned to say that the old man wasn't doing too well.

Billy sat in his rocker, staring straight ahead, as he used to do for hours at a time before he started playing the piano again. Caitlin had turned on the television and had paused on CNN for a moment. There was another report on the military activity in the Persian Gulf. The report said something about Marines, and Billy jumped up and told Caitlin not to change the channel. It was too late, the screen jumped to MTV and Billy slammed his fist on the table.

"Caitlin, dammit," he said. "I told you not to change it."

He got up and went over and took the remote from her and sat down to watch the report on the Iraqi invasion of Kuwait.

"I'm sorry, Daddy," Caitlin said, suddenly frightened.

She walked slowly to Lurleen and buried herself against her. Lurleen soothed her and everyone went about their business. Billy sat glued to the television set for the next hour, changing back and forth from CNN to the regular news. When the news was over, he went to the back of the loft. He opened the combination lock on his old footlocker, lifted the lid, reached inside and brought out a smaller wooden chest, about the size of a makeup case with a small padlock on it. He took the case up the stairs to the roof and turned on the light. Opening the case, he unwrapped the oily rag to reveal the .45-caliber pistol he had purchased as soon as news about Iraq's march into Kuwait began. From the bottom of the chest he removed the three full clips and laid them on the picnic table. He checked the action on the pistol, stripped it, and put it back together. Then he loaded a clip into the pistol and sat up on the roof as if he were on guard. He knew it was nuts, but something could happen any minute. The world was getting crazier and crazier. If Iraq kept it up there was going to be war, and then he'd have to go, just like before. Maybe he should just go down and volunteer. But they wouldn't take him because of his disability. He'd convince them that he could be helpful in some way. Then again, maybe he ought to stay close to home in case something broke out here.

Around one o'clock in the morning Lurleen came up to get him. When she saw the pistol she stood still, waiting for him to look up, recalling those times when she'd watched him consider ending his life. She finally lost her patience.

"You went back on your word about having guns around the kids," she said, walking to him.

"No, it's not like that, Lynn," he said. "Let me explain."

Billy began talking real fast about Iraq and Saddam Hussein and how everybody had to be real careful and watchful because something could go down at any moment. Lurleen finally calmed him down enough to convince him to come downstairs and put the pistol away. He reassured her that he was okay, that he wasn't thinking about suicide. Lurleen said she knew, but wasn't sure how much she could believe him. Billy explained that he was just anxious about the gig. He said that the other thing eating him up was that he didn't think Butterworth was going to make it.

"He's so sick, Lynn," he said. "Man, I just feel helpless. I'm taking him to the hospital tomorrow to check him in."

She held his arm firmly, her own hooked into his, as if at any moment he'd fly away from her. Carefully, concentrating with all her might, she guided him through every step of putting the pistol away and made him lock it up again. She brought him to bed and made love to him slowly until he was aroused, and as always he was all over her, forgetting himself in her embrace. In the middle of the night he woke up in a sweat and was back in Vietnam, in the middle of a firefight, whispering that the machine gun was jammed and shaking Lurleen. She woke up and held him until he again was relaxed enough to fall asleep.

The following day, Billy went up to Harlem and took Butterworth to the hospital to sign him in. Each day he stayed with Butterworth from mid-morning until late afternoon, when he came back home for the evening rehearsal. He watched the situation worsen in what was now called the Gulf War, each report making him more concerned about the Marines in Kuwait.

On Friday the seventeenth, Vidamía went with Wyndell to bring Pop Butterworth magazines and the papers, and Butterworth looked at them together and, in a raspy voice, said, "Damn, you two are the best-looking people I've ever seen."

And then he got very serious and spoke what Wyndell later termed "some strange shit." "Watch yourselves, chillun," Butterworth said, "cause the shadow man's gonna get you sure as God made split-pea soup."

Wyndell had laughed and said, "Man, you still talking stuff? Whyntcha get yourself outta that bed and let's play us some music so I can run your old behind into the ground."

Butterworth smiled weakly and said, the voice raspier than ever, and the effort making his eyes water, "I wish I could, son, but I can't. I'd like a favor if you could do one for me."

"No problem at all," Wyndell said, all serious so that it frightened Vidamía. "Just tell me what I got to do."

Butterworth motioned him closer to the bed and from around his withered, scrawny neck, the dark coffee-colored skin dry and ashy, he undid a key from a chain and pressed it into Wyndell's hand.

"That there's the key to my papers," he said. "They're in a bureau up at Mae Wilkerson's house in the Bronx. Third floor in the back. She knows where. There's a letter addressed to Mae explaining the whole thing. Whatever's in there is yours. Do what you want with it. If you can use the stuff, go on ahead and use it. If you can't, burn the whole damn thing."

"What is it, Pop?" Wyndell had said.

"My papers," Butterworth had replied. "A few tunes I wrote, that's all. There's no arrangements or nothing. Just the basic tunes, top and bottom. Get Billy to play them for you to see if you like them."

"Tunes?" Wyndell said. "That's great, Pop." And, turning to Vidamía, he pointed to Butterworth. "Can you believe this, the man is a composer!" Then back to Butterworth. "Man, you best get yourself well and get outta that bed so we can play some music, you understand what I'm saying to you? The gig at the Gate is in two weeks and you gotta be ready. Don't you wanna sit in with us? Billy's expecting it."

Butterworth smiled again, his long yellow teeth already showing death, and then shook his head and said he didn't think he could comply with the request at this time. And he was right, because as the illness, which the doctors had categorized as terminal, progressed, it began to incapacitate him further until the slightest movement caused him increasing pain.

Ultimately, as if paint remover had been applied, the illness, which had begun in the throat, stripped the many-layered coat of negrification that had been the source of the inhibitions of Alfred Butterworth and he'd drift in and out between civility and angry, foul language. At first he would be discussing something calmly and suddenly he'd say things like "motherfuckin' apostles" or "Sure the bitch was sucking Jesus' dick. Why you think they crucified his ass?" Precipitously, without warning, words tumbled from his mouth as if a large faucet had been turned and turned, and turned some more, allowing a dam to release its captive waters.

When Vidamía, her extreme curiosity hungering to decipher the mystery of Butterworth's now aberrant mind, received nothing but psychological mumbo jumbo from her mother in a waste-of-time telephone conversation, she went and looked into the big Spanish–English dictionary at the library across the street from Tompkins Square Park. Hoping somehow to get at the Latin roots of the word "repressed," she ran across the word *represa*, which in Spanish means dam. The irony of the bilingual coincidence made Vidamía initially laugh, but then the more she thought about it the angrier she grew, thinking of poor Mr. Butterworth, so quiet in the past, his body becoming skeletal, and yet as bony and skinny as he was becoming, his voice, up to now raspy, now acquiring a different timbre and an almost crystal-like resonance, the words coming out clearly, everything up to that time withheld rushing out of him, indicting everyone and everything that had ever wronged him or in his opinion had hindered his vision.

Vidamía tried holding Butterworth's hand, but to her consternation, other than the occasional curse word, the old man simply smiled at her and invariably fell asleep, snoring lightly, his face placid in repose. But when her father came to see him, which he did every day, sitting in the room for hours, something quite different happened. His good friend and the person for whom he felt the same filial devotion he'd had for his father, behaved quite differently when Billy held his hand. The old man would immediately start discoursing, or, as Mae Wilkerson said on one of her visits to the hospital, sermonizing. Once, to ascertain whether her observation was accurate, Vidamía called her father out of the room. As if an electrical circuit had been disconnected, Butterworth turned off in mid-sentence. But as long as Billy held Alfred Butterworth's hand, the old man discoursed, so that all Vidamía could think about was Wyndell's tenor saxophone in full flight reciting eloquently chorus after chorus of musical ideas, each one more complex and beautiful than the previous one and everything up-tempo, evoking all his musical heroes. When Butterworth spoke he did so clearly, his voice no longer ravaged by age and the cancerous polyps in his throat.

One day he began at two in the afternoon, and at six, when they brought him his evening meal, he was still going—

What you think you are, you silly-ass mothafucka? You made the heavens and the earth? So mothafuckin' what! And you're the Almighty what? Don't talk shit, okay, man? You understand what I'm saying to you? Do you, you pasty-faced son of a bitch? You sitting up there in mothafuckin' white Heaven, dictating to niggers how they should be. Suck my dick. Suck my limp, useless mothafuckin' dick, you faggoty-ass punk mothafucka. You did what?

And, turning to Billy, as if he couldn't believe what he was hearing back, he said, *Check this mothafucka out, Solomon.*

Nobody ever figured out who Solomon was, but that's what Butterworth said when he looked at Billy Farrell holding his hand. Mae Wilkerson said maybe Pop Butterworth was appealing to the wisdom of Solomon, implying, one could imagine, a sort of a biblical legal brief, that is, arguing the case. *Did you ever hear such shit? What am I gonna tell him? I got no choice, do I, Solomon?* And Billy'd nod his head, as if he was agreeing with Butterworth, the sadness spilling out of his eyes in big, thick silent tears. *I gotta tell him, don't I?* And, turning away, he'd start talking at the ceiling, removing another layer of his repressed negritude.

You fulla shit, you know that? Where in the fuck did you get your ideas, you stupid-ass mothafucka? Yeah, right. Can't make up your mothafuckin' mind, can you? You feeling creative one morning after you make the world, so you figure you gonna make people. Outta clay so the shit gotta be coming out their asshole all the time. And you make a man and you wanna call him Ken or some stupid-ass white name like that cause you know your clay man Ken can maybe do stuff and carry your word forth into the mothafuckin' desert some fuckin' where. And looking at this puny mothafucka standing all naked and pale as a mothafuckin' ghost you say: Sheet, his name should be Kent cause he look like he ain't gonna be able to do diddly-squat. So you're madder'n a wet hen and pissed off to boot and you say, Agh Damn! And that's what you name the nigger. Aghdamn.

One day you spend from sunrise to mothafuckin' sunset watching Aghdamn sneaking around the bushes, either jackin' off or trying to find him a goat to fuck. You so pissed off you hit on the idea to get this pasty-ass mothafucka some pussy cause otherwise Aghdamn's gonna keep fuckin' the goats, and already there's some half-boy and half-goat critters been born and they look like hell and all they wanna do is fuck, too, and everybody from the chickens to the mothafuckin' monkeys in the vicinity's going around covering up their ass. So you wait till he's asleep, rip out a rib from his side, and put together a fine-looking mama. You give her some titties, a nice round behind, and then you look at her and she look like some big-ass Barbie doll all smooth between her legs. What am I gonna do now? you say. So you take your ugly ole index finger and you dig her up a pussy snatch and you say: I'ma call this bitch Denise so this dumb-ass Aghdamn can do his hammer some good. And then you change your mind again and say: Denise? That sounds like some poet's name. What I make this bitch for? For Aghdamn to stop beating his meat and stop fuckin' my goats, so I'ma call her Evenin so this silly-ass mothafucka can get some sleep cause he's starting to get on my nerves.

And you take a look at this mama laying on the ground, still asleep but looking fine, her legs spread where you'd dug her up her

675

pussy snatch and back you go up in there fingering her and you say: Uwhee, that feel good, all soft and gooey. My man Aghdamn's gonna have him a partee! But that pussy look all red and ugly and you say: I better dress it up. So you take some hair from the bitch's head, roll it around between your palms to make it curly, and stick it on her snatch to cover it up and then you dip your hand into the sea and bring up some seawater and lock it into the bitch's snatch and say: There, so this silly-ass mothafucka can smell it and stop thinking about the goats and start thinking about swimming and fishing and create surfing, scuba diving, and fishing shows on TV instead.

But he ain't happy, is he, Solomon? No, suh.

"No, he ain't," Billy said, squeezing Butterworth's hand.

And Butterworth, his eyes lost in his private vision, went on.

You get up one morning and Aghdamn's done fucked Evenin all of two times in ten days and Evenin's pulling at his johnson and the thing's taken the day off and don't wanna hear it. And the next night Evenin's pulling at him again. Aghdamn? Nothing. The silly-ass white man is oblivious. That's right. He hears her hummin' but he ain't comin and is in a state of total disinteresation. This goes on for a couple of weeks, and Evenin's fit to be tied, bitching at Aghdamn and making his life so miserable that he goes off and hides on the other side of the garden, and to pass the time he sets to inventing beer.

The weeks pass into months and pretty soon you start to fret cause these two silly-ass white fools are supposed to procreate and they ain't doing the thing. So you think and think and think some more and then you say: Let me fuck with these mothafuckas. You go down to the swamp with nasty ole gators and snappin' turtles and you stick your big ole hand in and from the bottom of the mothafuckin' swamp you take some of the blackest mud you can find and make yourself a nigger. You give him big ole lips, some nappy hair, and a big dick. You borrow you some mothafuckin' juice from the goats and stick it up his ass so all he wanna do is dance and fuck and you set him loose in the Garden of Eden. And what you call him? Right. Deuteronomy

Jackson so that just like Evenin became Eve and Aghdamn became Adam, the nigger becomes Doit. And he does.

First time Evenin lays eyes on this big ebony mothafucka with that thing hanging offa him, she say: Oh, baby, baby, baby, and they go at it, starting at sundown and still going at it at sunup and Doit's hammer still harder than Chinese Algebra and Eve coming so much her orgasm be echoing up in the mothafuckin' hills.

So what happens now? Aghdamn see this and gets jealous as a mothafucka and he goes to Eve not with the intention of kicking her ass, but in a conciliatory mothafuckin' mood and he says: Excuse me, dear, but we got to talk, we got to discuss things, we got to come to some understanding about this here thing, because I strongly feel that there has been a breakdown in communication. And Eve, totally fucked out, but always looking for a thrill, scoped down and saw Aghdamn's johnson starting to act up, getting thick and long and says, bold as she can be: Aghdamn, cut the shit and let's fuck.

And sure as Ritz crackers they go at it for almost twenty minutes. And you know what? Nine months later the bitch has twins. One black as night and the other white as snow. And you look at these two boys and you name them. The black one you call Amabelate, cause lookin' at him all grinnin' and squirmin' around you know all he gonna wanna do is play around and whenever he has to be somewhere he's gonna be late. And the white one you name Callhimin, cause he look all serious and whatnot, his face all scrunched up like he's interviewing people to be the head honky. He a funny mothafucka, ain't he, Solomon?

Butterworth turned from the ceiling to look at Billy, his eyes sort of closing but then opening up again, then looking back up with his face a mask of anger.

Fuck you! Don't tell me I'm blaspheming. Mama, tell him to keep outta this. I don't give a mothafuckin' hoot if you a minister. Take your black ass back to Waco or Savannah or wherever you came from and go pick yourself some cotton. Don't be comin' around

677

fuckin' with folks, tellin' them they's blaspheming. Yeah, go ahead and go for your belt like you always do, cause I ain't a kid no more and if you lay a hand on me I'ma take a ax handle and hit you upside your nappy mothafuckin' head. That's right. Go ahead and try it and see if I don't. Yeah, you fulla shit. Oh, kiss my ass, reverend. You the one blaspheming. Talking all that shit on Sunday and the rest of the week you trying to bunghole young girls in barns. Get outta my face, reverend.

And then, looking beyond his memory and once again berating the Almighty as if he were determined to secure himself a place in the subbasement of Hell, Butterworth resumed his diatribe.

You had to go do it, didn't you, you silly mothafucka? Amabelate and Callhimin. Black and white. You coulda stepped in and said, fellas you gotta sublimate your aggression. Here's a bunch of melons and that there's a brand-new peach basket I made. You stand a ways off and shoot the melons into the peach basket. I took out the bottom. Whoever get the most melons in the peach basket wins. What you win? The melons, you stupid mothafucka. For what? To eat 'em. They ain't gonna do me no good layin' on the ground broke open. But you don't. You make one white and the other black and let them go at it.

Butterworth then began going back and forth from one voice to the other, as if two people were having an argument.

She's my motha. She ain't you motha. She white like me. Oh, you skinny ass, pasty-faced fool. Look at her pussy snatch, the hair all black and crinkly like my hair. How come she don't have lanky blond hair growin down there? Oh, you nothin' but a black-ass nigger and you ain't got no motha. And Evenin payin her two boys no mind and just runnin' around all distracted cause she can't find her pocketbook with her credit cards so she can go shopping for shampoo and hair spray.

And that's how it happen, Solomon. You understand what I'm telling you? That's exactly how it happen. Exactly how it happen.

There wasn't no snake, you mothafucka. That faggoty-ass Genesis wrote some bullshit with snakes and whatnot. There wasn't no mothafuckin' snake that was supposed to be the Devil. That was nearsighted mothafuckin' Genesis seen Doit's johnson and said: Aha, it's the serpent, and made up this silly-ass story about some damn snake tempting Eve with an apple from the forbidden tree. All bull-shit. That was the nigger's johnson, you myopic mothafucka. His johnson. There was no fuckin' apples involved. That was the nigger's nuts. Eve just took a liking to Doit's vampin' on her vaj.

So the deal's that one thing led to another and one day Callhimin got pissed at Amabelate and called him a black, river-bottom, no-count nigger and Amabelate gave his honky brother such a bad whuppin' that Callhimin went and got him a Uzi machine pistol and went after that boy. Went after him like a starving man at a chittlins convention. Walked up to him right in the middle of Lenox Avenue and opened fire. All that bullshit about the jawbone of an ass. It mighta looked like that, but I was standing right on the fire escape and Callhimin shot Amabelate about twelve times. But you know what? Amabelate survived that shit. That's right. He got his sorry ass over to Harlem Hospital and they said: Damn, you one holy motha-fucka. You look like Fearless Fosdick from the comics you got so many holes in you. And they start stitchin Amabelate up on Saturday mornin' and they don't finish till Tuesday night he so fucked up.

So Callhimin's happy as a pig in shit cause he done kilt the nig-ger. He so happy that he start inventin' things and in one afternoon he invent toilet paper, movies, hair cream, and milkshakes. Damn, Solomon! This is one inventin' fool, ain't he? He go into work from nine to five and he just invent till he drop. They ain't nothin' on Earth that Callhimin didn't invent. Damn, he's good. If shit wasn't natural he woulda invented that, too. Television, airplanes, Xerox, opera, long pants, checking accounts, and a whole bunch of other useless shit. And one day when he got a headache and can't think o' nothin', he invent rope. And that was the best invention of all cause one day he turn around and the mothafucka thought he was goin' crazy cause here come Amabelate Jackson, none the worse from lead poisoning, with his sons Jesse, Reggie, Michael, Maynard, Samuel, and their big sister Mahalia and their little sister Latoya, the prettiest niggers you can imagine and all of them smart as a whip. You never heard people talk shit like these Jackson folks.

And immediately Callhimin's head start sending him evil fuckin' messages and he says: Damn, I shot that mothafucka and he still alive and not only is he alive, but he been out fuckin' some high yeller bitch and she done whelped these pups. So he said: That's it. No more fuckin' around. So Callhimin grab him some percale sheets he invented and made some silly-ass uniforms and put on hoods and wrote on the uniform KKK which stand for Keep Kookin Kitty, or Kant Katch Kunt, or Kiss Krist's Keister, or Keep Kosher Kike, or maybe Kaka Kaka Kaka. And then he talked to some of his white friends who was all good ole boys disguised as rednecks and crackas and he say to them: Boys, let's have us some fun and string up a few niggers. And Callhimin give himself a title like Grand Imperial Dragon like he a Chinese restaurant somewhere in Alagadamnbama or some fuckin' place. The thing is that they said: 'Hey, we invented rope so let's string up the niggers and that's the end of it. And while we at this let's burn some crosses to show the niggers that we ain't gonna be fucked with. How's that gonna show we don't wanna be fucked with, Uncle Callhimin? Joe Bob, don't test my patience, son. Just build the cross and we burnin' it. Don't ask me what it mean. It mean just what I said. Christ died on the cross, so niggers better watch their sorry ass. Can't argue with that logic, can you, Solomon?

"No, you can't, Pop," Billy said.

And he let the shit happen, Solomon. He let all this shit happen, didn't he? Let it happen. And I ain't talkin' about the fool that started the whole thing. I ain't talkin' about Him. Hell no. He sittin' up in white Heaven playin' Super Mario Brothers or some shit like that and done lost control of the whole thing a long time ago. Amabelate let it happen. You think he'd wise up and see these silly mothafuckas comin' with the rope and dressed all strange in white robes with hoods, lookin' like they all playing being Li'l Red Ridin' Hood and forgot to paint the outfits. You think seeing this he'd wise up and say: Damn, these crackas mean business. I best get me somethin' to defend myself with. At least a shotgun, but better yet a writ of mandamus to stop these mothafuckas. But hell no. This silly mothafuckin' Amabelate rememberin' his ole man's reverence for the silly mothafucka who made him from river mud, sets to prayin' and singing hymns and talkin' about brotha this and sistah that and reverend this and deacon that and just like the mothafuckin' KKK, he and the rest of the silly-ass churchgoing mothafuckas, they start dressing the women in white. What they gonna do, fool the Klan into believing that they friends, or they just trying to turn the women over to them?

No, Mama, you can't tell me to hush. It's the truth. It's the damn truth. You just don't wanna hear it. I'm sorry, Mama, that you and the resta y'all don't wanna hear this. But I gotta tell you anyway. I got to. If I don't I'ma die the most unhappiest man that ever lived. These mothafuckas treated me like dirt. Every day of my sorry-ass life they treated me like I was shit. "Nigger" this and "nigger" that and me feeling ugly and thinkin' maybe it'd be different if I was lighter or maybe if my hair was straight like Cab or my nose nice and straight and white-lookin' like Lena, but that didn't make no sense because when I was around the music I felt so good that nothin' mattered, Mama. Nothin'. I'm sorry I wasn't a good son, Mama. I never did nothin' that woulda made you ashamed of me. Maybe I drank a little too much, or smoked some reefer and even snorted some blow or laid up with somebody's wife, but I never killed nobody, Mama. I never stole nothin' from nobody, Mama. The only thing I did was turn my back on the church, Mama.

And you know why, Mama? Cause it hurt us. Oh, Mama, the church hurt us. Believing all that stuff about God hurt us, Mama. Who? Don't "who" me, Mama! You know who they are. You can't sit around and blame it on the white man. There's black folks that don't give a fuck about you or me or anybody else. They figure this is the land of opportunity so you should be able to make it because there

681

is equality and that's the important thing. But it ain't. Equality don't mean shit if you go there and they look at you and because your skin ain't the right color they figure you don't know nothin' and you an ignorant nigger or a spic or a chink or a feather bonnet or a raghead.

No, Mama, don't tell me I got to trust the Lord. The Lord ain't shit, Mama. And don't tell me to be careful. I got to tell her, don't I, Solomon? Mama, he full of shit. Yeah, Mama, I know he calling me, but I ain't ready yet. No, Solomon, don't try to shut me up. If I shut up the shit's gonna go on. I got to tell him, otherwise I ain't shit. What you want? Yeah, yeah. You're God the Almighty. You know something. I don't give a rat's ass what they call you. They wanna call you Jehovah or Allah or Buddha or Winnie the Pooh, that's okay with me. I don't give a fuck, cause you fulla shit. Lying to people like you a used-car salesman and telling them they gonna go to Heaven and stuff.

There ain't one mothafucka I know of that done come back from this Heaven and said: Pop, Heaven's a mothafucka. You like chitlins and some nice turnips greens and a nice piece of barbecue? Man, hurry up and die because they got some serious eats up here in Heaven. Or somebody come down and tell you: Yo, Butterworth, you think pussy was good when you was down there fuckin' around with them skanky bitches you ran with, wait till you get up here and get your johnson into these heifers. Damn, brother, hurry up and give your soul a rest. No, sir. You wanna hang on as long as you can. One more pork chop or one more reefer or one more drink o' whiskey or one more dickin' some fine woman. So why you talking about Heaven? Check this mothafucka out, Solomon. I'm headed for eternal damnation and if I don't hurry up and die you gonna send some of your most fundamentalist believers to talk sense into me? Man, eternal my dick, you silly-ass fool. You think you look like some Hebrew prophet with that beard, but you look more like a ole, dried-up, shut-tight cunt with gray hair. Fuck you and your threats, punk.

The following day around three o'clock in the morning Alfred Butterworth, an unknown alto saxophone player, passed away peacefully in his sleep. There was no jazz memorial for him at St. John the Divine, and nothing at the Citicorp Church. The nurses said there was a little smile on his lips, like he had been having a wonderful dream. Mae Wilkerson got in touch with his people in Alabama and had his body shipped there for burial. Billy said a prayer, and thought about his father and Joey Santiago.

61 Combat Readiness

The further the summer went along and the closer Fawn got to the date of her operation, the more frightened she became, until she hit a place where the paralyzing horror simply stopped. All she could feel then was a coldness and something similar to a shell developing around her, enclosing her in a hazy uncertainty. She had no idea how she had allowed Vee and Cookie to talk her into going to the beach. She changed her mind at the last minute knowing it was a bad idea. They were two real bitches even if they were her sisters. She was sure they knew about the yin-andyango. Sometimes they looked at her and whispered together and laughed. They knew that if she put on a bathing suit the thing would show through, lumped up. Everyone would be able to tell. Big joke, ha-ha. Look at Fawn's dick. They were so cruel. It didn't matter before, because she was little and the thing kind of folded next to her thigh, and she always had that little skirt on her bathing suit so nobody could tell anyway. But now they didn't make that kind of swimwear and she'd seen what it looked like with a regular bathing suit. God, she might as well have a big ole dick hanging from her all bunched up like she was a guy. Everything bulging out, top and bottom. She was a mess of bulges. Her boobs and her bee-hind and hips and the fucking yinandyango hanging there. She hated everything about herself and wanted to dig her eyes out so that she wouldn't have to see the stuff sticking out of her. Maybe she could ask the doctor to cut everything off and make her a little girl again with nothing sticking out and then she could start over.

Vee had yelled at her to come back, saying she was sorry and she didn't have to wear a bathing suit if she didn't want to, she could just wear shorts—"But come and hang out with us, okay?" She had told Papo she was thinking of going to the beach, but if she didn't go, she'd meet him over by the Pitt Street Pool. She crossed Essex Street and headed there, walking along Houston Street, the anger making her face hot and her heart beating more rapidly than usual. She was aware of her boobs bouncing as she walked. She looked at her watch. It was nearly eleven o'clock. Walking rapidly around the periphery of the grounds, she looked for Papo, but he wasn't there so she sat on a bench. Guys came by and smiled at her, but she stared them down like girls in the neighborhood did when they didn't like somebody. If they talked to her, she just turned her head away and ignored them.

When she had almost given up, Papo appeared. He said he was sorry he was late and did she want to take a walk to the Village? Maybe they could go to a movie.

"Like what?" she asked.

"*Pretty Woman*," he answered. "It's suppose to be good. It's funny and shit."

"You saw it?" she said.

"My cousin Marisol tole me about it. She said I should go check it out. You got any money? My moms was supposed to leave me some money but she forgot and left the house."

"I got twenty dollars," she said shyly, already feeling funny.

"Bet," he said. "Let me go tell my grandmother where I'm gonna go. Walk me over to B?"

They went over to Avenue B, where he told her to wait for him. He then went upstairs to a building and five minutes later he was back and they went over to the Village and walked around with the Saturday crowd. Around one o'clock they ate at McDonald's on West Third and then went across Sixth Avenue to the movie theater. During the film she let Papo kiss her a few times. She closed her eyes. He smelled like a hamburger, but she liked the feel of his tongue in her mouth and the warm feeling it gave her. She liked resting her head against his arm or his shoulder like she'd seen Cookie and Vee and her mother do, but a couple of times his hand casually wandered too close to her breast; she sat up straight but didn't say anything. He'd pull her back gently to rest against him and she'd reluctantly return to the position, only to go bolt upright again. Finally, she said if he kept it up she was leaving. He stopped then and contented himself with kissing her, which she began liking more and more, until she forgot about his touching her. The next time she laughed at something on the screen, she realized that his right hand was on her breast. She said nothing this time.

When they came out she asked him what he thought of the movie, wanting to discuss it as she and the family did when they went to see a film, talking about the performances of the actors and the plot and the significance and everything, which she liked doing because it was fun to hear what other people had to say. Her mother always said that if ten people saw something, they'd all have a different story, and it was almost more important to hear other people's observations of events than what one perceived.

"Did you like the movie?" she said, as they sat in the pizza shop. She felt more relaxed after being in the dark with him.

"Yeah, it was okay," Papo said, his mouth full of pizza.

"Just okay?"

"Yeah, da guy was trying to eat up the girl's mind, right?"

"No, she was a call girl. A prostitute."

"A ho? No way. She was a nice girl. How the niggah be buying all kinda shit for a *puta*? Niggah don't buy a ho expensive shit. He kick her ass. If she was a ho, niggah woulda kicked her ass."

"No, really. She was a prostitute in the movie."

She tried explaining the film and how the male character had hired the call girl to go places with him. Papo interrupted her and said that's what he was talking about.

"Dat's the point I'm bringing out," he said.

"What?"

"Dat he wanted to date her so he bought her stuff. You have to do dat with nice girls."

"He wanted her to look nice," she said, feeling exasperated.

"Because he was gonna marry her. She was pretty."

"Right, that's why they gave the film the title," she said tersely.

"You saying she was a ho because she was pretty?"

"No, I'm not saying that at all."

"Cause you pretty and you ain't no ho, right? My pop always be callin' my moms a ho."

"I thought you told me you'd never seen your father?"

"When he was around I remember. Anyways, my moms wasn't no ho. And if the bitch was a ho in the moobie, the niggah shoulda got his gun and shot her."

"There was no gun in the movie," she said, her annoyance increasing with each sentence he uttered. "Anyway, we should go back. It's getting late." He was so stupid, she thought. God, he was almost fifteen. The reason he had been in her class was that he kept getting left back. He was cute, but he was stupid. Maybe he couldn't help it, she thought, and then felt bad for him. She smiled painfully at him and stood up.

Papo nodded, and they began walking east on Bleecker Street.

The other three had literally salivated when Papo came into Frankie Cabeza's apartment where they had set up their head-quarters while Frankie was doing a bit at Rikers for assorted breakings of the law. Papo said he was taking the little bitch to the movies and whatnot, but he was going to call them later in the afternoon and that they should just hang loose.

"You gonna call here?" Pepe said.

"No, I'ma call across da street. Go ovah dere so you can hear da phone ring," Papo said.

"Why you gonna call across da street?" Pepe said.

"Pepe, shutup," Pupi said, taking out the bolo knife he'd pur-chased at the Army & Navy store. He spit on a whetstone and began sharpening the blade.

"Niggah, I just wanna know where he gonna call," Pepe said.

"You a retard, bro," Pupi said. "Niggah's gotta call here, okay? How we gonna know he calling if he call someplace else? Anyway, chill."

"Yeah, so, like, chill here and I'ma a call and we can get us some pussy," Papo said.

"Word. You want me to bring Macho Man?" Pupi asked, re-ferring to the pit bull his uncle had given him and which he had personally trained.

"Yeah, bring him in case she don't wanna give up no pussy. Scare da shit out of da bitch."

"Yeah," Pepe said, baring his teeth like a dog. "Macho Man scare da bitch in her pussy."

They all laughed at Pepe and fived and whatnot and off Papo went, but now it was after three o'clock and da mothafucka was still gone and he was probably fucking da bitch by himself and making her all dirty and sticky, man.

"I'ma get me a Uzi and Jacuzzi da shit outta da niggah if he pulling some shit, cause dat was supposed to be pussy for all da homeboys and he just gobbing it all up and whatnot," Pipo said, rubbing the ever-present diminutive erection through his baggy trousers.

And then about three-thirty the phone rang, and they were up, slipping into their sneakers and grabbing their dicks through their pants and brandishing them at each other, making pumping movements with their pelvis. Pipo took the brief phone call and hung up.

"Where we gonna meet him?" Pupi asked.

"Over on Eldridge," Pipo replied. "The empty building."

"What we gotta do?" Pepe asked.

"He said, just hang back and when he go in with da bitch, wait a couple of minutes and then come up to da fifth floor," Pipo said. "He said come to da apartment dat's got da couch where dey found dat niggah Nestor OD'd."

"Word," Pupi said. "I'ma go get Macho Man. I'll meet y'all in da yard."

They went out and bopped down the street in their fades and their baggy pants and pure white pumps, looking definite. Before he left, Pupi went into Frankie Cabeza's room and in the closet found the little silver pistol with the clip and put it in the waistband of his jeans, so that it felt cold at first. He pulled the T-shirt over his pants and turned his baseball cap around.

"Let's do it," he said as he came out of the bedroom.

Fawn and Papo walked east to Broadway and then downtown. He tried holding her hand as they crossed Houston, but she pulled it back, feeling uncomfortable.

"I'm sorry," he said. "Do you wanna see da puppies?"

"What puppies?" she said.

"My brother's pits. Vanna had six."

"Vanna?" she said.

"Yeah, like da girl on Wheel of Forshun," Papo said.

"That's the dog's name?"

"She's one of da girls. You'll like them. Maybe he can give you one, if I ask him."

"I don't know," she said, wanting to tell him she was scared of the dogs and had read in the paper that up in East Harlem a pit bull had crushed a baby's skull. "I'd have to ask my parents. I don't know if they'd want a dog."

"Anyway, dey're beautiful."

"Where are they?"

"Over on Eldridge."

"I guess," she said, shrugging her shoulders.

She went with him reluctantly, knowing that it wasn't such a good idea but as if something inside were driving her forward, urging her to do something reckless. It was like watching a movie or reading a book and wanting to know what came next.

The entire day, Billy Farrell felt as if something was going to happen. Things were heating up in Kuwait. The Marines had to intervene. It was going to happen. It was the same feeling he'd experienced when something was going to break while they were in-country, or sitting in a bunker at night. This was before he began to not pay attention to things and was fucking up and they'd sent him back to the base and the whole thing happened with Joey. Everything became very still, and you could hear the wind in the trees and the water rippling in a rice paddy and the insects buzzing around—except that it wasn't peaceful and instead everything was magnified. The young guys'd always ask what was going on and somebody would inform them that the shit was going to hit the fan. "How do you know?" they'd ask, and somebody like Grady, who'd been in the Corps since Korea, getting his stripes and getting busted and working like a son of a bitch only to lose his stripes again, would tell them he just knew, and they'd better tighten up their asshole or it'd be their shit that was going to spray everybody.

"Ten fucking times I've been a sergeant and ten times they took my stripes. And it was always some Mickey Mouse thing," he'd say. "Some wet-behind-the-ears louie telling me shit he learned from a book and me trying to explain to him that out in the field it wasn't like that and he insisting and me getting pissed until I'd finally lose it and cuss him out and he'd start talking insubordination and Article 15 and the brig. I'd fucking lose it altogether and smack him. One time I even pulled a forty-five on a captain. Thirty days in the brig and my stripes."

The feeling was like his heartbeat, steady, insistent, without awareness of itself, but animal and alive. He was sure now that something would happen. As the day wore on, the feeling of anticipation increased. The day Joey got it, however, he'd felt calm and something had happened anyway. Now, as his hearing became sharper and he could smell mud and grass and the sweet aroma of pot and the peculiar odor of gunpowder and firearms, he doubted himself for a moment. Immediately, he retracted his doubt and was again certain that it was coming and he had to be ready. He thought of the music, of the rehearsal that night and the way everyone was coming together, "beginning to be in the pocket," Cliff had said, sounding grown-up and hip. The remark made Buster Williams chuckle and nod approvingly. Cliff was a mystery to him. Other than his interest in girls he was like a blank slate. In music he was so gifted that it left you shaking your head how someone so young could cram so much in his head, but he didn't seem to have much ambition. It was almost as if he could take it or leave it as far as the music was concerned. Billy's own playing was becoming so smooth that when he sat back, comping behind Wyndell or Cliff's solos, it became effortless, the chords placed with exactitude. "Play so that the music accentuates the solos of the other musicians," Mae Wilkerson would say, "and provides the improviser a framework without intruding into the performance. When your turn comes, you'll be well within the chord structure of the tune and then you can let go with even more force. Do you understand what I'm saying, Billy?" "Yes, ma'am, I certainly do," he'd say, enjoying the lilting of his voice as he imitated the African-inflected language. It was like Joe Namath who went to school down south and even though he was from Pennsylvania talked like a southerner. Almost thirty years later he could still hear Mae Wilkerson's strong and loving voice. Pop said it had broken her heart when she heard that he'd joined the Marines. As Billy Farrell thought of those days, he was almost a hundred percent sure that he had made a mistake, but something still told him that if people like him didn't serve then there would be no country at all.

A few minutes before four, while he sat in his rocker, his body resting but his mind alert, he heard the elevator. Everyone was due back at seven for rehearsal, so it was too soon for that. Lurleen wouldn't be coming back from the video store with Caitlin so soon and neither would the girls. It had to be Cliff. The elevator doors snapped open and hit below and above with greater than usual force. Simultaneously, he heard Cliff calling him, his voice surrounded by fear.

"Dad, Dad," Cliff was saying.

Billy was up and out of the rocker, his heart suddenly racing, but his head clear. He threw the door open just as Cliff was about to put the key in the lock.

"What's wrong?" he said.

"It's Fawn."

"What about her? Are the girls back from the beach?"

"No, she didn't go with them."

"How come? They said they were taking her."

"She changed her mind at the last minute. Something about a bathing suit being too tight."

"What happened to her? Is she okay?"

"I don't know. She went into an empty building over on El-dridge with that kid."

"What kid?"

"You know. The one she likes, I guess."

"Yeah, okay. She's hanging out with him. He's friends with a pretty rough crowd, right?"

"Yeah, and they went in after Fawn went in with him."

"The same guys he hangs around with?"

"Yeah. And they had a pit bull with them."

"Like it was arranged?"

"Yeah, that's what I'm trying to tell you."

Cliff explained how he'd come from the subway station on Grand Street, turned the corner, and saw Fawn and the guy walking up the street. He'd wanted to call her, but didn't since she got so spooked by everything lately. He'd crossed the street, went into a *bodega* and made like he was going to buy something. That was when he saw Fawn and the boy go up the steps, and inside the building. He told his father that he then saw the three others open the broken door of the abandoned building and follow Fawn and the boy. Billy asked if they had seen him.

"No, I was gonna go in after them but figured I better come home and tell you."

"You did the right thing," Billy said.

"We should go get her, Dad," Cliff said.

"How long ago did it happen?" Billy Farrell said, ignoring Cliff's suggestion.

"Just now. They went inside and I ran the six blocks over here to tell you."

"What do you think?"

"They're bad. I told her she shouldn't be hanging around with those guys. They're into crack and holding people up and everything. I heard from some of my homeboys that they even killed somebody, Daddy. A Chinese man."

"Why didn't she go to the beach with Cookie and Vidamía?"

"I told you, she changed her mind. Something about a bathing suit. Cookie said she should wear shorts, but Fawn said the hell with them and they wouldn't understand and left the store. Vee went after her, but she just ran down the street. She's been acting weird lately anyway. What are we gonna do? Shouldn't we at least go and see if she's okay?"

"No, forget that. Call the police and give them the address and the description. They know how to handle situations like that."

"I don't know the address."

"Well tell them where it is, and we'll go and meet them."

"Should I call Mom at the video store?" he said.

"No, it'll worry her. Just call the police."

Cliff nodded, went to the phone, and dialed 911.

62 An Awful Kaleidoscope

Fawn and Papo came to the abandoned building on Eldridge Street, its windows smashed, trash surrounding the entrance to the cellar, and old sneakers and stuffed toys stuck on the iron spiked fence in front. She followed him, feeling apprehensive but thinking that she was just a big baby and maybe it was all about him wanting to kiss her and touch her again and that wasn't so bad as long as no one saw them.

"Nobody lives here," she said when they got to the top step.

"Yeah, that's why we keep the dogs in the building," Papo said. "C'mon."

"Is it dark?"

"No, don't be scared. It's okay."

But she was scared. The place was dark and it smelled of pee and caca and pot and garbage, and she felt sweat running from her armpits down past her ribs.

"Where are they?"

"On the top floor."

"Why?"

"Because they get sun up there," he said.

"Sun? For what?"

"Dat's how dey get bitamins," he said, having heard this bit of correct information from Pupi's uncle one day when Mike was talking to Pupi about taking care of the dogs.

"Vitamins?"

"Yeah, bitamins. Tru dere eyes, cause dey got fur all over dere body. And dey keep cool tru dere nose. Dat's how you can tell if da dog is sick."

"Yeah," she said, frightened but eager to see the puppies. "If the nose is cool they're okay, but if it's hot they're sick."

"Yeah," he said, stopping on the fourth floor. "One more floor. You wanna rest?"

"No, that's okay."

When they got to the fifth floor she avoided looking at the strewn newspapers, discarded boxes of Chinese food, and dried feces on the landing. Papo led her to one of the doors, opened it, and invited her in. It was an apartment that had been abandoned but was obviously used by people from time to time. Here and there she saw empty crack vials and under an old dinette table she saw a syringe. One of the walls of the apartment had been knocked down. On the other side of the room there was an old couch, and that's where Papo headed and plopped down. Fawn stood, looking at him, unable to figure out what she should do. She looked around at the apartment. It had been a six-room flat, but the roof had collapsed on half of it. The dwelling had been reduced to an empty room that faced the street, another room with a bathroom to its left, and the room they were in, the living room. Beyond that room she could see the open roof and the sky, the sunlight coming down and illuminating the destruction. It was as if someone had dropped a bomb on the roof. She saw pigeons roosting in the debris near the roof level.

"Come and sit down for a minute," Papo said, patting the dirty cushion next to him.

"Where are the puppies?"

"Dere in another apartment. Sit down and rest."

She sat on the couch and he was immediately next to her, kissing her. She allowed herself to kiss him back, enjoying once more the feeling of his tongue in her mouth. He repositioned her gently so that she was resting partly on his lap and partly on his arm. His hand was moving to her breasts, massaging them and watching the nipples rise through the fabric of the bra and T-shirt. She kept her legs tightly closed, the tight panties keeping the yinandyango safely tucked away between her peepee and her thigh. And then he was touching her stomach, but when he started playing with the belt and zipper of her jeans, she sat up, shaking her head, feeling the awful fear. She closed her eyes and took deep breaths, fearing that at any moment she would begin convulsing and start making faces and Papo would see how ugly she was.

He reached for her, smoothing her blond hair and telling her how much he liked her, how pretty she was. She kept her eyes closed, feeling as if she were drifting off into sleep like the time she had touched herself, and after a few seconds she let herself slip back down to his lap, this time feeling the hardness of his thing on her back. She was so bad, just like Cookie and Vee, who were doing it all the time. The feeling of relaxation was becoming greater and greater, extending downward from her head to her chest and then her stomach and below. And then she heard the door open. She sat up, this time her heart jumping and the fear making her shake, knowing it was someone else.

She turned and they were there, one of them holding the

leash to the largest pit bull she had ever seen. The dog's eyes were riveted on her. She turned to Papo and was about to ask if this was the puppies' mother, but the words hadn't come out of her mouth when she saw the dog's large red testicles hanging between his bowed legs.

"I should go," she said, taking a step toward the door.

"No, you gotta stay," Papo said, stepping in front of her. "Lock the door. I got da key."

Pepe moved to the door, put the padlock through the hasp and snapped the lock shut.

"Now you gotta stay," Papo said.

"I don't want to," she said, meekly. "I'm scared. Who are they?"

"My homeboys," Papo said, sneering at her. "Fellas, she wants to know who you are."

"We his homeboys," Pupi said, tapping the leather strap of Macho Man's leash against his leg. "I'm Pupi, the little one over there is Pipo and this doofus with the mustache is Pepe. Oh, this is our other homeboy, Macho Man." He petted the dog's head. "You Fun, right?"

She nodded and tried to go around Papo, but he pushed her chest.

"Don't," she said, tears welling up in her eyes. "That hurt."

"Just shut up, bitch," Papo said, his left eye ticking violently.

"Don't hurt me."

" 'Don't hurt me,' " he mocked her and then his right hand came up and slapped her face so that she fell back on the couch, dazed, the skin of her cheek stinging and the tears streaming down her face. "Didn't I tell you to shut up? Take off your clothes," he said.

She curled up in a ball on the couch, her eyes shut tight and her face beginning to twist, the muscles knotting up into her witch face. She was shaking now, her face contorting and her teeth grinding against each other. Papo and Pipo pried her hands away from her face and held each of her arms as she twisted, her head going from side to side and the dizziness of the movement making her nauseous. And then they noticed the disfigured face.

"Looka that shit, man," Pepe said. "She totally buggin'."

"Yeah," Pipo said, holding back the pitbull. "The niggah's ugly as a mothafucka."

"I have to go home, Papo," she said, the muscles of her face rigid, aware of how terrible she must look. A new awareness hit her and she thought that perhaps if she was ugly they would let her go. "Please, I have to go to the rehearsal." She had no idea why she said that and thought maybe she was going to go crazy. Why had she come up? She knew it was a mistake from the moment that Papo hadn't understood the film. He wasn't just stupid, he was bad. "I should go."

"Shut up, bitch," Papo said, yanking her arm backward.

"Okay, okay," she said. "Don't hurt me, please."

"We ain't gonna hurt you, honey," Papo said, mocking her. "Just take off your clothes."

"No, please," she said. "I can't."

"Let her go, homeboy," Papo said to Pupi, loosening his grip on her arm. "I'ma take dis bitch to school."

Pupi released Fawn's arm and Fawn once again shrank back into a corner of the couch.

"Stand up, bitch," Papo said, his voice quiet but menacing.

"No, please, please, please," Fawn said, crying. "You said you liked me."

The slap came with lightning rapidity, catching her right cheek before she could cover up.

"I said stand the fuck up!" Papo screamed.

She was up immediately, standing before him, her hands shaking in front of her lips as she peeked out over the fingertips. Pipo now noticed that the front of her jeans were wet and pointed at the spot. He tied Macho Man to a steampipe and came over and touched the front of her pants. This was an opportunity for them to laugh, pointing at the front of her and calling her a baby. It was then that she felt the urine running down her legs but couldn't help it and wondered if she would also poop in her pants. She couldn't. It would be embarrassing and would smell. She made up her mind that no matter what happened she wouldn't, and then they'd see that she was brave and let her go. That was it, she would be brave.

"You gonna take off your clothes?"

"No, please. I can't."

"You dissing me, bitch?"

"No, I'm not. I just can't. I don't want you to see me."

" 'I don't want you to see me,' " Papo mocked her in a squeaky voice.

Their hands were now all over her. Touching her breasts, her buttocks, and thighs, her arms and face, pulling her hair hard enough so that it hurt. When she protested they slapped at her. At one point Pepe punched her in the arm and Papo yelled at him to take it easy. "No punches, stupid," he said. The words gave her a little hope, but the feeling that she was being protected was gone before she had a chance to feel gratitude. They had now created a circle and were taunting her to try and escape. Each time she made a dash one way, they closed the circle and once again mauled her, at times squeezing her breasts and buttocks with such force that she whimpered, the tears bursting from her eyes. All the activity had caused Macho Man to bark and growl and strain to get into the action.

The four stopped and she stood in the middle of the room, rigid with fear. She recalled going back to Tennessee with Lurleen that one summer and one of her uncles talking about animals caught in the headlights of a car and how they stood paralyzed by the bright beams. That's how she felt looking into Papo's eyes. Why did he want to do this? She thought he liked her a lot. What was she going to do now?

"Are you gonna take off your clothes?" he said, approaching her.

"I can't, Papo," she said. "I thought you liked me."

They oohed and aahed and repeated her question, except that they pronounced the word "liketed." Again Papo's hand reached out like a viper striking its prey and the buttons on her blouse were gone, stripped. With another strike the white blouse was completely shredded from her. The sight of the naked flesh, the full breasts in the brassiere sent the four horsemen into a riot of lust and violence. They were like sharks in a feeding frenzy, their fingers eager to touch her, their movements crazed, primeval in their quest to feel her nakedness. In a second they had thrown her to the ground and mostly with their hands except for Pupi's final cutting off her jeans with the knife, they ripped her brassiere and white baggy jeans off of her. In the process she received a small cut on her thigh when they'd dragged her across the linoleum floor, and one of the carpet tacks sticking up scratched her.

"Get up, bitch," Papo said, recalling the Chinaman and already feeling that she was gonna end up the same as him. "Get up."

She stood up in her panties and her black Reeboks and white socks, her arms covering the front of her breasts, wondering if she'd pee again. The evaporating urine was making her feel cool down there and she imagined that they would soon notice the yinandyango stuck behind the cloth of her panties.

"You wanna get hurt?" Papo said, coming up to her.

"No, I really don't," she said, feeling stupid.

"Den go sit in the middle of the couch and put your arms over your head," he said.

"Why?"

"Do you wanna get hurt?" he repeated.

"No, please."

"Den go sit on da mothafuckin' couch and put your arms over your mothafuckin' head," he said, the words brimming with anger, each one spit out separately.

When she had done as she was told, he motioned Pepe and Pipo forward, and as if they had planned the entire thing, each one attached his mouth to one of her breasts.

"Now, put your arms down and make believe you're the mother dog and they was your puppies," Papo said.

"No, please," she said, shaking her head violently from side to side, making the two let go.

"You wanted to see puppies?" Papo said. "Dere dey are."

She continued to shake her head for a few moments and then there was a slap and then another and she stopped and they were once again on her breasts. This time she did as she was told, holding the two homeboys to her breasts, smelling their odors of sweat and poop, cigarettes and wine, pot and musk and incense and she didn't know what else, maybe garlic and gummy bears. They sucked on her nipples and she wished she could take them and kill them, crush them like cockroaches beneath her feet, but they had their things out and Papo said she had to take them in her hands. She did as she was told and watched as Pepe took his penis out and was trying to get Macho Man to lick it like he sometimes did with his mother's Chihuahuas. Papo saw him and told him he was a stupid mothafucka cause the pit was gonna grab his dick and swallow it.

She watched Pepe take his thing, which was real big, and begin moving his hand over it, pulling the prepuce back and forth so that the organ looked like a turtle sticking its head in and out of its neck. Papo asked her if she saw what Pepe was doing. She nodded and he said she ought to do the same thing to the homeboys. And then Papo was in front of her face, unzipping his pants and taking out his thing. It was so big and red it scared her so that she almost peed again. She looked into his eyes and saw the frightening, deadly fierceness and suddenly knew she was never going to see her mother and father again and she gave up.

He pried her mouth open and his thing was in her mouth and she could hear him say that she had to lick it. She moved her tongue around, hoping she was doing it right and they wouldn't hurt her too much. She closed her eyes and imagined traveling with Bobby McGee, playing her harmonica. She was drifting and then she felt the stinging pain and then the blow as Pipo bit her nipple and punched her in the stomach, as he had often struck his mother. The sudden movement made her expel Papo's organ from her mouth and her bottom teeth barely touched the underside of his glans but nevertheless made him wince. Once again he reached back and slapped her on the temple, making her head snap to the side and she blacked out momentarily.

"I'ma fuck her, man," Pipo said to Papo.

"Niggah, what da fuck is wrong wif you? The bitch almost chewed up my dick. And anyways, I was just about to shoot a load in her mouf."

"We came here to get us some pussy, niggah," Pupi said.

"Dat's right, Papo," Pipo said, thinking about his mother. Since she'd left nine months before he'd had no pussy and the shit was getting to him.

"Okay, okay," Papo said.

"She's gotta take off her Reeboks," Pepe said, coming over.

"Niggah, shut the fuck up," Papo said. "She gonna do it like them bitches in the movies. With her mothafuckin' shoes on."

"Word up," Pipo said.

She knew what was going to happen now, and she locked her legs together. When Papo saw this he slapped her again and she fell back against the couch.

"What the fuck you think you doing, bitch?" he said. "You a mothafuckin' ankle woman that give up no pussy? Take off your panties, *puta*. *Quítate los fockin pantis y enseñame esa criquita*

701

linda. Esa criquita rubita, mami." He spoke the Spanish sweetly, encouraging her to remove her panties and show him her little blond crack.

This time she fought back, striking at them. She couldn't imagine what they'd think if they saw the yinandyango. The fact that she would fight back excited them and they rained blows upon her body and head, cautioning each other not to mar her face. After a couple of minutes she was nearly unconscious, her head ringing so that she was hardly aware of where she was.

Pupi cut the panties away with the knife, told Pepe to hold her arms and then they laid her out on the couch. Pupi grabbed her ankle and brought it up over the back of the couch and held it there. Papo had said he would be first, so he grabbed the other thigh and spread her legs. And then they saw the red appendage hanging like a wrinkled finger from her pubic area. The sight intrigued them. They looked at each other. Pipo was the first one to speak.

"Oh, shit, man," he said. "Da bitch is like one of them freaks from da *Robin Burr Show*."

"Yeah, chicks wif dicks," Pupi said.

"Put your finger in her," Pipo said.

"You put your finger in, niggah," Pupi said.

"I'll put my dick in her," Pepe said.

"Oh, you niggahs is a bunch of faggots," Papo said. "Get out the way."

Fawn was now beyond the stage at which there is any reserve of dignity. She knew she would die and her mind had broken up into small confetti-like pieces. Her thoughts came to her disconnected, as if everything in her life were an awful kaleidoscope, fragmented and prismatic.

63 Where Have All the Flowers Gone

Cliff dialed 911 exactly as Billy had asked.

"Nine-one-one," the dispatcher said. "Where is the police emergency?"

"On Eldridge Street," Cliff replied. "Somebody took my sister up into an abandoned building. You gotta send the police, please."

"Sir, what address is the emergency at?"

"I don't know the address. It's over on Eldridge Street. Manhattan. Lower East Side."

"Well, sir, how can we send the police if you can't tell us the address?"

"It's between Grand and Hester."

"Is it Grand or Hester, sir?"

"No, no. Eldridge between Grand and Hester, but I don't know the address."

"Sir, next time please get the right address."

"Okay, sure. But please send the police. Please."

"Can you see the perpetrators?"

"No, I'm in my house. The place they got her is about six blocks away."

"Did you get a look at the perpetrators?"

"Yes, there were four."

"Can you describe them?"

"Yeah, the one that was with my sister is about five-ten and a hundred and sixty pounds. He's white, but Spanish. I think his name is Papo. He was wearing dark jeans with white sneakers and a blue T-shirt. He had on a Jets baseball cap. Green and white."

"What about the other ones?"

"Two of them were about medium size and the other was small. They all had baggy pants and sneakers with T-shirts and baseball caps. One of the medium-sized ones had a pit bull on a leash. The guy with the dog was wearing black combat boots. His pants were down over the laces, not like they wear them rolled up so you can see the boots."

"Now, what is your name?"

"Cliff Farrell."

"Is that Clifford?"

"Yes."

"And how do you spell your last name?"

"Farrell. F-A-R-R-E-L-L. Farrell. Cliff Farrell."

"And your phone number, Mr. Farrell?"

He gave the woman their phone number and was informed that he should be near the building in order to show the police exactly where the perpetrators were to be found.

Ten minutes after Cliff made his phone call, the message came into the local precinct from the 911 unit. The four-o'clock shift was just coming in. A full fifteen minutes transpired before the call went out that there was a problem at an abandoned building on Eldridge Street. Patrolmen David Gallagher and Eugene Vargas of the 7th, cruising west on Delancey Street in their patrol car, received the first call of their shift, turned on the siren, and headed for Eldridge Street.

When Cliff hung up the phone, he saw his father coming from the back of the loft. He was placing a pistol into the waistband of his jeans and buttoning his camouflage Marine shirt to conceal the weapon. There was a patch on the shirt with the name FARRELL on it. He had put on a Marine cap with corporal insignia on the front and was wearing combat boots. There was a set of binoculars around his neck. Anyplace else in New York, Billy Farrell would've looked out of place, but in the East Village / Lower East Side area he looked perfectly normal.

"What did they say?" he asked Cliff.

"They said they'd send the police over as soon as they could."

"What time is it?"

"Four-twenty," Cliff said.

"Shit!" Billy said. "They just changed shifts. Let's go."

"You're going up there?"

"Only if I have to," Billy answered. "The police can handle it."

As they got into the elevator, Cliff wanted to ask his father about the gun, but he could already tell that Billy was someplace else in his mind. By the time they got to the street they could hear sirens in the distance, but they soon faded. Something else was going on. When they got to the building and Cliff pointed out where Fawn had gone in with Papo, the police had yet to arrive. They went across the street to see if they could see anything, but saw nothing. Billy debated with himself whether he should go up into the building but decided to wait a while longer. Five minutes later sirens again, this time closer. Patrolmen Gallagher and Vargas screeched into the block.

Human beings who live in an urban environment, where they hear almost daily of beatings, muggings, murders, and rapes, commonly steel themselves to the constant attack on the senses, putting up a shield of disbelief around themselves. Each time something takes place, the shield becomes thicker, and the person begins to believe more and more that these crimes happen only to other people. When it does happen to us, it isn't quite believable. Cliff and Billy had two different reactions. Cliff was positive that any minute now Fawn would be coming down, smiling with embarrassment that she had caused such a fuss to be made around her. Billy, on the other hand, knew that nothing good would come of the situation. He had sensed something and now it had come. Now something told him he should act, but he waited until the police arrived. His father had been a cop and they had their own procedures that had to be respected. If the laws weren't respected by civilians, then everything would turn to chaos. They finally saw the patrol car enter the block and waved to it.

Cliff approached the police car as the patrolmen were getting out. As the two officers closed the doors two more police cars came into the block from the opposite direction.

"Officer," Cliff said, pointing to the building. "I called. They got my sister in there."

"Who are you?" Officer Vargas said to Billy.

"I'm the girl's father," he said, his face a mask of crazed determination.

"Well, wait across the street, please," Gallagher said. "The two of you."

And then they heard a shot. A crowd had gathered, and everyone looked up in unison. One or two people pointed at the building. Up on the fifth-floor fire escape, little Pipo was shouting that they had the bitch and they were going to kill her if they didn't let them go. The call from one of the patrol cars went out immediately informing all concerned that they had a hostage situation. Within a half hour the block was full of police. A sniper team, a hostage negotiation team, a SWAT team, emergency services, and big brass from headquarters had all converged. They set up a command post on the roof across the street and preparations for negotiations began.

At the same time that Cliff had been on the phone with the 911 dispatcher, the Four Horsemen of Avenue B, or the *Posse of the Pingo* as they referred to themselves, had taken notice of Fawn's yinandyango. They had argued that she was a chick and the thing was a dick. After much prodding, they'd decided that Pepe should touch it. Pepe was more than happy to do so. He took it in his hand, handled it, and then, bending it, attempted to slide it into Fawn. Fear had caused her to shrink, making it impossible for the limp yinandyango to either enter her or become erect. Pepe now put his finger in her, making Fawn wince. Her eyes remained closed, but she could feel the intrusion, the pain from the rough fingers. She squirmed automatically and felt the arms jerk at her legs forcefully.

"I'll fuck her," Pepe said.

"No way," Papo said. "She's my chick. I go first. I told you niggahs dat."

"You gonna fuck her with dat dick hanging there?" Pipo said.

"Hell no!" Papo said.

"Then what you gonna do?" Pupi said.

"Cut the mothafucka off," Papo said.

"You gonna cut off her dick?" Pepe said.

"It ain't a real dick," Pupi said.

"It's bigger dan Pipo's," Papo said.

"Niggah, fuck you," Pipo said. "You probably already fucked the bitch and you scared dat fuckin' a half-guy is gonna turn you into a faggot."

"It ain't a real dick," Pupi said.

"It's a real dick, homeboy," Pipo said. "Dere's bitches like that. Most of dem lesbian *cachaperas* got dicks. Why you tink dem women go wif each other?"

"Dat shit's gonna bleed and den no niggahs gonna get pussy," Pupi said.

"Dat ain't true," Pipo said, recalling the times he had raped his mother during her period. "You can fuck a bitch when she bleedin'."

"How you know?"

"I know, niggah."

"All I know is dat da chick got a dick," Papo said.

"Word," Pipo said.

"Prove it," Pupi said.

"Get Pepe to jerk her off." Pipo said.

"Go ahead, Pepe," Papo said. "*Hasle la puñeta.*"

"Okay," Pepe said, happily.

He grabbed the organ and started stroking it. A few minutes later, even though Fawn fought against it, the organ was growing and fully erect. The pseudo-penis wasn't very large, perhaps three inches at the most and about as thick as a man's thumb. Fawn was crying silently, her hips beginning to pain her from being spread so uncomfortably.

"Damn," Pupi said, reaching down to his trouser leg, lifting it and then unsheathing his knife. "Da niggah's right."

"It's a dick, Papo," Pipo said. "We gotta cut da mothafucka off if we gonna get us some pussy. You start fuckin' da bitch, she's gonna stick dat ting up your *culo* and make you a faggot for sure."

"Turn her upside down and bring her to da middle of the room," Papo said.

"Pipo, you grab her legs and I'll grab her arms. Pepe, you pull it and Pupi'll cut it off."

Pupi then made a suggestion.

"Y'all hold da bitch up and me and Macho Man'll take care of da shit."

Fawn had curled up into a ball on the couch, her features carved into a hag's face. They pried her arms and legs loose. She was no more than five feet four inches tall and weighed perhaps a hundred and ten pounds. They were holding her up at shoulder level with the front of her facing the floor and the yinandyango dangling from her, limp again. Pupi went over and untied Macho Man and brought him over and placed him beneath Fawn. The dog looked a bit confused but then Pipo took the dog's large head and pointed it at Fawn's appendage and urged him to get it. The dog immediately jumped up and grabbed it in its mouth and remained hanging for a brief moment, its legs not quite off the floor. The pain made Fawn black out momentarily. When she came to again she thought she would now scream for sure, but not a sound came from her.

"Cut da mothafucka, Pupi," Papo screamed.

In a flash Pupi had the knife once again in his hand. Placing his hand on Fawn's stomach he slid the knife across the pubic area. In one sharp, violent motion he made the cut, nicking her opposite thigh with the tip of the knife. The blood from the severed yinandyango flowed freely and the cut stung Fawn, who began once again to urinate. Pipo brought Macho Man back to the radiator, where he tied him up again.

"Where's the dick?" Papo said.

"Macho Man ate it," Pepe said, happily.

The pit bull, his large reptilian face dumb and dangerous and his meatlike tongue hanging from his jaws, sat in the corner licking the blood around his mouth, his canine penis protruding slightly. They had laid Fawn back on the couch and at Papo's urging Pepe used her ripped jeans to wipe the blood from her. The bleeding continued until Pipo, recalling having seen the stanching of a wound in a film, suggested that they hold the jeans on the cut until the bleeding stopped. Papo did so, asking for how long. Pipo said maybe five minutes. Five minutes later Papo removed Fawn's jeans and the blood had stopped flowing, the area within the blond pubic area raw, the hair stained.

"Pepe, put the mattress behind the couch," Papo said.

Pepe did as he was told. Papo then picked up Fawn in his arms. She was limp and sweaty, her skin cold and clammy. Her face had relaxed somewhat, but she appeared dead. He looked at her chest and saw that she was breathing. Maybe she was asleep. He brought her behind the couch, placed her on the mattress, and then told the others to go into the other room. They did as they were told. He unzipped his pants, but his organ wouldn't get hard until he masturbated himself. He spread Fawn's legs and attempted to enter her. Each time he tried, his organ would slip and he finally ended up masturbating and spraying his seed on her chest.

"Your turn, Pupi," he said, standing and zipping up his pants.

"Damn, bro," he said. "You shot your shit all over her."

"I didn't wanna get her pregnant, man," Papo said. "I don't want no kids."

"Word," Pupi said. "Give me a rag and go with the fellas."

Papo threw him a rag and Pupi wiped Fawn's breasts, hating their roundness and large size. When he was sure the others weren't looking Pupi turned Fawn over, propped up her legs, spread the buttocks, placed his penis on her and thrust violently, like he secretly did with Guango the *pato* over on Second Avenue, except that Guango always put Vaseline all over his dick and was always telling him, don't hurt me too bad, baby. The faggot paid him, so what was he supposed to do? He imagined he was a fierce pit bull mating with one of the females and he grabbed Fawn around her stomach, avoiding her breasts, which he didn't like touching. He thrust three or four times and he came violently, driving Fawn's body into the mattress. Her mind was blank. All she could perceive was a deep dull pain over her entire body. The yinandyango was no longer there, but the stinging pain where it had been, persisted.

When Pupi was done he turned Fawn over and spread her legs. She had no volition to protect herself or move on her own. Pupi stood up and called for Pepe, but Pipo showed up, claiming that it was his turn. Pupi said it was Pepe's turn. Pipo knew Pupi had Frankie Cabeza's gun and the dog and knew Pupi was crazy enough to use both. Papo eventually intervened and Pipo went at it, penetrating Fawn slightly, the violation no longer significant in his eyes. When he was finished he complained.

"Bitch's pussy was like sandpaper," he said.

"Yeah," Papo said. "That was some tight pussy."

"Word," Pupi said.

"I'ma fuck her good," Pepe said, taking out his large member, already erect.

The other three watched in wonder as Pepe got down, spread Fawn's legs, and pushed a little bit at a time. Papo got down on the floor and looked between Pepe's legs as the organ entered and then it was inside and the girl was pushing her hands against Pepe, trying to get him away from her. Pepe pinned her arms down and thrust violently. He was on her five minutes, pushing and grunting, and then his climax causing him to thrust six or seven times as he emptied himself. For the first time Fawn cried out weakly from the pain inside her. When Pepe got up the semen was still falling from his tumescent penis.

"Chiquita likes to lick it," he said, confessing to the others.

"Your mother's dog?" Papo said.

"You fuck it?" Pipo said.

"No, you know," he said, making a masturbating motion. "When I do it. She likes to lick da come. Anyway, da girl's got a good pussy, like da bitches in da moobies."

At this point they heard the sirens. They stood poised, listening for the sound to recede, but they came closer and then they knew the police had arrived. They now began arguing about what they were going to do.

"We'll just leave her," Pepe said.

"Shut up," Pipo said. "How we gonna leave her? She'll tell the cops what we did."

"Throw da bitch out da window," Pupi said. "She's a scummy lying bitch anyway. She got her a dick and she didn't say nothing."

"Den dey'll know we did it cause we in here," Pipo said.

"We gotta hit her," Papo said. "Like the Chink. Gimme the knife, home."

Pupi took out the knife from under his right pant leg and gave it to Papo.

"Y'all go in the other room," he said.

She was hearing everything, knowing it was going to happen. They were going to kill her. She shut her eyes as tight as she could and felt herself convulsing once more, her face tightening. It was going to happen, she thought. A second before Papo struck she heard her mother playing the dulcimer and the words of the song drifting to her from the black void that was approaching: *Where have all the flowers gone . . .* She stiffened and the initial pain came. As soon as they were gone Papo took the knife and thrust it violently into Fawn's vagina, cut downward into the lower intestine and then upward. He hit bone above and withdrew the knife. He then thrust the knife into her lower abdomen and holding the knife in both hands lifted upward, tearing upward, past her belly button all the way to the sternum, damaging her vital organs, ripping further into her stomach and eventually severing several arteries so that Fawn Singleton Farrell became comatose for a brief moment and then began dying, irreparably damaged so that had an emergency team appeared at that very moment and by some miracle they were able to transport her to an operating room no medical team could have saved her such was the violence which Papo brought to the act. When he was done his arms were bathed in blood and he was breathing heavily. His organ had been erect and he knew he had ejaculated because he felt the warm liquid running down his leg.

He found rags in a wardrobe and began to wipe himself, now feeling nausea and weakness in his knees. This was nothing like the Chinaman, or the kittens he had smashed against the wall in the cellar up in East Harlem with his cousins when they were kids. And then he heard the sirens and the others were running back into the room. The fear in their eyes was immediate as they stared at the blood on Papo's arms. They looked behind the couch and Pipo immediately ran and vomited in a corner. Pepe suggested that they bring Macho Man over to lick the blood. Papo smacked him on the face and called him a sick fuck.

"What we gonna do?" Pipo said, wiping the vomit from his chin and spitting. "Dere's too much blood, man. Dere gonna know you did it, Papo."

"We all did it, man," he said. "What you gonna say? You gonna squeal on me?"

"No, bro, it's not like that," Pupi said.

"We tell dem we still got da bitch and if dey wanna see her

alive, dey better back off," Pupi said. "We get dem to go away and den we book after it gets dark. What time is it?"

"Four-thirty," Pipo said.

"Shit, it's still early," Papo said. "I'm getting hungrier than a mothafucka."

"Wait here," Pupi said.

Pupi went to the front window of the apartment, pulled out the gun and shot into the wall. He then stepped out on the fire escape and shouted down at the policemen that they had the girl and if they wanted to see her alive they better be cool. He ducked back in and told them there were three cop cars out on the street.

"You tink dey'll come up?" Pupi asked, shaken and ready to go down and turn himself in. He couldn't stand looking at Fawn's body and went into the room off to the side. They heard more sirens. Pipo looked out of the window and saw that many people had now congregated in the street. There were more than a dozen cop cars and wagons downstairs. And then he saw them for the first time. The SWAT team people with their shields and dark uniforms. He came running into the other room.

"Dey got them SWAT mothafuckas up on the roof across the street, bro," he said to Papo.

"Fuck 'em," Papo said. "Go out dere and tell them we ain't coming out wif da bitch until dey clear out. Tell dem we want some food. Some chicken, pizza, and soda."

"I ain't goin out dere, bro," Pipo said. "They gonna shoot our ass."

"Go tell them," Papo said.

"Niggah, them mothafuckas are train snivers. They got periscopes on da rifles and whatnot."

"Pepe, help me wif the couch, man," Papo said. "This pussy mothafucka's scared."

They stood the couch on end and slowly maneuvered it into

the adjoining room so that it blocked the window facing the roof where the SWAT team was located. Standing behind the couch, his arms still stained by Fawn's blood, Papo now shouted his orders and told the police what they wanted. He could see them crouched on the other roof and heard the loudspeakers talking to them, asking them to let the girl go and give themselves up.

"No way," Papo shouted. "No fuckin' way, you *hara* mothafucka."

By six o'clock the police knew they had a genuine mess on their hands. They got a rope up to the fifth floor and in a bucket they sent food and drink to the four. The air had grown cooler in the last hour but everyone outside was still sweating. The brass had gone up on the roof, crawling around, everyone fearful of getting shot since the kidnappers were armed. No one could figure out why they had taken the girl hostage and wondered if they had any demands. Television crews from each of the major networks and the local stations had arrived and the mayor had issued a statement that the police ought to act with the utmost care to ensure no loss of life on either side, especially as it concerned the hostage.

64 Flashback

With each passing moment, as he stood with the crowd of people waiting to see what would happen next, Billy became more and more nervous, more impatient, more lost in the memories of combat. Gradually he was again in that strange zone where he knew that he had to act or everything was lost. At about six-fifteen he told Cliff to go back to the loft and make sure that when Vidamía and Cookie returned, they remained there and were safe. Cliff did as he was told and then Billy slipped away.

He walked down the block and around it so that he was now behind the block where Fawn was being held.

He went through the yards and over fences effortlessly, avoiding the police that had been posted at the back of the building, adrenaline feeding his drive forward toward the objective. At times he was crawling through the thick urban vegetation of ailanthus saplings and wild weeds that grew in the backyards and empty lots. He found the cellar door of the building locked. He inserted a thin piece of pipe between lock and hasp and pried the two apart. He was now in the dank cellar and like a shadow he was up the stairs stealthily. When he reached the fourth floor he took a deep breath, crossed himself, and continued. He was no longer thinking but acting purely on animal instinct.

When he reached the fifth floor his breathing was coming almost without effort and he could feel himself smiling, recalling boot camp and his DI telling him he was a killing machine. He had been trained to protect and attack and that's what he would do. They had no right taking his kid. He didn't care who they were. You didn't do that kind of thing. No way you did that. He felt for the extra clip in his pocket and then took out the .45 and held it down near his left leg and silently slipped the safety off. He went along the wall slowly, listening, and then he heard the voices and knew they were in there. As he approached he heard a dog growl.

There was an area within which if you fired a weapon there was a strong chance that you could destroy your target. The killing zone they called it, but he couldn't recall where he had heard the term. Now as he walked along the wall, the steel of the .45 snugly in his fist, he could hear them chattering, their singsong voices thin and incomprehensible to him, except that they were speaking English, interspersed with Spanish, but they might as well be the Viet Cong gook bastards that got Joey. Now they had little Fawn, and the police were down there, helpless to do anything about it.

Raising his combat boot he aimed a kick at the door so that the blow knocked the haft off the lock and sent the door practically off its hinges. He crashed into the apartment and immediately saw Fawn naked on the dirty mattress, her hands up near her face, the middle of her bloody where they had slit her open. Fawn's eyes were wide open, in complete shock so that she didn't even see him, he thought, not realizing, or perhaps not wanting to accept, that she was already dead. The dog came at him first, lunging violently on its hind legs only to be restrained by the thick chain. He blasted the animal above the jaw, ripping his skull apart so that the back of his head exploded against the radiator.

And then he saw them. They were like rodents scurrying for cover. They had gotten his father, then Joey, and now Fawn, all three of them helpless to defend themselves. They were moving in four different directions, but he knew what had to be done. He hadn't qualified as a rifleman and that's why he was a machine gunner, but he'd get these bastards if it took his life. The shots came in quick succession, the flashing of the muzzle of the big gun almost one stream of light as if the anger he felt in his body had become a beam that would destroy all that stood in his way.

The first shot crashed into Pipo's smallish chest, flooding his left lung with a cascade of blood that sent a searing black pain into his brain, causing him, mercifully, to black out and go into shock, sparing him the experience of watching his life ebb away as he sprawled into an almost comical position against the dirty armchair, stained by spilled food and dirty hands. Before Billy Farrell would fire his last shot, some thirty seconds later, Pipo would be dead. The autopsy would later reveal that the .45-caliber slug had literally blown his lung out through the back of his shirt, taking part of his heart with it.

Papo wasn't so lucky. Billy Farrell's next shot entered Papo's left cheek, caromed around in his mouth, destroying the left

lower mandible, entering the upper palate, and emerging upward through his right eye, so that he lost his stereoscopic vision
but retained consciousness. He was in effect blinded but fully
aware that the hell that he had been taught to fear had finally arrived. Miraculously, out of instinct, his right hand found Frankie
Cabeza's silver gun, which he had taken from Pupi when he'd
refused to speak to the cops. Papo was blasted by the next two
shots which shattered his right kneecap and his right shoulder.
Whether it was one of the shots or a combination of all three,
both bladder and rectum opened up, involuntarily sending hot
urine and feces tumbling out of him as had been the case with
Huang, so that for a split second he grabbed his stomach as if
he'd been shot there. Papo let go of his stomach just as he had let
go of Huang when he'd broken his neck and had smelled his involuntary defecation. All he could think about as he lost consciousness was that he would probably not receive anything for
his fifteenth birthday, and fuck them anyway, the creeps.

Pupi, whose huge knife had severed Fawn's useless penis,
and which Papo had used to murder her, had enough time to re-
act. Having had the knife returned to him, he raised it in a gesture of attack. It only took one shot but it was the truest of shots,
laser-like and accurate, so that it left a neat brownish hole a bit
left of center on Pupi's forehead. The back of his skull, brains,
bone, and hair traveled backward and slammed against a
slightly opened wardrobe behind him, leaving on the full-length
mirror a red-and-black Rorschach-like design which the
morgue personnel who came to place the bodies in bags argued
about. Some said it looked like Ringo Starr and others said it
looked like Sandy Duncan. One of the former changed his mind
and said it looked more like an octopus. They all agreed that it
was a fucking mess.

Pepe, the last of the enemy, dim-witted and perplexed by
what had taken place, attempted to make his escape through the
half-opened window to the fire escape. Billy Farrell perceived

his desperate exit out of the corner of his eye and shot at him. The bullet crashed into the fleshy part above the hip at enough of an angle to shatter the fourth lumbar vertebra, immediately paralyzing him as he attempted to step from the open window out onto the fire escape. His body went straight up and his hands, receiving no messages from his addled brain because of the spinal injury, flipped over the edge of the fire escape and began his five-story tumbling descent earthward. His body hit a protuberance on the first story of the building, causing a deep gash across his cheek which bared both upper and lower teeth. His body turned once more, then continued downward, landing at the front cellar entrance. In the distance Billy heard the thud of the body and the police loudspeakers as orders were being given. Pepe survived the fall, was in intensive care for two weeks, and began mending enough to answer the police's questions about the incident. A week later Pepe, now a quadriplegic, developed pneumonia and died.

The sound of the shots still reverberating in his mind, Billy went over and looked at his daughter's naked body, the face bloody from the times she touched herself where she had been wounded and, expecting a blow to her face, had covered up. Her eyes were open but he imagined the horror behind the eyelids, for the face was contorted in the grimace of the seizures which sometimes came upon her. He removed a large handkerchief from his back pocket and wiped the blood away, and then reaching down worked the still pliable face so that the muscles relaxed once more, and Fawn was once again a beautiful young girl.

In repose he saw now that of the three girls she resembled Lurleen the most and his heart nearly tore out of his chest from the pain. They had slit her open so that her insides were showing above her pelvis. The wound wasn't quite to the heart as it had been with Joey, but seeing the entrails produced the same visual effect for him. He looked at the men he had shot and was shocked to see that they were just boys. Already numbed by what he'd seen, he removed his fatigue shirt and covered Fawn's body. His olive Marine undershirt was wet with perspiration and his dog tags were stuck to it. He unstuck them and looked at the twin metal tags on the chain, the teeth notch reminding him of death. His name, serial number, blood type, and religion were on them.

And then he was back there again, walking into the deserted village, the machine gun on his right shoulder, and the .45, similar to the one he now held in his left hand, in its holster on his web belt. They had gone hooch by hooch, making sure the village was deserted. Sergeant Brecher, Lucky Weinreich, Parma, Billington, Joey, and himself. Everything was clearly in focus in his memory. Why hadn't he recalled this before now? When they were convinced that everyone in the small dwellings had left, the six of them sat down to smoke. He lit a cigarette, closed his Zippo, and as he blew the smoke out, he saw them standing in the doorway of a hooch to his right as he sat against the tree. It was a young girl, perhaps eleven years old, and two little boys on either side of her, one about seven and the other one four, maybe younger. The smallest one had no pants on and had his hand out, begging for something to eat. The children were scared out of their minds and they were dirty and looked as if they hadn't eaten in a week.

"Look, Sarge," he said, standing up and pointing. "Three kids."

"Shoot them," Sergeant Brecher said.

"C'mon, Sarge," he said. "They're just kids."

"You better do it, Farrell," Parma said.

"Don't do it, Billy," Joey whispered.

"I can't, Sarge."

"That's a fucking order, Marine," Brecher shouted, standing up. "A fucking order. Cock that fucking gun and shoot the little gook bastards."

"I can't, Sarge," he'd repeated, feeling as if the enemy were now Sergeant Colin Brecher from Sioux City, Iowa, or Omaha, Nebraska, or Salem, Massachusetts, or wherever he was from, and married to the Corps. Brecher had seen his buddies slaughtered by the Chinese at Inchon in Korea and just the sight or even mention of Asiatic people threw him into a crazed fit. For a moment, Billy thought of taking the safety off his .45 and shooting Brecher, but that, too, would've been wrong. He reached into a pocket, brought out a chocolate bar, and began walking toward the kids. The little one came forward, his hand still extended, his penis and testicles minute.

"Parma, Billington, Weinreich, Santiago."

The children were frozen again by Brecher's voice, so that now he saw them again as in a photograph, the images of hunger, sorrow, fear, and devastation two-dimensional, grainy, faded, and brittle with time, but still active. He knew immediately that he hadn't recalled the incident before this moment because in the next few seconds all hell broke loose and Parma and Weinreich had stood up and opened fire on the kids with their rifles. The bodies had flown back inside the hooch simultaneously, the littlest one seemingly with his hand still out.

He dropped his machine gun and ran to Brecher, shouting that he was crazy, telling him he had no business shooting the children. He struck Brecher with his right fist, bloodying the sergeant's nose.

"You're gonna earn yourself a court martial, Farrell, you son of a bitch."

"Yeah? You do that. Whatta you think's gonna happen when they find out what you did?"

"What did I do?"

"You had those three kids shot, you crazy bastard."

"Who saw what happened?"

"Every one of us," he said, sweeping his hand to include the others.

720

"Any of you see those kids make any funny moves?" Brecher said, turning to the others. "Like they was signaling someone?"

"Hell, no. The little boy put his hand out for food."

"Bullshit," Brecher said. "Everybody saw them signaling. Didn't you all see that?" he shouted at the others. They all said that's exactly what had happened, including Joey.

"Okay, Farrell?" Brecher said. "Now, you tell me. You want me to turn you in for insubordination, or you wanna forget this whole thing?"

"Fuck you, Brecher," he said. "You murdered those kids. What the fuck are you trying to pull?"

"Watch yourself, Farrell," Brecher said, looking him in the eye. "Watch your fucking self, partner."

"C'mon, Billy," Joey said, tugging at his arm.

By nightfall they had returned to their unit. When they were back at their bunker Billy couldn't eat or sleep. In the morning he confronted Joey.

"Why did you back him, bro?"

"Why do you think?" Joey said.

"I don't know. You saw what happened. He did those kids for nothing, man. They were skinny little kids, probably stuck in some tunnel and forgotten. They were just hungry, man."

"Yeah, I saw what happened. Damn right, I saw what happened. And if I hadn't backed Brecher they woulda killed you right there. That's one crazy mothafucka, Billy. Forget the whole thing, we're going back to Khe Sanh tomorrow for R&R and then we got a couple more months and then we're gonna go back to the States, man. Back to New York, bro. I'ma take you Latin dancing and you gonna play at all those jazz clubs you talk about. You're gonna meet my sisters and all their homegirls and it's gonna be great."

"But, Joey . . ."

"Forget it. Man, I feel terrible for those kids, but what the fuck are you gonna do? Them white boys . . . Sorry, man. I mean they're all gonna stick together against us."

"I hear you, man," Billy said, thoughtfully. "I hear you. Okay, man. I'm cool, man. I'm cool. We'll just forget it."

But he hadn't been able to forget. He went back to Khe Sanh in a daze, not responding correctly to questions. His lieutenant sent him to the infirmary for observation. His condition was diagnosed as stress and battle fatigue, and he showed no improvement as they fed him tranquilizers in heavier dosages. He'd wanted to talk to someone about the murders of the children, but worried about Joey, who was going back in-country. He talked to the Catholic chaplain, Captain Farrentino, and they had prayed together for the souls of the children. He'd asked the chaplain what he should do about Brecher. The chaplain got a very troubled look on his face and said that things like that happened in war.

"I didn't do anything to stop him, sir," he said.

"Technically, they were the enemy."

"Children? No little four-year-old boy's an enemy."

"How do you know they weren't a decoy?"

"The village had been swept clean. It was safe."

"It's never safe with the gooks, son."

"They were children, sir."

"God will forgive you," Captain Farrentino said.

He'd gotten up and left cursing, more confused than ever. As soon as Brecher had given them the order to waste the kids, he should have taken the safety off the machine gun and just blown Brecher away. The man was crazy.

Finally, after three weeks, Joey was back in Khe Sanh and came to see him at the infirmary. He told Joey about the chaplain, but Joey asked him again to leave the issue alone. And he had. Sergeant Brecher had come to see him and asked him if he was cool. He had nodded and made himself shake hands with Brecher. But the next day he went and spoke with Lieutenant

Dyer, and the lieutenant had brought him to Major Rittenauer. They had discussed the matter in great detail. Major Rittenauer hadn't been pleased with the report. Brecher had seen Billy subsequently but had said nothing to him. In fact he had been extra pleasant. Brecher probably knew that he'd ratted him out.

A week later, Sergeant Brecher had gone in-country again. Before the week was out word came that he'd been wounded and sent back, probably directly to Tan Son Nhut Air Base, and then flown to Japan on an Airevac plane. Before Brecher left to go back in-country, he must have contracted with the guys Castillo had talked about at the VA hospital on Twenty-third Street. Castillo had said the guy who was in on it had said they'd made a mistake. That they had gotten the wrong guy. He'd known it all along. It was him they were after and they got Joey. He saw it clearly now. He knew they were going to get him and he never said anything to Joey. So he was responsible after all. It was so clear now. He was a coward. A coward for not seeing the Miles Davis thing through, a coward for not wasting Brecher, and a coward for not warning Joey about what he suspected. He didn't know how he had known, but he had. And still he asked Joey to go with him. How could he have done such a thing?

He sat up against the wall across from where Fawn lay, her small mutilated body covered by his fatigue shirt. He had wanted to hold her, wondering for a second if she was cold, but her nakedness made him feel ashamed. It didn't matter. She was dead and probably already in Heaven. There was no sense living now. He had failed and would probably spend the rest of his life in jail for what he'd done. He'd let his daughter die, and he'd never be able to erase that from his conscience. All his training and he still let it happen. He was supposed to protect Lurleen and the children and he had failed. His only recourse was to die, as he should've died when Joey was killed. If he had he could've avoided all the trouble that followed him. But he couldn't die now. He couldn't, not now. He was playing the music again. No, he had to be brave. He had to be like everyone else and take his lumps. Everybody had it tough. All his life people had taken care of him. First his mother and father and his grandfather and grandmother. And then his father died and Pop Butterworth came along. And then in high school the brothers and lay teachers and coaches. After that the Marine Corps, and when he came out, his grandparents and his mother. After that Elsa tried, but she was too young, and then his grandfather had found Lurleen for him and she had taken care of him. And even Vidamía had taken care of him. Now it was time for him to take care of everyone with his music. Now he had to finally accept responsibility for his life. He took a deep breath and tried to think of the next rehearsal and the tunes they were going to play, but nothing came to him. He tried imagining the chord structure of "Moonlight in Vermont," but nothing appeared. He closed his eyes and tried to hum Monk's "Friday the Thirteenth" but could recall nothing of the tune and knew that he was back in the dark tunnel, and this time he would never come out. He wished it were different, but he had to go. Wherever it was that people like him went, he now had to go. He removed his hat and laid the .45 next to him. He closed his eyes and said a Hail Mary, and then an Our Father. When he was finished he heard the policemen coming up the stairs, the sergeant issuing orders. He knew he had to go now.

No matter what happened he had to act now. This time there mustn't be any mistakes. No more walks on the ledge of the roof or wandering out into traffic. The tears were flowing from him, but he was dead inside. Everything in his life had been too much suffering, everything tainted with a sorrowful dirge that followed him wherever he went. He heard the bagpipes again, skirling into the marrow of his bones as they had when he was a boy. He heard the drums and the pipes and inside of him he marched forward. His entire life had been pain. First his father, and then Joey, and now Fawn. The only thing that had taken the pain away was the piano and Lurleen, and he couldn't face her now. He had let one of the babies die. She'd understand, as she always did, but he couldn't face her. Couldn't face anyone. Playing the piano was no longer possible because now God had taken that away from him for good.

He heard the second wave of sirens, summoned by the shots. Pop Butterworth was gone, and he had gone out strong. He knew now that he had to go out strong as well and once again picked up the .45, put it to his temple, looked out at the hazy blue sky through the broken roof, and pulled the trigger just as the policemen, guns drawn, peered into the apartment. The loud booming sound of the .45 made them instinctively flatten themselves against the wall or hit the dirty, piss-stained floor of the corridor outside the apartment.

A red, opaque film of sound and darkness enveloped Billy Farrell. Lifeless, he slumped sideways, the pistol still firmly in his left hand.

Fourth Movement

The Drum

65 Mourning

Vidamía imagined a sturdy leather-bound photo album with a lock and key. It was in this album that she would keep the memories of her father. She would treasure them and store them in a private place in her life. Among those memories would be the one of her father's casket, the large American flag draped over it and the Marine honor guard in their dress blues standing at attention and then firing their rifles into the solemn gray sky. The rifles had fired blanks but she was certain even the sound was wounding something and once again she knew that no matter what happened in her life she would heed Maud Farrell's advice and never let a son or daughter of hers go to war, no matter what the circumstances. "Even if you have to break their legs, shoot them in the foot or blind them in one eye," her grandmother said, angrily, her face set in a mask of stone. Vidamía knew she'd never go quite that far, but she would raise her children lovingly so that when she spoke, they would listen, just like Lurleen, who didn't have to repeat things, the wisdom of whatever she said revealing itself immediately.

At the funeral Vidamía recalled that on July 30, 1990, about the same time that Wyndell notified her that he'd gotten an opportunity to play at the Village Gate, Iraqi tanks stood poised on the border of Kuwait waiting to invade the smaller country. As soon as the confrontation began to take shape, her father had taken a position in front of the television set. He remained in front of the set, taking in the reports, his eyes wild and his fists clenched.

During the entire three weeks of August, her father had been diligent about rehearsals. He was always on time, definitely focused, influenced by Buster Williams's serene attitude and professional demeanor, Wyndell's enthusiasm for his playing, and the fact that he wanted to regain Cliff's respect. But when he wasn't rehearsing, he appeared obsessed by the military action in the Gulf. One time at supper he mentioned that perhaps he ought to call the Marines and ask if they needed him to report for duty. Lurleen reminded him that he was forty years old, and, as if he were waking up from sleep, he shook his head, rubbed his eyes, and asked her what she'd said. When Lurleen repeated that he was forty, he said he knew that and why was she bringing it up. It was as if he'd been someplace else, his mind tuned to a different reality from the one they were experiencing. It scared Vidamía, but eventually Lurleen made light of the matter and they went on eating.

Vidamía still didn't know how Lurleen had managed everything, but she had gotten hold of the Veterans Administration and they'd sent a detail of Marines. After the coffin was lowered into the grave, the sergeant brought his saber down, two Marines folded the American flag into a neat triangle, and the sergeant brought it to Lurleen, who stood by the graveside, dressed in black, her eyes far away and lost.

Funeral wreaths with inscribed purple ribbons came from all over the United States, Canada, Ireland, and Australia, where the Farrell clans had settled. The Sandersons, the Meekinses, the McAlpins, and the Burrells—relatives from Tennessee, Mississippi, Missouri, and Texas—all sent wreaths and condolences. Garlande, Davina, and Dr. and Mrs. Ross also sent wreaths and a handwritten message to Vidamía. There was a wreath from Barry on their family's behalf.

Her mother, Elsa, was there with Barry, her demeanor betraying the confusion this new event had produced in her life. Vidamía observed her and couldn't tell whether Elsa was actually feeling genuine grief or, as she stood apart from the others, feigning sorrow. She no longer felt dislike for her mother or was even embarrassed by her lack of sincerity. Rather, she pitied Elsa and her attempts at genuineness. It was as if with the passing of time Elsa had forgotten totally her original identity and had invented herself from textbooks, lectures, magazines, and the influence of her profession. Everything that came out of her mouth sounded manufactured and without true meaning.

Vidamía declined to drive from the cemetery with her mother and stepfather. She returned to the Lower East Side with the Farrells, riding in Mr. Contreras's car, with Baby and Cookie. Lurleen, Cliff, and Caitlin rode in Mrs. Pitino's car. Mrs. Pitino was a friend of Lurleen's who taught at her school and had a brother who was a Vietnam veteran—now in a mental hospital in Pennsylvania. Barbara Pitino remained with the family for two days, helping to straighten things out, making trips to the supermarket for boxes and packing things away because Lurleen was thinking of moving. Barbara had suggested a roomy apartment in a brownstone owned by her father, not too far from Barbara's home in Brooklyn Heights.

When Vidamía had phoned home to let Elsa and Barry know about the tragedy, Barry offered to send a car. Vidamía thanked him but said she preferred taking the train back to Tarrytown. Her senses numbed, she rode the train staring blankly at the gray-green landscape, the absence of sunlight adding to her grief. When she reached Tarrytown, she got off the train and didn't bother with a taxi. Methodically, she walked home up the hilly streets in the steady late-summer drizzle, getting soaked and feeling with increasing awareness the heaviness of everything she thought about her father and sister. When she arrived, she went around to the back of the house like the deliverymen, the plumbers and electricians, the men who did the yard work, the black people who came and served whenever her mother threw a big party. Feeling like a stranger in the house she'd grown to love, she went in through the back door and into the kitchen. When she trudged up the two steps of the entrance to the kitchen and opened the door, Beanbag came up and greeted her. Usually, he came bounding up to her and banged heavily against her legs, wishing to be petted and played with. This time, however, he emitted a small whine of seeming grief, as if he understood and were offering his condolences. When she didn't even respond to that, he walked slowly away. "I'm sorry, Beanbag," she said. Sensing how drained of emotion she was, the big dog lay down outside the kitchen, his eyes staring sadly at her.

As soon as Mrs. Alvarez saw her, she opened her arms, and the two of them cried together. Mrs. Alvarez took her upstairs and helped her to take off her clothes and dry her hair. Mechanically, she changed, came downstairs, and ate some soup and a sandwich, the only things she had been able to consume since the deaths of Billy and Fawn.

She recalled the way Lurleen looked when she returned from identifying the bodies. Her devastation was so complete, the horror in her face carved so deeply. It was as if she were wearing a mask in the most profound of tragedies, something in which the words of the actors tear at your heart. Even Lurleen's eyes seemed etched in that granite of sorrow that humans wear when confronted with the immensity of such a loss.

Vidamía was alone in her room, choosing appropriate clothes for the funeral. She had just placed her "little black dress," which her mother insisted was good for any occasion, on the bed and was standing by the window, watching the rain, noting that the air was the color of gray-yellow metal, everything cool and moist, when her mother came into the room.

"How are you feeling, baby?" Elsa said.

"I'm all right, *mami*," Vidamía replied. "Numb, I guess. I don't know. I really thought he was going to be okay. But maybe Lurleen was right."

"What?" Elsa asked, her voice suddenly defensively inquisitive, betraying the profound jealousy she felt toward Lurleen. Over the half-dozen years Lurleen had been, albeit peripherally, in Vidamía's life, her blond whiteness, her quiet confidence, and her beatific attitude of suffering inspired greater and greater resentment in Elsa.

"What did she say?" Elsa now inquired.

"Oh, nothing. She worried that playing the piano again might make all his trouble resurface. I suppose she was right."

"Yes, perhaps she was," Elsa said, smugly, seeding Vidamía's shattered mind with doubt, her displeasure over the purchase of the piano the previous year surfacing once more. "Oftentimes having to relive a painful part of one's life will produce hatred and self-destructiveness." And then with little sensitivity for the import of her words, she added, "Perhaps in the larger scheme of things it's all for the best. He was a troubled man, a man filled with tremendous pain."

Vidamía turned from the window, feeling an overwhelming desire to scream at her mother that she was a phony and didn't have an ounce of sympathy left in her.

"That is so much bullshit, Mom," she said, sharply.

"I've asked you to please not use that kind of language, young lady," Elsa said.

"Don't tell me what to do, okay?" Vidamía shot back, going to the closet and getting her raincoat.

"Where are you going?"

"None of your business. Just leave me alone."

"We should talk about this."

"I don't want to talk about it. I'm tired of talking about it. Especially to you. All you know is how to judge people and look down on them from some self-proclaimed exalted state."

"Self-proclaimed exalted state?" Elsa said sarcastically. "Are you sure you're using those words correctly?"

"You are so screwed up," Vidamía said to her mother and shook her head disapprovingly. She then walked deliberately up to her mother and spoke in exaggeratedly enunciated tones, her nose no more than six inches from Elsa's face, realizing for the first time, that she was actually much taller, physically and otherwise, than her mother. "And another thing. Why is it you still insist on this idiotic 'baby, darling, sweetie,' or, when you're not feeling well, 'young lady' or 'Miss,' but never my real name? Let me introduce myself. I'm Vidamía Farrell, thank you very much. I've always been Vidamía, and I'll always be Vidamía. Just like my father wanted. Vidamía Farrell. I know you hate it, but that's the way things are," she said and turned to go.

Elsa laughed nervously. Vidamía turned back to say something else, thought better of it, and instead shot her a look of disdain and rushed out of the room, buttoning her yellow slicker and pulling up the hood as she ran down the stairs and out of the house again. Beanbag made a halfhearted attempt to follow her but with a simple look she ordered him back to the place where he was resting on the rug in Barry's den. The rain fell in a steady misty drizzle, giving the grass and the leaves and every surface it touched a gauzy texture, and producing a pleasant fragrance as if somehow each flower and tree and the earth itself had been blended to produce a sweet yet melancholy end-of-summer scent. Her father and Fawn, she thought, could no longer smell the fragrance of flowers or grass or rain as it fell.

Lurleen was absolutely right. Giving people hope of Heaven, or reincarnation only made them lack appreciation for the here and now. Oh, yes, it provided a bit of comfort, but after the loved one was dead, the rationalizations didn't matter. If all that non-sense didn't exist, then maybe people, knowing they would never see each other again, not in Heaven and not in their next lives, would appreciate each other more *now* and treat each other better *now*. Vidamía made a determination to understand her mother.

Through the mist of falling rain, she peered out from the other mist forming in her eyes, this mist caused by the awful, persistent pain in the middle of her chest. The tears came easily now, flowing freely from inside of her as if she had suddenly given herself permission to mourn her loss fully. She recalled Lurleen finding Fawn's diary and poetry and showing it to her after the funeral arrangements had been made. There was one poem in which Fawn had likened rain to the tears of nature as it mourned the death of trees and small animals.

Vidamía and Cookie had gotten off the D train at Grand Street after saying goodbye to Leslie Rosen and Betsy Fuller, Cookie's classmates at Performing Arts, with whom they had gone to the beach at Coney Island. They heard the sirens and the police cars screeching around the corner and followed them, since they were headed in that direction anyway. They walked fast, as if they were being pulled by the magnetic force of the destruction all the way to the building on Eldridge Street, following the commotion, never imagining that it had to do with their family. When they got there, at least thirty police vehicles had crowded into the block. There were TV cameras, reporters interviewing people, and patrolmen trying to keep the crowds away from the crime scene. Down the street in front of the abandoned building the police had cordoned off the area with yellow DO NOT CROSS tape to indicate that a violent crime had been committed and there was a police investigation under way.

"Yo, what happened?" Cookie asked a couple of homeboys standing around with their arms crossed. "Drugs?"

"Yeah, drugs," one of them said. "Some white *hara* busted the dudes. There was a whole lotta shooting. Beep, beep, beep. Automatic, right, Freddie?" he said, turning to his friend.

"Word," Freddie said. "Some blond long-haired dude with a mustache. He was across the street watching everything and all of a sudden he disappeared and went up and got the dudes. Had to be a *hara*."

"Oh, my God," Cookie said, pulling at Vidamía's shirt.

"We should go home, Cookie," Vidamía said.

"No, wait, Vee," Cookie said. "Wait. Oh, my God."

The two of them stood fixed to the spot as the doors of the morgue wagon opened and the police placed more yellow tape around the area and more policemen and morgue personnel went upstairs with empty body bags. Sometime later they came down carrying the bodies in their bags and then the doors of the morgue wagon closed and the vehicle pulled away and people started moving off, and Vidamía and Cookie were left staring at the scene until finally Vidamía, Cookie clinging to her arm, went over and asked a man what had happened. The man said a veteran had gone crazy and shot some people.

"How do you know he was a veteran?" Cookie said.

"People said he was dressed in soldiers' clothes," the man said.

"The veteran," Vidamía said, her voice trembling, "what happened to him?"

"They shot him," the man said, matter-of-factly. "You live around here?" he asked, his eyes going up and down the front of her like he wanted to undress her. She turned away without answering him and pulled Cookie away from the scene.

"It was him, wasn't it, Vee?" Cookie immediately said, the tears welling up in her eyes. "What are we gonna tell Mama?"

"You don't know it was him," Vidamía said, also avoiding

having to say the word "Daddy." "He didn't have a gun. Mama told me she wouldn't let him have guns in the house." She knew she was lying to herself, still hoping the truth could be delayed. She knew it was him because something inside of her had been torn away and already the place where Billy had been was empty and raw and the only image that she could conjure up was of that time in the desert with her mother and stepfather when she had wandered off and looked into the window of an abandoned house, at the stark desolation of the interior, and the absence of any discernible humanity tore savagely at the core of her soul. That is how the building and the block now felt to her as she led her sister away.

"I don't wanna go home, Vee," Cookie had said.

"We have to, Cookie. Mama'll worry."

"I just don't wanna go there and have him not come in and stuff, Vee. Please. I don't wanna go back."

"Fine, we won't go back right away," Vidamía said. She went into her bag, took out a quarter, and called Wyndell from a public phone. She spoke into the receiver, explaining that she was on the way to his apartment. "The machine's on, but we can go over to Wyn's apartment if you want," she said after hanging up the phone. "We can go there and wait."

"Maybe we should go back and see how Mama's doing," Cookie said. "Oh, God, what are we gonna do? What's gonna happen to us?"

"Don't think about it. It's gonna be all right. We'll be all right. Maybe nothing happened."

"It was him, wasn't it?" Cookie said, digging her nails into Vidamía's arm. "They killed him. The police killed him and now they're covering it up like they do everything else. You heard the man. Just like the stuff that happened over in Tompkins Square Park, when they went crazy and beat on everybody."

"No, stop it, stop it. You don't know. Let's just go home and wait. He's probably waiting there. You don't know. Maybe he's worried about us."

Cookie didn't say anything more as they walked down Houston and away from the direction of their home, not consciously, but as if needing to avoid the confrontation with the reality they both knew was inevitable. Toward eight o'clock that evening when the sunlight was beginning to fade, they made their way back to the loft, and it was worse then because when they turned the corner they saw that the police cars had returned and were now in front of their building, and then they knew that whatever they had feared, whatever they were to face, would be greater and more devastating.

A policeman tried stopping them when they attempted to go into the building. Cookie kicked the policeman in the leg and called him stupid.

"You fucking pig," she said. "You killed my father, didn't you?"

"Hey, take it easy," the cop said, feeling ridiculous for placing his nightstick in front of him to protect himself from Cookie. And then another policeman came over.

"Take a walk, girls," he said. "Just keep moving."

"We live here, you fucking pig," Cookie said.

"Stop it, Cookie," Vidamía yelled, her own voice on the edge of screaming out her own pain, the hysteria barely controlled. "Officer, we live here. Can we go up, please?"

"What's your name?" the second policeman said.

At that point a policewoman with sergeant's stripes named McGowan came out of the door. She saw what was taking place and told the other two policemen to let them up.

"They're his daughters," McGowan said. "I saw their pictures up there." Turning to Vidamía and Cookie, she motioned them forward. "Go ahead up. Your mother's gotta go downtown with us. I'm sorry about what happened. Your father did the right thing."

"No, he didn't," Cookie said, subdued now by the police-woman's voice, reminding her of her great-grandma Brigid, but younger. "You killed him," she added weakly.

"We wouldn't do that, honey," McGowan said, her voice almost soothing. "You know better. Go ahead up. I'm really sorry. Your mom's waiting for you."

"Okay," Cookie said, and all at once she was a little girl and she was crying full out, all the toughness gone out of her, her face soft and vulnerable, her nose ring and black lipstick looking out of place. As she stepped inside the door, she nearly collapsed, so that Vidamía had to put an arm around her.

"I'm sorry," she said to Sergeant McGowan. "I didn't mean it."

"I know you didn't," McGowan said, her eyes beginning to grow moist. "I know that. Go ahead up. Your mom needs help."

They had gone up on the elevator, the creaking of the cables and the machinery magnified in the deathly silence that was now Billy Farrell's absence, which they felt already without knowing the particulars of what had taken place.

66 Never Coming Home Again

When they came out of the elevator and into the loft, there were at least ten other policemen standing around, their expressions pained, perplexed. Lurleen was talking to one of them. Cliff was sitting in Billy's rocker staring out of the big factory windows at the failing light of dusk, the sun a huge red disk dipping behind the skyline of Downtown Manhattan. Caitlin was sitting on the floor, looking at a comic book. Cookie rushed over to her mother and, burying herself in her hair, sobbed, the pain coming out uncontrolled in long keening sounds that tore at the hearts of the young cops as well as those of the older detectives. Vidamía went over to Cliff, knelt next to him, and took his hand. Cliff began crying softly. After a few minutes, Vidamía bolted upright.

"Where's Fawn?" she said, starting to walk away from Cliff to look for her.

"They got her, Vee," he said, his eyes in shock. "They killed her. That's why Papa went after them."

"Fawn?" Vidamía said. "Fawn, too?"

"Yeah, some boys from Avenue B, the cops said. Papa shot them."

"And they killed him?" Vidamía asked.

"I think so."

"Oh, my God," she said and went over to Lurleen, who had now taken Cookie to her room and helped her lie on the bed, soothing her as if she were once more a colicky baby, talking to her in a sort of half-speech, half-lullaby whisper.

When Lurleen saw Vidamía she sat up on the bed and opened her arms, and Vidamía went to her, feeling her knees grow weak, and then collapsing and finally letting the pain out as Lurleen held her, smoothing her hair and saying, "That's okay, baby. It's gonna be all right. Your daddy loved you very much."

"I shouldn't have gotten him the piano, Mama," Vidamía said.

"No, no. Don't think that way. He loved the piano. You don't know how much he appreciated you getting that piano in here. What happened couldn't be helped. You know that. He was just trying to get Fawn back. Can you do me a favor?"

"I think so," Vidamía said, tremulously.

"Can you stay here with the kids?" Lurleen said. "I gotta go downtown and make sure it's them. Your daddy and Fawn. I'll be back."

And then Vidamía looked at Lurleen. She looked small and

shrunken, her eyes faded and beaten. Vidamía took Lurleen in her arms and hugged her and felt Lurleen stiffen and then sigh and after a moment say she'd be all right.

"It's a damn shame, ain't it?" she said, dabbing the corners of her eyes and sweeping the ash-blond hair behind her ears. "A damn shame." And then she turned away, nodded to the policeman, and was gone. Vidamía went over and sat down crosslegged in front of Caitlin, who seemed oblivious to everything around her. Vidamía sat and simply watched her little sister, creating a net of protection lest the pain that had invaded their souls intrude upon her innocence.

Fawn was buried next to her father two days later. While there was no viewing of Billy's remains, Fawn had lain in her white casket at the Ortíz funeral home on First Avenue, her pale face luminous and her blond hair brilliant in the candlelight. Friends from the neighborhood wanted to have a minister or a priest say a few words, first at the funeral home and then at the graveside, but Lurleen had stoically resisted, saying that she didn't want religion to be part of saying goodbye to her husband or daughter. Maud Farrell sat with Ruby Broadway next to her, and Buck Sanderson next to Ruby. Maud sat quietly with a rosary and prayed over the bodies. She didn't oppose Lurleen's refusal to have a religious funeral, nor did Lurleen oppose others grieving in their own way.

When a social worker from one of the Settlement Houses where the kids went for drama classes and arts and crafts came to the house and insisted on a service, Lurleen had looked at her, imploring her to stop.

"I think it would be the best thing to do, considering the circumstances—"

"No religious services," Lurleen said, firmly, her eyes absolutely cold and determined. "If that ain't good enough, then so be it."

"I was only trying to—" the social worker started to say.

"And I'm gonna tell you one more thing," Lurleen said, her efforts to modify her southern accent in order to adapt to New York now gone. "I'm a widow left with three children to raise. I'm tired, full of heartache, and damn near collapsed, but I don't want an ounce of pity. If you're going to sit around here trying to decide for other folks what's best for them, I'm going to have to ask you to leave my home."

The social worker slinked off, muttering as she left the loft. Lurleen put her head down and it was clear she felt worse for the social worker than she did for herself. The rest of the week was hell. Lurleen couldn't sleep for more than a few minutes at a time. Sergeant Mary McGowan returned to the loft and sat with Lurleen and told her exactly what the police had been able to piece together from their investigation. She had the reports of the autopsies, but said that Lurleen didn't have to look at them if she didn't want to. Sergeant McGowan hadn't wanted to show them to her, but Lurleen insisted and again, stoically, made herself read them.

Lurleen, knowing Vidamía would want to know the whole truth, no matter how painful, later told her that Fawn had been raped, and they had eviscerated her. Her father had shot the four of them and their dog and had then committed suicide. One of the four survived and had told the detectives what had taken place. Lurleen asked her not to discuss it with the children.

The worst aspect of the tragedy had been the newspaper coverage. Not because they had reported unfairly or inaccurately, but because people in the neighborhood invariably pointed at the family and stared at them when they went outside the loft. The *New York Post*, the *Daily News*, and *Newsday* all carried the story on their front pages with extensive coverage. There were pictures of "a distraught daughter of the deceased veteran being restrained by the police," and Cookie being handled very gently by

Mary McGowan in front of their building. They had gotten a photograph of Billy in his Marine dress uniform and a school picture of Fawn in the sixth grade which a classmate had given the newspaper. The four young men who had been shot by Billy Farrell had their moment of glory when their pictures, provided by their families, appeared alongside the accounts of the event.

There were sympathetic pieces written about the tragedy. *The New York Times* did an investigative piece on the backgrounds of the four young men, highlighting the fact that they were the product of four generations of poverty since the arrival of their great-grandparents from Puerto Rico in the 1940s. The actions of Carlos "Papo" Marcano, José "Pepe" Baez, Antonio "Pipo" Correa, and Henry "Pupi" Mercado, although the article didn't state this directly, appeared to point to the greater problems of overcrowded schools, lack of opportunities for youth, and a society that places little value on the needs of the children and parents of the poverty culture.

The television networks had a field day. Lurleen refused to be interviewed or to allow reporters into the loft. Several reporters attempted to speak with Cliff, Cookie, and Vidamía, but each refused to speak to them. The consensus in the media was that this was simply a case of a Vietnam vet who had gone to his daughter's rescue. Little was made of the fact that Billy Farrell had been attempting a comeback in the world of jazz. In fact the most commonly held belief was that the developing crisis over Iraq's invasion of Kuwait might have been responsible for Billy's problem. In spite of the clumsiness of the shot-in-the-dark approach by reporters, they weren't too far from the truth.

Talk shows, including *A Current Affair*, *Donahue*, *Oprah*, and *Geraldo*, attempted to get Lurleen to tell her story. Some promised considerable sums of money, but in each case Lurleen thanked them and simply requested that they not interfere with the family's mourning. Spurred by Mary McGowan, whose father, Terrence, had worked with Billy's father, Kevin, at the 23rd Police Precinct in East Harlem at the time of his death, police officers made sure the family was not disturbed.

During the first few days, some of the relatives of the four young men who died made unfortunate remarks about revenge on the family. The veiled threats got back to the police, who dealt with them with haste and efficacy, warning those involved that they would treat any attack on the family as if it were being perpetrated on the family of a police officer. Day and night, fearing retribution, there were at least two police officers in civilian clothes, parked in their own cars in front of the building, making sure the family was safe. They stopped Wyn a few times, but he explained who he was and was allowed to go upstairs.

The day after the funerals, Wyndell Ross went and spoke with Art D'Lugoff of the Village Gate.

"I heard something about it and kept hoping it wasn't the same Billy Farrell and then I saw the papers," Art said. "I heard he was doing real good. You still want to do the gig?"

"Yeah, I was kinda looking forward to it, but I don't know," Wyn said. "I'd have to find another pianist, and one of the musicians is his son. I don't know if he's gonna be ready. He's a kid, you know. Fifteen."

"Anyway, don't worry about it," D'Lugoff said. "Let me see what I can do. Maybe you can switch with the Brazilian group playing in September."

A week later the dates were switched. It was now a matter of finding another pianist, which should've proved easy, but everyone seemed to be involved in something or going out of town. Some could do the date, but didn't have time to rehearse. Vidamía returned to Tarrytown to inform her mother that she wouldn't be going to Harvard in September. Elsa began to protest, but Vidamía stopped her and explained that she had already called and asked for an appointment to discuss the matter with the administration. She would be going up sometime in the next few weeks. She had packed two suitcases and ordered a car to bring her to New York to stay at the loft. Barry was willing to help her, so there was no need to worry about money. He, at least, understood her loss. She sat with him in his den, her legs curled up under her on the leather couch, and told him how well her father had been doing.

"You did the right thing in trying to help him," he said. "Whatever happened is regrettable, but if there is one consolation, from everything you told me he was playing his music again, and I'm sure that wouldn't have happened without your persistence."

"But maybe if I hadn't pushed him, the rest wouldn't have happened," she replied.

"You can't think that way," Barry said. "Things have their own organic sequence. There are too many factors involved. All that you can do in life is make efforts on your own behalf and on behalf of others. As long as you keep in mind that what you're doing is for an ultimate good, then no one, including yourself, has the right to judge the outcome."

She got up, and he walked her to the door. She told him that what he said was difficult for her to accept, but that she would try. She hugged herself to him and remained in his arms, weeping softly. When she was done she wiped her eyes and smiled.

"Can I ask you something?" she said.

"Anything," he said.

"I can't call you Dad or Daddy, but could you be my father now?"

"I've always thought of myself that way," he said, smiling sadly.

"No, not my stepfather," she said. "My father."

"Of course," he said.

"I love you, Barry," she said.

"I love you too, Vidamía," he said. "If there's anything I can do, ever, don't forget to ask. Whatever it is, I trust you more than ever."

"Thank you," she said. "You don't know how good that makes me feel. I'll see you when I get back."

"I'll be here."

"Good night, *papi*," she said.

"Good night, *mijita*," he said.

That weekend, Vidamía stayed at Wyndell's apartment. On Saturday they had lunch at a Japanese restaurant nearby. When she announced her plans to go up to Harvard and speak with them about delaying her entrance, he told her about the postponement of the gig and his difficulty finding a pianist. Buster Williams had tried to get Kenny Barron and then Cedar Walton, but both of them had commitments.

"What about your friend in Boston?" she said.

"Rebecca Feliciano?"

"Yeah, she's a pianist."

"I didn't even think of calling her."

"Why not?"

"I guess because she's not in New York. She's pretty busy."

"When did you see her last?"

"Six months ago when . . ." Wyndell hesitated, as if he didn't want to reveal something.

"What's the matter?" Vidamía said. "Please don't do that. It's like you're trying to hide something from me."

"I'm not. I just don't want to remind you of things."

"What things?" she said, feeling the anger which had lately begun to surface with little provocation.

"She came in for her father's funeral about six months ago," Wyn said. "I saw her briefly. She was in pretty bad shape."

"I'm sorry," Vidamía said. "I didn't mean to snap at you. I'm all right. Really. Why don't you call her? Maybe she can do it."

"I guess I should."

They returned to his apartment and Wyn went into the bedroom and made the call.

She walked away from him and out into the garden and stood contemplating the wet yard. It had rained all night and she'd awakened to the thunder and lightning. They had spent the night together, but hadn't made love. Since her father's death she hadn't wanted to be intimate and Wyndell understood that. She had been unable to sleep and had remained awake wondering again about her part in her father's death. Now she felt tired and grouchy. Wyn came out into the garden, put his arms around her, and said he was sorry.

"Are you all right?" he said.

"I'm all right. Just thinking."

"I feel bad about your dad," he said. "He was really great, Vee. Really. Not just great for a white guy, but gifted as hell. We were just starting to blend. It would've been fantastic. I'm sorry."

He held her and she cried, softly at first and then violently, the racking sobs making her angry as she recalled once more the horror of that day her father had ceased to exist. And poor little Fawn. She couldn't figure out what they could've done differently to prevent what took place. Lurleen said Fawn had been apprehensive about the operation. How would she ever rid herself of feeling responsible for what had happened to her father? How could it have all happened? It was so horrible.

Most people were so cynical and she didn't want to be that way. They weren't content with destroying their own dreams but went out of their way to dash others' hopes and dreams to the ground, and, not content with merely shattering those dreams, they would step on the pieces so that only dust remained. They escaped through drugs, sex, booze, careers, family, and religion and never faced their personal responsibility. And then there were people like Lurleen, who felt a duty to help others become happy and healthy. What would she do? Poor Mama. Vidamía felt as if she had no parents now. As if her lifeline to those she loved had been truncated. She knew better, though. Barry loved her. He was her *papi* and Lurleen was her mama. Neither one of them her blood, but without question her parents. One Puerto Rican and the other American. That's what she was about, a blending of the two cultures.

She guessed she was one of those people, like Lurleen, who couldn't escape her responsibilities and had chosen to carry the burdens of the world on her shoulders. She had no choice. There was no other place in the universe where she could go. The Earth was it, and she couldn't hide from the horrors it produced. But why did it have to be so ugly? Why couldn't it let up? So much unhappiness, so much suffering, so much hate. She recalled walking with Wyn in the late evening the day before the funeral. It was nearly midnight when they'd gotten back to the loft. Lurleen was sitting in Billy's rocking chair. Caitlin, unable to sleep, was curled up on her lap in her long plaid nightgown. When she saw Vidamía she climbed down from her mother's lap, came over, and took Vidamía's hand.

"Don't be sad," Caitlin had said.

"I'm all right, honey," Vidamía replied. "Really, I am," she assured her, lifting Caitlin up and kissing her.

"Daddy's not coming back," Caitlin said.

"I know."

"You know why?"

"No, I don't."

"He's gone far away," Caitlin said. "To a happier planet."

"I guess he has," Vidamía said. "Would you like me to read you a story?"

"Okay."

Vidamía kissed Wyndell and Lurleen and took Caitlin off to bed with her. She had read aloud from *The Hobbit* until Caitlin fell asleep. A happier planet, she thought, and for the first time she accepted that Billy was gone and would never come back.

No matter how much anyone promised to cook or pay the rent, they had all blown it and Bill Bailey was never coming home again. Her father was gone, and accepting his death forced her to recall happier times with him. Her mind began to collect those memories like photographs in an album and to paste them securely in place.

67 The Gig

A voice came over the sound system.

"Good evening, ladies and gentlemen, and welcome to the historic Village Gate. Tonight we have a very special musical presentation—the debut of four up-and-coming and very promising musicians on the New York jazz scene. Please put your hands together and help me welcome the Wyndell Ross Quintet, featuring Buster Williams on bass. The Wyndell Ross Quintet, ladies and gentlemen."

The crowd clapped politely and then Wyndell Ross counted off the time and on the downbeat Rebecca Feliciano came in and right behind her everyone was blowing in a tremendous explosion of beautiful music, sounding better than Vidamía had heard them in rehearsal on Monk's "Straight No Chaser." She watched Cliff, dressed totally in black: a black suit with a red carnation on his lapel, and a black shirt, unbuttoned to the middle of his chest. He seemed taller and more handsome than ever, so stoic that it hurt to look at him. He looked exactly like their father, Billy Farrell, in photographs at the same age, except that Cliff looked invincible and their father had always looked so fragile.

Cliff stood listening to the music and nodding to the rhythm.

When his turn to solo came, he gave himself totally to the music, playing like he was J. J. Johnson, Frank Rossolino, Kai Winding, Bob Brookmeyer, and Curtis Fuller all rolled up into one, or so someone behind Vidamía said, marveling at the tone and richness of his sound, amazed by his virtuosity and technique.

What a mystery her little brother was, Vidamía thought, as she watched him begin another chorus. Cliff had always seemed older than his years, much as if he had understood early his father's vulnerability and knew that he'd be called upon to take on adult responsibilities while he was a boy. He had impeccable manners, never grew flustered, and was always ready to help someone in need. Around the neighborhood he was known as a fearless white boy, friends with everyone, and so tough that all he needed to do was stick out his hand to black, white, Latino, or Asian and as if by magic everything was suddenly cool. She couldn't figure out what it was about him, but perhaps it was a quality that made you decide that you'd rather have him on your side than against you.

Although he was almost a physical replica of their father, Cliff had never, to Vidamía's knowledge, experienced any major disappointment in his life until his father's death. But if his father's death was a serious blow to him, he certainly was masking the impact with remarkable grace. A couple of weeks after the funeral, Cliff had helped Vidamía close the store while Cookie was in rehearsal for the play at the Medicine Show. After they'd counted out the receipts and made out the deposit slip, they had called Tito Delgado, paid him, and ten minutes later, after pulling the gate down in front of the store and locking it, they were in Tito's car on their way to the bank. With Tito standing guard they had placed the receipts in the night deposit slot at the bank. When they were done they waved at Tito and continued walking. She asked Cliff if he felt like getting something to eat. He had nodded and they'd gone over to the Levee on First Avenue and First Street and had gumbo and corn bread and drank sodas.

Cliff was a little over six feet tall, blue eyes set deep in his head and dark blond hair that he combed back severely and parted in the middle. He was naturally muscled and incredibly sure of himself. When they entered the restaurant, every woman in the place devoured him with her eyes, going from his face to the front of his pants and his rear as he walked past them. Vidamía's older friends all said the same thing of him: gorgeous, sensual, irresistible. "He's one of those men you just have to have," Kathy Ward's sister, Nell, had said. Nell Ward was twenty-four and had just returned from getting a master's degree in literature at Oxford University.

"He's only fifteen, Nell," Kathy had said.

"Really?" Nell said, momentarily embarrassed, and then, after recuperating, "I don't care. He's lovely and I'd kill to have him."

He wasn't at all like their father, Vidamía thought. Just the looks. The person he seemed the most like was Buck Sanderson, except that wasn't true either. Perhaps in sexual allure, but he was just somebody very special, very perfect, someone women fell in love with and men wanted for a friend. Halfway through the meal Vidamía asked him how he was doing.

"Okay," Cliff said, smiling easily at her. "You?"

"Still hurting, I guess," she'd said honestly.

"Me too," he'd said. "I was pissed off lately at Dad, so my feelings about it are kinda confused."

"Are you still angry?"

"I just feel bad that he's dead. Mama was telling me how messed up his life was. I guess none of us ever knew how rough things were for him."

"Yeah, his whole life was full of violence. His father got shot, and then the war and everything. He was coming out of it with the music."

"Yeah, that's the part I'm gonna miss the most," he said, his face suddenly solemn. "He was so fucking good. Man, he could play piano."

"Cliff?"

"Yeah."

"What are you gonna do?"

"What do you mean? I'm gonna stay in school and then maybe go to Juilliard, or up to Boston, and learn more. You know, and keep gigging. Why?"

"I worry about you sometimes," Vidamía had said.

"I'll be okay, Vee," he said, smiling again at her.

"You sure? It's like sometimes I look at you and you remind me so much of Daddy that I think one of these days you're just gonna explode with anger like he did."

"Me?" he said, surprised. "I don't think so. I get angry, sure. But it's no big thing. I don't believe in violence just for the hell of it. It's a fucked-up way of solving things between people. I'm not saying that Daddy was wrong. Sometimes I think maybe if he was gonna do something he should've done it right away. I mean, *I* wanted to."

"Did you tell him?"

"Sure, I told him. When I saw Fawn going into the building with that boy, I came home and told him we should get her. But he said we should wait for the police."

"You think he was wrong."

Cliff nodded, his eyes still blazing with the cold anger she had always known was there.

"Sometimes I blame myself because I suggested it and maybe if I hadn't been along he would've thought of it himself. But I think he was trying to teach me to have respect for the law or some bullshit thing like that."

"And you don't? I mean, have respect for the law?"

"Oh, sure, but sometimes you gotta do what you gotta do and take your chances."

"You don't have a gun, do you?"

Cliff laughed, but he didn't answer her question.

"It was all really weird," he said, going back to the original topic of their father. "I feel sad about Fawn. Daddy, too, but mostly Fawn. She was real scared most of the time. But I woulda done what he did. Those kids were scumbags. Sometimes I feel like I don't wanna hear about guns and shootings. Other times I think that there's no other way. I don't want much, you know? I just wanna play music, maybe travel and meet people, and have a good time. But I definitely don't want people fucking with me. That's all."

"And if there's a war?" Vidamía said.

"Fuck war. Who fights wars? Kids. I ain't going. They'll have to put me in jail."

"And if somebody came in here right now and tried to hurt us?"

"I don't know," he'd said. "I don't think that way. I don't go around thinking shit's gonna happen. If it happens you deal with it."

"But suppose someone did. Suppose they came in and tried to hurt us."

"Well, they'd be one sorry bunch of mothafuckas," he said, seriously, and looking no different from the homeboys in the neighborhood, except with Cliff you could tell that he wasn't just playing a role.

"You have a gun, don't you?"

He laughed again.

"What you don't know can't hurt you," he said.

"You have one, don't you?" she said, suddenly frightened and at the same time exhilarated by his protectiveness. "Are you ever scared?"

"Yeah, sure, sometimes."

"You seem so cool and sure of yourself all the time."

"I'm trying to impress girls," he said, laughing easily.

As she listened to Rebecca Feliciano's solo, she still couldn't figure what Cliff was about. She thought—and immediately hated herself for thinking—of Cliff in terms of color, but she guessed he was like millions of other boys all over the United States, no matter their color, unsure of what they were going to do with their lives. She tried to imagine him at the different stages of life, but could not. This bothered her until she realized that she couldn't imagine anything about him because her little brother possessed enormous power and he and nobody else would decide what his life was to be.

"Straight No Chaser" came to a close and the audience exploded in applause. She sat in the middle of the din, moved by the outpouring of affection from strangers for people she loved. She watched the bandstand as Wyndell, without introducing the next number, snapped his fingers to count off the time. Her heart once again expanded to take in everything she loved about him. When he first came onstage ten minutes before, he had looked like the Wyn she knew, but he now looked monumental, his person filling the entire stage as the thick sound of his tenor caressed each note of "My Funny Valentine." As aggressive as her playing could be, Rebecca Feliciano handled the chord structure of the tune with subdued delicacy, her body leaning over the piano, her derby and black hair making a shadow of incredible beauty against the gleaming surface of the keys. In the background, David Weinstein's brushes seemed to still the audience against the fragility of the music. Cliff, as usual, produced an unusually melancholy sound as he punctuated the lyricism of Wyndell's interpretation of the tune with the rich tones of his trombone, while Buster Williams's bass gave each musical phrase a deep, dark shading to the ballad.

Tears once more came to Vidamía's eyes. Unashamedly, she allowed her heart to expand further, thankful that she could spend this time with the people she loved. In a few months she'd be away from New York and her family and the daily intimacy of her life with Wyndell. She didn't know whether she'd be able to handle it and had already worked out a schedule allowing for nearly weekly trips back to New York. She even suggested to Wyndell that he move to Boston, using Rebecca's recent success there as a possible incentive. Feeling already saddened by the prospect of the eventual separation when she went to school, she watched his discomfort as he told her that he'd have to think about it.

As she listened to the music she thought of the previous weekend. They had walked uptown through Washington Square Park, strolling with the early-Sunday-afternoon crowd up Fifth Avenue to America's for brunch. They sat at a table for two on the parapet along the left wall of the restaurant, watching the other people—couples in love like themselves, families, large groups of friends at the tables for ten or twelve—the coffee cups enormous and the menu so varied that it sometimes made her dizzy trying to decide what to order. When she did it was always too much food for her and she had to leave nearly half of it.

Wyn had no problem with his portions. A huge platter of Spanish omelette, Mexican corn cakes, and sausage with large pieces of bread and butter disappeared miraculously. She marveled at his appetite because the amount of food he took in didn't match the delicacy with which he consumed what the waiters placed in front of him, and she was invariably charmed by his Continental table manners, which he'd acquired during his time with Davina in Europe, the fork always in his left hand, the knife in his right hand, cutting and herding the food onto the fork.

There was no question that she loved Wyn. Sitting in the huge restaurant, she savored the moment, watching as he brought his Bloody Mary to his lips, and she basked in the magnificence and the boyish appeal that made him appear so accessible to women. If he took care of his health he'd be playing for the next fifty years—growing handsomer each year. They would be like his parents—his mother in the arts and his father a physician. Except with them the roles would be reversed and she would be the doctor. She promised herself again that she would stay with him through thick and thin.

They had finished eating, and, their arms around each other's waist, returned to the apartment. As soon as they were past the double doors of the entrance to the building and inside the door of his apartment, Wyndell placed his hand on her back and then slid it slowly inside the waistband of the loose silk skirt she was wearing, until his fingers were kneading her buttocks and she could feel him erect against her belly. They hadn't made love since her father's death, nearly a month before, and the sensation of his closeness made her eager for him. He kissed the corners of her lips, and then her closed eyes, and she was instantly aroused. Unlike other times, she didn't want to wait to be made love to but wanted him inside of her immediately, needing for him to be driving against her. She reached up with her mouth and sought out his tongue and with her right hand opened the zipper of his pants, searching violently for him, grasping the erect organ in her hand so that she felt him grow even more passionate.

Once naked on the bed with him on top of her, refusing his offer to kiss her clitoris slowly as he did until she was ready to climax, but feeling herself searching for him with her own sex, not letting him guide himself in or taking the heavy organ with her own hand, but seeking him out with her cunt until she found him and he slid in and she began moving slowly, grasping him in her and he moaning, calling God and her name, and her hips going, not being fucked by him but fucking him for the first time as if the threat of the upcoming separation were helping her establish a greater claim to his body and his being; no contraceptives or anything, knowing she was safe, the HIV test tucked away in his files, trusting him that he hadn't been with anyone since they'd met, feeling an almost blinding power of ownership; and now fucking him, lost in him, her hips moving violently as she thrust against him until the cry issued from deep within her and everything in the middle of her was ebbing away with pleasure, coming and going and coming, one wave after the other, her mouth open against his skin; feeling him then thrust against her, the head of his organ pounding against her cervix so that within the small area of pain there was also pleasure and then he was coming, going up into her so that her own pleasure began again and she stiffened out and hooked her legs around his ankles and rocked slowly and felt his chest expand, the wind from his nostrils coming in large spurts of sweet breath. And then she was crying inconsolably, the pain of her loss and of loving Wyndell magnified by the intense sexual release of her love, but also the knowledge that their time together might be over soon, overwhelming in its impact; knowing that she couldn't let him go so soon after losing her father. That had been painful enough and she didn't know how she would manage without Wyndell there every day.

Three days earlier she had flown up to Boston, where a car met her and took her to Cambridge. There, at Harvard, she spoke to an admissions counselor and explained why she couldn't begin in the fall semester of 1990. The counselor expressed her condolences and said that if Vidamía needed to take a year off she could enter the university the following fall. "No," she'd said, "just six months." If she could start at the beginning of the year and make up the work during a few summers, she'd be okay. She'd like to graduate with the Class of '94, if that was okay. The university agreed. She flew back to New York that evening and returned to the loft to help Lurleen out.

They finished playing "My Funny Valentine" and during the applause the quintet immediately went into "How High the

Moon," the tempo breakneck, Rebecca brilliant as she played chorus after chorus in her intense, percussive style, the piano shaking and her face so determined that she reminded Vidamía of the seriousness of a matador she had seen in a bullring in Sevilla with Elsa and Barry. She had been fifteen and had sat awed by the courage of the bullfighter as he faced the animal. As Wyn, Cliff, and Rebecca traded fours, Vidamía once again reflected on her relationship with her mother. In her attempt to improve the situation, Vidamía had asked Elsa and Barry if they'd like to come and see Wyndell perform one day during the engagement. She went up to Tarrytown one Saturday afternoon expressly to invite them. Neither Barry nor Elsa was home when she arrived, so she went upstairs, changed into more comfortable clothes, and helped Mrs. Alvarez with dinner. When she was done, she showered and changed again, putting on a dress, nylons, and heels. She made up and wore the earrings and bracelet Elsa had given her for her seventeenth birthday. In the meantime, Barry and Elsa had arrived and they sat down together to eat.

After they'd finished their supper, Vidamía asked them if they could have their dessert in the library. This was always a signal that something important was to be discussed. In spite of everything that had happened, their connection as a family was still solid enough to enjoy their private joke about the library: in every other library in the world people had to be silent, but theirs was a place to talk. As wealthy as they were, they sometimes joked that they should get one of those ninety-five-dollar dinette sets with the rubbery seats on the chairs for the library since any discussion of consequence in Rican tenement or project apartments always happened in the kitchen.

When they were seated Barry asked her how things were going. Vidamía replied that they were going well. She looked at her mother, and Elsa smiled at her. It was a different smile than she'd ever seen on her mother's face and Vidamía was suddenly reminded of being little again and watching her mother as she got ready to go out into the world—to school, or on a date, or to work—and how she'd always come to kiss her and hug her, trying her best to reassure her that she would return.

"*Mami*, do you think you and Barry might like to come and hear Wyndell and Cliff perform?" she said nervously, but getting immediately to the point. "I mean, Grandpa Justino's going to be playing too, so . . . I mean . . . I'll understand if you . . ."

Barry, taken by surprise, began to offer an excuse, but Elsa cut him off.

"That'd be kind of interesting," Elsa said. "Do you think it'll be okay, Barry?"

"Oh, sure," Barry said, suddenly relieved.

"Good," Vidamía said. "I'll put you on the guest list."

"Oh, no," Barry said. "We'll be fine. Save those places for your friends."

"Okay," Vidamía said. "That was easy. Thursday or Friday?"

"Thursday we're both in the city," Barry said.

"Sure. Thursday's fine," Elsa said.

Vidamía couldn't believe it. Opening night. She was already anticipating the tension of introducing Wyndell to her mother. Barry excused himself and started to rise. Vidamía thanked him and then went over and kissed him before he left the room. She then kissed Elsa.

"Thank you, *mami*," she said and began leaving the room. "I have to call Cookie to have her phone and make the reservations."

She was halfway out the door when she heard Elsa call her.

"Vidamía."

The sound of her mother's voice saying her name sounded odd. For a moment she felt apprehensive. When she turned, her mother was standing with her arms open. Vidamía ran to her with the same feeling she'd had as a little girl whenever she saw her. She held on to Elsa for a long time, letting her tears overwhelm the two of them.

"Oh, *mami*," Vidamía said, the emotion making her voice sound pure and innocent.

"Can you sit with me for a moment?" Elsa said.

"Sure," Vidamía said.

"I need to ask you a favor."

"Sure. If it's about Wyn, I understand. We'll go slowly."

"No, I'll be fine. I'm sure it'll be okay meeting him. It's my father I'm worried about. What am I going to say to him?"

"Grandpa? Oh, he's no problem. He'll be glad to see you."

"Are you sure?"

"Yeah, he's real cool. He's into his own world and nothing seems to bother him much. He's a day-to-day kind of person."

"Yeah, he was always like that."

"No, it'll be great, *mami*."

They spoke for the next two hours, at first skirting those subjects which at times had presented problems for them. After a while they ended up laughing at their efforts and relaxed into an openness they had both thought impossible. At one point Vidamía took off her heels and then her earrings. As she did so, for the first time, she thanked Elsa genuinely for the gift. At midnight they got hungry and went to the kitchen and had pie à la mode and continued talking.

Up on the stage the music was again subdued as the quintet played "Darn That Dream." The song was so sad that Vidamía almost had to excuse herself to go the powder room. She recalled that one evening during a break in rehearsal Rebecca had been playing the tune and Cookie came over, leaned against the piano and began singing the song in her torchy voice. Wyndell came into the room, picked up his tenor and began playing little riffs behind the singing. Pretty soon the other musicians joined in and Cookie, unfazed, sang on. When they were done, Wyndell suggested that maybe she should sing a few songs with them. Cookie shook her head and declined politely. As the quintet played now, Vidamía saw that her sister was mouthing the words to the song as she swayed to the music.

Darn that dream
I dream each night.
You say you love me
And you hold me tight,
But when I awake
You're out of sight,
Oh, darn that dream.

As the days passed, the memory of the day of Billy and Fawn's death becoming less immediate, her mind eased into the task of storing away the tragedy, as one does mementos of a time beyond reach. On those occasions when she couldn't avoid the memories and depression set in, Vidamía would go to the piano. Whether she was at the house in Tarrytown or at the Farrell loft, she sat down and played the blues chords that her father had taught her and which Wyndell had explained to her. There, alone, she let her fingers explore the keys and often found that she could improvise little melodies against the simple chord structure.

"I usually cry after I finish," she said to Wyndell when she explained how she played whenever the memories became too unbearable.

"I understand," Wyndell said, but he couldn't imagine her pain. He turned to look away, her sorrow enveloping him. Suddenly he knew no amount of talking about it or playing would cure her pain. It would be there forever, like a dark bird nesting within her heart.

Three weeks later, she and Lurleen were in the loft alone,

Caitlin asleep, and Cookie and Cliff at a party on the Upper West Side that Vidamía hadn't wanted to attend. They had taken a family vote and decided not to move to Brooklyn but to remain in the loft until things settled down and they could decide more calmly what to do next. Lurleen, embroidering a pattern on a shirt, again expressed regret that she had responded so harshly to the social worker about a religious service for Billy and Fawn the previous month.

"I was wrong," Lurleen said. "She was just a young woman trying to do her best. She was trying to help, but I can't stand people shoving religion down folks' throats as if that was the answer to everything."

And then she was truly angry. Her face became blotchy, the vein on her forehead thicker, as if it was going to burst through her skin at any moment. She turned her face to the wall to hide her sorrow and dug her fingers into the palms of her hands, wanting to hurt herself.

"Maybe it'd help if I believed in God," she said, turning back to face Vidamía, genuine doubt surfacing in her voice for the first time.

"No, it wouldn't, Mama," Vidamía said. She stood up, went over to sit next to Lurleen, and smoothed her hair. "You believe in better things. You believe in being honest and good with people, and you believe there's life up in the stars, and being around you makes people want to hope. If you believed in God then your mind'd be made up and you'd be just like every one of those TV preachers—smug and pontificating and pretty much unbearable."

Lurleen nodded and her gaze was once again far away. She missed Billy so much. War did awful things to folks, she thought. Donny Meekins, her own daddy, had been a paratrooper in Korea and had come back with half his leg missing and totally deaf; he couldn't hear her playing music, but he tapped his one good foot and grinned lovingly at her when she played. She'd gone back last year and watched him die, holding his skeletal hand as he faded, his wonderful smile replaced by a grimace. She had watched Butterworth's life ebb away in that hospital, and her Bill dying right along with him. She guessed losing Fawn had been too much for Billy. Where was God in all this?

"And you?" Lurleen said, looking up at Vidamía. "What do you believe?"

"Same as you," Vidamía said. "I'm your daughter, ain't I?" she added playfully, allowing the language to undulate so that if you closed your eyes she sounded like a southern white person or perhaps an educated, university-trained black person returning home to a working-class family and needing to fit in. Then she became introspective and told Lurleen that it didn't really matter. "It's an irrelevancy, a philosophical distraction at best. It certainly hasn't helped people get along any better, has it?" she added, using the language with the care that her mother had instilled in her, admiring more each day Elsa Santiago's dogged insistence on certain things. Expressing herself correctly and concisely was one of them.

"You're sure right about that," Lurleen said. "Those boys your daddy shot are dead, and I'm sure their mamas raised them to be God-fearing—just like your daddy was raised. But it had nothing to do with religion. Something else made those boys behave like they did. Something that doesn't have a name yet, but it's making everybody hate and be spiteful with each other. And then again, maybe it is religion. It can sure make folks smug and self-righteous."

They went on talking like that for nearly two hours, and then Cookie and Cliff came in with their friends. They turned on music and raided the refrigerator, the period of mourning now over and everyone going ahead with their lives as Lurleen had suggested. But Billy Farrell's absence was palpable and immense and each day Lurleen's loneliness grew until she began talking about returning to Tennessee and raising Caitlin back home. Vidamía had asked about Cookie and Cliff.

"What's gonna happen to them if you go back to Tennessee?" she said.

Lurleen opened her eyes as if she were returning from sleep, and said, "Oh, yes, I hadn't thought about that," and this was the first time Vidamía had observed that sort of carelessness in Lurleen. She always remembered the most minute details concerning other people and made sure, whenever possible, that the other person's needs were satisfied.

"You're right, darling," Lurleen said, her eyes gaining some of their usual brightness as she fought the desolation of Billy's loss. "Ole Lynn's gone out to lunch for a bit, but she's back. Not to worry about that. School's started and we're gonna have to get all the winter clothes aired and everything," she rattled on, part of her mind in the future and another part in the past, fighting the tragedy that had sabotaged her happiness, but the strongest part of her being struggling to remain pure and not allow hatred to pollute it, believing that this was simply a swing of the pendulum toward evil and that she was undergoing not a trial, as Christians believed, but a part of the natural process that will eventually result in a sane civilization.

Now, as Vidamía sat watching the stage, her eyes filled with tears that were a mixture of happiness and regret, she wished Lurleen had come to watch Cliff perform. But she hadn't wanted to. Once Lurleen made up her mind there was no moving her. "He'll be fine," Lurleen had said. "He told me I'd make him nervous being there." Grandma Maud had also decided not to attend the performance, not stating exactly why, but obviously still too shaken by Billy's death. Grandpa Buck Sanderson, dressed in a suit and a tie and looking healthy and full of life, came with Ruby Broadway. She was in a red evening dress and a gold brocaded stole. They sat at a table near the stage and beamed as they watched Wyn and the quintet.

68 Don't Let a Little Black Stop You

The quintet's music filled her with indescribable joy. She knew enough about jazz to permit herself the luxury of commenting that Wyndell and the rest were "in the pocket." She thought about her mother. The night they finally had their heart-to-heart talk which Vidamía had longed for, Elsa told Vidamía everything, unburdening herself of all she'd held in. She told her that when she was fourteen her sisters had taken her to a concert and she'd seen a group called Bobby Rodríguez y La Compañía perform the tune "She's a Latin from Manhattan."

"Back when I was a teenager I thought Bobby Rodríguez had written the tune," Elsa said. "I assumed that the song was about us. About Puerto Ricans living in New York."

"And it wasn't?" Vidamía said, incredulously.

"No, it was from some old Al Jolson movie. Do you know who Al Jolson was?"

Vidamía said she hadn't heard of him. As she told Vidamía about the movie, Elsa's mind raced back to those days. She took a deep breath and said that the previous night she had turned on the television. As she flipped through the channels she saw a black-and-white movie and was fascinated by the fast-paced dialogue and the women darting back and forth, emoting in the mechanical way they had in those days. And there was Al Jolson. He was singing and moving around in a tuxedo and top hat, with at least a hundred dancers behind him, dressed exactly like him. All at once the shot faded and they appeared again in blackface, with Al Jolson singing his wretched "Mammy" song.

"Do you want to hear this?" Elsa asked self-consciously. "Maybe this is too boring?"

"Oh, no, *mami*. I really want to hear it. But can we sit outside?"

"Sure," Elsa said. They went back to the library, turned on the outdoor lights, and, opening the French doors, stepped out onto the terrace and sat in two of the large redwood chairs. The night was clear and the sky filled with stars. A slight breeze was blowing across the side lawn.

Al Jolson's character was called Al Howard, and she watched for a while before realizing that this was the movie that had the song "She's a Latin from Manhattan." Of course. What was the movie? She went searching for the *TV Guide*. It was *Go Into Your Dance*, made in 1935. Fifty-five years ago. Everyone in the film was dead by now. No, maybe not Ruby Keeler. She had outlived them all. Elsa watched on, wanting to hear Jolson sing the awful "She's a Latin from Manhattan" song as she had on the tape back then when she had been obsessed with the tune.

What a disappointment it had been to learn that Bobby Rodríguez hadn't written "She's a Latin from Manhattan." At least someone had arranged the tune well and it had a good salsa beat. But Al Jolson made up like a black man angered her. Why would anyone want to be black even for a second? she thought. What was their need to get painted up like a Negro? But she wanted to hear the song, the awful song, and forced herself to watch the dopiness of the movie with its trite plot. Al Jolson's character wants to perform on Broadway again. No one wants him. So he gets a gangster to put up the money for the show. The gangster's wife has eyes for the Al Jolson character. The Ruby Keeler character is also in love with the Al Jolson character. It sounded like a silly soap opera, except everyone talked real fast.

"It was unbelievable," Elsa said. "This big Hollywood 'She's

A Latin From Manhattan' production with people doing a dopey combination of a tango and a samba, I guess. I couldn't help myself."

Elsa explained how she began laughing hysterically and rolled off the couch. The more they sang the song, the more she laughed. And then, in the next scene, Al Jolson is in his dressing room getting made up in blackface. Soon, there's Al Jolson in blackface, declaring his love for his white lady love. And then he's back onstage, still in blackface, singing "Go Into Your Dance." The song over, he's back with his beloved.

"And then," Elsa said, grabbing Vidamía's arm, "I almost died. He says, 'I'm so happy that if I didn't have this black on I'd kiss you.' And she says, 'Well, don't let a little black stop you.' As much as I had laughed, I was now totally out of my mind—with anger. I almost threw something at the television. When I woke up this morning I felt great. It was like I had six hundred hours of therapy in watching that movie. I can't explain it. I was really angry. Angrier than I've ever been."

"About the guy getting painted up?"

"Everything. I don't know. It was very confusing. Do you understand?"

"Yeah, it was a racist movie."

"Sure, this country has always been clumsy about that kind of stuff," Elsa said. "To them it's all one nonwhite group. Blacks and Latinos as one group, so that they don't have to deal with differences in people."

"No, I understand," Vidamía said, and thought about the arguments she'd had with Wyn. "Americans want us to forget we're Puerto Rican."

"Exactly. *I'm* the real Latin from Manhattan, a Loisaida homegirl with a Ph.D. in psychology, not that Al Jolson thing, or Chiquita Banana, Carmen Miranda, or Charo with all that *cuchi-cuchi* booshit, like the homegirls used to say. I'm the real thing. But I was thinking of the thing the actress said at the end when Jolson said he'd kiss her if it wasn't for the black grease-paint."

"What?"

" 'Don't let a little black stop you.' It's kind of what I've done."

"What do you mean?"

"*La manchita de plátano,*" Elsa said, using the Puerto Rican euphemism for the presence of African blood in one's back-ground—the "plantain stain"—which all Puerto Ricans suppos-edly share, no matter how white they may appear. "The little black doesn't stop you, does it?"

"You mean because of Grandpa?"

"Yeah," Elsa answered uncomfortably.

"No, I don't think about it," Vidamía said. "It's fine with me. In fact I'm kind of proud of having African blood."

"Good. That's much healthier than what I've done."

"Daddy had a little black, too, you know," Vidamía said mis-chievously.

"He what?"

"Oh, not like that. He had a little black man that he talked to. You know. Imaginary. He was mumbling to himself one day, and, kidding around, I asked him who he was talking to. He said it was Mr. McQuinlan, his black leprechaun friend."

"Sure, of course," Elsa said, seemingly unfazed by the story. "Bright people often have something like that. When they're children and they're lonely. They have imaginary friends. I guess Billy kept his."

"Yeah," Vidamía said wistfully, noting that her mother had also called her father by his name. "You called Daddy Billy," she'd added.

"Yeah," Elsa said, wistfully as she got up. "That was his name. I'm sleepy, baby."

They'd gone up the stairs with their arms around each other's waist. The large clock in the library struck three in the morning and Elsa checked her watch to confirm the hour. When they reached the second floor Elsa rested her head on her taller daughter's shoulder.

"I love you, *mami*," Vidamía said.

"I love you, too," Elsa replied.

"Good night, *mami*."

"*Buenas noches, negrita,*" Elsa said.

They kissed and hugged and went to get ready for bed.

Wyndell and the quintet were now deep into "Night in Tunisia," everyone blowing incredibly fast. Cliff was totally into the tune, one chorus after the next, the tones of his trombone throaty but clear. People were stomping and whistling and Rebecca was pounding the piano and lifting up off the piano bench as she accented a chorded phrase.

They had slept late and then at breakfast they continued talking. Elsa now revealed why it had been so difficult for her to use the name Vidamía—and, by extension, Billy's. She ended up telling her about her relationship with Billy Farrell.

"It was as if I had given much more of myself than I had intended. I don't know if you understand. Maybe I'm not explaining myself clearly."

"I understand."

"Like I had lost control of my life in getting pregnant. I never regretted having you. What I did regret is that I was too hasty in making the decision to break up with your father. He never abandoned us like I said."

"Really? You would've stayed with him?"

"I think so. He wanted us to get married. I have no idea what I would've done with two or three more like you, but he was very serious about it. Kind of dopey and idealistic, but he really loved me. He was a very passionate man, and believe it or not, I'm no slouch."

"Wow," Vidamía said, suddenly feeling the same lightness she felt when she talked about sex with Cookie, at the same time reflecting on the fact that her mother was, after all, only thirty-four and extremely attractive. "I guess my interest in the subject is in the genes, huh?" Vidamía added, looking at Elsa like a junior vamp.

"How are you spelling that, J-E-A-N-S?" Elsa said, and they both laughed.

"It was his idea to give you the name," Elsa said. "Did you know that?"

"Yeah, Grandma Ursula told me the story. I figured you were trying to sound mature and impress him with some sort of Latin passion."

"Sort of like that, except that after a while being with him was really powerful. But I really think that if we had been more mature we could've made it work," she said, her memories making her pensive.

"You really loved him, didn't you?" Vidamía said.

"I was very young, but I loved him," Elsa said. "I love Barry now, and that helps me to recognize that I did love your father. I guess that's why I didn't want too much contact with him. I didn't want to be reminded. It was all very crazy, but I did. I loved him. If I hadn't, I really don't think we could have made such a beautiful and smart daughter."

"Well, you had a lot to work with," Vidamía said.

"Thank you. And I'll tell you another secret. Smart and beautiful are okay, but it's always been your charm and wit that I've been jealous of, dear."

"It's the Irish part of me."

"Sure it is," Elsa said, dismissing the assertion. "Wait till you get a little older and the Latin from Manhattan starts making herself at home in your life. I'm sure you'll change your mind."

"Lethal combination," Vidamía said.

They went on talking until nearly two o'clock in the afternoon, Elsa speaking about her life honestly, Vidamía spellbound by this new mother who had emerged from her tragedy. At one point Vidamía asked Elsa why she had agreed to see her own father.

"I guess on account of what happened to Billy," she said. "It shook me up and I started thinking that my father could die and I'd be stuck with all kinds of hateful feelings toward him. I didn't want to feel that way. He can't help being who he is. He was never mean to me. I just resented him not being around, and I was afraid of his being dark and everything."

"And now?"

"Watching that movie helped. I guess I still feel pretty scared, but I want to go through it," Elsa said. Recalling how she had wished that her parents were dead, she then told Vidamía the story of Barbara Gelfand and the grief she had felt at losing her parents in the Holocaust. Vidamía got up and went to Elsa's chair and hugged her.

Vidamía imagined the fallen leaves covering the ground in Washington Square Park and the air growing cold and she and Wyndell apart. Maybe she wouldn't go to Harvard. Maybe she'd stay in New York and go to Columbia. She suddenly felt an overpowering feeling of desire as she imagined being with Wyndell again, but knew she had to follow through and go to Boston and attend school and do her best and get into the medical school.

Vidamía still couldn't believe that her mother was sitting a few tables away watching Wyndell play. No more than two hours before, they had been at dinner together. Elsa and Barry sat with Vidamía and Wyndell discussing life and art and movies after the four met and had gone to an Italian restaurant near the Village Gate.

"Vidamía has told me so much about you," Elsa said and conspiratorially she looked at Vidamía. The two of them smiled mysteriously, sharing the private joke of the times Vidamía had taunted her mother with references to their lovemaking. Both Barry and Wyndell were left wondering what the joke was and demanded explanations but were simultaneously told that it was none of their business. When it came time for Wyndell to return to his apartment to pick up his saxophone, Elsa did the most charming thing that Vidamía had ever seen her mother do. They were standing in the street, and Wyndell turned to her to say goodbye. Elsa stuck out her hand, and when Wyn took it, she gently pulled him forward and offered her cheek for him to kiss. Wyndell leaned down and touched his lips tenderly to Elsa's cheek. She returned the gesture, pecking him and lingering there for a moment before drawing back and winking coquettishly at Vidamía.

"*Vélalo bien, mija, que no te lo roben,*" Elsa said, warning Vidamía to watch him closely to make sure nobody stole him from her.

"Unbelievable," Vidamía whispered to Barry.

Barry snickered, and when Wyndell looked to him for support, Barry shook his head, told Wyndell not to pay too much attention to women, especially to his wife, and definitely not to his daughter. Elsa and Vidamía immediately slapped at Barry's arm and laughed.

An hour later, right before the first set began, at eight-thirty, Barry and Elsa came in and sat down a few tables away from where Vidamía was sitting with Cookie, Mario, and Meredith, Rebecca's lover. They had agreed that Elsa would meet with her father in between sets. Several times during the performance Vidamía caught her mother looking at her father, sitting near the stage, unaware that his daughter was behind him. Vidamía couldn't help admiring everything the quintet had accomplished in such a short period of time. She felt her head bobbing and her body swaying to the final strains of " 'Round Midnight." Wyndell was looking past Cookie at her, pleading with his eyes, asking Vidamía again to understand why he couldn't move to Boston. But just as he couldn't move to Boston, she couldn't pass

772

up going to Harvard, and he knew that. She'd told him she was going to find a place to live and begin getting used to school. They'd see each other on weekends and promised not to see other people.

A few days before the gig, Vidamía asked Barry why he thought there had been such a drastic change in Elsa's attitude toward her. They were sitting on the terrace outside the library, the late afternoon was warm and sunny. Mrs. Alvarez had brought them fresh lemonade. Barry removed his sunglasses and shook his head. He explained that Elsa was an extremely complex woman.

"I think once you became interested in Puerto Rican culture, it eased her mind," he nodded philosophically.

"Eased her mind? Explain. I know she was happy about it, but I never thought much of it."

"Elsa has always been concerned with the issue of color. Irrational as it seems, she was afraid that you'd be drawn to the black side of being American. Especially with Wyn."

"And once I got into Puerto Rican history and culture there was no chance of that?" Vidamía asked.

"Something like that."

"That is hilarious. *Mami* explained about her problems with race. It's like being Puerto Rican is an antidote to this black and white stuff that is such a hang-up with Americans. Brilliant. Wow! That's what I was trying to explain to Wyn when we were arguing about his wanting me to be black. In other words, being Rican means that you don't have to decide whether you're black or white."

"That's as good an explanation as any, and probably healthier than having to decide between black and white. That kind of crap damages this country."

"But why was she so distant and now she's so nice to me?"

"I don't know. I told her if she kept it up she was going to lose you. Elsa is a very competitive woman. I think it was a combination of your independence, your interest in P.R. culture, fear of losing your respect, and Lurleen's love for you."

"But *mami* loves me," Vidamía said with a mixture of pride and uncertainty.

"She loves you more than you can imagine," Barry said. "As long as I've known her."

"But she was so cold sometimes. She would never even call me by my name. I mean she's not like that anymore. She calls me Vidamía and Vee. It's cute. It's like she's one of Cookie's homegirls, but grown up like their mothers, but different. Sophisticated. You know?"

Barry nodded and drank from his lemonade. Putting on his sunglasses, he looked out at the expanse of lawn that led into the woods. Vidamía was certain that he was hiding some private hurt from her. Perhaps her mother had been so distant because being close to her would remind her, as she had said, that she should have stayed with Billy Farrell. She certainly was a complex woman. The air had grown chilly and the light of day dimmer. Vidamía and Barry rose from their patio chairs. Vidamía took Barry's hand, hugged him and kissed his cheek. She thanked him for clearing things up. He nodded, and they walked back into the library with their arms around each other.

69 Little Rootie Tootie

Cookie loved Thelonious Monk and sometimes called Mario her "little rootie tootie," whatever that meant. She and Mario were swooning over each other, pecking each other's lips, oblivious to everyone around them. As inspired as Wyn's solo was, Vidamía couldn't keep her mind from wandering. She thought about Cookie's confidence regarding everything she did. She had gotten a part in a movie and it didn't even faze her. Vidamía recalled her attitude after she went to the audition three months earlier.

"You think you'll get the part?" Vidamía said.

"Probably," Cookie answered, matter-of-factly.

"Did you meet the other people yet?"

"No, but my agent says I will when rehearsals start."

"And you play somebody in a girl's rock band?"

"No. I mean, yeah. She plays in this rock band, but she's in love with this boy, right? And he's, like, a jerk and everything. He's the friend of the boyfriend of the lead. They're trying to get Winona Ryder or maybe Molly Ringwald to do it. Anyway, my character really loves this boy even though he's a nerd, but very smart and everything. So she climbs up on the roof of the house."

"Her own house?"

"No, the boy's house. In the middle of the night. And she's up there playing stuff from Charlie Parker, and he loves Bird. So the police and the firemen come and it's a whole big deal. I'm gonna get the part. It was a good thing I had my ax with me the day of the audition, right?"

"Yeah, I guess. And you just took out your ax and started playing?" Vidamía used "ax" as she heard Wyn and other musicians refer to their instruments.

"Word. Surprised me, too, homegirl."

"Tell me, tell me what happened," Vidamía said, sitting cross-legged on the bed.

"No, nothing," Cookie said. "Like the man is talking and explaining the scene and all these girls are watching me and they're all, like, twenty-seven and maybe even thirty years old and trying to make themselves look younger, and he's explaining that this girl's in high school, plays the saxophone, and that she's a

775

very good student, which I'm not, as you know, but lives with her parents who are very poor and she has a dream of going to college and becoming a doctor, like you wanna do, which is totally weird and very *myoho*, like Rima would say about Buddhism. And the girl, Diana, plays in the marching band at school and on weekends plays with a rhythm-and-blues band, and they'd seen me walking into the audition to sign in. And I can hear these other girls talking about 'she's crazy and she's bringing props and why didn't someone say you had to play the saxophone and shit?' and I'm studying the sides, trying to understand the role.

"And this man's talking about how this boy, Harold, loves Charlie Parker and that's all I needed to hear, man. When they call my name to read I had my ax out and I walk in, blow the hell out of 'Ornithology,' all crazy and fast like Bird played it on his alto, right? You know what I'm talking about? The side where he's at Storyville in Boston in 1953, right? Wyn played that for us on the system one time at his apartment, and you know me, I hear any kind of sounds and I remember them."

"God, that was almost a year ago," Vidamía said.

"I dug what Bird was doing so I had practiced it. Anyway, I'm playing like a crazy person and when I finish after about three minutes, this one guy, who I found out is the writer, says to the guy running the audition, 'That's it, Murray. That's it. Look at her, she's perfect.' And the other guy isn't paying attention, and then he says, 'Take a look at this, please, and read the parts that are in yellow.' And I go, 'Right,' and don't even put my ax away. I just put the guard on and let it hang offa me. I go over the lines and they say something like, 'Harold, this may come as a surprise but you and I have very similar interests.' So, like, I think to myself, if this girl Diana knows Charlie Parker's music, she's gotta be pretty hip so I go into character and remember Dizzy Gillespie from that time we watched him on television and I say, 'Yo, Harold, like this is gonna blow you away but you and I dig the same kinda stuff and whatnot,' which I know Diz doesn't sound like that, but it kind of gave me some inspiration, thinking of him goofing on everything, and I felt like this girl would be like that, right?"

"Yeah, right."

"And this man goes, 'Thank you very much,' but the writer was smiling and nodding and winked at me. He was okay, not a hunk, but cute."

She and Vidamía had originally thought nothing much would come of the audition. Billy had been opposed to Cookie's acting career. Lurleen, however, had been quietly supportive and had spoken to their father about letting Cookie have a chance at something she evidently loved doing. And now things were suddenly changing. They had kept everything a secret from everybody until things finally materialized. Billy never knew how successful Cookie would become in a short period of time. A week before Wyn's gig, Cookie and Vidamía were in the loft alone, listening to music and talking about things in general.

"Are you really going to change your name for acting?"

"Yep."

"Flores Farrell like they introduced you in the poetry slam at the Nuyorican Poets Café?"

"No, *boba*. That's a joke. That's to mess with the homeboys."

"What, then?"

"You know. My middle name. McAlpin. McAlpin Farrell. I discussed it with the agent last week and that's what we agreed on. I got my glossies. Two hundred and fifty. I kept twenty to give to my fans," she said, laughing at the put-on. "You want one?"

Vidamía laughed some more, the tickly feeling of pride growing in her chest. And then Cookie brought out from her attaché case her new eight-by-ten glossies. Her sister Hortense "Cookie" Farrell looking like the foxiest young woman you'd ever want to see; her hair long now and coifed like a lady's, no longer spiked as it was three years prior, the nose ring hole airbrushed out and her complexion clearer than it was to begin with, her blue eyes bright and innocent in the black-and-white photographs. There, on the bottom of the picture in bold script, everything looking official and as if the name had existed forever: **McALPIN FARRELL**.

"Damn, homegirl," Vidamía said in her best, downtown, Loisaida, Afro-Rican accent. "You the real thing, ain't ya? Check you out, *mami*. You don't dare."

"I got it, honey."

"Now, don't be playing yourself. You gonna give some folks heart attacks and whatnot. *Te ves preciosa*, honey. You look beautiful. You gonna be the real thing."

"Thank you, *mamita*," Cookie said, her eyes becoming teary. "Who says you can't take the country outta the girl? I love you. You're the best friend a person could have, even if you're my big sister."

"I love you, too, you animal."

And then Cookie was jumping up and down like a little girl at Christmas when she's gotten the best present ever.

"Oh, wait, wait, remember about the magazine?"

"Yeah. Did you get the spread?"

"I called you yesterday."

"We were on the boat."

"Okay, wait right there," she was saying as she ran out of the room, yelling for her mother, "Mama, Mama where's the magazine?" And then, coming back into the room with the *Seventeen* magazine that featured her picture, full-length in a green-and-white print dress, her long, elegant neck accentuated by the makeup, and holding a large straw hat with a trailing green ribbon the same color as the dress, her sister looking totally in command so that you thought how much you would like to get to know this girl and help her any way you could. "It came out while you were up at Tarrytown talking to your mom."

Vidamía was speechless for an entire minute as she shook her head in disbelief.

"You're a cover girl," she finally said. "You're going to be famous. Can I still call you Cookie?"

"Sure, that's still who I am," she said, proudly. "Cookie Farrell from the Lower East Side. McAlpin Farrell's my makeup and whatnot. A fourth-wall disguise, as we say in the craft, my dear," she tagged on with a remarkable British accent. And then Cookie was very quiet. She sat down on the bed, turned to Vidamía, and said she was probably right, that she *was* going to be famous, but that it wouldn't mean much.

"You know what I mean, Vee?" she said. "With Papa gone and everything. I think he would've enjoyed seeing me doing well. I think he worried about me. He never said anything, but I think he worried that I was going to turn out bad and use drugs or get killed. But none of us use drugs, including Fawn, and she got killed anyway. Poor little Fawn. Life can sure be awful sometimes," she said and sounded very much like Lurleen. And then she was once again New York tough and determined. "As much of a bitch as life is, I'ma kick ass, homegirl. You-understand-what-I'm-saying?"

Then they were wrestling on the bed, trying to tickle each other and laughing like two crazy girls.

And now, sitting in the Village Gate and having Cookie—excuse me, McAlpin Farrell—sitting next to her, looking so stunning, Vidamía could understand how irresistible she must have been to the producers of the film when she had first auditioned for them nearly three months before. Cliff was now soloing on "Little Rootie Tootie." Vidamía couldn't wait to hear what had taken place earlier in the day. Cookie had returned for the callback, this time dressed with great elegance and style. What Vidamía didn't know, and Cookie later explained, was that the writers had thought it over and made this girl, Maggie—they changed the name of the character—a recent immigrant from Ireland. Without batting an eye, Cookie slid into an Irish brogue the likes of which they hadn't imagined. They couldn't figure out whether they were in the presence of some little punk girl from the streets of Dublin or someone so well trained that they had no choice but to give her the part.

"What did you say? Tell me, tell me," Vidamía asked as they sat waiting for the musicians to come onstage.

"They're gonna start any minute," Cookie said. "Rebecca's sitting down."

"Just tell me," Vidamía said, pushing her. "C'mon, Cookie. You gonna leave me hanging? I had to go eat dinner with Wyn and my parents."

"How'd that go?"

"Not fair, Cookie. I asked you about your thing first."

"Okay, okay," Cookie said. "*Coño*, girl, you get so bossy sometimes. And me a promising star of stage and screen and whatnot and you ordering me around like I was trash. Damn, lighten up a taste."

"I told you, girl, don't be playing yourself," Vidamía said, shaking her shoulders and turning her face away like she couldn't be bothered, even sucking her tongue and making a loud clicking sound of derision.

"Okay, okay," Cookie said, relenting. "So like when he says this bit about this girl coming from Ireland and whatnot and they already heard like I got this thick, Loisaida, badass P.R. accent and whatnot, they musta figured Cookie Farrell ain't nothing but a backward-type *jíbara*, right?"

"Yeah, okay."

"So right away I go into this Irish accent like Grandma Brigid from the auld sod, right? I go, Would you be minding if I tell you a wee story? And they go no, go ahead. A man and his wife are golfing one weekend. The man hits the ball into the rough and goes looking for it. He's in there no more than a minute when a leprechaun jumps up and says, 'Top o' the marnin' to ye, lad.' And the man says, 'You're a leprechaun.' 'That I am,' says the leprechaun, 'and ye have three wishes.' The man says, 'Okay, I want a Porsche.' 'No problem at all, lad. When ye go home tonight there'll be a Porsche in yer garage.' 'Okay, but I want a million dollars.' 'Done, lad. On Monday when ye go to yer bank there'll be a million dollars in yer account. Ye have one more wish.' 'I want to be a scratch golfer,' the man says. 'No sooner said than done,' says the leprechaun. 'From now on, par and under.' 'Well, thank you very much,' says the man. 'I have to find my ball.' 'Hold on, laddie,' says the leprechaun. 'Ye know we leprechauns are kind of mischievous. I see you're golfing with yer wife.' 'Yes, I am,' says the man. 'Now, would ye be minding if I went behind the shrubbery with yer wife for an hour or so?' 'I don't know,' answers the man. 'I'll have to ask her.' So the man goes to his wife and asks her. She says that she doesn't care about the car or the golf, but a million dollars is a million dollars and if he doesn't mind, she's willing. The man shrugs his shoulders and his wife goes into the bushes with the leprechaun. About an hour later they're coming out and the wife is brushing the grass off her skirt and the leprechaun thanks her. 'You're welcome,' says the wife. 'May I ask you a question, ma'am?' 'Sure,' says the wife. 'How old is yer husband?' 'Forty-two,' says the wife. 'Why?' 'He's a little too old to be believing in leprechauns, in't he?' says the leprechaun. And these dudes fell out and threw up their hands and said I had the part and did I have a lawyer or an agent because somebody ought to look at the contract."

Vidamía was shaking her head and grinning from ear to ear.

"You are too much, my sister," she said. "You are one crazy, twisted *niña*. Your mother's gonna—"

"Girl, don't you talk about my mama," Cookie shot back, hand on her hip and pouting like some badass *morena* homegirl from Harlem and whatnot, her accent so convincing that Vidamía was stopped cold. It was obvious that she was in the presence of someone of great thespian capabilities. And then Cookie was back to her true self, the down-home New York Cookie Farrell of the beautiful even smile and tender heart Vidamía loved with all her being. She began to say something, but Cookie shushed her and pointed and whispered that the musicians were coming up on the stage.

70 Santurce

The straight-ahead set went on for the next forty minutes, in all over an hour. Wyndell was standing in front of the mike in his Alan Flusser suit with flowered tie, handkerchief, and matching socks, smiling and talking easily to the audience as he introduced the band while they continued playing softly in the background.

"On drums, ladies and gentlemen, Mr. David Weinstein. David Weinstein on drums. On trombone, Mr. Clifford Farrell. Clifford Farrell, ladies and gentlemen. On piano, Ms. Rebecca Feliciano. Rebecca Feliciano on piano. And on bass, our mentor, Mr. Buster Williams. A special hand, ladies and gentlemen, for our connection to this great American music. Buster Williams. Buster Williams, ladies and gentlemen. Buster Williams."

Each time Wyndell introduced a musician the person did a few bars above volume. The audience gave each musician special applause. The applause, and some considerable whistling, went on for a while and then quieted down enough for Wyndell to address the audience again.

"My name's Wyndell Ross and at this point we'd like to ask a very special musician, a pioneer in the Latin music business and someone who's played with Tito Puente, Machito, and all the greats of salsa to come up on the stage and accompany the quintet in a tune by the late African-American composer, Mr. Alfred Butterworth. The tune is called 'Santurce' and has as its inspiration the town of that name on the island of Puerto Rico. Ladies and gentlemen, a big round of applause for Mr. Justino 'Tumba' Santiago."

And up on the stage went Grandpa Tumba Santiago dressed in his polyester white suit, white shoes, and red shirt with no tie—looking spry and very tropical, his kinky hair slicked back. His friends were whistling and his lady, Panchita—her blond hair newly peroxided, and amply filling her tight electric-blue dress—was smiling from ear to ear.

Vidamía looked back at her mother to share the moment. Elsa had grasped Barry's arm and there was a look of overpowering sadness and regret in her eyes. Vidamía mouthed the words "Don't worry," and Elsa nodded and smiled awkwardly. "Thank you," Elsa mouthed back.

Grandpa Tumba Santiago was now behind his congas and Wyndell was counting and David Weinstein came in on the cowbell and eight beats later Rebecca joined in with a lilting Latin melody that made half the audience want to get up and hit the dance floor like it was Monday night at the Village Gate and "Salsa Meets Jazz" was on the musical menu with Alfredo Cruz from WBGO holding forth as emcee.

Vidamía now heard the *pacatun-tun-tun* of Grandpa Tumba's congas and Wyndell picking up where Rebecca had left off. Underneath it all Buster Williams was laying down a carpet of rhythm and harmony, the bass traveling up and down, giving the tune its Latin flavor and people already whistling as Wyndell began improvising on the tune with Cliff beating out the *clave*, one-two-three, one-two, over and over again, the music rushing over the audience, and over Vidamía, reminding her of the surf long ago in Puerto Rico, when she'd sat hypnotized, watching the huge *marullos* coming in, one after the other, on the beach in Vega Baja.

The music was inside her, working itself into the marrow of her bones, into the sinews of her muscles, into the fiber of her being so that her soul soared, above the people and the city, higher and higher, until she could see the entire country from one coast to the other, and at that great distance no one was black or white, yellow or red, brown or beige, and there was no distinction as to who was better than another. She closed her eyes then and began to understand that her life would always exist in flux, changing forever into greater and greater insights. And yet one thing would remain constant, and this latest revelation gave her hope, because it appeared to be something that had developed naturally in her.

A glimmer of this personal quality, which she could not yet name, began to surface just that morning as she rose. She emerged from sleep unusually refreshed given the tension of the past month. No one else was awake in the loft, and as she washed up and got dressed she felt more excited than usual. Initially she thought that the excitement was a result of the upcoming dinner with Elsa, Barry, and Wyn and the subsequent performance at the Village Gate by Wyn and the quintet. After drinking some orange juice and making herself a cup of instant coffee, she let herself out of the loft and climbed the stairs to the roof. She set her coffee cup on one of the tables and surveyed the city, its skyscrapers and bridges, its patches of parks, the highways that lined each side of Manhattan, the traffic even at this hour moving steadily. It was then, as she looked at the sun rising over the northeastern part of Manhattan that she glanced at her watch and realized that it was not even seven o'clock in the morning. In the coolness of the new day, with a tropical breeze blowing behind her, she realized that her feeling of pride and well-being had nothing to do with the upcoming evening's activities.

Vidamía thought of Billy Farrell standing on the narrow

ledge of the roof, as Lurleen had related it to her when Vidamía pleaded to know everything about him so she might understand why he had ended his life. As if being pulled by him she had an urge to walk her father's steps, even looking at her shoes to see if they were safe enough to attempt what she was imagining. And then she saw Billy's face clearly. He was shaking his head, smiling at her as he had sitting in Katz's Deli when he told her she reminded him of Beara, the daughter of the king of Spain. She had forgotten about the comparison at the time, when she was so engrossed in getting Billy to play again, but later she got curious and went searching until she found a book on Irish myth, and there it was, Beara. She remembered her father telling her about Beara, who lived near the river Eibhear, which they said could be the Ebro River in Spain. In Irish legend she was to go to the river and wait for her husband who would be disguised as a salmon in shining armor. The salmon also represented wisdom to the ancient Irish.

She saw her father differently in her mind's eye now. The images were more sharply defined than she had imagined. For a while their roles were reversed and she had been the adult and Billy the child. As the parent she had been responsible for his well-being. She saw a little boy by the name of William Christopher Farrell, once a shy, gentle child who loved baseball and building model airplanes and worshiped his father, whose death had scarred him and left him with nothing but honor and duty and sorrow to hold on to. She saw him in his innocence, skipping up the sidewalk, a book bag slung over his shoulder and his straw-colored hair falling over his eyes. He was mumbling something to himself and then laughing freely without any awareness of being watched. And she saw the same William Christopher Farrell playing the piano, lost in that magical world of jazz he loved so much. And she also saw him walking through a jungle, firing his machine gun, the thick tree branches shattering before his fury. He was all those things: carefree little boy, wounded early in life, sensitive artist, and crazed soldier. Contradiction piled upon contradiction. That's what Billy Farrell was, and the knowledge made her reflect on her confusion over the events of the previous month.

She imagined she saw Billy shaking his head and smiling as if to tell her that she didn't need to prove her courage because she possessed that quality in great abundance. She understood that he'd also had great courage and whatever happened at the end, she was sure his choice had been the only one left to him. Whatever it was she felt suddenly at peace. She finished her coffee and sat to watch the sun rise higher in the sky. Like her father she had no choice but to go forward and take her chances. The challenge excited her and she smiled inwardly as she felt the weight of knowing that, no matter what happened, Billy would always be with her, his courage and strength passed on to her. "Goodbye, Billy," she said out loud as she raised her face to the warming sun.

As she sat in the club listening to the music and watching her grandfather giving himself to his congas, Vidamía thought again of the log that Kunta Kinte had gone looking for to make his drum. A strange notion passed fleetingly through her mind and she was at once in the club listening to the music and apart from that reality in a deep wood, aware that she had found the right wood for her own life drum.

Instantly, she felt free of her own background: white and black, African and European, Puerto Rican and Irish, southern and New York. She now belonged to the world, to life. And suddenly she was standing up with everyone else and applauding. She was glad Wyn had agreed not to mention her father. Wyn had wanted to dedicate the evening to Billy, but she insisted that it would have made Cliff uncomfortable.

She thought now about her own life and what awaited her.

The prospect of studying at Harvard was exciting, but she knew that from now on her life was set. Until she was ministering medically to her first pediatric patients and could call herself Dr. Farrell, she couldn't think of her life apart from her mission as a physician. When would that be? Ten years? Four, four, and two. That would be in the year 2000; she would be twenty-eight, and then she'd reassess her life. She hoped secretly that Wyn would still be there, but she had to stop thinking about it. Instead she thought about the salmon husband, the salmon of wisdom in Irish myth, and immediately knew that her wisdom would come from within and not from some outside source. Knowledge, information, facts came from outside. Wisdom developed inside. The thought sobered her momentarily, but the next moment tears were streaming down her face, and she was clapping and Cookie was hugging her and all around her there was light and sound and voices and through them she could hear her father, Billy Farrell, telling her that everything was going to be all right and whatever happened not to let them get you. As if she were speaking to him she said, "Don't worry, Billy Farrell, I won't."

And then unexpectedly they were playing the song, and she closed her eyes in desperation, her heart breaking. She turned to complain to Cookie, but her sister was gone, and Mario Wong and Meredith Brooks looked at her and shrugged their shoulders. She looked around the club but couldn't spot Cookie anywhere. When she looked again at the stage, there was Cookie, standing at the mike with Wyn and the rest—Buster, Cliff, Rebecca, David, and her Grandpa Tumba Santiago—behind her, playing the song. Her little sister looking grown-up and stunning, was singing in her smoky voice, "*Won't you come home, Bill Bailey* . . ." like nothing had happened and they were back together in the family band, playing in subway stations.

Cookie was singing, belting out the song, pleading for Bill Bailey to come home. Vidamía Farrell, wishing with all her might that her father had not left them, knew it was a useless plea. That beautiful time of innocence when everything was possible had disintegrated and in its place something more powerful had emerged and she would explore it and build upon it. As much as she loved her father, he was gone now. She had his courage, but more important she had herself, and as if a current of powerful energy were suddenly coursing through her being, she saw Ursula Santiago and Maud Farrell, her mother Elsa and her mama Lurleen, and knew they had endured enormous pain and had a different kind of strength than the men in the family and she'd continue to draw on their power. Bill Bailey was never coming home again, and the prospect of life without him made her ache. She smiled painfully and even though she knew the entire matter was a rationalization, she felt as if Billy had come home. He had left the horror of his sorrow and stepped out into life, with all its disappointments and pain, to do what he loved and play jazz again. She had helped him to accomplish this, and in return he'd filled her with enormous confidence in herself and her capacity to change her environment and the people in it. It was a confidence that she'd be able to use for everything life demanded.

She thought again of being small and wanting to be a little drummer boy in the Revolutionary War. And then she recalled little Fawn in Tompkins Square Park with her drum harness strapped on her shoulders, insisting she was a drummer girl. Vidamía didn't like the image of war. Instead she thought of struggles and knew that whatever threatened her dreams and those of others had to be resisted. One way or the other, she'd have to stand up against injustice without resorting to violence. Whether it was with her spoken or her written words, with her emotion or her intellect, her body or her soul, she would always fight injustice. Until there was no longer strength in her being or breath in her life, she would do battle and win against the things that prevented human beings from realizing their dreams. Not just the talented and gifted, but everyone. The greatness of the country could not be measured by those who were the best, but by how the weakest thrived.

Through the excitement of the music and the deafening applause Vidamía Farrell, daughter of Elsa and Lurleen, granddaughter of Maud and Ursula, saw herself returning with her log and knew that she had to get busy and make her drum.

Author's Note

The writing of this book began in 1987. It is now sixteen years since the initial idea occurred to me and I began writing about it. I composed the novel out of concern and affection for the variety of people I've known during my life, in my family and out. Their color or ethnicity never mattered in our relationships. My intent in the novelistic structure of the work has been to pay homage to two original art forms from this hemisphere: the Mexican mural and United States jazz. As such, the novel may be viewed as a mural or heard as a symphonic work.

My love of jazz began when I was a teenager. I am not a jazz musician so my knowledge of the music is that of a fan and a student. I arrived in this country at the age of thirteen, with little knowledge of the United States. At that impressionable age, I was tossed into an Irish neighborhood in the south Bronx, specifically 141st Street between Cypress and St. Ann's Avenues. I played football and other sports for the Shamrocks. My presence eventually caused the team name to be changed to the Rebels. The neighborhood accepted me with curiosity and warmth. My introduction to the United States was through Irish eyes. My inspiration comes mainly from my heritage. However, in understanding the United States, I also look to the Irish for inspiration since in many respects their pride in their ancestry is similar to ours as Puerto Ricans. There are other similarities. As is the case with us, their ancestral home has been subjected to invasion by a more powerful political entity. Our mutual love of language has impelled us to adopt the use of English as a way of combating the aggression. I have attempted to emulate this linguistic stand since English is not my first language.

My siblings married Irish. Last year, my daughter, to whom this book is dedicated, married a young man from Dublin. In that regard the circle has been completed.

In mid-November of 2004, several months after the hard-cover edition of this novel was in production, I was invited to the University of Puerto Rico to lecture and conduct writing work-shops. While on the island I called my favorite cousin, Sunchi Yunqué. She came to a reading at a café called Guajana and in-vited me to her son's wedding that Sunday. I hadn't seen Sunchi Yunqué in nearly twenty-five years. At the reception, she intro-duced me to her son and her three daughters. Her eldest one was a striking, green-eyed beauty who could've been a perfect model for Vidamía. That was remarkable enough, but then she intro-duced me to her three sons, ages eleven to seven. They were dark-skinned and curly-haired. When I asked their last name my second cousin said it was Murphy. I asked her if she had married an American serviceman. She shook her head and said her husband's family had been in Puerto Rico for centuries. I un-derstood then that perhaps this Puerto Rican Murphy may have come there with the original settlers in the fifteenth century. I felt then as if my connection to the Irish had now been estab-lished again solidly and directly through family.

Before I understood the English language, I was fascinated by its rhythms through the music on the radio. Popular music held a minor allure for me. Jazz, however, captivated my imagi-nation. Back then, in the mid-fifties, there were two radio pro-grams that I listened to after everyone else in our house had gone to sleep. One was "The Milkman's Matinee." The other was Symphony Sid's broadcast. They both played jazz. I was enrap-tured by the music and for a time, in high school, I attempted to play the tenor saxophone, with disastrous results and much dis-approval from teachers, fellow band members, and, more signif-icant, my parents and siblings, who had to endure my efforts at imitating the people I heard on the radio.

Over the years Charlie Parker, Dave Brubeck, Thelonious Monk, Dexter Gordon, Stan Getz, Miles Davis, John Coltrane, Duke Ellington and his orchestra, Billie Holiday, and other mu-sicians transported me to a world of mystery from which, fortu-nately, I have never returned. To all who form this pantheon of great jazz musicians, my undying love and appreciation. If I was introduced to the United States and its complexities by the Irish, I was introduced to its soul by jazz, and by the hundreds of jazz musicians who created this great and life-giving music. If there are errors in the technical aspects of this novel, or if I've created misconceptions regarding the music, please know that no one is to blame except me. Whatever the errors may be, they are unin-tentional.

Acknowledgments

Many people are responsible for the publication of this book. None deserve my thanks more than these three: My agent Thomas Colchie deserves the most credit for believing in the novel after it had been buried in obscurity for nearly a decade. For his friendship, good humor, strategies, and stewardship, my thanks. I will be forever grateful to his wife, Elaine Jabbour Colchie, who opened her heart to the book and her home to me. Her insightful suggestions have improved the work. I owe a special debt of gratitude to Robert Wyatt, whose words of encouragement and belief in my work helped to sustain me through some difficult times. To all three, my respect and affection.

My appreciation goes, as well, to the team at Farrar, Straus and Giroux for their support and the production of the book. Jonathan Galassi, John Glusman, Jeff Seroy, Susan Mitchell, and Ayesha Pande worked diligently to bring about the publication of the book. I thank them and their staff.

My children's mother, Patricia, deserves credit for suggesting I write a novel that would affect the United States. I hope I have accomplished her wish. To her, my eternal gratitude for help and encouragement with the first draft of the novel.

Two friends who are prominent members of the jazz community agreed to appear as themselves in the book. To Buster Williams and Larry Coryell, my special thanks. You are both an inspiration to me as artists and as human beings.

I have known Jayne Cortez, a great American poet and jazz lover, for more than thirty years. With enormous generosity she has permitted the inclusion of her poem "If the Drum Is a Woman" in the novel. My thanks to her.

Over the years, friends have commented on the novel and made suggestions. My special thanks to: Carmen Barnes, Jordan Elgrably, Dan Evans, Sherry Winston, Brett Khune, and Kat Kavanagh. A special thanks to Angela Carter, of the Irish Book Store, for help with research. My thanks to Nando Alvericci of WBAI for his help with the musical origins of "She's a Latin from Manhattan." My thanks also to Victor Escobar for the long talks we had regarding his life as a Marine. Earl Horton deserves my sincerest thanks for sharing his Vietnam combat experiences in the Marine Corps. My acknowledgment as well to my Vietnam-veteran students at Hostos Community College during the early seventies when they took my courses, "Vietnam" and "Six Twentieth Century Revolutions." Their experiences on the battlefield, and our long talks about their lost innocence, their regrets, and the nightmares they still endured, helped to give form to this book. As then, I honor your sacrifices.

During the period of time that I have worked on the novel since 1987, my companions during long days and lonely nights were the disk jockeys at WBGO Jazz 88. For their company, enthusiasm, good humor, and erudition concerning this great American art form that is jazz, my appreciation. Along the same lines, I owe a special debt of gratitude to the Institute of Jazz Studies at Rutgers University for permitting me access to their archives and to their wide selection of recordings.

My thanks to Kurt Hollander, editor of the *Portable Lower East Side* for first publishing part of the novel in 1989 as a work in progress, and to *Bomb* magazine's Betsy Sussler for publishing a chapter in 1992. My thanks to Tamara Straus, the editor-in-chief at *Zoetrope* magazine, for excerpting the first two chapters prior to publication. For this Picador paperback edition my thanks to Josh Kendall and Frances Coady.

The writing of this book was made possible in part by grants from the National Endowment for the Arts in 1989 and the New York Foundation for the Arts in 1990.

Ultimately, this work is my offering to the United States for sheltering me and mine.

The country and I have issues pending, but I hope we can continue our dialogue.